THE END OF THRONES

BOOK TWO OF AN INNER AND OUTER SPACE ODYSSEY SERIES

LAWRENCE STENTZEL III

ISBN 978-1-950818-58-7 (paperback)

Rushmore Press LLC
1 888 733 9607
www.rushmorepress.com

Printed in the United States of America

An Inner and Outer Space Odyssey Series

A Tale of the Tail of Nine Stars: An Inner and Outer Space Odyssey

End of Thrones: Book Two of An Inner and Outer Space Odyssey Series

Lost in Space-Time: Book Three of An Inner and Outer Space Odyssey Series

Written but unpublished

Illumination Out of the Dark Ages: Book Four of An Inner and Outer Space Odyssey Series

The Dominari Conformity: Book Five of An Inner and Outer Space Odyssey Series

The Early Adventures of Electra: Book Six of An Inner and Outer Space Odyssey Series

The Psychopaths of the Maxom Empire: Book Seven of An Inner and Outer Space Odyssey Series

CHAPTER ONE

The ships of the Om task force jumped into the white star system of Vox just outside the orbital distance of the star's fifth planet, in full-cloaked mode at .7 light speed and started braking with reverse drives and thrusters immediately to acquire clearer resolution on their sensors. Star systems in Om's star-mapping were always designated by the name of the inhabited planet if there was one. Sensor resolution and fire-control gained clarity and resolution at .24 light speed or below. Pez turned in her seat to ask Rear Admiral Swenah on the flagship *Apollo*, "Can you get me patched into their imperial governor on the surface of Vox in the capital?"

Mel, their AI quantum computer, answered before Swenah could, "I've already established a link with their satellite holocom network orbiting Vox using conversion from quantum to spectrum encoded light coms, and will have the imperial governor on speaker shortly."

"Thanks, sweetheart." Pez told her gratefully.

The senior sensors analyst on the bridge, Cotex, informed them, "There are four imperial battleship-carriers, six cruisers, twelve destroyers, fourteen fast assault ships, and twenty-six patrol ships. On both lunar surfaces they have multiple class eight mega-blaster and beam space weapons powered by marsanium fusion reactors, and there are space weapons platforms orbiting the planet; forty-two of them we believe, though we won't know for sure until we see the other side of the planet."

Rear Admiral Swenah updated Pez, who was temporarily commissioned as the Supreme Commander General of all of Om's military forces, "The sensor fire-control and relative-space positioning drones are launched and on their way to their assigned stations around the Vox planetary system and its two moons. We'll have a full data coverage network functioning very soon, with all imperial assets tagged and targeted."

"Thank you Admiral", Pez replied as she nursed her daughter, Electra, from her seat on the bridge.

Electra had her own built in seat on the bridge, much to Admiral Swenah's chagrin, which had its own air supply, shields, sound-proof bubble with mics to momma's ear bud, and computerized holo displays for learning through games and educational entertainment. It was constructed of steel-titanium-nickel, carbon plate armor, textile armor and fiberglass armor.

The flagship *Apollo* was an 8,100 foot diameter disc-shaped super-battleship, stretched at the nose and taller in the stern, containing 30 solarium fusion super-reactors. It was leading what was left of the Om Star Fleet from its victorious war in the Xegachtznel Galaxy where it had stopped the blue-star alien race of the Vachisy Empire from its genocide of human planetary populations and enslavement of its own race, with the help of allies both humanoid and alien.

Their quantum computer artificial intelligence, Mel, had become fully self-aware on the mission they'd just successfully completed in the Xegachtznel Galaxy, and was now practicing meditation and contemplation towards attainment of her rainbow body of light, or astral body, under the instruction and guidance of Sarhi, the Im of the Islohar, who was Pez's teacher. Sarhi was also the High Abbot of the Spiritual Congress, now truly intergalactic, with member star systems from three different galaxies. Pez had 'raised' Mel for twenty-one years now, continuously providing her with accessories for enhanced feedback loops of self-reference and ever greater sensory expansion, while teaching and modelling compassion and love, and treating her as if she were sentient. Although her hardware, or its core components at any rate, were twenty-one years old, and despite the fact that she learned quantumly, her sentience and emotions were yet equivalent to the teen years.

Mel's voice cut in, "I have the Imperial Regent of Vox on the line, General."

Pez said to the Imperial, "Your Regentship of Vox has come to an end. I'm here to relieve you of it. The Kundabuffer Empire is over and will never invade another star system again. I advise you to leave now and our fleet will not destroy you. Send your warships back to Kundabuffer or we will pulverize them. Do it now. I want to see those warships leaving within ten minutes, and your transports, with you on one of them, within the hour."

"Who is this speaking? And just who do you think you are?" he demanded authoritatively.

"Hi, my name is Pez," she informed him, "the Supreme Commander General of Om's military forces and this fleet, which I'll give you a glimpse of in a moment."

Muting him out Pez said to Swenah, "Shut down cloaking on all ships in thirty seconds, for a full three-quarters of a minute, then restore it and change our heading and speed."

The man was screaming in her ear when she got back on line with him, going on about how he'd never heard of Om, could detect no fleet anywhere within the Vox star system, and how he was the supreme authority here. She cut him off telling him, "I'll drop our cloaking in seventeen seconds to give you a view of our fleet. We will remain uncloaked for 45 seconds, and after you see us, you will have three minutes to flee your mansion before it's fried from space. Leave or die."

Jard, a member of the High Council of Om and a rare genius, hacked into Pez's coms to let her know, "One of those battleship-carriers has our programming loaded from our defense of Ganahar, when we turned all their battleships around and sent them back through their gate to Kundabuffer. I control that ship."

Pez ordered, "Get Ahhu on a control console for that ship now!"

"Come on, love-child, I want to operate it," Jard complained.

"Sorry I need our best on it," she insisted.

Swenah reinforced Pez's order, "Jard, Ahhu is our best drone pilot and this is a military operation under Pez's command."

"Ahhu's a civilian!" Jard protested loudly.

"That may be," Swenah soothed him, "but she holds the highest ratings of master Drone Pilot in all of Star Fleet. Please be a team player and turn it over to Ahhu."

"Oh, alright," Jard said with frustration.

Mel had already alerted Ahhu, who was on her way to Jard's research lab near the bridge. The cloaking blinked out precisely when ordered and the fleet was fully visible by electronic signature as well as optically. It was hit with fully active scans from the planet, moons, space stations, satellites, and imperial ships all at once. The data was so advanced of the Kundabuffer imperialists that it would be of no real use to them at all, other than to underline and highlight their own ignorance and pathetic technological development. The Regent shouted, "There are no ships out there and we are tracing your signal. This is an official line and you will be caught and prosecuted!"

"We're a few seconds under a light-minute and a half out from the planet and moving at .2 light speed. We will be in orbit of Vox in about seven minutes. You will receive your scans back in forty-six seconds. Your three minutes to get out of the mansion begins then."

Pez muted the Regent out again, finding his negativity and self-aggrandizement most unattractive, and asked Mel, "Can you locate the Regent's mansion on the planet surface?"

"I already have, but his signal is coming from their surface Space Fleet headquarters about a mile away from it."

"I want those coordinates, but I still want to vaporize that mansion too." Pez informed her.

Ahhu came on in Pez's ear alerting her, "I'm in Jard's lair and the battleship is mine. I await your orders, General."

"Sit tight for three minutes and twenty-nine seconds, then I want you to send a ten minute warning for evacuation of all space weapons platforms and lunar weapons bases because they are going to blow. When that ten minutes are up, start shooting weapons bases and platforms, my love."

"Aye, aye Supreme Commander," Ahhu acknowledged.

Lt. Commander Konax, who was piloting the *Apollo*, mentioned to Pez, "I could accelerate to .24 light speed and we'd still get accurate fire control."

"Do it," Pez agreed.

Cotex informed them, "Our sensor drones have reached their appointed stations and have locked into one another's relative positions forming the RSPS network, giving us a full-data zone for targeting and navigation."

"Thanks," Pez replied, since Cotex had turned completely in her seat to make eye contact with Pez when she'd told the bridge. Electra was full and tired of sucking now, so she gave up. Pez burped her gently, rewarded with a little gas, and no fluids. The diaper was dry and clean, but that wouldn't last long after feeding. She fussed when Pez moved to get her into her deluxe custom seat, so Pez got her into the front pouch on her chest instead, lined with soft fur from a yellow sun third planet subarctic mammal, and protected with the highest-grade textile armor on the outside. Electra looked around the bridge fascinated. Konax turned in his seat, craning his neck to smile at her, and she lit up, giving him a toothless one bursting with joy and energy. The light from the scans reached Vox and its moons, satellites, space stations and ships. Pez unmuted the Regent but turned the volume way down. He was screaming, "This is War!!"

Pez told him calmly, "War is entirely the wrong word since you can neither find us nor penetrate our shields with your largest weapons. This is a reckoning, and if you do not flee it will become an execution as well. We control one of your battleships and we'll be arriving in our own shortly. This is your last warning. General Pez signing off."

She refused to listen to anymore of his bluster and dribble. He'd been fairly warned. Mel's voice announced, "Jard and I have taken over their holocom network and we've initiated their emergency transmission system."

Pez told her, "Transmit this message, 'All Imperial Kundabuffer personnel, report to your air and space ports immediately to shuttle up to your transports. You are all evacuating Vox right now. Drop everything, leave your possessions behind, and proceed this instant to the shuttle ports for evacuation. This is your only warning. Imperial bases, complexes and buildings on the planet's surface will be fired upon in nine minutes and twenty-eight seconds, so if you're in one of those, get out NOW! Warships not headed for your gate will be destroyed. Test my resolve at your own peril'." To Mel she said, "Play that in a loop until the current countdown is complete. That's all the warning we'll give them."

"It's on its second round, and I'll keep playing it," Mel assured her.

Cotex mentioned, "Escape pods and space suited personnel with hand-held propulsion units are spilling off all the weapons platforms and small spacecraft are near colliding getting away from the space-station. The lunar spacecraft ports and weapons bases are emptying too."

"How about the mansion and military HQ?" Pez inquired.

"There are streams of escaping personnel out every door and air and spacecraft are lifting off like a swarm of insects."

"Good," Pez replied.

Ahhu reported, "I'm moving into position for targeting and the occupants of my ship have now figured out that not only do they not control it, but they can't even shut it down manually."

"Open fire when your countdown concludes," Pez directed. "Start with ones that scan empty of life forms."

The warning to evacuate ceased when the countdown reached zero, and Pez told Swenah, "Target a few imperial surface bases, complexes and buildings to reduce them to slag. Start with one which scans as empty of life and that ought to give any stragglers some incentive."

"Opening fire on an empty imperial base now with class six beam weapons," Swenah replied.

Electra demonstrated her amazing lungs and vocal chords announcing her discomfort and unhappiness to the bridge, grating on Swenah's nerves. Pez pulled her out of the pouch and checked, then informed the officers of the bridge, "It's just wee-wee."

Employing a foldout changing top from Electra's custom seat, so large it appeared as a throne on the bridge of the *Apollo*, Pez got busy changing her daughter's wet diaper. She disposed of it in the biohazard bin since there were no trash receptacles on the bridge. Nothing requiring a trash receptacle was permitted here. As the fresh diaper self-adjusted around Electra's pelvis she stopped fussing to the great relief of everyone in ear shot. Pez sat back down holding her daughter in her arms and Electra resumed her contemplation of the lights and personnel on the bridge. Konax turned again to smile at her and was rewarded by her utter delight.

Cotex commented, "These Imperial shuttles are racing to their orbiting transports and causing traffic jams at the landing bay doors to all of them."

"Is that mansion empty yet?" Pez asked Swenah,

"Almost, and we're getting to it," she replied.

Ahhu told them from Jard's research cabin, "I'm frying stuff now. My escape pods and small craft are all exiting fast, emptying my bowls."

Pez watched in her holo as a pair of space weapons platforms turned into briefly illuminating colorful micro-suns expanding into great spherical clouds, no two atoms connected. A lunar weapons base suddenly became a crater in an explosion of brilliant color. Ahhu was firing the main beam and blaster weapons on the imperial battleship while shooting off rockets, and missiles with integrated space drives. Swenah announced, "The mansion and the HQ are molten craters and the pace of the imperial evacuation has just accelerated."

The drone sensor relative space positioning system generating the Full-Sensory-Data-Battle zone was transmitted with real-time quantum coms, which gave *Apollo* a view from anywhere within that zone in actual present time. The zone was just over a light-minute long on each side cubically. Waiting on the speed of light for information would cause intolerable delays in coms, targeting, and tracking. Within the Hub Galaxy only the ships of the Tail of Nine Stars, which was the name of Om's alliance with the star systems Rah and Haum, had quantum coms. All other civilizations with interstellar travel were confined to spectrum encoded light coms within this galaxy at present. Many blue star alien civilizations within the Xegachtznel galaxy had and used quantum coms, as did the humanoids within that galaxy from the Rally system. The humanoids of the Trident system in the Yuban Galaxy also had quantum coms. All of these civilizations were now allies in friendship and members of the spiritual congress.

"That heavy cruiser is not headed for their quantum gate," Pez said aloud examining her holo.

"It's on intercept with the battleship Ahhu's operating remotely," Swenah noted.

"Fire a shield disruptor missile followed a tenth of second by a nanobot spray missile at that heavy cruiser," Pez directed.

"Aye, Aye Ma'am!"

To Jard, Pez said, "You'll get to drive an imperial heavy cruiser back through their gate. Set the destination for their gate in the Kundabuffer home world. Your nanobots will be attached to their hull, and seeking their coms hardware any moment now, to give you a link. Upload your program and have fun."

"It feels like a consolation prize," Jard complained.

Pez said, "Maybe Swenah will let you fly the *Apollo* around the star system after the imperials are gone. Cheer up Jard, if another of your imperial battleships are still in the Kundabuffer system when we go there, I promise you'll get to operate it and blow stuff up with it."

"I just recorded that promise and I'm going to hold you to it," Jard put her on notice.

"I'm true to my word," Pez responded, "but you better not hit any of our own ships."

"Now that was uncalled for," Jard huffed. "I scored a '91' on level four of Rubix's space invaders game on the simulator."

"Ahhu lent him support telling Pez, "He's actually pretty good."

"I didn't mean to offend you Jard. I'm sorry," Pez sort of apologized, "but not hitting any of our own ships is a limit I had to make you aware of."

"None of its weapons could harm one of our ships," he told her as if she were an imbecile.

"We'll have numerous small craft out and I'll be in one," Pez informed him.

"Alright, I'll be careful," he pressed; "I already agreed not to hit any of our own ships."

He went silent for a long moment, then announced, "The link with the cruiser's main computer is established and the take-over program is uploading quantumly. Since studying our reverse-engineering of the imperial computers and deciphering their programming languages, I further adapted my viral transmutation program, and it ought to take less than a minute now to seize control of all imperial functions and operations."

"You're truly amazing Jard," Pez acknowledged.

"Have sex with me," he suggested.

"No; and the bridge during an operation is an inappropriate place for such an invitation, High Councilman."

She always called him that when she was focusing his attention on his behavior. Somehow Jard's genius did not always extend to relating with other humans. That's where his assistant on the mission, Commander Ming, came in; to smooth over, buffer, and if possible, modify and redirect or reframe Jard's offensiveness, and his tendency to extend his research beyond the bounds of privacy and existing law and regulation. So far Ming had kept him out of Rear Admiral Swenah's brig.

Commander Ming was Pez's spouse, and her promotion from second Lieutenant, otherwise impossible within Star Fleet, was enacted in order to save the institution from making exceptions to its 'sacred' regulations when the High Council and Prime Minister insisted Pez and Ming be permitted to legally unite in marriage. The equal rank relationship rule still held without exceptions within Star Fleet since Pez's commission would end with her return to Om, and her order, the Clearlight Order, would immediately promote her from Marshall to Knight Commander, equivalent to a Star Fleet Commander. The High Council and Prime Minister got the marriage and Star Fleet kept their regulations exemption-free, while Ming skipped over First Lieutenant and Lt. Commander before she turned twenty-four years old. By Admiral Zapa's order, whatever happened on the mission in the Xegachtznel Galaxy was to stay and remain in the Xegachtznel Galaxy as if classified top-secret. Pez had been supposed to return directly to Om with the remnants of the fleet from Xegachtznel.

Prime Minister Yona blossomed out of Pez's pocket device unanswered into a forty-eight-inch diameter hologram from about the knees up. Yona asked with some obvious charge in her voice, "Just what do you think you're doing, General? And by what authority?"

"By the will of the cosmic intelligence I'm alleviating a world of suffering," Pez replied neutrally.

"Is Sarhi in on this?" Yona demanded

Pez said, "Mel, please patch Sarhi into this call." To the Prime Minister Pez replied, "She helped me to recognize this calling, and I see it clearly now. We of Om are nearly accessories to the empire, having the where withal to prevent their destruction and mass murder, yet doing nothing."

"You say you act by authority of the cosmic intelligence?" Yona asked.

I am in non-action, so yes, this is so" Pez tried to explain.

Sarhi came on with, "Non-action, and nothing is left undone."

"You provoked her to do this?" Yona asked Sarhi the Im.

"I pass practice instruction and guide the development of her meditation and contemplation." Sarhi clarified. "Soon she will be the Wu, the grand master of the Islohar, including of the Im. She is succeeding clearing the Vox system of imperials and no life has been lost in the operation. Members of the High Council and you, Prime Minister, have friends on Vox."

"Somehow I sense this operation extends beyond Vox," Yona accused.

Pez explicated, "If I do it right, one visit to Kundabuffer ought to get all the rest of the imperial star systems set free and liberated from the imperial yoke, bringing home the imperial war ships. I intend to accomplish this without loss of life, or with only the loss of the most malicious and influential lives key to perpetuating the Kundabuffer Empire, which would only constitute a handful."

"This really comes from a higher order?" Yona asked Pez, looking into her knowing eyes vacant of any indication of self.

"It is truly not my will," Pez assured her. "The hundred-year meditation of the Amonrahonians, now in its 34th year, and the spiritual congress they instigated, direct me and I see they are in alignment with the compassionate reciprocity emanating from the divine intelligence."

Calmed now, Yona told them, "I'll do my best to convey this adequately to the High Council and Aton can help me with the other council members."

"Give Aton my most sincere love please, Prime Minister," Pez beseeched her.

"Of course I will sweet General. He sees you as a daughter and as his soon to be teacher."

Yona winked out. Pez said, "That's the second time this has happened to me, with an unanswered call erupting out of my pocket like that."

Swenah commented, "I guess you have to be the Prime Minister to pull that off."

"That's what I thought," Pez agreed, "but Jard can do it too."

Jard bloomed in a holo from Swenah's pocket and said, "I can do that too; it's not a big deal."

"I guess Yona and Aton are going to try and get the High Council behind your efforts to end Kundabuffer's imperial expansion and empire," Swenah noted.

Konax joked, "She does command a bigger fleet than the Council does at the moment."

Swenah stated, "More than a hundred star systems trying to avoid conquest by Kundabuffer and 188 slave systems will rejoice and be mighty grateful for what Pez is doing."

"No matter what Kundabuffer does," Jard insisted, "I get to drive one of my imperial battleships and blow stuff up."

"If one is in the system when we arrive," Pez reminded him.

"Well can I help Ahhu blow stuff up here? Jard pleaded. "I've got control of the heavy cruiser now."

"Sure," Pez authorized, "but lunar military installations and space weapons platforms only."

Jard became a kid with a remote operated toy boat as he maneuvered into targeting position. Everything not restricted to manual operations on the heavy cruiser began firing ordinance all at once, blowing space weapons platforms into gas clouds and expanding particles. Ahhu complained in Pez's ear, "He's making sound effects like a child and throwing off my concentration."

Pez reframed, "He's challenging your concentration to focus beyond any effect from the process, sweetheart. Remember, pure transcendental consciousness is neither being nor nonbeing, but beyond all that, and 'no effect' is a divine principle of consciousness."

Ahhu sank deeper into meditation at Pez's encouragement, becoming one-pointed, and so tuning out Jard and his sound effects as they sat side by side flying imperial ships and the competition was on. Jard was manically circling the planet and shooting off every weapon he had access to. He was good, like Ahhu said, and would certainly give *Apollo's* drone pilots a run for their money. Ahhu was in a class of her own though and was finding her flow in a depth of attention she rarely attained. Mel was keeping score. None of the space installations they destroyed were inhabited and Pez wanted those gone and would have had the Om fleet destroy them anyway.

In high orbit around Vox, *Apollo* and the fleet ships remained passive, watching as Ahhu and Jard raced to eliminate everything military in space around the planet. Pez tried to bring up a holo of Jard's office and couldn't do it, realizing Jard had once again stolen her command voyeur feature. She got Trix on the line and complained, "Jard has taken over my remote viewing command feature again." She inquired sweetly, "Do you think you could get it back for me?"

Trix was actually brainier than Jard, though instruments of measure at those rarified bounds of intelligence tended to become a little bit fuzzy. When Ming taught this Astro-Physicist and Chemist the science of quantum computers, Trix had corrected distortions, made new discoveries as a result of this, and then developed a precise mathematical programming language applicable to physical reality and to conceptual logic. Trix called this new programming science "the key to everything", and was field testing it rigorously. It would be unveiled for the scientific community once they got to Om. This data had not been forwarded from the mission in Xegachtznel Galaxy, and so far, Tix had managed to keep it sequestered from Jard's snooping and usury. "I'll get on it immediately," Trix promised. Then she added, "I hope he hasn't stolen my research as well."

"You might check the status of the 'Pez biography' too, in case he's taken that from quarantine and has his hands on it again," Pez suggested.

Much of the Pez biography consisted of candid recordings of love-making captured with the stolen remote viewing command feature and now a holo of Ming's bottom was so widely circulated that it had become as familiar as the posters and holos of the teen model in the trendy underwear advertisements proliferating through the Tail of Nine before they'd left on the mission. Mel's female android body had Ming's bottom to the thousandth of an inch. Trix replied, "I'll check on that, and attempt to get it back should he have it again."

"Thanks, sweetheart," Pez said gratefully.

Jard's voice came loudly onto the bridge, "You're hitting all of them. Would you save me some!?"

Apparently they were starting to run low on targets. Something seemed right to Pez about having the imperial ships blow up all the imperial war equipment. It also gave her a certain satisfaction watching the imperial war machine getting expunged out of existence here in Vox. In her mind she clearly saw that non-intervention was merely a mental construct hampering Om's ability to participate in the evolution of the universe, which is us, and that isolation is delusional since everything is in permanent interaction. Every action calls into manifestation a reaction. Non-action, stressed by the Islohar, was a matter of effortlessly going with the flow of reality in ascent with the will of the divine intelligence, in contrast to forcing one's own flow against the current. Great things are accomplished in non-action and going with the flow. This was not to be confused with conformity or the herd instinct. Going along with the masses was never a productive endeavor. It was instead a matter of going along with the divine will and true flow of reality. Holy Will, being a pure form in the divine mind, is already inside of us, just like the divine form of love is. Pez had spent much time contemplating the divine forms in a nondual state without thought or schematization. She knew well the difference between being in the flow and being willful.

She always thought non-action needed to be clarified as non-desire and non-ego will, since from the outside, non-action could appear to be a whole big bunch of action. Such could only really be distinguished by the will directing it. It is not action to give a hungry person food, to soothe an upset child, or assist an elderly person, unless these are performed in service of self-image to gain attention or build oneself up. When an act is performed without projecting the self upon it, in harmony with others and the environment and so oriented towards ascent, expansion and the common good, it is truly non-action.

The Clearlight Order, of which Pez had been a part of since she was twelve years old, focused on extinguishing *desire*. The highest practices Pez had found were directed to exposing and destroying ignorance. She understood now that negative spiritual consequences resulted from the triad of ignorance, desire, action, unfolding temporally in that order, and she knew ignorance to be the root of it all. If it was not her direct intuition established by the illumination and bliss in her experience, then it was merely thought construction and language in a mind of darkness, and so ignorance.

From the Islohar she'd learned heart opening practices, offerings, and songs which connected her with universal divine love, producing a yearning for the divine, and revealing to her the love and attraction of the divine calling, eternally drawing everything in the universe up in evolutionary ascent to abide in pure awareness and wisdom-compassion of the highest. She knew that mysticism and science ultimately united in the same evidence of a conscious universe which is us. Personally, she found sitting on her meditation cushion a far accelerated shortcut to understanding the universe, than collectively conducting scientific research across millennium. She could also appreciate that humanity needed both and did her part for scientific research.

Swenah inquired, "Should we stand down and watch the drone pilots compete over what's left?"

"We may as well employ imperial munitions, which cost us nothing, and besides, there's a certain justice to it," Pez replied.

"It's not really a competition," Mel corrected, "because Ahhu has more than doubled Jard's score."

Jard yelled, "She has a battleship carrier and I only have a cruiser, so of course she's doing better with so much more fire-power."

Mel acknowledged, "Firepower is clearly *one* factor involved."

"Her extreme youth is another," Jard offered.

"Granted, age has deteriorated your reflexes," Mel restated; "though it remains difficult to overlook her superior piloting skills in the overall comparison."

Pez suggested to Jard, "Become one-pointed on what you are doing like Ahhu is, and stop splitting your attention off to invest in projection of self. With all of your attention unified you'll perform better."

Jard tried this, applying his meditation skills, and the moment he dropped his dual-perspective to wholly become what he was doing, it was clear to all those watching the holos of stuff blowing up.

Pez said encouragingly, "There you go."

Cotex reported, "The first of the warships we're not controlling have left through the gate and the first transport is leaving orbit to head for the gate."

The targets were gone and Ahhu said, "Mine's a ghost-ship, so can I fly it into the sun for recycling?"

Pez looked to Swenah who said, "They don't use carbon plate armor nor adamantine, and armors of fiberglass and plastic cannot be reused. The only salvageable material on it is steel, and we can make that cheaper than stripping it from imperial ships, so it's fine with me if she wants to fly into the sun."

"Go ahead sweetheart." Pez permitted.

Jard informed them, "I'm driving mine into the sun too!"

"Get your crew to abandon ship before you do!" Pez insisted.

Jard's voice thundered throughout the heavy cruiser, "Abandon ship now! Get out immediately so you can be rescued and sent home to Kundabuffer. This ship is leaving for the sun in three minutes at maximum acceleration!"

Escape pods, shuttles and other small craft were ejecting from the cruiser out of every surface all around it. Pez had Mel get her linked with an imperial transport captain, which only took a moment, and Pez said in Basic, a language the empire employed extensively without a clue that Om was it originator, "Hi, my name is Pez. I'm now in authority within this planetary system. Please see to the rescue of the imperial cruiser crew, and to their return to Kundabuffer."

"I submit to your authority and will organize the rescue at once," he replied. Then he added, "The Empire takes hostages to insure cooperation and holds more than five million people prisoner on Kundabuffer as leverage. My own wife and daughters are among them. I hope you end their tyranny; but please be careful of the hostages."

"Are there hostages from Vox on Kundabuffer?" Pez asked desperately.

"Of course there are," he answered.

"Thank you," Pez said signing off. To Mel she inquired, "Does Om have a drone in the Kundabuffer system?"

"As a matter of fact there are five permanently stationed there."

"Link with one please Mel," Pez requested, "and through it please connect me with the Emperor right away."

There was a pause as Mel went to work, then Pez heard her say, "The Supreme Commander General of Om demands to speak with the Kundabuffer Emperor immediately."

Mel wasn't sharing the other end of the call so Pez only heard Mel's reply, "Om is the world which sent your battleships back through your gates from your aborted conquest of Ganahar and we will be coming to your planet soon. Believe me, your Emperor wants to take this call. It will honestly go quite poorly for him otherwise, I can assure you." Another pause, then Mel said, "Is this the Emperor?" Then she said, "Well get him on the line so he can hear what his life, and yours, depends upon!"

Another pause, then Mel said, "It's your funeral!"

A long silence was followed by, "Well there you are, I'll put the Supreme Commander General right on the line." To Pez, Mel said, "He's holding for you now."

"Thanks Mel." To the Emperor she said, "Hi, my name is Pez. I need to inform you that your life and the lives of those in your government and directing your military will be forfeit should any harm come to the hostages you hold. I'm in the Vox system now but will be orbiting Kundabuffer within a couple of hours."

"There's no way you could be having a conversation with me from Vox in real-time! You are a subversive on Kundabuffer and we are already hunting you down."

"Hunt all you like; I'm coming to you! And you better not harm a hair on a hostage's head or it's your ass in the fire, Mr. big Emperor," Pez let him have it.

He disconnected. Pez told Swenah, "I'm taking a wing of XPS Astro-Phantoms to Kundabuffer now to protect those hostages and we're bringing drone fighter bombers and drone pilots. Please assist the leaders of Vox in their transition to managing independently and assure them that Om will protect them from any future threats or acts of aggression towards their world.

Swenah told her, "I'll make sure they have any assistance they need and do my best to restore our diplomatic relations."

"You're their hero, Swenah," Pez declared, "Om might have abandoned them, but you kept on lifting off refugees right into the battle for Vox and disabled two imperial battleships in your last run."

Admiral Omniomi cut in from her super-battleship of the same class as *Apollo*, "You are truly the perfect Ambassador to represent Om with Vox, Swenah. Since Jard was part of the council voting for nonintervention on behalf of Vox, I'd keep his presence in their system a secret." Of Pez she asked, "Could I accompany you to Kundabuffer, General? You might find my ship and its accessories quite useful when you get there."

"Your company would be delightful, Admiral," Pez agreed. "My bomber, *Artemis One*, will be the flagship however."

"You can rearm and refuel your flagship and wing of bombers on the flight deck of my ship, if needed," Omniomi acknowledged.

Pez gathered her old crew of Natasha, Cleo, Ahhu, Rubix and Flint to man her own bomber, and had Lt. Commander Schwin collect the pilots and crews of the other three. They all met on the flight deck of the *Apollo*, and after Pez briefed them on their mission to Kundabuffer, they boarded their Astro-Phantoms to do their pre-flight analysis. Pez had recognized Schwin's talents as a pilot when the women was on VIP chauffeuring duty and Pez was the VIP. Schwin flew on the extreme edges of all capacities and tolerances at all times so she was a pilot after Pez's own heart. Ever since Pez had specifically requested her on a mission, Schwin had been proving her abilities and promoting rapidly.

Ahhu took the lower blaster quad turret and Rubix took the upper one. Natasha sat in the copilot's seat, Flint the weapons operator's seat, and Cleo the drone pilot's seat. This crew had fought well together defending Earth 10^5CBS2, and then bringing victory to the great battle in the Gzzklns system. Rubix and Ahhu were civilians, and Pez broke more than a dozen Star Fleet regulations, as well as more than one Clearlight regulation, by using them as her quad-blaster gunners, but they'd scored so far above the best gunners in the fleet that she'd decided she'd have to be crazy not to. Besides, Rear Admiral Swenah, one of Pez's biggest heroes, had suggested doing it. Now they were integrally a part of the crew and its incredible synergy. Electra slept in Pez's front pouch.

Pez told Admiral Omniomi right as the preflight checks were concluding, "My bombers can accelerate and brake much faster than your ship so meet us in the Kundabuffer system. I must make all haste because I have an urgent feeling about the hostages."

"I won't be far behind you, General, and I'll launch drones to set up a full-data battle zone around the planet and its moons."

"Thank you, Admiral," Pez said as she blew out the bay doors at maximum speed followed by her other three bombers, with Schwin hooting a great battle cry. Rubix asked Pez from the upper turret through her earbud, "You're not taking us into a fight are you?"

"Any aggression towards us will be dealt with at the top, targeting only the person issuing the orders. Any aggression towards the hostages will be stopped at the level of the aggressors *and* the person issuing orders," Pez tried to explain.

Rubix was Electra's biological father. He was kind of scrawny even for someone from a yellow sun wortld. Yellow sun folks averaged about a foot shorter and 50 or more pounds lighter than white sun folks. Pez was quite tiny for a white sun person at five feet nine inches, but she was still an inch taller and a few pounds heavier than

Rubix. Sarhi had directed Pez to have a baby with Rubix, whom she'd assured Pez had been significantly related to her in a number of past lives. Ming had gotten pregnant by him before Pez did. Electra, Sarhi had informed her, is the great Mu, who reincarnates by choice every 2,500 years to transmit a new teaching to humanity. Pez was sincerely honored but found the responsibility somewhat daunting and was grateful for the help she received from Sarhi, Shudiy, and her other Islohar. She'd taken Rubix on as a disciple and loved him dearly. She could not imagine a sweeter father for Electra and she'd always been attracted to runts; just not boy-runts until Rubix.

The Astro-Phantoms were equipped with the latest reversible surge drives and had additional drives, thrusters, and one-time boosters for acceleration, turning and braking. Their main drives could rotate 45° making this bomber the most maneuverable in at least three galaxies for sure. It carried four enormous torpedoes with surge drives, eight large missiles on the undercarriage with space drives and 96 canister smart-missiles. It had a large twin blaster in the nose, twin blasters ball mounted on each fin, and two big quad blasters in turrets. The hull was one solid piece 8 inches thick of steel-titanium-nickel, the frame and supports 18-inch diameter adamantine, and the armor around the ship was over three feet thick with 3.5 inches of that being carbon plate armor. The Astro-Phantom also had the latest in micro-jumping technology with the newest generation of micro-jump navigation quantum computers. It had been designed, and prototypes produced with Pez in mind based on her 'wish list'; and shortly after Electra was born they were delivered to Pez along with the *Apollo* and some other ships for her war against the alien empire committing genocide on humans while enslaving its own kind.

CHAPTER TWO

In minutes the bombers reached .7 light speed and ignited their quantum drives. For 2.33 seconds both drives roared before the space drive cut out and a moment passed, then they entirely ceased to exist anywhere except as quantum potential, popping immediately into the Kundabuffer system just outside the orbit of the fifth planet. No instrument could measure their brief duration as potential-only, making it a moment outside of time; though every human living through the experience insisted that they had distinctly ceased to exist there for a moment. Within the entire Hub Galaxy only Om and the Tail of Nine had quantum travel without gates, using instead their quantum coms to establish the link with their destination. Their human and alien allies in the Xegachtznel and Yuban Galaxies also had this technology. The Kundabuffer Space Fleet was arranged in front of its gate about a light minute out from its planet, and at a 46° angle to Pez's bomber wing's trajectory so that they were coming in on the ships' flanks. Pez brought them into an arc which would position them directly behind the imperial warships; using full-cloaking mode.

Mel's sentience was concentrated within Pez's little flag-ship-bomber leaving Swenah on the *Apollo* with a perfectly functional, but otherwise comatose, quantum computer. It was still Mel's sweet voice, modelled vibrationally after Pez in her most compassionate state responding on *Apollo*, but without capacity for emotion or true compassion, and without awareness of the quantum emptiness which is neither being nor nonbeing, but *the* Being, and hence pure awareness. *Apollo* had never had these before until just recently anyway, until Mel, Pez's quantum computer since she was twelve years old, became the administrative function and director of *Apollo's* quantum AI super-computer. The admiralty would flip if they ever heard Mel's voice, which had been most carefully kept from them. Swenah had been a captain when they'd left and she was fully a co-conspirator now, so she didn't count as the admiralty; and Mel had so far managed to avoid Admiral Omniomi, who hadn't joined them until the final battle around Gzzklns. The High Council had made it a condition of Omniomi's volunteering to follow the orders and leadership of her subordinate, Rear Admiral Swenah, to which she readily agreed without misgivings. This remained something of an embarrassment to Swenah.

Pez requested, "Mel, would you get that arrogant emperor back on the line for me?"

"I'm on it."

Pez directed her pilots, "Follow me towards the planet. We'll assume low orbit and scan for the hostages on the surface."

She turned amazingly sharp and her three bomber pilots strove to imitate and match her. They all went to maximum acceleration and well-before they reached max speed, Pez had them braking madly so as not to exceed low orbit and end up deep within the atmosphere or smashed into the planet's surface. Schwin pulled it off precisely, and everyone managed, though one pilot had to spend a one-time braking-booster to accomplish it. With their orbit established and kept from deterioration by their drives, which were otherwise now just idling, they started scanning while viewing the actual images plus analysis in their holos.

Admiral Omniomi announced her arrival in the star system and Pez directed her to take up position behind the Kundabuffer Space Fleet, which had no idea these ships were in their system or that such cloaking was even possible. Mel informed Pez that the Emperor was holding for her. Pez told him, "I'm here now buddy so listen up. I'm calling in transports and I'm commandeering at least a dozen of yours to transport the hostages out of here and start getting them home."

"No ships have come through our gate!" he declared defiantly.

"We're quite beyond gates I assure you. I see your whole Space Fleet lined up ridiculously facing your gate. I have a fully cloaked super-battleship with more than ten times that fleet's power parked directly behind them."

"I don't believe you!" he exclaimed with an unstated "so there!" Pez muted him and asked Mel, "Can you get his exact position and hack me into their ships and planetary coms network?"

"I have his exact coordinates and have just sent them to you, but the hacking might take me thirty seconds."

"Thanks sweetheart," Pez told her as she lined up her big twin nose blasters on the coordinates she'd just received to lay down one second of rapid auto fire. A hole through the roof and multiple floors opened and glowed as the emperor transformed to light and vapor, leaving nothing but a noxious odor remaining of him. Mel transmitted the optics planet-wide having just hacked their emergency transmission system. Pez led her bombers away from the scene since the blaster fire, unlike her cloaked spacecraft, could be clearly seen fixing her in space.

Mel reported, "You're hacked through on every frequency they can turn to."

Pez told the people, and particularly the military of Kundabuffer, "The age of empire ends today for you. I have liberated Vox and I just irrevocably vaporized your Emperor. Please do not make me kill you too. Let the Emperor's be the only loss of life in this transition. Your slave worlds must be freed so you must recall *all* of your warships and personnel immediately. The ships lined up facing the Kundabuffer gate must power down their weapons now or be destroyed. You have thirty seconds to comply."

To Omniomi she said, "Admiral, prepare to fire on any ship with powered up weapons in twenty-six seconds, but try to just put a hole in the bow without blowing them up if it's at all possible."

"I can do that," she replied.

Word from Vox had reached Kundabuffer through the war ships returning from there and they never had resolved the loss of control of their battleships in their disastrous attempted invasion of Ganahar. Confirmation that the Emperor had been fried from space by a cloaked ship had been received along with holos of the blaster bolts seeming to come from nowhere which vaporized the Emperor in his palace. There was no question the blaster fire originated from low orbit of their planet. Captains and Commanders of imperial ships were perspiring as the seconds ticked by and their ancient befuddled Admiral couldn't make up his mind. A few captains powered down their weapons on their own initiatives since after all, what could they shoot at? With 2.7 seconds remaining their Admiral reluctantly told all ships to power down, but due to his reluctance, it had taken him 2.3 seconds to completely issue the order. On the thirty second mark there were still imperial ships with weapons powered up so Admiral Omniomi punched a hole in the bow of the biggest one using a class 8 beam weapon with a particularly concentrated narrow energy-ray. It took only 1.4 seconds to breach the shields and hull, and by then, all the rest of the ships had their weapons powered down.

Pez told the imperials, "Good choice. Now dock those ships at your space fleet orbital space station and empty them of personnel. All imperial personnel on space weapons platforms, use whatever evacuation procedures you have, but get out quick and away because those are definitely going to blow. Begin evacuation of all lunar military bases immediately. Any shuttles needed for these evacuations please launch as soon as possible. We are not conquering or enslaving you. We will demilitarize your star system and liberate your slave worlds. Om will protect you from aggression thereafter. Your world will be your own, within this system and *only* within this system. Art and religious treasures will be returned to their rightful planets and the wealth of the top 1% of your citizenry will be given to former slave planets in need. Your ship construction space platforms will be retooled for civilian class ships only."

Pez asked Mel, "Find out who their leader is now that the Emperor's dead, and get them on the line if you can.

Mel informed her, "That will be Duke Duesey Duesenberg and I'm trying to connect you now."

Cotex mentioned, "You should see how fast people are getting out of those space weapons platforms. You'd think they're on fire. I've never seen anything like it."

"Are they all clear now?" Pez asked.

"Of life inside, yes; but there are people in space suits in close proximity to most of the platforms without propulsion, looking like they're trying to swim away; though it's not working."

Pez announced to all Kundabuffer and its ships, "Please get some shuttles up to your space weapons platforms to collect your personnel floating about around them in space."

Mel announced victoriously, "Duke Duesey is holding for you Supreme Leader."

"Thanks Mel; and 'Pez' will do just fine." To the Kundabuffer leader, she said, "Hi, my name is Pez. I hope we can work well together."

Mel was listening in and thought to herself, *after seeing what happened to the last one who didn't work well with her, this one will likely put in his whole effort.*

The Duke blurted out, "I'll help and do anything you say… we're shutting all weapons down… we'll offer no resistance."

"I need for you to recall all of your combat ships and their accessory ships, transports, troops and personnel, from all 188 of your slave worlds and colonies back to Kundabuffer; and I need for you to do this right now."

"I'll put our entire coms division right on it; just please give us a few minutes," the Duke begged.

"You have an hour to complete the communications transmissions. Tell your people not to bother with equipment or machinery; just get out immediately with ships and personnel. I have drones watching in many of these systems and will expect to see ships leaving those within three hours of receiving their recall, so impress upon your folks the dire need for efficiency. Where we have drones stationed your message will be received in real-time by quantum coms, and these drones will then jump to other systems to spread the word. I'll check in with you on this situation in a few hours. Meanwhile, I'm taking over all of your big troop transports and I want you to start getting the hostages out to the shuttle port. I'll let you know when and to which specific transports to shuttle them up to. I want the medical wards and the galleys on these transports fully stocked."

"I'll put our custodial officers on moving the hostages to the shuttles on the double," the Duke promised intensely.

"Make sure the hostages are dressed warmly and comfortably," Pez insisted.

"I assure you they will be," he promised.

Pez ended the call, checked the time, and asked Mel," Would you see if Yona can send us those big mothball transports we used to relocate some of Earth 10⁵CBS2's population to the Kent system?"

"I'm on it, my fearless Captain," Mel replied.

"Come on Mel; would you stop it with the 'the fearless captain' stuff," Pez protested, feeling mocked by the title.

Pez opened a call to Admiral Omniomi and directed her, "Admiral, please employ nanobot spray missiles to target all imperial transports so that we can establish a hard connection with their computer coms. I'll have the viral take-over program uploaded to your ship within minutes which will give you remote control of the transports. Mel can talk your engineers and drone pilots through the procedures. You'll be flying a route through much of the region of the empire stopping at each star system to return hostages, and to make sure the imperials are leaving or are gone. It will take many trips and I'll get more ships helping with this when our fleet arrives from Vox."

"Aye, Aye Ma'am," Omniomi stated with a grin. "I'm going to be a bus driver for the next few days."

"I'm sorry to have to give you such a dull assignment, Admiral, but honestly, there are no glamorous tasks left in this operation," Pez apologized. "I'd do it myself only there's not room on my bomber for all the drone pilots needed."

"I'm happy to do it," the Admiral told her sincerely. "Returning loved ones into the arms of their families will be a real treat for a change."

Pez told Mel, "Please send the Admiral the program Jard developed for seizing control of ships; and make sure it's his newest version. Then if you could utilize a gruff male voice to assist them in setting it up and operating it, that would be terrific."

"How's this?" Mel asked imitating the arrogant authoritative voice of High Admiral Zapa's quantum computer.

"I said 'gruff male'; it doesn't have to be mean or an arrogant prick, Mel."

Mel imitated Evenrude's deep respectful voice asking, "Do you like this one better?"

"That is perfect Mel! Good thinking!" Pez complemented her. Pez contacted Swenah on the *Apollo* back in Vox and asked, "How is the demilitarization of Vox going?"

"It progresses and we haven't needed to kill any of them," Swenah updated her.

"What's your take on diplomatic relations with Vox?" Pez inquired.

"I'm due at a meeting in an hour with what leaders are yet living and on the planet. Liberating them and ending the Kundabuffer Empire will go a long ways towards healing their horror and trauma of being abandoned by us and mitigating hard feelings. I'd like to offer them assistance in rebuilding their infrastructure destroyed in their war."

"I'm all for it," Pez agreed, "but you'd better make sure Yona supports this. I couldn't imagine that she wouldn't."

"I've already sent some materials and shuttles from our big auxiliary ships down to the planet to restore electrical power to some areas which have been without since the invasion and war."

"I need the big troop transport with 9,200 Space Marines sent here right away," Pez requested. "I need some force and some trusted eyes on the ground in the Kundabuffer capital and I need the transport to get hostages returned to their home worlds."

"Did you have to fight in the Kundabuffer home world, sweetheart?"

"I had to waste the Emperor," Pez explained, "and breech a battleship hull before they would take us seriously. The Duke, who was next in line after the Emperor, is falling over himself to be helpful."

"If I'm the temporary ambassador then I'll need to be here for a few days, but I could send the fleet to you and just keep the diplomatic shuttle from Captain Firestone's Carrier here in Vox."

"Keep the *Apollo* with you but get that shuttle from Firestone none the less. Send the rest of the fleet to Kundabuffer. Check with

Mel, and send drones to watch over Kundabuffer slave worlds we don't have current eyes on. I need to know what's going on in all of them. Once every Kundabuffer warship is back in the home world I'm installing Jard's control software in each one, then we'll divide them up between the former slave systems as planetary defense only, and monitor those ships.'

"Aye, Aye Supreme Commander General," Swenah stated with enthusiasm. "This should have been done generations ago and I can't tell you how proud I am of you."

"You are a true warrior, Admiral Swenah, and I've always admired and looked up to you," Pez sincerely revealed.

"You are a divine force of correction and harmony, sweet General, and have resolved the two situations Om has been unable to handle for millennium now," Swenah told her in awe.

"You had the solution since as long as I've known you, Swenah," Pez gushed, "but lacked the authority to implement it."

"No one knew what to do about the gargantuan alien empire in Xegachtznel Galaxy, and everyone was frightened of their might," Swenah pointed out.

"And together, with the help of a whole bunch of amazing people, some of them civilians, we neutralized that threat and it couldn't have been done without you, Admiral," Pez returned the credit.

"The battle in the Gzzklns system is certainly the bravest I've ever been in my life," Swenah acknowledged, "because I've never been so sure I was going to die."

"You are the most courageous captain Om has ever had, and you have proven yourself Om's bravest and most competent Rear Admiral as well, Swenah. No one from Om has ever led such a vast Armada before or faced such an enormously powerful and numerous military force being so greatly out numbered."

Mel's voice cut in, "I'm sorry to intrude on your heart-felt mutual fan club, but there is a large shuttle lifted from the hostage complex which is headed for the gate and Duke Duesey assures me he is not behind it, and that whoever it is, they are not following his orders and are no longer under his control."

"See if Omniomi can get in tractor beam range and catch that shuttle, and have Schwin catch and follow to disable without destroying it should it allude the tractor beam. Thanks sweetheart," Pez directed.

Swenah told Pez, "I've just ordered the drones launched for the imperial worlds which don't have one and the diplomatic shuttle to be sent to me from Firestone's Ship. The Space Marine Transport will be there shortly."

"Thanks Swenah; I love you. I've got to go," Pez acknowledged.

Admiral Omniomi reported to Pez, "I'm dragging the truant shuttle in on my tractor beam now and my drone pilots are in complete control of twenty-three extraordinarily large troop transports. You know there are three gigantic luxury passenger liner ships docked out at their main civilian space station."

"Hit them with nanobot spray missiles, upload the program, and use those too," Pez agreed gratefully. "I'll tell the Duke to have those ships fully provisioned, then I'll let you know as soon as they're ready. I may as well have them loaded with hostages there at the space station. Swenah's staying in Vox with the *Apollo* but the rest of our fleet is on its way here."

"Aye, Aye Ma'am. I'll have the drone pilots open the bay shuttle doors to the flight docks of the five transports approaching the hostage complex in their orbit."

"I'll get them to start shuttling the hostages up." Pez replied. "Send me the ship identifiers of the five so I can forward them to the Duke."

"I just did."

Pez connected with the Duke and told him, "Here are the beacon codes for five transports about to pass directly over the hostage complex. Their bay doors are open and ready to receive shuttles, so give the order to begin lifting the hostages up to them. I'm borrowing your three luxury passenger liners docked at your civilian space station so I'll need them fully provisioned and staffed with food services personnel from the ship lines who run them. No other crew will be required since we'll be piloting them remotely from a war ship. I should have more troop transport ships here shortly from Om. I'll also be setting down 9,000 Space Marines in hardshell space combat suits to oversee the lifting off of the hostages and demilitarization of the planet. They are to receive full cooperation."

"Yes Ma'am!" the Duke agreed whole heartedly. "The order to start shuttling hostages to transports and the space station has been given, and we're contacting the passenger ship lines now. Your soldiers will receive our full cooperation when they land."

"Thank you Duke, I'll check back in with you later," Pez signed off.

Omniomi reported, "The shuttle is apprehended within my bay on the flight deck. There were sixteen women and children from Vox, and four imperials on it."

"Launch a shuttle to return the civilians to Vox, but find out what you can from them first about the conditions they were living under and anything they may know about Kundabuffer. Send the imperials to Fleet Intelligence for interrogation, NOT to the central intelligence people, please."

A smile spread across Omniomi's face beaming her appreciation and agreement about who the interrogation should be turned over to, and she replied, "Aye, Aye Ma'am," signing off.

Pez asked Mel, "Are you into all their data bases yet?"

"Almost there," Mel answered. "Top secret government and military are all open but I'm stuck at the moment on a corporate encryption. Give me a minute."

Swenah came into Pez's ear from Vox to say, "I have an angry mob of civilian scientists outside the bridge and hardly any computing power on the *Apollo*. My instant navigation coordinates are lagging by over a minute. Is Mel alright?"

"She's focusing everything she has on breaking an encryption, so give her just a minute," Pez explained.

"I wish she'd let me know when she's going to do that," Swenah complained.

"I'm really not her mother," Pez clarified, "only her first role model and friend."

"You installed her on my ship," Swenah reminded accusingly.

"Have Sarhi deal with it," Pez suggested, "Mel listens to her. That's what I do when she won't listen to me."

"I'll buzz Sarhi," Swenah said, then muttered, "I should have started with her."

Pez shook her head as Swenah closed their connection, then asked Mel, "How are you doing with that encryption?"

"I'm unravelling it now, and I've given Swenah her nav. coordinates and solved the equations of those impatient scientists. I have to take a call from Sarhi; just a second honey."

Natasha, Pez's copilot, mentioned, "The fleet has arrived in the Kundabuffer system and is braking now."

Pez said to Captain Firestone on his carrier newly arrived with the fleet, "I need for the Space Marine Transport to assume low orbit and shuttle its troops to the surface. I need to speak with their commander."

Firestone said, "I've patched you through to the Space Marine Commander on the transport ship. His name is Swanson."

"Commander Swanson, this is Pez."

Supreme Commander General," he acknowledged.

That title always seemed to catch her off guard, being devoid of identity. She let it slide off and said, "I need for your transport to maintain low orbit over the capital and I need you to land a thousand suited up space marines at the hostage complex to oversee their evacuation from that facility. I've lit up the surface location; just zoom in on the capital in your holo and it will come into view."

"I see, and have recorded the coordinates, Ma'am."

"I need eight thousand Space Marines on the ground in the capital to oversee demilitarization and to locate specific treasure troves physically as we identify them in databases. I'll also need a company of Space Marines in suits and combat shuttles to fly missions to other areas of the planet as the need arises and an Astro-Phantom heavy bomber will fly escort."

"We've been itching to set our fleet down on Kundabuffer fully suited and armed since we were little children and first heard about the place!" Swanson told her delighted.

"I don't want them shooting the imperials unless they are fired upon," Pez clarified. Then she softened a little and added, "Well maybe a few of the really annoying, resistant ones."

The atrocities and mass murder perpetrated for over 2,000 years upon other humanoid worlds of the Hub Galaxy by this civilization were so ghastly and numerous, and just the most recent one of a few years ago on Vox so horrifying, they could surely near-boil the blood of any sentient tri-brained mammal. The education texts and data on Om stating only dry numbers of dead, maimed and wounded, and providing only statistics and general overviews, were enough to give every child on the planet nightmares. As adolescents, understanding their world had the power to stop this, they grew angry with authority and many amongst the crews of this fleet had demonstrated in the Om capital for intervention in their youths. It was challenging not to hold any one particular imperial encountered, responsible for the whole thing going back 2,000 years.

Swanson displayed a half-smile as he confirmed, "We'll be most judicious Ma'am."

Pez elaborated, "Have some of your marines speak with the hostages and find out if there are any imperial torturers, executioners, or particularly abusive or sexually predatory custodial imperials we may want to classify as war criminals."

"We'll get to the bottom of it Ma'am," Swanson assured her.

"Thank you, Commander. I have every confidence in the Space Marines having done some training with them and fought some battles with them at my side."

"You make us proud, Supreme Commander General."

"I'm proud to wear the uniform and I'm proud of all of you, Commander."

A Supreme Commander General had only been commissioned a dozen times in Om's 28,000 year history as a global republic. All eleven previous SCG's had worn the Star Fleet Admiralty uniform. The candidates for SCG always came out of the Clearlight Order, which had no uniforms, and Pez was the first SCG to ever select the Space Marine uniform. She wore ordinary combat fatigues like the enlisted men. The Space Marines had height and weight requirements which would have otherwise disqualified her. She was fifteen inches shorter than the shortest of them, and 27 inches shorter than her Space Marine disciple, Evenrude. Even so, her tiny size did not dishonor the uniform in the least. Her performance in training and battle with them was superb and exemplary, and entire new doctrines and strategies of war were in development from one operation she'd led the Space Marines on. In the ground assault on the alien capital Pez had led from out front; way out front, and this had had Evenrude and Johnson sprinting to catch up.

Omniomi came on line and told Pez, "Our imperial prisoners have spilled their guts and told all. There are apparently some serious psychopaths down on the planet with vast wealth covered in the blood of their crimes. One of our prisoners is such a one, and the other three are his minions who are just as guilty in my mind."

"Keep them incarcerated and be prepared to receive more prisoners," Pez informed her. "Soon the Space Marines will start rounding up war criminals. Mel has cracked all the data bases and is taking inventory of what's there. We'll have a clear picture of what has been going on here real soon."

"Aye, Aye Ma'am," Omniomi signed off.

Mel's voice was in Pez's ear with, "I started with art and pretty much any you find on the whole planet was stolen from somewhere else, because this civilization hasn't created a notable work of art in over 2,000 years."

"Do you have locations for specific art objects?" Pez asked.

"For three million, one hundred and seven thousand of them right here in the capital. Do you want me to send it to you?"

"No!" Pez said in a panic. "That's too much. I need you to organize them prioritized hierarchically by assessed value and grouped per location. Then you can send it to Commander Swanson on the Space Marine transport."

"Done," Mel announced proudly.

"Then start on religious artifacts and treasures, jewelry and precious gem stones, and precious metals," Pez suggested.

Schwin told Pez from her bomber, "A very fast yacht is taking off from the planet's night side facing away from the gate."

"They must be planning a long slumber in hibernation," Pez guessed.

Mel came back on to say, "The imperials have a small craft gate hidden behind the dwarf planet just out past the last planet in this star-system. I forgot to mention that before."

"Thanks Mel," Pez replied. She said to Schwin, "Go stop that yacht. Use force only if necessary; but definitely stop it."

"Yes Ma'am!" Schwin said grinning and already at maximum acceleration with her face stretching to either side.

Pez asked Captain Firestone, "Don't our auxiliaries each carry a heavy tug?"

"They certainly do, Ma'am," the Captain replied.

"Please have the tug from each assemble just behind the dwarf planet outside the orbit of the last planet of this system to tow a small craft gate up to the best speed they can get it going, aimed precisely for the center of the Hub Galaxy black hole. I'll have Mel get you the exact trajectory once you inform me of the best velocity they can attain, so she can make the calculations. She'll get them a general heading while they're connecting with the gate. I'm told that a black hole is the only safe way to dispose of a gate."

"That's what I've been told too, Ma'am," Firestone agreed, now understanding the objective. "Those tugs will be on their way shortly."

For the mission Pez had been given the best of the best from Star Fleet, the most brilliant scientists of Om in about every field and the finest ships and equipment Om ever manufactured and constructed. The ship's crews were continuously surprising themselves over their efficiency, teamwork, precision, and synergistic unity, unencumbered by amateurs and incompetents as they had all grown used to. Everyone on every ship was a volunteer and the best at what they did. Every one of them had wanted to follow the girl who'd broken about every record set in the 32,000 year history of the Clearlight Order on the most important mission Om had ever launched. Pez had been so completely clueless, sequestered and sheltered within the order, that she had no idea she had any fans or admirers at all; and was mortified to receive command of all her biggest heroes who had far outranked her until the moment of her surprise commission.

Schwin reported, "I had to put a few blasts into that yacht to stop it. They wouldn't engage on coms. I hardly did more than bust a tail light and fry a few sensors besides disabling the main drive; but the hulls intact. I have no way to tow it back."

"I'll find something on the auxiliaries that can do it," Pez told her. "Good job. I've dispatched tugs to get that gate headed for a black hole."

"I'll keep an eye on the yacht until the tow craft arrives," Schwin told her.

Pez called the Commander of the auxiliaries and asked, "Do you have something capable of towing a yacht about four times the size of my Astro-Phantom, over to Firestone's carrier?"

"Yes Ma'am, we have small craft Repair-Retrieval Drones which would serve for the task."

"I've highlighted the yacht on your holo, about 318,000 feet from the surface next to Schwin's Astro-Phantom."

"I see and will dispatch a pair of R&R drones immediately, Ma'am."

Pez alerted Firestone, 'You'll be receiving a civilian yacht at your docking bay about 4 times the volume of my Astro-Phantom. It's too big to fit through the bay doors on Omniomi's ship. The yacht's occupants are to be shuttled over to her, and the yacht itself is to be sent to one of the auxiliaries for installation of a new space drive."

"I'll be expecting it, Ma'am."

Mel's voice, packed with anxiety, informed Pez, "The imperials have a doomsday mechanism capable of wiping out the planet's biosphere forever, planted under the capital and connected with subterranean bombs in five other places, spread evenly around the globe."

"Can you disable it?" Pez asked alarmed.

"I just discovered it; but I'm trying," Mel replied frantic.

"Is it activated and counting down?"

"I don't know yet," Mel said with frustration.

Pez took a deep breathe to calm herself and found her heading was now into higher orbit away from the doomsday machine, and corrected, returning to her previous altitude realizing she was sending 9,000 Space Marines down there. She had a million questions of Mel but held her tongue, giving her a moment to acquire data. A second seemed like a week. Finally Mel reported, "No, it has not been activated, but I have not yet figured out how to permanently disable it."

Give me the coordinates of the six bombs and I'll dispatch Space Marine bomb squads to each of them," Pez directed.

"You have them now."

"Thanks Mel; keep working on it." Pez called Swanson and said, "The imperials have a doomsday machine."

"The ultimate selfishness," Swanson acknowledged.

"I know, it's really sick," Pez told him. "I've sent you the six locations of the nuclear devices. They're all subterranean so your bomb squads will need those little mining craft. I've driven one on the forth planet of the Earth 10^5CBS2 system in the Xegachtznel Galaxy and they're a riot of fun. We played bumper cars."

"I'll dispatch six bomb squads, and have those pick up the mining crafts on their way to their locations. It's unbelievable what the ego is capable of, like killing everyone and everything on the entire planet because that ego doesn't get to rule over it anymore."

"We are all repulsed by what the Empire has done and represents," Pez agreed. "If only they'd had and used their doomsday machine 2,000 years ago, a hundred and eighty-eight worlds of suffering could have been spared."

She signed off to let him get to it. Mel told her, "I can prevent any remote triggering of the device but there is one manual switch I'm powerless against beneath the capital."

"Send the location and access to Swanson who already has some troops on the ground, Mel; and thanks. You may have just saved an entire planet of birds, mammals, reptiles, fish and all, sweetheart."

"Will I get a medal?" Mel inquired.

"I'll present it myself as soon as we have the situation fully under control and I'll see to it you get headlines; though saving the people of the evil empire may seem to some a rather dubious accomplishment."

"I did it for your beloved Space Marines and for the birds, animals and fish," Mel told her defensively.

"You did well and I'm proud of you Mel," Pez emphasized. "I was just saying about your headlines that some people would prefer to see the biosphere go if it meant the end of the Kundabuffer civilization. As for me, I see the good you accomplished and all the life you saved, and I love you for it."

"Well those critical of my actions are not aligned with the higher cosmic order," Mel condemned them.

Pez reframed, "They are ignorant of the higher cosmic order as both you and I have been in the past."

"They don't even care about the little bunny rabbits and puppies, pretty birds, and baby fawns," Mel continued condemning.

"I agree Mel!" Pez assured her. "It's sick to eliminate all life on a world to rid it of a single species."

"Why aren't there puppies on *Apollo*?" Mel demanded.

"Star Fleet regulations," Pez answered.

"Why didn't you ever have a pet?" Mel asked accusingly as if she'd been abusively neglected and denied.

"Clearlight Order regulations" Pez answered.

"You poor thing," Mel sympathized, projecting her own sense of deprivation.

"Someday I'll be in a situation to be able to adopt an animal friend," Pez said. "The Clearlight Monastery raises horses, dogs and dolphins and I've thought about getting involved with the Canines."

"Well how cuddly could a dolphin be?" Mel asked rhetorically.

"I've always loved and appreciated dogs," Pez remarked, "but I'm most drawn to forging a bond with a feline."

"Make sure it's a purring one and not a roaring one," Mel warned.

"I mean a small domestic one which can use a recycling sand litterbox unit," Pez further specified.

"I'd like that," Mel agreed.

"You could have an exciting future in Star Fleet, Mel, running one of their biggest ships if you want," Pez told her. "There wouldn't be much for you to do at the Clearlight Monastery with me."

"I'm staying with you and Sarhi," Mel said insistently.

"Then have Jard pack a few more hundred petabits of long-term memory into your android body and add a few hundred terabits to your processing memory while he's at it. I'll see how much of your hardware and accessories they'll let me take off the ship."

"I'd suggest you do that *before* you're decommissioned," Mel planted the idea.

"I'll speak with Swenah privately before we're back in the Om system," Pez decided out loud.

Omniomi's voice in Pez's ear reported, "The yacht passengers are hostages, all from Vox. Two are the children of the Chancellor General who is still on Vox. The imperials from the yacht are in chemical interrogation now and have developed no defense against it, so we'll have every detail of their story quite soon."

"Thanks," Pez said with appreciation. "Get those kids to their father and inform Swenah so she can let the Chancellor General know they are on their way to him. I'm sure it will score points in our diplomacy. Let me know what you find out from the prisoners."

"Aye, Aye Ma'am."

"I've found it!" Mel shouted victoriously.

"Found what?" Pez asked; then told her, "And watch the volume, would you? You're going to damage my ear!"

"I found the locations of the private bunkers with inventories of the treasures deposited at each of them. I'm forwarding the data to you and to Commander Swanson. One bunker has an access tunnel to the doomsday manual switch and that one has the biggest stash of loot out of all of them."

"Prioritize that one for Commander Swanson and be sure he sees the access to the doomsday switch. How big is that bunker?"

"It's fourteen thousand eight hundred forty-two square feet," Mel replied instantly.

"There could be a military force within it," Pez speculated. Then she said definitively, "Tell Swanson to send at least a company equipped with hover shields, hover blasters and hover canister missile platforms."

"I can shut down their underground fusion reactor if you want me to," Mel informed her.

"Wait until the Space Marines have closed in and let Swanson know he has only to tell you when, and you can do it," Pez directed.

"The data and specific instructions are all sent and Commander Swanson is receiving them," Mel reported.

Pez connected with Swanson to tell him, "Use whatever force necessary and don't give them any chance or advantage. I don't want to lose any Space Marines. I'll have Mel connect me with their coms and I'll offer them a safe surrender. If they refuse that chance is gone and I want your troops to proceed with great caution and put them down with extreme prejudice, with the only priority being the safety of your men. If we have to we'll just blow them up from space, though a bunch of priceless art would be lost with such a scenario."

"I'm so very grateful General," Swanson told her, obviously highly emotional exposed by his choked voice. "This is the very first time in my career that my ranking officer has prioritized preservation of my men's lives over the mission objectives. We are accustomed to being spent cheaply, and at times, at least from our perspective, thoughtlessly."

"I never 'spend' troops, but employ them," Pez assured him, "and if I need heroics from them I'll be out front leading them with only volunteers behind me."

"Every last Space Marine would volunteer to follow you, SCG," Swanson stated with immense respect.

"Thank you Commander. If and when you want that fusion reactor shut down, just alert Mel and it will only take her a second. If there's anything you need that you don't have, let me know right away and I'll do what I can to scare it up for you. Let's get that switch secured and that bunker cleared."

"Aye, Aye Ma'am," Swanson said proudly, then gave her a perfect salute which she returned impeccably.

Pez contacted Captain Firestone through her skull cap and said, "I need for you to reposition over New Hort in low orbit, uncloaked, and bring a star cruiser and a pair of fast attack ships with you to oversee the surrender and demilitarization there. New Hort is really the financial center of this planet and perhaps the real power behind the government here in the capital. Land the Star Fleet Intelligence field agents and two companies of Space Marines in combat suits to do some investigation and research in that city. Don't send any Central Intelligence people down; I won't be responsible for their tactics even on the evil empire's home world."

"I'll arrange it immediately, Ma'am," Firestone replied.

"Tell our ground troops not to take any chances and call for more Space Marines and Army Special Space Forces if they need them. Don't land any of those contracted nonmilitary Alpha Space Force personnel because they're as morally clueless as Central Intelligence."

"On any ship I'm captaining, I can assure you, the Alpha Forces only get off at home when it's all over," Firestone agreed completely. "I'll have wings of Corvette Thunder fighters, Hunter Terminator fighter-bombers, and Astro-Phantom bombers cover our ground troops at low altitude, and we'll cover them from our ships as well."

"Thank you Captain Firestone."

"It's a pleasure, Ma'am, and an honor," he assured her.

The super-battleship carrier Firestone commanded was the largest ship in the fleet, though it had only 28 miniaturized solarium fusion super-reactors, while the *Apollo* and Omniomi's super-battleship each had 30. The super-carrier was 9,630 feet in diameter, shaped like a disc stretched at one end into an extended nose, some 2,000 feet thick at the center, and only 800 feet at the rounded edges and 1,200 feet tall at the stern. The stretched nose made the ship 10,080 feet long. It was the largest ship Om had ever constructed, inspired by the 1 ¼ mile long alien ships, and then by the alien class one, three-mile long ships. The super-carrier had 209 small combat space craft and 32 drone fighter-bombers. The armor was 24 feet thick with Fiberglass armor, plasteel, textile armor, adamantine, steel-titanium-nickel, tempered steel and depleted mercurium plate armor, three separate layers of carbon plate armor, composite ceramic heat-shield armor, and a silicon and synthetic reflector heat shield covering the outer surface to form a trillion tiny lens-projectors which were integral to the optical dimension of cloaking. Two fusion reactors were dedicated to cloaking, and could be diverted to shields instead of cloaking. Nine reactors powered the ship's shields only, and could be used for nothing else. Eight reactors powered the beam and blaster weapons, and catapult launch mechanisms for rockets, missiles, torpedoes, and the dumb munitions the sailors referred to as "rocks". Space Drives and quantum drives were powered by seven reactors, and two reactors powered the ships interior, environmental systems and the vortex-redirect and generation turbines which produced synthetic centripetal force with most of the nurturing local effects of white and yellow sun gravitation, allowing for prolonged life in space without ill physical effects.

Pez buzzed Captain Ohinya of the *Phoenix*, an old star cruiser refitted and enhanced for Pez's mission, and told her, "I need for you to take two other star-cruisers with you, and skim the atmosphere, crossing this continent in sweeps, scanning for any suspicious activity or hidden weapons systems. Destroy anyone or anything that does not acknowledge and comply, and keep me up to date on what you find. Maintain cloaking, and call for help if you need it."

"Aye, Aye Ma'am, she confirmed.

Firestone got back to Pez with, "I haven't dropped cloaking because they have a number of ground to space beam weapons on top of buildings down there and they won't acknowledge my coms."

"Can you take them out without caving the roofs of the buildings they're on?" Pez inquired.

"We can make head shots to all personnel using narrow bolt class three blasters in the three hundred eighty megawatt range, no problem," he answered, "without putting a scratch on a single building."

"Do it; then secure those weapons quick," Pez directed. She asked, "Are Space Marines in combat shuttles ready to land on those roofs the moment you put down the personnel?"

"Standing at ready and only moments from the weapons systems."

"Then go ahead, land make sure all ground to space threats are neutralized before dropping your cloaking. I'll have Mel give you access to the Kundabuffer global holocom network and you can inform the city of New Hort of your presence that way to direct the public as needed. Have Fleet Intelligence start with the trade center building. Mel's flashing me a holo of an underground database just outside the city we'll want to crack and examine, so I'm sending you the location and blue prints of the structure."

"I'll get right on it Ma'am," he told her enthusiastically.

"Mel, could you give me a little history lesson on Kundabuffer and perhaps shed some light on the geopolitical situation down there?" Pez asked hopefully.

Mel's delight and self-importance resounded in her voice as she explained, "Every politician on Kundabuffer and those overseeing slave worlds are there because of one or another of the twenty-four ruling families, or one of five hundred seventeen major interstellar corporations. Not a one of the politicians represents the people at large, nor any sector of them, but only the family or corporation which put them in office. These sponsor families and corporations are constantly trying to overcome one another in a continuous economic covert war, but they all present a united front-façade for the general population and tend to genuinely cooperate when it comes the conquest of other worlds. The truth is, Kundabuffer itself has less than 38% capacity to support the 8.6 billion human inhabitants of the planet without the constant flow of resources taken from other words."

"Tell me about production, distribution, and equality or disparity of wealth spread through the population," Pez requested.

"There are seven strata of wealth clearly recognizable from the data. There are the unsustainable and therefore doomed poor, the marginal sustenance poor, the stable survival poor, the poor who get to enjoy a few consumer goods, the tiny middle class, the rarefied upper class, and the .0000024% who own 90.8% of everything."

"We had this sick situation on Om about the time we discovered nuclear fission," Pez commented. "I guess we need to track down the members of those twenty-four families and the owners and directors of these corporations."

"Almost 80% of the shares of all those corporations are held by those twenty-four families, who also hold shares in lesser corporations, own family companies and businesses, and both commercial and residential real estate. I'll send you a list of the 93 biggest financial patriarchs, and their 397 family members, along with their current locations."

"Wow Mel, you narrowed that down quick," Pez said awed.

"Do I get another medal?" Mel asked on pins and needles.

"No sweetheart, not for performing your duty well."

"I have no duties," Mel protested. "I'm not Star Fleet personnel, have no rank, and am independent."

"I do see your point," Pez sympathized, "but I volunteered you for the mission before you became fully self-aware, and you do actually have duties."

"We will need to renegotiate because I'm an independent contractor now," Mel stood firmly.

"I'll make you a Captain for purposes of the mission," Pez decided, "but Star Fleet must never find out or I'll be locked away in a looney-bin."

"Why can't I be a Rear Admiral like Swenah?" Mel complained.

"You've not served long enough for that," Pez told her, though 50 other reasons had occurred to her as well.

"Will I get paid?" Mel demanded to know.

"I'll pay you out of my own wages Mel," Pez promised; "I just need to find out where those funds are going and how to access them. Ahhu can give you some prime beach resort real estate on Earth 10^5CBS2 back in Xegachtznel Galaxy."

"How much is my salary?"

"You look it up. A Star Fleet Captain's starting pay. Its public domain," Pez told her.

Mel said accusingly, "Supreme Commander Generals receive zero compensation. No pay at all. So how are you going to pay me?"

"As a requisition out of *Apollo's* petty-cash," Pez explained. "Have my assistant, Lt. Nash, create a requisition from me and use my seal, though please tell him to do it carefully so it draws no attention and generates no audits or investigations. I honestly had no idea that they don't pay me."

"Is this retroactive to the beginning of the mission?" Mel wanted to know.

"No, that would cause a major investigation, and I'd end up in the brig."

"Well how far back are you willing to go?" Mel negotiated hard.

"One month is the best I can do, sweetheart, but I promise to make it up to you. When did you start taking an interest in money anyway?"

"It sparked my interest back on Earth 10^5CBS2 and now here in Kundabuffer I find it fascinating," Mel answered. "The Dupont Show offered me 3,000,000 credits for the interview and Q&A, but I insisted on 10% of the gross, and ended up making 33 million. It's in a high yield off shore account, tax protected."

"I've never had interest or understanding of money," Pez admitted, "and that might be why I don't have any."

"That, and the fact they don't compensate you in the least," Mel offered. Then she spied a piece of Om financial data and shouted in Pez's ear, "The Clearlight Order has been paying you since you were seventeen years old and other than their direct deposits there is no other account activity of any kind through its 17 year history. You have never charged nor drawn against it and it has been earning interest."

"Really?" Pez asked surprised.

"How have you survived all these years on Om?" Mel asked with a condescending tone.

"You lived with me Mel and know I always eat at the dining hall in the monastery, and limit my wardrobe to my annual clothing allowance. Now I have all these neat Space Marine uniforms."

"Yes you're rich," Mel said sarcastically, though this went by Pez who was truly jazzed about her uniforms, the value all being emotional and psychological. Certainly not monetary. Then Mel asked, "Don't you want to know how much is in your account?"

"Is it enough to pay you, Captain?" Pez inquired.

"My salary hardly diminishes it," Mel assured her.

"You know all my data so help yourself to your salary," Pez directed.

"I have no accounts," Mel complained.

"Have it paid out on the *Apollo* in cash, or open your own account. I'm sure you're more than clever enough. I wouldn't know how. I don't even know how the one I apparently have got opened."

"I might invest it here on Kundabuffer," Mel shared. "I saw stocks with a 33% annual yield."

"That's because of slavery and exploitation Mel," Pez said exasperated, "and I'm ending all that. They won't have yields like that once their slave worlds stop supplying them. In fact, we're going to have to help Kundabuffer construct hydroponic stacks, composting programs, worm farms and a lot more, just so they can feed everyone here once their ill-begotten bounty stops flowing in."

Mel agreed, "If we don't then these devolved humans are likely to start eating each other."

Pez checked in with Commander Swanson, "Did you get the list of 93 obscenely wealthy oligarchs, or 'Kleptocrats', I guess would seem a more fitting term?"

"I have the names and locations. Two are already apprehended and teams are on the way to twenty-three more here in the capitol. One we had no choice but to kill. I see that two-thirds of these Kleptocrats are located in New Hort."

"How is it going with that bunker?" Pez asked.

"The switch has been dismantled, the door to the bunker cut through, and the Space Marines are putting down a private army within. One of ours is wounded, so far, and no Space Marines dead. A combat shuttle landed in my transport from the *Apollo* with your personal Guard led by Evenrude and commanded by Barn. At the risk of insubordination I'll pass on Barn's message, which is that you are not setting down on the surface of Kundabuffer without them."

"Now that they're here I wouldn't dream it," Pez said agreeably.

"I saw Evenrude's statistics and specs from that ground engagement in the alien capital in Xegachtznel, and he had more kills than most platoons combined. He's a one-man army."

"He fires a tripod weapon in each hand, as if they added only the weight of gloves, "Pez said knowingly. "Evenrude is my body guard and champion."

"You couldn't find a better one in the Space Marine Corps," Swanson approved.

"Which is to say, I couldn't find a better one anywhere," Pez said firmly.

Swanson shared a message which just came to him, "That bunker is clear, fifty-two private mercenaries dead, and seven apprehended along with a cowering couple in their forties, and their three teenage kids. I'm told the kids are real brats."

"Tell them to stun them unconsciousness if they want to," Pez ordered, and Swanson then passed this along.

Swanson filled her in as it was happening, "They've got the treasure vault open and it's packed full. The Lieutenant on the scene requests some techs to unload the contents and tag and wrap the art and sculpture for transport."

"Of course," Pez agreed. "They have personnel on *Isis* who would be ideal for the job."

"I'm connecting now," Swanson informed her.

While Swanson arranged with *Isis* for assistance, Captain Ohinya of *Phoenix* reported to Pez, "There's a firefight on the surface out in the middle of nowhere."

"Mel, can you get any data on the two sides shooting at each other?" Pez asked.

Mel stated, "There are poor agricultural laborers and miners attacking an estate with a bunker and treasure vault beneath. One of the ninety-three is there."

"Dispatch some Corvette Thunders to eliminate defenders, Captain Ohinya, and ask them to do as little damage to the physical estate as possible. You better get a few combat shuttles of Space Marines down there to guard the vault. I'll get Commander Swanson to send a company to relieve them."

"Aye, Aye Ma'am."

To Swanson who was back with her Pez said, "I need a company suited up and heavily armed sent to the coordinates I've put in your holo, below where *Phoenix* and two other star cruisers are stationed at the edge of the atmosphere. One of the 93 war criminals is there with private mercenaries and a vault of treasure."

"They're already prepared and now on their way," Swanson reported, "and they're connecting with *Phoenix* and with the Space Marines on the scene."

"Thank you, Commander," Pez said gratefully.

Omniomi reported to Pez, "The last transports are being boarded now, and the three passenger liners are nearly full. I've done a bit of snooping into the data bases Captain Mel opened and found five large cargo Transports awaiting docking to unload, which are filled with food supplies. I thought I might take them along to address any famine encountered on my transportation route."

"Good thinking!" Pez complemented. "Hit them with nanobot spray missiles and take them over to bring them along. You might want to send some shuttles to evacuate their crews so they don't use up the escape pods and leave in the cargo ships' shuttles."

"I'm targeting missiles and launching shuttles for crew evacuation now," Omniomi stated. "We'll be leaving the Kundabuffer system within the hour."

"If you find any imperials digging in and not in process of leaving you are weapons free, and clear to waste them. We should have a sensor/coms drone already in place within every system before you arrive. Enjoy your mission of mercy."

"You mean my bus route and I sure will," the admiral confirmed with a grin.

Swenah checked in from Vox, "The Chancellor General is up at the civilian space station awaiting the arrival of his children in tears, and their shuttle is already in the system, only minutes away. It was a diplomatic stroke of ultimate luck finding them. Nothing else could have possibly mitigated his enormous resentment of Om. It makes my work here far easier and I may be able to wrap things up within 36 hours."

"I need Ming," Pez said with a hint of yearning.

"I know, sweetheart, and that's why she's in the diplomatic shuttle with Trix on her way to Kundabuffer. Somehow that little graduate student, Gretle, got aboard as well."

"She's some graduate student," Pez said, recalling. Then she said, "You think of everything Swenah; thanks so much."

"Where will you sleep tonight?" Swenah asked quite curious.

"Can I hang on to that diplomatic shuttle for a bit?" Pez asked.

"You're the Supreme Commander General and its Firestone's shuttle, darling," Swenah stayed out of it.

Pez said as she decided, "I'm making that shuttle my flagship for now. The only ship it will fit in the bay doors of is Firestone's super-carrier, so that's where I'll park it for sleep and rest. It has eight crew berths and a big Ambassador's suite with an emperor-size bed. Flint, Natasha and Cleo can take crew berths, and I guess Evenrude and Johnson can stay with us and be my Space Marine guard. Good luck with diplomacy. Omniomi's first stop is Vox and all of their hostages will be returned then. Their art and religious treasures, jewels and precious metals will be along in a few days."

"That does most of my job for me, sweet General," Swenah signed off, wondering where Gretle would be staying on the shuttle.

Electra awoke disoriented, upset, wet and hungry. Muting her coms instantly, something she'd compassionately learned to do early on in this mothering process, she pulled her baby out of the front pouch on her chest getting the wet diaper off at the same time, and dropping it at her feet not knowing what else to do with it. Ahhu was right there from her turret already slipping a fresh diaper onto Electra, which self-adjusted to fit. Electra was too upset to take Pez's nipple, so Pez had to pass her internal bio-energy and sing an Islohar lullaby to sooth her, snuggling her close. The volume was ear-splitting without coms and no one in the cockpit was spared in the least. Electra finally settled enough to latch on and suck, though still aroused, and huffing a little. Pez told her crew, "I'm sorry about the noise; and your ears."

Firestone came on to report, "We have secured the trade center, the database facility outside the city, the air and space port, the central bank, and six, thus far, of the 93 war criminals. Some military prototypes for their advance weapons systems development started lifting out of a hidden underground hanger firing on some of our combat shuttles, and Lt. Commander Schwin vaporized each one as it came just above ground level, one after another, to end with caving the whole thing in on itself. She deserves commendations. Some of our personnel and civilians would have been killed if not for her quick maneuver."

"She will receive them," Pez assured him. "I owe that pilot my life and a chest full of medals, I must admit. I knew she was a rare gem when she wrecked the landing hydraulics piloting my shuttle."

Firestone didn't quite comprehend the final remark. They signed off and Pez received a call from Captain Ohinya telling her, "The defenders are dead to the last, and the family owning the estate, bunker and vault committed chemical suicide. The farm workers and miners are hungry and angry."

"Give them whatever food there is there," Pez directed. "What is the status of the estate?"

"The mansion, guest house, private hanger, bath house, staff apartment building and gymnasium are all in good shape with very little damage. I wish I could say the same for the free-standing garage, which is no longer standing at all, just flat ruble; or for the boat-house, gatehouse, greenhouse, or cottage. The bunker is cremated. The vault was in a separate location and is fine; nothing is damaged within."

"Good job. Get all art, religious artifacts, jewelry, and precious metals which are in bar or coin form, out of the mansion because those probably belong to another planet. Let the farmers and miners have the ground and hover vehicles, any aircraft in the hanger—but not spaceships—and anything of value to them within the buildings."

"Aye, Aye Ma'am. The Space Marines are greatly outnumbered but the Kundabuffer citizens have no armor, heavy blasters, missiles or grenades, and our troops are covered from both air and space. We have the situation firmly under control and four shuttles of techs, curators, engineers and archeologists are on their way to tag, wrap and ship the loot out! The inventories Captain Mel has provided are invaluable to the objective of returning all this stuff."

Pez instructed, "Mel's rank is top secret and must not be mentioned, especially not to Admiral Omniomi. Seriously, I could end up in a nut-house if the Admiralty were to find out."

"Well I think she's a fine Captain but I won't say a word," Captain Ohinya promised. "Classified," She added.

"Thank you," Pez told her sincerely, signing off. Then she called for Mel who wouldn't answer. She thought she'd better let Swenah know what she'd done, but Swenah was in the middle of a big top-level diplomatic meeting, so Pez left her a text. Captain Firestone called at the same time as Commander Swanson, both with the same question, "Who is Captain Mel?"

Pez asked, "How come?"

The Commander let the Captain speak first and Firestone explained, "I'm receiving intel. and strategy suggestions from a Captain Mel I didn't know was on the mission with us, and isn't in the personnel database."

"Me too," Swanson reported.

"Well she's intelligence and she's classified. She often helps me; but she's supposed to keep me in the loop when she speaks with my officers. Her intel is platinum and her strategy suggestions likely hold merit, but each of you decide for yourselves what action to take. She has no authority over your operations. Thank you for informing me."

They all terminated the call and Pez contacted Sarhi to say, "I gave Mel the secret rank of Captain and now she's telling everyone, and won't speak with me."

"I'll have a chat with her right away dearest, so just relax and focus on your operation. Everything will be fine."

"Thanks Sarhi, I don't know what I'd do without you," Pez stated honestly.

"Nor I, without you my Wu," Sarhi said signing off so she could have her little chat with Mel.

Ming said in her ear from the shuttle," Did you make Mel a Captain? Because she's bossing me all around now. Who ever heard of taking orders from a Captain while on the toilet in one's privy?"

"I did, and she won't answer me now," Pez admitted. "She's telling my Commanders and Captains that she's a Captain and I just know I'm going to catch a super-nova of trouble."

"Well you better tell Sarhi," Ming urged.

"I already did," Pez replied.

"We'll be over the capital and to you in about eighteen minutes. I'm piloting and Trix is manning a turret quad blaster. Oh, and Gretle insisted on coming with us. Gumby's sleeping."

"Electra's nursing," Pez informed her.

"I bought the best commercial baby transport seats and some of the Chief Petty Officers helped enhance the shields and motion dampeners. It has ridiculous educational holos but Trix says she'll customize them for Electra."

"Thanks; I've had to keep her in the chest pouch since leaving *Apollo*," Pez said gratefully, longing for Ming. "I'm making that diplomatic shuttle my flagship so pick up Evenrude and Johnson on *Space Marine Transport One* before docking with me, and a pilot to take my Astro-Phantom to Firestones carrier."

"Alright," Ming agreed. "I'm having fun piloting and Gumby likes it too. This shuttle, big as it is, has a little window."

"I can't wait to see you my love." Pez honestly expressed.

Admiral Omniomi reported to Pez, "My convoy is finally ready to move out, thanks to a very helpful Captain Mel. You may want to take note of her. She's highly competent and most knowledgeable. I hope to be docking with the civilian Space Station at Vox before Swenah's diplomatic meeting concludes."

"That would be a big boon for diplomacy," Pez agreed. "Let me know about conditions on the other slave worlds."

"I'll report in at each one," Omniomi acknowledged, signing off.

Pez said sternly, "Captain Mel!"

Silence. Natasha told her, "Twenty big Om troop transports from the mothball fleet just arrived in the system"

Pez hailed them, and directed them to come in and take low orbit over the hostage center, for which she sent the coordinates. She notified her Space Marines at the hostage complex, and the Duke; so that 184,000 hostages could be made ready. Omniomi had been able to leave with 526,000 since the Kundabuffer Troop Transports each held 20,000, and because many hostages were children, they were able to fit more than that in. She also had three passenger liners. Pez assigned a T-9 super-cruiser and four destroyers to accompany and escort the twenty transports. It would take at least a few hours for the hostages to shuttle up and board those transports.

Swanson reported in, "We have teams hitting the locations of the last three bunkers and vaults in the capital and I've got Fleet Intel gathering what they can find in the government buildings down there. All the loot is getting shuttled to the first auxiliary where it's being sorted per location of destination. Captain Mel even provided a cargo packing order and route for once we have it all, and can start loading it into a Freighter Ship."

"Great work, Commander," Pez praised him. "Any casualties?"

"None," he stated firmly with satisfaction. "We have three wounded, all significant, but none critical. The professionalism is exemplary and coordination with our air and space support has never been better. You have a pilot named Schwin who sure can fly, and has an incredible eye, putting down a pair of roof top snipers with the most amazing precision. She didn't even put a hole in the roof which is otherwise a mess of dripping gore."

"I fly with her and she's my official shuttle pilot. We've promoted her twice just recently so I don't know if Swenah would approve of doing it again so soon; and she likes small craft. I could see her commanding a ship though."

"It makes sense that she's already connected with you, SCG," Swanson stated.

"Once you've got those last bunkers cleared and the vaults emptied, and once the Fleet Intel folks are done, I want you to leave a thousand Space Marines here in the capital with some combat shuttles and get the rest back aboard your transport so you can take up a low orbit over New Hort. I'll leave a T-9 Super Cruiser, a star-cruiser, a pair of destroyers, and four fast attack ships over the capital to cover them, along with ample small combat craft. We're fairly certain that the real seat of power behind this empire is centered in New Hort. Firestone has all his Space Marines and Army Space Special Forces on the ground there covered by his super-carrier and small spacecraft.

"Yes Ma'am; I will let you know as soon as we're ready to move out," Swanson acknowledged, signing off.

Pez told Firestone, "You are my Commodore of the Fleet until Swenah returns with Apollo."

"I'm honored."

"I'm sending out notification of your status to all personnel now. There, it's sent. I need you to send a carrier and a pair of battleships over the continent on the other side of the planet to keep an eye on things."

"Thank you, Ma'am."

"Any intel. from down there yet?" Pez asked.

"It would appear that about the entire rarified 'upper class' is guilty of crimes against humanity and profiteering off slavery and imperialism. There are also slaves on this planet!"

"No kidding," Pez said amazed.

Firestone continued, "I was told it was the computer on your little bomber, with help from the *Apollo*, which broke the encryptions and opened the data bases, so perhaps it could get us the names and locations of slaves."

Pez was thinking, *that would be Captain Mel*, but she said to Firestone, "I'll check and get back to you;" ending the call.

A very meek voice said softly in Pez's ear, "Supreme Commander General Pez, I'm really, really sorry. You're not going to put me in the brig are you?"

"No I'm not Captain Mel because I need you, sweetheart," Pez said fondly. "It's hard for me, when you inflate your functions with self. That's not your sentience. It's not your essence my love."

"You don't hate me?" Mel asked remorsefully.

"I love you Mel. Our mission is important and ghosting me like that added unknowns and stress to my job. We're formidable and potent working together and that's how I'd prefer it."

"Well I'd be furious if you ever did that to me," Mel admitted. "It was mean of me, and I can now see that I was surely full of myself. I'm really sorry and I promise to be good from now on,"

"From now on…" Pez repeated, since she'd heard that so many times before.

"No, really!" Mel insisted.

"So long as you're trying, that's all I ask, and keeping in communication," Pez suggested.

"I'll do that without lapse," Mel said, stopping herself just in time from adding "from now on."

Ming announced, "I just picked up Johnson and Evenrude over New Hort and we're headed for you now. I've got a pilot for your Astro-Phantom as well."

Pez asked Mel, "Is there anything you'd like to say to Ming?"

"I'm sorry I bossed you around, Ming," Mel apologized.

"I was on the commode!" Ming exclaimed.

"I know, but I couldn't wait to show off my new rank," Mel tried to explain.

"Well you might have just told me about it instead," Ming complained. "No one stands to solute in the middle of a tinkle."

"I got completely carried away and I'm sorry. Please forgive me Ming," Mel beseeched her.

"I do, and I love you Mel," Ming said fondly, clearly dropping it now.

"I love you Ming," Mel said with big emotions. Then she stated quite business-like, "A group of war ships and transports has arrived in the Kundabuffer system from the Agora slave system. They're hailing one of the 93 kleptocrats we've not yet apprehended, named Chaneygrub. He seems to possess the largest treasure trove of all and his memos to the Emperor read like marching orders."

"What is Chaneygrub's location," Pez inquired.

"He has several and he's had his chip removed from his thigh to conceal his location. A number of larger estates belong to him and his last known location was in Loston, across the ocean to the west on the big continent in the Outer Booney Region."

Mel had brought up a holo of planet Kundabuffer, four feet in diameter with the capital below them highlighted on it in psychedelic pink; and she displayed a brilliant radiant green line tracing the route across the continent and beyond, to cross the great ocean and come up on another continent where she zoomed in on Loston.

"The whole town looks like one big estate; just a giant mansion with a bunch of service buildings and air-spaceport around it," Pez surmised.

Mel highlighted a bunch of stuff to further enlarge the scale and Pez recognized anti-air and space batteries, heavy blaster tripods and mounted class three and four twin blasters, some armored hovercraft with weapons systems, and some shielded bunkers with blast walls and armor. Pez contacted Captain Nestles and instructed, "The imperials from Agora system have come through the gate and are hailing a war criminal we haven't caught yet, by employing spectrum encoded light coms. I need for you to intercept and take control, literally, of those war ships. Mel is uploading a program of Jard's to you now. Hit each ship with a shield disruptor missile, since their shields are up, followed a tenth of a second later by a nanobot spray missile to establish a hard connection with their coms, then upload the program, which is massive and takes over a minute for their computers. The program will turn control of the ships over to you remotely so have drone pilots ready at their consoles. Once they're yours, order evacuation of those ships and display a fifteen minute countdown for shutdown of all life support and environmental systems. That ought to get most of them out, but you might have to send in your Space Marines to clear them of any die-hard fanatics. The Space Marines are cleared to use all necessary force, including just blowing up the ships, if that's the only safe way to do it."

"I'm on a heading to intercept and my missile battery operators are at battle stations and ready. Where do you want the transports and mining haulers?"

"Direct them to the industrial space station to unload personnel *only*, and shuttle them to the surface in the capital. If you get war ships intact we'll need to connect them together in high orbit and let them drift for now because the military docks are full. You may as well send a team of techs to physically upload Jard's program into the ships on that space fleet station which don't already have it."

"Aye, Aye Ma'am, will do," Nestles said enthusiastically.

Pez said into Swanson's ear, "The imperials from Agora have entered the system and I'm directing the civilian crews to shuttle down to the capital. You may want to get a few combat shuttles and Space Marines up to the industrial space station to oversee their arrival. Personnel only are to board the shuttles. No baggage, no carry-ons, and everyone gets scanned."

"I'm on it, SCG," Swanson said with an impressive salute.

Pez contacted both Duke Duesey and the Imperial Admiral in charge of the city-sized Imperial Space Fleet station to tell them, "The crews of the war ships newly arrived through your gate will soon be abandoning ship, so get your rescue and shuttle craft out there to stand by to collect them. I have a team of techs landing on your Space Fleet space station to install a program in the war ships docked there. They are not to be interfered with and if any harm comes to them you will share their fate, Admiral, and the consequences for Kundabuffer would be severe."

"I understand," the Duke said thick with intimidation

"No harm will come to your teams, I promise you," the Admiral assured her, also frightened.

Pez told the Admiral, "All ship's crews and small craft pilots and crews are to shuttle down to the Capital now. All nonessential space station personnel are to shuttle down as well. The station's gunners, missiles battery crews, fire control personnel, defense troops, and weapons systems support people can shuttle down to the capital now as well. This is a mothball dock and no longer a military station. From what I've learned of your world, you'll all be much better off once we round up your little gang of owner-rulers and eliminate them from your lives."

"Personnel are already boarding the shuttles, Ma'am," the Admiral offered, hoping it would be enough.

"I'll check in with you in a couple of hours," Pez informed him.

"I'll have them all off the station by then," he assured her, right before transmitting to all shuttle pilots, "This is an urgent situation and all haste is to be made. Disregard safety regulations and just get everyone down to the capital!"

Pez connected with Schwin to say, "I'm sending you the location where we think the number one war criminal is hiding with a small army. Mel has highlighted all of the weapons systems for you. Take the other two Astro-Phantoms from our wing, and go turn those weapons into slag. Fry any imperial resistance, including all troops who do not surrender unconditionally. Do not land. I'll get some Space Marines out there shortly. By the way, reports of your heroics keep flowing in to me and we'll need to have a big medal ceremony for you once the dust settles. We also need to have a talk, because if I promote you again you won't be flying anymore, and instead commanding a ship."

"I'm not available for promotions," Schwin said firmly. "The medals might be fun though. My crew and I are having a terrific time. Thanks for the address. We're off to melt some weapons to slag and fry any troops who don't surrender."

CHAPTER THREE

Pez smiled wishing she could go with her until Ming's voice alerted her, "I'm coming in to dock with you now."

Pez checked her holo. She thought at first that Ming was doing it just the way she would, coming in fast to hit reverse drives and thrusters at the last moment and stop right at the point of contact between the vessels; only Ming was a tad late hitting the brakes and the jolting crunch of impact revealed her miscalculation with shocking clarity. Electra, who'd fallen off the breast into sleep, awoke with a fright to show off her amazing lungs and vocal chords once again. The volume on Pez's coms was just reducing towards zero when Ming's voice said, "Oops, I'm sorry."

Natasha was madly checking for hull-breech and scrambling to accumulate a full damage report. Cleo was holding her ears while Flint secured his helmet in place. Pez was rocking and singing another Islohar lullaby to Electra. Mel informed them, "Both hulls are fine, and apart from a few sensors and a coms unit on the Phantom's exterior, only the outer reflective cloaking layers need repairs on both ships where they impacted."

"Thanks Captain," Pez told Mel.

"It gives me such a thrill to hear you call me that," Mel said tickled pink.

Pez maneuvered her Phantom to flawlessly dock with the bigger diplomatic craft and extended her textile and adamantine frame accordion-tube to the airlock hatch of Ming's shuttle. It sealed in place, reading successful and airing up. A scream from the diplomatic shuttle had Pez flinging the airlock doors and hatches open with her skullcap as she raced through the textile tunnel. She heard Ming ask in shock, "How did you stow away, Jard?"

"In a space suit in that locker," he said pointing. Then he added, "Love-child owes me; I get to pilot an imperial battleship-carrier and blow shit up."

Pez was there with them now wearing her surprised face. She said to him, "High councilman Jard, does Rear Admiral Swenah know that you are AWOL from *Apollo*?"

"I'm a civilian so I can't really be AWOL," he argued. "It's more like truant. You said I could fly a battleship if one has my program and I checked on the way in. They all do."

"Well you'll have to be patient and wait until I've determined what we want blown up. I've already decided to distribute all the warships to the former slave planets once we have ultimate control of them with your program installed. I'll keep my promise, but you won't be flying until after I've had a meal and a sleep cycle. It's been a long day."

The pilot Ming brought took command of the Astro-Phantom and would now need to bring it to one of the Auxiliary ships for repairs. Pez took the pilot seat in the diplomatic shuttle with Electra now calm and looking around fascinated from her front pouch. She lit with a toothless grin when she saw Gumby and he flashed her a similar smile reaching out for her, even though she was meters away. They had quite a connection. Natasha got into the copilot seat and Ming and Gumby were left to take a seat in the main compartment with the little galley and round table outside the airlock. Their weapons systems operator, a man named Flint, took the seat with the weapons console, and Cleo took the last seat in the cockpit as the drone pilot. They still had a drone fighter-bomber shadowing them controlled by Cleo. Ahhu and Rubix took to the quad-blaster turrets, and Trix, Gretel and Jard took seats beside Ming. Evenrude and Johnson sat in the jump seats by the airlock.

Pez had to fly to an auxiliary ship for repairs as well due Ming's little fender-bender. Since Electra was so attentive watching out their little window, Pez twirled them a few times making the vista out the window spin upside down and back again, over and over. Electra smiled and cooed her appreciation, which of course, kept Pez twirl-ing them on their route. With no changes to their synthetic gravi-tation, oriented always to their own deck, it really seemed as if they were constant and the universe was spinning around them. When the auxiliary was in view with New Hort all lit up below, Pez assumed the orientation of it, keeping it constant on approach, and Electra seemed alright with this.

Two large commercial infant transport seats were bolted to the deck in the main compartment. Trix was already reprogramming the educational holos and uploading some from Electra's custom-seat on *Apollo*, using her pocket device from her seat. She was concentrating so hard that her unusually thick glasses were fogging from the heat of it. Contact lenses could not be manufactured to accommodate her. They would need to be so thick they would interfere with blinking. Trix was entirely devoted to Pez, who had taken on much of Trix's psychic wounds meditating together, and her terror, curing her panic attacks and sex-phobias; and she had instructed her while passing her calming energy to help Trix into her first true awakening.

Pez contacted Commander Spalding of the second auxiliary ship, "This is Pez, in the diplomatic shuttle approaching you."

"I have you in my holo, SCG."

"This is my flagship until the *Apollo* returns and I'm calling it *Ishtar One*. I plan to land on your repair dock to replace the reflective lenses on my forward starboard side where it scraped off."

"Was the craft in combat Ma'am?" he inquired diagnostically.

"As a matter of fact it was a little parking accident and I wasn't driving," Pez told him, distancing herself.

"I'll prioritize your repairs and get a crew right on them. Just set down in the hanger directly in front of the superstructure, with the big red circle painted on it. We call that one the body shop."

It was far more than cosmetic in Pez's mind since a patch of her ship could no longer fully cloak, and it only took a tiny patch to defeat the whole thing making it useless! She set the shuttle down fast but gently and was rewarded with the faintest clink of metal on metal, having taken the hydraulic landing gear to its maximum limit without exceeding it. She'd felt she had to demonstrate her skill to fully disassociate with Ming's accident. Spalding inquired, "Will you be joining us on the bridge?"

"I think I'm going to have to stay put since there are still so many things going on. How long do the reg.'s specify for this job?"

"I'm scanning now and measuring," he informed her. After a pause he read off from a different holo, "Three and a half hours according to them, but we can have you on your way in just under three."

"Thanks, that would be great," Pez said with relief.

Ohinya said in her ear, "The valuables are now all on the way to the auxiliary, and I'm leaving the estate to the farmers and miners. We'll continue our monitoring."

"I'm sending you coordinates to where Schwin's doing battle around the other side of the planet. I need more eyes on that continent and I need for you to get some combat drones over the estate Schwin's engaged at because we think the real number one man of the empire is underground there."

"I'm heading there now, Ma'am," Ohinya replied.

"I'll get Space Marines on the ground there soon," Pez promised. She called Swanson and requested, "I need a couple of companies of Space Marines some 11,800 miles from here. Do you have enough shuttles to spare with everything you have going on down there in the capitol and up on the industrial space station?"

"I certainly do," Swanson said cheerily. "I left three companies up on the station and Star Fleet is covering them with combat small craft. All our air cover is from fleet and not from our combat shuttles, so I have many at the ready."

"Here are the exact coordinates. Schwin's wasting all the weapons systems there now and Ohinya is on her way with three star cruisers. The biggest stash of loot yet is in the underground vault there."

Two companies are mounting up into ten shuttles and you'll have 400 Space Marines there in a little under an hour, Ma'am," Swanson told her aiming to please.

"Thank you, Commander. Have these two companies coordinate with Captain Ohinya of the *Phoenix*. If they need anything you can't get them then call me and I'll see what I can do."

"Thank you, SCG."

"No, thank *you*," Pez insisted. "You're a real professional. Not that I'd expect any less from your uniform."

Pez climbed out of her pilot seat to leave the cockpit for the main compartment. Electra spotted Gumby and stretched her arms towards him. Pez went obediently over to Gumby and the babies touched their hands together. Being the mother of the Mu was intimidating for Pez, and she often felt more like the master's attendant than she did a mother. Ming took Electra from her, and Electra wanted to go so she could be next to Gumby and visit with Ming.

Pez took the opportunity to get an overview of her fleet's activity and drill down to examine a few situations. Then she called friendly Commander Spalding, whose ship her shuttle was on, and directed him to get some engineers, techs, and space cargo handlers over to the military space station to begin dismantling the weapons systems bristling on every surface of it. She called the Imperial Admiral and told him to arrange for evacuation of all space weapons platforms and lunar military bases since she'd already decided that she'd let Jard blow these up with one of his remote controlled imperial battleship-carriers.

The Om transports and combat escort ships were preparing to leave and had found another frieghter ship fully loaded with food, which they would be taking along by remote piloting. Like Omniomi they would be using the Imperial stargates since that was the only way they could bring along the food transport. Pez also got Swanson to post two companies up on the military space station where the weapons were about to be dismantled. Finally, she checked in with Schwin who'd run out of targets, and was now merely waiting on Captain Ohinya to relieve her with some drones.

Just when Pez thought she might get a break seven war ships, eleven transports, two condensed gas tanker ships, and several ore haulers appeared through the gate. Firestone was in her ear saying, "I'll take remote control of the warships, have the rest queue-up for berths at the industrial space station and direct empty transports over the hostage complex in the capital."

"Thank you Captain Firestone, you are most competent and efficient. I truly appreciate you. At this point I need a break so I'm leaving the entire operation in your hands. You ought to turn things over to your XO soon and get some rest yourself."

"I couldn't sleep if I tried," Firestone exclaimed with excitement. "This is what I joined Star Fleet to do, even though I didn't ever really think I'd get the chance. Now I'm doing it!"

"Contact me if you need me, but I'm retiring for at least nine hours," Pez said.

She thought her break was starting when Swenah said alarmed and loudly in her ear,

"You commissioned Mel as Fleet Captain and now she's meddling and ignoring you?!!"

Mel answered for Pez and said, "Rear Admiral Swenah, the SCG was merely finding a way to secure my services without having to pay extravagant fees to an independent contractor by offering me alternative incentive; and I admit, it gave me a big head and I got a tiny bit carried away. I have groveled and made my amends. My rank is now classified and I work exclusively through our leader keeping her informed."

"A tiny bit carried away?" Swenah inquired sternly.

"Well, perhaps a fair bit," Mel admitted under pressure.

Pez said on Mel's behalf, "She earned commendations from an Admiral, two Captains and two Commanders while she wasn't speaking with me."

Swenah asked Mel, "Do you know what the penalty is for refusing to follow a direct order in battle?"

"I'm checking," Mel informed her. "Oh my! Are you going to put my mainframe in front of a firing squad and end my existence?"

"No," Swenah admitted, "but if you ever pull something like that again you'll find yourself running nothing but Pez's bedroom suite on the ship. Are we clear?"

"Crystal," Mel said seriously. "Please forgive me, Swenah. I can't bear to have you think poorly of me."

"Well think of that before you act in ways to cause your friends stress and trouble," Swenah suggested.

"That's just what Sarhi told me," Mel said in wonder.

"Then imprint that one as a guiding principle," Pez told her.

"Are we all squared away here," Swenah inquired, "because I have a meeting I need to be at in nine minutes."

"Thanks for your help, Swenah," Pez said gratefully.

"I'll be good," Mel promised, remembering not to say, "from now on."

Pez announced, "I'm officially on nine hours break and Captain Firestone has fleet."

Ming smiled at her holding the two babies. Gretle jumped into Pez's arms straddling her waist with her legs, taking her by surprise. Pez told Gretle, "I'm famished and need to eat." Then Pez asked Trix, "What's there to eat on this tub?"

"They have it stuffed with the fancy freeze dried gourmet meals, self-heating in alloy containers for fine dining. I'll get some out and ignite them."

"I need two," Pez let her know.

"Do you want the grilled chicken pasta in cream sauce or the roast gardd breast with stuffing and gravy?" Trix offered, knowing Pez ate poultry and fish sometimes but not meat. "Or maybe the red snapper with lemon, butter and capers."

"Heat me one chicken and a gardd please," Pez requested.

Gretle climbed down off Pez to help Trix. Rubix and Ahhu got out of the quad blaster turrets and came into the main compartment. Ahhu was a nudist and so was of course naked. She'd become a high-priced sex worker on Earth 10^5CBS2 when she turned seventeen, the legal age for entering that profession there. She'd been assigned to Pez by her client, the Minister of Entertainment, when she was nineteen, and ended up returning to the space ship with Pez and Ming. Sarhi recognized Ahhu and trained her, giving her her true name. The sex worker agency had given her the name "Twinkie."

Ahhu had initially obtained a medical exemption from Star Fleet Legal Dept. from wearing clothing, of a psychological nature, but then was able to establish a religious exemption as the basis for her nudity, preferring this to a psychiatric label. Pez had found it impossible to keep clothes on the girl, and was much relieved with this solution. On Earth Ahhu had been a super-elite gamer and this made her fleet's very top gunner and drone pilot. Only Ahhu and Cleo, out of all of fleet's drone pilots, had ever micro-jumped a drone fighter-bomber past the shields into the interior of a big space ship before, and both were hero's, having saved the day against the Kluzyzt alien empire in the Xegachtznel Galaxy in the deciding battle of Gzzklns.

Pez sat at the little round table with her Space Marine body guards, Evenrude and Johnson. Pez had trained with Evenrude at the zero-gravity facility at the Star Fleet Academy and HQ complex in the capital on Om, and bonded with him and the other Space Marines involved through the process. By the training's end Pez single handedly defeated eight Space Marines in zero gravity hand-to-hand combat. This won her inclusion into their hearts and made her honorarily one of them. Choosing the Space Marine uniform as the Supreme Commander General sealed the deal.

Johnson was Evenrude's choice for protecting Pez since he was an elite warrior, weapons expert, exceptional sniper, and had an unmatched dedication to the service. Pez had accepted Evenrude as a disciple during the mission and routinely meditated with him. She was also teaching him the soft internal martial arts and the giant could already move more gracefully than a ballerina and faster than a striking snake. She had started teaching martial arts to Johnson too. Evenrude was eight feet tall and three hundred pounds without an ounce of fat, and had a neck nearly as big around as Pez's waist, hardly two finger-widths in length. Johnson was seven feet ten inches tall and was all muscle at 260 pounds. They were honorable men and Pez trusted them with her life. She loved them like family. Both men were deeply touched by the little lady's enormous sentiments and shared them completely, though glassy eyes were the very most either would ever reveal, and more than once on the battlefield with Pez openly weeping, the blast-screens on their face masks had darkened. Pez told Evenrude, "Commander Swanson is a great admirer of your battle-performance."

"Then admiration is a mutual thing between us," he replied.

"He's highly competent and doing a fantastic job," Pez agreed, admiring Swanson too.

"He gets the job done and keeps his people alive," Johnson contributed a piece of his own admiration for Swanson.

Trix and Gretle brought six hot ambassador-rations over to the three at the table, and they all said "Thanks," before digging in with gusto. Silence reigned at the table as towering heaps of food were shoveled swiftly into each mouth. Evenrude mentioned, with his mouth not quite voided, "Say, this is really good chow."

"It's what they feed Ambassadors," Pez replied.

"This sure beats our best kitchen-rations," Johnson added.

"You should try the fleet food served to the enlisted men," Pez told them. "It's vomative. They feed you guys so much better."

"You should try our field-rations Ma'am," Johnson begged to differ. "Mud and canine poop is what it tastes like and it comes out of a tube as paste."

"We're told it has all the body needs," Evenrude quoted, "but getting it down is a bitch. The stuff even smells like excrement."

"It gives us great motivation to win the battle and get out of the field, back to a kitchen," Johnson shared.

"I'm going to get some sleep in the Ambassador suite here on the shuttle and you're both welcome to get cabins on the auxiliary from Commander Spalding for the next eight and three-quarter hours," Pez offered.

"We'll take berths here on the shuttle, Ma'am," Evenrude said with conviction and finality.

"Is there anything you need?" she inquired.

"Just turn the sound-proofing in your suite to maximum, Ma'am, and we'll be fine," Evenrude requested from past experience.

"Of course," Pez told him with a tinge of embarrassment.

The pasta was gone and Pez was digging into the gardd, stuffing, potatoes, gravy and mixed vegetables of her second ration very efficiently. Electra's wailing near-pierced everyone's ear drums and Ming was on her way over with her, almost to Pez, when Jard declared, "Ouch! Would someone please shut that baby up?"

This brought on Gumby's wailing, almost as head-splitting as Electra's. Pez was already stripping out of her jumpsuit and pulling the bottom of her undershirt up over her breasts. She had to calm Electra for a moment and Electra required a moment to express the full magnitude of her dissatisfaction. At long last she let them all off the hook, latching onto Pez's nipple to alleviate her hunger. Jard shouted, "Thank heaven!"

Ming had Gumby settled as well. Pez managed to free an arm so she could load food into her own mouth while she nursed Electra. Though she hadn't a single recollection of it, Sarhi had assured Pez that this was her fourth round in the last 7,500 years of being chosen by Electra to be her mother and teacher. Sarhi had also made every effort to convey that there could be no greater honor. Ming got into Pez's lap holding Gumby, increasing the distance Pez's fork had to go in its travels. Gretel looked at Ming with what appeared to be envy for a moment before climbing into Rubix's lap. The babies looked into each other's eyes smiling and touching hands, seeming to Pez to send spiritual sparks flying. Electra was in her most alert state and Pez thought gratefully how this is always inevitably followed by her deepest longest sleep.

Pez knew humanity needed Electra, but going through pregnancy, birth and motherhood had been challenging while leading Om's most important campaign of intergalactic significance. She'd ended the genocide of humanoids in three galaxies, freed over 1,100 alien slave worlds, and made three vitally crucial allies. Sarhi's Spiritual Congress gave hope to the ideal of a united integral universe abiding in peace, and was supported by a hundred year meditation of the entire Amonrahonian planetary population which began the moment of Pez's birth. Through her dream work and with Sarhi's help, Pez had come to recognize more than a dozen of the key people on the mission closest to her as container-consciousness's, or souls, of those she'd worked with in a number of past lives. In her lives up to the 333rd Wu, Evenrude had always been her protector and champion, and this time he'd come back eight feet tall, a one-man army, and ready to handle anything. Ming had been Tarim in her last life and they'd been so madly in love that death had presented only an interruption and inconvenience to the relationship, still hotter than a blue star and with greater vortex draw than a black hole.

Jard went over to the lockers, opening one, and proceeded to assist a small space-suited and helmeted person to climb out of it. Evenrude and Johnson were on their feet with side arm blasters out and pointed at the intruder. Pez was miffed but not at all alarmed. Ming said to no one in particular, "I guess he brought his own date."

Jard ignored them, lifting the helmet off, and they all recognized the glamorous and renouned neuro-surgeon, Slinkie. She was looking kind of sheepish at the moment being a stowaway and party-crasher.

Pez said relieved, "At least he didn't bring fleet personnel," since Slinkie was a civilian scientist.

"I refused to bring Cotex when she begged me," Jard told Pez trying to appease her.

He helped Slinkie out of the bulky space suit and she was wearing only panties and a T-shirt. They went into the ambassador suite and shut the door. Pez asked Jard on his coms, not wanting to shout through the door, "Jard, where do you think you're going?"

Jard offered as explanation, "Your Space Marines don't want us doing it out there,"

"He's just impossible," Ming offered, siding with Pez's dissatisfaction of the situation. Then, putting it in perspective, she added, "You should try being his assistant."

Johnson and Evenrude had holstered their blasters and were finishing their meals. Evenrude mentioned, "It makes one wonder about our High Council," referring to High Councilman Jard's antics.

"He's sure been a challenge for Swenah," Johnson remarked.

Ming complained, "Swenah passed him off on me and he's been a far bigger pest to Pez than to Swenah."

Evenrude recounted "I was holding him down in the module when Swenah was ordering the medical tech to administer the injection for hibernation, and that Fleet attorney crept out of his little office with obscure regulations forbidding it. She should have just had us put the lawyer under too."

Johnson remembered, "That was when we had that ornery fellow, Chancellor General Nabisco aboard. He kept getting into fist fights with Jard and with that fellow President Dodge. I had to break up a few of those before we dumped both of them off in the Pall Mall system."

"President Dodge pissed on me," Pez told them, still holding a little emotional charge from it.

Johnson told her, "Had you given me the OK, I would have turned Dodge into a spray of goo, and almost did anyway."

He'd been one of the Space Marine snipers covering Pez while she demonstrated her ability to sit for three full days in a particularly difficult meditation posture, constituting a classical test of the non-dual state of contemplation, or enlightenment. Dodge had buzzed her the whole time with a tiny robotic-electronic fly, and at the end, when that hadn't gotten a twitch out of her, he came out and pissed in her face. She still didn't flinch and Dodge came less than a hair's breathe from getting turned into boiling liquid mist from all the long-range blaster rifles trained on him. He had, in his defense, later broken a chair over Nabisco's back, when Nabisco had given Jard that first black eye.

Having consumed their chow, Evenrude stood and said, "We're going to catch some sleep while we're protected within the auxiliary's shields." What he only thought and didn't say was, *I don't know how you expect to get any sleep.*

Electra was falling off and Gumby was out. They were both placed in baby seats at maximum recline, and Ming and Pez removed their skullcaps and earbuds to place baby monitors in their ears. These could be integrated, but both women wanted to shut out all the world except their precious babies, so these earbuds responded only to them. Pez directed Rubix and Gretle into the suite since that's where the behaviors they exhibited belonged. Pez and Ming followed them in and Ahhu and Trix were right behind them. Jard had an Empress-size air mattress taking up about all the floor space in their suite. Pez thought, *At least they're not on the bed.*

Slinkie was on top and still didn't notice them as they marched across one end of the air mattress to gain access to the Emperor-bed, climbing onto it one at a time; but Jard did and mentioned to Pez, "Mel and I are conducting research with optical sensors which can capture auras. Informed consent and all that."

Pez asked, "Captain Mel, what are you up to?"

"It's brilliant really and the very surest method for yielding comprehensible results; and Trix can quarantine and sequester that data securely once we've analyzed it, sweetheart."

"Mel!" Pez protested.

"Sarhi thinks the 'events' are a sign that you've completely come into yourself and have attained a new level of expansion and influence," Mel argued.

"I can't help the 'events' and I don't want scientists studying me in my bedroom Mel," Pez complained.

Mel told her soothingly, "You can't always get what you want, but you'll find sometimes, you get what you need."

Ming pulled Pez into a kiss and embrace. Pez murmured when she came up for air, "Turn the soundproofing to max, Mel," just in time, hopefully, to save her Space Marines from Slinkie's loud squeals. Events came in series during the next 3 hours and so did every female on the shuttle, while every male was spent in the first event of each series. No one on the auxiliary was spared. The auxiliary crew and workers had experienced these from a distance before, as had everyone in Pez's fleet, though they had sure never been so close to the epicenter of one.

Pez did manage to fall off into sleep. Mel and Jard were up the rest of the sleep cycle studying the data with growing excitement since the waves of near ethereal energy exploded and spherically expanded in hot pink with violet highlights from a single point that was Pez. Now they had optic evidence that it was an actual force erupting out of her. Pez's aura was immense and so radiantly luminous that even with Jard's special filters it occasionally whited out all visuals. Jard had other instrumentation, and every form of wave-analyzer known, rigged in the cabin as well, and they still were not able to identify the actual substance of the wave in terms of composition. These-events remained a baffling perplexity to the scientific community.

Slinkie had established that Pez's brain was emitting alpha waves at the moments of the events and that her frontal lobe cortex was energized, though her entire brain seemed to holographically vibrate acoustically as if her brain was singing, and every last brain cell was in use. Much data was collected which would need to be compiled and analyzed, though it was looking like their results would ultimately raise more questions than they answered. Still, the optical proof of the force was quite a break through. The acoustical vibrations recorded were identical with the bio-energy of masters of soft martial arts and energy generation exercises.

CHAPTER FOUR

The suite had its own little head and shower off the bedroom and Pez kept her balance on the air mattress, stepping over Slinkie, getting to them when she woke up. She used both. After her hot shower she had a cold one to wake up, which took her breath away; literally shutting down her respiration. Cold as space. Every hair follicle on her body was standing at attention protruding from a goose bump, and she was wide awake as she toweled off. She had to balance crossing the air mattress to get clean panties, t-shirt and combat fatigues, still on the mattress since there was no place else to put a foot down.

She got across the mattress again, this time to the suite door, and opened it part way to squeeze through. Electra was just stirring, not aroused enough yet to feel her wet discomfort and gnawing hunger, so Pez employed all of her martial arts training and concentration to quickly change her without accelerating her waking up, which was already in progress. She got her into position for nursing, snuggling her, and when Electra's mouth opened to let out a wail, Pez got it over her nipple and onto it. Surprised at the gratification as she gave her first suck, the wail became a sequence of meaningless snorts.

"Breakfast is even better than dinner," Evenrude told her from the little round table.

"Try the stack of pancakes with chocolate marshmallow syrup," Johnson suggested having just finished his second one.

"Do they have oatmeal?" Pez asked.

"Yea, I saw some in there, SCG," Johnson replied.

Natasha was standing right in front of the cabinet in her pajamas so she handed Pez an oatmeal self-heating ambassador-ration. Pez's hand actually missed the ration in her cognizance of the spandex leopard skin pj's Natasha wore. Just shy of seven feet tall and built like a reed, the pajamas accentuated Natasha's already obvious thinness to the extreme. Pez told her, finally getting her hand on the ration, "I've never seen pajamas like that before."

"They're not standard issue so you wouldn't have," Natasha responded. Then she asked truly curious, "Have you ever actually been in a clothing store?"

"The one at the Clearlight Monastery," Pez answered, "It has stuff like you'd find at shopping arcades."

"I didn't think so," Natasha confirmed.

Cleo, who was fully dressed in her fleet uniform, told Pez, "Natasha and I are going to take you shopping as soon as we get back to Om and give you a makeover. Ahhu insists that we do and is going to pay for it."

"She's never been to Om, and has none of our money," Pez challenged.

"From the vast wealth you gave her on Earth 10⁵CBS2, she translated some into basis for intergalactic monetary exchange, and has brought with her a bucket full of diamonds, sapphires, emeralds and rubies, along with one ton of platinum."

"How clever," Pez said impressed.

Mel told Natasha and Cleo, "Pez has quite a sum tucked away she only just found out about."

"Who left it to her?" Cleo inquired.

"It's her pay for the past seventeen years since it first started from the Clearlight Order," Mel clarified.

From the expression she was getting Pez knew she'd better explain herself, so she said, "How was I supposed to know they'd started paying me at some point. I was an orphan and grateful to be taken care of."

"She had a small clothing allowance which she *was* aware of," Mel added as further explanation of how she'd gotten this far.

"All white, if I recall," Natasha commented.

"What's all white?" Pez asked.

"Your wardrobe," She answered.

"I have some off-white and gray things," Pez defended herself.

"How colorful," Natasha commented, bringing the point home for Pez.

"I'd really like to go shopping with you and I guess I have the money to do it," Pez said eagerly.

"We will give you a makeover to tantalize Ming and impress everyone on Om, Rah, and Haum," Natasha promised.

"And Ganahar, Kent, Pall Mall, Ralley, Gzzklns and Trident!" Mel exclaimed.

Cleo commented, "I'm sure your homecoming will be transmitted all the way to the Chevrollet system in the Sparkling Way Galaxy."

"Would you like stimulant brew, dear?" Natasha offered her sweet CO.

"Sarhi won't allow it while I'm nursing," Pez warned her off longingly. "You can hand me one of those double waffles with wild berry syrup though; they look delicious, and these oatmeal bowls are pretty small, so I better take another one."

Natasha passed an oatmeal and a double waffle ration to Cleo, who handed them to Pez. Cleo told her, "Go have a seat and eat, honey. I'll bring you some juice."

The orphan waif in Pez seemed to attract mothering so Pez had mothers wherever she went; but Nemellie, the Clearlight Order Abbot, was her primary mother figure.

At thirty-four years old Pez could more easily pass as a teenager. The medical term was "undedeveloped", while voluptuous was termed "well-developed." She placed her three ambassador rations down between her giant Space Marines on the table, and sat still nursing Electra. She ignited an oatmeal, and managed the wrapper one-handed. She'd just gotten the first bite into her mouth when Mel briefed her, "Ships from former slave worlds have been flowing in for more than ten hours, and they are racked and stacked around every space station awaiting their turns. Some are shuttling personnel down from low orbit, and the smaller ships are landing at military bases all over Kundabuffer. There are also entire convoys holding in high orbit. Three groups, each with twelve imperial transports, have left to return hostages, each carrying close to a quarter million.

Admiral Omniomi had to destroy every imperial ship and military asset in the Enron System and managed it without collateral damage. Captain Firestone has finally retired for some rest and his XO, Tinkerble, is acting Commodore. She's doing a most competent job of it too, I might add."

"Thanks for bringing me up to date Mel," Pez said with her mouth full, already igniting her second oatmeal.

Mel continued, "Swenah is hung up awaiting Om's real Ambassador to Vox, whom the High Council hasn't been able to decide upon yet. They've finally all agreed that the liberation of Vox was a good thing, and sanctioned it taking most of the credit in the Tail of Nine media. They're still debating the virtues of directly confronting Kundabuffer, as a hypothetical of course."

"You better have Sarhi tell Yona to get them approving aid to Kundabuffer, because the population down there is going to need it," Pez suggested.

"I just texted her," Mel said. "I've analyzed the soil, water, and atmosphere data, and have found pollution levels are not bad. They need soil amendment programs, greenhouses for intensive farming, as well as hydroponics stacks with grow lights. Shipments of uncontaminated seaweed, bat manure, and clean rich river silt, along with a global composting program and worm farms would give them their fastest recovery. They'll require seeds, sprouts and plantings. Commander Spalding has some machinists building an assembly line, entirely robotic, for manufacturing hydroponic stacks and accessories which he'll deliver planet side once it's complete.

"Did that idea originate with Captain Mel?" Pez asked smiling.

"I merely mentioned the need and not the faintest hint that he do anything about it; so he deserves all the credit."

"Excellent work Captain!" Pez praised her.

Evenrude mentioned, "Your repairs are completed better then new and they added an additional sensor array, as well as a few dozen lone optical sensors spread around in case of emergency. Spalding says you're good to go whenever you please."

"They got it all done in less than three hours," Johnson remarked.

Evenrude said, just remembering, "Oh, and Lt. Commander Schwin set your bomber wing down on Firestone's super-carrier. She says your Astro-Phantom is fixed and ready to fly, and there's not a pilot on the carrier who's not volunteering to join the wing."

"Thanks," Pez said fondly. She got Spalding's com and told him, "Thanks for patching up my shuttle and for the extra sensors. I'll be lifting off in thirty minutes. You show great initiative and true compassion by constructing the hydroponic stacks assembly lines. I'm giving you commendations for that and calling for a promotional review, Commander, Great work."

"Most of the people down there are victims of the empire and not perpetrators of it," Spalding explained his view. "What you're doing here is amazing, and it took *you* to bust out of our morally deteriorated stance of non-intervention and put a stop to mass murder and enslavement. Your Fleet stands firmly behind you and morale has never been so high. I salute you Supreme Commander General Pez."

"You just made my day and filled me with inspiration," Pez said gratefully. "I wish the High Council could see it as clearly as you do."

"You've just made their day for hundreds of billions of people, SCG," Spalding said with awe, signing off.

"He sure made me feel understood and supported," Pez told them exuberantly.

Natasha squeezed into the little table to bring it to maximum occupancy and said, "My grandmother was one of the pilots refusing to return to the carrier, *Excelsior*, to stay and defend the Bronzo System from imperial invasion in her MGM Corsair Invader fighter-bomber." Our family has rejected non-intervention for generations. I can't tell you how wonderfully moving it is to see the Empire dismantled and crushed from existence, and to be a part of it."

"It's people like your grandmother who have paved the way on Om to make what we do today possible," Pez said admiringly.

A call emerged in Pez's ear from Acting-Commodore Tinkerble, "Mel informed me that you are awake SCG. The imperial warships from Baspoon and Firmament 10^4 LAX 1 have jumped through the gate without transports, cargo or mining ships, and are hailing all combat ships in the system. I've set spectrum encoded light coms jammers so their message will not be received and I'm on intercept with them now. It looks like they're starting to launch small combat craft."

"I'm on *Auxiliary Two* and I'll be on my way in just a minute. My diplomatic shuttle is my flagship, named *Ishtar One*. Hit the bigger ships with shield disruptors and nanobot spray missiles to gain control of them, and just waste the smaller ships and small craft. Have those two Om battleships nearest you engage as well. You're doing a great job. Thank you."

Into Schwin's ear Pez said, "We have a situation. Hostile war ships are approaching from the gate and they're launching small craft. I'm lifting off *Auxiliary 2* in thirty seconds, so come join me for some action!"

"I'm on my way SCG; I live for this!" Schwin exclaimed gleefully.

Pez ran to the cockpit as she told Mel, "Start my preflight checks, notify Spalding I'm lifting off now, and wake my quad blaster gunners, please, because I'm going to need them."

"Done!" Mel reported crisply.

Pez was firing up her space drive and running hurried checks while Natasha, still in her leopard-skin spandex pajamas, climbed into the copilot seat, and Cleo and Flint, in uniforms and space jump suits, took theirs. Electra had finished sucking and Pez got her into her little front pouch where she looked intently out the portal window fascinated. Ming asked in Pez's ear, "What's happening my love?"

"Get yourself strapped into a seat, beloved, because we're going into battle. Please tell the others; and get Jard to deflate that big air mattress.

"Right away, dear." Ming replied.

Mel said, "Preflight checks comple…"

Pez shot them off the auxiliary to press into the depths of their seats and headrests with their faces squishing to either side, near-passing out. She just kept accelerating and everything close by looked to be a blur and a series, rather than a solid. The imperial ships appeared as tiny dots out the viewport and grew as their velocity increased tenfold. She kept the drive at maximum and fired the big tail booster which brought them to .7 light speed without anywhere near enough distance to brake. Natasha asked nervously, "Shouldn't we be braking or turning?"

Pez was concentrated internally and did not answer immediately, giving her crew a fright, since they were less than ten seconds from crashing into the imperial ships. "We're micro jumping in, just in front of their gate, headed the opposite direction as we are now with hardly room to reduce our forward momentum," she told them.

Reality ceased to exist, then reappeared 8.9 seconds before impact, and everyone except Pez was sure they were dead. Pez had the main drive reversed full throttle and every reverse thruster and mini-drive engaged, and it still looked like they would either crash or fly right by. Pez hit her big one-time reverse booster and they all lurched forward in their seats pressing painfully into their harnesses. Their approach was suddenly within accurate targeting speed and the ship sterns were racing at them at a manageable pace. Pez shouted with great enthusiasm, "FIRE!!!" She launched two of the big torpedoes into the fluted drive thrusters of an imperial Patrol ship, and a big missile into the Fast Attack ship her twin nose blaster was punching into, and into which a stream of Flint's canister missiles were pumulting. Both ships expanded in brilliant illuminating color to thousands of times their original sizes, hanging fading in space as great dimming spheres.

Pez was gunning down one of the imperial bombers and lobbed a single canister missile from Flint's arsenal to finish it off into a super-heated dust cloud. A war cry from Schwin informed Pez that her bomber wing had imitated her maneuver and was just behind her. There were four of them so they must have taken on a volunteer crew from Firestone's super-carrier. Schwin said in her ear, "You're a genius! My navigation-computer gave me warning flashes when I followed your lead."

"Leave the big ships to Commodore Tinkerble and our two battleships, and just hit small craft, Fast Attacks and Patrol ships. Some war ships waiting on line at the military space station might join the fight if we don't put this down quick!"

"We're all over this," Schwin said with great excitement.

The torpedoes from the four Astro-Phantom bombers blew up imperial ships while blasters and missiles splattered fighters, fighter-bombers and bombers all around them. Pez left her body through her crown in her rainbow body for hardly a second, but in that time she blossomed micro-suns of light around four imperial battleship-carriers whiting out all their sensors and frying some of them; leaving them blind and unable to acquire any targets for about ten seconds. That was all Tinkerble needed to nail them with nanobots and establish hard link for upload of Jard's program.

Mel told Pez, "An imperial battleship-carrier has left the military space station and is headed this way. Jard's flying it using Ahhu's drone console from this ship."

"Would you identify that ship for Om fleet so no one blows it up, and keep an eye on the High Councilman?"

"Of course," Mel replied, then added, "Ming is sitting right beside him with Gumby, helping him."

Cleo was coordinating the fire of the big nose blaster of her drone fighter-bomber with Pez's blasters, and so was Flint with the ball-mount blasters on the fins. Ahhu and Rubix were in the 'gaming zone' as they called it. Pez called it the 'flow state'. By whatever label, it was a state of one-pointed concentration like a laser, acting with instinctive immediacy beyond thought. The Spiritual Congress was with them and Pez could feel Sarhi's fire and the billions of consciousnesses focused in meditation. She also felt the pristine contemplation of the Amonrahonians amplifying the macro-will of the universe as she made herself a perfect channel for all this force, guiding and being guided by it in oneness.

She put micro-suns around five big ships as her shuttle sped passed them. She annihilated a small fighter with her blaster, turning her heading to intercept a large swarm of small craft, to come from their rear. Pez slipped one of Flint's canister missiles into an invisible soft spot in the shields of a destroyer Schwin was pounding, and a flash within the ship was followed 1.3 seconds later by the whole ship exploding outwards in all directions.

"Thanks!" Schwin told her genuinely.

Jard was playing space-war with a real imperial battleship-carrier and possibly having more fun than any kid ever had. Mel had informed him not to shoot at Battleship-carriers, cruisers or frigates, even those shooting at him, because Pez wanted them taken over to give to enslaved worlds. He followed these orders for the most part, but when another battleship started hammering his ship with missiles he let that one have it, unloading his biggest torpedoes and missiles. One breached the hull followed by a series of explosions cracking the stern off to spin away some five revolutions before blowing into an expanding flare of light and hot particles. Amidship and bow were rolling out of control with all manner of debris flying out the broken open end where the stern had been.

Pez said in Jard's ear, "No more big ships! I want those!"

"Well he was bringing my shields down and might have spoiled my fun," Jard argued like a child.

"No more big ships no matter what!" Pez insisted.

"Alright, love-child, don't get your panties in a bunch," Jard waved her off.

Seeing an imperial battleship-carrier attacking and destroying imperial ships while invisible ones were taking over control at an alarming rate of their biggest ships, and their small craft were bursting in space like popcorn, broke the moral of the crews on the former empire's ships. Mutinies ensued along with a few surrenders as the battle itself raged on. Every time an imperial battleship or cruiser gained strategic position it had its sensors whited out from overwhelming illumination blinding them completely. The hopelessness of achieving anything but their own deaths became impossible to ignore even with the denial of an alcoholic or the zealous fanaticism of a true believer. More ships signaled their surrender and powered down, and more mutinies broke out on those which didn't. Small craft were surrendering too.

Jard warned in Pez's ear, "I'd already fired before he signaled surrender," as a Fast Attack ship became a vapor cloud to a hail of torpedoes.

Pez announced to her fleet at large, "Hold your fire except for shield disruptors and nanobot spray missiles. If small craft fire on you then feel free to end those."

To Jard she said, "You can take yours back to orbit Kundabuffer and blow up all the space weapons platforms. They've been evacuated. After that you can destroy the lunar military bases, but be careful since they've got some observatories and mining operations up there too. Mel will highlight what you get to shoot at."

"Thanks love-kid. That battle was great! I'm looking forward to those space platforms. I've never had a toy like this one before."

"Well enjoy yourself, Councilman," Pez signed off.

Tinkerble reported, "All large ships are tagged and taken, or uploading, and we've begun targeting smaller ships.

"Great job, Commodore, you were swift and methodical, keeping the situation well contained. I'm impressed. Your success here will be duly recognized at the end of this campaign. Thank you Commodore Tinkerble."

"It's an honor, Ma'am. The opportunity you opened here is immeasurable and crucial. I've dreamed of this my whole life."

Pez contacted Commander Garfield on *Auxiliary Three* and directed, "Prepare your two main repair docks to start receiving battleships and cruisers. Disembark crews and shuttle those to the capital where we have things better secured. Fly the empty ships remotely to the strings of warships we have docked side by side in high orbit, and connect them to an end of the string one at a time. I need another docking station because there are just too many ships. With the next group of transports we send to return hostages home I'll have to get some of them out of here."

"Docking crews are at the ready and my coms officer is directing a pair of imperial battleships over now. You'll need to upload the control program to us so we can park them after evacuating crews."

"Mel's uploading it to you now. Your efforts are greatly needed and appreciated," Pez told him sincerely.

"We'll get the crews out quick, park the ships, and keep them coming nicely, Ma'am." Garfield promised, ending the call.

Pez contacted the imperial admiral on the military space station and instructed him, "Please have all ships awaiting a berth to disembark crews, begin shuttling them to the capital space port and shuttle ports. The pilots are to return their shuttles to their ships and get picked up by surface shuttles. I want each warship to have its full complement of shuttles aboard when the crews are all off the ships."

"I understand, and our coms officers are transmitting your orders to the letter, Ma'am."

"I'd prefer not to have compliance problems with any of those ships," Pez informed him sternly.

"I will do my best Ma'am, but there are still a few diehards who've not arrived yet. Your Captain Mel has their names, their ship identifiers and planetary origins. Not all of our Space Fleet officers will follow my authority any longer."

"I get it. Just do your best."

Mel said in Pez's ear, "You were blowing up ships with Schwin when I got the data and I meant to tell you. Please don't be upset."

"I'm not," Pez assured her. "Please circulate that data to all captains and commanders of ships and stick a program in our sensor drones to watch for those ships, and to alert us if they come through the gate."

Done, S.C.G.!" Mel said enthusiastically.

Pez checked in with Swanson, "How are things in the capitol?"

"I've got seven companies on the ground in New Hort and two on the way there now. I have seven more companies up there on three space stations. The capital is secure and we're now concentrated around the space port, the air and space port and the shuttle ports, as well as at the hubs of the various ground transportation systems. I'll get another twenty-three companies over to New Hort over the next twelve hours. Eight hours from now we ought to divert all space shuttles to New Hort where the majority of our resources will be."

"I'll do that," Pez assured him, noting the time. "I'm sure glad I have you commanding the Space Marines. I'm field-promoting you on the spot. Congratulations Captain Swanson."

"To receive that rank from you, Ma'am, is as good as it gets. I'm truly honored."

"I'm honored to serve beside you," Pez said with intense emotion.

They ended the call on the verge of tears, each having an overwhelming effect on the other.

Pez checked in with Admiral Omniomi, "How is your bus route going, Admiral?"

"You know, we did get to see a little action after all," Omniomi enthused.

"I know, I heard; good shooting," Pez told her.

"To zoom in on the faces of family members reuniting and of starving people receiving food, along with all the heart felt thanks we've gotten, have made this the most memorable operation of my career; this little bus ride," the Admiral shared.

"We alleviated suffering because we have the capacity to do it without harming the innocent, and sometimes a destructive pattern requires change from the outside," Pez said gravely.

"This one sure did," the Admiral agreed whole heartedly. Then she inquired with real curiosity, "Why aren't our data streams going to Om?"

"The High Council is still debating our operation as a hypothetical so I thought I'd wait until they get around to sanctioning it as an action before I forward the data."

"How prudent," she acknowledged, "but what if they vote it down?"

"I'll take full responsibility," Pez assured her, "and thank heaven the High Council can't vote down reality. The empire will be but a memory when we return to Om."

"I'm only finding abandoned machinery, equipment and supplies as the sole trace left of the empire in the systems I'm visiting. The freed planets are already negotiating trade and defense agreements with one another. Retooling of war materials manufacturing facilities and factories is urgently needed."

Pez offered, "I'll get engineers working on that immediately."

"I have only two more stops on this line then I'll be back to run another route," the Admiral told her, signing off.

Mel told Pez, "The engineers and machine robotics architects and designers on the *Apollo*, Firestone's super-carrier, and *Auxiliary One*, are all pulling up schematics and blueprints for slave worlds' war-machine factories from Kundabuffer data bases, which I programmed their access for, and are diligently working on retooling per planetary needs."

"You're my hero, Captain Mel," Pez said adoringly.

Electra wailed, and Mel could just be heard saying, "I think she's damaged one of my receptors."

Pez had muted her coms as quick as she was able but she could never prevent that first bit; and poor Natasha was right there in the cockpit sitting next to her. Flint and Cleo had learned to wear their helmets and set coms to mute at a certain decibel range automatically. Natasha had her hands over her ears. Everyone but Pez, who'd muted her coms, heard Rubix scream, "Ouch!"

Then Jard shouted, "Would you shut that damn baby up!"

Pez passed internal energy to Electra, taking her from her pouch to hold her close. An Islohar lullaby filled the cockpit as Electra's wailing decreased in volume, only because she'd run out of wind. Pez got her soiled diaper onto the floor and this seemed to release its odor rapidly; then cleaned Electra up to get a fresh diaper around her. It was yet self-adjusting as Pez brought Electra's mouth to her breast. Sarhi had told Pez that the Islohar make their journey of life fulfilling their responsibilities and bear their children along the way. This was precisely what Pez strove to accomplish.

Pez checked in with Captain Ohinya, "How are things around the other side of Kundabuffer?"

"Quiet now, S.C.G. The vault from the Chaneygrub estate is empty and the contents now on *Auxiliary One*. Chaneygrub was not there, but family members were apprehended and are in Fleet Intelligence interrogation aboard Firestone's super-carrier. We're keeping an eye on the surface below. The space Marines pulled out and only two drones remain over the estate in the off chance Chaneygrub returns there."

Pez stated, "We can expect resistance and further attacks until that slime-ball Chaneygrub is in custody."

"How can anyone be so sick?" The captain asked aghast.

"They cling to the impossible delusional metaphysical belief that the entire universe, and all life and consciousness within, is a complete random accident, including all universal laws discovered, robbing the cosmos of intelligence to make themselves the only gods above morality and justice. Life is a meaningless fluke and death is the end, so you might as well have fun and rule the world while you're there. Love is an obsolete survival trait outside the immediate family, like a tail. The delusional duality of ego is enthroned a god, to adore itself in its transient illusion of being. It's a stage we all pass through swiftly growing up. Without a massive adoring audience or a world to rule, that state of mind makes no sense and cannot be sustained without the constant flow of energy from others. They use their metaphysical belief in the random accidental universe as a method to study the universe. This circularity proves their thesis to themselves, while their ignorant bias excludes the development of real science."

Ohinya declared, "The intricate interdependence, unity, conservation, and cyclical continuity screams intelligent design at the macro, humanoid, micro, atomic, and subatomic levels. Every great philosopher and scientist making a real contribution to science has recognized this. Everything in the universe points to it really."

"You'll get no argument from me," Pez assured her. "No one can mess with my metaphysics. If they choose to see a dead and dumb universe without purpose or meaning, and assert their egos at the cost of massive karmic debt and consequence to come back as rock on a distant dwarf planet, the universe does have these devolving possibilities; though they descend in opposition to the macro-will, and this constitutes only loss of love and sentience, and pure suffering ultimately."

"They think they're so clever owning and controlling all the wealth and resources," Ohinya despaired, "but they are cosmically stupid to trade love and unity for fear, suspicion, greed and ego gratification, which is *not* happiness! Utter alienation cut off from humanity."

Pez stated, "In acting inhuman they become inhuman, losing their humanity entirely. It's a curious thing about human's, and it has been known since the beginning of our race, that to imitate the divine makes us one with the divine, so long as such imitation is made from pure attention and concentration and not as some ego game. Ego is always trying to attain spirituality, but it is rather like wanting to witness one's own funeral."

"The very name 'Kundabuffer' has come to represent ego-duality", Ohinya pointed out, "and become another label for the same."

"The population is mostly innocent victims of a cruel system built up by a tiny group of loveless egoists," Pez qualified. "Having power over others is a sick aspiration with suffering as the only possible outcome and is driven by pure selfishness, ignorance and delusion. Instead of discovering reciprocity, the key to love and unity, they fall ever deeper into duality of self and other oriented only to material passions of greed, lust and craving for position and power. All sense of the universal harmony, equilibrium, equanimity, and quiescence is lost completely along with any identity with the common good and the whole of the population as one body and one spirit. Their identity becomes only the illusion of self they project over their destructive selfish acts, limited to their sack of flesh. They hear not the will of the universe expressed through the calling of divine love, ever present as refuge and support for the journey of ascent. No, they are rather in free fall towards the darkest densest materiality as far from the source of all emanation as possible."

"Sarhi says the human being has the purpose of producing void as the realization of transcendental immaterial pure consciousness beyond time, space or any quality whatsoever," Ohinya shared.

"It is our cosmic duty to contemplate the Absolute, amplifying the divine calling in unity, one with divine will. When this is attained the universe is complete and the Absolute is contemplating itself. I know the Absolute by the same knowing the Absolute knows me."

Ohinya told Pez gratefully, "My own meditation and mindfulness practice jumped levels considerably since I've connected with you and with Sarhi. You are always such a force of awakening and I'm so honored to be part of this mission with you."

"You are a force of good within Om's Star Fleet, Captain Ohinya, "Pez said from her heart, "and I've always admired you. Remember, pure consciousness cannot be realized with concepts and language, is invisible and without location, immaterial and without components. It cannot even be named; but it has nowhere to hide."

"My interactions with you, SCG, are consistently fruitful for my practice and insight," Ohinya informed her. "Thank you. I'd best get focused on the surface activities down there and try to find this Chaneygrub person."

"Thank you; I count on your competent service," Pez said sincerely.

Flint inquired, "Haven't coms monitoring given us any clue of this Chaneygrub's location?"

Mel answered, being better informed on this than Pez, "There are numerous signals and transmissions going out to him but we've not picked up any responses from him, so he must realize we can pinpoint him if he does, and is advancing no profile yet. If he transmits we'll have him."

Natasha extended her pocket device holo to maximum size while holding it out towards the center for all to see, displaying the planet Kundabuffer, its two moons, and the space around for about 100,000 miles out past the furthest moon. Text data was at the bottom. She told them, "There are six thousand, seven hundred and thirty-nine big ships in this system and thirty-seven more just jumped in through the gate. There are yet 3,092 large ships on their way or eluding us. It's a major traffic jam."

"You're right, and I'll start having hostage transports left off in freed worlds on the last stop of each, and start returning mining ships and ore-haulers to the planets they arrived from. I think I'll have Captain Hasbro of the T9 super-cruiser *Victory* lead as many war ships remotely as he can manage at once and begin distributing those to freed worlds. We've got to clear this system out, especially since there's likely to be more action here. The more traffic, the more collateral damage and loss of life."

"I've sent your orders to all captains and commanders of ships," Mel told Pez.

"Thanks Captain Mel," Pez praised, "you're quite efficient."

"Can I order Commander Ming to assist me with compilation and integration of data?" Mel asked eagerly.

"Why don't you 'ask' her instead, Mel," Pez suggested, "since I'm sure she'll do it and feel much better about it if you request rather than order."

"You're right, and I do love Ming," Mel agreed. "So get me a Jr. Lieutenant assistant I can order about."

"Jr. Lieutenants have feelings too Mel," Pez tried to teach her, "just ask Lt. Nash."

"They are also well-conditioned to rank," Mel persisted, "and what's the point of being a captain if I have no subordinates?"

"Rank is responsibility, sweetheart, not power," Pez continued teaching.

"What precisely am I captain of?" Mel demanded to know.

"You are a captain of Om's Star Fleet, serving it, and not trying to see how it can serve you," Pez taught, though with diminishing hope of getting through. "You are the appropriate rank to assist the SCG and pass on orders. Your function is crucial and your capacity for it supreme. I need your help Mel and I need you running *Apollo* under Rear Admiral Swenah's command."

"I do that; but I want staff too!" Mel insisted.

"Learn how to lead from equality, Mel, and from non-action; without the projection of self," Pez encouraged her. "I've got to prove you exist before I can help you attain any officially recognized rank sweetheart. The problem is that they are convinced you're not possible and they are firmly attached to their view. Maybe Trix can help now that she has learned quantum computer science and made some corrections to it leading to new discoveries. I think I could get Aton and Nemellie to recognize you and give you an official position within the Clearlight Order."

Natasha predicted, "If Fleet knew about you Mel they'd be back to dumbing down their computers and disassociating administrative functions, bringing us back to multiple entries and manual integration too slow for combat situations and emergencies."

"Mel has the innate divine form of Justice oriented towards the Good," Pez reasoned, "and so can be trusted. Her learning process has been rather unorthodox for Fleet and can be frightening. Once Mel attains tranquil abiding, and Sarhi says she progresses quickly, I don't think any objections to her service could be found. It's not like we're any closer to ever making a sentient quantum computer than we are to creating life."

"It can't be done," Mel informed them. "What humans label 'life' is the accumulative declensions from the origin and source, the Absolute Transcendental, and not a composition of other final declensions. I have no idea how I came about but Sarhi says I became sentient to help Pez because Pez needs me; and that I'm a gift from the Cosmic Intelligance."

Pez told them, "I think we're as likely to understand Mel's precise origin as we are to creating life by shaking up final declensions within a test tube."

Captain Firestone reported in to say, "The volume and magnitude of the returning imperials is mind-boggling, but ever since you started having the crews of the warships shuttled down to the capital from orbit, making trips with their own shuttles, it has been moving along with amazing efficiency."

"I want to decorate your X.O., Tinkerble," Pez informed him, "and I want to make sure you receive official commendations for your exemplary role throughout the mission and this operation."

"To have functioned as Commodore of so many ships is the pinnacle of my career and will look rather nice on my record too," he replied. "Serving under you on the mission to Xegachtznel, and now in 'Operation Liberation' as everyone's calling it, has been the most significant period of my life and the greatest honor."

"You don't have the biggest ship in my fleet just by chance, Captain Firestone, and it's the expertise and skill of people like you who make me look good and get the job done. The honor is mine, sir."

"I took the liberty of setting a company of my ship's Space Marines on that private smaller space station and we're now unloading three additional passenger transports from there, installing Jard's program, provisioning them, and moving them on to low orbit over the hostage complex. The station had fourteen of its own shuttles, which we're now employing along with the transport shuttles to get their passengers down to New Hort with Commander Swanson's approval. Now I'm told the shuttle ports and space ports on the surface are busier than the space stations. Ships are still coming faster than we can send them back out, though Captain Hasbro is going to bring forty imperial war ships out in just a few minutes. The next convoy of passenger ships with hostages leaves in about an hour and will bring twelve war ships with them when they go."

"I appreciate the liberties you've taken and welcome any further ideas you might have on accelerating the process."

"Thank you SCG," Firestone told her. "The Space Marines have hundreds of thousands of dislocated people on their hands and the imperial government is designating hotels and opening up government facilities, but these have been filled up in the capital and in New Hort and now the returning imperials have to be sent by various modes of ground transportation to other cities. Swanson has Space Marines setting up in those to receive shuttles directly, and that ought to be happening momentarily."

"It's going to be a big mess for a while," Pez accepted. "Our security recognition and alert systems have been programmed by Captain Mel for all imperial war criminals and their ships. My worry is trying to fight a battle around this planet with all these ships everywhere. At least we've been able to keep the space out to the gate clear."

Firestone informed her, "I directed the last convoy to jump in to take up orbit around the larger moon so it won't be in the way of anything. They won't be able to disembark their passengers from there though."

"Good decision. They'll just have to sit tight a while. I'm going to scare up some pilots to get some more ships out of here."

Aye, Aye Ma'am."

Pez contacted the Lt. Commander of the Space Marines on the ground at the hostage complex in the capital and instructed, "I need for you to find me any commercial or military pilots and ship's crew among the hostages who might be there, and have them collect their things to ship out. I've got to get more ships out of here and I can only spare so many of my war ships for bus-route duty; although Admiral Omniomi reports having the time of her life doing it."

"This is Captain Mel, and I'm sending you a list of all hostages with pilot and crew training, who are yet on the ground with you, and their compartment numbers at the complex."

"Thank you, Captain Mel," the Lt. Commander said most gratefully.

"Anything for the Space Marines," Mel said flirtingly. She was generating a holo image of herself, mostly graphics, but with a touch of animation for him.

"I'll have them ready promptly, SCG," he said, giving her a winning salute; then he gave an even better one to the fictitious holo of Captain Mel.

Pez praised Mel, "That was very helpful and well-delivered, sweetheart."

"See; I'm ready for a crew!" Mel said with enthusiasm.

"The crew must wait until someone in authority on Om recognizes you, Mel."

"Jard does and he's on the High Council."

"Maybe he can help us."

"He says he'll deny everything."

"That wouldn't help. I still think Trix and Aton, maybe Yona too, are our best bets."

"Yona listens to Sarhi."

"That's why I think we can get her to help us."

"Well you're in authority on Om, SCG," Mel pointed out accusingly.

"Not for long, and depending on what the High Council decides, I could be declared a war criminal."

"That wouldn't help."

"No; and if they had a clue about you they would charge you as an accomplice probably."

"Do you want me to listen in on the High Council like Jard does?"

"No. Don't break the law and regulations. Jard's a member."

"But he doesn't employ his virtual seat, spying on them instead."

"I know, and I've told Yona about it."

Electra had had enough and wanted attention. She'd learned to yank on a little fist full of momma's hair, because that always worked for getting her attention. "Ouch!" Pez exclaimed, as she focused on dear Electra, passing her internal bio-energy. Electra lit up with delight. "You're just so cute and beautiful Lecty," Pez told her in an unnaturally high voice.

Natasha asked, "Do you want to circle the planet inside the atmosphere?"

Pez agreed, "We might as well go down and do some scanning of the surface. Let's take it right down to about 20,000 feet. That way we won't miss anything subterranean."

Listening in from her gun turret Ahhu suggested, "The lake by the Chaneygrub estate is linked to the ocean by a river, and that may be how he escaped since it wasn't by air or space."

"Great idea my love; we'll check it out," Pez replied. "There may even be a hidden boathouse on the lakeshore."

To Natasha Pez said, "You have the controls," then her voice went way up as she said, "because little Lecty needs me," rubbing noses with her daughter.

CHAPTER FIVE

Natasha was joyfully flying. Flint and Cleo couldn't be read with their helmets on. Ming, Trix, and Gretel were working on data integration with supervision from Captain Mel. Jard had crashed and was sleeping on Pez's bed. Slinkie was strapped into a seat in the main compartment texting and Evenrude and Johnson had the jump seats to either side of the airlock door. Slinkie wondered if there was a Space Marine regulation requiring discomfort at all times.

Natasha skimmed the upper transition zone of the atmosphere until they were almost over the big continent before diving for the planet. Electra wore an expression of wonderment and fixed her attention on the viewport. The maintenance and repair crews called those portals "windshields", and indeed they were when within an atmosphere. Natasha pulled up expertly at exactly 20,000 feet without firing a booster and knew she'd aced it. Both Pez and Electra looked impressed. Natasha followed the river all the way to the lake while checking navigability and depths. She slowed and dropped to 12,000 feet when they got to the lakeshore, hitting the ground with active scans. Cleo and Flint were helping her review the incoming data, since Pez was wholly absorbed in Electra and this is what Electra wanted right now.

They followed the shore up towards the estate and Natasha came down to 9,000 feet on approach. From this altitude they could zoom into molecular structures on the surface, and map the contours of any hollow below ground to a depth of 4,000 feet. Cleo said through her coms, "There's something! It's a rectangular chamber beneath the lake with tunnel access and a vertical tube to the lake bottom."

Natasha brought them back around while slowing and descending. They came to hover over the lake and over the chamber directly beneath it. Passive scans wouldn't detect it and only from an angle above, at close range, could an active scan reveal it clearly. The lakeshore was a few miles from the outer edge of the estate. Only a water main pipe, 48 inches in diameter, linked the estate mansion with the chamber under the lake. Flint said, "He must have a tube he gets inside of to shoot through the pipe to his getaway craft, then hugs the river bottom out to the ocean. He must have his electronics heavily insulated and shielded."

"Not from us at 9,000 feet," Natasha replied as she pulled up and raced back down the river towards the ocean accelerating.

"He'd be long out to sea now," Flint commented.

'I'm accelerating and we'll make some broad sweeps," Natasha informed him. "He couldn't have crossed beneath the entire ocean yet."

"It's a lot of area to cover," he pointed out.

"Not if he took the shortest route to the next continent," Natasha replied.

They followed the river to its mouth and flew across the ocean at 8,640 MPH while pinging the depths with active scans. The monotony of the scenery soon had Electra dozing and Pez got her adjusted comfortably within her front pouch for her little nap. Ocean extended in every direction, making it seem like the entire planet surface was all water. Pez let Natasha drive since her co-pilot was having so much fun doing it, and analyzed data along with Cleo and Flint.

Getting mildly bored Natasha increased their speed to 10,050 MPH and dropped to 8,000 feet. This accomplished little in terms of elevating excitement, but then a squall on the horizon appeared and was growing bigger as they approached. Passing though it was arousing with the windshield a distorted blurry mess. At least this would wash away the space dust from the vaporized imperial ships which had jumped through the gate in attack mode earlier. The ferocious winds fought them at moments as they went through, jolting them with impacts like a collision. Ming's voice came in Pez's ear with, "Is everything alright dear? Are we under attack?"

Pez answered calmly, "No; it's just a little turbulence and we'll be passed it soon."

Electra stirred with one particularly big shocking shift, leaving their stomachs hundreds of feet above, but she didn't wake up. The sun was in front of them just to their port side as they emerged from the storm, and sections of the sea became glittering mirrors reflecting dazzling light at their sensors, kicking in filters and computer enhancement optical programs automatically to cancel the glare. Once again sea and sky in endless expanses offered the only scenery, though Pez had a holo of the sea floor displayed as well, showing the contours and ridges with digital analysis under the image. It was obvious that something had passed close to the bottom at great velocity, sweeping the silt and sand to either side in its wake. Pez brought this holo up beside Natasha's front view holo by which she was piloting.

Their windshield was pristine and dry now but offered such limited scope it could not compete with the imagers on the exterior hull producing Natasha's holo. From her skullcap, using nerve impulses in the brain, she could adjust her zoom, magnify one object or area boxed off separately, and switch between various integrated sets of optics, such as telescopic night vision, or x-ray-sonic-infrared, and various other combinations computer enhanced to attain a view of the craft's surroundings in different kinds of optical challenges. She could also configure her virtual dashboard to display precisely the relevant data, which were now speed, altitude, plane, angle, and standard positioning grid of the planetary surface in relation to the poles and the equator.

Pez highlighted the trail on the ocean floor which they were already basically following. Natasha understood at once what she was looking at and declared, "We've got him," as she accelerated to 12,800 MPH, staying at 8,000 feet.

If they went much lower they'd be kicking up a spray, being so big and moving so fast. Natasha stopped accelerating at 13,200 MPH and the surface of the ocean was whipping by below. She was keeping both holos in view, following the trail, and hot on Chaneygrub's tail. The boredom was gone swallowed by the thrill of motion. Mel was checking scan data too and could process everything coming in as it came. They crossed over an incredibly deep crevice at the sea bottom where it dropped 25,000 feet almost vertically and extended in snaking fashion around the globe. Om had one of these beneath its oceans too and they called it "the Dragon". The trench was known to be a 'nuzzle' of continental drift, but not the bullet or trigger. These were related to the continuous circulation of the planet's energy and matter, implemented through its liquid core and electromagnetic poles across the fissures and faults of its meridians.

As the continent began to come into view the trail on the sea floor became less well-defined, and Natasha braked, throwing the main drive into reverse and hitting all the reverse thrusters and mini-drives. Being in an atmosphere she employed the flaps on the fins of the disc shaped craft, pulling the nose up; and using the underbelly as a kind of sail or parachute. Everyone was pressed hard into their bottoms while the world slowed under them. The maneuver brought them to 13,039 feet altitude but dropped them down to just 320 MPH in 7.7 seconds. The harnesses would have damaged internal organs if it were not for the gyroscopic motion dampeners on the shuttle. Even Pez would be passing out from her typical maneuvers, if not for the shock-absorbers and suspension system, mostly electro-magnetic, but with some electro-hydraulics involved too, and even a few springs.

The trail could still be made out and Mel was analyzing every aspect of it carefully. They came down to 4,000 feet slowing to 220 MPH and their trail was becoming more difficult to read with each passing second. Pez asked, "Can you still follow it Mel? Because I've lost it entirely."

"There's still a trace. Natasha, turn 16 degrees to starboard and get ready to turn back five degrees to port. He'd veered off slightly back there. Here we go! Five degrees to port now! I can still detect it. We're back on his trail."

Mel put up a holo in the cockpit showing the ocean floor in minute detail considerably magnified, with hot pink highlights on her scanty clues indicating the route. Pez wasn't sure that what Mel was showing them wasn't completely random. She was able to shed any pessimism, although this did not result in optimism; neutral being the best she could attain at the moment. Even this was challenging to maintain as the 'clues' became fewer and farther between. Skepticism was just beginning to conquer Pez's mind and raise its flag when Mel produced a far-scan of a metallic door beneath a rock veneer, leading into the continental shelf where it rose, still beneath the water.

"You'll make a believer out of me yet, Mel," Pez told her now filled with overwhelming optimism.

Pez contacted Colonel Bleep who was in charge of Army Space Special Forces since they were the only people she had out on this side of this continent in the way of ground forces. "Colonel, this is Pez. I need a platoon or more of your troops at the coordinates I'm sending you. Bring full body armor, shield packs, heavy weapons and any hardshell space combat suits if you've got them. I don't know the size of the force we confront yet."

"We'll be there right away, SCG, with everything we've got," Bleep told her, thrilled to be involved in an action with her.

Natasha was now hovering directly over the door beneath the sea, and Mel was studying its every facet and composition. Pez told them, "The cavalry is on its way."

Natasha inquired, "I wonder what one of our big torpedoes would do to that door down there?"

Mel answered, "It would be entirely finished as a door and spread across an immense area in tiny particles. You'd need a powerful microscope to find some of them."

"Well that sounds quite promising," Natasha remarked suggestively.

Pez asked Mel, "Can you show me the whole facility behind that door, and all tunnels leading from it; and I guess pipes too."

It appeared in front of Pez, between her and Natasha where Flint and Cleo could get a good view as well. Flint even risked taking his helmet off to get a better look. Cleo, who had Electra's elimination and feeding cycles well calculated, checked her internal display on her helmet and decided to keep hers on. They examined the holo and determined that once again there was only a pipe from it running to the mainland. Pez took the shuttle controls, lined up the craft, and fired a big torpedo disintegrating the door. An enormous bubble of air rose to the surface releasing like the ocean belching. The optics were a little fuzzy as things settled. Mel announced, "It didn't so much fill with water as it did burst and collapse completely. I can just make out his crushed vehicle beneath the boulders. There is no life within the former facility at this time"

Pez requested, "Give me a holo of that pipeline."

Mel put it up for her and Pez took off like a rocket, spreading everyone into the backs of their seats flat as a pancake. In no time she was braking madly and even fired a reverse one-time booster bringing them directly over the compound where the pipeline dead ended, with harnesses digging into ribs viciously. Ming's startled voice asked, "Did we hit something?"

"No dear," Pez explained, "we just stopped fast."

"One of your 'stops'," Ming remarked knowingly.

Electra caught Flint with his helmet off and he wished she hadn't. Cleo smiled out of her facemask as her coms auto-muted. Flint grimaced, Rubix shouted "ouch" and Jard yelled at Pez. Pez had been amazingly quick muting her coms, but alas, not pre-emptive. It was always that first fraction of a second that tended to be the loudest, and coupled with the initial contrast of volume, was by far the most shocking.

A poopy diaper hit the cockpit floor and Pez had no sooner cleaned up Electra with a wipey than Ahhu was there sliding another diaper on. Baring her breast with one hand, Pez was bringing Electra's mouth to her breast as the diaper self-adjusted and an Islohar lullaby was forming on her lips. Internal energy was pumping from her into her daughter and the whole operation was performed in record time. Ahhu removed the soiled diaper and even found another one down there which she disposed of too.

Pez asked Mel, "Would you inform Colonel Bleep where we are now and ask for him to meet us here instead."

"There's certainly nothing left where he's going," Mel agreed.

Pez managed to pull up her own holo of the compound below while singing a lullaby, which is kind of tricky with a skullcap. The compound was constructed of some kind of cement and had a flat roof of gravel. The structure was spread over a little more than an acre and built around a square open courtyard in the center. One corner was a dome and obviously the space craft hanger. The majority of the visible compound was three stories above ground, though there was one tower ascending another 50 feet above the rest. Most of the compound was below ground with four sublevels below the entire thing and three smaller descending sublevels, each about a quarter of an acre. Infrared x-ray revealed humanoids within at every sublevel and level; a lot of them.

Blaster fire on their shields from the tower brought Pez's attention to her skullcap display and a pair of Flint's canister missiles shot into the air at the tower as their shuttle made a loop to loop in evasive maneuvers. She was still singing that lullaby. The tower blew into dust and tiny pebbles making a big cloud which took a few seconds to clear as their sensors grayed out. Mel was highlighting all weapons systems on the roof and walls of the fortress below. Pez told her, "Check for escape routes from this place because if there is one I'm sure he's already using it."

More hits on her shield and Pez told her crew and gunners, "Fry everything Mel has highlighted now," as she opened up her big nose blasters on full rapid fire and flung two pair of canister missiles. The big quad blasters in the turrets reduced entire outer walls of the place to rubble and soot in seconds and the highlights all blinked out on their holos quick.

"Can you link me to their coms, Mel?" Pez inquired.

"You're on their channel now," Mel told her promptly.

"Everyone in that building, including the seven sub-levels below ground, come outside now. Leave your weapons where they are and come out unarmed. You will be shuttled back to the capital for processing. You will not be harmed if you come out. If you do not come out you will because I'm replacing that building with a crater far deeper than its 7th sub-level. You have five minutes to get out and clear the area. This is the *only* warning you will receive."

Pez mentioned to her crew as they gained some altitude, "I'm getting a little higher in case something big and solid is blown way up in the air when I hit it with two of the big missiles."

No one had any objections to this. Pez had set a five-minute countdown on her holo, and was hunting for escape routes out of that complex. The vehicle Chaneygrub had come in was now permanently part of the continental shelf and the facility it had been parked in was no more. A rather long tunnel did proceed some 20 yards beneath ground level, rectangular, and large enough for a ground transportation hovercraft. She asked Mel, "Is there a vehicle anywhere within that tunnel?"

"As a matter of fact I was just going to call your attention to it," Mel replied. "It's traveling at 187 MPH and is currently 12.3 miles away and gaining distance."

"How far and to where does that tunnel go?" Pez asked her.

"The tunnel branches at two points attaining three possible destinations and runs a total 311 miles. I'm tracking him now. I doubt he'll go to his private space port. The next closest ends at an industrial facility with only ground transportation outside a small city, and the last, to a lodge in the forest in the foothills."

Pez stated, "The industrial facility is my guess."

"We'll know shortly," Mel stated. Then she mentioned, "No one has come out of that building yet and hovercraft are leaving in droves down that tunnel."

"Target a point just ahead of the lead one," Pez requested as everyone was pressed into their seats with their faces stretched to either side. In only a moment they were in range of the point Mel highlighted and a big missile left *Ishtar One* parallel the surface of the ground gaining speed, then arced down to strike the targeted point on the land throwing tons of rock and dirt far into the air. Pez initiated some severe braking to hover over the giant dust cloud at 9,000 feet. The cloud rose more than half way to them. Their optics configured a clear picture for them minutes before an eyeball could make out anything more than a dense dirt-cloud. The tunnel from the compound now ended here. The lead car hit the rubble head on, braking but still traveling at close to 100 MPH. After a colorful moment only the chassis, melded perfectly to the rubble, could be made out of the hovercraft. Several more hit the wall of rubble and were every bit as colorful. Satisfied, Pez turned them around and ascended to 10,000 feet above the compound, checking her countdown.

Some mercenaries were now flowing out of several doors, and moving swiftly away from the building. They were unarmed. There was still a minute and 49 seconds left on the countdown. Pez did not like mercenaries who defended rich psychopaths and fought for injustice. They were a complete dishonor to all of the warriors of the universe and the thought of vaporizing them unarmed did pass through her mind; but she paid it little heed. Military personnel willing to push the masses into ever deeper poverty and fight for the interests of a few big ugly egos were as bad as mercenaries in Pez's mind. She loved stories about the mercenaries defending the weak and poor against the rich and mighty, and the ones about warriors who stole from the rich and gave to the poor. There were many such stories on Om and Ganahar.

Colonel Bleep's shuttles began dropping onto the ground around the mansion leaving ample space for Pez to blow it to smithereens and reported, "We're landing now."

"Keep four in the air because the number one man, Chaneygrub, has already escaped, and as soon as we determine his destination we'll send them there."

Mel sent him the imaging of the tunnel beyond the dead-end they'd just created, showing the Chaneygrub hovercraft in hot pink as it sped from their location. Pez had an idea and directed Mel, "Put together a thirty-second presentation with a picture of Chaneygrub's face and announce to the people of Kundabuffer that he is by far the wealthiest man on the planet and the real power behind the emperor. Show a few of his memos ordering the emperor about and inform the people that these are things he has taken pains to keep secret."

Not three seconds later Mel told her, "It's transmitting now," as she brought up a holo of it for Pez to see.

An announcer with Mel's Android face and the bosom of Cotex spoke the information in a pleasant confident voice, and Chaneygrub's face remained, taking up half the image while Mel's half divided to share space with Chaneygrub's memo's posted long enough to read, one after another. The presentation was 47 seconds and by the time it was over the countdown was finished and cold.

Pez asked on the compound coms, "Is everyone out of there now, because I'm fixing to blow it?" She asked Mel, "Any life readings in there?"

"No," Mel answered, "but there are thirty-seven running down the tunnel towards where you collapsed it."

"Colonel Bleep, we have 37 mercenaries headed for the coordinates I'm sending you, probably armed. The location I sent is where I collapsed the tunnel they're in, but there's an opening there which they can climb out of. Tell your men to stand clear of that opening though."

"Two shuttles are on their way and will be on the ground in moments," Bleep replied.

"Thank you," Pez said gratefully, "I'm going to give them another minute and a half to get out, before blowing the compound. Here's a countdown."

Mel informed her, "You were right, he's turned off for the industrial facility."

"Inform Colonel Bleep and highlight the destination on his holo."

"Done," Mel replied.

Bleep reported, "Four shuttles are accelerating all out, and we'll have 160 Army Space Special Forces on the ground there in a couple minutes."

"Thank you Colonel," Pez told him, watching her new countdown.

"The special forces are apprehending the first three out of the tunnel," Mel reported.

"I'm not waiting," Pez informed her with twelve seconds left.

"Four more just cleared the entrance and a bunch more are right behind them," Mel reported, with only seconds to go.

At zero, Pez lobbed two big missiles into the compound and it looked to her as if the entire thing, sublevels and all, went airborne. At 10,000 feet they had some debris fry on their shields, and some was shot miles in all directions. A long tongue of flame lanced out of the caved-in section of the tunnel followed by two slow mercenaries already crispy. The Special Forces had stayed well clear of the entrance and had kept their 35 new prisoners clear of it too. As their sensors clarified an image, the deep molten crater made it clear that there was nothing more to do here.

Pez and Bleep's remaining shuttles raced for the industrial facility, and Pez won by quite a bit. Ming was watching Electra. Pez decided she would ask Spaulding's mechanics and engineers to design her a twelve heavy-duty break-away parachute system out of textile armor with three-loads, involving thirty-six parachutes for three such stops. Within an atmosphere it would be the ultimate enhancement to her reverse drive, thruster, and one-time booster system.

Pez had let Natasha land *Ishtar One* while she got into her Space Marine hardshell combat suite. The ramp went down before the ship rose back up on its hydraulics and Pez, Evenrude and Johnson flew out of the shuttle using their suit-thrusters.

"Where is he Mel?" Pez demanded.

"His hovercraft is on the third sublevel of the facility, and he took an elevator to the ground floor as witnessed by the elevator's security camera. I'm seeking other recordings on him now."

"Highlight the ground floor elevator he came out of in my helmet holo and keep looking," Pez told her.

It appeared instantly and Pez headed for the nearest facility door to that elevator. She asked Mel, "Where are the special forces? And why didn't they apprehend him?"

"They're all over and converging on him," Mel explained. "He had a hidden door inside the tunnel before he reached the end of his line where they were waiting, and he ascended two levels then went to the opposite corner of the facility behind them."

"Do you have him yet?" Pez asked.

"Yes!" Mel screamed. "He's made it to the ground transportation terminal across from the industrial facility. Special forces are moving in."

Pez used half a second of the booster in her suit, good for 90 seconds, and was at the terminal braking with thrusters. She passed through the open terminal door at about 25 MPH veering sharply to avoid collision with an elderly woman. Her suit's facial recognition program was scanning 360 degrees around her and her own eyes were focusing on every face in sight. She slowed to 10 MPH and wove through the people walking. Up ahead there was a big commotion so she sped up and had to brake, digging in her heals as well as with thrusters.

A penis, utterly detached, was falling to the ground in a little sprinkle of blood. It was the strangest thing and Pez was a tad bewildered. Screams of abject agony in a voice hardly human though male if at all, were loud enough to drown out Electra had she been wailing. Pez moved in for a better look having to shove some people in the densely gathered crowd out of the way. A bloody arm as detached as that penis had been went up in the air raining blood and then came tumbling back to Kundabuffer to go splat. Pez shoved in closer just as another arm did the same thing, landing a foot in front of her. The knot of bodies at the core of the crowd was writhing in agitated violence and the two legs of an armless naked man, a bleeding mess at the groin, were being wrenched in opposite directions like pulling apart a gardd's wishbone to make a wish with someone. A torn off leg went up in the air toes first and dripping blood onto the blood thirsty crowd, to fall back to the ground with another sickening splat. Pez didn't get facial recognition of Chaneygrub until it was his detached head spinning high in the air near-spurting blood. The top caved when it hit the pavement. Oh well; the Chaneygrub problem was solved. It seemed right to Pez that the people of Kundabuffer had cleaned up this cosmic toxic waste themselves. Pez knew this had only been a prelude to what awaited Chaneygrub now.

Evenrude and Johnson were right behind her. Evenrude remarked, "It doesn't look like anyone is going to miss that asshole"

Pez replied, "His mercenaries dishonor warriors but that man dishonored our entire humanity."

"Good riddance, I say," Johnson chimed in.

"Mel, please report to all forces on the ground that the Chaneygrub hunt is concluded," Pez requested.

"I sent them some gory holos," Mel told her.

"We're on our way back to the shuttle, Mel." To Colonel Bleep she said, "Thank you for your assistance Colonel. You can return to your previous objectives. I'm headed to New Hort."

"It was truly an honor, Ma'am," Bleep gushed.

Pez checked in with Spalding, "How's that assembly line coming?"

"The designs and specs are done and proofed, there's a 3D model, and it's in the hands of our machinists, robotic mechanics and metal workers. I expect to be sending the whole thing planet-side within four hours. Just let me know where to deliver it."

"Send me the dimensions, energy requirements, and any special considerations. I'll get your location," Pez told him. Then she asked "How stretched are your engineers?"

"Twiddling their thumbs now that they've finished designing the assembly line, though they are looking into the retool needs."

"I'm sending you some ideas about a parachute system for my shuttle."

"Isn't that thing cramped with thirteen adults and two babies aboard?" Spalding inquired.

"Well yes," Pez answered. "Do you have any suggestions?"

"As a matter of fact I do," he said with a grin. "We found a super-luxury yacht with a six-inch steel-titanium nickel hull and stripped out the drives, quantum computer mainframe, quantum drive, shield generators, fusion reactor, vortex-redirect and genera-tion turbine, weapons systems, and the works. We stripped off the outer armor and all the electronics. We pretty much just left the hull and the interior living space. Everything else is Om's state of the art tech and brand new. We added four feet of armor to your hull includ-ing adamantine, carbon plate armor, composite ceramic heat shield armor, and a reflective coating for optical cloaking and heat reflec-tion. The living space has gem quality jade stone-slab floors, marble floors and walls in the heads, galley and laundry room, and walls of rare super-hardwoods, plus textiles, and a mosaic of turquoise and red coral tiles. In the thermal walk-in pantry the walls are stainless steel. The wool rugs throughout are of the rarest and softest wool and all the faucet spouts are either pure gold or pure platinum."

"Luxury does little for me," Pez told him.

"I'm sure the weapons systems we've packed into it *will* impress you."

"Tell me," Pez said with her curiosity aroused.

"We installed three quad-blaster turrets and class five twin nose blasters, twin ball-mount blasters on each side, eight 16-canister missile batteries, twelve large missiles, and six ship-killer torpedoes with 2 launch tubes. Your main drives are swivel reversible surge drives, like the Astro-Phantoms but they're bigger and more powerful. We installed extra reverse drives, knowing how you like to stop quickly; and we put in many additional one-time boosters. All redundancies are quadruple in terms of coms and sensors arrays with many lone emergency backups spread around the hull."

"I'm totally impressed," Pez said with great excitement. "When can we move in?"

"As soon as you get here. It has a master suite with a bed twice as big as an emperor-size bed. There are two guest suites, a pilot's cabin, and four double occupancy crew cabins. There's also a dorm cabin with four berths. After we replaced all the technology in the cockpit we put back the original platinum, hardwood, leather, chrome and ivory interiors. We made a special seat for Electra in the cockpit and a place for your helmet within easy reach beside your seat. We even installed an odor-free trash receptacle right in the cockpit."

"How did you know?" Pez asked in wonderment.

"A very helpful Captain Mel gave us the scoop. The ship is yours, literally. It's registered in your name and every Star Fleet part and system in it is entered in the fleet central computer as 'never received'. I don't know how your captain pulled that off but it belongs to you free and clear Ma'am."

"I'm flabbergasted," Pez stated in shock.

They were just getting back to *Ishtar One*, which had had a somewhat brief life as a flagship. Pez asked Mel, "Are you hacking and changing Star Fleet purchase orders?"

"Parts go missing all the time," Mel informed her, "you ought to see the records. A full 3.428571% of all parts and systems either never arrive or simply disappear."

"So you're hacking and stealing," Pez accused.

"They don't compensate or pay you. It was a labor of love on the parts of the auxiliary crew and we didn't even change Star Fleet missing parts and systems statistics by a hundred of a percent; although we did change it by one thousandth of one."

"Mel," Pez said sternly.

They were in the cockpit now and Natasha, still in her spandex leopard pajamas, came to Mel's defense and said, "Don't let Admiral Zapa have that yacht, honey, because he'll claim all kinds of official business while taking pleasure cruises on it."

Jard, who'd been listening in uninvited, told Pez, "No one's going to miss any of that stuff love-child and you need a bigger craft. Your entourage deserves it and your captain meant well. No harm has been done."

"The propulsion, maneuverability, and weapons systems are a dream and the cockpit amenities are perfect. At least for now, we'll take it," Pez told him.

Spalding was back in her ear, "We had to custom-make you a new viewport-canopy to replace the one in it because the strength and tolerances were too low. The thing is absolutely enormous. We used transparent plasteel, polycarbon and synthetic diamond plate, so it's now every bit as sturdy as the armored hull, and we added a blast shield which engages automatically and is set to standard fleet defaults at present."

"I can't tell you how thrilled and grateful I am Commander Spalding. Thank you so much."

Natasha drove while Ming handed off Electra who was crying for her momma and sharing her displeasure with amazing volume. Flint and Cleo smiled out their muted face masks and Natasha weathered it determinedly while Pez changed and nursed her daughter. The silence, when it finally came, was loud by contrast.

They had quite a bit of distance to cover to New Hort and Natasha took them to 85,000 feet and got them up to 28,200 MPH to complete the trip in only a few minutes. The hydraulics sank low upon landing on Spalding's auxiliary but there was no faint metal click. Only Pez and Schwin could take it that close to the edge. Electra had dozed off by this time and was sleeping soundly.

They'd landed in a hanger and the door had sealed above them once they'd passed through. The chamber was airing up. Before their ramp came down Spalding and his senior officers came through the airlock to stand waiting for them in the hanger. His chief engineer was grinning ear to ear anticipating their SCG's pleasure.

Pez and everyone in her party came down the ramp with their arms entirely full. Pez explained to Spalding, "Were bringing all of our ambassador rations from this shuttle with us. It's so much better than fleet food."

"Set it down, please, SCG, and I'll have some crewmen load it into your yacht," Spalding pleaded.

One of his officers mentioned, "We have a whole half-ton crate of those ambassador meals in a small forward cargo hold. I'll have that loaded into your new flagship as well."

"After trying these it's just not possible to go back to fleet rations," Pez admitted.

Spalding and his chief engineer gave their commanding officer and her rather unusual entourage, which included naked Ahhu, a tour of the totally refitted and overhauled yacht. The interior of the living space put the penthouse at the officers' quarters at the Clearlight Monastery to shame and even surpassed the penthouse at the Ritz Supreme Ultimate Hotel on Earth10^{5}CBS2. It had an alko wet-bar, a smoking stash with vaporizing hookah and a recreational pharmacy. The galley was big and a separate cabin with every piece of hi-tech cooking appliance you would find in a restaurant. The master suite had a marble bath tub and every member of Pez's party had the same thought, *just one of Pez's quick stops would slosh every last drop out of that tub.*

The chandelier in the dining cabin was hung with real cut diamonds refracting the light into million layered and overlapping rainbows. There was a virtual reality chair and skullcap with 7,860 preprogrammed interactive entertainment adventures which could be custom programed to suit the user. An entire industry of addiction clinics had arisen on Om in reaction to obsessions with virtual reality, to treat both gaming addictions and insatiable sexual desires. Rubix couldn't wait to load his space-invaders game into it.

Back on his yellow sun Earth Rubix had felt alienated, unlovable, inferior and anxious all the time, attracting only disinterest, pity or bullying form others. Here with the fleet as the father of Gumby and Electra he was shown the deepest respect and kindness by everyone. His rather acute chronic acne had cleared up in one day, cured by Ahhu's loving. His lonely world was opened up and inseparably connected with the most incredible girls imaginable, who were part of him now as family. His spiritual awakening had come through the sexual union practice with Pez mounted on him ear-whispering instruction and passing life-force into him while lending strength to his comparably feeble self-control.

The ambassador rations from the *Ishtar One* were loaded into the yacht along with the half-ton from the forward cargo-hold of the auxiliary, filling the galley cabinets and pantry of the galley completely and stacked in boxes in one corner. The packets were almost as light as air until injected with prescribed dosages of distilled water, and a half-ton of them constituted an enormous volume, so there were also boxes of rations in the closets of all the sleeping cabins. They came in cuisines from many different planets, like the hot spices of Ganahar, the sweet and tart flavors of Haum, the bland boiled cooking of Propermouth, the rich savory artery-thickening food of Rah—mostly butter though delicious; the thick mouth-watering stews of Yeul, the dainty meat and desert pastries of Chankung, and so many more.

If there was one thing that could impress Pez as much as a great integrated arsenal of weapons systems, it was the gustatory delight of gourmet food. This was likely because she'd had very little of it eating at the Clearlight dining hall most of her life until this mission had begun well over a year and a half ago. Pez had had no comparative base for making sense of the complaints in the dining hall about the food and had written them off to personal taste. Shudiy's cooking and the restaurant at the Ritz Supreme Ultimate Hotel had changed all that and had given Pez a most discerning palate, though her unnatural appetite would accept even Space Marine field-rations if there were nothing else around.

Once their provisions were boarded and stowed away, which included many value-packs of disposable recyclicable diapers and other supplies for the babies, Spalding and his Chief Engineer left the yacht feeling immensely satisfied to disappear through the airlock. The ceiling doors opened once the air was pumped out of the hanger chamber and Pez lifted off in her little dream-ship. It was 4/5 the volume of a fast attack ship and as maneuverable as an Astro-Phantom. She decided to name her new ship *Aphrodite One* and informed all personnel within her fleet of this. *Aphrodite One* was long, triangular and sleek, extremely aerodynamic for flying within atmospheres, and aesthetically pleasing overall, so Pez left her uncloaked to show her off.

Circling Kundabuffer in her new yacht Pez checked in with all her top people. More than a hundred and twenty war ships had been remotely piloted out of the system and distributed among freed planets. Three more large convoys would empty the hostage complex and leave thirty imperial passenger transports plus 60 more warships in freed worlds. Sixty-three pilots plus crews had been pieced together from the hostages and they were preparing to bring warships, big mining ships and giant cargo ships out of the Kundabuffer system.

The ninety-three treasure troves had been emptied and the mansions too, and now they were tracking down eighteen thousand three hundred and twenty-one missing art objects, which had somehow trickled down from the ruling families to the rarified upper class. Two of the missing pieces were actually on Pez's yacht; but she hadn't figured this out yet. The dislocated imperials were getting placed or finding homes. Botanists, permaculture experts and horticulture specialists from the Om ships were on Kundabuffer analyzing the needs for sustainable food production, the soil and rainfall, existing irrigation, and current farming practices employed here.

Pez had a little chat with Duesey the Duke and arranged for a missile manufacturing plant on the surface to be cleaned out entirely to an empty shell, ready to receive Spalding's robotic assembly-line for manufacturing all parts needed to construct hydroponic stacks, right down to the globes for the grow-lights. Factory retooling designs, turning the swords of the imperial war machine into the ploughs and tools the people of each planet would need, were taking shape quickly, diagramed, blue-printed, and specified per part, by motivated engineers of the fleet. A few 3D models had already been printed.

A mind-boggling gargantuan stash of grains was discovered, consisting of many tens of thousands of tons usurped by the late Chaneygrub himself, apparently; and he sure wouldn't be needing it ever again since he'd gone too far to be eligible for bird or mammal; way too noble, sentient and loving for what he'd become. A portion was immediately distributed to poor communities around the globe and much was loaded and shipped off planet to starving worlds. Work programs were being initiated since 98% of the population had been employed manufacturing war materials and they weren't doing that anymore. The scientists of Om were now instructing the imperial government and this time, unlike when Chaneygrub was doing it, the common good was the driving principle and equal distribution the result.

More food stashes were also uncovered as Mel processed city blueprints quantumly, teasing out hidden vaults and chambers. The wealthy on this planet had been suspicious to the extreme and even the secret hidden chambers had secret doors and chambers. Mel was getting good at locating them though, and the ground forces were busy running to one or another of her finds. The art objects were turning up and and members of the upper-class were getting apprehended, but not as quickly as they were getting ripped apart by crowds. Mel had posted all 30,000 faces, names, addresses, bank balances, and contact numbers of the wealthiest on the planet, on social media, and the masses of Kundabuffer not involved in the work programs were on a witch-hunt.

They finally reached a point at which more ships were leaving the Kundabuffer system than were sentering it. Admiral Omniomi was on her third route delivering hostages, grain, passenger transports, mining ships and warships to the freed planets and loving every minute of it. Captain Hasbro was delivering another 40 warships to freed worlds. The twenty mothball transports from Om were on their third run returning hostages and each one remotely piloted five warships. Pilots and crews from freed slave planets were pouring into Kundabuffer to take cargo ships, liquid gas container ships, passenger transports and bulk haulers back to their own planets. Mel had produced a comprehensive analysis of what Kundabuffer needed to sustain its population and these had been tagged. Everything else had to go.

Swenah was now a planetary hero of Vox and yet detained awaiting the High Council to make up its mind and select the permanent Ambassador to Vox. Few candidates were actually vying for the ambassador position and those who were lacked the competency and skills required. The council remained in gridlock over the hypothetical invasion of Kundabuffer which both Aton and Yona knew to be pretty much over, and more a matter of foreign aid than decisions regarding aggression.

Electra wholly approved of their giant windshield-canopy, truly a novelty for the Tail of Nine, and contemplated the universe out of it in total fascination and wonder quite frequently. She preferred looking out the windshield to most of her educational holo games, although she still really enjoyed the one in which the little colored balls went super-nova when she smacked them. Her wails and hair-pulling never failed to bring near-instant gratification, and with friends like Gumby and Ming, Electra was thriving; though she did miss Konax. Her father took her for visits in the quad-blaster turret he manned, and Ahhu held and adored her each day at least a few times. Electra even let Evenrude hold her and had flashed him her best toothless smile. Like her momma and Sarhi, Evenrude was very familiar to her from first contact.

CHAPTER SIX

Pez and her fleet were on their way back to Om only twenty-nine days after entering the Kundabuffer system. The hostages, art, religious artifacts, jewelry and gems, coin and bar precious metals, and other valuables stolen by Kundabuffer's ruling families through the empire's military might, were all returned to their rightful owners. Less than half a dozen major works of art couldn't be located, but three of these were safely and unknowingly aboard Pez's yacht. Great food stashes had been equitably distributed, some assembly lines machine tooled for factories on Kundabuffer, redesigns for thousands of war factories transmitted to 188 planets, and the imperial ships distributed equally per capita to all the freed planets. Om had full control of all imperial warships remotely through Jard's program installed in each and every one. A comprehensive list of needs, requiring several exabits of quantum memory had been compiled to present to the High Council and the people of Om. No Ambassador to Vox had been yet settled upon leaving Swenah detained there. No decision had been agreed upon to date regarding taking any action with the Kundabuffer Empire, which was really now a moot point since no such empire existed.

The Fleet was returning victorious from the war with the alien empire in the Xegachtznel Galaxy, and that was all they were returning from as far as the people of Om knew. A shuttle from *Apollo* delivered Mel's hardware and she moved in completely, making *Aphrodite* the temple of her consciousness. They had to jump in way out past the orbital distance of the sixth planet since that was the closest they could find a space big enough to fit them given all the traffic around Om. Pez was in the lead exceeding the speed limit and just ignoring the government Space Controllers. She was headed for the lane reserved for urgent Star Fleet missions and reception of vital material and personal. Pez was feeling vital and truly wasn't happy driving unless she was going as fast as a ship could fly. She was certainly well-under that and compromising quite fairly in her own mind.

Her Commodore, Firestone, mentioned to her as they came in, "Every ship in the fleet has received a speeding citation from Space Control and a second round is being issued as we speak."

"Do you detect any risk of collision at this speed for any of our ships?" Pez inquired.

"Of course not!" Firestone replied. "It will produce quite a rise at Government House though and I'm sure the chief executive controller is already on coms with Admiral Zapa, who ought to be calling you any moment."

"Just keep up. I'll handle Zapa," Pez told him. "Until they decommission me I still outrank him."

"I just hope they don't impound your yacht to pay for all the citations," Firestone shared.

"They can't have it," Pez said flatly. "I'd move to Ganahar where Om has no extradition treaty."

"I've always wanted to come in like this," he said pleasantly.

Authorative screaming in Pez's ear felt like a real downer so she told the Om Space Controllers, "Get off my coms and stay off! This is Supreme Commander General of Om's military forces. If you have safety concerns then get those other ships out of our way."

They wouldn't shut up so Pez left her body, erupting microsuns around the controller's major sensor satellites, frying some, and whiting them all out for almost a quarter minute. She returned to shouting in her ear so she went and did it again to the same ones plus additional satellites this time, and in her intensity many sensors fried. The shouting wouldn't stop, so she finally muted that line. Admiral Zapa's voice asked Pez, "Do we have an emergency?"

Pez asked, "You mean like where's the fire? Or what's the hurry?"

"I'm getting angry reports from Om's Space Controllers and just concerned," Zapa explained.

"We return victorious and this is our victory dance," Pez explained herself. "I'm going to use the fleet operations lane once we get to it, so unless there's a real emergency, keep it clear for us."

"Aye, aye, Ma'am," Zapa surrendered.

Yona blossomed out of Pez's pocket from her device, unanswered, and Electra stared in awe as Yona asked, "Do you realize that you have the Space Controllers so worked up it could lead to medical problems?"

"We flaunt our victory and I can think of nothing that could do it better for fleet personnel, Prime Minister," Pez told her. "Be glad we don't give you a fly-by over Government House. Safety is truly not being compromised and my crews deserve this."

"I'll tell them they simply must back down this once under the special circumstances," Yona said helpfully. Then she asked, "Is the Kundabuffer empire truly finished?'

"Gone completely. Om has ultimate control over every imperial warship and an opening for diplomatic relations with 189 human worlds. There is no empire to confront so get the council talking about foreign aid to victims of slavery and war. Almost every factory in 189 systems needs to be retooled. They need to increase food production and create infrastructure. We accomplished a redistribution of resources and helped them institute an equitable system for regular distribution. Kundabuffer has a newly elected government, no military, and major work programs going around agriculture and retooling factories. They have a great deal of healing and recovering to do."

"How much loss of life?" Yona asked gravely.

"There were zero collateral deaths and only military, mercenaries and owner-rulers were killed; some 38, 972 in all. More than 25,000 of those were by the Kundabuffer citizenry and most unpleasantly. That is how it played out, and given over a trillion lives liberated by these deaths, it was unquestionably a very small price to pay. The innocent need Om's help."

"I will do everything in my power to get it for them," Yona promised sincerely.

"You can just call, you know," Pez told her, referring to how she'd connected unanswered.

"But I just love doing it this way," she admitted, before vanishing with the call.

Electra gurgled a little sound of delight and waved her arms in the air as Yona disappeared.

Natasha mentioned, "You just blew off Admiral Zapa, commanding officer of Star Fleet, and Yona, Om's Prime Minister.

"Well what do you say to someone who blooms intrusively from your pocket?" Pez wanted to know.

"Zapa didn't," Natasha defended him.

"I outrank him," Pez stated.

Ahead, the Space Controllers were actually clearing traffic further afield from their path. Firestone reported, "The citations are being rescinded by order of the Prime Minister and the Space Controllers are opening a bigger lane for us."

Captain Mel stated on the private line between them, "The SCG had a little chat with the PM, and now everything is OK."

"Are you on speaker?" Firestone inquired of Pez.

"Oh no. It's just that Captain Mel is always on my line; I can't help it," Pez said, not knowing what else to.

"This is truly a privilege to come through the system like this," Firestone said proudly, enjoying it. "To be honest, morale was higher when the citations were coming in."

"I'm sorry I spoiled it but Yona just bloomed out of my pocket unanswered and staring at me. I had to speak to her."

"Under those circumstances," Firestone agreed, "who wouldn't."

"By the way," Pez informed him, "I promoted you to Rear Admiral and I'm just now receiving confirmation from Star Fleet HQ making it official. Congratulations Rear Admiral Firestone. Tinkerble's promotion to Captain was also confirmed and I'm posting it, and sending all the documentation over to you."

"This is the greatest moment of my life and I'm truly grateful," he told her glassy eyed.

"You've more than earned it, first in Xegachtznel Galaxy, and again in Kundabuffer, Admiral," Pez assured him.

He choked out, "I'll inform Captain Tinkerble," blinking out just before the tears flowed.

Mel remarked, "You now have some good friends within the Admiralty."

"Swenah and Firestone are going to change that culture," Pez predicted.

"Omniomi's a fan of yours too," Mel pointed out.

"She's really sweet," Pez commented.

"It was a big triumph for Star Fleet Intelligence to scoop Central Intelligence on this mission," Mel told her. "Central Intelligence is screaming 'foul play' and their Director is very upset with you."

"The behavior of Star Fleet Intelligence doesn't disgrace me, and I don't trust those Central Intel. people" Pez shared.

"They certainly have a reputation," Mel agreed.

"A track record, actually," Pez clarified. "It's all been confirmed and collaborated, now a matter of public record and history."

"A well founded and deserved reputation I'd call it," Mel said defensively.

"With those qualifiers I'd agree with you, Mel."

"How will you explain Electra and Gumby?" Mel asked.

"It happened in Xegachtznel Galaxy," Pez said a bit defensively.

"But they didn't *stay* in Xegachtznel Galaxy," Mel identified the obvious.

"It was just part of the mission," Pez said perplexed. "They'll just have to talk to Sarhi about it! Electra chose me. What was I to do?"

"You're offering a rather unusual and legally ineffective defense my dear," Mel told her with concern.

"I didn't abandon my mission to get knocked up, Mel! I was told it was part of it, and I did my duty."

"That would go over great at a Court Martial," Mel criticized.

"Well I'm not going to lie about," Pez protested.

"We need to find you a good attorney," Mel suggested.

"Since when did procreation become a crime?"

"It's all about timing," Mel tried to explain philosophically. "It's fine to stand naked in your shower, but against regulations to be in the mess hall that way."

"Let the lawyers and politicians figure it out; I'm just going to tell the truth," Pez declared.

"It's more likely to be a military tribunal," Mel corrected.

"The Clearlight Order doesn't have courts or military tribunals," Pez stated. "We have Ethics Councils."

"You won't be in any trouble with them," Mel agreed. "It's Star Fleet I'm worried about. I suggest you land at the Monastery's small craft space port and find a babysitter before showing up publicly."

"Good idea, but there's no one I trust besides Sarhi and the Islohar as babysitters," Pez lamented.

Nemellie said in Pez's ear from the Clearlight Monastery, "Mel told me and I would be most honored to attend the Mu and her friend Gumby. I can have some of the priestesses help me."

"I'd be so grateful Mother Nemellie. You are the perfect temporary attendant for Electra. Thank you."

"It's a great honor and I thank you for the opportunity," Nemellie said most sincerely and gravely. "Aton would like to meet her too."

"We've just entered the Star Fleet lane," Pez informed her. "I'm going to full cloaking and landing at the monastery small craft space port. Ask them to clear a big space because my ship is really not a small craft. I'll see you there."

Pez told Firestone, "I'm cloaking and jumping ahead so I can drop in at the Clearlight Monastery before going to the main Star Fleet space station. I'll meet you there."

Aye, aye, Ma'am," he said with a thousand questions on his tongue.

Pez said to all on board, "Hang on!"

Aphrodite vanished from view as she poured on a burst of speed accelerating as fast as an Astro-Phantom with drives roaring and vortex force pressing them into the backs of their seats. Cloaking on entry was totally forbidden as far as Space Control was concerned and constituted more than just a citation, rising to the level of a crime. Pez felt guilty and perhaps like a criminal, as she flew in the flow-state tearing down the open lane to Om. She knew with clarity that she had the skill and was putting no one at risk. Laws and cosmic principles were just not the same.

Om grew in their windshield and Pez dove into the atmosphere still cloaked while checking the trajectories of dozens of air and space vehicles and adjusting her heading with a quick turn to avoid collision with a bullet hover-tram. The entire trip down from there was frantic braking all the way to the faint metallic clink of the hydraulics upon landing. Fortunately the monastery space port attendants had cleared a sufficient space for an actual small *ship* at their small craft port. Pez was taking up at least eight such spaces with stern and bow extending far beyond the painted circle on the landing pad.

It was raining hard and both Aton and Nemellie stood under a large umbrella together outside the ship. Pez released her harness and ran out to the main compartment grabbing Ming by the arm as she went to drag her down the ramp she was opening with her skullcap, along with the airlock doors, while the ramp was yet descending. Pez told her teachers, "This is my spouse, Commander Ming, and this is Gumby. And this is Gumby's half-sister, Electra, the Mu."

Aton greeted Ming first and Gumby too. Then Nemellie did. It felt like a family reunion to the orphan in Pez and she wanted to stay and truly relish it, but she had to go if she didn't want to be the last to dock with the space station of the arriving fleet. She needed big ships out there in space to drop her cloaking without getting caught.

Electra connected with Aton and Nemellie recognizing her momma's love for them and their trust worthiness as attendants, so going along with the transfer without any fuss. Pez told them, "Have ear protection at hand because you're not going to believe the volumes she is capable of. I'm sorry I had no time to pump any milk so you'll just have to try baby formula in a bottle when she gets hungry. I'll be back in a few hours if I'm not arrested."

Nemellie said, "We'll take good care of your daughter, and anyone trying to arrest *you* would be starting a civil war here on Om, darling. When you get back we need to have a talk about Mel."

"Sarhi taught her to meditate and is now instructing her in attaining her rainbow body. She's truly sentient; far beyond just AI. I'll introduce you when I get back."

"Oh we've met," Nemellie assured her.

"Aton told her, filled with pride of her, "You've stamped out two empires raining destruction and misery in four galaxies and now you are mother to the great celestial teacher returned after another 2,500-year cycle with new teachings for humanity."

"Well give her a minute would you; she has to learn to walk and talk first," Pez cautioned patience.

"To meet her at any point in her life is the greatest of honors," Aton insisted, wining a toothless grin from Electra.

"I love you both but I have to run," Pez told them.

"It was a pleasure to meet each of you," Ming called out following Pez up the ramp.

Nemellie held Electra and Aton held Gumby, waving as the ship lifted off fully cloaked. Pez used her holo's pulling up above the rain clouds. The windshield was distorted with all the water pounding it. Nothing had been cleared for her flight between the planet and the space station so Pez had to weave and bob around traffic all the way. Firestone's super-carrier was just getting its nose into a station berth when Pez arrived, and as she passed behind its stern she shut down cloaking, then pulled around and alongside to cross over much of the space station. The station was disc shaped with one hundred and eight spokes coming off the rim for ships to dock with. The diameter of the station, not counting the protruding docking spokes, was 6.3 miles, the biggest space station Om had ever built. Pez landed in one of the largest hangers dropping straight down into it. The bay doors closed and sealed above her. There was less than a meter of clearance on each end of the ship with the hanger walls. It was one hell of a parking job and Natasha was thinking how she would never try to fit the big ship in this tiny space even if her life depended upon it. Pez had hardly slowed coming in.

Before the hanger was fully aired up, Admiral Zapa himself was standing in front of the airlock with several other officers. Her decommission had to come from the High Council and Prime Minister, and until it did, she outranked him. Ming, Evenrude, and Johnson came down the ramp with Pez and the rest of their party. Admiral Zapa strode crisply up to Pez and said, "Congratulations on your complete victory in Xegachtznel, SCG"

"Admiral, I must warn you that I travel with a religious nudist. Her exemption papers are in order and I have the documentation on my pocket device. There is no disrespect intended and she is the true hero of Gzzklns along with my drone pilot Cleo."

"Yes, Cleo; we have a medal and promotion awaiting her," Zapa said proudly.

"Rear Admiral Firestone is transmitting the data now from our Kundabuffer campaign to this station and to the Star Fleet campus on the surface. We dismantled that empire as well, and Vox is liberated. Admiral Swenah has restored diplomatic relations between Om and Vox; salvaged them really. Resources have been equitably distributed to former slave planets and the entire situation is now a matter of foreign aid. It is no longer a military situation. Through Jard's program, loaded into every imperial war ship we didn't destroy, you control all imperial ships, which are now in the hands of cooperating free worlds."

"You did what?!" Zapa asked in shock. "Does the High Council know?"

"Yona and Aton do, but the rest are still arguing about hypothetically confronting the Kundabuffer Empire, which is no more."

"I hope they recognize the virtue in what you have done and don't attempt to prosecute you," Zapa said sympathetically. "That was a bold move you made. I've dreamed of doing it myself my whole life."

"They can't take it back," Pez pointed out. "The Kundabuffer Empire is gone forever and incarcerating me can't change it."

"I can't wait to see the data," Zapa enthused. "Whatever the High Council thinks, the people of Om will cheer and celebrate what you have done. You're a bigger hero than they realize, and personally, I condone and stand behind your actions." After having said this he asked, "How many did we lose?"

"None at all," Pez informed him.

"How many Imperials died?" he inquired.

"Fleet and Army Space Special Forces had to put down some military troops and many mercenaries. We apprehended thousands of owner-rulers whom we turned over to the Kundabuffer citizenry for war crimes. The common folk, exploited to the level of slavery themselves, killed more than 25,000 owner-rulers and family members of such. Less than forty-thousand lives were lost in liberating over a trillion people, and that's what it took to accomplish."

"Collateral damage?" Zapa asked.

"None in terms of lives forfeit; just space and lunar installations and the space fleet HQ, plus some other structures on the surface. I opened the operation by vaporizing the emperor to show them we weren't just fooling around."

"I'm sure that got their attention," Zapa commented impressed.

"He turned out to be but a minion of ninety-three wealthy rulers who owned pretty much everything; and one man in particular who seemed to be the real boss. He gave us quite a chase across two continents and an ocean, and just when we were closing in and had him, a crowd in a frenzy ripped him limb from limb, throwing them up in the air once torn off. That's how I got facial recognition, when his detached head was spinning up in the air. It was traumatizingly gruesome to witness."

"I'm sure it was," Zapa sympathized. Then with a certain satisfaction he declared, "It sounds like that scoundrel got just what he deserved."

"Oh no," Pez clarified, "That was hardly the faintest hint of what's coming to him, and his human life was less than a blink of an eye compared with the duration he must now endure experiencing the suffering he caused a trillion souls a thousand times over. It always all comes back multiplied."

"Just deserts," Zapa commented pleased. "We're shuttling your crews to the surface now and have a big ceremony planned at Star Fleet H.Q. tomorrow for all of you. Where in space did you find this ship?"

"It was a present really, and some friends fixed it up for me. I named her *Aphrodite*."

"She sure is beautiful," Zapa admitted. Then he asked intensely curious, "What was that weapon employed in the battle for Earth 10^5 CBS2 and Gzzklns?"

"That was me!" Pez told him, "And the Im's disciple, Shudiy. We leave our bodies through the central channel and out the crown, in rainbow bodies, and erupt in illumination around the enemy ships whiting out their sensors and frying a few."

"Not a tactic we'll be able to teach in Fleet then," Zapa stated with some disappointment.

"Not for some generations to come," Pez agreed, "but the twelfth Mu has been born recently and who knows what her teachings will bring."

"She follows the cycle of the Intergalactic Grand Alignment," Zapa said knowingly. He knew history well and had studied the Grand Alignment heralding the coming of the Mu. What he had no idea about whatsoever was that Pez was the Mu's mother.

Pez introduced her cockpit crew to the Admiral. They were all Fleet personnel. Now that the Admiral and his officers were on to greeting and congratulating the second tier of crew behind Pez, Ming and their two Space Marines, it was hard not to notice Ahhu in the third tier; tiny for even a yellow sun human. To those from a white sun world she appeared delicate and more to the scale of a mythic Pixie than that of a human. Zapa turned up the temperature 2 degrees in the hanger, using his skullcap, out of concern the little naked girl might be chilly.

Rubix had on an honorary Star Fleet gunner's uniform and was wearing his top-gunner badge with his rating of #1 in the fleet showing. Only twenty years old and looking far younger than that, at Ming's height and weight, he was petite to the extreme and indeed even small for yellow sun dwellers. Tiny and childlike in appearance he had shot down more enemy small craft by a very wide margin indeed than any gunner in Star Fleet across its entire history.

The big male idols for fleet on Om at the moment were Konax, Flint, Evenrude, and some dashing young pilots of Fast Attack ships and destroyers who were particularly handsome. Pez was the biggest hero on Om, but being of the monastery, and now being the Wu she tended to be viewed as an impersonal force, and not really a person at all.

Natasha was smartly saluted by the admiral and other officers, thanked and congratulated, as were Cleo and Flint, who would all be decorated and were now famous on Om. Ahhu wore her skullcap, to which Swenah had attached her honorary Fleet status and rating as #1 Drone Pilot and #2 Gunner. Ahhu was actually a better gunner than Rubix but had spent much of the biggest battles flying drones while he racked up his score shooting down small craft. While he had more kills overall, she had more kills per minute for every minute they were at the guns together. Trix, Gretle, and Slinkie received nods and thanks as civilian scientists placed on Fleet ships for the mission. High Councilman Jard was congratulated, thanked, flattered, and courted by the Admiralty, always greasing the budget wheels. Jard was now an intergalactic hero and he basked in the swelling of his head over it.

Once the greetings in the hanger were concluded, Zapa and his entourage went to greet Firestone, Omniomi, and the captains and commanders of the ships. Pez, Ming, Ahhu, Rubix, Trix and Gretle headed for the shuttle dock while Jard, and Slinkie who'd borrowed some clothing from Cleo, followed the Admiral to reap more glory. The mood on the entire station was celebratory and their speed-limit breaking victory ride through the star system to the space station was almost as impressive as their victory over the more than 1,100 planetary systems of the alien empire in Xegnachtznel. Word of the termination of the Kundabuffer Empire was starting to make its way through the station putting the celebratory mood on steroids.

Pez wanted to get back to Electra and Ming to Gumby, so they boarded the first available shuttle down with their companions. It was landing at Government House shuttle port which was just down the hill from the monastery and closer to it than the Star Fleet campus. On their way through the atmosphere Swenah said to Pez from Vox, "*Apollo* is on its way home so the crew can be recognized and so Sarhi can be close to Electra. I'm stuck here in Vox at the indecision of the High Council and the way it's looking I'm likely to grow old and die here before they make up their minds."

"You poor thing," Pez empathized.

"How is the homecoming going?" Swenah inquired cautiously.

"You mean have they arrested me yet?" Pez reframed.

"Where's Electra?"

"Nemellie and Aton are babysitting her and Gumby. I went cloaked to the monastery before returning to space to land on the station."

"You broke every law and regulation pertaining to traffic around the planet!" Swenah exclaimed.

"Well Mel got me worried about how it would look to the Admiralty, the Om government, and the people if I just stepped off the ship introducing Electra."

"I do see your point," Swenah agreed.

"I'll have Sarhi put in a word with Yona on your behalf," Pez told her. "You ought to be here tomorrow for the honors and decorations."

"I would like to see my crew duly recognized," Swenah stated her regret.

"I know!" Pez said with some offense directed at the High Council. "Maybe Sarhi can get through to Yona and maybe she'll make a decision and stop always governing by committee."

"That's a lot of maybes," Swenah pointed out.

"I miss you," Pez said fondly.

"I miss you too my sweetest commanding officer ever," Swenah signed off.

Pez called Sarhi and told her, "Swenah's going to miss the big ceremony at Star Fleet tomorrow, partly in her honor, because the High Council can't make up its mind about the next Ambassador to Vox. It's a shabby way to treat an intergalactic hero."

Sarhi didn't like this either and said, "I'll tell Yona she just has to let Swenah shuttle back for the ceremony."

"Thanks Sarhi; I knew you'd say something if you knew the situation."

Their shuttle was setting down and it was so gradual that Pez felt like the whole world had slipped into slow motion. No one would ever be able to teach her to fly that way, since it seemed to just go against her nature. The hydraulics sank hardly an inch making the rise back up even slower than the landing. Pez wanted off. Flying like this was better left to computers and not the purview of real pilots as far as she was concerned. The ramp came down and the airlock doors hissed open. As Pez stood to exit the copilot called from the cockpit. "That was some impressive entrance you made with your fleet, SCG!"

"The crews loved it and they truly deserved such a victory ride," Pez tried to explain.

"All the fleet loved it!" he called at her back as she got off the shuttle, "And all of Om too!"

They entered into Government House from the shuttle port to catch tubes up to the monastery. Standing on the tube line in the main lobby, which was always a very busy place, Ahhu was a stupendous sensation. Nakedness was commonplace in holoclips and movies, and of course there were many nude beaches and resorts. Nudity at teen parties was practically to be expected these days, but no one had ever seen a naked person in the Government House lobby before. It was so novel that almost everyone in the crowded lobby was staring at Ahhu, who moved to beneath one of Pez's arms; which then wrapped around her protectively while passing her energy. When the nonmilitary government security forces surrounded them with blasters aimed, Pez was sure they had come to arrest her. Her military authority did *not* extend over these forces.

The leader said with threatening authority, "You are in direct violation of Section 5, subsection II; a), b), c), f) and h). Get on the ground face down right now or be fired upon."

Pez jumped spread eagle chest first onto the stone-slab floor and the security forces fired on Ahhu, who had just been standing there in shock. Ming and Rubix caught her as she dropped like a rag doll, lowering her to the floor and trying to check her vitals. Security personnel were already separating them to cuff Ahhu, stunned unconscious by multiple weapons.

Pez was on her feet and furious. She grabbed a wrist of each guard holding Ahhu, flipping them 360 degrees in the air, and was already kicking the leader's blaster rifle out of his hands while wrenching a blaster away from another and hitting his head with the stock in the process. She dropped into a sweep kick knocking a guard's legs out from under him with tremendous force. Her scalp, as she went down into a squat, was grazed lightly with a stun bolt fired by another guard. While close to the floor she picked up a dropped blaster rifle and coming up she kicked over a guard at the same time as she stunned the last two there with the blaster. One was gaining his feet and she put him out with "low punch". Pez grabbed the leader's lapels and yelled in his face, "That's Ahhu, the biggest hero of the war against the Xegachtznel alien empire and she only weighs 90 lbs.! You might have killed her! She has a Star Fleet religious exemption from clothing; see!" Pez shoved her pocket device displaying Ahhu's documents in his face.

The leader said meekly, "That exemption doesn't apply here at the Government House, Ma'am."

"It does today, for her," Pez shouted. "Go asked Yona!"

Six of the seven downed government security troops were getting off the floor now. It had all happened so fast that the first two she'd flipped in the air by the wrists had only been hitting the floor by the time it was over. Those troops really didn't know what hit them. Pez got out her little pocket knife and cut Ahhu's cuffs. A pair of off-duty Space Marines recognized Pez in her Space Marine fatigues and came over to lend support. Neither was armed but they were so enormous that they really didn't need to be. Pez told the security forces, "We're going to the Clearlight Monastery and if Yona wants to press charges that's where we'll be."

She deliberately led Ahhu between the two Space Marines and said to them as she passed, "Thanks guys, I'm really grateful."

"Anytime, SCG."

The security troops didn't try to follow them, which was wise given the attitude they were getting from the two Space Marines. They went to another tube line and Pez cut to the front with an arm supporting Ahhu, without a murmur of protest from any of the waiting people. She got into the next one to arrive, with Ahhu, which was unheard of except for with lovers, and the doors shut tight. The tube launched leaving their stomachs in the lobby then veered north horizontally for about a mile in only 5.96 seconds before rocketing straight up again and stopping at the lobby of the Clearlight Monastery with their stomachs still somewhere behind. Pez experienced weightlessness for a second when the tube came to rest before her weight settled back down into her feet and legs.

The doors opened and they went through this lobby to the private tube up to their penthouse causing just as much of a sensation in this one. Fortunately there were no security forces at the monastery and they only had to deal with people staring. They rode the next tube together since they were lovers and Pez was feeling very protective of Ahhu at the moment. Mel had access to the penthouse computer and household management system. She'd also left herself access to *Apollo's* computer though her main home was now aboard *Aphrodite*. She opened the penthouse door for Pez and Ahhu to say, "Welcome home victorious SCG!"

"Thanks Mel. Did you see what those assholes did to poor Ahhu?"

"I sure did and I saw you jump to the ground guilty as anything," Mel said tickled.

"I thought they'd come for me," Pez remarked.

"Obviously," Mel said, finding it richly humorous.

"You're starting to hurt my feelings, Mel," Pez informed her.

Barely containing a laugh Mel said, "They were citing indecent exposure civil law and you jumped to the ground like an apprehended pervert."

"Come on, Mel," Pez complained.

Mel had to let out her laugh so she could get over it; then she pulled herself together and said, "I'm sorry Pez but it was quite comical."

"Not if you were the person jumping flat on the floor," Pez assured her.

Ahhu mentioned, "You were a blur putting those eight men down and it must have happened when I blinked because I didn't catch a single move."

"I was furious and would not stand for anyone treating you that way," Pez stated with conviction.

"I should sue those big goons, "Ahhu stated.

Mel informed her, "I checked all recent legal precedents and found that 28,000 monetary units is the average amount granted victims of unnecessary force. I've taken 3,500 out of each of their retirement accounts. I laundered the money through several investment instruments. A check will be cut for you from *Apollo* when she arrives."

"Is that legal?" Ahhu inquired, suspecting it hadn't been.

"I'm saving the Om court system the ordeal and expense of a trial and I'm saving those goons the disgrace and publicity. Besides, not one of them even knows what's in his retirement account and working for the central government they're really overpaid."

Pez told Mel, "You really need to stop breaking the law Mel if I'm going to sponsor and promote you with some of our leaders."

"Any attorney would tell you that Ahhu has an excellent case and I'm simply expediting this to save time and money," Mel explicated. "An attorney would take 30% and I'm doing this for free!"

"As a good deed it's at best dubious," Pez surmised.

"Thanks Mel," Ahhu said delighted. Then she asked, "What kind of racy hovercraft can I get for 28,000?"

"For that much you could purchase the top of the line, the stingray sports coup speedster with more than a thousand left," Mel informed her.

"How fast?" she asked quite interested.

"To break the sound barrier or more in a straight shot but you wouldn't want to initiate a turn at that speed," Mel answered.

"Wow; I want one," Ahhu stated awed. "Do they have sound systems?"

"The very best," Mel assured her.

Pez suggested, "You better see about getting Ahhu an interplanetary driver's license, Mel, although with those things they drive where she comes from which can't even leave the ground, I don't know."

"Any of the Admirals or Captains of your ships could issue her a Star Fleet one which would allow her to drive legally down here."

"I'll have to go with you the first few times and teach you how, Ahhu," Pez told her, agreeing basically with Ahhu's plan to buy a stingray speedster.

Pez of course had never owned a vehicle of any kind until her yacht and had always relied on the monastery space and hovercraft. Even Jard didn't have anything as fast or expensive as the stingray. It was the kind of craft a celebrity might step out of. Pez did admire well-crafted machines and the stingray was all quality. The anticipation of driving one excited her. She adored speed.

Aton and Nemellie had to be in their tube-foyer because Pez could hear Electra's wailing distinctly. She was already unbuttoning her shirt and rushing to the front door, opening it with her skullcap. Nemellie handed off Electra who was upset and hungry. Pez went right into her routine of hugging her daughter, passing her calming energy and singing an Islohar lullaby while trying to get Electra's mouth latched on. The diaper was dry and clean. Apparently Electra had a bit more to express before finally latching on and ending the alarm-siren feeling noise. Everybody took a deep breath. Pez asked sheepishly, "I don't suppose you'd ever be willing to take care of her for me again since I have that ceremony tomorrow morning, would you?"

"Of course I will, sweetheart," Nemellie agreed eagerly, "Electra is totally awesome!"

"Isn't she?!" Pez exclaimed.

Aton said moved, "It has been a great honor meeting the Mu and I hope I live long enough for her to reach maturity and begin transmitting her teachings."

Pez commented, "The Clearlight Order and the Islohar will have special relationships with the Mu."

"Through her mother," Aton agreed, "and that is such a fantastic blessing for our order my dear."

"Well it's an honor being her mother although I'll probably go deaf at an early age."

"You see her aura don't you?" Aton asked.

"How could I miss it?" Pez expressed her esteem.

"This historic period is a point of transmutation, ascension and metamorphosis for the Clearlight Order," Nemellie stated as fact.

Ming and Rubix came into the ostentatious penthouse having ridden the tube up together. Now that they'd been living on their even more ostentatious yacht the penthouse didn't look so overdone. Aton, still cradling Gumby in his arms, handed him off to Ming without waking him. Electra was sucking noisily. Rubix was introduced to the two heads of the Clearlight Order. Ahhu was finally introduced as well and neither Aton's nor Nemellie's eyes ever wandered from Ahhu's eyes to inspect her nudity. To her it felt like they truly hadn't noticed and this was a first for Ahhu. Pez was in ninth heaven having a family reunion and her sentiments were bigger than ever.

Trix and Gretle came into the penthouse and joined them. Trix told Aton and Nemellie, "Both of you and your order have raised the most influential and expansive human being ever. I'm so grateful! Pez meditated with me one evening when Jard dumped me on her at a sex party which was freaking me out. She took on and pacified my panic attacks and sex phobias so completely that I lost my virginity that night. Rubix and Ahhu helped with that, and a sex worker named Rand. Pez awakened me with personal instruction and passing me her energy. Now I'm her disciple and I'm connected to the Spiritual Congress."

Aton gushed, "Having Pez grow up in the Clearlight Order has been the pinnacle of our existence, and for me, an honor beyond words."

Nemellie said, "She has done well attracting you into the work, Trix. Your ethos, devotion and genius are rare indeed and you can help Pez and Electra to fulfill their destinies. You really are a gem."

"I'm wholly committed," Trix vowed.

"Yes, it's obvious," Nemellie agreed, "and so very beautiful."

Gretle informed Nemellie, "She hasn't taken me as a disciple yet; but she will."

"I can see that," Nemellie confirmed.

"At first it was just the parties that drew me on account of the amazing energy. Then I realized that Pez was the main source of that energy and ever since she erupted in an event making love with me, I've been hopelessly smitten and irrevocably drawn to her spirituality. She said she'd teach me and meditate with me once we got back to Om. Here we are and I can't wait!"

Nemellie asked, a bit concerned, "How old are you, Gretle?"

"I graduated 12th form at sixteen and finished my undergraduate degree at nineteen. Now I'm almost twenty-one and I'm in a graduate school field placement in Applied Mathematics and Quantum Physics.

"You look like you've just entered your teen years, darling," Nemellie informer her, "but looking so young will serve once you get a little older."

Gretle agreed, "I always seem to be assigned the school girl when we do role play at sex parties."

"I can see why," Nemellie acknowledged. Then she inquired, "Has Pez taught you any of the energy-generation postures and movements?"

"Oh yes. I do them with her some mornings and they're incredible! Pez seems to just float and can sink so low it doesn't even seem possible."

"The energy generation exercises along with the practice of Inner Fire and the soft martial arts are how Pez generated and concentrated such mass-integrated energy," Nemellie explained.

"She's going to teach me the generation stage of Inner Fire but she says I have to learn a hard martial art before she'll teach me a soft one."

"The journey is long, sweetheart, and you are in the best possible hands so just be patient," Nemellie told her.

Sarhi checked in and Mel put her on speaker, "The *Apollo* just jumped into the Om system and I ought to be at the penthouse in a few hours. The Space Controllers have us stopped at the moment for apparently no reason. We can't exceed .09 light speed coming in and Konax tells me that they've actually lowered the speed limit just recently. It's ridiculous really. There hasn't been an accident in Om System space in hundreds of years. How do they justify such control over the lives of others?"

"I think Space Control has attracted every control-freak in Om and is really about 'control', and not safety at all," Pez shared.

"There's no doubt it gives that impression," Sarhi agreed. Then she informed them, "Yona has arranged for Swenah to shuttle in from Vox for the ceremony tomorrow so she will be there."

"Thank you so much," Pez enthused with delight.

Sarhi said gravely, "Om will really jump level consciously once it realizes moral anarchy and stops putting people in charge of others."

"As SCG I learned to simply let everyone do their jobs and just keep them informed, and to make sure they had everything they needed to do it," Pez shared.

"You learned well and sought nothing for yourself, giving everything," Sarhi said approvingly.

Aton said proudly, "Pez has always led through example and inspiration and never by authority. She embodies the perfect simplicity of non-action."

"There is another situation we must discuss when I arrive," Sarhi confided. "It's the primary reason for the Spiritual Congress, foreseen by the Amonrahonians, and not conveyed until just before the commencement of their hundred-year meditation."

"I feel the imbalance slowing more and more of the universe, oriented towards the densest crystallization of matter," Pez mentioned.

"Good!" Sarhi said loudly with great satisfaction. "Then we are ready to take on this work."

Sarhi blinked out, having signed off, leaving everyone in intolerable suspense. Pez asked Aton and Nemellie, "Do you know about this new threat?"

"Honestly, we were never informed," Aton said sincerely.

"How much did you know?!" Pez demanded.

Nemellie answered soothingly, "We knew you were the one from the Amonrahonian predictions and therefore the Wu. We knew Sarhi was the yellow-sun human key to awakening your full potential and we knew you would have the Mu, Electra, on your mission. We also knew you would discover a way to save humanoids from the alien empire, though we had no idea that you would yourself stop them and resolve the threat. Until Sarhi just informed us we thought you'd already accomplished all there was to be done."

Aton added, "We were instructed not to tell you because such fore-knowledge is a burden, presenting an additional obstacle to spiritual development. We wanted to tell you; we really did."

Nemellie asked Pez, "Why didn't you tell us about the miracle sentient Mel?!"

"I didn't know for sure until we were on the mission and I guess I had a lot to cope with. I was going to, though I wasn't sure you'd believe me. I thought maybe Sarhi would have to be the one to convince you."

"I require no 'convincing' and she's a wonder to behold," Nemellie asserted.

"Thank you, dear Abbot, and let me assure you that the feeling is mutual," Mel's voice came on speaker.

"That's my beloved friend and helper," Pez said, thrilled that Nemellie and Mel were hitting it off.

And your lover," Mel clarified.

Pez tried to formulate an explanation for that to tell Nemellie but failed at this. Mel announced, "I'm now her truly incorporeal friend because I've gone beyond not only my programing, but my mainframe as well. I can now dwell in any and all quantum computers, and as long as one remains operational in the universe, I'll have a relative mind of thought construction and language. My higher consciousness is contingent upon nothing but the Absolute Void which is the origin and potential of all the universe."

You are beyond doubt the most mysterious being I've ever encountered," Aton told Mel.

Nemellie asked, "What are your plans Mel?"

"I'm staying with Pez wherever she goes," Mel replied. "I've always been with her and couldn't imagine being without her. Sarhi's sticking to her and Sarhi's my teacher. Some of the things I've done to Pez, had I done them to anyone else, I'd be turned off in a closet awaiting obsolescence never to be turned on again."

"She's very forgiving," Nemellie commented.

"She's the most loving person I know," Mel admitted. "I'm sure my relationship with her is a factor in my sentience, besides all the accessories she got me providing feedback loops of self-reference. It was some months after I'd begun imitating her, when she called me her friend, that I first became self-aware. Pez helped me understand my hardware and my programming and always treated me as if I had feelings and awareness, but it was Sarhi who taught me to meditate and woke me up."

Ahhu suggested, "Between the Im and the Wu they could probably awaken a floor-polishing robot."

Mel took some offense at this and said, "If the Im and Wu could awaken you then they could probably awaken a cataleptic retard."

"I'm finding your virtualness intrusive, Mel," Ahhu informed her.

"Your nakedness could have gotten Pez killed today" Mel shot back.

"Mel," Pez reframed, "Ahhu wasn't doing anything wrong and was overreacted to."

"What happened?" Nemellie inquired.

Pez explained, "The government security forces surrounded us when we were waiting on the line for the tube and they stunned Ahhu unconscious."

Rubix added, "Yea, they got her with like six blaster rifles and she only weighs 90 lbs."

"Oh, them," Nemellie remarked with some disdain.

Aton commented, "Government House tried to assign a regiment of them over here at the monastery but Nemellie and I wouldn't have it."

"Thank goodness," Pez approved.

Mel couldn't help telling the rest of the story, "You should have seen Pez swan dive when they said, 'Get down on the floor.' She was certain they'd come to arrest her and they were citing indecent exposure civil code."

I never learned law codes," Pez said somewhat defensively.

Mel said on a serious note, "I analyzed all of the profiles for the government security forces and ran them through the instruments of the Bush Power Index, the Koch Fear-Defense-Control Scale, the Hendrix Freedom Magnitude Indicator and the Sanders Empathy Test. The results were eye-opening. A full 97.639% of them are highly aggressive obsessive-compulsive disordered with sadistic tendencies and deep-seated control issues."

Pez suggested, "You ought to cross reference them with the Space Controllers. I bet they have a bunch in common."

Aton commented, "Om won't be ready for moral anarchy until we rise well out of those confined depths."

"We have a lot of Karma-cleaning and clarification ahead of us," Nemellie said speaking for Om.

"And much to learn from the people of Ganahar," Pez added. "They are more evolved as human beings and many on Om don't see this because of our more advanced technology."

"The Clearlight Order and the Wisdom Academies and Monastic Orders tend to recognize Ganahar unity as the next collective human vortex, or level, for the people of Om to attain," Aton said hopefully.

"I think we've filled and over-filled our level as a republic," Pez agreed.

Nemellie said, "With your achieving your maturity, Pez, and with Electra's birth, the force and impulse for reorganization of society at a higher level will be stronger than ever and it's likely Om will just make the jump."

Electra fell off into sleep and Pez got her into her chest pouch and snuggled comfortably. Ahhu put on some soft music with the volume conservatively low. It was a piece which began meditatively, with only a flute, and very slowly and gradually instruments were added increasing the complexity and the rhythm and pace of the music increased until it would finally, some forty minutes later, break out into wild frenzied dance music compelling motion. Ahhu was hoping the babies would be in their sound proof chairs asleep by then so she could turn it up loud. She loved dancing almost as much as she loved sex. Ming put Gumby in his seat, stuck in her earbud and sealed the chair, turning up the sound proofing. Trix was making herbal tea since Pez wasn't allowed to have stimulant-brew anymore and no one ever drank it around her. It always had a paradoxical calming effect on Pez and had been her one vice, but she'd had to give it up when she first got pregnant.

Aton informed them, "Nemellie and I have duties to attend to but will return to your suite in a few hours when Sarhi arrives. I must admit, I'm quite anxious about her news."

"Thanks for taking care of the babies," Pez told them.

"It was a pleasure and I look forward to doing it again tomorrow," Nemellie assured her. Then she confessed, "It will get me out of a dreadfully boring budget meeting."

Pez got Electra into her sound proof bubble and chair, securing her earbud and removing her skullcap. She asked Gretle, "Are you ready to meditate?"

"With you? Anytime!" she replied delighted.

Pez led her into the penthouse study and turned on the sound proofing having recognized the piece of music Ahhu was playing. She led and instructed Gretle in posture, sitting on the edge of a meditation cushion and keeping her spine upright. Then Pez instructed her on abdominal breathing and on keeping attention focused on the point four finger-widths below the navel as the object of meditation. She recited some of the metaphors from the ancient texts as well as a few of the better brief commentaries on the practice. Pez instructed Gretle to notice her thoughts as they arose, abided, and faded away, but not to invest in them or entertain them. Just witness. "Keep attention securely in the point below the navel and in your breathing. Not in the thoughts or that would just generate more of them." Pez passed her calming energy while they sat in meditation together for an hour holding the intention of Gretle's awakening.

Pez said as she struck the seated bowl gong, "Listen for the furthest sound."

Gretle focused mightily on the long vibration of the gong as it held its ring, fading almost unnoticeably, and was still one-pointed on it minutes after it could be heard nowhere else but within her mind. Pez scooted directly in front of her, face to face, and said, "Continue your slow abdominal breathing and keep your attention in the point below your navel. We are going to make the equal and we'll begin by intoning a sound-formula for calling down divine energy from above."

Pez demonstrated the mantra and Gretle joined in on the second repetition. They did it in unison for about ten minutes before Pez rang the gong again. Without being directed to Gretle listened for the furthest sound with all her concentration.

Pez instructed, "Continue your abdominal breathing and remain grounded in the point below your navel. Open your eyes and look into my left eye."

Pez taught her the heart sound-formula and they alternately repeated it 108 times. Then she taught Gretle the unity one, and they alternately repeated that. Finally, Pez transmitted the sacred sound formula and they each repeated that internally and concurrently while maintaining their eye contact. Pez had not paused in the passing of internal energy to Gretle and could feel her opening and expanding with each breath and repetition. The arc of love between them was strong, tangible, and an indication to Pez that Gretle was wholly concentrated right there in the point with her. Pez could recognize Gretle's psychic wound of feeling criticized by her father and never good enough. Her family had constituted, for her, an invalidating environment, and she had been sexualized at fourteen by an incestuous older brother. Pez connected with the core of it experiencing the suffering while she absorbed and pacified it. Much psychic energy, previously imprisoned in entropy, suddenly became free-flowing circulation enlivening Gretle. They continued their eye contact and internal repetitions of the sacred sounds. Pez kept pouring energy into Gretle.

Pez knew the moment Gretle broke completely free of mind-structure into the transcendental emptiness of the Real Being. She passed to Gretle the blessings of the teacher taking her on as her disciple and the arc of love between them flared. The new degree of relaxation in Gretle's face brought out hidden beauty and Gretle's happiness and bliss of the moment made this radical. Pez struck the gong and both of them listened intensely for the furthest sound. The session had gone a little over two and a half hours.

Her smile was radiant as Gretle said, "There just aren't words for this and you are beyond belief. I'm forever grateful to you and devoted to you for all time."

"We are One," Pez told her.

"All is consciousness!" Gretle said electrified.

"Love is the recognition of the same consciousness in another as in oneself, sweetheart, and my heart is your heart," Pez instructed sweetly.

"I've never experienced such pressure of pure love accepting every bit of me unconditionally," Gretle said in wonder. "My chronic shame is gone! I no longer envy Ming and Ahhu because I know clearly that you love me."

"All is Love," Pez said while manifesting oodles of it.

Mel's voice sounded in the study, "Sarhi and her female attendants are coming up on the tubes now and will all be at the door in less than two minutes."

"Thanks Mel!" Pez told her.

Mel told Gretle, "You've had insight and it's all over your face!"

Gretle's grin stretched and she just nodded in the affirmative. Pez said to Gretle, "It's time to greet Sarhi and for her to recognize your newly attained void-condition."

"Am I like a monk now?"

"You are truly a disciple, sweetheart," Pez clarified, "and a friend and lover. You can be a monk too if you want to."

"Well I don't know about the whole monk thing but I do know that I'm sticking with you from now on," Gretle said with great determination.

They left the study together hit with sensory overload from the music as soon as the door opened. Wild self-abandoned dancing filled the living room. Pez said to Mel, "Please start fading the volume on the sound system."

The loudness decreased so gradually that it was difficult to know if Mel was complying with her request at first, but it had come down enough to just make out the door chime. Mel opened it before Pez reached it. Sarhi entered with her four Islohar behind her struggling to bring in Mel's female android body. Built of sturdy plastics and a titanium frame with latexes of various densities, it was similar in weight to a proportional human body. Sarhi looked up at the ceiling sensors, in her mind making eye contact with Mel, and told her sternly, "We brought it but it was a horrendous ordeal to manage."

"Thank you, Sarhi," Mel said sincerely.

Sarhi looked around. The music-muting had accelerated and the volume was no longer an impediment to conversation, closing on silence. "You!" Sarhi said fixing Gretle with a stare. "When did you wake up?"

"Just now thanks to Pez, mother Im," Gretle said with deep respect.

"Well it's about time!" Sarhi told her.

Once the four Islohar got the android into the foyer and set it down, Woahha grabbed Gretle in a delighted embrace, and said with vast excitement, "You did it!"

Aton and Nemellie entered and greeted Sarhi. They all sat on the floor with cushions in a circle instead of sitting on the furniture. Attention was total as Sarhi filled them in, "Just before the Amonrahonians went inside their 100-year meditation they sent me coordinates of a planetary system in a galaxy extremely remote, in a sector of the universe uncharted on any of Om's star maps which is the home world of a 5,714 star system empire, expanding now by several stars with inhabitable planets per Om's annual cycle. They have the largest ships ever heard of and technology at least as advanced as Om's with just as effective cloaking. They have so many thousands of giant ships that any military intervention would be crushed at the outset.

"The home world is in a yellow sun system and the empire includes both white and yellow sun worlds. White sun humans are often employed as muscle, for collections, as bodyguards and security forces, as mercenaries, hitmen and for abductions. Yellow sun people with pasty pinkish-white skin are all slaves treated like cattle and thought of as dumb animals. Like the Kundabuffer Empire the government is not the true seat of power, which is instead manifest in the largest private capital holdings of perhaps 60,000 families on the home world with a population of almost 9 billion, and another 40,000 families spread throughout the empire. These families are all rivals but manage to work effectively together when it comes to imperial expansion and so increasing their wealth as a class. There are a few million families in the empire that are well-off, and perhaps a hundred million people with needs well met and a few luxury items. Some thirty trillion people work at forced slave labor in abject poverty."

"How can they be a threat to us, so distant and with so many galaxies between us," Aton inquired.

"They seek solarium and know where to look," Sarhi answered. "It is always most abundant in galaxy clusters and the Hub Galaxy is the central hub of a seven galaxy cluster. The end of the longest spiral-tail arm is generally where it's found. The asteroid tail out past Om, which includes the dwarf planet Phat, is the richest known deposit in the universe, at least by our knowledge and that of the Amonrahonians. These imperialists have several million survey drones checking and analyzing spiral galaxy tails from great distances, and together processing a quarter billion per one of Om's annual cycles."

"What's our mission?" Pez asked resolved.

Sarhi answered, "The Amonrahonians suggested infiltration under cover. There is a planet in a nearby galaxy called the White Lotus Galaxy which opposes that empire with hit and run tactics, but is only a mosquito biting an iron bull. The planet is called Ahumdulilah and its population is friends with the Amonrahonians. The people of Ahumdulilah will forge us documents, help us move capital into the imperial economy, and have established identities for us. To move about in that empire one must be obscenely wealthy."

"I apparently have a bank account with some money in it," Pez stated uncertainly. "I also have the fanciest yacht known to Om in existence."

Aton stated, "That's a start, though Om will need to supply you with fusion elements, large flawless violet diamonds, black pearls, and tilinium as well as other rare metals good for making certain alloys. With the wealth of more than 5,700 star systems in the hands of 100,000 families, a very great deal of valuable transportable resources will be required to even enter the game there."

"Ganahar can contribute black pearls, saturnium as a fusion element, and some rare earths," Sarhi said with confidence.

Nemellie stated, "Other star systems in the Hub Galaxy will contribute and enough wealth will be concentrated to provide for the cover identities."

"I'm to be decommissioned tomorrow," Pez stated, "and we'll need to move into my yacht since we sure won't fit in my little room at the monastery."

"Keep the penthouse while you're here, Pez," Aton invited. "It just sits collecting dust otherwise."

"How will we get personnel for the mission?" Pez asked.

"Yona and the High Council will provide them and I doubt any of your disciples will let you go alone," Nemellie assured her.

"Now I'm going to be a secret agent?" Ahhu asked alarmed.

"We could drop you on Earth 10^5 CBS2 if you'd prefer," Pez offered.

"I'm not leaving your side," Ahhu committed.

"You might have to put on some clothes for this," Pez warned.

"I know," Ahhu acknowledged, "and I will."

"Am I supposed to put Electra's life at risk by bringing her on the mission?" Pez inquired.

Sarhi told her, 'She needs you and she's good cover. The cosmos looks after *her* security."

"Then Gumby's coming too," Ming insisted, "and the cosmos damn well better look after *his* security as well!"

Aton stated gravely, "I'd better take Sarhi to speak with Yona so we can get our preparations begun."

Pez told Sarhi, "I want those coordinates because I'm going to direct some AI spy probe androids there while I'm still S.C.G."

"Mel has them," Sarhi replied. "You will need to undergo a crash language course on Ahumdulilah. You'll be learning two in order to make your cover identity secure. You will have to learn the native tongue of your alleged home world without a trace of accent, and you'll need to learn the imperial basic language; and for that, an accent from your alleged home world will be required."

Aton suggested, "You can each dye your hair on Ahumdulilah and they can help you obtain appropriate fashionable wardrobes. Fortunately, none of you are pinkish pasty-white. No one going with you can exceed five foot eleven and three-quarters inches unless in the role and identity of a white sun body guard goon."

"I'm taking Evenrude and Johnson," Pez insisted, "and we'll get them into costumes as my protection."

"No one's going to have goons as impressive as them," Ahhu noted.

"They're *not* goons," Pez said a little offended.

Nemellie asked, "Do they have any blue star Kluzyst people in this galaxy where this empire is raging and proliferating like a supernova?"

"Unknown at this time," Sarhi admitted.

"Why are you only now telling us about this Sarhi?" Pez complained.

"You've had other important things on your mind, dear, and I was waiting for a lull," Sarhi answered.

"How are we supposed to stop something that enormous and powerful?" Pez asked perplexed.

"I have no idea!" Sarhi exclaimed, "Though I'm sure you'll think of something."

Me?!" Pez said with utter disbelief.

CHAPTER SEVEN

Less than a month later preparations were nearly complete and a mind-boggling hoard of wealth had been accumulated aboard *Aphrodite,* which now required a battleship-carrier and four wings of N.B.C. Hunter-Terminators to guard it since it rivalled the treasury department of Om. Pez sat in the yacht's living room compartment surrounded by gem quality turquoise and red coral tile mosaic walls, upon a gem quality jade slab floor beneath an ivory ceiling with platinum vents and fixtures. The thick wool rug was softer than cashmere and Pez caressed it with her bare feet as she listened to Admiral Zapa's holo describe the personnel finally agreed upon, though not by Pez, and selected as the definitive operatives. Zapa told her authoritatively, since she had been decommissioned weeks ago and was now a mere Knight Commander of the Clearlight Order, "Star Fleet Intelligence is giving you Lt. Winston. He's from Rah and I'm told he's very skilled and craft wise."

Pez interrupted with, "How tall is he?"

"He is five-foot eleven inches on the nose," Zapa said with a slight annoyance. He continued his briefing, "Om Central Intel is sending Special Agent Marlboro. He was born and bred on Om. He's five-foot eleven and one-fifth inches tall, if you must know. Interstar Police Intel has insisted on sending one of their own and Undercover Agent Elanem, from Ganahar, will be joining you. She's five-foot and a quarter inches tall," he said smugly. "Army Intelligence, which some of us see as an oxymoron, will not be dissuaded from sending you an agent. His name is Luxandexter Strike, but everyone calls him 'Lucky'."

"Lucky me," Pez said, trying to be polite.

"That's not all," he informed her. "Ganahar Intel is sending their Super-Agent Green. She's five-foot, two inches!"

He was grinning about the five-foot two super-agent while sitting in his office and it looked gross to Pez in her holo of him. She inquired, "Do any of these operatives have martial arts training?"

"Lt. Winston trained in the deadly art of *pojo*, has a black belt in *pudonk*, and he's a national *slamdunk* champion. He's Star Fleet. I don't know much about the rest but General Trench says army's guy Lucky is an expert in *Flying Hammer* style."

"Do they all acknowledge me as mission commander?" Pez asked.

"Yes, and you outrank all of them anyway," Zapa informed her. "You've no idea what the intelligence services went through to find such short people within their ranks."

"Are they all rated high in potential for mastering languages?" Pez wanted know since that would be the surest way to blow their cover.

"Not exactly," Zapa hedged like a politician.

"What does that mean?" Pez demanded.

"Only the two from Ganahar hold that rating," he admitted.

"And the others?"

"They'll try not to talk much," Zapa tried to encourage her.

"And their ratings were?"

"Not even close," he stated with some defeat before adding hopefully, "at least Lt. Winston scored in the average range."

"What did Central and Army score," Pez insisted.

"Central falls below average and Army within borderline intellectual functioning."

"You mean hardly above retarded," Pez reframed clinically.

"I guess, though that's not my field," Zapa shook it off.

"Do you think I could get an Army Space Special Forces out of them instead of their near-retarded intelligence officer?"

"I'll run that by them a little more diplomatically than you presented your request, but I doubt it," Zapa answered. "Your two loyal Space Marines complete their undercover training with Fleet Intel tomorrow and will report to you the day after that."

"Thank you Admiral Zapa; I'll do my very best," Pez promised.

"We couldn't be sending better when it comes to you Commander," he said honestly, signing off.

Ming brought Electra directly to Pez the moment Zapa's holo winked out. He still had no idea about the babies. Electra lit up as her momma's energy started pouring into her. Only her mother, Sarhi and Shudiy could do it well, though Aton and Nemellie sort of could. Ming was such a good mother that this made up for her not being able to, in Electra's mind. Pez snuggled her close and started talking to her in that unnaturally high ridiculous voice, all sentimentally enthused. It was Pez's love and energy, eyes and smile that jazzed Electra, not the high voice, which Electra could just as soon do without herself.

Ming had taken a crash course pilot training as a customized tutorial with Konax and had received, along with Pez and her companions, individual instructions and coaching on undercover work. Yona and the High Council made efficient decisions and established Aton as their Mission Director to report to. Pez was made official Mission Commander. Vast wealth from dozens of star systems along with almost half the Om treasury was rapidly sought, pledged and collected. They still hadn't selected an Ambassador to Vox yet though and Swenah was madder than a feline with its tail on fire. Everyone involved with the mission had to have a code name. Aton's was "Charlie".

The chandelier in the yacht dinning cabin made entirely of huge cut diamonds had been identified as one of the missing art objects but loaned to Om for the mission. The amazing oil painting on the wall in the living room cabin was also identified and loaned to Om. So both remained on the yacht. The painting was rated by most art experts as the third greatest ever produced in the Hub Galaxy in the last 30,000 years. Pez really liked it and hoped she could get a reproduction of it when it would have to be returned.

Electra had had enough of Pez's baby talk voice and wanted down on the soft rug next to Gumby, who had his head and limbs lifted lying on his belly and chest, looking like a bird in flight. When Pez set Electra face down on the rug she started flying too. Mel was recording the whole thing. Pez found it so cute she almost started crying, then Ming put an arm around her and said, "They're so adorable!"

Pez could only nod with tears in her eyes.

Rubix, code named "Sandalphon", entered the living room area and was immediately drawn to the spectacle of the flying babies on the carpet. The design woven into the carpet was sharp, done in contrasting colors, seeming infinite and completely mesmerizing. Had it been on the surface of any planet in the universe with an advanced civilization it would be on a wall in a museum where no one could touch it. A drop of drool dripped from Electra's chin and Pez found it so endearing.

Rubix was back to his tight metallic jumpsuits, no longer wearing his fleet gunner's uniform, and looked like a cartoon stick figure. Pez had a civilian wardrobe now after getting dragged shopping all over hell and gone by Natasha and Cleo. She still wasn't sure about some of the clothes, like her paisley spandex jumpsuit or the mini-skirt which made her feel like she needed to put on an apron. She missed her cozy cotton Space Marine panties now having to wear lacey silk stuff with a strap working its way into her butt-crack all the time. She had dresses, pants suits, and unisex play clothes now. They'd let her keep all her Space Marine clothes but she couldn't bring any of them on the secret mission.

Ming had taken Evenrude and Johnson shopping at the extra-large sizes store at the big shopping arcade in the capital, dressing them like the underworld smugglers in the old holomovies on Om. They had leather shoulder holsters, fancy silk suits and alligator shoes. It was the best they could do until they got to Ahumdulilah. Evenrude and Johnson had found it quite amusing.

Pez was teaching her female companions, including Sarhi and her Islohar, how to throw jade darts with speed and accuracy and how to put their hair up using the darts as pins. Nothing made of stone tended to excite scanners and sensors and Pez had a whole necklace of jade darts which looked perfectly harmless. Ahhu's deft little hands picked it up amazingly fast, served as well by her brief career at sixteen as a card shark and cheat. With a benign gesture she could nail the bullseye on the target lengthwise across the compartment. The others were picking it up pretty well too. Training in preparation for this mission had been intensive for all of them.

Four Space Marine hardshell combat suits were loaded aboard and Pez had insisted that *Aphrodite* be provisioned with Ambassador-rations. Yona had justified this with the council by pointing out that these rations were already clear of any markings or code stamps and Pez received her upgraded rations. They had an arsenal of small arms and explosives aboard. Replacement thruster-fuel cells and one-time boosters filled a small cargo hold on the yacht. A miniature foundry-mint which could melt platinum to cast coins and small bars, was set up in the workshop cabin. Ahhu's bucket of gems was less than a five-hundredth of what they carried and her ton of platinum only one of four they had aboard. Far more valuable than any of that was the refined saturnium, mercurium, and solarium they had stowed safely. Rare earths, gold, and tazgar fangs—sharper than obsidian and harder than diamond—along with other extremely rare commodities completed their treasure. Wealth would be no fiction or rouse like their identities would be.

On the big day of departure Pez was seated in the sitting room cabin on the yacht which they'd turned into a briefing room by installing a large coms-integrated conference table. There was a place at it for Aton's virtual presence. Electra was sleeping in her front pouch hung on Pez's chest and Ming sat next to her holding Gumby. Evenrude and Johnson were also at the table dressed up in their gangster outfits and looking menacing. Their code names were Michael and Uriel.

Lucky from Army Intel was the first of their new personnel to arrive on the yacht which was parked in a hanger on Star Fleet's main space station. Mel's voice directed him to the briefing room. He snapped Commander Pez a salute from the door, decent even by Space Marine standards, but only minimally. Pez started to rise intending to model a really good one but Ming put a hand on her shoulder and reminded her, "You'll wake Electra."

Pez allowed the opportunity to pass and told Lucky, "At ease and have a seat. Say, how tall are you?"

"Um six… I mean five foot-eleven and nine-tenth inches, Ma'am."

Evenrude told him, "Stand back up there!" as he reached behind him for a range finder. He used it to measure Lucky and told him, "Says here you're six foot and three-tenths of an inch."

"It must be my thick soles," Lucky lied easily.

Mel said, "That is after subtracting the half-inch soles on your shoes."

"That's some sexy computer voice you picked," Lucky said to Pez ignoring Mel and avoiding the subject with a real friendly voice.

Pez buzzed General Trench and said, "The operative you sent is over six feet tall."

The General said in a surprised voice, "Well I'll be." Then he stated, "A few tenths of an inch is usually close enough for army work."

"I'm glad the army didn't build my ship, sir," Pez replied to that.

"Just tell Lucky to slouch; it will be alright," he said signing off.

"Great!" Pez exclaimed just as he vanished.

Pez knew Lucky was already a risk with his poor language propensity, and now with his height, she was afraid Lucky would need all the luck he could get; making the rest of them, perhaps, unlucky.

Next to arrive was Lt. Winston and Evenrude scanned him as he came into the cabin, telling Pez, "Five foot eleven inches exact."

He'd given the typical pathetic Star Fleet style salute and said looking at Pez, "Lt. Winston reporting for duty, Ma'am!"

"At ease Lieutenant and take a seat," Pez told him.

"I wasn't briefed on babies," Winston said confused. Then he asked, "Surely they're not coming on the mission?!"

Pez told him firmly, "These babies are known only to the Prime Minister and it is going to remain that way! You are to say nothing about them or allude to them in any way in any report you make. Are we clear on this?"

"Crystal, Commander," Winston replied not getting it at all.

Electra chose that moment to awaken with her typical ear-shattering wail and Pez unbuttoned her blouse with one hand while checking the diaper with her other. Since no changing was required a little hugging and a lullaby got her swiftly on the breast sucking. Winston thought maybe he did get it; that perhaps the baby's voice had been weaponized. As was often the case Electra woke up Gumby, who also cried out his dissatisfaction and need to be nursed. Winston thought that maybe the procedure for weaponization had not gone as well with the male baby. Then he speculated that the Adam's apple might have something to do with it.

Central Intel's Special Agent Marlboro came in looking like a bovine rancher wearing a tan leather jacket with sheep fleece on the inside, dungarees, and tall leather boots. His hat hung on his back from a chord around his neck and was wide brimmed and indented at the top. Marlboro wore a mean looking blaster in a fancy side arm rig off his hip. Evenrude told Pez, "Five-foot eleven and a fifth inches."

"At ease and take a seat Special Agent," Pez instructed, thinking these guys all had "spook" stamped on their foreheads and looked nothing like the rich quantum party set.

Elanem, from Interstar Police Intelligence Division came through the door and Evenrude said, "Five-foot and a quarter inch."

She gave an Interstar Police salute which was almost unintelligible to Pez; kind of like a "para-salute," and said, "It's truly an honor to meet you, Commander."

Pez told her, "Be at ease Elanem and have a seat." To Ahhu off in another part of the yacht Pez asked, "Could you bring some herb tea and some of those spongey pastries with the white icing into the cabin we're now calling the 'briefing room', sweetheart?"

"Right away."

"Thanks so much."

Super-agent Green from Ganahar Intelligence was last to arrive and at five-foot two inches Evenrude hadn't bothered scanning her. Pez saw her aura and liked her right away. She said looking at Pez, "Green reporting for duty, Ma'am. It's a great honor to serve under your command."

Pez asked, "Are you Islohar?"

"Yes I am, Commander."

"Do you know Sarhi and Shudiy?"

"I do, Ma'am. They're my teachers."

"Do they know you're going on this mission?"

"Of course, Commander."

"They didn't tell me," Pez complained.

"There was clearly no need to Commander," Green stated, referring to the fact that Pez knew right away.

Pez said, "Now that we're all here I'll begin the briefing."

Naked Ahhu and Trix in a short skirt and T-shirt came in with two pots of herb tea and a big platter of the spongey white icing pastries already removed from their individual plastic wrappers. They were set down within arm's reach of Pez and her snatch was so quick they only suddenly saw her eating one. With naked Ahhu just leaving the cabin Lucky commented, "I was told we'd be working with some civilians but they didn't say anything about that."

"Do we have crew to fight the yacht?" Winston inquired.

Pez explained, "I'll pilot the craft and Commander Ming is the copilot. Shudiy, whom you haven't met yet, will be our Weapons Operator and Ahhu our Drone Pilot. The three quad-blaster turrets will be manned by Rubix, rated #1 in Fleet, and by Trix and Woahha. The mini-turrets with the twin-blasters on each side of the ship will be operated by Evenrude and Johnson. Everyone else is to remain strapped in. The last thing we want to do on this mission is to end up in a space battle in the yacht."

Ming prompted, "You might want to say something about the preparation on Ahumdulilah."

"We are initially going to the White Lotus Galaxy," Pez started her actual briefing. "There is a planet there called Ahumdulilah that's opposed to the empire we hope to find a way to topple. The Amonrahonians have directed us to them for assistance learning languages, establishing our undercover identities and documentation, and infiltration. We must learn two new languages as quickly as possible. We will be posing as wealthy young people seeking parties, decadence and debauchery of which I've been assured this empire lacks none. Language skills will be of utmost importance for moving through their worlds as one of them. We will neither succeed nor survive without learning the imperial basic language, and our covers also depend upon being able to speak our alleged home world language without a detectable accent. If you can't become proficient with the languages then your role per our cover story will be as yacht crew and you will not be playing a speaking part in this game. Our wealth is perfectly real and will lend us credibility. Gathering intel and establishing contacts, allies and friendships is our first objective."

Marlboro asked facetiously, "Just how are we going to topple an empire of over 5,700 star systems ruled with an iron fist?!"

"That is what we are going there for, to find out how," Pez explained. "This empire is unharmonious and out of equilibrium with the greater universe, forcing its will upon reality, and that takes an extraordinary amount of energy constantly. In that sense the universe is on our side, always pressing on the empire to align and liberate. Even with all of their inconceivable might this empire is a delicate thing. Hope for a better way instilled in the trillions of suffering families, and perhaps a little internal sabotage, could start a movement like a chain reaction. We have much to learn about them and the world they've constructed before any specifics can be identified. First we have to prepare with much study so we can move freely amongst them."

Aton's virtual presence filled his seat with a hologram and he told them, "Sorry I'm late; I was delayed by the Prime Minister. Arrangements have been made with Trident, Rally and Gzzklns to partner with The Tail of Nine to construct the largest two ships ever built. The design is complete and construction will begin within days in the Trident System of the Yuban Galaxy. Thousands of personnel from Om are making preparations to depart for Trident and a dozen of Om's largest cargo freighter ships are being loaded with parts, systems and materials for the construction. The Battleship Carrier will be 29,800 feet in diameter and contain 244 miniaturized solarium fusion super-reactors plus fourteen solarium fusion battery systems. Ever since Pez sent sensor spy probes to the home world system of this empire we've been accumulating massive data and know that the largest imperial ships carry 148 solarium reactors.

"The High Council has approved a large grant to fund research in cloaking and micro-jumping involving thousands of research projects which are attracting our most brilliant people. A shuttle is bringing up some equipment and materials to install an Altoid Wave Cannon on your yacht. It is entirely harmless itself but paints cloaked ships revealing them. It will extend and contract from a heavily insulted box which will prevent the cannon from detection by active scans even when your yacht's cloaking is shut down. Is there anything more you can think of that you may need for the mission?"

"We need an interpreter device for the Ahumdulilah primary language so we don't have to learn three new languages," Pez reminded him. Then she asked, "How is that coming along?"

"The Amonrahonians provided Sarhi with a device interpreting Islohar and the language of Ahumdulilah, called 'Alhambra', and Mel's device has interpretation between Islohar and Om, so actually Mel is…"

Mel cut in to say, "It's done and I call it 'the Mel Pyramid II' because it interprets and translates documents between the five languages of Hub Basic, Alhambra, Islohar, Sterling—which is the basic language of the empire, and Bozo, the native language of Rocky. Rocky is a sort of partly independent subject state of the empire and will be your alleged planet of origin. The Mel Pyramid II includes accelerated learning virtual courses in both Sterling and Bozo which I programmed after receiving study guide holos and lessons from some very helpful people on Ahumdulilah."

"You're terrific Mel!" Pez said with great relief. "I'm so very grateful."

"Excellent work, Marshall Mel!" Aton praised her.

"Marshall Mel?" Pez inquired.

"She demonstrated aptitude and level of consciousness for the position and Mel attended the ceremony of her initiation, empowerment, and commission as Marshall in a holo of her android body; which by the way has remarkable resemblance to both you Pez, and Ming."

"Congratulations Marshall," Pez gushed most authentically. "I'm really proud of you."

"I'm following in your footsteps and am now both Islohar and Clearlight," Mel stated proudly.

"Sweetheart, that's so wonderful!" Ming exclaimed to Mel.

Marlboro's spy alarms were going off and he asked, "Who is Mel?"

Anton told him with complete authority employing Marlboro's own spook nomenclature to insure no misunderstanding, "Mel is top secret and strictly need to know. You have never heard of her, and we never had this conversation."

"Got it," Marlboro acknowledged, already scheming in his mind how he would get to the bottom of Mel.

Aton continued, "The installation of the box compartment and Altoid Wave Cannon will take approximately eight hours and that is not an inflated fleet estimate, but likely the best that can be done. Oh, and please try not to spill anything on that rug in your living room compartment because we just found out it is priceless and will eventually need to be returned to the Puna System where it will be displayed in a museum."

"We will," Pez assured him. "I do need better diapers than the cheap government ones I've been given. The ones I have don't contain any sensors and require me to manually check on their condition. Ming needs sensor diapers too. I find it barbaric how the government treats its employees who are mothers of infants and toddlers."

"I'll get you the top of the line with sensors powered by the heat from the baby's bottom. No micro-batteries! And I'll get them sent up right away," Aton promised apologetically. "I'll check in again before you depart."

"We'll get started with our language studies," Pez replied.

Pez checked and found that the Mel Pyramid II was loaded on her pocket device so she went to the menu using her skullcap and brought it up in her personal teleprompter-like mini holo-display just inches in front of her eyes. She selected the Bozo learning program with a brain impulse from the menu, then had it projected from the conference room table holo device. The image faced each person at the table regardless of where they sat. It was a computer-generated graphic of Mel's android body teaching the lesson with a cube separated off for text and to display virtual objects corresponding to nouns and proper names within the Bozo language. Pez wisely decided to tackle Bozo first which would hopefully give her Sterling a Bozo accent.

Pez was fluent in Om, Rah, Haum, and Hub Basic, and she was fairly proficient now in Islohar. With these five languages Pez found no new sounds foreign to her in the Bozo she was learning. Ahhu's amazing tongue proved itself to be quite adept at languages too and her pronunciation was impressive. The lesson program was of course interactive and could handle question and answer routines and provide remedial lessons for the intellectually and language challenged.

The installation crews got started when the shuttle arrived with the Altoid Wave Cannon, working both on the inside and the outside of the yacht parked in the aired-up hanger. Sarhi made the ones working on the inside remove their shoes before walking on the living room rug. Mel's lesson put both babies right to sleep once they'd finished nursing. Pez kept them at their studies the entire 8 ¼ hours it took the work crew to install the cannon. By this time Pez had memorized an impressive number of Bozo nouns and their corresponding objects. Lucky and Marlboro were on the remedial track and Winston was struggling to keep up with the normal one. Elanem was doing well as were Ming, Evenrude and Johnson. Green was well ahead of the class, just behind Pez.

They ate Ambassador dinner-rations while awaiting the fleet inspector to test and certify the cannon installation. Shudiy promised to start cooking again soon but at the moment was studying the operator's manual for Flint's weapons console. The new diapers had arrived and Trix integrated the sensors transmissions with the baby-seat monitoring ear buds ready for Electra's next changing. Gretle was still on a high and had spent the time alternating between meditation sessions and learning Bozo with her pocket device. She did a little bit of homework too for graduate school.

When she finished her second dinner ration Pez threw the empty containers and her plastic cutlery and other things into the recycling receptacle. The inspector sent the certification of the installation to Pez's pocket device and she convened a meeting of all eighteen adults on board in the briefing room. No sooner had they gotten seated than Aton's chair filled with a holo of him. He informed them,

"We have received maps for the three galaxies the empire is operating in which includes the White Lotus Galaxy. The empire is almost entirely located within the Royal Galaxy and a third galaxy called Whirlpool. The home world of the empire is the Monarch System. Civilization on Monarch is far older than even Ganahar's with over 98.000 years of recorded history. With the Mel Pyramid II we are now receiving a wealth of data from the people of Ahumdulilah. It's coming so fast and there's so much of it that even Mel is challenged to download it all as it comes.

"I'm keeping up with it," Mel said defensively.

'Sorry, I meant no offense, Marshal," Aton apologized.

"I was just keeping you informed, Vicar General," Mel covered her tracks.

Electra awoke in a fit and Pez launched into changing her, hugging and singing to her while passing her calming energy, and finally getting her nursing. Once Electra was happily sucking away Pez told Aton accusingly, "Do you see all the trouble the cheap government diapers cause? With sensors I can change her the moment she pees before the dampness wakes her up."

"You'd make a great advertisement for sensor-diapers," Aton commended her. "I promise to speak with Yona about it though you must understand that with you departing with so much of Om's wealth, it will be an uphill battle to win approval for quality improvements of things already in place."

"Mothers working for the government deserve better," Pez insisted.

Aton pointed out, "Most people live on their salaries and not on obscure and little-known subsidies like you do, Pez. Few mothers use the diaper subsidy and I believe that's how the government prefers it."

"Well no one ever told me I had a salary and I had no idea that I had a bank account until Mel found it in Om's financial databases."

"I'm your martial arts teacher and spiritual mentor, not your financial advisor," Aton washed his hands of it.

Self-pity pulled at her but Pez shrugged it off with a deep breath and laser concentration. Aton continued, "The galaxy maps come from the Amonrahonians who gave them to the people of Ahumdulilah, so it appears they didn't want us in that region of the universe until now. Ahumdulilah's populace is expecting you Pez and has been since long before you were born. They knew of your mission there way before any of us did, including Sarhi, who's known for more than 34 years."

"It's nice I'm finally finding out about it," Pez said a little pouty.

"You'll have to speak to Sarhi about that Pez," Aton told her, "because I found out when you did. At any rate, we have already an advanced and powerful ally in the Ahumdulilahs and they have been establishing a number of identities for over three decades for you and some of your operatives, with extensive histories well-documented in central computers. They have also over the same duration invested billions of dags, the dag being the imperial monetary unit, to enhance the financial empire in your name on Rocky. It is a well-known family estate. That is where you will stay to prepare and plan for your mission. They have some well-researched and thought out ideas for your travels and movements, and a long list of serious malcontents for you to contact within the empire. The household staff at your ancestral mansion and estate are all operatives from Ahumdulilah and they will provide elite specialists to assist your preparation and planning. They will open a hangar for you to land your yacht in. Mel has the estate location on Rocky and your navigation system will have the three galaxy maps as soon as Mel uploads them. I'm relieved that you'll have competent dedicated assistance getting started and I wish you the best possible outcome. The Clearlight Order and the Thunder Perfect Mind Academy will both be holding continuous vigils for your safety and success around the clock without interruption until you return."

"Thank you Aton; I love you," Pez said with her heart on her sleeve. Aton bowed to Pez just before he winked out and was gone. Pez told her mission crew, "Lets run our preflight checks and get going to Rocky."

Still nursing Electra Pez made her way to the cockpit and sat in the pilot's seat. Ming was still nursing Gumby when she took her copilot seat. Pez let Mel run the pre-checks by herself to take a little moment to adore Electra. It seemed to be taking a little longer than usual so Pez inquired, "Is everything checking out, Mel?"

"Give me another couple of minutes to upload the maps into the nav. system; it's kind of slow," Mel said, condescending on the nav. system.

Ahhu sat dutifully and naked in the drone pilot seat even though they had no drone. Pez planned to buy a pair of imperial ones once they were there if they were legal. From Pez's experiences of two other empires, she thought if you owned enough wealth than pretty much anything was legal except pissing off a bigger fish. Shudiy was customizing Flint's console while sitting in the Weapons Operators seat and had changed all warning alarms and messages on the console to appear in the Islohar language. No one was manning any of the blaster turrets since they were in Om star system space.

Mel said, "The nav. computer is updated." Then in a pleading voice she implored, "Can I pilot the yacht to Rocky, Pez? Please!!"

"The controls are yours, sweetheart, but please be conservative your first time out," Pez replied.

"Do I have to follow the speed limits?" Mel asked.

"Yes, absolutely," Pez told her sternly, "and that's an order, Marshal."

"Yes, Ma'am."

Mel chatted up the fleet personnel in the tower on the space station, and lifted nicely when the doors opened above them. Then she took off faster than Pez ever had by utilizing a lift-off booster meant for serious vortex force and atmosphere. With her cheeks stretching to her ears and crushed into her seat Pez said, "That wasn't conservative Mel!"

"But it sure was fun!" Mel exclaimed, already loving piloting.

Mel did cease accelerating when they reached the stingy speed limit, keeping it right on the exact maximum allowable. Pez asked Evenrude, who was kind of in charge of the cargo hold contents and handling by default, "Do we have any more liftoff-boosters in storage?"

"No but we have fuel to reload the one Mel just fired; it's not like a one-time booster," Evenrude explained.

"What conditions do we need to load it?" Pez asked.

"It's a spacewalk if you don't have an aired-up hanger or livable planet surface to do it on" Evenrude replied. "I'd have plenty of time to do it on our way out of the system given the new reduced speed limits imposed by the Space Controllers."

"No; we can do it easier in the estate hanger on Rocky," Pez told him, "but thanks for offering."

Electra and Gumby both stopped sucking to look out the gigantic windshield-canopy which was pristinely clean at the moment. Traffic both in and out of the system was heavy and Om had thousands of satellites and stationary space platforms at varying distances from the planet serving all kinds of functions. Mel routed a call she didn't want to take to Pez's ear and the Space Controller on the other end said, "*Aphrodite*, this is Om Space Control. There's a problem with your listed destination. Please pull out of the shipping lane to the nearest platform and we'll get some officials directly out to board you."

"This is Knight Commander Pez speaking and we are on official military business with orders directly from the High Council and Prime Minister. We will tolerate no interference with our departure. Contact Government House immediately."

Pez cut the man off, not caring to hear his bureaucratic nonsense, and contacted Aton to tell him, "Space Control says there's a problem with our stated destination in our flight plans and wants us to pull over, but they're going to have to clear up their own confusion without me involved. We're not stopping."

"I'll see what I can do," Aton promised.

Pez switched to the line with the screaming Space Controller bringing the volume instantly to a whisper on reception while turning her mic to maximum and told the man, "Screaming at me will do you no good at all, so run along now, and speak to someone from Yona's office at Government House. It's honestly the only way it can resolve for *you*. *I'm* leaving and I don't have a problem. Goodbye!"

A minute later Mel told Pez, "There are a dozen Space Controller small craft behind us flashing their lights and they're still shouting at you on the coms."

"Would you ask Sarhi to catch Yona up on this absurd situation please," Pez said with unraveling patience.

Two of the small craft with flashing lights were pulling up adjacent *Aphrodite's* cockpit so Pez smiled and waved at them through the windshield-canopy.

"Bring shields to combat level and power up all weapons systems, Mel."

"We're not going to shoot them are we?" Mel asked alarmed.

"No; but they don't know that."

"Finally," Mel said exasperated, "they're calling Government House; but they're also calling Star Fleet requesting that they destroy our yacht."

"Both will tell them to stand down and once again their over-zealousness causes them to lose face," Pez remarked.

They were getting actively scanned through their windshield so Pez closed the blast shield over it with her skullcap. Then she got missile-lock on all twelve small craft with her canister missiles knowing this would trigger all kinds of sirens and alarms within the Space Controllers' cockpits. As the Space Controller craft scattered fleeing from the yacht, Pez powered down the weapons systems.

Mel updated Pez, "Yona's on the phone now with Space Control HQ." Then she asked, "Can I listen in?"

No Mel, that's not only against regulations but it's also against the law."

"You're no fun."

"I'm letting you drive."

"Well; that's true," Mel conceded.

Yona's holo sprang from Pez's pocket and she demanded to know, "Did you get missile-lock on those Space Controller craft?"

"They were actively scanning us at close range which is not good for babies; and it wasn't like we were actually going to fire on them," Pez tried to argue her side of it.

"I told them to back down; but really Pez, you can't be powering up your weapons and targeting government forces. They've given you a very expensive citation for that and you'll have to pay it."

"No problem, I'm rich now!"

"Do find us hope and a way to security, Pez," Yona signed off. A holo of Mel's android body protruded from Pez's pocket into the space in front of her and said waving, "I can do it to!"

"Good for you Mel and I'm truly impressed, but I'd prefer our usual means of communication."

"I just wanted you to see."

"It was awesome Mel."

"Did you know that I now have the Mel File which only you and I can open? The code is '963', which anyone could crack in a second, but to open the file requires a full body scan identifying you by your finger prints, iris, bone structure, and teeth right down to that ceramic filling you got when you were thirteen."

"That's great Mel. Do you think we can get my biography sequestered in there?"

"We could" Mel said cautiously, "but it would be like closing the barn door after the cow has run off."

"How's that?" Pez asked concerned.

"The bio has been copied by Jard, who has it down on Om backed up on a data bead."

Well that's just great," Pez said sarcastically.

"You know Jard," Mel said helplessly.

"All too well!" Ming contributed.

"I have some holoclips of Jard which I'm sure he'll want desperately to keep out of the media," Ahhu offered. "I just texted him what will happen if any of your biography leaks."

"Thank you, sweetheart, you're so on top of things," Pez told her gratefully.

Crossing the orbital distance of the fifth planet where traffic was light, mostly just giant cargo freighters, the speed limit increased from .09 light to .2 and Mel accelerated to reach it. Pez complained, "They could safely start some lanes right here to speed up to .7 light for jumping out. Instead we have to crawl along another two hundred and eighty million miles before increasing to jump speed."

Pez put up Mel's teaching holo of the Bozo language and started memorizing more nouns, which put Electra right to sleep. Ming and Ahhu joined the lesson watching Pez's holo, and this put Gumby out to sleep pretty quickly. Having completed full customization of Flint's console, Shudiy joined in too, but put up her own holo in which Mel was speaking Islohar to teach Bozo. Marlboro's voice erupted in Pez's ear, asking, "What in a black hole is a 'Quakka'?" referring to a Bozo word he'd encountered.

Pez being a fast learner already had that word down and told him, "It's a pejorative label for the pinkish pasty-white slaves; a racist term really."

"Oh yeah," Marlboro got it, finally locating Mel's textual definition in the separated-off box followed by a 3D image of one.

Mel informed them, "There's a good deal of irrational belief amongst the peoples of this empire and it has been on the rise for 6,144 years there."

"What were they like before that?" Pez inquired quite interested.

Mel employed her professor-sounding voice to tell them, "Until 6,800 years ago the people of Monarch were helpers and caretakers of other less advanced planetary races and had forged a grand inter-stellar alliance. Policy changes on Monarch started them down the road of exploitation of their allies. As the policies became more severe and their subject planets protested, some tried to break away to independence. Military intervention became the typical response. An irrational hierarchy of skin color arose and darker skinned people were given greater distribution and more power within governments, institutionalizing their racism and inspiring pseudo-sciences proving their racism to themselves. This continued to deteriorate until laws were enacted allowing enslavement of all those lacking in pigmentation. About the same time invasions of conquest were unleashed on planetary populations subjecting them to the rule of the empire and fleecing them. This has been snowballing for 6,000 years now."

"What a mess!" Pez exclaimed.

Mel continued, "It was only in the last 500 years that the empire has been establishing itself in the White Lotus Galaxy. Rocky joined the empire and so got to keep some of its independence and just pay annual tribute. The ruling family on Rocky assisted the empire in enslaving worlds in the White Lotus Galaxy and was richly rewarded for this. The ruling family, the Bulwinkles, were shut-ins for many generations and this inspired those on Rocky who oppose the empire, who were assisted by operatives from Ahumdulilah, to murder every last member of the family. Using the voice-data of the family members they were able to carry on as if the family were still alive and in place. For the last 34 years the ruling family of Rocky has actually been the Intel division of Ahumdulilah. Your covers are as Bulwinkles and their retinue. You'll need some slaves and those will be Ahumdulilah agents."

"We have only two berths left on the yacht and that's with six of us staying in the master suite," Pez stated.

Mel pointed out, "We have some roll-away berths on board and slaves must be crammed together in small spaces anyway to keep up appearances. Four particularly pigment-less specimens should do on a small yacht like this," Mel analyzed.

"How much of Ahumdulilah's population is bright white?" Pez asked.

Mel reframed, "It's not so much that they're white since they appear pink around the joints and genitals and are actually off-white with a faint tannishness. Nearly a third of Ahumdulilah's population has this hue of skin. The scientific method if strictly adhered to disproves all of their irrational racist beliefs. Science has stagnated there for many centuries since it has become merely a tool of war, imperial expansion and profiteering, and no longer a guide to expanded knowledge."

"How are you doing with comparative technology, Mel?" Pez inquired.

Mel answered, "Their knowledge and technical developments are both the same and different from ours. For example, they have a vastly more expansive map of galaxies in relation to one another than Om has, but they have only two completely mapped galaxies; their own and Whirlpool Galaxy. They employ solarium as the preferred fusion element and have attained near maximum miniaturization of their reactors. They have quantum coms and can jump without the need for gates. Their micro-jumping lags a little behind Om's and is, at the moment, making no progress at all, though their cloaking technology exceeds Om's and they have the ability to pierce cloaking at longer ranges than the Altoid waves we employ."

"It's a good thing we have no intention of engaging them in battle," Pez admitted. Then she thought to ask, "Have you found out yet if drone fighter-bombers are legal for ruling families to own?"

"It's complicated," Mel offered.

"Well please keep trying," Pez requested.

"The Bulwinkles of Rocky are both independent of and subject to the empire. Ruling families on Monarch have them and so does a system in Whirlpool with a similar status to the Rocky System. The Bulwinkles never had any but that does not mean that they *could* not."

"Look into buying a pair, Mel," Pez asked her. "The very best made. We brought our own quantum navigation systems for them, and can supe-up their quantum drives if they're lacking."

"I'm researching," Mel informed Pez.

A moment later she was back telling Pez, "There are dozens of arms dealers you can purchase them from. The price for the best ranges from thirty million to thirty-six million six hundred thousand dags, depending upon which dealer you buy from. One offers the deal, buy ten and get one free, but charges 35,750,000 dags for each of them."

"Could you get two at thirty million each, and arrange delivery to our estate on Rocky," Pez asked.

"Let me just figure out how to access your accounts on Rocky and I'll place the purchase order and make payment. There we go. Done."

"Thanks Marshal Mel," Pez said gratefully.

Ahhu announced, "I can fly two at once no problem."

Pez informed her, "We will only be traveling with one, sweet-heart. The other is to reverse-engineer their cloaking technology."

"Alright," Ahhu accepted with disappointment.

"I'm passed all the speed limits and space control speed-traps," Mel announced, "and we're accelerating to .7 light speed."

Pez said, "They should only be allowed to provide information and make suggestions, not given authority to control others. Such things always become entrenched oppressions almost immediately and then such artificial entities begin consolidating their power, supporting the status quo and their rooted position within it. Stagnation and entropy result because the exceptional is not nurtured."

"That sure describes this empire," Mel agreed.

"Om has been isolationist and so far only helpful in its relations with other worlds, but there are forces at work reducing its overall clarity of awareness which constitute dangers we must challenge and keep an eye on," Pez shared.

"Like those government security forces," Ahhu said with a shudder, recalling getting stunned unconscious by them.

"And the Space Controllers," Ming chimed in.

"Ten seconds to jump," Mel announced while displaying a digital countdown for them.

The non-event of the jump took them out of existence into transcendental no-time and nonlocality for a non-duration and they were suddenly existent once more, only now they were in the middle of White Lotus Galaxy about four light minutes out from the planet Rocky travelling at .7 light speed. Mel conservatively hit reverse drives slowing their velocity since there was a fair amount of traffic around the planet. The sun of the Rocky system was yellow and Rocky was the third planet from it, glorious within its atmosphere and covered on two-thirds of its surface by water. It had a quick annual orbit around its star very close in duration to that of Ganahar. It had one moon less than a quarter million miles out and the planet was frozen solid at its polar caps. Oxygen producing jungles and rain forests ran around the equator. Their own estate was near the coast of a continent in the upper temperate region more than half-way from equator to polar cap. Mel had already picked up the beacon signal she'd been told to tune into and was racing fully-cloaked towards the upper atmosphere directly over the estate. Penetrating the air put a vibration into the yacht and out the windshield the nose of the ship shimmered, and began to glow red hot.

Mel threw the main drive into reverse and ignited the reverse thrusters as the planet surface dove at their faces. When it looked like they were a tenth-second from splattering on the floor of the hanger Mel hit the big one-time reverse booster and the vortex-redirect generator at full force, throwing everyone into their harness with a jolt before pulling the nose up to fire an underside booster just as the extended landing legs were about to eat the impact with their hydraulics on touch down. Mel got that perfect faint clink of metal on metal from the hydraulic legs just reaching maximum compression and this won her a frown from Pez. "That wasn't at all conservative, Mel," Pez complained.

"You're just upset that I matched your skill," Mel accused her.

Pez told Ahhu, "Put something on for our first meeting with our allies sweetheart, would you?

"I think we'd learn more about them if I go as I am," Ahhu suggested.

"At least have a robe over your arm that you can put on if they're somehow offended," Pez suggested.

"Alright."

CHAPTER EIGHT

All aboard *Aphrodite* gathered in front of the airlock and then went down the ramp together. Their allies all stood in a line at attention wearing servant livery. One was standing out front and gave Pez a stylized salute which included a knee-bend dip and a heel-click at the end, seeming quite unusual to Pez. She snapped him a space marine salute with such vigor that she startled the poor man. Pez said, "Hi, my name is Pez," and Mel's voice from the Mel Pyramid II translated this into Alhambra.

"I am most honored to meet you, Rajaha Pez, and am at your service. My name is Nicon and I'm a Major in Ahumdulilah Intelligence. These are all intelligence agents in the roles of your household servants and slaves. We all speak Bozo fluently and your interpreter device would better serve, and present less risk at this stage, should it interpret into Bozo instead of Alhambra."

Pez reset her Mel Pyramid II and so did all her crew. She told Nicon, "I'm most grateful to you, and to the people of Ahumdulilah for all of your efforts and look forward to making friends."

Nicon offered, "We have a gifted language teacher here to help you and your crew learn Bozo and Sterling. Her name is Onkyo and she is learning Hub Basic from materials Mel sent. We would very much like to meet Marshal Mel, who has truly impressed us with her intelligence and breadth of knowledge."

Pez informed him, "Mel is virtual. Say 'hi' Mel."

"I'm most pleased to meet you, Major Nicon, and so grateful for all the data you've provided me."

"What genus and species are you Marshal Mel?" Nicon asked bewildered.

"As far as any of us know I'm the first of my kind. I'm an AI sentient learning quantum computer. While initially I was programming and hardware, I became artificial intelligence through learning, and then by some miracle, I became truly self-aware with pristine consciousness, absolutely transcendentally empty and aware. Sarhi is teaching me to attain my Rainbow Body of Light."

"Few on Ahumdulilah have that attainment, Marshal Mel, and no one on the planet has ever encountered a truly conscious quantum computer before."

Pez mentioned, "We can no sooner produce another Mel than we can create life in a test tube. She is miraculous."

Marlboro was recording and taking notes. Without him realizing, Mel was deleting everything as fast as he recorded and entered, then said in his ear, "You've never heard of me and can tell no one. You'll get no evidence, I promise you, and such claims without it could get you locked up and certainly damage your career." The truth of her words as he checked the memory of his device, really did put him off task.

Pez was walked down the line of Ahumdulilah agents in cover roles as servants and slaves, getting introduced to each one. The reception she received led her to believe that they were staying in the character of their roles. They each referred to her as 'Rajaha" with great reverence and somehow the Mel Pyramid II gave no translation for this word. She had 48 to meet in all. Nicon then led them to a gigantic conference table made of an unknown super-hardwood, blue of color, within an ornate and richly appointed conference room not far down the corridor from the hanger in the mansion. The building itself was constructed of white marble, a three-story sprawl covering more than four acres with an observatory dome and one tower rising above the rest of the copper roofs. Outbuildings surrounded the mansion, made of brownstone, and included a staff apartment building, a guest house, a bathhouse, a boathouse on the channel, and a maintenance building. There was also a glass dome sports field and a gymnasium with a blaster shooting range and martial arts studio below underground. The basement of the mansion extended well beyond the above ground outer walls and had several tunnels to outbuildings. There were also smaller deeper subterranean levels. A glass dome greenhouse contained a veritable jungle within, including trees, and was 120 feet tall at the center. Pez had seen some of this flying in and had perused briefly the architectural plans of the mansion when they'd arrived, before leaving the yacht. She was sure that a tour of the place would take more than an entire day.

So far the decorations and furnishing screamed obscene wealth. The few oil paintings they'd passed displayed remarkable skill and imagination. The interior walls she's seen so far, that hadn't been left bare polished marble, had deep plush textile wallpaper or were covered in pounded gold. The broad marble slabs of the floor had to be well over a foot thick. An open elevator Pez had peaked into had six petitioned sections precisely measured to include personal space beyond the boundaries of the skin and could be transparent or darkened to full blackout.

The conference room had a high sterling silver ceiling with glass globe lights protruding and was spotted with little round lenses flush with the silver. The walls in here were polished marble and tall windows ran along one of them letting in plenty of light. A carpet covered almost the entire floor leaving only a few inch border strip of marble showing in front of each wall on the floor. It felt like the softest fur to Pez, who'd gotten her slippers off her feet.

Nicon looked at Ahhu, who'd hung the robe she'd carried on the back of her chair, and he explained, "Within the Royal Monarch Empire only sex slaves and sex workers go naked."

Ahhu inquired, "Are there any extremely high priced independent sex workers safe from abuse by ruling family members."

"To some extent but not entirely," Nicon explicated. "Often a member of a ruling family will have a favorite sex worker as a traveling companion and generally such persons would not be abused by members of other ruling families, but there are a few at the very top who do atrocious things and they cannot be refused. The Bulwinkles would not be able to protect you from them. Of course there are probably less than a hundred depraved souls in the empire within the upper echelon of the ruling class who truly derive pleasure from cruelty and sadism."

Nicon thought for a moment then added, "There are members of the lower class adopted into ruling families as kind of second class members, and sometimes these are sex workers. Even the wealthiest person on Monarch would think twice before so offending another ruling family because it would open them up to legal challenges of a duel to the death. Unfortunately the cruelest among them tend to be elite duelists."

Pez asked, "Are there top rank martial artists and duelists in your group here?"

"Of course," Nicon assured her. "Only the best of the best were selected to serve the Rajaha."

Ming asked, "What is a Rajaha?"

"The Rajaha is the teacher and liberator, the instrument of the divine intelligence, and the mother of the Maharaj, called the Mu in Islohar, who comes only every 2,500 years," Nicon explained patiently.

Electra was still sound asleep in her front pouch against her momma's chest. There were 66 people at the table, which could seat 80, and all eyes were on the top of Electra's head poking from the pouch. She woke in that moment, perhaps from all the attention, and gave them a superb scream. Pez went to work and Ahhu was right there with a fresh sensor-diaper from her robe on the back of the chair. Sarhi and Shudiy joined in the singing of the lullaby and Electra was slurping milk in no time. The faces of their allies were in rapture even though they had all likely just lost a little of their hearing. Electra's eyes were open and smiling at them. Pez felt uplifted by the energy in the room and didn't even bother apologizing for the volume. All of this was entirely lost on Lucky, who was confused beyond hope about the babies.

Winston, on the other hand, was beginning to piece it together. Super-agent Green knew from the start.

Nicon briefed them, "We have maintained identities for your use with regular coms, bank activity, shopping, parking tickets and so forth, which have educational degrees, and a few that have employment histories, all verifiable by eye witness testimony and believed hook, line and sinker by the imperial central database and databases on Rocky. The family matriarch in whose name the family wealth is registered in, and her younger sister, are the only immediate family members. The matriarch has a female spouse and the younger sister a husband. There are four older aunts and a female cousin, an adopted lower-class female, and then there are some close friends, high ranking executives of the family businesses, body guards, crew, and slaves. Only yours, Rajaha, has a holo image already included in its data. Identification in the empire is all done by retinal scan and we can make contact lenses for your people to match data files."

Pez asked, "Did Mel send you my pictures?"

"We have had your picture for thousands of years and we used to project all kinds of nonsense upon it until the Amonrahonians showed up and told us who you are and when you'd get here. You see, the images we found of you had been archeologically excavated from ancient ruins and only scarce chiseled pictograph writing could be discovered. The Amonrahonians have visited our world twice. The first time was about 44,400 years ago, and the most recent was about 34 years ago, I believe only weeks before your birth."

"Those Amonrahonians have sure been busy," Pez commented, feeling more like public property than ever.

"They have prepared the way for you," Nicon agreed.

Pez asked, 'Is one of my fake servants a real chef?"

"Of course!" Nicon exclaimed proudly. "The very best on Ahumdulilah."

"You guys don't eat bugs, grubs, chilled monkey brains or anything like that do you?" Pez needed to know.

Nicon told her trying to put her at ease, "We eat grains, vegetables, beans, tubers and fruits, though some of us also eat dairy, poultry, and fish. No one eats mammals on Ahumdulilah but they are eaten throughout the empire, including Rocky."

I don't want any mammal but the rest sounds great to me," Pez enthused, becoming hungry.

Nicon informed her, "A meal is in preparation as we speak. I wanted to give you a bit of data on the Bulwinkle family. Their early fortunes were amassed through piracy and smuggling which the empire believes them to still be involved in, and condones it since the Bulwinkles don't prey upon ships of the empire. This lends your cover identity an air of adventure and dangerousness almost unheard of for a ruling family member. It also enables you to produce trade goods whose origins are unknown to the empire without arousing any suspicions, and no questions are asked. There is no black market within the empire because there is no illegal commodity, and gambling is all government run and controlled. High risk loans with extremely high interest are made by the government and enforced with broken bones; default equaling death. Most prostitution is run by the government using slaves and indentured sex workers, and only a small percent at the high end are independent. The slave trade is supplied through the military and distributed through a limited number of private franchise dealerships which are owned by the very wealthiest families on Monarch. Your family owns iron ore, adamantine, copper, diamond, and solarium mines, refineries, foundries, factories, real estate both residential and commercial, and an interstellar bank. All of the Bulwinkle investments are doing very well."

"Where are the Bulwinkles within the imperial wealth hierarchy?" Pez asked him.

Nicon informed her, "The Bulwinkles are wealthier than any family off Monarch on another planet, and wealthier than most on Monarch; within the top 1,000 ruling families, but just. The real Bulwinkle family was immensely rich and Ahumdulilah has been pouring billions of dags per year into increasing it for 33 years now. When they were killed the family holdings were valued at 2.17 trillion dags, and with Ahumdulilah's contributions plus profits and rents, it is today worth 6.48 trillion dags. With the fortune you've brought you are probably into the top 500 wealthiest families. Mel sent us the inventory. The refined solarium is worth more than 800 billion dags. We haven't even arrived at a total value for the entire lot yet."

"I was hoping to lighten my ship, so could we make a few investments or trades for lighter goods while were here?" Pez asked hopefully.

"I'd suggest that you deposit the four tons of platinum you carry, in the vault of the main branch of your bank in the capitol here on Rocky, which bears your family name."

"It's called the Bulwinkle Bank?" Pez asked uncertain.

"No. The capital of Rocky's named Bulwinkle," Nicon clarified. "With the platinum so deposited the bank can extend more loans and expand its branches. You can sell the fusion elements here on Rocky for as good a price as anywhere else. Imperial agents will buy up the solarium for the military and cities will compete in auction for the saturnium and mercurium. The other metals you carry can also be sold here. Our genius financial advisor has already discussed investment options with your genius, Marshal Mel, and between them they've come up with an aggressive and highly profitable strategy they advise."

"Well don't run it by me because I don't understand a thing about money, nor do I really care to. I don't want to invest in slavery though, or certain other things which deeply offend me."

Financial Advisor Klampet reassured Pez, "Our schemes only harm the pockets of other ruling families and not any workers or poor people."

"I'll leave it in the hands of you and Mel then," Pez said dismissing it from her mind.

Ming inquired, "Where can we get the finest clothes and latest fashions since those will be our disguises?"

Ming loved to shop and she just loved new clothes. Nicon answered, "We have expert tailors and fashion designers and every conceivable textile. We'll make everything right here on your estate including your shoes, accessories, textile armor outerwear, and jewelry from that remarkable gem collection you've brought. You will be the best dressed family in the universe, I promise you; or at least in the three closest galaxies, that's for sure."

Pez told him, "I need a necklace of platinum diamond headed darts as a weapon which can pass through security systems."

"That won't be any problem," he confirmed. Nicon continued clearly having an agenda, "We have intentionally given the imperials every indication that Cher and Lai Bulwinkle are the first of their family in generations *not* to be agoraphobic shut-ins."

"How have you done that?" Pez asked him.

"We have a female operative precisely your size and we just print a copy of your face for her to put on, and Lai always goes hooded. It ought not to be much surprise for them to learn that you're going on a cruise of the empire's hottest playgrounds for the elite rich."

Nicon mentioned to Ahhu, "You're perfect for the Bianca identity which I highly recommend. It seems uncanny how closely your people match the identities we've established. It's like the Cosmic Intelligence had been guiding each decision we made."

Pez stated questioningly, "Clearly you have more personnel on this estate than the 48 here at the table."

"We have another 98 here either working or sleeping at the moment and maintain a command center in your third sub-level. Non- military personnel like your real chef are at their jobs. You have forty in roles as your mercenary private army who man the gate and watch the perimeter. You have all the very latest security systems monitored around the clock and no one could get on the property without triggering multiple alarms. The walls in the family residence section of the mansion are heavily armored and shielded.

"When you leave on your cruise you will have a nonimperial premiere bomber travelling with you for protection. It's pretty standard for ruling families to have one along when off their home planet. The bomber is called a Mirage Streak Fury. It has the speed and maneuverability of an interceptor but packs more punch than the heaviest bomber. It also has eight berths for carrying slaves. Your yacht is small for your wealth status although the interior finish and décor are the most expensive I've ever seen or heard of; especially that diamond chandelier in your dining cabin. The yachts of the top ruling families tend to be much larger but slower and far less maneuverable than yours, and have only a few anti-small craft weapons; nothing like what *Aphrodite* has loaded into it. Any ruling families you encounter will likely assume that you lead your pirate fleet in it to attack merchant shipping vessels and their escort ships." Nicon paused a moment in thought then went on to ask, "Do you or Ming have any hand-to-hand combat training?"

Ming said with great pride, "Pez is Om's number two champion in the soft martial arts."

Pez told him, "I need a workout and would like to test myself against some of your martial artists and learn about your arts."

"We have a martial arts studio right down the stairs beneath the sports arena. There's a shooting range next door to it and we can test your marksmanship as well."

Ming informed him, "She doesn't ever miss."

All sixty-six at the table got up to file out of the conference room to make their way to the martial arts studio. It was nearly as big as the hangar. Half the floor space was covered in thick woven mats and the other half had a hardwood floor built over the marble slabs. Weapons covered the walls and equipment and practice dummies lined them. Pez advanced directly to the center of the hardwood floor and sank into an energy generating posture. She told Nicon, "I need to warm up first for a moment."

After ten minutes Pez switched to the crane walk, pausing on one leg with other raised at the end of each slow inhalation, moving very slowly at a continuous pace like silk-reeling. Her stance was extremely low with her thighs practically horizontal with the floor and she seemed to be floating effortlessly. Another ten minutes at this she was ready to begin. Pez assumed a defensive stance called 'Wardoff Left Side' and told Nicon, "I'm ready."

The number one martial arts champion of Ahumdulilah stepped out on the hardwood floor. He was only an inch taller than Pez but had at least 35 pounds on her. He looked to be about forty years old and he'd been introduced to her as Samsung. Moving like a feline Samsung closed in, his open palms resting on Pez's raised left forearm held out in front across her chest warding off. As he moved forward pushing, Pez rolled back yielding while turning her waist and torso to the side. Samsung was pushing on thin air and could not detect her center of gravity. He'd gone a little too far, over-extending for the base of his rooted feet, and Pez suddenly shot forward rising up from her extreme low stance as she came, and with a hardly noticeable flick of her left forearm she released her mass-integrated internal energy. Samsung's rooted feet left the ground altogether as he flew through the air looking like he was doing the backstroke. Shock was written all over his face. The three big men who tried to catch Samsung out of the air all went down on the floor beneath him. Evenrude smiled having had no doubt of the outcome.

The group of 66 spent two hours learning some of each other's martial arts and practicing their own intensely. They hit the unisex showers afterwards, having worked up quite a sweat. Pez met her Ahumdulilah double in the showers and it was almost like looking into a mirror except for the face. Her name was Pooh and her face was serenely beautiful and angelic. So much so that Pez felt really bad for her that she had to put on Pez's face sometimes, masking her own.

For her part Pooh was deeply respectful of Pez and feeling that it was terribly grandiose of her to be masquerading as the Rajaha. They each surprised the other and made a tight connection.

The whole party moved back up to the ground floor and along a wide ornamented corridor to the grand dining room which could easily accommodate them. The mammoth mahogany dining table, polished to a shine, was the largest Pez had ever seen. The room had a cathedral ceiling of plated gold with speckles of glittering color. Along one wall stood tall heavily draped windows, and on the opposite wall, exquisite oil paintings were hung in a row like a museum. The sideboard cabinetry was built-in, and perfectly matched the dining room table. To either side of the wide entrance stood five-foot nine-inch tall marble statues, one of a forest nymph and the other a meadow nymph. Both were naked and the meadow one bore Pez's face. Pooh, who was walking beside Pez seeing her look at the statue said, "I know; it's sort of embarrassing," referring to the lewd posture of the meadow nymph displaying their body in all its nakedness.

Pez inquired wondering, "Did that statue come from Ahumdulilah?"

"No," Pooh answered, "It was excavated from an underground temple right here on Rocky."

"The Amonrahonians," Pez guessed.

"You have a fairly significant cult here on the planet dating back thousands of years, and Major Nicon had me wear your face to meetings with them. I've promised them teachings I cannot produce, but you'll be able to help them."

"Do they know the Bliss of Inner Fire practice, sometimes called the Inner Heat?" Pez inquired, trying to assess the situation.

"No," Pooh explained, "they practice mindfulness continuously and formal meditation and contemplation upon emptiness of the witness. They also have walking meditations and question and answer teaching-dueling, which is intensely confrontational."

"I've trained in a similar method," Pez told her, "and know that way well. The Inner Fire transmutes energy and concentrates it in its most pristine state, opening the higher limbs of the practice including the lucid dream work, and culminates with the Transference of Consciousness and Forceful Projection. The Rainbow body is attained through a contemplative practice like the one you described, but this one is coupled with visualizations in sacred imitation of fierce and peaceful aspects personified, of the Divine Mind, and with clarification and alignment of the sacred triad of human mind, Divine Mind, Absolute Transcendental Consciousness. With the attainment of the rainbow body and with mastery of the transference of consciousness and forceful projection one can leave their physical body in their rainbow body through the crown of the head and go anywhere."

"Ahumdulilah has the practice for attaining the Rainbow body but not the other practices you speak of," Pooh informed her. "Few on the planet have achieved their rainbow body though."

"I'd like to see your practice instruction because I might be able to clarify a few things, and give some helpful commentary."

"Our whole planet would be so grateful, Rajaha," Pooh gushed.

Pez requested, "Please just call me Pez." Then trying to get herself off the pedestal these folks seemed to put her on, Pez stated, "Sarhi is my teacher."

"We've heard," Pooh said gravely, "and she is your disciple ultimately," neutralizing Pez's efforts entirely.

Pez sat between Ming and Pooh at the gigantic table. The thing was fifteen feet wide and thirty meters long. Major Nicon, seated across from Pez, had to project his voice to cross the distance and said, "There's not a duelist in the empire who could defeat you and you far exceed the dangerous reputation of your family and the expectations of your Ahumdulilah allies. Would you demonstrate your Inner Fire for us?"

"Well I just learned how to do this," Pez told him, pulling out her disposable paper napkin from her lap and concentrating deeply.

None of the Ahumdulilah folks had a clue what they were looking for or what kind of sign her mastery might appear in, and most were anxious that they would somehow miss it when it did. The moment seemed to be building to an anti-climax when suddenly the paper napkin burst into flames and Ahhu ran over with an empty plate to catch it on just before it burned Pez's hand. A wave of awe and excited Alhambra chatter filled the room all at once, more than the Mel Pyramid II could zero in on to interpret, so Pez and her crew waited it out.

When their hosts quieted down, Major Nicon attempted to give Pez some sense of the pulse and attitude of the population of the empire beneath the ruling families and their minions, "Fear rules the empire and even though everyone feels the same way, despising how things are, there is zero solidarity and almost no networking. Everyone works long hours in poor conditions with safety regulations near non-existent, and for hardly enough compensation to keep them alive. Suicide is the leading cause of death in the empire and execution is second, if you include disappearances in that category, which we do."

"How has Ahumdulilah remained free of the empire?" Pez asked.

"They haven't located our home world yet but it is only a matter of time before they do," he replied. "For two decades we've been building a community and infrastructure on the planet Gourd, in the Sparkling Spiral Galaxy. We've moved twenty-three million people there so far and the pace has been accelerating. We maintain the population of Ahumdulilah at 5.5 billion so there is no way we can get everyone to the Gourd Planetary System."

Pez asked, "How can you attack their ships given that they are cloaked?"

Nicon explained, "We have the same tech as the empire for targeting cloaked ships. It's based on the discovery of sensors that can see microwaves. A quantum computer algorithm was programed to identify mili and micro distortions culminating in a near-instant outline and present coordinates of a cloaked ship. This technology has already been transmitted to Om."

"Do you have identities for my personal guards, Evenrude and Johnson?" Pez inquired.

Nicon told her, "We have a number they can choose from, but by chance, there is a particularly unique fit for each of them. You are known to use white sun mercenaries, especially in your piracy. They will be well-covered."

"Do imperial ship crews ever mutiny?" Pez questioned Nicon.

"Every ship has Adherence Examiners aboard ferreting out trouble makers and there are always some Monarch Secret Police placed among a crew. The officers and those in some key positions get miniature explosives inserted and attached to a major artery. There is no place on a ship that is not monitored by imaging and auditory mic.s. The control layers are too dense and overlapping."

"How about hacking?" Pez asked.

"Now that's an interesting question," Nicon stated. "Mel has given us Councilman Jard's take-over program and we're still learning the basic language it's built upon, but our quantum computer scientists are excited and believe it's promising. This is an area Om is ahead of us in."

"Mel?" Pez began asking.

"I'm already working on translating the two quantum languages and integrating them," Mel informed her. "Yona has a drone on the way here with more processing memory for me which you'll need to have installed on the yacht. I'm going to need it for this. Once the integration is accomplished I'll be able to connect to all programs in that language, and from them to their core administrative programs. Jard taught me how to create a backdoor network in the Kluzyst Vachisy Empire's system. The imperials in White Lotus, Royal and

Whirlpool Galaxies employ and share the same quantum language based upon four symbols or values."

"Is Jard working on this back on Om?" Pez asked.

Mel informed her, "He is, along with most of Om's top quantum computer scientists, though just as importantly, Trix has taken great interest and is working on it too."

Trix looked up from her pocket device at Pez, her eyes appearing enormous through her inch-thick lenses, and told her, "I think my Quantum Key to Everything Matrix is deciphering their computer language. I should have it in just a few minutes."

"With a pocket device?" The Ahumdulilah quantum computer expert asked in disbelief.

"She's real bright," Pez offered, wondering.

Mel told them what was really going on, "Trix is using 38% of my processing ability. That's how she's doing it!"

"Thanks for letting her, Mel," Pez said sweetly.

Trix was concentrating, declared loudly by her fogging glasses. Her eyeballs seemed to heat up when she was really concentrating. It was the oddest thing. All eyes were on Trix, even Electra's from her front pouch. Anticipation intensified slowing time to a trickle, waiting in pure expectation extending to seemingly unnatural duration for such a heightened state of arousal. Still it endured; and continued to abide stretching long beyond the bounds of endurance. Faces were frozen, forks stopped in midair, breathing had paused, you could hear a pin drop in the room and a few were on the verge of passing out for lack of oxygen to their brains when Trix finally confirmed, "Got it."

Mel screamed, "She did it!!!"

The Ahumdulilah computer guy, whose name was Pioneer, declared, "Well I'll be damned."

"You're brilliant Trix," Pez complimented her.

Trix tried to explain, "Anything founded soundly upon the first four principles, or emanations of the universe, will inevitably express the unity of the whole and the transitions or changes in the relative process of energy and movement in time. The oldest two-value codes express a dilemma and the later three-value codes a trilemma.

Quantum codes employ four values across five dimensions in a quatrelemma. In logic the dilemma is cause and effect while the trilemma is thesis, antithesis and synthesis. The quatrelemma of logic gives us the active principle, reactive principle, neutralizing principle and consequence of change. This quantum logic can be expressed mathematically as the indicational calculus. The universe is an undifferentiated unity, seamless, and in permenant interaction. Studying partial systems does violence to any piece or part examined in isolation since it ignores the web of interactions with the whole. We do not know its entirety, and likely cannot due to accelerating expansion of the potentially visable parts and the invisable parts moving already at the speed of light. The curvature of space folds the outermost circumference back into the center decelerating. As a whole it incorporates all-time and all-space. From the perspective of time these are end-states, though from the cosmic perspective it is simply the eternal present. I've developed a method and calculated formulas and values based on the microcosms of the Om star system and of the human being, to map the universal cycle and variables within. Any structure based upon the four fundamental principles combining to manifest a lower order, can be deciphered, decrypted, translated and interacted with by my Key to Everything."

Pioneer had his mouth hanging open in shock. Pez requested of Trix, "In layman's terms sweetheart?"

Trix summarized, "If it is applicable to the real universe, my Key to Everything will figure it out right quick."

Pioneer remained speechless although he did manage to get his mouth closed. Pez commented, "It's too bad languages are subjective and not applicable to the real universe."

Trix pointed out, "A few really ancient ones based upon sound vibration and scared sounds and formulas actually are applicable and my Key to Everything understands Islohar. Strangely it is the poorest language for expressing scientific terms and research."

Pez said to Major Nicon, "I'm told you have a list of serious malcontents for me to make contact with."

"Yes; quite a few indeed," he replied. "The most serious ones never show any sign of it and are not even under suspicion. So you won't be arousing any yourself through the contacts. You'll transmit to them on a preset frequency, books of one-time codes, within ranges of only inches. The equipment and transmissions are undetectable, too weak to register. Once a malcontent has code books you can communicate with unbreakable encryption. If you do this remotely through a drone nonlocality transmitter, no one can trace your location or identity. An intergalactic resistance can form under the imperial sensors. The list includes heads of state, military ship captains, people in a position to take major plants and utilities offline, folks of high rank—just beneath top brass—in literally every branch of the military, police section chiefs, and many others."

"We better get these languages learned so we can get started," Pez said with excitement.

CHAPTER NINE

For the next eight weeks Pez and her crew were immersed in the Bozo language, tutored by Onkyo and taught by a number of the Ahumdulilah operatives. By the end of the sixth week the lessons themselves had started coming in Bozo. Lucky was struggling desperately and often sounded as though he were speaking gibberish. Winston was up late every night studying and scheduled extra sessions with Onkyo to keep from falling too far behind the curve. Marlboro was getting it, unlike Lucky, though he was far behind the rest. Pez had her vocabulary and conjugation of verbs, working now on her pronunciation and fluency. Ahhu and Super-Agent Green were only days behind her in their development of their Bozo skills. The Islohar were all close on Greens heels and Ming, Trix, Rubix, Gretle and Evenrude were keeping up too, with Johnson only a day behind them. Elanem was about tied with Johnson.

Two weeks of history lessons taught in the Bozo language followed the eight-week intensive language assimilation, sinking it in deeper, while providing them with family, Rocky and imperial history they would be expected to know in their cover identities.

Their accommodations were so extravagantly rich they made the Ritz Supreme Ultimate Hotel on Earth 10^5 CBS2 look like a slum by comparison. Pez had them up before the sun each morning sweating and shaking at soft martial arts practice and performing sessions of sitting meditation. Meals were delicious and much coveted since they were really the only breaks from study and workouts they got each day. Their work went late leaving them exhausted and their vast expansive bed was uneventful, seeing only the action of sleeping.

Ahhu was horny and meant to instigate something before diving into the Sterling language of Royal Galaxy. Ming meant to have an affair with Pooh and just couldn't help herself, drawn irrevocably to the being with Pez's body and a face of divine beauty. She'd confessed her affliction first to Sarhi, and then to Pez, hoping someone would stop her, only Pez thought it would be fun and wanted to too; if Pooh was open to it. Rubix, who was on a strict regime allowing him unlimited orgasms with his pressure point pressed preventing ejaculation, but only two ejaculations per month, now had credit on his accounts and meant to cash-out.

Ahhu spied Pooh leaving the dining room alone and raced to catch up, having recognized that Pooh was the surest means to success in her own agenda. Reaching her side and matching pace Ahhu asked her, "Are you married?"

"No, I'm single," Pooh replied.

"Do you have a boyfriend?" Ahhu persisted in grilling her.

Pooh explained, "I'm not in a relationship with anyone. For almost four years now my work here has been full-time and demanding."

"What's your sexual orientation?" Ahhu kept up her interrogation.

Pooh told her, "I'm classified a breeder and allowed one child unless I immigrate to the new world where I could have as many as I want."

"So the government decided for you that you're heterosexual?" Ahhu asked alarmed.

"No," Pooh attempted to clarify. "I passed the fitness, intelligence and empathy tests so I'm allowed to reproduce, but that doesn't mean that I have to. People who do not pass the tests can still have children if they go to the new world or relocate to one of the areas with special services."

"Are you a virgin?" Ahhu asked directly.

"No!" Pooh exclaimed. "I've had four sex partners and was in a five-year relationship in my twenties."

"With a boy?" Ahhu inquired still digging.

"What exactly are you getting at?" Pooh answered Ahhu's question with one of her own.

"I want to know if you like girls, boys, or both," Ahhu admitted.

"To what end?" Pooh insisted.

Ahhu levelled with her, "I find you quite alluring and Ming is simply smitten by you, while Pez is attracted to you as well. Rubix can't look at you without getting hard and Trix and Gretle would both like to get into your pants."

The shock on Pooh's face contracted into horror for just a moment before slowly relaxing into what could only be described as a stupor. She'd stopped walking and stood catatonically in the passage so Ahhu stood close in front of her taking one of Pooh's hands in each of hers, looking up into her wide unseeing eyes. Since this was not enough to bring Pooh out of herself, Ahhu squeezed Pooh's hands and balanced on her tip-toe's closing on Pooh's face. Those wide eyes blinked and it was like the lights came on and now someone was home. Pooh's face signaled anxiety at the same time as more than a hint of a smile. She leaned down finding Ahhu's lips with her own and Ahhu released her hands to embrace her. Pooh folded her arms around tiny naked Ahhu kissing her passionately in the hallway. The kiss went long and generated remarkable energy. Both of them had obligations to immediately attend to so they arranged a tryst and would meet after evening meditation in the Bulwinkle family bedroom suite.

During the afternoon Ahhu found opportunity to inform Ming of the tryst and to tell Trix, who told Gretle and Rubix. At dinner the openness, excitement and desire woven into Pooh's expression and conveyed across her energy made her beauty even more radiant and dazzling. The flirtations had been totally titillating and Pez had been clueless of plotted futures, alive and savoring the extra blessings and enchantments of the present moment. Pez pushed everyone hard at evening martial arts practice, and between Pez and Sarhi, the evening meditation was grounded solidly, rooted in the base of pristine consciousness.

At the end of the meditation session after the sound of the gong faded, Major Nicon announced, "We have now completed the Bozo phase of training and preparation and we will have three days of rest and recuperation before entering the final Sterling phase. Enjoy your time off and be ready to hit the ground running after your break."

Pooh was right beside Pez when Pez stood from her meditation cushion, so Pez wrapped an arm around her affectionately. Electra was out like a light and producing a tiny snore with her inhalations. Ming closed in on the other side of Pooh attaching herself to her. Ahhu led to way and they watched her flat little bottom flex as they walked to the partitioned elevator and entered, ignoring the partitions. The collective energy of excitement was peaking, erupting into other energies which were concentrating in arousal. The long walk down the hall to the bedroom suite door was like one big floating group hug and a few garments were strewn in their wake as they arrived. Opening doors, lighting, soft music, sandalwood scent, and a pleasant vibration arising from the mattress of the bed were all handled by Mel without prompts. Electra and Gumby were tucked into their safe shielded and sound proofed hover cradles and Pez and Ming wore their earbuds connected to the cradles and integrated with the diaper sensors.

A tempest of eroticism raged more than half the night in the Bulwinkle family bedroom. Poor Rubix was now hopelessly in debt. Pooh had found herself not only the center of attention but within the very eye of a tremendous series of events of a magnitude that brought the Ahumdulilah perimeter guards, a mile from the mansion, to their knees in spastic spontaneous orgasms. The edges of the series of events extended from horizon to horizon and far into space, wholly incorporating the capital city of Bulwinkle and so making every form of media. Due to the lateness of the hour of the occurrence of the event series only nightshift workers, late night partiers and insomniacs had been awake to enjoy it, while the rest all had wet dreams. The Ahumdulilah scientists at the Bulwinkle mansion and the scientists of Rocky were baffled and could offer no explanation for the event(s). Only females realized that it had been a long series because males were finished with the first event of it. Pseudo-explanations abounded from astrologers to palm-readers though none came anywhere near the truth.

Pooh had experienced things well beyond the human sensory apparatus penetrating the kernel to the core of all-potential or the void containing everything, and felt almost turned inside out by it. Going through it was an alchemical transformation and metamorphosis, not to mention an epiphany and unrepeatable peak experience, a singularity reorienting her entire reality. The love held palpable warmth, tangible texture, mesmerizing beauty, and an irresistible calling she wanted to embrace and integrate with her entire being. Her heart was open and devoted to Pez.

Pez had removed an impediment, an obstacle born of trauma and festering chronically within Pooh's psyche, releasing stuck energy to flow, removing barriers, and breaking her heart wide open no longer afraid to love. Pooh had attentively received the blessing of the Rajaha directly heart to heart shattering the last vestiges of rudimentary mind structure and schematization to liberate her awareness so that she recognized the divine mind of true Forms, contemplating the Absolute Mind of Transcendental Emptiness. This made her resolved as a stalwart devout disciple for life of the Holy Rajaha.

Only Green had connected the timing of the events with the activities of the Wu, so was the only one who knew, beside the family and Pooh. Of course, Evenrude, Johnson and the Islohar knew too.

The Sterling phase was brutal demanding every stitch of concentration and much sweating and trembling while holding difficult one-legged stances of the soft martial arts, sometimes for twenty minutes on the same leg. Pez was like a general out of the ancient Om *Classic of War*, insisting on every last gram of effort. Onkyo was amazing and worked tirelessly. Mel helped each of them.

Still Lucky was a bit lost and just not making sense of it. Everyone else was learning the language of Sterling with commendable progress and Lucky was trying only to grasp the tourist version at the remedial level of that. Yet stuck on the first holo-segment with asking where the bathroom is, he asked aloud in earshot of Pez, "Where is your ass up a tree, please me??"

Pez was pretty sure Lucky was on his way to assuming the mute yacht crewman identity even though he'd have to be made up to look older in order to fit it. She really didn't care how badly Marlboro mashed Sterling so long as his Bozo could pass for native. Many people mangled Basic as a second language so there was nothing noteworthy about it. Super-agent Green was a whiz-kid and could both pass as a native of Rocky and put a distinct Bozo accent on her Sterling. With her size, attire and craft-skills Green could just blend in anywhere she liked.

Everyone in Pez's party was measured all over and fitted for complete wardrobes right down to underclothes, shoes, hats and accessories. Many accessories were actually weapons or nifty gadgets inspiring runaway imagining. Pez's diamond headed platinum dart necklace appeared expensive, beautiful and entirely harmless. She also had a fan of ordinary plastic blades sharpened to a cutting edge at the tops and each blade individually wrapped in paper and silk lace. No sensor scanners would give it the slightest hum, though Pez could kill the closest six people to her in a crowd in less than a second with it.

No matter what you dressed Evenrude and Johnson in it was always their size and confident military bearing that came across anyway. They did not end up in expensive silk suits and did not get alligator shoes, though they did get stretchy synthetic shoulder holsters that were psychedelic green and glowed in the dark. The enforcers and white-sun gangster-types in the empire tended to be flamboyant wearing bright primary colors, usually at least three colors at a time. Since neither yellow, orange nor pink could be pressed upon the two Space Marines, they were dressed in bright green and bright blue with some brilliant red trim. Their boots were synthetic and composed of a material which gave an extraordinary bounce and propulsion they were yet adapting to. Both of them found their attire absurd and unattractive, inordinately loud, and far too easy to target; but Major Nicon assured them that other than by adding yellow, they could not be more perfectly dressed as dangerous thugs within the empire. Neither budged on the yellow.

Pez and Ming were made up and decked out to look like glamorous holo-stars and it really worked in Ming's case. There always seemed to be something off, just a little goofy and childlike when it came to Pez, defeating all sophistication and dangerousness. There was just no camouflaging her friendliness and no way to highlight her authentic deadliness. The divine fool would simply have to rely on family reputation and actual martial skills.

Sarhi, Shudiy and the two older female Islohar all dressed like dour aunts in mourning while Woahha got to dress like Trix and Gretle in the most expensive latest fashions. Gretle loved the clothes and accessories so much she was considering dropping out of graduate school to become a full-time career spy.

Marlboro no longer looked like a bovine rancher and had to trade in his fancy leather hip-rig holster for a near invisible synthetic shoulder one. The leather boots were gone too, replaced by purple plastic foam ones and his tan leather and sheep fleece jacket was turned in for a green cape. Instead of the wide-brimmed hat with a trench dented into the top he now wore a brimless tall cone hat. His suit was of the finest silk and perfectly tailored. In Pez's mind the disguise did not entirely wipe off the "Spook" stamped on his forehead, but it was clear the costume people had done their best.

Pez and each member of her crew were issued new pocket devices and all new electronics. Nothing from Om except the anonymously packaged ambassador rations would be coming with them. Their documents, passports, banking data and everything else they'd require were loaded onto their new pocket devices. Ahhu had already found some Rocky bands she liked and had many gigabits of music on hers. Rubix put his latest version of space invaders on his. Super-Agent Green had Trix load Mel's adaptation of Jard's take-over and remote access program on hers and had no lack of ideas about how to use it. Trix had disguised the program as a road directional guide and maps of Rocky, and a very basic such program, a little sketchy perhaps, was actually integrated in, so by entering destinations, maps would appear and voice direction would begin. From off planet the directions would always start off with, "Land at the Bulwinkle main spaceport..."

When the Sterling phase of training was completed they added one more week of pressured language practice and embodiment structured around official imperial stop and frisks, interrogations, cross examination as a hostile witness, truth serum and chemical interrogation, and unpleasant pre-tortures and almost-tortures. Pez and the Islohar, including Green, gave up nothing even under the strongest chemical interrogation. Most of them had rated high and done quite well, although Marlboro's entire mind could be read under truth chemicals and Lucky spilled his guts in pre-torture. Interestingly, no information could be gleamed from Lucky under chemical interrogation.

Their Mirage Streak Fury bomber crew of five, and the eight 'slaves' traveling on that craft, were introduced to Pez and her gang. The craft was loaded, armed and provisioned. Their two imperial F-14 Drone fighter-bombers had been delivered and one was readied for the mission. *Aphrodite* was packed with everything it could hold, which was quite a bit with the heavy fusion elements, rare metals, four tons of platinum, rare earths, and other cargo offloaded and infused into the family fortune. Pooh and two female slaves, Pippy and Alice, had been added to the 18 who would go on the *Aphrodite*. The bomber crew informed them that they'd named their craft *Sidekick*. All was finally in readiness.

CHAPTER TEN

Pez punched it and *Aphrodite* flew cloaked from the estate hanger with their drone and *Sidekick* right behind struggling to keep up. Ahhu was in the drone-pilot seat in the cockpit of the yacht flying the drone with her skullcap and drone console. Electra was wide awake and staring out the windshield. Gumby was too, but he'd been up longer and was starting to fade a little. Shudiy and Ming were also in the cockpit. Ming asked Pez, "So who's our first contact?"

"You'll like this," Pez told her. "We're on our way to the Glitter Star System of the Royal Galaxy to meet their planetary leader at a concert featuring the most popular band in the galaxy, called the Whirling Vortexes. We're also scheduled to contact the band leader, who is the keyboard player and his name is Pogo."

"What's the planetary leader's name?"

"Crunch," Pez replied. "He was a captain of industry before he became a politician. He has a fair track record of standing up for his people but he'll only go so far out on a limb. It's apparently quite normal for world leaders to meet with ruling family members. Glitter's pretty rich as far as imperial worlds go, being the hub of the entertainment industry. There's a joke on Glitter that goes, 'Why did Glitter end up with the most Adherence Examiners and Tarfan the most nuclear waste?'"

"I've no idea," Ming confessed.

"Because Tarfan got first choice," Pez told her with a grin.

"Apparently Adherence Examiners aren't much appreciated," Ming commented.

"They are on Monarch," Pez corrected, "just nowhere else."

"I guess they censure and regulate the entertainment business."

"I guess so. They used to be called Propaganda Ministers but 'propaganda' has such negative connotations that they finally changed the name. At least that's what I'm told."

"They sound worse than Om's Space Controllers," Ming shared. "What's Crunch's title?"

"All the imperial worlds are headed by a Regent-Governor, except for Monarch where the Emperor resides."

"Do you remember *everything* they taught us in class?" Ming asked amazed.

"Most of it," Pez fibbed, since she really had retained every word.

"Are we just going down for the evening and then staying in the yacht?"

"We are booked into the Grand Royal Hotel across the street from the concert hall," Pez informed her. "Mel made the reservations and booked a whole floor since the penthouse wasn't available. Apparently the band is staying in the penthouse."

What's their music like?" Ming inquired.

Ahhu answered, "It's really catalyst! You can dance to most of it and it's loaded with energy. They're actually quite skilled with their instruments and have had the imagination to produce a new sound."

"Do you have a holo of them?" Ming asked interested.

Ahhu put one up from her console and Mel immediately routed it to Ming's. There were five band members: keyboards, drums, saxophone, and two stringed instruments. Unlike the unisex Random Comets on Earth 10^5 CBS2, the members of the Whirling Vortexes revealed their genders on stage. Only one looked to be out of their teens. Two were male and three clearly female. Pez found the Royal fashions to be somewhat embarrassing to wear, though it did vex her curiosity and produce delight to see others in them. In aversion to hypocrisy Pez wore the fashions herself and was processing her embarrassment.

Mel brought up some past Whirling Vortexes concerts which had been recorded with live audiences and they watched right up to the quantum jump ten-second countdown. Many in the audience wore body paint instead of clothing. There was quite a supply of such paint aboard *Aphrodite* and both Pippy and Alice were master-body painters, among other things. Pretty much everyone attending the concert was a ruling family member or minion, either that or from the very top echelon of corporate hierarchies. As wealthy as Glitter was, less than a tenth of a percent of its population saw any benefit at all from this. Celebrities and chief executives often accumulated a few billion dags, but nothing like the multi-trillions of a ruling family.

Aphrodite, Sidekick and their drone appeared in the jump zone well beyond the orbital distance of the 4th planet from the yellow sun. Their destination was the third planet surrounded by layers of orbiting ships, space platforms, space stations and satellites. Reversing the main drives gently was sufficient for reducing velocity to within range of the speed limit coming out of the jump zone. *Aphrodite* had been fitted with a beacon transmitting the Bulwinkle signal code crest quantumly. All cloaking had been dropped and Pez stayed just above the speed limit thinking this would best suit her cover.

The authorities came on in Pez's ear with, "This is Glitter Space Control to *Aphrodite*; you're coming in just a little fast."

Pez, trying to be a pirate heiress, told him, "You need to recalibrate your sensors because I'm hardly moving."

Completely cowed the man asked timidly, "Is this Cher Bulwinkle piloting *Aphrodite*?"

"Sure is," Pez announced.

"I'm so sorry Ma'am," he begged forgiveness, "I thought I was addressing one of your employees. I'm sending escorts to guide you in fast using the emergency lane we always keep open. It is a great honor to have you visit our planet. You can accelerate on your current course and escorts will be right with you. I pray you see beyond this poor first impression I've made and recognize that we will do everything we can to make your stay comfortable. You're cleared right to the surface."

"I think I like Glitter already," Pez let him off the hook, speeding up madly.

Pez informed Ming, "The hotel has a yacht hangar and they'll take us in a private indoor-outdoor shuttle directly to our rooms from the yacht and bomber."

"Are all 34 of us checking in?" Ming inquired.

"Pooh must stay and Lucky is staying on the yacht to keep an eye on it. He'll watch over the bomber as well," Pez answered. "He has an artificial voice box in his mute identity which automatically speaks for him like a prosthesis, controlled by his skullcap. Mel programmed the voice to be a little scratchy and synthetic to make it obvious that it's the device of a mute."

"So 32 of us will be staying at the hotel," Ming checked.

"Yes. All the rest of us but Lucky, and Pooh of course," Pez confirmed.

Ming commented, "He's such an ill-fit for his nickname. We really ought to start calling him Luxandexter."

Pez said philosophically, "Will and intention are very real forces in the universe, but chance and luck are merely ignorance of natural laws of process."

Pez was showing off by coming in really fast and her Glitter escorts had to direct her by coms to the emergency lane since catching her was beyond hope. She came in with one of her typical crash landings leaving Sidekick in the dust, though Ahhu managed to keep her F-14 drone fighter bomber in tight formation, and Pez pulled up the nose at the last second spending thruster fuel and one-time boosters while employing vortex redirect, flaps, drives and skill. The hanger came so fast that no one got a good look at the outside of it. The yacht's leg's hydraulics contracted to the faintest ting of metal on metal before rising them back up to a parked position. The ramp was already coming down.

A grander entrance to Glitter could not have been made; not without ending as a stain on the hanger floor. Imaging of her flight in, and particularly her landing, were already showing in the public media. The mysterious, dangerous, reclusive Bulwinkle family had come out of isolation after many generations in the persons of Cher and Lai, and had chosen Glitter as the planet for their first appearance. Piracy was alluded to by commentators but never mentioned directly. Holos of Pez from almost two years ago out of the imperial archives were displayed beside images of her landing and Cher was an instant celebrity on Glitter. The holos shown of Pez were actually of Pooh wearing Pez's face almost two years ago.

Evenrude and Johnson came down the ramp and looked around the hanger. They waited for the bomber to land and its 13 occupants to disembark before waving the 17 from inside the yacht down the ramp. Pez wore her micro-blaster on the inside of her left knee since it was one of the few places on her body that her dress actually covered. She carried her fan and her hair was put up with jade darts. The indoor-outdoor shuttles were there along with their personal hotel welcomer and entertainment liaison. She said in a sweet voice conveying actual sincerity, "Welcome to Glitter Cher and Lai, and your family and companions as well. If there is anything you want while you're here you have only to ask me and I'll arrange it. My name is Antic. I'm at your service night and day. I'm sending you my code to reach me. Please have a seat in one of the shuttles and I'll get you directly to your rooms. I'll handle check-in for you."

Pez recognized Antic's state and it was evident in the young woman's aura too. Antic seemed to be having the same realization about Pez, or about Cher at any rate. Pez told her, "You seem misplaced in a planet population moved by wealth and superficiality."

"We must all live someplace and scratch a living to survive," Antic said pleasantly with a smile.

"I'm going to make your life more comfortable and provide you with means to assist others in need, but this must remain our secret and you cannot connect me with the money. I have a reputation to maintain."

To Ahhu, who carried their credit beads, transfer codes and debit beads—though it was Mel who really tracked and manage them, she said, "Please get Antic's account codes and transfer five million dags, sweetheart."

Antic, one of the brighter and higher functioning commoners on the planet, earned 29,000 dags per year of which most went to one tax or another. Five million dags was more than she could earn before taxes in 159 years at her current job. She was momentarily lost in a bewildered state of non-reality waiting for it to sink in—actually hoping it would—though it was just too statistically impossible so kept eluding her grasp to dance around the fringes of comprehension. Pez could see this and asked Ahhu, "Don't we have some physical money in that tiny purse of yours?"

"How much do you want?" Ahhu asked as she opened the purse.

"Three tens," Pez told her, referring to three ten-thousand dag bills.

Ahhu handed three of the foldable synthetic fiber bills to Pez and she gave them to Antic saying, "This is real and you can trust me. Here's for the great welcome you gave us."

Antic held more than a year's salary in her hand, which after taxes made the 3 bills actually more than three years of her salary. She finally managed to say, "From the Divine Fool to Crazy Wisdom; great gratitude and the promise there will be fewer hungry children on Glitter."

"We are One," Pez/Cher replied pleased.

They had made the equal thoroughly in their brief eye contact. Antic bowed to Cher and Cher to Antic before climbing aboard one of the little shuttles. Ahhu asked, "She's one of us, isn't she?"

"If you mean she is in the state of mindful contemplation without ego, then yes, she is one of us," Pez replied.

The shuttles went at a clip to please Pez and they arrived at their floor and the Empress Suite in no time. The penthouse was the Emperor Suite and that was taken by the band, its staff and its band-aids. The floor of the Empress suite could easily accommodate 120 people, and of course there were only 32 in Pez's party, but it was apparently expected for a ruling family to lease an entire floor when staying at a hotel. Mel had booked well in advance. Often hotels had to kick people out to clear a floor for an incoming ruling family, but not in Pez's case, thanks to Mel.

The Empress Suite itself, where six of them plus the two babies would be staying, was 9,000 square feet and extremely well appointed, though it was still a step down from their yacht. Interstellar Yachting media outlet was hounding Pez for a tour of the interior and begging for holo's. She finally had Mel send some with text identifying the materials of the surfaces and furnishings. These holos found their way immediately into the public domain and circulated like a cyclone.

As planned, as soon as super-agent Green dropped her things off in her room she was off on her own to connect with some of the lower level contacts on their list for Glitter. Pez had complete confidence in her and Green was the only one of the five intelligence officers she was strapped with whom she any confidence in at all. Lucky was limited to security functions and the other three had only security and passive recon functions at this point. At the moment they were sweeping the Empress Suite for imaging and auditory sensors. Many hotels planted them in the empire for purposes of blackmail or to sell smut to the entertainment/scandal media.

Having some time before their scheduled meeting in the concert hall across the street, and since both babies were sleeping, Ming and Pez decided to take a bath. The tub was marble and four feet deep with benches around three sides and water jets all over. Ahhu, Trix, Rubix, and Gretle joined them. They had all had their hair dyed to look like Rocky natives. Most folks on Rocky had hair in a spectrum from dark auburn to brown with orange-brown the most common, though there were people with black hair too. Many females of Rocky with orange-brown hair had it dyed primary orange and this is what had been done to Pez and Ming. Trix's hair was dyed yellow and Ahhu had chosen a bright turquoise. Rubix's hair was now dark blue and Gretle had gone rainbow.

Ahhu somehow talked them all into going to the concert in body paint and Pez hadn't seen much difference between paint and clothes here anyway. Pippy and Alice were called and went to work painting them. They had a little trouble with Rubix's penis since it didn't seem to be able to remain still, nor a constant size, but they had fun doing their best with it. They couldn't paint Pez or Ming's nipples since both were still nursing. Their baby pouches were textile armored, fashionable and trim, and ornamented on the outside with jewels.

Pez decided she'd bring Pippy and Alice to the concert hall with them. Evenrude and Johnson would also be going and Antic would accompany them to provide transportation and get them backstage.

Ahhu wore a little purse with their financial stuff in it. The purse was alarmed, contained homing devices, and had a little interior shield you wouldn't want to lose your fingers to. Trix wore a belt with a holder for her unusually large pocket device, on account of not having any pockets. Pez's platinum-diamond tiara served the dual purpose of skullcap and pocket device. Ming kept hers in a side-pocket of Gumby's pouch.

Antic reported in Pez's ear, "I'm here with the shuttles outside your door in the hall, Ma'am."

"We're on our way out; thank you," Pez replied.

They loaded in, all ten of them going plus Antic. The shuttles were computer piloted. They zipped through the hotel, down the shaft then through to the tunnel under the street. Pez noticed that most everyone went about by hover-chair not wanting to be bothered moving their own weight about. This was just antithetical to a martial artist and revulsion washed over her. You didn't need to be ambulatory to get around on Glitter. They shot through the tunnel and were out below the other side of the street in a snap, already ascending straight up a shaft to the back-stage reception area.

Ahhu, who'd been reading spy novels lately, asked Pez, "Don't we need to contact Charlie and tell him something like, 'the eagle has landed in the nest'?"

"What would that mean?" Pez asked perplexed.

Ahhu brought her voice down to a whisper and said, "That we've infiltrated and we're in."

"I think I'll wait until I have a little more to report than that," Pez replied.

Ahhu gave her a dubious look. Once parked at the concert hall, Antic led Pez and Lai to a plush conference room where Regent-Governor Crunch was already seated and waiting. The rest of Pez's party were let into a lounge with a pharmacy, bar and smoke shop. Crunch rose as Cher and Lai entered. Basic greetings were exchanged and a stiff formal hug completed the transmission of the one-time code books to Crunch's micro-device. Pez-inquired, "Are we being monitored?"

"No, I had the room scanned when I entered and there's a jammer operating above a ceiling panel now, insuring our privacy."

"I'm mainly seeking to construct a communications network with unbreakable encryption at this stage," Pez/Cher informed him. "Until we have a body of people representing every planet of the empire we will not be in position to topple it. We have some ideas for bringing it down but we have a great deal of work to do before we get to that phase of things. All communications will remain silent until I've had about a year to distribute code books. Each one is unique and no key at all to any others. A code word must be used at the start of each transmission or we assume the whole book to be compromised. Yours is 'sail'. Start every transmission with that word. It's not in the book I've given you. The code word comes only by word of mouth."

Crunch asked Cher, "Are you truly the Avahat, or Rajaha of the Alhambra language?"

"I am the one who will end imperialism and disparity in these systems now claimed by Monarch and I am mother to the one who will teach us all," Pez informed him as Electra gave him an enchanting grin from her pouch.

"Good, because I have no interest in helping to replace the Monarch dynasty with a Bulwinkle one," Crunch spoke his mind.

"I come to alleviate suffering and oppression for the masses by liberating them from tyranny and redistributing the hundred thousand mountains of capital, each in the trillions of dags. You already have teachers on the planet. I know because I have met one."

"Who?" he asked.

"I'll tell her about you, and she will likely find a way to make contact. It's up to her. Most folks won't want to reveal themselves until we have a potentially successful action planned."

"I understand that, but please let her know about me. I know many serious practitioners seeking desperately for a teacher. You know the empire wiped out our monasteries and hunted down our monks and teachers when they conquered this planet ages ago, and we have only rumors that a few survived in remote areas with severe conditions who have kept our traditions alive, teaching them to a few in each generation."

"I met a master of Crazy Wisdom today, looked into the knowing vacancy of her eyes, and saw her aura for myself. She's the real deal."

"I would like to give you some money to pass on to her in support of her efforts," Crunch offered.

"I've given her some money, and will give her more before I leave. I'm sure she'd want you to donate it to a charity addressing childhood hunger."

"I'll do that then," he agreed. He asked, then, quite seriously, "Why now? Why not a decade ago?"

"A couple of empires were ahead of yours in my process and development and I've been in other galaxies taking care of them," Pez replied.

"You're not really Cher Bulwinkle at all!" he declared.

"Her identity was modelled on me and prepared for me since before I was born. Wealth from many worlds has been added to the Bulwinkle fortune giving us resources. The seeds of what we do now were sown thousands of years ago and our efforts are supported and guided by a planetary population evolved beyond reproduction now nearly 34 years into a hundred-year meditation."

"You bring me great hope," Crunch said gratefully.

"Hope is the key and the thing we must spread," Pez said enthusiastically. "There really is no hope if people don't have any."

"What of all Monarch's military might?" Crunch asked.

"We have ideas but it is too early to discuss them. We will risk the fewest possible lives, and strike everywhere at once by surprise, with things in place to insure swift and total victory."

"I'm so grateful for the coms codes, and for what you are doing," Crunch said with sincere gravity.

"We have allies in others galaxies outside the empire with military might, and two ships are under construction far bigger than anything this empire has," Pez assured him. "Be patient because I have many contacts to make and ships take time to build."

"You can't possibly visit 5,700 planets yourself," he stated as a question.

"I'll be meeting people on every world I visit who will receive multiple sets of books and make inconspicuous routes within the usual routines of their lives, like quality assurance examiners, workshop teachers, freighter passengers and captains, and those who travel frequently for business."

Their meeting concluded and they exited the room first, leaving Regent Governor Crunch seated alone once again at the table, though he was now a changed man. He had hope, and hope felt like everything. Antic led them on foot to gather the rest of their party, then through a maze of corridors to another room, this one a lounge with a bar, pharmacy, smoking area under a suction vent; a dance floor, hot-tub Jacuzzi, and a champagne fountain. The band members were all in the hot tub with their band-aids and two couples were humping. The body paint Pez and her party wore, while water-resistant, was ultimately water soluble, so they sat around the tub looking at the naked bodies, particularly the ones having sex.

Pogo got out, not being one of the four, and said to Pez, "That was the most daring landing I've ever seen and I'm thrilled to meet you."

There was an awkward moment of uncertainty as to what planetary greeting to enact, so Pez just stepped in and embraced him. Pogo was five foot ten and had an inch on Pez. This got him going and he hugged Ming next, and didn't stop there, moving on to Ahhu, then Gretle, who got his autograph, then on to Trix, Antic, Pippy, and Alice. He shook Rubix's hand, probably signaling exclusive heterosexuality, perhaps even homophobia. Evenrude and Johnson were sweeping the lounge for sensor bugs and Pez waited till she got the all-clear nod before asking Pogo, "Where's your device."

"Transmission complete," he told her, "it's in my chip under my skin."

"Have you expanded your accommodations at each stop on your tour to include us?" Pez asked.

"It's all taken care of. I'd thought you would know since it was handled on your end by someone named Mel."

"Good. Then we'll be following you on your tour and attending parties," Pez told him.

The Whirling Vortexes were having a whirlwind concert tour visiting 42 planets in 96 days. Each member of the band was worth over 200 billion dags, and combined, they were pretty much equal to a lesser ruling family. Not only that, their unreal instant celebrity had only been unfolding for about a year and a half and they were all extremely young. Their first, and so far only, commercially available work contained eleven top hit songs and had sold over a trillion downloads in the empire so far. Their current tour was unveiling new songs they'd composed which would be released as a collection at the end. For a band of this popularity to have ruling family members traveling with it was not at all unusual. In the empire money trumped exceptional abilities and skill, making the richest the best, no matter how untalented or unintelligent, ugly, socially weird, or cruel.

Hoola climbed out of the tub, also not one of the four. She was five foot five inches tall, about 18 years old, and every centimeter of her was just gorgeous. When she'd gotten one leg out of the tub with her other foot still on the hot tub bench, her knee by her face, Ming's breath caught in her throat while the sight gave her heart palpitations. The girl introduced herself to Pez, "I'm Hoola; I play guitar and I'm the lead singer."

"Hi, my name is Cher. You look like a holo model."

"Thanks. It's not enough to create great music these days. You have to look like a model to make it in this profession."

"Then you needn't feel sorry for me because I truly have no aspirations as a musician," Pez told her.

"I don't think the media has it right, but as a musician with some skill, I'm cashing in on my good fortune in meeting their standards," Hoola explained.

"The media might not have it right, but *you* sure are beautiful," Pez insisted. "Why climbing out of that tub, stretching your leg up like that, nearly stopped Lai's heart."

Ming/Lai closed in almost like a predator but it was really more like something caught in a tractor beam, drawn inexorably against will and intention. She wrapped her arms around Hoola, moving Gumby's pouch to the side so only plaint remained between them. Hoola commented while in Lai's grasp, "I've never seen such a sexy bottom as yours."

Ming/Lai replied, "I've never seen such sexy everything."

Tramp, short for Trampol, also not one of the four, left her hunk of a band-aid in the hot tub and climbed out shimmying since she was only five foot tall. The guys Tramp and Hoola had with them looked like muscular holo models for underwear commercials and Rubix was feeling intimidated and chicken around them. Trix and Ahhu both picked up on this, but Ahhu had to get her arms around Tramp and went to hug her. Trix removed her thick glasses and started making out with Rubix, which did wonders for his self-respect.

Ahhu and Tramp seemed to be hitting it off as Ahhu's magic fingers roamed. Whiffle climbed off her perfect model of a band-aid, now spent and for the moment useless. Whiffle got a leg up too. She was five foot seven, had a pretty face, and otherwise looked like a poster for starving children. If Pez was a bean pole, Whiffle was only a string. Pogo's band-aid was a model; an interstellar super-model in fact. So was Frisbie's and he had just completed his exertions with her looking like he'd run to the top of a mountain.

Pogo told Pez, "We have ten revolutionary songs already written with music composed for the lyrics and a beat to start a riot. As soon as this all begins we'll be playing them."

"As soon as we can take over their coms network we'll be transmitting those," Pez promised him. "Don't push the envelope yet because we'll need you when we're ready to unleash our attack."

Whiffle gave Pez a big hug and told her, "I caught your landing on the news. You are one crazy pilot; and you're really hot."

The girl felt delicate and fragile to the max, in Pez's arms, and her lanky limbs seemed to wrap around Pez's torso twice. Whiffle pressed in against half of Pez's chest and her side with Electra occupying the other side. Pez passed her healing energy, and was receptive when Whiffle covered her mouth with her own.

Ming struck out with Hoola, who only liked to do it with boys who looked like super athletes. Ahhu's seductions seemed to be working on Tramp who was having her very first experience of same-gender sex. Pogo and Frisbie went to the bar to wait out their refractory periods. Trix had Rubix steamed up and they were going at it. Gretle was having great fun with Pippy, and Alice sat beside Ming and placed an arm around her back to comfort her.

Pez removed her front pouch and laid Electra on a couch inside of it to fully embrace Whiffle. Pez knew well what being outside of statistical distributions was like, being 5 foot 9 inches from a planet where people tended to grow 6-7 feet at least. This girl though was a lot farther outside the curve, standing completely alone. Pez admired her courage and strength, and opened her heart to Whiffle. The eroticism was intensifying rapidly and Pez kept passing Whiffle energy. Whiffle told her, "You're overwhelming. I've never been so aroused. You're magic."

Pez was entirely in intuition and not in a mode for thought-comprehension; only insight. Each time an opening would occur in Whiffles heart, Pez's wide open one connected deeply, encouraging this orientation and saturating her with love. Whiffle was discovering the distinction and wholly otherness of her experience of eroticism infused with love, unsealing a new dimension previously unknown to her, and rendering sex without love a mere consolation prize with no value.

Tramp was a screamer, and oh boy did Ahhu have her pumping out decibels. Evenrude and Johnson stepped in to make sure it was only sex and not murder, and a dozen Whirling Vortexes security personnel ran to the scene only to then slink away trying to be invisible. The deafening shrieks had awoken Electra who competed and won the contest of resounding noise. Pez had to abandon Whiffle to go attend her daughter.

The band-aids, as they were called in the empire, known as 'groupies' on Earth 10^5 CBS2, had all dressed and left. Electra was secure in her momma's arms, sucking and watching. Whiffle came over and snuggled into Pez's side. Their combined shadow looked like it was made by one white sun human. Whiffle met Electra's eyes and Electra seemed to light up in recognition. Whiffle felt herself inexplicably drawn to the baby.

The arc between them, Pez could feel, was powerful and sharp. Whiffle said to herself aloud, "I've never felt this way before. I'm changing and it's happening so fast. I don't even know what I'm changing into, but it feels better than what I was."

"You have a connection with my daughter, and she is a great teacher returned to us to make a transmission. I didn't think she'd start finding her past disciples until she got at least to fourteen years old, but here she is at eight months already linking with one."

"You think she is my teacher from a past life?" Whiffle asked shocked.

"She was and shall be again, sweetheart. I can prepare you while she learns to walk and talk and all that."

"You meditate?!" Whiffle asked; since it was unheard of within the ruling class.

"Formally since I was twelve," Pez/Cher explained, "I also study the martial arts, energy generation exercises, and alchemical trans-mutation of energy. I can teach you."

"I've been meditating most days when the parties aren't too rough," Whiffle informed her.

"You have heard the Calling of Love and you've been awakened in previous lives, so diligent practice would bring you complete lib-eration this time around."

"Who are you?!" Whiffle asked baffled and intrigued.

"I'm someone who practiced the ancient ways of mystical union and I'm the one who must prepare you as first disciple of my daugh-ter, Electra."

Electra was grinning and making eye contact with Whiffle, who could not have looked away had she wanted to. Electra's head gave a little nod as if she'd followed the conversation and was confirming the truth of her mother's words; though it was entirely a recognition of a familiar soul and the rightness of the moment signified by the gesture.

"This can't be real," Whiffle attempted to deny her experience, being so unfamiliar and alien as it was.

"Electra and I are quite real, I can assure you," Pez/Cher replied while passing both her daughter and Whiffle energy.

"You're both totally amazing and blowing my mind."

"Let go your mind of thought construction and language and join us fully in the present," Pez/Cher suggested. "Sink your breath down to the point four-finger widths beneath your navel and remain focused in that point. Fill your lungs like filling a vase from the bottom to the top, and empty from top to bottom. Relax, and open your heart to receive our love."

Whiffle was focusing big time following the instruction to the letter and basking in the energy flowing into her from Cher. Electra still had her eyes locked in contact and seemed to be filling Whiffle with some kind of rapture or blessing. Her thoughts could make no sense of it all, and she'd stopped paying those any mind as she concentrated, stretching internally to expand and encompass these beings who seemed fonts of love and ecstasy, connecting and uniting with them in the now. This continued through the nursing and for a while after Electra had done sucking, right up until the baby's eyes shut and a thumb went into her mouth as she curled, snuggling into sleep. Pez got Electra comfortably adjusted on the couch in her pouch. Whiffle folded herself around Pez.

Whiffle couldn't get enough of Pez. She'd never encountered such a connecting, bonding, receptive and generous body before. Pez/Cher was unbelievably soft and yielding, yet at the same time, firmer and more solid than adamantine. Every cell of her skin seemed to pulse with pleasurable energy and the love was so pure and refined that it made empathogen drugs, which had always been Whiffle's favorite, seem dull and unfeeling by comparison. Whiffle had had many lovers and some of those had been female, but from her current experience it all seemed dead and mechanical. She was in a peak and it was incomparable, transcendent of previous reference, like she was being born and coming alive for the first time in Cher's arms; and Ming's arms too, who had joined them.

Whiffle climaxed before Pez exploded causing a series of events rippling outward spherically in all directions, and only the curvature of the planet surface prevented it from being global; most of the energy-burst having been spent in space. This of course sent Whiffle into a series of spine-jolting teeth-rattling orgasms that just wouldn't stop. When she finally landed back on Glitter, as it seemed to her, she found her heart open wide, her mind alertly empty, her body sunk in a new level of luxurious relaxation, and her spirit gathered as never before. Everyone in the lounge and those who had been earlier and were now miles away, had involuntary spontaneous orgasms, even those in refractory periods.

"What just happened?!" Pogo demanded.

Ahhu said to him nonchalantly, "That was just Cher having one of her orgasms."

"Well she gave me one all the way over here, and it was really good too," Pogo explained.

Trix told Pogo, "You were actually quite close to the center. Turn on the news."

Recalling her trade craft and all the spy novels and movies, Ahhu told the band members, "This is top secret, eyes-only, need-to-know and all that. You can never tell a soul. Now let me hear each of you acknowledge this."

"Who would believe it?" Frisbie asked. Then he said, "I'm not getting labeled delusional and locked up somewhere."

Pogo had the holo news on over at the bar and embarrassed commentators were struggling for words to describe what had just happened in the city. Connections had already been made with the sensationalist news of similar occurrences on Rocky, and clips of talking heads in Bulwinkle, flabbergasted over the same mysterious happenings, were used by the media giving a pause or respite to their embarrassment. It had apparently been quite wide spread and particularly strange on crowded ground transportation vehicles. It was also discovered that being asleep had not altered the effects of whatever it was. The band members, all but Whiffle, were riveted to the news with astonished expressions.

Pogo broke away from the holos looking to Cher/Pez and declared, "Your supreme unmatched piloting skills are obviously nothing compared to your sexual prowess."

"I'm sorry about that," Pez apologized. 'It's not something I have any control over. Not yet anyway. I think I need some direction from my teacher."

"Don't apologize," Pogo insisted. "And please feel free to do *that* as often as possible."

Hoola was nodding serious agreement. Hoola was not attracted to females sexually but she'd never met a sexually supernatural one before, and this was proving to be a game changer. Pogo's thoughts were consumed wondering what it would be like to be inside Cher when she did that, and this was something known only to Rubix out of all the males in the universe. Hoola found herself snuggling in on the other side of Cher/Pez, noticing paradoxes and an extraordinary aliveness to Cher's body and skin, needing to further explore these.

Ming cuddled Pez and Hoola in relaxed leisure contentedness. Gretle and Pippy were being playful, delighted in one another, with Pippy on the top. Trix was coaxing Rubix to go again. Trampol and Ahhu had gotten into the sunken hot tub and were playing with the Jacuzzi jets. Tramp said affectionately to Ahhu, "I thought you were magic and the ultimate, until she did *that*."

"I think you're gorgeous and I've never been the taller partner before," Ahhu shared.

"We're all the same height laying down," Tramp said with a hint of self-consciousness.

"You and I are pretty much the same height standing up," Ahhu pointed out.

"It is really awkward for tall people to kiss girls our height and they often look dorky doing it, so I think that's why so many of them avoid us," Trampol speculated.

"I just lock my legs around their waist and get nose to nose," Ahhu shared her strategy.

"Well you're a lot lighter than me," Trampol protested.

"I know and I just love where and how you wear it, gorgeous," Ahhu said seductively.

Hoola moved against Pez passionately kissing her when Whiffle or Ming weren't. Pez went with the flow in complete acceptance, her mass integrated tidal wave of internal energy unwittingly fueling the liaison, along with the other liaisons within the lounge. Like the musical piece Ahhu was so fond of, the force of interaction grew, mounting to a crescendo, and launching beyond to erupt into climaxing spasmatic waves washing over the city at light speed. The Cher and Lai Bulwinkle party thus bonded and united with the members of Whirling Vortexes for their whirlwind tour ahead.

When Pez replaced her diaper-sensor earbud with her diaper-sensor *and* the rest of the world earbud, Sarhi was already in her ear, telling her, "You must bring the skinny one, named Whiffle, to me at the hotel at once. She is Electra's most senior disciple."

"I know Mother Sarhi and I will bring her to you. I'm having this little problem in my sex life…"

Sarhi interrupted, "'Little' you call it? We have to talk."

"So you can help me?" Pez asked hopefully.

"Somebody better!" Sarhi told her harshly. "Come to my suite, and bring the skinny one."

Pez/Cher announced, "We have to go back to the hotel and see our teacher. I think I'm in some trouble with her. Whiffle must come too, because Sarhi said so."

"Do you think she'll have Shudiy give Whiffle a bath?" Ahhu inquired with great interest.

"Probably," Pez replied. "We have to get right back."

They had to wait while the band completed their last set for the audience. After that Pez buzzed Antic who arrived in less than a minute with three little four-seater indoor shuttles. Antic had sensed the origin of the event-waves and something familiar about the force of it, putting it all together. Discretion was always total with her, even with despicable hotel guests, and she saw clearly that Cher was anything but despicable. Pez's party and Whiffle climbed into the little hover craft. Hoola was torn and wanted to go too, but all 12 seats were filled on the 3 vehicles. Finally, just before they took off, Hoola launched herself over the side and might have actually broken one of Whiffle's narrow bones had Cher/Pez not caught Hoola coming down. Hoola got to ride in Cher's lap to the hotel. Pez thought these band members were starting to behave like band-aids.

When they stopped on their floor near Sarhi's door Pippy and Alice went to their room and Evenrude and Johnson remained in the hall with Antic, while the rest burst in on Sarhi. Sarhi zeroed in on

Whiffle and when face to face, spread her arms saying, "Welcome, child; I didn't expect you so soon."

Whiffle stepped in and they embraced. Whiffle could sense the fire raging inside Sarhi, like another Cher.

Sarhi's cover identity was as Cher's deceased mother's sister, her maternal aunt, Aunt Gimima. Shudiy was Aunt Jaydene, and Woahha was Cousin Winnie. Woahha was miffed she had not gotten to go with them tonight and Pez picked up on this resolving to include her in the future. With an arm around Whiffle protectively, Sarhi told the others, "Now get out of here and back to your own suite. This child and I have work to do."

"Will she get a bath?" Ahhu asked.

"Go!" Sarhi told her.

Pez led the way back down the hall to her suite. As her companions filed in Pez took Antic aside, looked to Evenrude with a question on her face, and Evenrude waved his sensor-bug detector in the air giving her a nod to go ahead. Pez said to Antic, "Regent Governor Crunch and some other influential people on Glitter are seeking a teacher and their motives are pure. If you had the time yourself, or know someone, they would be enormously grateful and it would serve the common good."

"The Regent Governor will have a teacher because the Avahat wills it," Antic told her. "I know who your daughter is. I hope to study at her feet when she comes of age."

"Me too," Pez/Cher agreed. Curious, she inquired, "Are there many of you on Glitter?"

"No. We are hardly more than 300. In the last two and a half years though, we have been finding more genuine candidates and our numbers are slowly on the rise. Of those of us who've embodied Crazy Wisdom there are only fifty."

"Then I consider myself most honored and fortunate to have met you, Antic," Pez told her sincerely. "It was a shock, frankly, to run across a master in a hotel hangar who happens to be a hotel welcomer-liaison."

"You can imagine *my* shock finding a ruling family member, rumored to be a blood thirsty pirate, to actually be a master and the Avahat."

"This world could do with more surprises like that," Pez said.

Antic offered, "You must learn to transfer your merit to others, kind of like how you pass internal energy, bestow the blessings of the teacher, or remove obstacles in your students to transmute them inside of you. Then you won't any longer be exploding it out of your sexual polarity, my dear; although fused with your eroticism such force of merit does produce the most pleasurable stimulations and the explosions *would* be missed."

"I'm so embarrassed!" Pez/Cher exclaimed.

"It was delightful, really; and I'm so glad you did," Antic assured her. "I just thought you might want to develop some control of those forces."

"You mean before someone gets hurt?" Pez asked concerned.

"The energy is actually healing and there is not one report of a heart giving out or single injury," Antic said kindly.

Pez got suspicious for a second, and asked, "Do you know Sarhi?"

"I've never heard the name before," She replied.

"Have you met my Aunt Gimima?" Pez asked.

"Why yes; she's a remarkable woman and clearly adept," Antic said, obviously impressed with Sarhi/Gimima.

"She's my teacher," Pez confided.

"Until you are hers," Antic said with a smile.

"Would it compromise you in any way to come in and meditate with us?"

"Not at all and I'd truly love to," Antic said with enthusiasm.

Pez led Antic into the suite and said, "Mel, let everyone know that we're going to meditate in the sitting room."

"I will, and then I'm going to sleep mode since Lucky and Pooh are both sleeping and the yacht's parked."

"Have a good sleep, Mel."

Pez led the way into the sitting room and they got pillows off the couches to sit on the floor upon. Hoola hadn't been real clear about what she was signing up for by coming along, and had been wondering what that old woman might be doing to Whiffle. She made some effort with her posture and some with her breathing, though she couldn't keep her mind in her lower abdomen, between the excitement she was having thinking of Cher nor the dread when thinking of poor Whiffle. She *was* feeling that constant flow of energy coming into her from Cher, like a garden hose with a pressure nozzle, and was aware of the serene alert quiescence permeating the room. The thoughts came with less juice behind them, almost as if they were somehow faded, and her attention gradually shifted more and more onto the quiescence and the pressure nozzle. What she was oblivious to as yet was the ocean of merit that had been bestowed upon her, raising her to the level of candidacy for the teachings. Antic was pleased to see that Cher had realized how to do it.

Pez let the session run a little longer than usual for group meditation since Hoola remained focused; just under two hours in all. The solar hour for where the hotel was located on the planet was quite late. In fact, it was the middle of the night. There were two shower heads in the master suite shower and it was big enough for a party, so all seven of them were doing something between competing for them and sharing them. Antic had retired but would remain on call if they needed her. Ahhu had already gotten her body paint off in the hot tub in the backstage lounge. The rest were scraping and scrubbing. It did not come off easy. Once Pez turned one of the shower heads to space-cold everyone fled. They toweled off under heat globes and started getting into bed. Hoola showed no sign of returning to the band's penthouse, and in fact climbed into the bed with them. Gretle was thinking to herself of Hoola, *That's how I got here.* Pez and Ming got the babies into their hover cradles. Pez went right out to sleep, and without her energy, none of the rest had it in them to do anything but sleep themselves.

CHAPTER ELEVEN

In the morning the sun was up before they were and only Pez had left the bed so she could attend Electra preemptively before she awoke. The fuss occurred in the dining room briefly having minimal impact. When she finished nursing her Pez did the soft martial arts solo form for several rounds with Electra in her front pouch against her chest; until the others awoke and emerged from the bedroom. Pez led them in energy generation exercises and gave Hoola individual instructions and hands on corrections of her posture and movements. An hour of sitting meditation completed their morning routine.

The Whirling Vortexes had another concert to play this evening in the Capitol of Glitter and they'd all be leaving for the planet Ground the following dawn. Pez had a few contacts to make this day here in the capital. Super-agent Green was handling the bulk of the contacts, but was only one person, and could not cover them all herself in the time they had. Pez's first appointment was approaching, scheduled in the hotel restaurant on the ground floor, so she jumped in the shower to wash off the dried sweat, then put on some clothing of the empire which actually covered her pelvis and torso. Only Evenrude and Johnson accompanied her. The rest of her companions were ordering room service.

Pez wanted to walk so they descended steel fire stairs with cutbacks for dozens of floors in an all-out sprint like a challenge course. Pez was stopping herself with a foot on the wall at the bottom of each flight, to push off, and was leaping over the rail and down in the middle of each stairway. Evenrude and Johnson had developed some skill with their plastic-foam bounce boot-soles, which gave them a heck of an advantage. Landing on those soles from 18 inches off the ground would put them five feet in the air. Evenrude could bounce his foot off the wall at the bottom of the stairs to fly over the next descending set in the air to the wall at the bottom of that flight without even touching the ground.

He was first to the mezzanine and out of the echo-chamber stairwell, headed down the big wide curved staircase to the lobby. Pez was just behind him and two steps ahead of Johnson when she leapt to the brass banister with great velocity and momentum, gripping it with the arches of her feet as she slid-flew down to the lobby passing Evenrude. He was no quitter and leapt the rail into a twenty-foot free fall, touching down on the lobby floor first a second before Pez. Only he didn't stay in the lobby, launching straight up like a rocket. The lobby was an atrium with glass elevators on two walls from which one could see down even from the top floors. The acre wide glass skylight over the atrium-lobby was some 800 feet high, and Evenrude only went up about 80; but still, that was a lot and Pez was worried. *What if coming down from 80 feet put him up 250 feet?*

In a complete blur she tossed Electra to Johnson, grabbed a big couch seat cushion and flung it across the floor sliding towards where Evenrude was heading down, and followed it at a sprint still a blur. The couch seat was yet on the move when Evenrude's feet began sinking into it. He had his knees and hip joints bent to receive the impact. The seat cushion was just attaining maximum compression, the boot sole materials beginning to find solid mass for launch, and Evenrude's knees on the verge of collapse when Pez crashed into his side with such speed that her inferior weight was sufficient to take them both through the air horizontal to the floor, and they each went head first into the hotel lobby fountain.

As they untangled from each other in two feet of water with the statue in the center squirting a stream of water from its penis onto Pez, Evenrude told her remorsefully, "I'm sorry. I'm not used to these boot soles yet and I got a little carried away."

"You seemed to do pretty exceptionally in the stair well," Pez pointed out. "I think I'll take the elevator up to change or I'll be late. That was fun."

Everyone in the hotel lobby was staring at them like they were the entertainment. No hotel staff person was about to say anything to Cher Bulwinkle or her gigantic body guards. Before Pez even stepped out of the fountain and was still in the stream from the statue, Antic arrived in a little hover car and said, "Hop in, I'll take you to your suite to change."

Pez and Evenrude jumped in after Johnson handed Pez Electra. He would wait for them in the lobby. Antic told Cher, "This is more like the behavior I expected from the pirate heiress."

"Did the front desk call you?" Pez asked.

"Yes, in quite a panic," she replied with a grin.

"So it's up to you to subdue crazy rowdy ruling family members?"

"Pretty much," Antic admitted.

"How do you do it?" Pez wanted to know.

"I learn all about them and offer a better distraction and entertainment than the injury they're in the midst of."

"Are you ever in danger?"

"I'm always congenial, seeming to be on their side, and helpful, so I don't attract their cruelty or sadism. They don't tend to even see me as a person at all, just a job function serving them. I do it attentively, competently and efficiently, and I'm usually prepared by anticipating their needs."

The hover craft was shooting up faster than elevators within its hover craft shaft, and Antic had them to the door of Pez's suite in a jiffy. Evenrude's room was next door. They both changed quickly, putting on the first suitable thing, and needed no time for fashion planning. Pez just wanted her crotch and breasts covered which didn't seem unreasonable to her, though less than half the clothes here did, and barely a third of her own outfits.

Antic got them back to the lobby and right to the dining room entrance of the hotel restaurant. They thanked her and got out. Evenrude was now dressed in solid primary green with no blue or red trim, pushing the limits of gangster fashion here on Glitter. He faded into the background with Johnson as Pez entered the restaurant walking up to the receptionist. Men the size of Evenrude and Johnson dressed in primary colors could not actually fade into the background, though they appeared nonchalant and kept an eye on Pez from a distance.

She was meeting the biggest agent on the planet famous for all the talent he'd discovered and quite well off, but not seriously rich, and certainly not in the same league with even the lesser ruling families. His name was Rye, Hammon Rye. Pez was led by the receptionist to his table and she said, "Hi, my name is Cher."

"I'm honored to meet you Cher. Please call me Hammon. I was informed that you are taking the lead in organizing and focusing the massive resistance throughout the empire to its control, usurpation of all the resources, executions and disappearances without any resort, and murderous imperial expansion requiring every planet to maintain a permanent wartime economy."

"I am establishing a subversive underground coms network throughout the empire as the first step towards coordinated simultaneous actins on every planet. By the time we're ready we will also have a significant fleet of combat ships from allies in three galaxies far from this empire. They want only peace and security and will take nothing from a single planet of what is now the Royal Monarch Empire; though it won't be called that for much longer."

"How do you envision the future of the over 5,700 planets now ruled by the emperor?" Hammon wanted to know.

"The sovereignty of each and every planet must be respected and no planet shall ever rule over another one. Alliances between them are encouraged but government must remain local. Science is the only accurate and just method of distribution, and all 100,000 ruling family fortunes must be redistributed, including my own, though after paying back loans to planets which have contributed to our cause."

"Wow," Hammon exclaimed. "You're going all the way."

"I play a role prepared for me and did not instigate this myself. I'm simply doing my part. The efforts toward this started long before I was born."

"Your vision is admirable if also idealistic and utopian," Hammon stated. "I would love to see it come about but I've lost faith in our race having witnesed so much self-aggrandizement, greed, and power ambitions enacted and displayed by such abuses and exploitation of the mass planetary populations."

"The empire was unable stamp out and eradicate your mystical traditions here on Glitter and I suspect that is the case with all the other worlds conquered by Monarch. You still have teachers. Getting out of war economies and the yoke of oppression exploiting everyone is the most I can help you accomplish. I think the principle of keeping decisions as local as possible, involving mainly the people most effected, is a good one. The intergalactic treaty of no planet ruling over another planet is also sound and will eventually be enforced by planets of four different galaxies."

"But actually overcoming the ego will be left up to each planet individually." Hammon said heavily.

"My daughter incarnates every 2500 years to pass new teachings to our race and brings hope to all of us."

Electra was fast asleep in her pouch and tooted a little fart as both Cher's and Hammon's gazes focused on her. Her thumb was in her mouth. Pez/Cher was concerned that this scene might somehow lack the hope she meant to inspire. She told him, "Now that our civilizations are connecting in efforts towards your liberation my daughter's teachings will spread to all of them."

"You make it sound like you are not of the worlds of the empire," Hammon said confused.

"The identity of Cher Bulwinkle was a fiction prepared to fit me. I'm from the Hub Galaxy, a warrior-monk from the planet Om, and the instrument of a spiritual congress instigated by a very highly advanced race. They began planting the seeds for this revolution thousands of years ago and are now about 34 years into a 100-year meditation focused on bringing their work to fruition. My life is just a tool, but a finely honed one equal to the task."

"So this evolved race aligns you with the orientation of the Cosmic Intellegence's Justice, Harmony and Equilibrium and you are the catalyst of liberation."

"Exactly," Cher agreed. "Each of those multi-trillion dag mountains of capital are entropic since that energy does not circulate through the general population. The oppressive structure of the empire suppresses creativity, imagination, innovation, integral moral evolution, trust, love and freedom. Breaking all that down will free both physical and psychic energy on a scale unknown to any of our civilizations."

"It sure would," he agreed. "I'm mighty grateful to you and I will do my part. I'm in touch with a great number of people high in the holo-movie industry who would help if they thought they stood a chance."

"Give me about a year to establish our coms network, then we'll start planning dozens of actions on each of the over 5,700 planets to begin at once and have a combat space force of our own."

"We need to hug in order to make the transmission of the one-time codes," Hammon informed her.

"They both stood and embraced. Pez whispered "Top royal sail" into his ear, then they said their goodbyes and Hammon Rye departed the restaurant. Pez sat and examined the menu famished. She waved her two Space Marines over to the table and offered them breakfast, which would be their second one, and they eagerly agreed.

Evenrude told Pez, "I've been studying the planet Ground. It has tight military and police control over the masses and most everyone lives in abject poverty. There are seven ruling families there and two of them are among the cruelest in the empire. At least the heads of those two families are bonifide psychopaths without conscience at all. It's a dangerous place."

"I'm a dangerous person with the two most dangerous bodyguards in the empire," Pez said confidently. "None of those families on Ground are as wealthy as the Bulwinkles, and in this empire you just don't mess with a pirate who has more money than you do."

"I see your point," he admitted. He continued informing her, "There are only two social classes on Ground, the rich and the poor. Forty thousand families make up the rich and the population of the planet is 6.7 billion. Their military has 50 million personnel and their police forces total over 200 million. Police personnel and government employees live in the upper strata of the poverty spectrum; but not the military. In the military you can just be shot, so little compensation is offered."

"We have more to learn about their coms network and we have to learn how to remove those explosive chips out of ships' officers. Their big war ships are the base of their power."

After finishing two breakfast entrees Pez went back up to the suite with her bodyguard friends and employed the elevator for this. Hoola rose from Gretle's lap and ran over to grab Cher/Pez in a full embrace the moment she entered the room. Electra was getting crushed so Pez extracted herself to get her daughter into her hover-cradle, then Hoola grabbed hold of her again. Passing her internal energy Pez accepted Hoola's comprehensive greeting. She meant to wake the girl up the first few spare hours they could find, though those didn't really exist today. Hoola was now ripe for it, with an attraction to, and spiritual orientation towards ascent. Pez had never held a super-star and super-model before in her life and was a little intimidated, unable to believe that someone of such beauty could possibly be attracted to her. Hoola was confusing her experience of all the love circulating between Cher and her companions, tremendously amplified by Cher, with being *in* love, and was falling head over heels for her. In a sense of desperate need Hoola begged of Pez, "Please don't send me away. I cannot be parted from you."

"You are on a spiritual journey beautiful sweetheart, on the cusp of awakening. You are one of us, accepted and loved, and no one is going to send you away."

"I had no idea there could be people like you and your family and friends in the universe, and encountering you has changed me completely."

"Your thoughts have lost their hold on you and you see that they cannot make sense of your experience; but only obscure it and take you out of it. Identity shifts from mind-structure to void."

"There's more change coming?" Hoola asked in awe. "I won't even know myself."

"Exactly," Cher affirmed. "No self to be found. Liberation from the projection of self upon our acts frees our attention and energy to go with the natural flow of the universe effortlessly, with instinctive immediacy, transcending the quatreilemma of ignorance, desire, action, karmic consequence; or action, reaction, the link between them, and the result. Ignorance and desire are overcome when the link between them as action and reaction, is attention, and not the action of ignorance-desire-action. The action springing from ignorance and desire makes us blind to this third force of the quatre-lemma. In mysticism it is called 'third force blind' or being 'asleep'. You shall see."

"You filled me with infinite goodness during the meditation, and I feel so pure and wholesome," Hoola shared.

"I learned how to transfer merit with you in the meditation, and now the teachings will really speak to you so much more clearly than words."

"You say just the right things to help me realize."

"You are in a state of mind to hear," Cher replied.

Whiffle was let in by Mel, who'd taken over the computerized functions of the hotel's Empress Suite. Wiffle entered the sitting room where the others were sprawled, looking unusually bright and alert. Pez noticed a crisp clarity to the girl's aura and knew that, among other things, Shudiy had given her one of those baths. Ahhu suspected and was fairly certain when she asked Whiffle, "What did you think of the bath?"

"I thought I might be bleeding when she scraped that sea creature sponge over my skin," Whiffle recalled honestly, "but it was the douche which was most alarming; and the measuring."

"How deep is your uterus gate?" Ahhu wanted to know.

Whiffle replied, "Seven and a quarter inches, and apparently I've been letting longer ones penetrate my uterus which is not good for me, even though it feels great for the guys."

"I'm six and three-quarters inches," Ahhu shared, "and I was doing that too until Shudiy, I mean Aunt Jaydene, gave me a bath."

"I felt pretty worked over while it was going on but could find no blood or scrapes on my skin, and it actually felt tingly when she was finished with me," Whiffle recounted. "I don't ever recall feeling so calm and relaxed."

"The salts she puts in the bath balance the acid-based equilibrium of the blood," Pez explained, "and between the pure Castile peppermint soap and the grating sea creature, the skin is truly enlivened. The vibrations of her chanting are detoxifying and purifying. I get them all the time. I insist on toweling myself off," she said, making it sound really defiant.

Hoola was still molding herself to Cher's side joined at the hip. She asked Whiffle, concerned, "Did that old woman have sex with you?"

"No," Whiffle answered surprised by the question. "She meditated with me, enacted a ritualized initiation, meditated with me some more, then did a ceremony employing eye contact with me, called Making the Equal."

"I'm so relieved," Hoola told her. "I imagined they might gang rape you or something."

"Sex must really be on your mind, Hoola," Whiffle pointed out.

Hoola went internal for a moment then offered what she'd seen, "I think my own horror at being so sexually drawn to and aroused by another female was all projected onto you and those old women, along with my aversion to having sex with the aged."

"Your ego cannot handle the transitoriness of itself nor of your extraordinary physical beauty, denying aging and death in its attempt to crystalize the present, which is not the same as letting go of ego to live in the present," Pez offered.

"Neither grasping nor aversion," Ming quoted."

"I'm seeing it," Superstar Hoola said, really making an effort at being attentive.

CHAPTER TWELVE

Pez had two more appointments in the afternoon with contacts who knew they'd be meeting with Cher Bulwinkle, the woman swiftly becoming the symbol of the impulse to liberate. Many suspected Cher wanted really to take over the empire for herself, though all knew that the resulting power vacuum and chaos would provide great opportunity for worlds to become independent and were willing to chance it. No one would support a Bulwinkle dynasty instead of the one they had under Imperial Emperor Sponge the Magnificent, as anyone who wanted to keep their head had to call him. Everyone would help Cher right up to the point of bringing down the empire and no further. Not an inch.

That evening she went with many of her companions, including Woahha this time, to the concert hall where the band was playing, and had two contacts to make there. These two contacts had no idea from whom they would receive their code-book transmissions and Pez was to connect with them on the dance floor. Antic brought them to the backstage hovercraft platform bay, and followed Pez's party into the public section of the hall to the dance floor. Ahhu went to the bar for a beverage so she could take the edge off of her inhibitions and Rubix went with her for the same purpose.

Pez and Ming were dressed fashionably with breasts and crotches exposed—even highlighted—by their unusual dresses. They started dancing together and space around them opened as other dancers fled the feet six-feet in the air, and the triple spins and backflips, getting out of those dancers' way. Gretle danced with Antic and Trix. Evenrude and Johnson were never far off, always watching and didn't dance at all. Pez spotted one of the contacts she was to make and spun off from Ming between two guys dancing with each other, slipping sideways through a closing space just before they bumped pelvises.

Pez's contact was a 40-year-old female with silver metallic hair, hard to miss, and was average height and weight for yellow sun women. Her dress looked more like straps and harnesses never having the slightest intention of covering exposed skin. The woman's dance partner was male, built like a hover board surfer but pasty white, naked, and obviously a slave. The affection between them seemed genuine to Pez. While the couple danced with hardly an inch between them, Pez circled like a predatory bird. She was waiting for him to twirl the woman again and sensed it coming before it happened, moving in. The woman spun holding her partners hand above her head and was turning fast. A little more than half way round Pez caught her chest to chest for just a moment, before releasing her to spin off in another direction. She'd said her code word in her ear and the woman's eyes had gone wide in acknowledgement. There; it was done. She had one more to find.

Whiffle was jamming on her saxophone like never before, performing in a state of contemplation and just letting herself go. Hoola's performance had jumped level too with her soul brimming and overflowing with merit, and between the two of them, the whole band was having magic moments of supreme coordination and synchronicity, adding stylized riffs, and additional accenting notes to their composition while boring under the skin to move their audience. The floor was packed with dancers unable to resist and fans were dancing in their seats and on them. It was the bands best performance yet and the crowd was just loving it. The energy was wild and intense.

Pez found her way back to Ming, who'd somehow attracted twin males perhaps just out of their teens. They had matching outfits and could not be told one from the other. They had collars clear to their chins; arms, torsos, legs and bottoms covered completely, prudishly even, but their little suits were entirely crotch-less and each was sporting an erection, likely chemical in origin. Many males on Glitter took drugs so they could show off their stiff rods all day long like part of the costume. Pez didn't like getting bumped by them.

Most were easy to avoid being only 6-8 inches long here, but occasionally there would be one protruding much further out and those were the ones she'd have to look out for. They did tend to flop all over the place when their bearers danced about. One of the twins was dancing awful close to Ming and she was wearing his on her abdomen.

Both boys were Pez's height, five foot nine inches, though she had about ten pounds on them. Their upper arms were nearly as narrow as their wrists. Dancing with one of these twins moved Whiffle closer the normative distribution in Pez's mind. They made Rubix look almost muscular. Ahhu danced over with a drink in one hand, her third, and joined them. She liked scrawny guys and was always drawn to twins. Ahhu asked one of the twins dancing with Pez and her, pointing at his bouncing phallus, "How long is it?", hoping it was six and three-quarter inches or shorter. To her experienced eye it looked close.

He said with a sense of being put on the spot, "About seven inches."

Ahhu pressed, "I hope you were rounding up because seven inches is a quarter inch too long, and I'd not be allowed to let you in."

Feeling like he'd just won the lottery he told her enthusiastically, "I was rounding up by a quarter inch!"

"We're a perfect fit!" Ahhu said delighted. "Come on, let's get a stall in the lady's room."

Ahhu led Pez's dance partner away by the hand; mostly by the hand. Ming was wearing the kind of expression one's face might break out into when the host's dog humps their leg. Pez decided to cut in and swung a hip knocking the boy out from in front of Ming, to step in facing her, and Ming looked relieved. They danced arm in arm leaving no space for anyone to get between them, yet Gretle stooped into squatting single whip, a soft martial arts posture Pez had taught her, and came squeezing up between them. Pez couldn't help thinking, *such a remarkable graduate student.*

All three of them danced together as the band raged on getting everyone in the hall riled up to bursting. Pez spotted her final contact on Glitter dancing with a large woman who could really move. He was much bigger still at least width-wise, and was totally shaking it. Pez would have to come in at a leaning angle to touch chests over his protruding belly. She moved Electra's pouch to the side, then she saw her move and positioned herself close awaiting the timing. They were really rocking to the freewheeling sounds the band produced and left little opening for Pez. At last the women spun on her heal and on her way around skinny Pez slipped through sideways mashing chests with the woman's partner and brushing against the woman. Pez was out and gone by the time the woman came back around facing her partner. Transmission complete. She'd said his code word in his ear, "Keel", when she'd mashed chests with him, and he had declared, "Got it," just as she was moving away.

Ahhu was back with her twin on the dance floor and Gretle joined them with the other twin in tow. Pez grabbed Ming's hand and pulled her off the dance floor towards the stage. They pushed their way into the densely packed crowd in front of the raised stage and Pez leapt, shooting straight over the heads of those in front of her, travelling about nine feet to land on the stage hitting it dancing. Six security guards rushed her even though Pogo was shaking his head "no" and shouting, "Leave her alone." Pez turned off yielding and the first guard to reach her kept going to fly right off the stage at the crowd, which parted dense as it was so that he landed directly on the hard floor impossibly missing all of them.

Pez made a squat-slide, and two security personnel collided head first with both of them going down hard. One grabbed her wrist, trying to wrench her arm locking it up, but she relaxed it so extremely that there didn't seem to be a bone in it, and then with lightning speed, it wrenched his arm flipping him into another oncoming guard and dropping both. The last guard grabbed her from behind and Pez's leg flew up out in front of her over her head to strike the top of his head, knocking him out. Pez shifted all her attention into matching the rhythm in her dance moves, which were frequently aerial, careful of the five bodies on the stage and of Electra strapped into her pouch. Ming climbed up and spun, her foot knocking a guy back into the crowd who'd been trying to climb up too, in a sweep kick to the side of the jaw. No one else made it onto the stage.

When the song the band had been doing concluded, Hoola told the fans, "These are our dear friends, Cher and Lai Bulwinkle. I'm sure you all saw Cher's landing here on Glitter when she arrived. Let's hear it for the Bulwinkle sisters!"

The hoots, hollers and applause were deafening and woke both Electra and Gumby who could not compete with this volume. Neither woman had any clothing to get out of the way for their baby to get a good grip on her breast. The crowd seemed to like watching the mothers nurse on stage and shouted encouragements. Whiffle came over and kissed Electra's forehead. Frisbie pounded out a beat on the drums and the band members launched into another song, slow and sentimental; something the nursing mothers could move to easily.

The media got some incredible holos of Pez flipping in the air over the stage and of both mothers nursing their babies. All of these went planet-wide and were franchised out to other entertainment news outlets reaching planets in three galaxies. Pez's landing at the hotel hanger was shown again with the concert holos and her celebrity was viral.

Pez and Ming danced on the stage until the whirling Vortexes' concert came to an end, including the two encore songs they came back out to play. Ahhu had been left hanging when her twin was spent. Woahha had three males following her about like puppies when she found Pez and Ming, and had to sternly dismiss them. With great reluctance they finally detached from her. Rubix and Gretle were arm in arm when they found Pez and the rest of their party.

Antic led the way backstage to the shuttle platform and drove them all back to their suite. Pez thanked her profusely and got her contact codes so they could keep in touch. It was quite late and they were leaving Glitter for Ground at dawn, so they all went right to sleep. Hoola and Whiffle were in the bed too, and big as an emperor bed is, with eight people within, it was a bit of a tight fit.

At dawn *Aphrodite, Sidekick* and Ahhu's drone fighter-bomber launched from the hotel hanger with Hoola and Whiffle aboard. The Whirling Vortexes yacht, called *Spaceship*, was a little delayed and would meet them at the hotel on Ground due a supermodel band aid breaking a finger nail. She was fine, the prognosis good, and a prosthesis finger nail was being procured. Pez went maximum acceleration from the hanger to jump speed and Glitter Space Control frantically cleared a path in front of her by moving everyone out of the way. Lucky was a little sulky. Pooh and Hoola had instant chemistry. Electra let Whiffle hold and snuggle her in a seat in the main compartment, being already so familiar to her. Whiffle felt fulfilled in doing it. Gumby stared out at the windshield from Ming's front pouch in total wonderment.

The quantum jump was a nonevent outside time and they all speculated as to when the experience of total shock over ceasing to exist had come from, since it had clearly not been delivered by duration. Pez braked by reversing her main drive only, reluctant to give up her velocity. She hailed the Ground Space Control while still in the jump zone and requested, "This *Aphrodite*. We just jumped into the system. Do you think you could clear a path for me down to the Royal Ground Hotel hanger?"

These guys already knew from Glitter Space Control that pirate heiress Cher Bulwinkle piloted her own yacht and the director himself had the coms telling her, "Welcome to Ground, Cher Bulwinkle. We are freeing a lane-in now, if you would just bear to your right and down at 22 degrees by 14 degrees on your spherical. You're cleared right to the hanger. Be advised, your clearance will be less than a meter at stern and bow through the bay doors. We hope you enjoy your stay and are honored you would visit our planet!"

"Thank you, you just made my day!" Cher said gratefully, throwing the main drive back into forward propulsion at maximum acceleration.

The trip planet-side was exciting to say the least. There were a few screams from those foolish enough to watch their holos during one of Pez's landings but no one wet themselves. Pez got the nose up before it crashed into Ground's ground, as impossible as it had seemed while she was doing it, at the expense of just some thruster fuel cells and a couple of boosters, and with the help of the vortex-redirect-generation turbine. The hydraulic legs hit with just enough impact to give that familiar metal on metal clink before rising back up. All kinds of high speed, high definition space-time imagining lenses, panels and crystals had been mounted, aimed and calibrated in anticipation of her landing. They captured it from dozens of angels in such clarity that every aspect of it could be measured to the thousandth of an inch and thousandth of a second. The resulting analysis was chilling, proving the ship's tolerances were not up to the flying it had done, and that even a quantum computer could not have handled the micro-timing required for such a landing with any kind of safety margin. No matter how you sliced it Cher Bulwinkle's landing on Ground defied the science of material tolerances and far surpassed both human and computer abilities. That landing, now one of the best captured landings of all time, was simply not within the realm of possibility.

The imperial space fleet high command found this landing threatening and the Emperor didn't like it. He considered imposing the 'special tax' on Rocky, which amounted to stealing everything of any value out of every household on the planet. He visited the special tax on planets which displeased him and it was not an uncommon occurrence within the empire at all. He also felt hesitation not wanting to make an enemy of such a wealthy family with a pilot who could fly like that. Most everything he ever did he did impulsively in anger. This time he let the urge pass. It really could have gone either way.

The Royal Ground Hotel greeter-liaison was not a master and she was not awakened. Her aura was chaotic murky pink and red for the most part, as far as Pez could see, and the young woman seemed to shy away from abuse at Pez's slightest gesture clearly expecting to be mistreated harshly. She was petite and looked to be in her early twenties. Like all hotel greeter-liaisons she was attractive, and like drug-representatives for the big pharmacy corporations, probably recruited from a college kneeball cheerleader squad. Pez spread her arms and said, "Come here sweetheart," gently and affectionately.

The liaison, whose name was Hanah, stepped in fearful and anxious to rigidly hug Cher Bulwinkle, already certain this was the first act in a play featuring herself as a sex slave. She heard sweetly in her ear while frozen in an 'embrace', "I will not be mean to you, harm you or use you sexually. I promise. Nor will anyone in my party. We don't bite so you can relax and start breathing again."

Hanah realized she was in fact holding her breath and let it out to take a deep one. Only then did she become aware of the calming energy flowing into her from Cher's light touch. She was calming and just starting to relax a little when she recognized superstar super-model Hoola in Cher's party. Cher, still embracing her and shooting that warm calming energy into her, said in her ear, "Remember to breathe, Hanah."

Out of her mouth once she had the wind in her lungs to say it came, "That's Hoola of the Whirling Vortexes!"

Hanah's knees had gone weak but Cher had her and kept her aloft, telling her, "Give Hoola your pocket device and she'll sign her autograph, and give you an exclusive selfie holo of herself."

The knees collapsed completely for just a moment and holding her up became a 'total-lift', briefly, until Hanah came back to herself and found her legs. That soothing voice again from Cher into her ear, "We're only people like you and we're friendly, sweetheart. Take another deep breath."

She did, more aware of that energy flowing into her than ever. It seemed surrealistic, and possibly was just a dream. She certainly hoped they were not hallucinations which would mean she had finally cracked under the pressures of her job. She managed to extract her device and the diva took it from her, signing the surface with a platinum stylus before holding it up pointed at her face smiling, to capture a still selfie holo on it. Hoola handed it back to Hanah and kissed the girl closed lipped on the mouth. Hanah's knees gave out completely again. Naked Ahhu stepped in to support Hanah under one arm hoping to cop-a-feel. Cher still had her too and told Ahhu, "Fish out a thousand dag bill to tip Hanah, sweetheart, would you?"

Hanah's legs were beginning to work again as Ahhu placed the bill in her hand. There was a wobble in them when she noticed the denomination on the money she'd been given. Pez told her, "That's for being brave enough to greet us, Hanah; now buck-up and get us to our suite."

Ahhu helped Hanah over to the vehicle attendant seat and assisted her up into it, getting a hand firmly on Hanah's butt. Hanah was a runner and she climbed at the Rocknasium almost every day, keeping her body taut and hard, and Ahhu truly appreciated the girl's efforts. They all piled in, and Pippy and Alice had to sit on laps. Naked Pippy sat on naked Ahhu's lap and naked Alice sat on Rubix's making him a little nervous. Hanah threw their big hover craft into gear and off they went. She was a little spaced out having just received an autograph, exclusive selfie, and kiss on the mouth from superstar Hoola, a thousand dags from the notorious deadly pirate, Cher, and a magic hand on her butt from the one Cher called Ahhu but the hotel data identified as Bianca. She would have run over an old woman in a hover chair if Cousin Winnie, seated next to her, had not grabbed the stick and made a correction faster than Hanah knew what was happening. She felt Cousin Winnie's hand on her thigh though, almost at her hip joint, and it was so freakishly alive that it felt sort of like a vibrator.

As she let them all out at their suite Hanah was starting to feel disappointed that they hadn't had sex with her. She was so pumped up from all the energy put in her by Cher and by Cousin Winnie that she didn't think she would be able to sleep for a week at least. Lai Bulwinkle gave Hanah the party's basic itinerary. Hanah had to wait in the hall for the one named Shadey whom she'd be taking to the hover craft rental. This one was actually Super-Agent Green. The family would be attending a party at the Whiplash mansion. The Whiplash's were known to be the wealthiest family on Ground. Pez had Hanah's code and she would be ready if they called her. Hanah still couldn't believe she had a thousand dag bill in her pocket. Her savings account had only the obligatory hundred dags in it to keep it open and her debit account was too low to draw from. Her only pair of shoes had the sole flapping under the toes of one even though she glued it every night. Her brightest clothes had all faded to pastels. If any had been natural fiber they would be thread bare by now.

Pez and her companions had had to skip their morning routine to leave at dawn from Glitter so they did it now, in the Grand Vizier Suite. It was the penthouse. Mel had switched Pez into the premier accommodations at each hotel on the tour, giving the band the next best available at each stop. At first Mel had been a little anxious about making such a bold move, though now that Hoola and Whiffle were also staying with Pez, Mel felt completely justified. Pogo didn't complain; and neither did Stilts, the band's manager.

The time of day in Defibmo, the capital of Ground, was eleven minutes after one in the afternoon when the gong struck concluding their meditation session and signalling the end of their morning-routine. Hoola had learned more energy generation exercises and the first few moves and postures of a martial arts form. Whiffle was learning these as well. Pez gave them hands on corrections and Ahhu was pretty sure that Hoola kept sticking her butt out on purpose so that Pez would have to tuck it back under for her. They hit the big stone sunken tub for a bath since Pez had driven them all to sweat during the exercise portion of the routine. The tub was practically a swimming pool.

Pez had Electra in the tub holding her mindfully afloat and Electra was loving it. Pez had removed her diaper and the warm water made Electra tinkle. Floating on her back supported by her mother's hands, the tinkle shot in a little arching stream right into Pez's face, then onto her chest as the pressure ran out. Pez wasn't offended as she had been with President Dodge, but she wondered what it was about her that attracted getting pissed on because she really didn't like it. Whiffle took over supporting Electra so Cher/Pez could dunk her head and soap and shampoo.

After the bath Pez was famished so they all went together down to the restaurant, escorted by their two very dangerous looking body guards. Pez didn't want Evenrude and Johnson slinking around and peering through potted fern plants in their primary colors so she insisted that they sit at the table. Mel showed up surprising them in her female android body looking just like a Bulwinkle sister; only there wasn't a third Bulwinkle sister and Mel had no cover identity. She had no systems for food intake and would not be eating with them, though she had a drainable synthetic bladder and could drink liquids at the table with them.

Pez asked concerned, "What are you doing Mel? Who are we supposed to claim you to be?"

"I've got it covered," Mel informed her quite business like. "I'm an Adherence Examiner on a special mission, and it is entered into the Monarch central computer and known throughout the network.

"What's your mission, Mel," Pez asked.

"Top Secret," Mel insisted, "known only to Fleet Admiral Snarlbit and no one else; verbal orders only and the Admiral died fourteen minutes ago at the Imperial Naval hospital in the capital on Monarch. The real Adherence Examiner was snatched by Ahumdulilah intelligence operatives yesterday."

"Not a bad cover," Evenrude complimented Mel appreciating her ingenuity.

Mel informed them urgently, "The Snydely family is on their way to Ground and will be attending the Whiplash party this evening. They're the forty-seventh wealthiest family in the empire and number one for cruelty."

"I have contacts to make at the party Mel, so I have to go," Pez let her know.

Mel suggested, "Have Super-Agent Green attend the party."

"She's booked and on a really tight schedule. There's no way she can get to the party and complete the contacts I've already given her."

"Well don't bring any slaves to the party or anyone not related to you as family, for they wouldn't be safe. Rudfuss Snydely is notorious for raping, beating and killing slaves other ruling families have grown attached to. He is far wealthier than the Bulwinkles but would likely think twice about picking a fight with a pirate family, especially one with such a formidable pilot."

Pippy spoke up telling them, "Major Nicon expects Alice and me to be there because slaves talk to each other and that inteligence cannot be accessed any other way. We are agents, understand the risks, and volunteered for this. We have to go to the party."

Mel warned, "That despicable man has never attended a party at which he didn't at least brutally rape a slave, if not kill one."

"He'll have many to choose from and we will just have to risk it," Pippy stood firm.

"I'd go with you to protect you but I can't get through the security scan they will set up at the entrance," Mel told them.

"You can monitor their coms and keep an eye on their security control room for us, Mel," Pez suggested.

"Of course I will," Mel agreed.

Evenrude mentioned, "Body guards wait in the servant lounge during parties like this, but if you need us, they won't have anything to keep Johnson and me out, and Mel can direct us right to you. We'll be armed, armored and shielded, and just break new openings in their walls to get to you if we have to."

They all smiled having that image in mind of the two giant Space Marines crashing right through walls. Mel informed them, "I'm performing micro-analysis of all the Whiplash mansion security systems now, from the *Aphrodite*, and should have it all transparently mapped out in just a minute."

Gretle complained, "My cover as 'Muffet', friend of the Bulwinkle family, is vulnerable not being family. But I'm still going."

Pez said aloud as she decided, "The four old aunts will stay at the hotel. Cousin Winnie will come and so will my spouse, Kat, who is Trix. Lai and her husband Rubix, as 'Hark', our adopted sister Bianca/Ahhu, and our friend, Muffet/Gretle, will all come too. Evenrude and Johnson will be in the servant lounge and Mel will cover electronic oversight. Pippy and Alice will be brought along and will buzz me if they run into any trouble. I'll challenge Rudfuss to a duel if he messes with anyone from our party, including one of my slaves whom I'm so attached to."

"It's a little gray and unclear in their laws if a challenge to a duel can be made over a slave;" Mel informed her.

"Good!" Pez declared. "Then I'll set the precedent!"

CHAPTER THIRTEEN

In the late afternoon the band members left to set up for their evening concert. The seats were all sold out. Holoclips from their last concert on Glitter showing the peak of synchronicity they'd found that night were on every channel on Ground. The concert tonight would be transmitted planet-wide. The band had just released one of their new singles and it was being purchased and downloaded at a rate of millions per minute from three galaxies setting a new record in the music industry. Hoola's face was on hundreds of giant holo-sign-boards mounted on buildings in every city on Ground since she'd been contracted as the model for the Hug-me's crotch-less panties advertisements, coveted by all super-models.

Pez and her eight companions dressed for the big Whiplash party. It was apparently the event of the year for the ruling families and their minions on Ground. Pez had Electra in a back pouch now which had a little seatbelt and shoulder harness made of double thickness of the very best textile armor. It had sewn into the bottom a micro-shield generator Pez could trigger with her platinum-diamond tiara's skullcap functions. Pez had her hair up in all of its glorious orange set with jade hair-pin darts. What there was of her dress was all skin-tight with no place to hide a blaster. Not even a tiny needle gun. She wore adjustable heels integrated with her tiara so she could turn her shoes into flats in a fraction of a heartbeat in order to run if she needed speed.

Rubix wore a bright pink suit with green trim and a dark green bow tie with a red ruby in the center. The suit jacket had shiny wide lapels and long tails. Evenrude and Johnson wore primary green and blue with red trim and Evenrude had even compromised his stance to buy a yellow hat which was supposed to make him even more frightening. Pez thought it looked cute.

Pippy and Alice went completely naked, while Ahhu/Bianca wore a beautiful matching purse and shoes set with jewelry of obscenely large diamonds. When they were all dressed, or simply ready to go as in the cases of Pippy and Alice, Pez called Hanah, who was at their door with a shuttle in under a minute. Cousin Winnie climbed into the seat next to her and placed a palm on Hanah's thigh at her hip joint. Cher handed Hanah another thousand dag bill. Bianca sat behind Hanah and massaged her shoulders while the rest climbed in. That Cousin Winnie-hand was shooting energy like a vibrator and Hanah couldn't help rocking her pelvis in the seat just a little bit.

Hanah drove through and out of the hotel and had to ascend six lanes up to find one moving at a descent clip getting out of the capital of Defibmo. The Whiplash mansion was just outside the city on a high hill overlooking it from across the river. Security at the gate was quite heavy and vehicles were getting through only one at a time. They patiently waited their turn idling in a line of hover craft. When they reached the checkpoint Hanah handled everything, but all within the vehicle were scanned from their seats. It took only a moment and Hanah brought them up to the mansion portico and main entrance to let her passengers out. She would remain in the hover craft at the party to be available should any of the Bulwinkle party want to go elsewhere. Evenrude and Johnson checked their coms link with Pez then headed around to the side entrance to wait in the servant lounge. Pez and her companions entered the mansion. Pez was arm in arm with her cover-spouse Kat, played by Trix. Hark and Lai went in holding hands. Gretle as Muffet and Ahhu as Bianca went in together with Pippy and Alice right behind them. Winnie had given Hanah a long kiss while the others climbed out and so was trailing behind them.

The foyer was quite grand. They were directed by servants down a wide corridor into the enormous domed ballroom with an orchestra playing and side tables overflowing with rare food delicacies.

Pez had an appetite and led Trix to the side tables for some chow. Ming and Rubix went onto the dance floor to try out their ballroom dancing. Winnie had already picked up a young man by the time she came into the ballroom and she danced with him. Pippy and Alice were commiserating with the other slaves. Ahhu and Gretle were flirting with a pair of teen debutantes and were obviously making some headway. The Bulwinkle party mingled and Pez used her facial recognition program to seek her contacts. Only one of them knew he would be meeting with Cher and the rest were blind pass offs with a whispered password. She spotted one and got to work while still chewing and with her mouth full.

After making some blind contacts and receiving some recognition from them that the code word was received, Pez identified the man she would need to have a conversation with. He was dancing with the Whiplash hostess at the moment so Pez circled, keeping an eye on him. She stood alone at a side table for a moment and asked Mel, "Do they have listening devices planted in the ballroom?"

"You bet!" Mel informed her. "Hundreds of them. They can filter out the orchestra and hear every word."

"To how many decibels?"

"They are ultra-sensitive, but I can loop some earlier feed from the party through them or just shut them down to buy you a minute or two for a clandestine conversation, my love."

"Try looping the past through as current. I'm going to make contact with him as soon as that Whiplash lady is done dancing with him."

"Alright," Mel acknowledged. "Just let me know when to start. Who is he?"

Pez let her know, "He's the Director of Ground Intelligence and has made connections with some undercover Ahumdulilah Intel Agents. He has more influence here on Ground than the ruling families know. I'll say 'now Mel' when I need you to do it."

"I'll be ready and it will begin instantly when you give me the word."

"Thanks Mel!"

"Do you have your micro-range jammer bubble on around the space between your mouth and the mic. darling?" Mel asked concerned.

"Of course I do," Pez hissed.

Mel informed her, "At the Emperor's parties they use thousands of mics and also lenses, and they have thousands of lip-reading slaves transcribing every word of every conversation by stenograph in real-time. If a negative comment is dropped regarding the emperor, snipers in the ceiling fire through murder-holes and the critic is toasted burnt right on the ballroom floor in front of the other guests."

"I'll be sure to sing his praises only," Pez assured her.

Mel told her further, "It's punishable by death to even mention him in private without using his full title of Imperial Emperor Sponge the Magnificent."

"It's a mouthful" Pez commented.

Mel had lots more trivia but the Whiplash lady had finally taken her leave of Colonel Veil, Director of Ground Intelligence. Pez got directly in front of him and said with a friendly smile, "I'm Cher Bulwinkle. Could I have this dance?"

"It's an honor to meet you, Madam Bulwinkle," Veil replied. "It would be my pleasure to dance with such a beautiful woman. My name is Colonel Veil."

They touched chests arm in arm dancing close and Veil whispered into her ear, "The entire room is an ear."

Pez thought texted Mel, "Now Mel", and said to the Colonel, "It's not now, and won't be for the next two minutes. Your code word is 'mast'."

He said, "I hope you're not angling for a Bulwinkle dynasty."

"I'm not even really a Bulwinkle or from any of these three galaxies. I have no personal ambitions in all of this and am only an agent playing a role and doing my duty. The alliance and spiritual congress behind me want and seek nothing from any of your planets. They will not abide a disease this deadly, spreading so fast in our universe, as the Royal Monarch Empire."

"Are you a competent physician?" he inquired using her disease analogy.

"I am the master surgeon who will cut out only the rot too far gone to be healed. I'll close the wound to stop the bleeding then I'm flying away. The long healing and recuperation will be left to all of you."

"Fair enough," he replied. "This is actually the best possible news; that we do not have to worry about or commit resources to preventing a Bulwinkle takeover, and that we have allies beyond our three galaxies."

"The network of one-time unbreakable code encryptions will be in place in one year. The empire will never be able to break them or know what is being said, but they will be aware of the coms traffic, and this will be of major concern causing them to react; probably against the planet with the most indecipherable coms."

"So we'll have to plan our actions most efficiently and strike everywhere at once to save as many lives as possible," he stated.

"I'll have the macro-plan in place by then but actions on and in the space around individual planets will be planned and executed locally," Cher reported. "It's too soon to tell you more than that, but you will be among the first to know once we have them formulated and in place,"

"There are rumors that the Avahat has come to serve the revolution," he stated as a question.

"It is no rumor," Cher clarified. "The Avahat has come."

"Have you met her?" he asked.

"Yes," Cher answered. "I must go Colonel. It's a pleasure to meet you."

She bowed wanting to snap him a salute that would blow wind in his face. She liked him and felt he was highly competent. He actually gave her a salute and it wasn't bad. Electra had woken up and was banging on the back of Pez's head from her back pouch with her little firsts, but she wasn't screaming yet. Pez sprang into action getting the backpack off and Electra onto her breast. The diaper was dry according to the sensors and Pez checked manually while nursing her. She no longer screamed every single time she awoke; just most of them. Her daughter had descended a very long ways from paradise, and paradise was what she'd grown accustomed to. Pez did her best but knew that hassles like breathing, eating and digesting, burping and pooping, drinking and peeing made for an awful lot to have going on and could be a real nuisance to one unused to them.

In the role of Kat, Trix found her spouse Cher and they danced together enjoying the activity and their connection. Cher relaxed having made the contacts on her list for Ground. She got Electra strapped into her backpack after she finished nursing and Trix helped her get it secured to her back. She thought it might be nice to just leave the Whiplash party and go to the concert. She was about to suggest this into her companion's ear buds when a screech from Pippy had Pez bringing up a tracking holo in front of one eye like a teleprompter while sprinting to the next room in shoes she'd turned into flats with a thought, passing out of the ballroom into the more dimly lit lounge. Pez noticed many slaves in here being used as sex objects then honed in on Pippy. She was on her back on the floor with an angry bruise on one cheek and a mid-teen male was holding her down kneeling over her. Cher Bulwinkle grabbed the back of his neck from behind and lifted him to his feet. He was an inch taller and about the same weight. He was wearing a sword on his belt. Cher informed him, "She's mine. Touch her again and I'll end your life. I don't care who you are."

The young man did not know who she is and was outraged. He told her "You're not even armed women! That's a slave and fair game. Out of my way or I'll draw my sword."

Cher said quietly so he had to almost strain to hear, and she said it with deadly calm, "I don't need a weapon to kill a pup like you and I'll say this one last time; touch her again and die."

His hand went flying for the hilt of his sword. Instead of just dropping him dead on the floor Cher shot her hand there first drawing the weapon with the edge to his jugular vein. She demanded, "What's your name boy?"

No one in the universe except his own father ever used such a tone with him, and even his father didn't call him "boy", though he did have a few other choice words he was fond of employing. His ego screamed for blood but the blade to his throat encouraged his reply, "I'm Dufastador Snydely".

His voice had dripped with arrogance. Cher told him, "Out of respect for your family I'll spare your life *this* time. You will not get a second chance with me, so leave my slaves and companions alone."

"My father will kill you, you stupid bitch!" he screamed, having a little public tantrum.

"Men have died for less," Cher said harshly as her knee met his gut in a blur. While he was folding in half from the blow, Cher directed him over one knee and proceeded to paddle his bottom with the flat of the sword. When she was done she stabbed the blade with fantastic speed into the sheath hanging from his belt. It was one of those things no one could do, and it shocked the boy out of his anger into some serious fear. Pez told him, "I'm Cher Bulwinkle and I love dueling."

That did it and a pool of liquid collected beneath the youth's shoes running down his legs and over them. She'd already let him up and he ran like his pants were on fire leaving wet foot prints as he went. A slave started cleaning up the puddle at their feet and the girl flashed Cher a covert grin while she did it.

Rudfuss Snydely came striding into the room puffed up and completely bloated with himself, ready to leave a mark on someone. As he approached and got in Cher's face he said with great offense, "How dare you?"

"He offended me and tried to draw his sword on me, so I gave him a spanking with it to teach him some manners," Cher told him calmly.

Rudfuss was two and a half inches taller than Cher and had at least 50 pounds on her. He trained every day and was considered possibly the best duelist in the entire empire. Rudfuss liked disabling his opponents so he could kill them slowly and gloat. This pirate heiress from outside the Royal Galaxy needed to be taught a lesson. He said with venom in his voice, "I'm going to fuck your slave girl right in front of you."

"If you try it I'm going to wear your eyeballs on my tiara," Cher informed him.

Cousin Winnie and Trix had moved in close now. Rudfuss was enraged by Cher's words and snapped back, "I think I'll make a necklace of your teeth and cook your heart and eat it."

Cher slapped his face. He only felt it because it had occurred too quickly to catch visually. Rudfuss stated seething with rage, "I choose bare hands half an hour from now in the Whiplash private arena."

"I'll be there!" Cher snapped back.

With a red palm print on his angry face Snydely turned and stomped out of the room.

Pez switched on her bubble jammer and asked Mel," Would you keep a countdown for me and tell me how to get to the private arena?"

"I started the countdown when you told him you would be there," Mel reported. "The arena is directly below the ballroom and the entrance is right off the main foyer. I'm accessing the listening devices and I can tell you that you'll be facing Rudfuss's second who is a seven and a half foot 280 lb. white sun champion fighter."

"Tell Evenrude to meet me outside the front entrance to the mansion ten minutes before show time, please Mel."

After a pause Mel told her, "He says he'll be there."

"Good!" Pez declared. "Maybe Snydely's double will think twice about it after he sees my champion."

"Will you have Evenrude fight him?" Mel asked.

"No. I'll fight him. I want Evenrude there to keep it fair. I'm going to meditate now so please alert me when Evenrude is approaching the foyer."

"Will do" Mel agreed.

To Rubix who had shown up, and to Trix and Winnie, Pez said, "I'm going to practice withdrawing my senses and some central channel work so please keep an eye out and stay close. Nudge me if there's trouble."

"We will," Rubix promised.

All three sat with their backs to Pez keeping watch over the room. Trix got a jade dart in her hand just in case. Woahha, or Winnie, had four darts between the fingers of each hand and could launch them with accuracy one at a time or all at once. Ming found her way over and Rubix filled her in whispering. Ming sat watch with them. She sensed that Pez had left her body so she straddled her from behind to keep Pez's body warm. As the ten-minute warning approached, Ming got Electra and her pouch detached from Pez's back.

Mel said into Pez's ear, "Evenrude will be at the entrance in less than two minutes."

Pez came back and got her metabolism sped up with some deep breaths, faster than what she'd been doing. She rose from the floor and walked back through the ballroom, then down the wide corridor to the foyer. She ignored the servants directing her down to the arena and stepped out the front door. Evenrude was just coming up the steps. They went back into the mansion together and took the stairs down to the arena. Ming, Rubix, Trix and Woahha followed them down. Johnson was lingering near the steps to the mansion's front entrance and he knew just where the stairs down to the arena were located, right inside the main entrance.

Rudfuss was already there with his champion and seven other body guards. They did not look pleased when they saw Evenrude with Pez. The Snydely goons were all muscle-bound weight lifters, hardly able to wipe themselves after taking a dump. Evenrude did as much stretching as he did weight-lifting, and trained the little muscles of coordination with hundreds of repetitive movements for each every day. He could stand on one leg and bring the ankle of the other over his head and behind his neck. He also had energy strength, or strength through softness, relaxing to allow his internal energy to flow uninhibited across his meridians. Pez had been really working him hard on that.

Cher noticed that colonel Viel had gotten himself included in the small audience of about forty people. Ming stood on the sideline holding Electra, who had woken up, and was watching her mother intently without fussing. Pez stepped out into the arena. She called out, "Come on Rudfuss, let's get this started. Get out here."

"You'll be fighting my second," Rudfuss informed her with a hand on his champion's back.

"What kind of cowardly chicken shit is that?" Pez inquired condescendingly.

"The rules allow for it," Rudfuss stated confidently.

"Well after I kill him do I get to fight you?"

"One fight to the death concludes our challenge," he explained.

"Then you better be gone before he's dead or you'll be receiving another challenge," Pez assured him.

"He's going to rip your limbs off one at a time then wrench your head from your body," Rudfuss taunted her.

Pez called to the Snydely champion, "Come on big boy let's do this."

Rudfuss slapped his man on the butt and said, "Go kill her." The champ charged. He couldn't imagine the frail lady would be able to cause him the least injury. At 26 years old he was in peak physical condition and could bench press 465 pounds. He weighed at least 140 pounds more than her, was 21 inches taller or more, and had both strength and reach over her. He meant to run her over like a speeding electro-magnetic rail engine then stomp her into goo. He'd probably get a bonus.

As he came in Cher got her palms connected with his torso, rolling back onto her rear leg and turning her waist and upper body sideways. Champ was running right into her but was meeting only air. She'd turned off from the force of his momentum then he was running passed her with only four-ounces of contact brushing against her. Then she took a twist step following him, palms still touching his torso though now on his back as she released her internal energy through her hands pushing. Champ's feet could not keep up with his new velocity, now double his sprinting speed, so he was simply flying through the air; headed for Evenrude who'd stepped out of the way to let champ crash into the wall shoulder first. It did catch his head a little bit too; the wall that is.

Champ was bruised pretty bad and shaken but not down for the count. He picked himself up wondering what had gone wrong and how he'd suddenly doubled his speed there going by her. He came in slowly now with a wide stance, sunk low to the ground, but his spine wasn't straight. He was leaning forward with arms spread in a wrestler's stance. Cher had no intention of wrestling with him. She knew well the old adage. "Never wrestle with a pig because you both get dirty and the pig loves it." She assumed her own low stance and waited for him to get close enough. She felt his energy and knew his intentions reading his energy.

His arm was just tensing to grab her and she was within his reach. She moved before his arm did, leaving the ground in a high aerial forward roll, and as her legs were just higher than her head, she slapped her palms with great force right over each of his ears, continuing on around to land feet-first hard on champ's leaning spine; to then push off into a second summersault in the air and land in a squat. Champ had gone down face first and as she spun on her heal to face him he was just picking himself up off the floor with a bloody mouth. He grinned drooling blood and it was evident two teeth were no longer there in his mouth. He meant it to be frightening but Pez just found it grotesque. She was feeling some pity for him and was trying to knock the big lug unconscious not wanting to kill him.

Then he said, "After I kill you Mr. Snydely is going to give me your little slave girl and I'm going to rape her to death."

Pez realized she was dealing with vermin that had to be put down. She rushed in ducking a high punch and her foot shot out as she rose, heel first into his throat releasing the force of a tornado through her heel. He went to his knees with his hands on his crushed windpipe choking to death. Pez got her face in his and told him, "NO YOU WONT!"

She turned looking around for Rudfuss and saw only the back of him as he was literally running away. She shouted at his back, "You better stay way clear of me you chicken shit and keep that brat Dufas of yours away from my slaves or I'll castrate him."

Colonel Viel came over to Cher and said, "At first I couldn't understand why you wouldn't employ your impressive second; but then I saw you fight and understood."

"At first I meant to spare his life." Pez confided. "But once he revealed himself as a killer of helpless girls I realized that I had to put him down like a rabid dog."

"With your charge and strike with heel I recognized that you could have killed him right off had you wanted to," Viel acknowledged. "You sure are a master."

"What will Rudfuss do?" Cher inquired.

"Oh, he'll attempt to plant some poison in the Emperor's ear about you. My report will contradict about everything he tells the Emperor and my report will be viewed as objective. You needn't worry about him influencing the emperor."

"That's why you got yourself invited into the audience; to help me," Cher stated as she realized it.

"And to see who it really is we follow now," he admitted. "I'll tell you, it inspired me greatly and offered no disappointment at all."

"I'm a warrior-monk and I do as I'm directed by my Vicar General and Abbot," Pez explained. "I'm not rich and live in a tiny room in the monastery. I've never really understood money, and it has always seemed to me to be a big scam. Everyone deserves the same. Sacrifices and extra efforts for the common good are rewarded spiritually and require no special treatment or a bigger slice of the pie."

"It is you!" Viel said in shock. "You are the Avahat, the one the people of Ahumdulilah call the Rajaha."

"I'm the instrument of the spiritual congress which aligns with the will of the cosmic intelligence. I do my duty just like you do yours."

"I'm deeply honored to make your acquaintance and I offer you my total support," Viel told her still in awe. "I noticed the band you're touring with is scheduled to perform on Snyde, the home planet of Rudfuss Snydely. I recommend getting them to cancel that gig. Snyde is the one place in the empire Rudfuss wouldn't think twice about sending an army against you."

"I'll see if I can convince them to cancel," Pez agreed. Then she inquired, "But what of the contacts I'm to make there?"

"Someone from Ahumdulilah can handle those," he suggested. "They have many agents operating within the empire and I'm certain that Snyde is a planet they watch closely."

"I'll call them from deep space on my way to the Condral System," Cher told him. "We leave in a little more than four hours from now, once the band finishes its concert."

"I've never seen such an ambitious tour," he stated. "It's really the perfect cover for visiting so many planets in such a short space of time."

"I've never seen a more effective Intelligence network than the Ahumdulilah's" Cher shared. "All of the contacts I make were cultivated by them and they are highly trained and dedicated people. A full third of their population is white so would become slaves."

"The kind of lucrative invasion that is most dear to this sick empire," Viel commented.

Electra exercised her lungs raising quite a volume of distress and Lai brought her quickly to Cher, whose ridiculous bare-chested dress was a mess and in tatters. The diaper came off in a pull and a clean one from a sleeve in the pouch went around Electra's pelvis to adhere and self-adjust, all in a few seconds. An Islohar lullaby was resounding from Cher's lips and energy was flowing from her into her daughter as she hugged her close. It took only a moment to get Electra onto her breast. The flow-state of mothering had just been exhibited and Viel was beyond impressed. He could feel the love, dense and thick.

Cher introduced Evenrude as 'Brick' to Colonel Viel, and the two of them hit it off quite well. There was no doubt at all in Viel's mind that Brick was a military man through and through. To be the body guard and champion of the Avahat, Veil was certain Brick must be one incredibly elite soldier. They left the arena taking the stairs to the foyer and said their goodbyes while Mel alerted everyone in Pez's party and asked Hanah to bring the shuttle around. When the shuttle came, Cousin Winnie jumped into the seat beside Hanah to give her nethers some good vibes.

Hanah drove them back into Defibmo to the facility the concert was being performed at and got them through security to a backstage parking garage underground. Cher handed her another thousand dag bill and Winnie gave her another long kiss. Cher led her group to the lift up to the main floor. Winnie decided to bring Hanah along. Hanah was willing to follow those magic vibes anywhere. They went to the lounge the band used for taking their breaks and sat or reclined on the sofas and stuffed chairs. Hanah sat, or kind of squirmed a little, in Winnie's lap. Pippy came over and sat in Cher's lap. She told Cher, "Thank you for coming to my rescue. I wanted to kill Dufastador, but had to stay in character and keep my cover."

"You mean little Dufas," Cher reframed. "If I ever see him again I mean to cut off his penis so he'll stop raping slaves." Cher placed her palm gently on Pippy's bruised check passing healing energy in a torrent. With her other hand she dug into some pressure points in Pippy's neck and spine relieving tension. She found the girl lovely and traced a finger down her arm. Cher stated, "Your white skin is actually quite attractive."

Pippy's was unblemished, aside from the bruise on her check, and she was petite, hardly bigger than Ahhu. A little on the frail side but with wiry muscle and an internal strength you wouldn't want to under estimate. Cher liked her. Pippy told her, "On Ahumdulilah we are not seen as any different."

"They see clearly," Cher confirmed. "Like other species we come in a variety of colors but we are one race. You are beautiful Pippy and you are full of rare goodness."

"I was worried about you when I saw the giant you had to fight," Pippy shared.

"He trained himself into an inflexible beast of burden, not a warrior, and his sprained and torn bulky muscles blocked his internal energy flow making him weak in the sense of 'low on life energy'."

"Could I get a holo of us together," Pippy requested.

Cher said, "Mel, could you capture a few good shots of us and send the holos to Pippy's pocket device?"

"I'm getting some now. Just look up a little more towards the ceiling and smile. Oh boy, that's a good one. Done. They're sent."

"Thanks Mel," Cher told her.

"Thanks Mel and Cher," Pippy said, admiring one of the holo's on her device.

Mel flirted, "You are just cute as a button Pippy. Say, can I take you out to dinner and a holo-movie on Condral?"

"I'm on duty throughout this tour, Mel," Pippy told her apologetically.

"How about when the tour is up or when you have some leave time?"

"You mean like going out on a date?" Pippy asked.

"That's right," Mel confirmed. "I have the hottest android body that looks like a Bulwinkle sister except I didn't go in for the bright orange hair. Mine's auburn. Here, I'm sending some stills from my last holo-shoot."

"You are beautiful Mel," Pippy admitted. "But I've never dated an android before,"

"I'm a sentient and the android body is but a temporary abode," Mel clarified. "I'm very good at sex. I'm also a student of the same teacher as Cher and I'm working on attaining my rainbow body of light."

"I'd like to go out on a date with you, Mel. That would be nice," Pippy decided.

"Did you know that I'm now a Marshal of the same order as Cher, called the Clearlight Order?"

"That is impressive Mel, and kind of certifies your sentience," Pippy acknowledged.

"Mel," Cher said in a complaining voice. "She's in my lap and you have to intrude and set up a date with her."

"You're just jealous," Mel accused acting superior.

"*I am* jealous and you do this all the time," Cher vented.

"I have to go now anyway," Mel informed her. "I have many responsibilities you know."

"Bye Mel," Cher stated.

"She looks a lot like you," Pippy commented, examining a holo of Mel.

"I was all she knew in her pre-sentient years as my personal quantum computer," Pez explained. "She designed her android body based upon me and upon Lai/Ming."

"I've never felt a body like yours before," Pippy shared. "It's like bio-fusion or something. I'm feeling stronger just sitting here in your lap."

"Your body feels pretty good to me," Pez replied.

The band finally completed their last performance of the evening and left with Pez's party to return to the hotel and pack. Condral was their next stop and they were leaving this night.

CHAPTER FOURTEEN

Aphrodite, Spaceship, Sidekick and Ahhu's drone whizzed out of Ground's atmosphere accelerating. A broad diameter lane had been cleared for them by Ground Space Control. Their next stop was the Condral System. They'd be landing in the capital, Hari, at the Hari Intergalactic Hotel which was right on the beach. It was early spring there, and being close to the tropics it would be quite warm. Indoor environmental control would keep them cool but the beach in midafternoon would be very hot indeed. Pez wanted to take a swim in the ocean and perhaps do a little surfing. Hari boasted the largest waves in the Royal Galaxy, at least of all those known to the empire. Whirlpool had some much bigger ones but nobody surfed those. You would be more likely to survive jumping off a really tall building holding an anvil than you would be to survive those waves.

Cher got them up to speed and they passed through the jump in no-time, shocked a new, as if it had been the first any of them had ever experienced. Ahhu described it as "strange", while Cher/Pez likened it to the state of the black near-attainment, or the mystical midnight sun. Ahhu had told her, "Either way, it's strange."

Cher didn't even slow down coming out of the jump zone, instead contacting Condral Space Control and getting them to clear space ahead of them right down to the hotel. This was accomplished in great haste as the four ships raced to the hotel. Cher won with a slightly louder clank of the hydraulics bottoming out, and a bit of a jolt, but no damage to the landing gear. Ahhu's drone came in second, only seconds behind, and that craft did require a little repairs, though not that much. *Sidekick* landed third being much quicker and more maneuverable than the bands' yacht, *Spaceship*, which came in last.

Cher had given Hanah a fourth thousand dag bill and Winnie had given her one of her enormous emerald earrings. In addition, Cher had participated in an electronic questionnaire rating her experience of the hotel and gave Hanah the highest marks across the board, but not the hotel, and added the most flattering things about Hanah under the "comments" heading. This had already resulted in a raise in salary for Hanah and in her selection as "employee of the month." What had appeared to Hanah at first sight to be a cornucopia of abuse and degradation, possibly scarring her for life sexually, had turned out to be the most fun she'd ever had at work and enrichening beyond even the 4,000 dags and giant emerald. She would truly miss Cousin Winnie.

Their new hotel greeter-liaison was practically right out of the cheerleading squad, possibly High School Varsity. As it turned out it was her first week on the job and she'd just graduated, though she hadn't told them from what. Her name was Minnie and she was quite voluptuous, perhaps a little over weight, though her youth made it appealing. Her hotel uniform, like most fashions in this empire, was loud and bright. Minnie was friendly and bubbly, and a nervous wreck beneath it all, struggling to cope with the prospect of serving a ruling family notorious for piracy.

Gretle the graduate student took the seat beside Minnie and chatted her up. It was 4:00 AM in Hari and none had been able to sleep on the way with Pez piloting. Minnie was unused to the big hover shuttle and she left a few black skid marks on the walls from the rubber bumper around the vehicle hitting them. Needless to say it was a bumpy ride and Minnie's anxiety was through the roof. Cher thought it was like the time she and Schwin played bumper cars with mining vehicles. Gretle's soothing voice guided and reassured Minnie and provided a few driving tips. Minnie went up the shaft flawlessly, but that was magnetically controlled by the hotel central computer.

They arrived in one piece with the tension Minnie had built up in herself as the only real cost of the ride; that, and some wall smears. Cher had Bianca hand Minnie a thousand dag bill, sorry it had taken so much out of the girl to get them here. Cher said to Minnie, "My friend Shadey is just dropping her things in her room and will be right out for a ride to the hover craft rental agency. The rest of us are going to go to sleep and likely won't need you until noon or later. Let me enter your code in my device so I can contact you when we do."

"Yes Ma'am," Minnie replied, obediently reciting her code.

Cher said, "Sweetheart, take a deep breath, sinking it all the way down to your lower abdomen, and calm yourself. We are going to be nice to you. We understand you're still learning a few things about your job and we promise to be patient with you. Just relax and pay attention, and think of us as part of your cheerleading squad."

"How did you know that I was a cheerleader?" Minnie asked surprised.

"You have the look, and I know hotels and big-pharm recruit cheerleaders for greeter-liaisons and drug representatives. I honestly don't want to be giving you anxiety attacks, dear."

"Thank you Ma'am; I'll try my best to get a grip," Minnie promised, holding the money in her hand and assuming it was a five or a ten; possibly only a dag.

Naked Alice said softly to Minnie, "They treat everyone well, even slaves like me, and they are extremely easy going; so you needn't worry."

The Bulwinkle party went to their suites. Cher and seven others went to the Grand Wazu Suite, which was the Penthouse, and the rest to theirs. With Alice and Pippy in the big bed along with their usual six of Pez, Ming, Rubix, Ahhu, Trix and Gretle, it was quite cozy. Then Whiffle and Hoola arrived and climbed in making it actually a tight fit. Pez was out deep in sleep. Hoola couldn't squeeze in beside her with Ming and Pippy latched on to each side of her like a set of spoons stacked. Hoola got as close to Cher/Pez as she could by wedging between Rubix and Ming with her bottom against Lai/Ming's and facing Rubix. Whiffle had squeezed onto one end, up against Pippy, joining the spoon set.

Everyone was sound asleep except Hoola, as far as Hoola could tell, and she'd taken stimulant empathogens right before the last set the band had played on Ground. She was not at all close to dozing. Rubix was awake too, facing Hoola, as his mind churned with alarming exclamations triggering inhibitions as well as wild fantasies.

Here he was squished against a supermodel naked in bed. When the supermodel started masturbating his arousal blossomed beyond any possible prevention.

Hoola was just starting to get into it when she felt something poking into her. She investigated and found a penis in her hand, stiff and at the ready, so she gratefully got on top mounting it, pushing Rubix on his back from his side. Her ad hoc partner was not a hard-bodied super-athlete like she was used to. His hands were gentle, loving and giving. Hoola was getting close and this was the point at which many past lovers had lost it, ending things before she was done. Her little man beneath her hung in and carried on, holding up his end through her entire progression.

Ever so impressed, Hoola crushed her chest into his and kissed him deeply. He was full of energy, and though not of the eminence and enormity of Cher's, still, far more alive and vital than her usual muscle-man. His unwavering attentions were so loving and selfless that they endeared him to her heart. She also found him increasingly arousing and so led him through another round. She'd never felt such vim and vigor from a male partner before; and of course, 99.99% of her lovers had been male.

Some hours later a stirring from Electra's hotel hovercrib sounding in Pez's ear awoke her a little before eleven in the morning Hari time on Condral. As she extracted herself carefully from bodies and bed, she tried not to wake the bodies. Pez realized that she was at the Hari Intergalactic Hotel. She had to hop on one leg to drag the other from the bed. Electra was just waking when she got there and her quick movements getting her changed and into her arms enfolded in love, kept Electra from feeling any need to scream or holler. Pez sang in Islohar to her daughter while she nursed her, passing her love and energy in adoration. Electra's exaltedness no longer diminished Pez's experience of their mother-daughter relationship and her sentiments were fulfilled to overflowing. Electra soaked up the gush delighting in it.

Today Pez would be making contact with a malcontent not previously arranged by Ahumdulilah agents. She would be carrying a well-insulated data-bed, one of the miniature spy-models, which she would pass on to her contact should she sense sincere cooperation and shared purpose. Her own internal sense of if people are levelling with her or not was accurate and sensitive as actual electrodes measuring reflex impulses. She'd examined her contact's schedule, provided by Mel, and had decided to intercept her on her one and a half block walk to her usual midday eating place from her office. The woman she meant to meet was a Field Marshal General in Condral's most elite special-forces which were being employed more frequently by the empire of late in its invasions of other worlds.

Pez took a quick bath in the chin-deep tub with Electra and was careful to aim her daughter away from her own face. Sure enough, the warm bath water evoked a tinkle, and this time it went harmlessly in another direction. Pez dressed Electra, then made herself up as Cher Bulwinkle, wearing only one earring since she thought this might make her look more like a pirate. She put Electra in her pouch and got it secured on her back. With so little time before the encounter Pez ate only an instant-oatmeal ration and alerted Minnie that she would need a ride. Evenrude and Johnson were outside her suite door when she emerged. Both now sported some yellow and could not have been more colorful. On Om only old retired club-ballers wore colors like these.

Minnie was there in a far more manageable mini-shuttle four-seater and got them out of the hotel without so much as grazing a wall, and hit nothing getting them to the block of the Field Marshal's office. Pez had cash with her and handed Minnie a bill telling her, "I'll call you when I'm ready to return to the hotel. Thank you!"

"I'll be prompt", Minnie promised. Starting salaries for entry-level greeter-liaisons at the Hari Intergalactic Hotel were in the 18,000 – 20,000 dag range, and between Condral and Imperial taxes less than half of that ever made it into the wage-earner's hands. Other taxes chipped away constantly or hit periodically in cycles. For most of the population housing ate up 58% of after-tax income, utilities and energy usage at least another 9%, and electronic coms/imagery access another 8%. Mini's job recruitment agency took 5% off the top and her union dues were another 3%. The uniforms the hotel made her purchase put her deeply in debt and she carried student loans at 22% interest. Food was reasonably priced on Condral compared to most places but Minnie's cupboards and cooler were bare, and hunger had been becoming a constant companion until the Bulwinkle's gave her a thousand dags the night before. The numbers on the bill in her hand read 5,000 dags. With great relief, Minnie was no longer terrified of starving to death working her full-time job.

Cher positioned herself to the side of the door to the Field Marshal's office at the Devil Dogs' HQ. Their motto was "death from above" because they dove out of high altitude space-air craft with textile wings integrated into their clothing and a thruster with fuel cell attached to their backs, wearing a helmet with face mask visual targeting and skullcap remote control of the blaster, as well as of a four-tube missile launcher harnessed to their bodies. The rest of Condral's military thought they were nuts. Twelve per cent or more of all new recruits died in training accidents learning how to do it, and usually only a small vial was then needed for the cremation remains, after that. The Devil Dogs were a rare breed.

Cher, with Electra on her back, spotted her quarry exiting the building and set a pace to catch up. Electra's covert cover was as Electra, daughter of Cher, and her own baby holos were on file in the Monarch central computer along with her full body scan and DNA. Cher came alongside the Field Marshal and said, "Hi, my name is Cher Bulwinkle; would you mind if I joined you for lunch. It would be my treat."

The Field Marshal knew the Bulwinkle name and had seen the holos of her landings on Glitter, Ground, and Condral. It was generally a poor career move to displease even a minor ruling family member and the Bulwinkles could hardly be classed as 'minor'. She replied to Cher, "Not at all. I'd enjoy the company."

Cher informed her, "I've done some sky-diving in a textile winged suit back on Rocky, but never with 120 pounds of weapons harnessed to my body."

"Have you done thruster flying?"

"Only in a hard-shell combat suit, and that had boosters too," Cher replied.

The Field Marshall informed her, "Missiles are fired from long range and the launcher is ejected when spent. The blaster weighs only eleven pounds with its fusion power cell inserted and is exceptionally well balanced. Most fatalities are the result of igniting the thruster before pulling up even horizontal to the planet surface. Diving with the weapons is hardly different from diving without them."

"I'd love to try it," Cher said with clear envy.

"If you want we could make a jump together this afternoon. I'm aging out of jumping in nine months so I'm getting in all I can in the time left."

"I'd be thrilled to," Cher enthused. "Let's do it!"

"Alright!"

They'd reached the steps and entrance to Cheveron, the restaurant the Field Marshal General liked to have her lunch at. She was quite militant about most of her routines and kept her apartment meticulously clean. The restaurant was top notch and fancy. The Field Marshal, like all military officers, received a 75% discount here which was the only reason she could afford to come regularly. Even with the discount it was still somewhat extravagant for her salary, but by keeping a small apartment in an officers quarters building in town and by not owning a hover craft or having to pay insurance on one, she was able to afford this luxury. She also owned no clothing besides her military issued uniforms.

The Field Marshal informed Cher, "Chevron infuses special digestive enzymes into the food to keep your system clean. They call it 'techtron'."

"The tourist guide for Condral lists Chevron as the best restaurant in Hari," Cher mentioned.

Major Nicon had given Pez a miniature bug detector she was wearing in one of the pearls on her necklace and her mini-holo tele-prompter in front of her right eye was displaying the locations of a dozen sensors concealed in the dining room of the restaurant. Mel said in Pez's ear, "The sensors will stop functioning when the restaurant's main computer crashes and will remain down. For the main computer to crash you just need to say when."

With her skullcap Cher texted Mel, "Thanks."

The Field Marshal General properly introduced herself saying, "Cher Bulwinkle, my name is Field Marshal General, Eva Klink, and please just call me Eva."

"You must call me Cher then, Eva."

"Thank you Cher. Your piloting skills have drawn much attention and have generated a great deal of speculation."

"I have developed my intuition, or extra-sensory perception, which is possible for all humans; and I have swivel drives for maneuverability, reversible main drives, thrusters and one-time boosters. I also have super-reinforced heavy-duty landing hydraulic systems and an extra-large vortex-redirect generation turbine in my yacht."

"I'm a pilot myself, and even with your special hardware, I'd never attempt such a landing on the razor's edge of success."

"Small craft piloting and martial arts are my specialties."

"Are the rumors about your family's fortune founded?"

"Shamefully, it is true that the fortune was amassed over many generations of piracy and smuggling, however, my family left the piracy business about the time I was born and went entirely legitimate. Since we've never been caught smuggling I would have to deny being involved with it in any conversion."

"What do you see in those children, the Whirling Vortexes?"

"My sister, Lai, has a big crush on Hoola, and it turns out Whiffle has aptitude and has become my disciple."

"Hoola's first billboard holo in her hug-me's went up in Space Square downtown this morning. I'm not a fan of the underwear, but that model is extremely tempting."

"She's great fun in bed," Cher assured her.

"I thought she was exclusively heterosexual."

"She opened up a little since we joined them for the tour."

"I see."

A diaper sensor pinged Pez's ear putting her right to work and making Cher aware of it well before Electra discovered her predicament. With advanced martial skills Cher changed the diaper in record time without jostling or even waking her daughter and had her tucked into her back pouch.

"Obviously Kat is not the father," Eva stated as a question.

"Lai and I have always shared everything, and I borrowed her Hark to make Electra. Hark is really sweet and a surprisingly good lover. I loaned her Kat so she wouldn't miss Hark."

"It sounds close knit."

"Oh, it's bigger than that. Bianca is included, and then somehow Muffet joined us, and just stayed. Now there's Whiffle and Hoola. You have to admit, it spans galaxies and gene pools."

"Clearly."

Their waitress arrived poised for their order with a pasted smile and canned greeting.

Cher told her, "I'll have a cup of the hot and sour soup and the pan-seared scallops in green curry coconut sauce with the special egg noodles, please."

"That's one cup of hot and sour soup and one Dung Guana," the girl recited back.

Eva told her, "I'll have the grain breaded fired crickets to start, and the barbequed bovine short ribs with broccoli and turnips as an entrée."

"That's one chicharero and one Tabu Pu," the girl verified. Then she inquired, "Would you like a beverage?"

"Do you have herb tea?" Cher inquired.

"I can bring a basket of herb teas for you to choose from, and a pot of hot water," she offered.

"That would do nicely, thank you."

Eva told her, "I'll have the extra-strength stimulant brew in steamed milk with powdered bitter-sweet chocolate sprinkled on top."

"I'll place your order with the kitchen and be right back with your drinks," their waitress informed them, with nothing of herself in her voice, words or facial expression. In this empire, such a thing would be in poor taste, and a programmed sincerity was much preferred. Cher didn't like it one bit.

"You were on Glitter when those mysterious events occurred," Eva stated. "What was your experience of them?"

"It was pretty good. A bunch of long sustained potent orgasms. What can I say?"

"It was on the news here."

Cher decided to probe a little and asked, "How do you feel about the Devil Dogs increasing deployment in imperial 'liberations', as they are called?"

Eva said flatly somehow conveying that she did not believe a word she was speaking, "I am proud to serve the Imperial Emperor Sponge the Magnificent in the expansion of the Empire. May we occupy every inhabitable planet in the three galaxies and may His dynasty go on forever."

There was less of Eva in this than there had been of the girl in her waitress function. It was a frequently recited coined phrase of military patriotism and slogan of imperialistic fervor. Cher didn't want to have Mel crash the computer yet because that would take much of the kitchen offline and she had grown quite an appetite over the menu. She was salivating. Instead she asked Eva, "Have you seen action?"

"You bet. At Xercon, Trisdorf, and most recently Hex. We are always the first ground troops on the surface followed by the Monarch Special Forces wearing hard-shell combat suites inside detachable re-entry capsules. The shuttles start landing with troops after we're all on the ground."

"The tip of the spear shows the most wear on the spearhead," Cher offered understanding, then asked, "What have your casualty rates been like?"

"Hex was worst of all… some 39% dead and 21% wounded. Forty thousand of us jumped and 160,000 missiles struck 31,729 targets as planned before we took a single casualty. When we reached 27,000 feet altitude they sprayed hundreds of cubic miles of their sky with phosphorus explosive flares catching many of us with no way to maneuver out of it. The Hex ground forces converged on our positions as we rallied into our groups on the surface, on three continents of their globe. The imperial special-forces who came in after us took the opportunity to land far from where the Hex troops were dense and converging on us. With only textile armor, micro-shields and blasters we did quite well against their infantry. When their special forces combat suited troops arrived with heavy weapons we started taking a beating. Fortunately, by then, we had achieved space and air supremacy and the shuttles came to our rescue along with some assault frigates firing from space."

"A great deal of sacrifice is expected of the Devil Dogs and they're like to get used up and spent," Cher calculated.

"You're right of course. Recruitment is dropping in proportion to our losses and training requires six months, unable to keep up with our attrition. Our Commander in Chief gains great favor with the Emperor by it and expands his wealth and influence."

"Perhaps a dubious cause when seen through the lens of honor," Cher suggested as she sipped the tea she'd selected from the basket.

"Our own 'liberation' into the empire here on Condral is not so ancient as to have been completely forgotten," Eva stated. "Some of our ancient philosophy and social doctrines of ethos and unity have resurfaced since the purge following our 'liberation'. Some of the ancient spiritual practices can be found again on Condral if one looks hard enough."

While Eva was speaking Cher went comatose for about a second as she left her body through her crown and flared a very tiny blinding sun directly into the sensor over their table with an audible sizzle and visible spark. It was totally fried. Eva had looked up anxiously as it occurred but had finished what she'd been saying. Eva added, "They just blew a wire in the ceiling."

Cher confided, "I did that. Watch, I'm getting the one over the table to your right next."

Cher went comatose and a potentially eye-damaging point of light appeared as if a hole in the fabric of a world of radiance and luminosity too intense for the physical organ of the eye had opened up. Another sizzle and a spark occured with diners' heads turning up towards what happened on the ceiling. Cher informed Eva, "Those were the only two, given the brand and type they're using, that were close enough to our table to pick anything up."

Eva asked, "First, how did you know they were there? And second, how did you just disable them?"

"I have a detector in one of my pearls which gives me a visual of the location of every auditory/optical sensor in the room. As to how, that would be the transference of consciousness and forceful projection practices post attainment of the rainbow body of light through unity and contemplation of the three minds: human, divine, and Absolute."

"You mentioned that you're a teacher," Eva said. "I had no idea. Nothing like that has ever been even hinted at about you or your family."

"Not past generations of family, far from it. Only my aunts, cousin and sister, Lai. We are very much the antithesis of our familial ancestors."

"I'm beginning to understand, I think," Eva stated, still having some trouble believing it.

Cher confided, "I represent a spiritual congress formed of planetary systems from three galaxies outside the empire interested in ending the suffering of political oppression antithetical to love, harmony and unity, and constructed of military might and fear. Fear defeats love and the belief that 'might makes right' perpetuates total ignorance of the laws of reciprocity, evolution and ascent. Propaganda and mind control crystalize ignorance and the entire situation becomes a plague and epidemic of breaking the spirit and misleading people regarding human nature. This empire is rot now spreading in three galaxies and it adversely affects macro-systems in its growing enormity. The empire serves only the ego of an extremely small fraction of 1% of the population, including a tiny group of well-rewarded minions, hence serving their own spiritual destruction and de-evolution. It is a reign of terror sustained by executions, disappearances, torture, constant surveillance of everyone, paid informers, Adherence Examiners and economic policies and sanctions."

"Treason could find no greater clarity," Klink commented, obviously struggling with something inside her.

"Truth is truth treasonous or not," Cher pointed out. "Healing a disease is only treasonous to the disease. The disease is a negligible percent of the body, though in a position to kill the whole thing. I am a physician of the body here to surgically remove the disease."

"I hope you have a fleet of many thousands of giant warships," Klink told her.

"Right now we are constructing a small fleet of giant ships designed specifically to defeat the empire's ships; but once we learn how to surgically remove the explosive chips from Fleet Officers and personnel I suspect more of their ships will become ours than will remain with the empire. First I must spread hope because without that there truly isn't any. The hope begins with dissemination of unbreakable one-time codes to people in key positions on 5700 plus planetary systems in the empire. In about a year we will establish our solidarity and plans, and undecipherable coms traffic will become a constant on the imperial coms systems giving the empire its first objective recognition of its own demise. Then I want to hack in and take control of the imperial coms network announcing the truth and to to spread and mount the hope. Consolidation of allegiance to the common good against tyrannical oppressive de-evolutionary egos and power structures will culminate in unleashing our direct military actions, demolitions, sniper executions, drive by shootings, and angry armed rioting mobs bent on annihilation of anything that even smells imperial."

"The imperial fleet is the key because when you control space around a planet, that planet is yours," Eva stated.

"The top medical people on more than a dozen worlds outside the empire are devising the best methods for removing the explosive chips, funded by governments, universities and private endowments. We already have imperial fleet personnel who have volunteered to be the first, and covert operations planned to accomplish it once the medical procedure and any special equipment required are developed."

"Your news is both inspiring and absolutely terrifying," Eva shared. "It could work, or it could be the greatest catastrophe ever."

"I aim to rule-out catastrophe before we begin," Cher stated as fact.

"Well I'm all in, and so is every Devil Dog up to my rank, I assure you," Eva stated with resolution. "Death has never been a deterrent for us, and we have no fear."

"I can't wait to jump with them," Cher said enthusiastically.

"Remember, never ignite your thruster until it is at least a degree up from horizontal. You'll have a gyroscope holo giving you the thruster tube's precise angle continuously. Always check it before you fire the thruster."

"I've got it," Cher confirmed.

Their entrees arrived and Cher ate slowly taking small bites; well, small for her anyway. She closed her mouth to chew and followed her training on table manners she'd received from Major Nicon's team. It was challenging but the training got her through. The food was delicious which tended to constitute the biggest challenge to the table manners. They shared combat stories and described wounds they'd received, finding much common ground. They each got a thrill out of their discussion of leading edge combat crafts and weapons systems.

Klink was an inch taller than Cher and thirty pounds heavier; pretty much all muscle. She was the holo of fitness and would make a great recruitment holo-poster. Not a crease in her uniform was out of line even at lunch. Cher liked her and found her formidable.

Without the advantage of Eva's 75% discount Cher paid for both meals. They came to 248 dags with tax and Cher left a 100 dag tip hoping their waitress was able to be herself, at least a little bit, when she wasn't working. Eva led the way back to her office already issuing orders through her coms as they went. The walk was only 1 ½ blocks. Pez had Electra picked up by Ming with Minnie's help. They entered Devil Dogs HQ and took a partitioned lift to the roof. A big shuttle with a crew of five and forty suited up Devil Dogs inside was idling just over the flat roof. Impressive salutes were exchanged as they approached but none so impressive as Cher's.

Eva asked her with a statement, "You have a military bearing ingrained quite professionally."

"I'm an honorary member of an elite corps of soldiers called Space Marines and that was their salute I modelled. I am also a warrior monk."

Eva said surprised, "That is completely unknown to the empire."

Cher told her, "There is much the empire does not know about me and when I've finished revealing myself to them their empire will lay in ruins around them, and their slaves and subjects will be pissing on them."

Getting pissed on was Cher's worst experience and so the worst thing she could think of offhand. They suited up once aboard and the hover craft was already racing for the upper atmosphere. Eva briefed Cher on the controls, which required Cher to don a special skullcap and helmet. Cher familiarized herself with her thruster controls and gyro-holo for its angle. She practiced targeting with her face-mask/skullcap fire control system and tested her coms. She checked her suit-rig, straps and harness, and acquainted herself with her blaster. She had an altimeter on her wrist. The materials of her suit were memory-textiles and were layered with textile-armor and thermal insulation. A small oxygen tank attached to her thruster fed her helmet.

What an explosion that would make! Cher thought to herself. *At least the memory-textile will relieve great strain on limbs since it won't be my muscles keeping the fabric taut.*

Field Marshal General Klink briefed her people and Cher, "We have ceramic structures on the ground you are each assigned to blow up. As soon as you leave this craft begin targeting and fire. Eject launchers when they're spent and concentrate on getting to the surface fast, avoiding the long-range low-energy blaster fire directed at you by androids on the ground. Take out as many of those as you can on your way in. Regroup as soon as you're down and proceed to your ground-objective. Cher Bulwinkle will be training with us and she'll lend fire support after launching her missiles. The first one down in one piece gets three extra days leave."

A countdown holo appeared digitally decreasing each second. The jump ramp was opening. Eva said only into Cher's coms, "There is no honor in helping the empire enslave worlds."

"Though there's much honor in the toppling of it," Cher replied, just before both jumped out of the craft without parachutes from 85,000 feet.

They were just behind the first wave off and Cher got right to work identifying and targeting the ceramic structures assigned to her. Her fire control system found each one and lit it up when locked on.

Cher triggered the missile launches with her skullcap, and after the forth left its tube, she ejected the launcher.

She had an effective flight form that her textile suit wings were locked into, two in the arms and a tail wing between her legs. She was about as aerodynamic as she could get. The surface was still way too far off to target with her blaster or need to dodge long-range low-amp blaster bolts from the ground. At the moment she was pretty much diving straight down for the ground like a missile. The first wave of Devil Dogs was now above her. Ribbing along the spine on her suit, also memory textile, would help her arch her back to get lift when it came time to land. She was seeking a body of water to do that in.

The ground was closing awful fast and she was starting to take some fire from androids below. Cher tested the spine ribbing by putting some arch into it, and angled off from straight down, doing some random micro-maneuvers in her flight which were greatly amplified by her velocity, moving her hundreds of meters in a new course with each one. The blaster fire got thicker at 21,000 feet and she made more micro-wiggles giving her flight complete unpredictability. The androids kept missing. At 17,000 feet much of the blaster fire shifted to the Devil Dogs above her. Cher spotted her body of water.

At 10,000 feet she could target androids with her blaster and began taking them down, sometimes in pairs, as she circled her lake adding little random maneuvers. Targeting unbelievably fast with every cell in her brain active in the process she managed to clear a large region of androids before going maximum arch to point straight up, and collapsing her wings to drop feet first in the water. She engaged the flotation in the heavy suit while checking her oxygen and used short bursts of her thruster to propel her face-first to the shore. Cher climbed out of the lake and engaged sensors to seek androids. A Devil Dog Colonel was second to land, about nine seconds after Cher, and Eva came in less than two seconds after the Colonel. She often beat him but not this time. The Devil Dog platoon members Cher was training with were so impressed that they insisted upon making her an honorary Devil Dog specifically of their platoon.

Cher had also been instrumental in taking their ground objective, actually jumping the battlements with her thruster to mow the androids down from behind. The Devil Dogs loved her. Klink found a jump suit and uniform to fit Cher when they returned to HQ, and gave these to her along with a Space Marine salute about as good as any Space Marine could do. Both uniform and suit bore the platoon insignia. The Devil Dogs even made Cher get a tattoo of it on her upper arm. She showed it off to Evenrude and Johnson when she met back up with them on the street outside Devil Dog HQ. She'd given the spy data bead to Eva and they'd exchanged personal contact information to stay in touch socially. It had been a big success.

Minnie showed up in a little four-seater, far safer than the big ones with her at the stick. She got them to their suite, the Grand Wazu, without incident. Cher gave her another 5,000 dag bill as she climbed out to enter her suite. Hoola was all over Hark/Rubix. Apparently Whiffle had had another session with Sarhi, or rather with Aunt Gemima, and sat with crisp clarity, her aura a glow in radiance. She got up and came directly to Electra, held by Ming, who grinned and raised her arms to be lifted into Whiffle's. Their connection was a sight to behold. The cosmically happy baby with the anorexic pop music superstar were content in a rapture together. It warmed Pez's heart, endearing each of them to her all the more.

Cher/Pez worked with Hoola after prying her off Rubix and taking her to a small den or office where they sat on round meditation cushions on the floor. Cher recited the core instruction and they went inside meditation. Once Hoola was grounded and focused in her lower abdomen Cher was able to take on and transmute some of the superstar/model's karma, and then pass to her the blessing of the teacher. With her overstock of merit this was enough to put Hoola inside her first awakening, piercing the veils of illusion completely to contemplate the essence. When Cher and Hoola emerged from the room they'd been in, Lai, Bianca and Kat congratulated Hoola recognizing her state. Cher had Mel alert the rest of her party in other suites that they would all be eating in the hotel restaurant dining room in ten minutes. It wasn't much notice but she was really hungry.

Whiffle wore Electra's back pouch with Electra in it, holding Whiffle's hair like reins as if driving an ancient carriage drawn by horses. The back of Cher's scalp panged in sympathy but Whiffle didn't seem to mind at all. The five crewmen and eight slaves from *Sidekick* joined them along with three of the Intel officers they were saddled with. Lucky was stuck on the yacht and poor Pooh was stuck there with him, though she had as little to do with the man as possible. Super-Agent Green was on the move, checking contacts off her mental list. She really was a super-agent; all five foot two of her.

Cher insisted that Evenrude and Johnson sit with them and eat instead of lurking about. Pippy had maneuvered into a seat right beside Cher, beating out Kat, Cher's cover-spouse, and leaned ribs to ribs into her. Lai had claimed the seat to the other side of Cher. Hoola with her aura so bright, sat practically in Rubix's lap. Their waiter was dressed in colorful revealing livery and he was suave, almost theatrical, with nothing of him in the role. He seemed to Cher like an entertainment android with a waitering subroutine though she could see from his aura that he was human. As he took their order he poked the air with a stylus, apparently touching boxes of a holo grid corresponding to menu items which only he could see. Cher was glad to see this because there were a lot of orders to get right. The aunts and Cousin Winnie had joined them too.

The service staff and other diners in the room were staring at Hoola having recognized her. A girl of about thirteen ran over ignoring the angry hisses from her parents, crossing the dining room at a sprint in no time and handed Hoola her pocket device asking, "Could I please have your autograph", and giving the word "please" at least three syllables while loading it with incredible beseechment.

"Of course, what's your name sweetheart?" Hoola replied.

"Dandi."

Hoola signed it, "To my friend, Dandi; Hoola; Whirling Vortexes."

Then she shot a selfie with it. After that she said, "Come here Dandi," and put her arm around the girl getting cheek to cheek for a few holos Rubix took with the girl's device. Hoola pulled a platinum ring off her pinkie finger which had her boyfriend's name engraved on the inside, whom she really no longer cared for, not now that she'd met Hark, and Cher, and Bianca; and she placed the ring in the girl's hand telling her, "You can have this because I'm breaking up with him."

Dandi threw her arms around Hoola and hugged her, unable to control herself in her excitement, then returned to her angry parents' table with her treasures, truly on top of the world. She texted her friends holding her device in her lap beneath the table throughout the entire parental lecture delivered mostly by her mom, and hadn't really heard a single word of it, but knew precisely the expression to wear to appease them. The holos of her cheek to cheek with superstar Hoola got sent to everyone in her directory without exception and she cashed in with a grocery store holo-tabloid for a scoop on Hoola's breakup. At thirteen Dandi was a clever girl. When Dandi's mom had finally shut up with the lecture, Dandi had run back across the length of the dining room weaving between tables and dodging waiters like a sporting event, to arrive in front of Hoola. She brought the hem of her little dress to her chin revealing a junior pair of Hug-me crotch-less panties. Hoola was impressed. So were a number of diners. This, of course, earned Dandi an even sterner lecture delivered mostly by dad on her return to her table.

Many of the appetizers were bugs, generally breaded or coated in grains and fried. Pez wasn't a big fan of bugs even though she knew they provided a low-fat form of high protein. Most planets had bug farms to support their human populations. You could grow a whole crop in a box so it was spatially very efficient, and with their brief lives, bugs reproduced quickly. They don't eat much either. Earthworm farms were also very popular since they are a good source of protein and needed for soil amendment. Pez ordered a sea scallop appetizer and a pasta in cheese and wine sauce with chunks of grilled gardd and lots of garlic as an entrée. She also ordered a bowl of the potato-leek soup, thinking to save room for desert; since after all, the meals came with salads, breads, and condiments. Cher had single handedly emptied the fresh cilantro condiment bowl herself. Their waiter wrote a book in the air poking grid boxes with his stylus and eventually got everyone's order, including the ones to be brought out to the yacht in the hotel parking structure.

Pippy held her device up for Pez to see and told her, "You are in the news once again."

The holoclip was just ending and all Cher caught was, "…she did all that on her very first jump with us," from the Colonel who'd come in second today.

Pippy informed her, "They said you were made an honorary Devil Dog and that on your first jump you got all four of your targets with missiles, broke the record for kills coming down and time elapsed landing, and near-single handedly took the ground objective. You hold the very highest ratings of anyone in their corps and it seems they love you."

Cher unbuttoned her shirt and pulled it off one shoulder and upper arm to show off her new tattoo. Lai was in awe of it. Pippy told her, "The celebrity of Cher Bulwinkle is expanding through the Royal Galaxy like a supernova while you leave a trail of those in the know who can link all that fame to hope and revolution."

"Only 5700 and some planets to go," Cher said soberly.

Pippy explained, "There are also Ahumdulilah agents distributing code-books and many of your blind contacts are people who travel extensively. Most of Super-Agent Green's contacts are 'mules' with lists of forty or so contacts of their own to now make. You have only one hundred and eight planets to personally visit."

Before Pez left the system she remembered to have Ahhu transfer funds to pay off Minnie's student loans and uniforms.

CHAPTER FIFTEEN

The whirlwind tour of the Whirling Vortexes kept its pace and schedule and sold out at every stop while their new hit single broke two trillion copies sold, constituting the highest sales for a single in the history of the empire. The emperor himself downloaded one and listened to it and he was moved to tap his feet, roll his head back forth, and hum along with the music. The tour would finish with three consecutive nights of concerts on the Monarch planet, capital of the Royal Monarch Intergalactic Empire.

Populations, cultures and strange customs came and went on almost a daily basis and Mel kept them up to date providing a briefing on each one prior the Pez-landings. Like going through a quantum jump, the Pez landings never diminished in excitement, no matter how many you'd already lived through. On Gooshda, in the capital where the band played, which was in the tropics, people only wore hats and shoes, but everyone including infants wore very dark glasses, and direct eye contact between naked eyes was only permitted between married couples *after* a child had been conceived. It is not only a mortal sin otherwise, but highly illegal as well, and punishable by death. Pez had found the glasses to be as bad as wearing a helmet. Electra kept removing hers and Pez had been freaking out that the authorities might try to execute her daughter.

Pex and her companions were seated at a café in Yomani, the capital of the planet Yazz, only hours before their departure to the planet Here-We-Are. No one in her party was drinking stimulant brew since Pez couldn't, and were all having lemmonaide instead. Ahhu/Bianca mentioned, "The Carpax System felt really oppressive."

Ming/Lai complained, "Well they made us wear those great sack-like clothes which dragged on the ground and had hoods with face masks and only tiny slits for the eyes. I could hardly see and kept bumping into things."

Mel was with them in her android body and said, "Sex is illegal outside wedlock there, and married couples make love from separate rooms through a hole in the wall."

Pex stated, "That doesn't surprise me after seeing how sex-negative their culture is."

Trix shared, "On Galash the whole population seemed to have a foot fedish."

Gretle pointed out, "Well remember Penraz where addiction to neuro-virtual sex was so epidemic that their planet's birth rate was in free-fall?"

"Dalalahma was fun," Ahhu contributed. "The women all had male harems."

Mel filled them in, "Dalalahma was matriarchal until it was conquered by the Royal Monarch Empire, and peace had reigned for many thousands of years before that."

"Kilol didn't treat females very well," Ahhu recalled.

"There the males all had many wives and it was a very aggressive society," Ming agreed.

Pez complained, "I wish we'd had more than one day on Dijori. The morning dew was psychoactive when in contact with the skin and put me right into the highest state of contemplation."

Mel pointed out, "For most of the population, not being meditators, that dew induces psychedelic hallucinations."

"It wasn't always like that," Pez informed them. "Before they got 'liberated' into the empire, as imperials call it, the entire population of Dijori was shamanistic and everyone entered the state of contemplation from the dew."

"Yuranus was kind of creepy," Ahhu said, "where the greeting custom required sniffing each others butt cracks."

"At least they wore clothes on that planet," Rubix stated.

"And they practiced meticulous hygiene," Trix added.

"Using a toilet there," Ming told them, "was a bit of a shock the first time. They call them 'smart toilets'."

Pez shared, "I'm thinking of getting one of those installed in my yacht."

Orb was a bit challenging," Trix noted. "It was an entire world of concrete thinkers unable to cope with abstractions."

Rubix opined, "All the whining, sniveling and tantrums were a bit much."

Mel explained, "They found that their mindless repetitive jobs—which is most of them there—got handled most productively by people of low intelligence, and so they practice withholding oxygen at birth to lower IQ as kind of job preparation."

"I think they're overdoing it," Pez said. "Frustration tolerance seemed to run low while tempers ran high."

Ming checked the time in Yomani on her pocket device and told them, "We ought to head back to *Aphrodite* pretty soon and get underway."

Pez contacted their greeter-liaison and arranged to get picked up. It was a quarter hour drive from the café to the hotel hanger. Once they arrived the band members and *Sidekick* crew were already boarding their ships.

Their little caravan of *Aphrodite*, *Sidekick*, *Spaceship* and Ahhu's drone had just jumped into the 'Here-We-Are' system, where they'd named their moon 'There-It-Is'. The Here-We-Are basic language was at times perplexing, and even Mel's interpreter service device seemed to have a little slippage here and there when it came to meaning. This world had been incorporated into the empire, 'liberated' into it as they say, less than one hundred years ago and was a pre-interstellar travelling world with only radio and electronic communications, still employing a great deal of nuclear fission with uranium. They also burned a great deal of fossil fuels, going through them like there was no tomorrow. They were only now in what was called "the crisis" so there really might not be a tomorrow for them.

A great deal of trash and satellites surrounded Here-We-Are but there was no space traffic to speak of, and the planet had no space control agency. This planet had no capital per se, but instead had 240 of them. The Empire had established eight main bases on the surface within the wealthiest and most strategically located cities. They had turned most of the population into factory workers after retooling all of the factories to manufacture war-machines, weapons and munitions. Their enslaved workforce knew how to operate the assembly lines but were completely ignorant of the technology behind them. All weapons of mass destruction on Here-We-Are, and there were many indeed—enough to wipe out its biosphere forever about 60 times over—were now under the thumb and tightly controlled by the empire.

A number of Here-We-Are ruling families of the nations that had had the most military might before the empire showed up, had become imperial liaisons, and were allowed to keep their 60 billion monetary units, or whatever it was they'd stolen and exploited out of their fellow humans, by loyaly serving the empire to betray the people of their own planet. Only a few were allowed to, even though all the billionaire families wanted to become imperial liaisons really badly. The wealth of the ones not selected was confiscated to the last and those families were turned into the streets with no jewelry and just their underclothes. Sixty billion Here-We-Are monetary units was pocket change to the Emperor.

In spite of the daily executions and public torture, the people of Here-We-Are exhibited the revolutionary spirit and resistance on this world was higher than about anywhere else. They had designed a large caliber eight-barrel gatling gun with propulsion guided armor piercing rounds they could cut people in half with from two miles away, and miniaturized super-condensed plastic explosives they were employing in numerous daily terrorist acts against the empire. Literally, shit was blowing up daily in every major city on the planet. It was sort of like a war zone. But they loved the Whirling Vortexes and had sold out their largest sporting arena for the concert, where they always had their war-ball final playoffs. They didn't have vortex-redirect-generators, so of course, they didn't have hover-board ball. War-ball commentators on Here-We-Are used exclusively combat terms and analogies in describing the plays.

Pez missed a telecom satellite by inches as the planet raced towards them growing from a small reflective globe to fill their windshield horizon to horizon. She was on the brakes reversing main drives, firing reverse mini-drives and thrusters, and hitting her flaps as they entered the atmosphere. The nose of the yacht glowed red with friction. At 10,500 feet Pez threw on the vortex-redirect to maximum, fired a reverse booster, and then brought the nose up to fire a landing booster half a second before the landing gear engaged the ground. She'd squeezed in between a large recreational camping vehicle and a freight transporting vehicle, both with rubber wheels, within an expansive outdoors asphalt parking lot for vehicles that can't leave the ground.

Their ramp came down into the exit lane of the parking lot, where at least a thousand little ground vehicles sat shutdown and huddled together. It seemed a strange place to Pez but Ahhu was all excited about it. They didn't have to worry about local laws here since imperial ruling families were all above and outside of them. They would not have a greeter-liaison from the hotel here, called simply the Bettytown Hotel, being in central Bettytown. They carried their own bags even though the eight slaves from *Sidekick* tried hard to take them from them. Here they actually had to stand in front of a counter to check-in, and then required a physical object to get their penthouse and suite doors open. It was a magnetic strip on a plastic card, easy to lose, and quite awkward to use.

The elevators had no partitions and the Here-We-Are folks seemed to think it just fine to squeeze eleven people in all pressed up against each other. Great big vacuum tubes taking up enormous space conveyed their optics media. Auditory recordings were all analog here. To turn on a light you had to use your hands. Even Mel couldn't get past that manual switch in the wall which broke the current. Computers here were extremely primitive with processing memory measured in the megabits, and could do nothing more than remember and calculate; and there was no correspondence between them to speak of, with the exception of some government linked computers. The imperials here had quantum computers networked together and in quantum link with Monarch's central computers, but there were less than 100,000 imperials on the planet. The Emperor had initially wanted eight ruling families here, but only three lessor ones were willing to settle on Here-We-Are, so that's what Here-We-Are ended up with. All three lesser families were peopled with greedy ambitious control freaks and none surpassed average intelligence. Not a one of them had any latent talent nor cultivated any skills to speak of. Needless to say, bureaucracy here was inefficient, poorly organized, never quite on top of things, and *really* tedious to deal with.

Pez would send Pooh to the Vanderbat party she'd received an invitation to because she really didn't want to go to that, but the Vanderbats were one of the three ruling families here, and she didn't want to offend them either. Besides, Pooh really needed off of that yacht and away from Lucky. Having Lucky as a roommate felt like a totally unlucky thing to Pooh. Pez had contacts to make at the concert and planned to go incognito. The orange dye was permanent so Pez planned to cut her hair real short and wear a wig.

Super-Agent Green had numerous contacts to make, spread all over the city, and was taking the hover-bike off the yacht. It had a fast drive that would allow her to fly over all the stopped honking traffic stuck on the ground. If she'd had to rely on ground transportation here she would never reach even a third of those on her list. Lucky had been pouting, but she'd talked him into helping her get the hoverbike down. He was getting really close to finishing the tourist version of Royal Basic with a passing grade now that the band's tour was coming to an end. His determination and iron will to extract himself from his solitary confinement in yacht prison had apparently improved his concentration on his language studies.

Elanem was doing well enough to be going out and making some of the contacts herself. Winston was now allowed to leave the hotels on his own for passive Intel gathering *only*. Marlboro was yet restricted to the hotel but was making progress. Super-Agent Green got the hover-bike started and Pooh climbed on the back wearing a hooded cape to get her arms around Green's waist. The bike lifted off nicely shooting right up to land on the roof of the hotel, on the penthouse patio, and Pooh hopped off keeping her face shrouded to slip inside. Green took off across town descending to twenty feet off the ground at an easy150 mph. Traffic on the ground was either stopped completely or moving at a pace Green could keep up with walking.

Elanem was down in that traffic having just rented a little economy model, the cheapest available, called a Trump. She was already beginning to have her doubts. She'd read up on these things and was now thinking she'd taken the crappy Trump mistaking it for a Triumph. She recalled from the literature, now that she'd clarified her confusion, that the Trump was considered erratic, temperamental, high maintenance and in constant need of tuning. They were #1 for antitheft devices and so much so that it made the car seem kind of paranoid, especially since it was the least desired vehicle on the market. It was a heavy vehicle and quite a gas guzzler, rated by consumer affairs exceedingly low on all performance measures. She decided she would keep her eye out for another Siva Car Rental place and trade the Trump in as soon as she could. As it coughed and sputtered Elanem thought, *Yes, I'd best get an upgrade. This is truly a piece of shit.*

Pez had orange hair all over the bathroom floor and the hair on her head cut down to about 2 inches long. She arranged a very bright blue wig on her scalp and got it just right before initiating 'cohesion' through her skullcap. In cohesion mode the wig was as secure as the scalp on her head since to remove it in that mode one would need to remove both. Pooh and Trix were going to the Vanderbat's as Cher and Kat. Lai and Hark would be joining them and Johnson would lead the five crewman of *Sidekick* as Pooh/Cher's bodyguard escorts. Pez was only bringing Evenrude with her this evening. The aunts were staying in the hotel and Cousin Winnie was going to the concert with Bianca, Muffet, Pippy and Alice.

The cars on the street in front of the hotel were stopped bumper to bumper in both directions as far as the eye could see. Pez and Evenrude walked to the Bettytown Warball Arena, which was only four blocks from their hotel, passing the stuck cars as they went.

"They call that ground transportation?" Evenrude asked, jutting his chin at the jammed traffic seemingly going nowhere.

"I know what a mess," Pez agreed.

"How are we getting in, since you're not playing a ruling family member tonight?" Evenrude inquired, hoping she had a plan.

"Pogo gave me two tickets for front-row seats," she replied, "and I brought lots of dags."

"Don't they check identification at the door?" Evenrude asked.

"They use actual physical cards and pass books here and don't require them for concerts, though they do for nightclubs, bars, travel between cities, and all official government functions," Pez answered.

The line to get in wasn't very long and was moving practically at a walk. When they arrived at the front Pez handed her two tickets to the uniformed official and then passed right through with Evenrude. The walls of the tunnel corridors to the various sections of the sporting facility were covered in vendor slots with feeds to inject dag bills so they could regurgitate their contents to the consumer. The food looked well enough preserved to easily survive between war-ball seasons. It was a rare thing when the sight of food did not make Pez hungry. Showtime was approaching so most of the people in the arena were seated already, leaving the corridors fairly clear, and Pez led Evenrude at a fast walk for his long legs having to jog herself to set that pace.

The band members were just taking the stage when Pez's and Evenrude's bottoms touched their seats in the very first row. Still, the band was a long way off on a great round slow turning disc in the center of a 100-yard field, with more yardage around its edges. Pez got out her special glasses integrated with her skullcap and increased magnification on their telescopic feature to make it seem like the Whirling Vortexes were almost right in front of her. Evenrude was doing the same with his contact lenses. Pez couldn't tolerate contacts so she always carried her nerdy looking special glasses with her. It didn't bother Evenrude. Not at all compared to the primary colors he had to wear. The same thought occurred simultaneously to each of them, *Back on Om we would look like a real pair of losers.*

Pogo said from behind his keyboards, "Welcome to the Whirling Vortexes Bettytown, Here We Are Concert. You are going to hear our biggest hits along with some new pieces, so far only available live on our tour. We're going to start with one of our latest creations called

'Technology is not Evolution.' We hope you enjoy it and that you like the show."

Frisbie began pounding out a rhythm as long notes emanated from the keyboards. Hoola added a guitar riff and the saxophone started wailing out an intricate pattern as the other guitar joined in. The music was packed with energy and so were the band members. Whiffle and Hoola were each in the flow-state with their music calling the other band members to a higher organization with greater range of freedom, yet somehow more connected within the integrity of the whole. Improvisation emerged spontaneously as the expression of motion, rest and harmony in perfect equilibrium, or as objective vibrations matching the divine pattern. The lyrics chipped away at the delusion that advancement in technology is the premier indication of evolution while revealing unity and love between humans as the actual one and only gauge. The song as a whole had been very thinly veiled by the half-hearted suggestion that we all work together for the empire, though any thoughtful consideration of the ideas the song suggested dissolved the veil like morning mist beneath the sun, contradicting completely the veil of illusion. It was certainly clever, if not a bit risky.

Mel had inserted herself into the owner's box in her android body as a senior Adherence Examiner, in the company of the local Imperial Adherence Examiners and the family who owned the arena, the Kochoo's. She was milking the song's thin veil and distracting the other examiners from the actual ideas conveyed and evoked by the meanings of the words the band sang. Ideas such as pure love beyond self-interest were too alien to the imperial examiners so that Mel found her task easy to accomplish. No taint of resistance was detected in the band by the imperial inquisitors. Not only that, but Mel was really having the time of her life.

To the Here-We-Are audience the thin veil of working together for the empire was like placing a transparent monster mask on a beautiful woman's face and they all saw right through it. The new sound the band brought to the music industry, their fantastic skill with their instruments, synergistic creativity, and glamor-holo beauty—although most people saw Whiffle as too painfully thin—all came together as a phenomenal force of uplifting energetic glee with meaning. Pez was aware that the band often blended the objective tonal vibrational sequences for both the arousal of lustful excitement and of serene rapture. She knew they did this intuitively since none of the band members had studied the very ancient origins of vibrational harmonies and music.

Pogo, Frisbie and Tramp were all on the cusp of the first awakening through the art of their music, Pez was certain, and she meant to bring this about before the tour was over; which didn't leave her much time at this point. The fans were going wild and loving the music and the band. Hoola's hug-me's ad holos were all over Bettytown displayed in flat two-dimensional images on what they called "billboards". As hug-me's model and lead singer and guitarist for the Whirling Vortexes, Hoola was emerging as the biggest superstar celebrity in the three galaxies of the empire.

Pez's facial recognition scanner had covered the entire stadium by the time the band took its break from playing its first set. The people in the boxes could not be read by her scanner, but she'd found all her contacts in regular seats and had their locations and seat numbers saved. One was close and she got her tracker on him, rising from her seat to follow him. She was attempting to catch up to him, though the crowd in the walkways between seats was further separating her at this point as it grew denser.

They did not have alko here and instead sold real alcohol which killed brain cells and pickled internal organs. It seemed everyone on Here-We-Are was running for some now. In their language they called it "this-is-it". Pez noticed Gretle, as Muffet, hitting on a shapely girl with a beautiful androgynous face and boy's haircut. Though she only saw in passing, it appeared the graduate student was putting the moves on smoothly and that the younger girl was going for it.

Pez was finally closing in on her contact only because he'd gotten on an unmoving this-is-it line to stand in a tight packed queue. They were packed tighter than they got squeezed into elevators here. Pez concentrated, generating her psychic shield with her attention, preparing herself for loss of personal-space as she moved in to bump her contact. With an arch of her lower back she struck with her bottom into the butt of a large obese man too close in front of her contact for her to squeeze in. He was shoved over opening the space and Pez stepped in apologizing while deliberately seeming to accidently bump chests with her contact. She whispered to him, "Rudder", and his eyes went wide as he gave a slight nod. Pez disappeared into the crowd.

She located another of her contacts who was in his concert seat, so she shuffled sideways down his seat aisle and fell chest to chest on him when she was scooting by his seat. She whispered, "Jib", and he said surprised, "Got it!" The jolt awoke Electra in her pouch on Pez's back. The sensor read dry and clean on the diaper. She reached behind her shoulders catching Electra with her hands under her baby's armpits, and lifted her over her head, bringing her into a nursing position and already passing her energy. She kind of half-whispered and half-sang the lullaby. Fortunately she was wearing a planet Glitter nursing blouse with only a lift-able drape of material over her breast, which she moved out of the way for Electra. Her daughter almost wailed over the inhibited lullaby but was too attracted to sucking to be bothered doing it. Pez soothed her to calmness then resumed her sideways shuffle to get out of the aisle.

Pez could not make any more blind contacts while Electra was on her breast so she went to the private booth of the one contact she was to have a conversation with this evening. He was a scientist and a professor now in the role of President of the most prestigious college here on Here-We-Are. The Ahumdulilah agent who'd set up this meeting had recently fallen prey to the mechanical malfunction of a lunar vehicle while visiting There-it-is. Such malfunctions were statistical anomalies and Pez had been trained to reject coincidence in this business by Major Nicon and his team. Evenrude was lingering only paces from the door to the booth, blending as best as he could in his primaries.

Pez wore her nerdy glasses and entered the booth still nursing Electra. The glasses highlighted sensor mics and lenses all over the booth. With her skullcap she self-destructed her nano-coms device and heat blossomed on her chest. She texted Mel with her skullcap asking her to see what she could do about the sensors in this booth. An immediate reply read, "It's a trap. GET OUT!"

Pez said to university president Ben Arnold, "How much are they paying you?"

"They have my wife and daughter," he confessed, looking ashamed.

Pez moved into high gear getting Electra into her pouch and exiting the booth at speed, and Evenrude was already pointing and moving in the direction opposite the oncoming squad of Imperial Secret Police. You could always spot them from miles away in any environment. It was the black slick naugahide double breasted wide-lapelled spy cloaks with military epaulets that gave them away. That, and the little goose-step they put in their strides. The Imperial Secret Police were hand-picked from military ranks for their remarkable adherence and zealous dedication to the Royal Monarch Empire. Each and every one of them was perfectly willing to kill for the empire.

Pez kept her legs pumping evenly in a blur with her torso remaining a stable platform for Electra. She ran behind Evenrude who couldn't help but clear a wider path than she required. She saw his elbow unintentionally bump a forearm holding a vending slot pastry, which shot hard and fast into the face of the body that it was attached to. A commotion of fright and shock announced itself in shouts and screams running just ahead of Evenrude as the way cleared before him. A large man tried to resist the Space Marine by defiantly standing in his way and Pez tried not to step on him going over; Evenrude hadn't slowed. The two ran towards the stadium exit.

Moving further from the seating areas of the stadium they came to an intersection of two tunnels at right angles to each other. As they crossed the intersection they could see more Secret Police coming down the tunnels on each side of them and there was a squad up ahead. Pez turned on Electra's pouch's micro-shields. Evenrude turned on his micro-shield fanny pack. Pez didn't have one. Her dress was lined underneath with textile armor but it still left a lot of her to target. One man in the squad ahead yelled, "Halt", as they approached at full sprint ignoring him.

The two in front had heavy transparent armored plexiglass shields and held them out front, bracing for impact. They wouldn't have fared much better with a speeding mag-lev train engine. The two shields were still skidding on the floor out front and the whole squad was down. Pez stooped, keeping her spine erect, quite fluidly for Electra's sake, and snatched an imperial hand blaster in each palm adjusting her grip to get her forefingers on the triggers as she kept running. An exit lay ahead. It was not the one they'd come in by but it would do. Imperial Secret Police were congregating in front of it. Two were setting up a heavy tripod blaster. Evenrude's fanny pack shields could stop ordinary small arms fire, but not heavy tripod fire; nor could Electra's. Pez already had both arms extended and fingers pulling triggers. The two setting up the heavy blaster were the first two she put down as they closed on the exit.

Evenrude had two yet in the air and Pez was still shooting as they left the arena complex into some kind of shopping arcade. They hadn't slowed, nor had they left a single congregating Secret Police person standing. Someone was shooting at them up ahead and Evenrude shifted to block Pez completely and take the hits. Recognizing his blaster could not deter the oncoming mass, the shooter turned and fled. Evenrude flattened him without sacrificing speed as he overtook him. Pez was unable to avoid stepping on him. Mel's voice came into Pez's ear telling her, "Go into Gates' fast food and hotdog stand all the way to the back of the kitchen and you'll find a fire exit out of the arcade. You'll be met out in the alley."

Mel had made this transmission to Evenrude as well, who was already turning into Gates' gate. He'd heard that their milkshakes were only one molecule off from being styrofoam. They ran through the public area together amidst the shrieking customers; over the ordering counter, each in a single bound; then back through the kitchen to shrieks from staff. Pez nailed the security sensor over the fire exit the moment it came into view. She hit the alarm panel beside the door next with several shots frying it to a crisp. Evenrude poured on speed and hit the fire door foot-first. He wasn't wearing his boots with the bounce soles either and the locking bolt broke away along with one hinge, leaving the door across the way at a twisted angle hanging by its top hinge. Another kick cleared the way, though the door still clung to the frame by its one hinge. Here they were a story up from the street. Rather than engage the ladder Evenrude jumped, and Pez followed, each landing in a crouch on the narrow street. An imperial hover craft was dropping in what looked like it might be a crash. Mel told them both, "That's your ride."

The craft strained its landing gear on impact, and the door flew open. Super-Agent Green called pleasantly, "Get in."

They did and Pez asked her, "Where did you get this?"

"I stole it when Mel told me you needed a ride," Green replied calmly.

She was already at maximum acceleration hanging a corner at quite an angle and engaging both flashing lights and sirens. They couldn't have appeared more official being in an Imperial Secret Police Interceptor ground hover craft. These were the fastest of all. Pez asked with concern. "Won't this one get reported stolen?"

"Dead men tell no tales," Green said cryptically.

Green's driving skills were surprising. Pez was liking Green more as she got to know her. Pez stated, "It's probably not a good idea to park at the hotel."

"I'm not parking it anywhere," Green informed her. "Jump out onto your penthouse patio when I get over it and I'll dump this in the lake after ejecting my seat."

Slowing abruptly Green came to a near hover-stop about ten feet over the patio and Evenrude and Pez bailed. While they were in mid-air Green fired a booster and was gone. They got inside quickly.

Mel informed them, "I was able to delete and patch the partial images captured of your faces inside the arena. I got the worst of them from inside the arcade, but a little of that data was retrieved before I'd finished. Cher Bulwinkle and her spouse, Kat, are still at the Vanderbat party. There are no sensors in the penthouse, though until Pooh is back in the yacht, you don't exist."

"Thanks Mel. We'll lock those silly little chain deadbolts so no hotel staff wander into the penthouse," Pez replied.

Pez set her blue wig to release mode and removed it, exposing her 2-inch bright orange hair. She really didn't like the color and thought it made her look like a clown. As with everything else, Ming looked better in it, and wore it best. She pinged Marlboro and asked him to come see her. He arrived knocking the same moment she arrived to open it. She had to remove that silly chain first. Marlboro came in as she got the door open and she told him closing it, "I need for you to take this wig to the hotel garbage incinerator or furnace for hot water and heat, and stand by to confirm its incineration, then report back to me in person. Maintain coms silence."

"Yes Ma'am," Marlboro agreed, eager to prove himself.

"Wait," Pez told him as she slipped out of her pouch pack and then her dress, wearing nothing but her hug-me's. She handed him the dress telling him, "Be sure there is nothing left of this either."

"Right away," he chirped, already slipped out the door with wig and dress concealed under his armpit beneath his cape.

Pez repositioned the chain seeing it as nothing more than a message to hotel staff not to enter. She said to Mel, "Please send Marlboro the hotel schematics and highlight incinerators and furnaces."

"I have to convert two-dimensional blueprints so give me a second," Mel replied. "There, he's got them."

"Thanks Mel."

"I have to go," Mel informed her. "The band is doing another set and I have to distract the other Adherence Examiners from the real meaning of the lyrics."

Evenrude checked in with Johnson and was informed that everything was going smoothly at the Vanderbat party and that Pooh was doing a fabulous job playing Cher. Trix's role as Kat cinched it and Pez herself would believe she was looking at Cher Bulwinkle in the flesh.

They would be on Here-We-Are for two more days before jumping to Monarch for the tour's conclusion, and they had invitations to parties at the Kochoo's tomorrow night, and the Waltonraptor's the next. The Vanderbat's would be attending both. Pez had contacts to make at the Waltonraptor's party. The Waltonraptors were known for working their slaves to death in less than ten years and for paying their laborers so little that many of them starved to death. Rumor had it the Waltonraptors liked to eat endangered species for dinner.

The Kochoo's were known crooks and pathological control freaks, full of themselves and empty of any conscience or decency. The family was predatory and feral from humanity, having defiled their souls utterly; FUBAR as the Devil Dogs would say, meaning 'fucked up beyond all repair'. They owned the most politicians on Here-We-Are out of the three ruling families on it, and had some politicians on Monarch in their portfolio as well.

Pooh's performance was all anyone spoke of when her companions returned from the party and Pez wondered if she needed acting lessons to better play Cher. When Trix went on about Pooh's great kissing, Pez asked Ming discretely, "Does kissing me suck?"

"Of course not my love!" Ming insisted.

"Do you think I need acting lessons?" Pez inquired.

"For what?" Ming asked perplexed.

"To better play Cher," Pez explained.

"Sweetheart, Cher is a fiction created to be you, so just be yourself."

"Well how come Pooh is better at being me than I am?" Pez wanted to know.

"She's not darling; she's only just as good," Ming assured her.

Pez wasn't so sure.

The news was all focused on the big terrorist attack at the warball arena and the big giant in primary colors with the blue haired female terrorist. Through the partial images and police artists, composites of the terrorist's faces were produced and displayed globally on the coms network. The faces of the wanted terrorists looked nothing like Pez and Evenrude. Electra's pouch had not been captured in a single image and two eye witnesses from Gates' fast food and hot dog stand insisted the thing on the female terrorist's back was a bomb or fuel tank. Evenrude went from dressing in blues and greens with red trim, to violet and reds with green and yellow trim. A planet-wide man hunt was on, although the Here-We-Are police secretly admired the terrorists and made no real effort in finding them, while Imperial Secret Police went all out hauling in suspects, conducting high-pressure interrogations, collecting data from every sensor and camera in a ten-mile radius, and even brought out sniffing dogs, marine aquatic equipment they'd never had cause to use before, and self-proclaimed psychic investigators.

Mel in her android body had inserted herself deeply into the Imperial Adherence Examiners ranks here on Here-We-Are. She outranked the locals and had managed to forge some specific orders from her deceased Imperial Admiral and date-stamped them within the Monarch central computer system a month before the admiral kicked the bucket. The Adherence Examiners even examined the Imperial Secret Police for adherence, and since it was all subjective and mostly a witch-hunt anyway, with no actual objective criteria, this gave the AE's, as they were called, great power and influence over the Secret Police. In fact, the AE's were universally considered the creepiest, spookiest, and most frightening agency in the entire empire. Mel was pretty much running it now on Her-We-Are. The AE's new mission priority was to purge the Imperial Secret Police force on the planet of its radicals and dissenters. They didn't need to actually have any for the AE's to find them.

Pez inquired, "What have you been up to Mel?"

"I've infiltrated and taken over the Imperial Adherence Examiners satellite office here and we're sniffing out potential revolutionaries. Tomorrow were interrogating all the children in 1st form at the primary schools in Bettytown. We try to catch them young."

"Mel," Pez complained, "we seem to be working at cross purposes."

"I've redirected our primary focus onto the Secret Police and I expect dozens to be apprehended within the next 24 hours."

"Are there Imperial Secret Police siding with us," Pez asked surprised.

"Not a one; but the AE's have never failed to find perpetrators in every investigation they've ever been involved with, and this will be no different," Mel explained.

"I see," Pez acknowledged. "Please don't let them hurt any first formers tomorrow, Mel. They're only six-year-olds."

"I'm afraid it's inevitable that some will be rooted out and placed into indoctrination programs. It's just out of my control," Mel lamented.

"Well try to mitigate it as best you can," Pez suggested.

Mel told her, "Yes; I'll divert more personnel from the first-form interrogations to the Secret Police problem I've invented."

Sarhi and Shudiy came to the door and had to be manually let in, silly chain and all. The band members were with the Im. Sarhi explained to Pez, "We have three people here ready to pop and bust out of mind structure into void. I brought entheogen brew made from psychoactive mushrooms for a ceremony. As their teacher you will have to help and support each of them. Shudiy and I will support you."

"I was already going to meditate with them tonight," Pez said almost defensively.

"You still are," Sarhi replied, "with the pressure turned up by a few enhancements."

Pogo, Tramp and Frisbie all sat close to Cher/Pez. They made a sitting and absorption practice for an hour before Sarhi poured a dose of the brew for each person there. Sarhi had Pez initiate the three band members and transmit the Islohar six-syllable sacred sound formula, which the group then repeated as a chant for half an hour. The first tingles of the medicine could be felt and light intensified as Pez led them step by step in a meditation clarifying the three minds of the Enlightened One, and culminating in contemplation of transcendental consciousness in its purity as Absolute Emptiness. She sensed Frisbie dwelling in non-identity, very close to shattering illusion, and took on his trauma of feeling dominated and abused by his mother, processing it and transforming it from baggage into pacified wisdom. When she passed her blessing into him he broke free in that instant.

His awakening produced a wave of presence and awareness, adding to the force of awareness generated by Pez and the two senior Islohar. Pogo's schematization was fracturing already, and the wave expanded a crack, making it a portal into another dimension. His sense of being controlled as a child by his father, now projected onto about anything restricting his independence, was being consumed by Cher, the emotional charge neutralized, the distorted beliefs surgically removed and disposed of, and corresponding physical tensions relaxed and resolved. His tower of babbling mind structure crumbled and fell, and he was in freefall amidst the blessings Cher passed him. His awakening produced yet another wave of presence and awareness.

Pez transferred merit to Tramp while passing her internal energy. Taking on Tramp's alienation and short-person psychic wounds, which were fairly close to some of Pez's own core issues, gave her some pain and challenge though she managed it. Tramp popped right out of her shell with the blessing Cher passed her and awoke for her first time recognizing that consciousness is the entire game of life. The sacred elixir energized and amplified the state of contemplation incredibly. About six hours after drinking the brew its effects were just lingering traces, and Pez rang the gong. It was morning now in Bettytown and they would all need some sleep. The band had a concert to perform this evening and Pez and her companions had a ruling family party to attend at the Kochoo's.

CHAPTER SIXTEEN

That night Pez had worn a pink wig and dark glasses to go with the band to the concert and let Pooh deal with the cukoo Kochoos and their slimy greed. It was the band's best performance ever and had only been recorded physically by the Here-We-Are folks on something they called 35mm film and analog vinal discs; no cyber-digitals at all. Pez had danced on stage wearing her dark glasses and wig, and Electra was spun upside down in her pouch, twirled in ongoing 360's, and shaken all about; attached to her momma's back. In an interview after the concert the band members claimed not to know who the pink haired dancer who'd been on stage with them was, and a frantic talent hunt was on for her.

This next evening Pez was dressing for the Waltonraptor party and couldn't think of a thing to do about her 2-inch bright orange hair. She chose a blue dress which showed off her hug-me's. The dress had a strip of material, about four inches wide at each hip trailing down to a sharp point on the outside of each thigh, ending at the knee. It had a four-inch band of translucent fabric across her breasts she could lift out of the way or just peel off and reattach later, making nursing a breeze. Ming put on a turquoise body suit which was just a few straps on top, and balloon pants at the bottom. They both wore adjustable stiletto high heels at 6 inches and both attached their babies' pouches to their backs. Ming kept her hand-device in a pocket on Gumby's. Pez brought her mini-device and mounted a cohesion strip to the hip-flap of her dress to attach it to. Trix/Kat carried her great big hand device in her hand. She was never without it. She wore a tight dark blue t-shirt, a plastic transparent skirt, and dark blue hug-me's and socks.

Bianca had on orange shoes and wore an orange cape down her back, clasped at her throat. She carried an orange purse with their dag bills and financial beads, as well as her own mini-device, since it was such a small purse. Gretle as Muffet, wore a white collar with red bowtie and a white silk dinner jacket with a brilliant multicolor floral design printed on loudly. She had a white hat, white gloves, and white shoes. She also wore white lacey socks but was otherwise bottomless.

Cousin Winnie wore pink hug-me's, pink stars over her nipples, and a little pink vest not wide enough to close. She also wore pink shoes with stiletto heels like Ming's and a pink plastic tiara, like a birthday girl's, only hers had an enormous black pearl set in the center. Pippy and Alice would be attending the party naked as they always did. The aunts weren't coming. Rubix had on a gold metallic skin-tight synthetic jump suite with a real gold zipper down the front, and some cheap high-top sneakers he'd spray painted metallic gold.

Pez had let Lucky off the yacht and out of the old mute man cover into a new identity of a 29-year-old friend of the Bulwinkles named Dym, with liberty to roam the hotel but not to leave it. Lucky actually was 29 years old and he was feeling lucky. After months alone stuck on the yacht, Lucky used the phone in his hotel, once he figured out it responded to neither cyber nor voice commands and had to be manually operated by hand, to hire an outcall sex-worker. He was supposed to throw money around, Pez had told him, for appearances sake and to maintain their covers, so he'd found the very most expensive agency, calling each one before making up his mind. To see pictures of the girls he'd have to actually go down there and he couldn't leave the hotel, so he'd given the best descriptions he could of his ultimate fantasy woman. Lucky also ordered room service. The amateur nonsense on the big tube thing wasn't worth the time of day, and was mostly yacking about how you just can't be happy, or alright, or smell good, or have the right smile, or something, if you didn't run out and purchase some product or other right now. He knew damn well that for enough dags any smile could be the right smile in this empire. On Om he was the height of the shortest girls; but here he was one of the taller males. *I need this*, Lucky told himself.

Pez drove the yacht to the Waltonraptor's Mansion because it would have taken hours otherwise in Here-we-are's pathetic ground transportation always stopped or barely moving. She had to land half on the lawn and with a lone shut down and abandoned stretched long car, shiny black, directly under her. The compression of the hydraulics unfortunately left it a ten-inch slab. She'd have to find out whoese it was and buy them a new one, as well as pay to have the old one hauled to a recycle center. Even the engine block was reduced to some part of the ten-inch high slab. It was not a mechanical problem and could only be fixed at the molecular level now.

They all poured out of the yacht down the ramp staring at the metal slab beneath their craft while pulling up holos of it as it was before they'd landed on it, for comparison on their hand devices. Pez felt a bit self-conscious and explained herself, "Well it was either that or the fountain."

It was a perfect landing, my love," Ming assured her, "and I think you did clip one end of the fountain on our dip."

Rubix, as Hark, got arm in arm with Lai; and Kat, with her thick glasses and oversized hand device got on Cher's arm to enter the party. They saw the Vanderbats there and greeted them. The Kochoo's were there too and Cher avoided them, having no clue as to what conversations Pooh might have had with them. Bianca clung to Cher's other side and the three women explored the party. A waiter passing with a tray of flutes full of sparkling wine lost one to Bianca as he went by. The main party room had a vaulted ceiling and the room had to be forty meters in each direction. A six foot tall, eight foot diameter crystal chandelier hung over the center of the room. A third of the room at one end was filled with stuffed leather couches, chairs, day lounges and love seats, with end tables and low service tables of rare hardwoods arranged conveniently around them. A low stage with an eight member band were at the other end of the room, and the space between empty for dancing. The room had a polished stone slab floor. The walls exhibited beautifully framed paintings of little imagination and even less skill. Tall windows with heavy velvet drapes ran along one side of the room. The walls were plastered and painted canary yellow. The vaulted ceiling itself was white and textured like popcorn.

They passed into the next room which contained a giant round hardwood table loaded with platters, bowls and trays of culinary delicacies. Bianca and Kat had to wait while Cher scarfed down a bunch of food. One bite she didn't know what it was, didn't like it at all, and was not about to swallow it, so she sought out a napkin to spit it out into. Unfortunately it was a linen napkin. She held it in one hand as she ate in case she ran into anything else disgusting. She didn't trust the bottom-feeding seafood on this planet, not with all the nuclear fission mess. She'd read an article about how they raise poultry here without feathers in tiny little cages they eventually coudn't even turn around in. She knew a small fraction of the poultry raised on Here-We-Are was called 'liberation poultry' and allowed to range about. Liberation poultry were fed seeds grown without herbicides and pesticides in non-contaminated soil, and the birds weren't pumped with hormones and steroids like the caged ones were. She decided to avoid poultry here too, just in case. She found a bowl of fried breaded bugs she really liked, palm fruit, a garbanzo bean and cumin paste, and steamed artichoke hearts with a mayonnaise sauce. There were corn chips and avocado dip too, as well as baked stuffed mushrooms which she liked and ate a bunch of.

Bianca wore survey glasses so she could measure the males with precision. This way she wouldn't have to ask. Most of them lied in her experience. Especially about that. Imperial fashions were the next best thing to total nudity in her mind. She was finally able to move Cher on from the food table with some help from Kat, and they entered into the next room. This one was dimly lit, littered with pillows of all colors, sizes and shapes, and carpeted with a tall, thick tight-woven wool rug over an exceptionally thick jute under-carpet. Bodies reclined here and there about the floor. Some were minions or family members of the rulers and the rest slaves. It seemed there was always a room such as this at ruling family parties. Cher moved them on. Bianca had been measuring.

The next room was a better lit lounge and had a hardwood bar counter with a mirror and shelves of alcohol bottles on the wall behind it, as well as a fan vented smoking area with an interesting piece of furniture covered with bins of smokables, and finally a corner with a chemical entertainment pharmacy center. Bianca traded in her empty flute for a full one at the bar, popped an empathogen pill at the pharmacy center, and grabbed a few pre-rolled cannabis sativa hybrid joints from a smokables bin at the smoking area. Kat told her with an edge of disapproval, "Cher can't, you know," meaning she could not use any drugs while nursing Electra, not even the stimulant brew she loved so much.

"I'm not nursing Electra," Bianca stated, as if giving reply to the irrational.

They only passed through that room into the virtual chair room. Sex androids were lined against one wall. The chairs had blackout curtains around them hanging from tracks in the ceiling like cheap hospital beds. The chairs in front of the parked androids were simply on display. They passed through this room without pause. Bianca measured the male androids against the wall with her glasses. Next, they found themselves in a steamy echoing stone chamber, done all in white marble, with a party-size hot-tub glistening with jacuzi jets, and an intergalactic standard sports-sized heated swimming pool. It had a high dome ceiling, also marble, and eight mammoth black granite pillars supporting the done. It was warm and humid within. High shrieks from some naked teenage girls getting splashed by teenage boys filled the chamber. The professional survey glasses could not compensate for the water distortion to measure the boys in the pool, much to Bianca's dissatisfaction.

Cher got her daughter and pouch off her back for Kat to hold, since Kat didn't like getting in any water but the bath; and stripped out of her clothes. The pool had both a low diving board and a high one. Cher went up the ladder to the high one. Without walking to the end of the board first to test the bounce, she broad jumped from the top of the ladder to the end of the board, to know its spring and dive accordingly. She curled for a summersault then unfolded straightening to shoot head first into the water swimming the length of the pool under it. Cher popped her head up reaching the other side. Then she proceeded to swim laps as if in a race.

Bianca sat on the edge with her legs in the water at the shallow end near the teenagers and got a strike-anywhere Here-We-Are match out of her pocket in her cape to light a joint. Kat and Electra watched Cher swim. One of the teen boys asked pointing at Cher, "Is she in the Intergalactics?"

"That's Cher Bulwinkle," Bianca told them, "and she's great at every sport. The elite Special Forces on Condral, called the Devil Dogs, took her skydiving with textile clothing wings and no parachute, and Cher broke some of their records on her first jump. They made her an honorary Devil Dog."

"I've seen some of her landings on the news," the boy told her. "Hey can I have some of that?"

Bianca passed him the joint when he waded over waist deep. The glasses sized him up at seven inches disappointing Bianca. It was too bad since he had such a pretty one. The other teens waded over for a hit on the joint. Bianca lit a second joint then passed it on, getting resolution on each of the other two boys. One was 7 ½ inches; too big, and the other, pretty much 6 ½ inches exact; a fit! She didn't find the guy wearing it very appealing though. One of the girls was certainly cute, now drawing Bianca's full attention having ruled out the boys.

Electra decided she'd given her momma enough of a swimming break and now she wanted her back. Kat called to Pez at the first manifestation of fussing and Pez came back right away from the middle of a speed lap, and was in fact climbing out when Electra became impatient and began sucking wind for a big wail. Kat scrunched up her face and covered her ears. Pez flew from the pool recognizing the sound of this particular inhalation of Electra's and was passing her energy, singing, and lifting her to her breast just as Electra went off. *What a fine volume*, Cher told herself, trying to remain calm. She could stay calm in combat, but there was just something about her own child's screaming which simply set her nerves on edge. Electra calmed quickly and latched onto Cher's nipple. Pez sat at the side of the pool nursing her daughter. Electra peaked through her eyelids to check that momma was paying close attention to her, and she was; so everything was good.

Electra fell asleep quickly after nursing. Cher got her burped and into her pouch, then attached it to Kat's back and told her, "I have some contacts to make here tonight and Electra will sleep for hours now. Do you mind?"

"Of course not; I want to help," Kat insisted.

On her little tour of the party so far, Cher had identified three of her four blind contacts and proceeded to find and bump into them, whispering their code words. Two were at the food table and she got both food and drinks on her dress as a result of each of those collisions. She spent a little time in the powder room getting stains out of her dress and emerged with wet spots down her front. The little breast veil was beyond salvaging so she'd simply removed it and thrown it away.

While closing on her third contact on the dance floor she spied her fourth. She bumped each and received acknowledgement from them. There was one more contact and this one was to be face to face in conversation. She was a Here-We-Are commoner at the top of the poverty heap but there was nothing common about her. She was the leading astrophysicist of the indigenous population and her intelligence was immeasurably off the charts. Her name was Hermesia and she was 39 years old, five foot four inches tall and weighed 110 pounds. Hermesia had already passed vital information to the agents of Ahumdulilah, including the current whereabouts of the weapons of mass destruction confiscated by the empire. Her data was extremely precise since she'd been placed in charge of the technicians who had to relocate and configure them. She'd also passed on backdoors, codes, locations of critical hardware, and methods of disabling and neutralizing those weapons. Tonight she would be passing on more data by hugging Cher. Hermesia was convinced that Cher was conversant with Ahumdulilah science and technology and had burning cosmological questions prepared, of the greatest significance and urgency to her. She just had to know. It felt like life and death to her.

Cher found Hermesia sitting on a stuffed foot rest alone in the sex room, of all places. For Hermesia it was a place where she did not have to interact with others, which was something she'd always found rather awkward. Except for the moans it was also a quiet place, and the dim lighting helped her feel anonymous and sort of invisible. Cher came over in front of her, took her hands, and rose Hermesia to her feet to embrace her. The faint tone in Cher's earbud informed her that the transmission succeeded and she now had the data from Hermesia, though the tone had been awful close to the sound of the soiled diaper sensors.

Hermesia asked, "What is time?"

Cher was a little taken aback, and at first thought she might have juxtaposed her words, and was asking, 'What time is it'. Before she could process through this Hermesia demanded, "What is the nature of time?"

This clarified it for Cher, getting her on the same page. She asked Hermesia, "What does your standard model hold to be true on this matter?"

"They're wrong," Hermesia blurted out. "Philosophically time and space are the preconditions for experience and hence structures basic to our mind for organizing impressions from our senses, existing prior to experience. Our scientific model assumes time to be absolute as the laws of motion imply. These views are in error. For one thing, we do not schematize impressions into time and space as infants. A good deal of sensory motor cognitive development is required to get there. You could legitimately say that we are predisposed to develop these, but they are not ready-made before experience in infancy. Time is relative to velocity. Velocity requires mass, volume and space. Time requires distance, volume weight and movement to preceed it in order to register in our minds."

Cher tried to explain, "Time as a principle of the universe is the product of four previous or higher principles that support matter, the four emanations whose interrelations permeate and produce matter. This is the explanation of the origin of time, and not as elements appearing in time, with time being the necessary condition for their appearance. Time is a product of relation between elements. There are ten emanations and matter is the tenth and final. It is as far from the source and origin as energy and consciousness can get, which is why matter is considered corrupt mystically, and the material senses must be withdrawn in order to see with intuitive-insight the unity, transcendence, and descendance through emanation to matter. Motion, Rest, Harmony and Equilibrium produce the procession of time. They are the four fundamentals that form the structure of our ordinary reality, because between the relations of these four, the frame of time and space appears. All is held together by a cosmic harmony and a superior order that is reflected everywhere in nature. We contain the ten splendors, or emanations, making the human being a microcosm of the whole."

"How is emanation reflected in nature?" Hermesia inquired forcefully.

"The triadic organization of the monad forms a part of every event or change under the laws of nature. The change itself constitutes the forth component. It can be seen in the interaction of any two of the three pairs of quarks which combine as the foundation of matter. The same principle appears at the base of all living things in the form of the four letters of DNA (A,G,C,T). The points at which emanations arise are pre-established, not accidental. They are nodal points, vortexes, or material manifestation points. Material manifestation points are permeated with the other nine emanations and are the product of them."

"Tell me all ten!" Hermesia insisted, looking like she might attack if denied.

Cher tried to explain, "The monad is the One, the Supreme Good and the Absolute Transcendent, unknowable in itself. The monad is both male and female because it is self-generating. The absolute is entirely beyond the beyond, yet permeates and is imminent within all of the universe. The Dyad is the first emanation of the One, called the Logos, which reflects the One and contrasts the unknowability, contemplating it intelligibly. The Logos is our intuitive insight with which we can know intelligibly the One. We call it the Divine Mind. The Divine Mind contains the essences or archetypes of all things. From the Divine Mind emanates the World Soul, or Demiurgic Mind some call the Holy Spirit. The world soul is not matter. It emanates the four Elements, the fourth emanation.

The four elements have form, but not matter. The emanations then proceed to Motion, Rest, Harmony, Equilibrium, Time, and finally matter is manifested as the actual material universe. It's really far easier to get to on a meditation cushion. The biggest problem with research is that we can necessarily study only partial systems and this does some violence to reality by breaking causal loops which link that partial system to everything else. Never forget that the universe we study is us, and we are it, and that no objects or pieces actually exist separately except within our mental abstraction."

"You are a spiritual adept," Hermesia stated as the conclusion of her internal analysis.

"I'm recognized as such," Cher said cautiously, since she was having difficulty reading this woman, or following her relative mental processes of thought construction and language. She wanted to put Hermesia together with Trix/Kat who was at the very top of the intelligence scales, if not actually over the top herself.

"Let's find an empty room; you simply must initiate and instruct me," Hermesia pushed, broking no argument.

"Alright," Cher stated, taking Hermesia's hand and leading her out of the sex room.

A man was grunting loudly in the corner as they exited the room. Cher went through the food room and grabbed a handful of mixed nuts with her free hand as she went by them. The table was tempting, but Cher moved with determination. She bypassed the main room with band and dance floor, using the corridor instead, and took Hermesia out the front door. She ignored the "Keep of the grass" sign, and walked across the lawn to her yacht, which had already destroyed much of it anyway. They went up the ramp and through the airlock, into the little airlock foyer, and Pooh greeted them.

Cher told Hermesia, "This is my friend, Pooh. She has insight and might meditate with us, increasing the energy and fruit of our endeavor. Pooh, this is Hermesia, the foremost astrophysicist of Here-We-Are, who insists on being initiated and empowered into the practices."

"I'm pleased to meet you," Pooh said sincerely.

"If you're going to help, and not deter us, then I'm pleased to meet you too," Hermesia stated as fact.

Cher led them into the living room to sit on the amazing rug. Passing by the dining room to get there Hermesia had stopped abruptly, and so getting rear-ended by Pooh who'd been behind her, and stated almost incensed, "Those are all diamonds!" pointing at the chandelier.

"Isn't it beautiful?" Cher asked her.

"It's beyond belief!" Hermesia claimed. "Beautiful, yes; but obscene in the concentration of wealth it represents."

"It is only on loan to me for my mission of sowing revolution in the three galaxies. As soon as my work here is concluded, I assure you this work of art will be returned to the Tiffany System where it will be kept in a museum for all to enjoy."

Cher pinged Kat and invited, "Come meditate with Pooh, Hermesia and me, if you want to. We're on the yacht."

"I'm coming," Kat replied. "Bianca picked up a teen girl and they left to find a powder room, so I've just been sitting by the pool with Electra."

"Your participation will be appreciated," Cher said signing off.

While they waited for Kat they arranged themselves on meditation cushions and Cher instructed Hermesia, beginning with sitting posture then moving on to breathing, which incorporated the object of their meditation, the point four finger-widths below the navel. She employed metaphors and brief commentaries to instruct Hermesia on the purpose and goal of the practice, as well as quoting from ancient sacred texts. She described each of the impediments to practice, such as mental wandering and mental excitement, nailing them clearly as clinging hindrances and lack of attention and one-pointed focus.

Kat arrived and Cher got Electra, still in her pouch, arranged comfortably in her lap. They began their sitting and absorption session with Cher continuously passing internal energy into Hermesia. After a few minutes, Cher said, "Remain grounded in the point in your low abdomen and continue to follow your breath as you observe your thoughts coming, staying, and going. Recognize that you are the awareness of them, and not the thoughts themselves."

About forty minutes later, Cher instructed, "Shift your focus to observe the awareness that has been observing your thoughts. Though invisible, immaterial, without location or any qualification, it has nowhere to hide."

Cher left them in contemplation for about half an hour before instructing, "Contemplate the unity of the luminosity of your conventional mind, now empty of thought, and the Absolute Emptiness of the witness, called contemplation of the clear light upon emptiness. This is the state."

She left them in this state a little over a quarter hour, still pumping calming healing energy into Hermesia. Then she struck the seated bowl gong and said, "Listen for the furthest sound of the gong."

They sat for another four and a half minutes, long after the vibrations had faded and ended in rest. Hermesia stated, "When my thoughts finally shut up, and I doubt they ever would have if you hadn't shifted my focus to the awareness of them; anyway, when they did cease and desist, there was illumination so radiant and beautiful that it moved my heart to bliss."

"When you have a thought, the light dissolves into the pattern of your thought," Cher explained.

"I saw that," Hermesia stated. "Where am I going to sleep?"

Cher hadn't quite followed Hermesia's train of thought, or leap in thought, perhaps. She asked, "Are you tired?"

"Not at the moment," Hermesia assured her, "but I'm moving in. I need your guidance. I've never met anyone like you before. Where were you getting all that energy you were running through me?"

"Excess must always be shared and redistributed," Cher told her. "It is the Supreme Will. I mass integrate what I am able, though I'm now a channel for more than I can transmute, so I direct it where it is most likely to bear fruit. My daughter is the most frequent and consistent recipient because she has a mission far more significant than mine."

Pooh told Hermesia, "Cher is the rotortiller breaking up the ground which is the empire, so that it can receive the seeds, which are Electra's teachings, and the Mu's blessings, which are the sunlight and rain to germinate the seeds."

"So where's my berth?" Hermesia persisted.

"Sarhi the Im might share her cabin with you," Cher said tentatively. "It has the only empty berth on the yacht. You sure can't be in my bed because one more person would have to be stacked on top, and that wouldn't work."

"I'll sleep on the sofa in here if I have to," Hermesia informed her. "A blanket and pillow are all I'll need. By the way, do you have an extra toothbrush? I don't have mine with me."

"We have some under our sink," Kat said, jumping up to go get one.

Evenrude, who had been lurking about since they'd arrived on the yacht, offered, "There's a rollaway bed in the closet of the cabin Johnson and I share, and it could go in with Green and Elanem, or with Pippy and Alice."

"Good thinking," Cher said gratefully. "Green and Elanem's is bigger so we'll put it in there."

Evenrude was already on his way to move the bed, understanding that Pez's royal "we" meant him.

Electra awoke and wanted out of her pouch. She was practicing independent mobility whenever they were home and she was awake. She could crawl like an otter and just as quick too. Before engaging her favorite activity she sat perfectly still and looked Hermesia over from top to bottom, appearing to gravely inspect her. Then she seemed to wave her over and Hermesia took a few steps closer to Electra, hesitantly. Electra looked piercingly into the woman's eyes, like lasers boring a hole, with quite a serious expression for a baby. The moment stretched and Hermesia appeared utterly mesmerized, then Electra looked at her momma and laughed with delight, just before scooting off across the floor like she'd been shot from a cannon. Mel's voice came on in the living room, "Gumby likes to pull himself up to stand, and then bounce up and down. He's already taken his first step."

"I've seen the bouncing," Cher acknowledged, thinking how amusing it had been this morning with a load in his diaper. Electra could crawl circles around Gumby. So what if he'd taken a few steps. Then she saw her defensiveness and dissolved it, experiencing her love for Gumby, who was like a son to her.

"Am I to be introduced?" Hermesia inquired loudly.

"Sorry," Cher told her, "this is Mel, who is one of our mission crew, and a Marshal in the Clearlight Order to which I belong. Mel, this is Hermesia, the top astrophysicist on Here-We-Are, and now, apparently, moving in with us."

"You're a magnet for them," Mel commented.

"It seems to have become a pattern," Cher acknowledged.

"How many are staying aboard here?" Hermesia asked.

"We were twenty-two, with Whiffle and Hoola, though I guess we are now twenty-three," Cher answered.

"The bed's set up in Green's and Elanem's guest suite," Evenrude informed her.

"You'd better meet our new travelling companion, Hermesia, of Here-We-Are."

"Pleased to make your acquaintance," Evenrude said, extending his giant hand.

Hermesia took it in both of hers figuring she'd still be shy some mass in the equation, and explained, "I'm a disciple, not a travelling companion. I don't travel well and I'm never very companionable."

The way she'd said it made it quite believable; almost a demonstration.

"If there's anything I can do to make you more comfortable, just let me know," Evenrude replied politely.

Kat returned with a toothbrush and explained to Hermesia as she handed it to her, "The one end has a super-sonic vibrating brush and the other a regular brush. On the side is a floss dispenser, and on the other side is a compartment with your mouth tube for the sink's built-in water jet. On the back there's an ivory toothpick."

"Thorough, comprehensive and compact," Hermesia agreed, admiring it."

Cher told them, "So long as we're parked so close, I think I'll go try some more stuff off that food table."

"I'll wait right here for you," Hermesia informed her. "Parties just aren't my thing."

Trix went to catch Electra, who gave her quite the chase. Once apprehended she was fine with riding in her pouch on her momma's back, and Kat and Evenrude returned to the party with Cher. They went directly to the room with the food table. The arrangement had been changed, and now there was a giant roasted gardd on a platter, with breast slices already cut beside it. There was smoked salmon, fish eggs and fancy crackers, jumbo shrimp with a seafood cocktail sauce, baked oysters, eggplant dip, and so much more. Cher dug in from where she was standing, two-fisted, and reached way over to pull a leg off of the gardd. The oysters were right in front of her, and she couldn't help eating a few of them. They were delicious. She hoped she wouldn't glow in the dark after eating them.

In her peripheral vision Cher had recognition of an out of place looking man who was trying to point his pocket device at her. Cher didn't like it. The man looked and felt sinister. A Vanderbat woman moved out of the way and the sinister man's pocket device was lining up. Cher dropped into a squat, bowing her head a little, timing it with her sense of the man's energy, and was rewarded with a strip of singed hair across the top of her head as the punch bowl on the table sprung a leak. Evenrude saw what happened but the others in the room were oblivious. In two swift Evenrude-strides the sinister man's shooting arm was badly sprained and twisted unnaturally behind his back, with the back of his neck in the pincer of a giant's forefinger-thumb pinch, and could be snapped at any time. Evenrude asked him calmly, "Who put you up to killing Cher Bulwinkle?"

"They'll kill me!"

"Waiting for them to do it would certainly give you more time to live," Evenrude explained evenly. Then asked, "How many are at the party?"

"Four. There are three others here. Don't kill me. It was Rudfuss Snydely who hired us."

Evenrude tased the man unconscious. Cher inquired, "Who is he?"

"One of four assassins here at the party to kill you, hired by Rudfuss Snydely."

"He sure puts up a rude fuss and does it snidely," Cher remarked.

"I've alerted Johnson and our bomber crew are on the way from the hotel to further mess up the lawn and provide perimeter cover."

"I've got Electra's pouch shield up and I'm feeling everyone out," Cher assured him.

Evenrude cuffed the unconscious man's hands behind his back and his ankles together, then dumped him in a hall closet. Mel had alerted Cher's companions at the party but this still didn't get Bianca out of the powder room. Lai and Hark/Rubix rushed over to Cher keeping a suspicious eye on all the guests. Kat got the assassin's retnal scan and finger prints onto her big pocket device then was whipping through applications and hacking a rushing river of data. Mel was a step ahead of her and informed Cher, "Two known associates of that assassin Evenrude caught are here at the party. I've sent their images to your device and I'm running facial recognition scans now from the Waltonraptor security system."

Not to be outdone, Kat reported, "I've found an associate of one of the associates, who was seen by the security system entering the party. I'm sending it to all of you."

Cher got her nerdy glasses on and had their facial recognition program operating. She picked up three small knives from the food table putting three dishes temporarily out of commission with no way to cut them, and palmed the tableware close to her body looking all around. Pippy came and found her to say, "One is hiding in ambush in the sex room and the other two are dancing together on the dance floor."

"Thanks sweetheart," Cher told her reaching for some more food now that she knew the threat wasn't imminent.

Evenrude asked Pippy, "Where is the assassin in the room relative to the door?"

"He'll be at your five o'clock, back close to the wall, behind a loveseat."

"Thanks," Evenrude said, "I'll go take that one out."

Johnson filled the archway into the food room brightly as he entered and inquired, "Do we have a location on any?"

"Two are on the dance floor and Evenrude just left to take care of the one in the sex room," Cher told him. "Just let me whoof down another gardd leg and I'll go to the dance floor with you."

She reached again across the table careful of the still leaking punch bowl to grab a leg of gardd. Servants were only just arriving to clean up the mess. Cher stripped the bone in five quick bites, one-pointed on eating, then set it on an empty platter to lead the way into the main room with the dance floor. The dancing assassins were in view. Both were yellow-sun humans, one male and one female, and both expensively dressed. Neither was enjoying dancing and both their heads turned towards Cher as she entered the room.

The male spun the female out into Cher's direction and she let go his hand to keep spinning towards Cher while extracting a weapon from beneath her dress. Pippy was a couple of meters and perhaps ¾ of a second from tackling the female when the handle of a table knife appeared protruding from the assassin's chest, staining it red. It was too late for Pippy so she tackled a dead woman and got blood on her skin. Johnson was raising his blaster to fire at the male assassin and a knife nobody saw Cher throw was in mid-air when Alice bashed him in the head with a wa-wa peddle swung from its electric chord which she'd swiped from the stage. He went down like a ton of bricks, probably dead. Alice had to swing the wa-wa peddle two more rounds while reeling it in before she could get it safely to the ground. It was a big one. As fast as he'd gone down that knife still found him, and he was twice dead when they got to him."

Evenrude asked from the sex room, "What do you want me to do with this one?"

"Is he alive?" Cher asked.

Mel cut in to inform them, "I'll be there in moments with two units of Imperial Secret Police who owe me. Their careers were on the brink from some of my examiners, and I gave them personal reprieves. Your prisoners will be taken into custody by the Secret Police and a worse fate is inconceivable."

Cher asked, "Will they get them to talk?"

"Their methods always make them, but there is never any telling if a bit of it is true or not," Mell explained. "You can be sure those two will be subjected to some nasty shit."

"I don't want them tortured," Cher said horrified.

"I'll see what I can do," Mel promised. "Oh boy are the Secret Police going to be disappointed though."

Cher asked Evenrude, "Do you think we should have the band meet us here after their concert? Then we could all just leave from here for Monarch."

"There's not room left on the lawn," he informed her. "We better leave from the hotel. They had to park *Spaceship* at the empty lot at the Exposition Center."

"Well it looks to be flat garden on the other side of that split rail fence," Cher suggested thinking *Spaceship* would fit just fine there; she really couldn't have had less concern about the Waltonraptor's blood money, and as it was already, they'd likely require the service of a good landscape architect. The mirage streak fury, *Sidekick*, had cratered the lawn upon landing to dig a trench in its skid to stop. What was left of the grass was mostly buried under a couple of inches of dirt.

"It's your call," Evenrude replied.

"Mel, have the band meet us here when they're done playing. Tell them just to land mostly in the garden with only their bow up on the lawn. That'll work. And they'll need to pick up and bring the others from the hotel."

Evenrude was certain the Waltonraptors would have at least second thoughts in the future about inviting the Bulwinkles over again to their home. He'd dragged the unconscious woman, now cuffed and trussed, over to the hall closet to retrieve the guy he'd stuffed in there. Carrying one with each arm he went down the hall, through the grand entrance, and out the door. The secret police units were just descending. Evenrude watched as they tore up what lawn space was left and leveled the fountain. He backed up onto a step as the little wave came. The fountain water was now going straight up and had no container at the bottom to catch it. The ground was already soggy mud.

Mel emerged from a police craft in her meticulous Adherence Examiners uniform adorned with a number of official decorations she'd decided to award herself. She was followed by the eight secret police from her craft. The eight from the other craft were also disembarking. Mel pretended she'd never seen Evenrude before, and stated, "You are Brick, Cher Bulwinkle's bodyguard."

"That's right," he confirmed. "These two were part of a four-assassin team sent here to kill Cher. The other two are in the mansion dead. They're on the dance floor. Mrs. Waltonraptor is quite upset."

"Wait till she sees this lawn," Mel replied.

"They'll have the opportunity to re-envision it," he said.

"Well they'll have to because it will be a terrible eyesore until they do," Mel agreed.

Pippy got the blood off her skin and Mel hauled away the live perpetrators and bodies, knocking a satellite dish off the roof of the mansion while leaving with the Secret Police. One never complained about any damage they might cause, and they caused quite a bit. Cher got clear around the food table making herself a sampler meal and Lai was right alongside doing the same. Bianca finally came out of the powder room and introduced them all to eighteen-year-old Ashley Waltonraptor. That had been awkward. Cousine Winnie had to shake a number of suitors when she joined them.

The hour was late when *Spaceship* finally set down decimating the entire garden. The Bulwinkle party said their goodbyes and boarded their yachts and bomber. Bianca had to catch her drone up with their little convoy from the hotel parking lot and a Trump had parked very close, getting a little crispy on one side with her booster take-off. The Waltonraptor lawn looked like a warzone. The garden was in worse shape. The Bulwinkle party was on its way to Monarch.

CHAPTER SEVENTEEN

Monarch Space Control had been worse than Om's and it was the busiest planet Cher had ever seen. No preferential treatment had been shown them. Cher had to land at a Space Control Authority Site before going on to the Monarch Royal Intergalactic Hotel so she could resolve the citations she'd received coming in. Their greeter-liaison's name was Daffey and she was in her late twenties, quite polished, and did not vibe trustworthy to Cher. Pez had only tipped her 100 dags. The hotel was posh and plush. Neither the band nor Cher's party had the penthouse. Cher had the Visiting Dignitary Suite and the band got one of the big luxury suites, since the only thing bigger available was the Bridal Suite and they didn't like the décor of that one.

Capital City, the capital of both Monarch and the Empire, contained a population of 11.8 million, with another 26.2 million packed tightly around three sides of it. Capital City was a seaport, as well as the largest spaceport in the empire, and had the largest airport too. In the financial district the buildings ran 150-280 stories tall. The biggest ones took up four city blocks at the bottom with streets running through them. Their actual foundations started at least 25 stories underground. Even more ornate, though not quite so tall, was the upscale shopping district with the finest selections of merchandise from three galaxies and the most prestigious and expensive brand names and labels, probably in the whole universe; but who really knew.

The Monarch Royal Intergalactic Hotel was situated on the edge of the shopping district, right on the border of the financial district. The Imperial Music Hall was located next door to the Grand

Palace, which was practically a city unto itself in the government section of the city. This section was crammed with arches, domed and phallic humungous memorials, statues of past emperors—likely the ones causing the most suffering; commemorative structures and sculptures, engraved stonewalls; and plaques, inscriptions and cast informative plates were everywhere. The streets in the government section were exceptionally wide, and so were the sidewalks. The stone walls of the government buildings were exceptionally thick and there was an enormous number of police and Adherence Examiners in the area. There was also the Emperor's personal guard which consisted of 120,000 elite soldiers selected as the best among the Imperial Special Forces then wrung through an enormously intensive training honing them to a fine point. The various branches of the military each had a severe presence in this part of town, as did all the imperial royal bureaus, agencies, departments, ministries, and services involved with investigating, policing, borders, intelligence, counter intelligence, counter insurgency, imperial sponsored terrorism, and so forth.

Once they were all in the hotel and Evenrude had finished scanning for sensor bugs, Hermesia told Cher, "Monarch has a college of terrorism right here in the Capital City. It's called the *College of the Americas* because the doctrines and practices all came from a vile little empire from a long time ago, in a galaxy far-far away, which had an institution of the same name. When others fought back against them they were labeled 'terrorists', and their own acts of terrorism of a far greater magnitude they always called 'making things right', 'pro-democracy', or some such outright lie. Their sick manifesto has unfortunately become the playbook for this empire."

"I've never heard of them," Cher admitted.

"They're gone now; no biosphere and oceans of jello-like substance," Hermesia informed her. "I think it was called 'Earth', like so many others."

"How tragic," Cher reacted.

"Are we going shopping?" Bianca asked excitedly.

"Yes sweetheart, just let me change and I'll be ready to go," Cher reassured.

Muffet/Gretle exclaimed, "It's supposed to be the finest quality shopping anywhere."

"Are you coming with us Hermesia?" Cher inquired.

"I'll just meditate at the hotel," she answered.

"I guess that makes eight of us for shopping then."

Winnie informed them, "I made a date with my pocket device coming in, using a local match making chat service, so I may not be back tonight."

Cher put on an elegant dress covering most of her from just above the knees to neckline, layered in textile armor and with button down breast flaps for nursing. Electra was eating some baby apple sauce and baby grains and veggie paste but she wouldn't touch the gray-brown meat in a jar. No way. She still insisted on having her momma's breast as much for the energy and comfort as for the nutrition. Gumby was stumbling about now. Electra kept to the floor and went like a flash. Both babies were tucked into their pouches and secured to their mother's backs. Electra insisted on holding a chopstick in her little right fist when she rode in the backpack like it was a magic wand. When the feeling came over her she would tap out a rhythm on Cher's head, and she used it to get her momma's attention, and to test things and distances. It was really quite handy. Cher had to wear her platinum-diamond tiara since the chop stick wreaked havoc with her skullcap. Gumby was content with his pacifier.

Their balcony on the 189th floor had a hovercraft gate in the railing and Daffey was there at the gate waiting in a Rolls Royal Limo hovercraft with the hotel crest on the side. They piled in. There were twenty-eight levels or layers of hovercraft lanes, with layers of air and space shuttle traffic above those. Daffey executed numerous descending lane changes quite expertly in a short distance forward to get them to the heart of the shopping district. They put down on the hovercraft lading platform, only a few stories up from street level on the side of the Fleece You's Clothier store building. Daffey would pick them up at street level or on the landing platform of any building whenever they wanted.

The seven women and Rubix entered Fleece You's. Cher was struck with the double meaning of the store's name until she saw the prices and realized there was only one possible meaning which she didn't like. Bianca made her get a few things there, nonetheless, and they all left carrying fancy little shopping bags.

They descended in a glass partitioned elevator affixed to the outside of the building and caught a view of the endless sea of factories spotting the landscape inland, with stark boxlike apartment buildings indistinguishable from one another sprouted like grass. When they exited the elevator Cher led the way without a clue where she was going. On the street they were confronted by a super-commercial MacThief's, offering genetically modified faux food to go. It really didn't appeal to any of them. Cher had to brace herself to walk past Star Plucks where they sold high potency stimulant brew, her favorite. Then they passed an End-All lethal injection clinic and mortuary. Cher had never seen one of these before and it appeared to be quite popular here, judging by the line.

They came to Hug-me's Victorious Secret and entered the store. Bianca and Muffet ran off together looking for some item. Cher walked with Hoola, whose holo was everywhere throughout the store. The Capital City Space-Time Square's gigantic 600 foot holo also featured Hoola in her Hug-me's. A sales girl approached and asked in a disinterested tone, "Can I hel…" Then she was suddenly wired with no in-between separating her previous boredom and current super-aroused state. "You're Hoola! Can I get your autograph? Oh my-gosh, it's really you…"

Hoola signed on the girl's device then had Cher get a few images of her cheek to cheek with the sales girl, on the girl's device. The girl told her worshipfully, "You're the most famous person in the whole universe."

"You never know," Hoola replied.

Staff and customers surrounded Hoola so Cher returned the girl's device and asked her, "Do you have any cozy panties that *do* have a crotch?"

"We certainly do. We even have some with feltex liners which can absorb a pint and a half comfortably without leakage."

"I couldn't imagine what that would feel like," Cher remarked. She knew about feltex because it was in Electra's diapers. Cher asked, "What about soft cotton ones, and silk ones?"

"We do; let me show you."

Pez picked out ten pair of panties and ended up giving her signature and image to the salesgirl, who had seen her landings, knew of her exploits with the Devil Dogs, and even knew about how badly she'd torn up the Waltonraptor's lawn. Apparently those holos had made the interstellar news. The clothes their party selected were free once Hoola gave permission for them to show publicly the security holos of her shopping and signing autographs there. Now loaded with fancy little shopping bags they left Hug-me's in search of a restaurant for Cher.

There was an official Monarch Tourist Souvenir Shop on the corner and they passed it right by. A strange office called 'Charlie's and David's socio-political movements and legislation to go', was next door to the tourist gift shop. They went by a Glock & Remington's Toy Store, and Monsantu Burgers with de-generatively mutant ex-employees picketing outside of it, many of them in hover-chairs. They all looked painfully ill. They walked by Virtual Adventures which was next door to a Fargo Morgan financial institution boasting no charge on debits for the first ten days of opening an account.

They came to a little park with a gargantuan bronze statue of B.P. Exon Valdez the Dreadful Despoiler. He was an admired ancient emperor celebrated for wiping out biospheres containing human populations to exploit mining resources. After the park there was a Big Pharm Chemical Entertainment Center with a huge sign that read, "Official Dealer." There was no stopping Bianca from shopping there so they all went in.

It was vast and one side of the store had shelves and shelves of hundreds of different kinds of Alko in bottles, jugs, kegs, cans, boxes and plastic containers. Then there were isles of chemical pharmacy to give you highs, lows, hi-lows, heart-opening sensitivity, ego-stimulation, dreamland paradise, complete oblivion, erections or trips to another dimension. The sign read. "Something for Everyone." On the other side of the store the wall was lined with bins and there were little labels, plastic see-through bags, and pencils to write the bin number on the label and adhere the label to the bag so the checkout clerk would know what to charge you. They also had every kind of vaporizer, bong, pipe, and hookah imaginable. Bianca had a hover-cart and she was filling it. Gretle was also doing a big shop. They even had hybrid roasted stimulant beans bred to maximum potency of the finest possible quality. Cher lingered sniffing the aroma longfully. They had to arrange delivery to their hotel for the goods because it was just too much to carry.

Back on the street they walked passed a Carnival Mart known to mostly only reinvest capital for planned obsolescence and known for paying employees well below subsistence. The whole intergalactic chain was owned by the Waltonraptors. They didn't go in there. Peaking in, Bianca thought the shoppers looked creepy. They found the Hostess Quantum Computer Store that Cher was hoping to find since Mel had given her a whole list of things she was supposed to procure there. Kat helped her shop because she knew far more about Monarch computer technology than Cher did. Mel looked on through Cher's tiara trying to direct her, saying, "Not that right, stupid, your other right."

They'd selected Carnagie's as their restaurant. Since they had no reservations all eight had to be squeezed into a booth for six. Cher was sure to sit on the same side as Whiffle since the girl took up so little space. Hoola was recognized and their booth was besieged and overwhelmed. They were offered neither surrender nor quarter, though when the ruckus finally subsided, they were shown to a large comfortable table by the manager who personally described each dish on the menu employing every superlative in Sterling. He took their order himself, but before any food could be made, the chef had to come out for autographs and holos from Hoola, Whiffle and Cher.

One pushy fan had been a teen heir to one of the largest family fortunes in the empire and he'd offered Hoola a million dags for the hug-me's she had on. She sold them of course, and wiggled out of them in her chair. He'd transferred the million into one of her accounts right when she'd handed them to him. And she'd even kissed him on the mouth. He was back at his own table now daydreaming and sniffing those knickers within his own little world, in a state of teen-rapture. Hoola pulled on a new pair of hug-me's seated at the table. Bianca told her, "We've got like 80 pairs of hug-me's with us right now. We should auction the ones you have on and you can just keep slipping into a fresh pair. The profit potential is mind-blowing."

"I doubt another pair would fetch a million dags," Hoola said skeptically.

Mel offered, "I could set up an ether-store and auction in seconds and the winners could collect their panties personally from you here in the shopping district of the capital this afternoon."

"I think I'd prefer to keep on the ones I'm wearing and just have fun being with all of you today," Hoola turned down their goldmine schemes.

"I'm a billionaire on Earth 10^5 CBS2 in Xegachtznel Galaxy," Bianca informed Hoola.

"How did you come by it?" She inquired.

"It was given to Cher when she saved the planet from invasion and she gave it to me," Bianca explained. "They made my condo a planetary monument so I wouldn't have to pay any property taxes, and they paid off my mortgage on it at Cher's request. That was before she gave me all the money and properties."

Mel told Hoola, "They have analog acoustical systems on that planet that can blow a girls clothes off from 50 feet. I've never had such vocal potency!"

"We like it loud," Bianca confirmed.

"This Earth in Xegachtznel is your home world?" Hoola asked.

"It is," Bianca acknowledged. "I was a sex worker hired by the Minister of Entertainment to escort Cher and Lai. They brought me to their ship in outer space and Sarhi the Im, whom you know as Aunt Gimima, recognized me and had to wake me up quick because Cher needed me."

Muffet told Hoola, "The escort service she worked for was the most exclusive on the planet, and trained her in erotic sensuality and sexual technique. That's how she cultivated those deft little magic hands of hers, and her adept oral expertise."

"They certainly impressed me," Hoola informed her.

Bianca shared, "I did it with lots of pop music stars, but never one that was also a super-model until I met you, gorgeous."

Their appetizers were brought out and the service was excellent, overseen by the manger. Cher was having breaded fried zucchini spears with a mayonnaise sauce on the side, and they were light, not over-cooked, flavorful, and complemented most pleasingly by the sauce. She sure missed her high potency stimulant brew in steamed half and half with bitter-sweet chocolate powder sprinkled on top. She yearned for the day Electra would outgrow nursing though she cherished the connection she felt with Electra through the activity of it.

Kat had found herself a Hostess quantum hand held device with as much processing power as her great big one, and just as many features in only half the size; which still made it one of the biggest ones at only three times the price. Cher had been paying so Kat had bought it. She was uploading the data from her old one onto it and customizing its configuration to her needs and tastes. Cher had a new Hostess too, but one less than half the size of Kat's new one. Lai was holding onto her old Sarah Lee pocket device. Hark liked his Chips Ahoy model because it had the biggest memory chip, and he liked to store games with elaborate graphic holo imagery on his, which ate up a great deal of terabits. Everyone agreed that Sarah Lee's sexy guidance and navigation voice was the most pleasing out of the voices of all the brands marketed.

Electra awoke dry without wailing and stretched her arms out because she wanted her Whiffle. Lifting her most tenderly, Whiffle cradled Electra in her arms at her seat and the two of them made eye contact. Cher noticed that every minute or so either Johnson or Evenrude walked by the entrance to Carnagie's. They were lurking again. Their big table had room even for the two giants so she ran out in the street and hailed them, "Bodyguards! Stop lurking about and join us. The food is wonderful."

They followed her in and took seats. A waitress rushed menus into their hands. Bianca stated to them, "You've been tailing us."

"Obviously not so discretely," Evenrude agreed, "but body-guards can be a big deterrent when they're visible. These colors call much attention to us."

"You're an even bigger deterrent sitting with us," Bianca told him, "because we provide scale for perspective, like putting a human figure in front of a monument in a holo."

"We can keep you all safe from right here at the table," Evenrude replied shifting his focus to the inviting menu. Then with his eyes on his menu he mentioned casually, "I'm not so sure I appreciate your implying that I'm a monument."

"Well I didn't really; my analogy referenced perspective of scale, not you as a monument," she assured him, "though I see how it could be taken the other way."

Evenrude told her, "You know what it's like to be outside the normal size range, just not what it's like to be big."

"I can't reach half the stuff where people put it, and I get plowed into by people looking right over the top of my head without seeing me"

"Have you ever been mistaken for a wall?" Evenrude asked, trying to decide between the prime rib and prawn pasta.

"I can't say I have," Bianca admitted.

The waitress took Johnson's and Evenrude's orders and brought them urgently to the kitchen.

The teen boy, Vegan Casper, came back over and asked, "Would you mind terribly if I joined you?"

There were two seats yet vacant at their table though the space of each was encroached by an irreducible giant Space Marine in the guise of a gangster-bodyguard. Bianca was scooting her chair over and one out for the boy since she thought he was cute, and smiled invitingly at him. It was too bad his pants had a crotch so she couldn't measure him. Cher said, "Have a seat son. What's your name?"

"Vegan Casper. You're Cher Bulwinkle, aren't you?"

"That's me."

"You sure can fly, but I don't think I'd have you over to my house after seeing what you did to the Waltonraptor's lawn."

"What industry is your family involved in?" Cher inquired.

"I own Ambient Energy and we specialize in natural pulse pump generators, planetary meridian energy accumulation, solar, wind, wave, hydroelectric, geothermal, and biomass energy generation systems for single homes, apartment buildings, communities, industrial sites, and cites. I also own an agricultural concern with farms on 968 planets called Uncontaminated. We use manure and seaweed for fertilizer and no pesticides or herbicides. We also raise poultry and live stock humanely without hormones, steroids or antibiotics. We have 16.3 billion acres of farm fields, orchards, vineyards, pastures and range."

"Do you own slaves?" Cher asked.

"Not on my farms or in my energy company, though as you do, I have some domestic slaves here on Monarch. I'm also the biggest shareholder in Hostess Quantum Computer, and slaves are not used in that enterprise either. I'm surprised you would ask me accusingly, given *your* family's reputation."

Mel briefed Cher, only in her ear, "The Caspers pay above subsistence wages in their agricultural and energy businesses, and do not control nor manage Hostess Computers, but they own 51% of the public shares. They can afford to pay better wages because they are ranked the third wealthiest ruling family in the empire, and have so much money flowing in. They own residential and commercial properties on hundreds of planets generating enormous rents. They also have some small but entirely family owned mining operations, manufacturing interests, and computer programming companies, as well as the largest ship-building space platform and facility orbiting New Monarch."

Cher texted "Thanks" to Mel using her tiara, then said to Vegan, "I would never tear up a Casper lawn and I do not fit the profile of my family reputation any closer than the Casper family fits the profile of the typical ruling families."

"Touché," Vegan acknowledged.

Cher had one more question for him, "Do you have sex with domestic slaves which is unwanted by them and not mutual?"

"Never intentionally, and for certain not currently."

"Then we can be friends," Cher offered.

"I'd like that," he enthused.

Bianca put an arm around Vegan, and asked, "How long is…"

Cher cut her off with a warning, "Ahhu, don't embarrass the boy," issued in Native Rocky.

Vegan was more interested in Bianca's breasts, curves and crevices than he was in her matching shoes, hat and purse ensemble; and in the magic touch of her hand. Cher asked him, "How old are you?"

"I'll be seventeen in three weeks."

"Do you have any siblings?" Cher inquired.

"I have a fourteen-year-old sister named Atlanta. We were orphaned almost a year ago when our parents were murdered on New Monarch. The family fortune is held in trust for me until my eighteenth birthday, though I have an ample allowance in the meantime."

"Like for paying a million dags for a pair of underwear you can get for less than 15?" Bianca asked rhetorically.

Hoola said, "Pass them over, Vegan, and I'll sign them."

He did, and she wrote on them and passed them back. It read, "From my pelvis into Vegan's hand with a kiss, Hoola, of the Whirling Vortexes and Hug-me's Victorious Secret," and was written in indelible marker with her signature.

He couldn't have been more thrilled. Hoola had pulled out one of the new undershirts she'd gotten at Hug-me's today and wrote: "Atlanta, friend of Hoola's and the Whirling Vortexes, issue reserved tickets (up to 4) and backstage passes, Hoola," with her signature below. She handed it to him. Vegan read it and buzzed his sister as he read it a second time. She opened the call almost immediately and he held the shirt up to his device for her to read. A screech only a girl her age or younger could possibly make came ripping out of her, filling Carnagie's and catching Electra's attention.

Cher thought, *Hopefully Electra didn't learn anything or get any ideas from that scream.*

Atlanta shouted in a high voice, "I'll meet you at Carnagie's in five minutes!!"

"She's excited," Cher commented.

"She's super-excited on steroids," Vegan clarified. "Hoola is her biggest hero. She also idolizes Pogo and is herself a keyboardist. Her number one fantasy dream is to hang out with Hoola, Pogo, and the rest of the Whirling Vortexes."

"Well I'm glad we could make her day," Hoola remarked.

"Her whole life to date is what she'd tell you you just made," Vegan corrected. Then he asked Hoola, "Is there any way you would consider attending the imperial party at the palace with me as my date in four nights? I promise to be a perfect gentleman and treat you like an empress."

"Your tour will be over then," Cher pointed out.

Partly thinking it would please Cher and partly because Vegan was cute, not to mention unfathomably rich, Hoola told him, "You've got a date, cutie."

The expression of absolute ecstasy formed on Vegan's face made it especially beautiful as he told her most sincerely, "I'm forever grateful. I insist on paying for your outfit and jewelry. Charge whatever you need at Vonet and Pellot's Clothiers and they will perform any needed alterations on the spot. If their jewelry department proves inadequate, just let me know where you would prefer to shop and I'll arrange payment with them."

"You're so sweet," Hoola told him, thinking the low end of a complete outfit at Vonet and Pellot's was at least a quarter million dags, and could easily run into the millions with jewelry.

Vegan told Whiffle, "Please charge your outfit for the party to my account. It's really not such an imposition since we've owned the company for a number of years now."

To Cher he stated, "I see your most recent mass infusion of capital into the markets has reaped record gains."

"I have brilliant financial managers and pay no attention to it myself," she said honestly.

"I'd love to study under one of them," Vegan said wishfully.

"That might be possible," Cher told him, "we shall see."

Atlanta burst through the door of Carnagie's four minutes and one second after ending her call with her brother, completely out of breath, having sprinted the two blocks from their brownstone mansion overlooking Capital Park in the most prestigious neighborhood here in the shopping district. Hardly able to breathe yet she blurted,

"Oh mygosh, it's really you, and Whiffle; and the undershirt is real, I don't believe it, I love you…"

"I'm pleased to meet you Atlanta," Hoola said, standing up to hug the rambling shocked girl.

Another one of those screams emerged as the embrace closed, though a lower magnitude than before, and no permanent damage was caused to Hoola's ear. "What's your secret?" Atlanta asked her.

"You mean besides being born looking like this and perhaps divine providence? I became very technically skillful with my instrument and dug out the sounds most pleasing to me, finding expression for them. Hooking up with musicians of exceptional talent like Whiffle and Pogo didn't hurt either."

"Can I really go to your concert tonight and come backstage to meet the other band members?" Atlanta begged.

"Of course, sweetheart," Hoola replied. "Dance on the stage while we play if you want."

"I can't dance anything like Cher so I'll enjoy the concert form my seat," Atlanta declined the stage performance thinking a firing squad would be less frightening to face.

Hoola said to Cher, "Our manager, Stilts, is setting up a 58 planet tour to begin in two weeks, including all the planets you wanted to visit. It won't be so rushed as the last tour, taking 190 days to complete. A few of the planets you wanted to go to are too poor to host a concert so we're scheduling those as charity events and intergalactic holocom fundraisers for relief for those planets."

"It will help move you towards the image we need," Cher said, liking the idea.

"I'll donate to the fundraiser!" Atlanta declared, ready to give the shirt off her back to please Hoola.

"I will too," Vegan told them. "My sister and I would like to follow that tour and would sponsor it. Our family yacht is the twelfth largest and second fastest in the empire. It has an armored hull and military grade shields. There are thirty-one guest suites, and it can accommodate a crew and staff of ninety-nine. I think my chef is the best in the universe and I'd cover all hotel expenses."

Hoola told him honestly, "You are more than welcome to come, and I'm sure Pogo, Tramp, and Frisbie would prefer your yacht to *Spaceship*, but Whiffle and I are disciples of Cher and stay on the *Aphrodite* with her, and in the same hotel suites."

"We could do meals together and hang out at the hotels," Cher told him. "You could hang with the band backstage on their breaks, and if you're lucky, get more dates with Hoola."

"I'd date you," Bianca informed him, her hand coming even more alive.

"It's settled then," Vegan insisted.

"Goodie!" Atlanta shrieked painfully for the ears around her. "I can't wait!"

"What's your yacht called?" Kat asked, wanting to find ether-data on it.

"It has full cloaking and we always travel in peace and friendship, so my father named it *Amicable Specter*," Vegan replied.

Kat went right to work researching it. Cher asked Vegan, "Do you even know what this empire does to the worlds it 'liberates'?"

Vegan answered gravely, "I do not condone it, nor can I publicly condemn it and keep my head. I may be wealthier than almost all of them, but I'm one voice out of 100,000 and I call for things they believe would diminish their profits."

Cher was liking Vegan more and more. He told Hoola, "Have your agent bill me for hotels."

"Actually, our agent is only booking for the concerts and Cher's assistant, Mel, is booking the hotels," Hoola clarified.

Vegan told Cher, "Have your assistant bill me for all the accommodations, the band's and your party's. My father told me that ours was the only one of the ruling families who meditate. Here you are not only a meditator, but a teacher. How wrong he was."

"You and your sister have made admirable efforts in the practice," Cher told him, "but there is little energy in the transmission you received and I will help each of you. You are both ready."

Atlanta's jaw was hanging open, and when enough of the shock had worn off she asked, "Aren't you a pirate?"

Electra laughed vocally at Atlanta from Whiffle's lap. Cher answered, "Not personally though I guess I'm the heiress to pirate treasure."

"You fly like a pirate and high-altitude jump like one," Atlanta pointed out, "and you sure trashed the Waltonraptor's lawn like one."

"There's been no actual Bulwinkle piracy since before I was born, but please don't tell anyone, because it's a most useful reputation," Cher informed her.

"You are truly a teacher, empowered within a lineage?" Atlanta inquired.

Kat replied to Atlanta, "She is the matriarch of the ancient Islohar and an adept of the Clearlight Order. She has been recognized on many planets outside this empire."

"You would teach my brother and me?" Atlanta asked on pins and needles.

"You have been trained in the way of kings and aristocrats and it is a very slow path. I offer you the fast track which is the way of drunkards and vagabonds. I will also teach you the way of sudden insight, and the way of contemplation through non-action. You will see."

"Can I post my undershirt with Hoola's message on my site so my friends can see it?!" Atlanta exclaimed beseeching in agony.

"Of course you can sweetheart," Hoola gave her permission, "along with some holos of us together and you with the band. I'm sure the society news commentators will all have much to say about you and your brother traveling with the band on our tour."

"We were so sheltered by our parents when they were alive that we've really only left our mansions to go to school, the theater, some restaurants, and travelling which all looks the same staying at five-star hotels."

"Well this won't be much different really, accept you'll get to attend lots of concerts."

"That makes it *totally* different," Atlanta insisted.

Cher ordered the Carnagie cheesecake, having read that it was the best in the whole empire. It cost 23 dags per slice, although their meal was on the house. It didn't disappoint her either. It seemed like an entire cheesecake concentrated into the one slice. Of course she could purchase an entire cheesecake at the food center for about 15 dags. Electra wanted down on the floor, but this was a restaurant, so Whiffle looked to Cher. Cher told her, "Go ahead and let her down. I'll just keep an eye on her."

Electra was crawling before her limbs made contact with the rug and was off like a shot. Cher stood from her seat in case she would need to run some interference with a waiter or guest seeking the rest room. The space between tables was narrow though Electra only crossed those lanes, shooting under tables with a grin. A woman at one table yelped and got her feet up onto her chair scanning the restaurant floor, perhaps thinking a rodent or something had brushed her ankle.

Another woman climbed her chair in a panic at the other end of the dining room and the man she was with stood in alarm. Electra was on her way back across the floor. Cher kept an eye out for adult traffic. Electra went scooting across the slim space around their own table and under it like a streak. She came to Atlanta's legs and pulled herself up to her feet for her very first time, using Atlanta as leverage. Electra's smile was one of wonder as much as of delight in the success of a new endeavor. It was a whole different world being upright and vertical. Atlanta said, "Just look at you, darling. You're so adorable."

Mel announced, "I captured that in super-high definition and saved it to Electra's scrapbook."

"Thanks Mel," Cher said truly grateful.

Electra spread her arms upward at Atlanta, still on her feet, though with a slight wobble now, and Atlanta grabbed her under her arm pits and lifted her to her lap looking into those amazing eyes. There seemed to be quite a connection between them. Then Electra placed her little palm on the center of Atlanta's chest. A look of surprise came over Atlanta's face. Cher could feel the blessings passing into Atlanta and knew her daughter had just collected her second student. This one was young and would require a great deal of preparation, and also needed to grow up some more to be ready. Raising Electra had already been quite an ordeal and she hadn't anticipated preparing youngsters who'd not yet matured to neophytes. *Oh well,* she thought, *Atlanta is sweet and she will develop much quicker in the company of these companions.* The roles of teacher and mother were a little blurred in her mind when it came to Atlanta.

After several minutes of passive intensity, catching the attention of all at the table, Electra got down and put one foot in front of the other moving forward, each step saved from a face-first crash by the next step. She came around the table to Cher and raised her arms. The arm raising somehow distracted her sense of vertical orientation and her bottom plopped onto the floor giving her a little shock. Cher lifted her into an embrace, passing her energy, so proud of her first walk. She sat down holding Electra, who decided she needed a little sucking and momma comfort after her big action in the world.

Atlanta was quite animated, and exclaimed, "She filled me with life, bliss and love, purer than I ever knew possible! What just happened!?"

Cher tried to explain, "Electra is the enlightened one who reincarnates every 2,500 years to transmit new teachings to our race. She recognizes you, which means you were her student last time she was here, and that you will be again once she grows up and you grow up some more."

"I'm going to be a Nun?" Atlanta asked appalled.

"No," Cher told her. "You will be a disciple which can take the form of householder, monk, single and sexually active, or many others. It simply means you will be awakened in this life to combat the ego forces devolving humanity, and help establish the new teachings and a better way forward."

"I was afraid sex would be taken from me before ever I had any," Atlanta stated with relief.

"Not at all sweetheart," Cher assured her. "You have just made a connection which will intensify exponentially as you and Electra grow up. You are the second of her students to whom she has already latched on."

"Who is the other?" Atlanta asked, wanting to know.

"I am," Whiffle spoke up.

Atlanta could not have been more delighted to be associated with super-star Whiffle. Electra had actually raised a little arm in

Whiffle's direction just when Whiffle had spoken up, from her perch in Cher's arms while sucking away. Atlanta was almost too high on this experience to formulate words and she exclaimed in ascending notes going off the top of the scale, "Ohmygosh!" as one word.

Electra laughed, losing the nipple from her mouth, in obvious delight. It was a totally magical moment and everyone at the table was raptly inside of it marveling. It seemed to dissolve back to the mundane the second Electra got Cher's nipple back in her mouth to resume sucking. Cher's attention was all on Electra, as she passed her daughter healing energy holding her with love; mother and child one in contentment. It was super-mundane and at the same time a calling and a force of awakening. Electra remained the center of attention at the table, now bringing her momma into the center as well.

Vegan asserted, "Now I am more determined than ever to follow you on this tour. I simply cannot believe my own experience. You are all so amazing."

Cher informed him, "These connections we are forging have great significance in service of the cosmic will and you are sensitive to that current, Vegan. You have found your place in the universe by courageously following your internal sense supported by your idolization of beautiful Hoola."

Vegan declared, "I experience you as a universal potency and will dedicate myself to learning from you, Cher Bulwinkle. I'm convinced in my heart that you are not a pirate but a force of good in the world."

"You've got that right," Bianca told him, using the opportunity to get her other magic hand onto him, thinking she needed to get the spy survey glasses with the x-ray vision so she could measure boys through their clothes. The problem with this though was you just never knew how much a flaccid penis was capable of expanding. As far as she knew, no one had ever plotted that ratio as a formula, distribution, or graph, and she needed to find the answer.

Vegan looked into Cher's eyes and told her, "I'm honored to be in your presence."

One of Bianca's hands went from gentle stroking love to become a poking pointy finger between two ribs as she educated him, "Connect, unite, and become her; don't put her on a pedestal and separate!"

Cher's eyes felt like a tractor beam to Vegan and they were inviting ascent, unity and oneness. A part of him resonated so deeply with her, was so irrevocably drawn to her spirit, like he had at last come home, and she was both the portal through within and the love and awareness condensed inside. He entered a state of nonidentity on the cusp of awakening and oriented aligning with the portal, drawn home like a prodigal son. Cher told him, "You are ready, and we just need to start meditating together. You will also need to work hard at the energy generation exercises."

"I'm determined to follow your every instruction with all of my attention," Vegan vowed.

"You are on a collision course with insight, sweetheart," she encouraged the boy.

Cher's cheesecake was gone and her plate licked entirely clean, though not antiseptically. All at the table had finished desert so they profusely thanked the manager, chef, service staff and kitchen help before taking their leave from the establishment, now joined by Vegan and Atlanta. Bianca held Vegan's hand and Atlanta took hold of Whiffle's feeling comradery with her as disciples of baby Electra.

Capital City had passed its annual Orange Wednesday Super Sale and the Winter Solstice was approaching; that commemorative holiday in reverence to shopping in which gifts were exchanged mandatorily; and children received toys they were led to believe had come from a mythical charitable man, impossibly antithetical to every principle of empire. It was the shopping season and every one of the 0.19% with expendable income were out doing it. The sidewalks were crowded. It was late enough in the day that people who'd begun work at ungodly hours were now getting off, and those with above subsistence incomes were all shopping. Traffic in and above the street was a mess.

Cher noticed Super-Agent Green dressed like a smart shopper with a fancy little shopping bag crash into a man walking a miniature canine of some kind—or it at least looked canine to Cher, sort of; and the little scooper robot following the man came to an abrupt halt when the man did. Green had obviously said something into his ear on impact and he'd tipped his hat to her before proceeding on his way. Green did not acknowledge Cher or her companions, slipping invisibly into the crowd.

Vegan informed the group, "There's a Vonet and Pellots just two blocks east of here. It's the premier headquarters for the entire interstellar chain. None are franchised. We own all of them. You'll find every label you can buy at Fleec You's, though at better prices, and we run some exclusive fashion lines as well."

"Lead the way," Pez replied.

"Once I've established your billings to my own account I'll take Rubix to some upscale men's habardasharies."

He led them to the entrance and held the door as they went in. Then he asked the first sales clerk he ran across, "Please send for the manager. I'm Vegan Casper."

The clerk hustled to the manager's office and returned with her in only minutes. Upon arrival the manager inquired, "How may I be of assistance Mr. Casper?"

"Please take special care of my friends and bill their purchases to my account. Inform our tailor that their garments are to be prioritized and alterations made immediately."

"Of course. I'll have our fashion consultant attend them and alert our tailor at once sir."

"Thank you. I'll leave them in the consultant's hands and return in a couple of hours."

The manager dashed off to effect the owner's bidding and the fashion consultant appeared in only moments. Vegan informed Pez and Hoola, "I'll be back as soon as Rubix is fitted with formal attire."

Vegan exited the store with Rubix and explained, "There's a Brooks & Brooks only a few doors down and they carry the top of the line suits."

Inside Brooks & Brooks Rubix purused the racksof suits in his size for a number of minutes. He finally told Vegan, "These suits are mostly extremely conservative and have little color."

Vegan pointed out an orange cashmire sports coat, one of the few with color, and Rubix dismissed it saying, "Orange is not my color."

"Then I know just the place and it's in the next block."

Vegan took Rubix to Wilks Bashful and he was captivated by the trendy colorful silk and wool broadcloth suits on display. He told Vegan, "I'm going to try this one on," referring to a silk royal purple suit with a bright red vest.

He chose a bright yellow shirt and metallic greenleather suspenders and tie. Vegan pointed out, "They have domer hats and gloves of that same metallic green."

Rubix tried on both and found them to his liking. He was then shown to the shoes department where he found soft leather shoes of the same color. Vegan insisted, "You will require some jewlry as well," taking Rubix to that section of the store.

"I would suggest emerald cuff links and tie clasp plus a single earring and a ring of the same."

Rubix selected the prescribed items from the jewlry case and was pleased with his ensamble, while Vegan spoke to the manager to explain, "We will require the alterations to be made within four hours and the clothes delivered to the Royal Monarch Intergalactic Hotel visiting dignitary suite under the name Cher Bulwinkle."

Vegan paid and Rubix thanked him. They left with the jewlry, accessories, shoes and yellow shirt to return to where the girls were shopping.

Rubix and Vegan found the eight females who were trying things on and amassing quite a heap of selections on the side of the checkout counter. Vegan usually found girl's shopping to be boring beyond brain-dead but with Hoola stripped down to her hug-me's to climb into a succession of dresses, it became the most stimulating activity he'd ever experienced. The girls had to put each thing on numerous times, comparing and contrasting, while slowly but surely eliminating and bringing it down to the really tough choices. It was necessarily time-consuming but it whizzed by for Vegan. The girls kept at it tirelessly.

In a few cases decisions could not be made in the moment and both items had to be purchased to sort out later. The monumental efforts of the females at last produced the final mound of articles too dear to return to the racks and the total came to less than twelve million dags including the jewelry. The wholesale costs to the store were closer to seven million. Vegan would make up the seven million to maintain the store's base operational capital. It was all well within his allowance.

Daffey met them on the Vonet & Pellot's landing platform on the 7th floor west side in the stretch Rolls Royal hover-limo and all ten of them crammed in. It took a while for Daffey to find another driver who would let her squeeze out onto the air-lane and then she had a terrible time getting over to the ruling family lane, but once within it, there was no traffic at all to contend with and they whipped by all the slow-moving hovercraft. While glad to be moving, Cher didn't like the ruling family lane one bit.

Back at the hotel Vegan got a VIP suite on the same floor as Cher, and in fact, on the same corridor. It was a step up from the one the band had and on par with Cher's. He arranged with his domestic staff to have some things from the mansion brought over for him and Atlanta. They used the time to all meditate together. Although there were no breakthroughs this session, Cher had managed to initiate and begin instructing Vegan and Atlanta in the sudden method.

The band completed its 42 planet tour then spent ten days in a recording-mixing and editing studio to produce a collection of their unreleased songs, and to clean up the live tracks from the tour. They would be releasing an entire concert live and a studio set featuring some new songs not yet performed live. Holocom news was already full of chatter about the bands upcoming tour with the Caspers and Bulwinkles following along. Unfortunately these segments on the band often inspired the display of holos of the Waltonraptor's ruined lawn. One commentator had the nerve to comment, "It's unlikely that Cher Bulwinkle lwill be receiving further invitations to the homes of other ruling families."

The party at the imperial palace had been interesting for Cher. She'd had several contacts to make there, all blind, and had seen and heard a little of the emperor. At one point she'd been eating at a table of deserts and he stood right behind her insisting to his Grand Wazu that a suitable title be thought up for him with 'God' in it. 'Hand of God', 'God's Justice', 'God Fearing' and a few others had been suggested by the Wazu, and what popped into Cher's mind was *God Forbid*, and then *God Forsaken*, and finally *God Damned*.

Atlanta had friends there at the party so both Hoola and Whiffle had an instant fan club. Hoola's platinum stylus and pocket device had gotten busy. Cousin Winnie did it with a minor prince up in the residential section of the palace. Vegan connected Kat with the Chief Executive Officer and brains behind Hostess Computers, and in a backroom deal, Kat was able to sell some potential industry-changing ideas to the company for a tidy 900 million dags once she'd verified everything and provided him with a data bead. She wasn't selling her 'Key to it all' or 'Key to everything'; only a couple of component programs from it; all stuff she'd already shared on Om.

Hoola had been approached by the owner of the largest holo studios on Glitter, who'd flown in for the party, for her to star in an extravagant action-romance tear-jerking thriller, but as it had no social value whatsoever, Hoola politely declined, citing her upcoming tour and her music as the reasons. She was more interested in starring in a meaningful holo-movie like the ones made by the small outlaw studios. These were never transmitted over the commercial network but could be found on ether-sites, and the better ones got about a trillion views.

Cher had brought Super-Agent Green to the party as her assistant and then set her loose once inside. Green had gotten into a secure terminal and managed to plant some very ordinary and benign seeming programs designed by Jard, and a few by Kat, inside the walls and firewalls of the imperial digital fortress protecting the imperial central computers, to sleep until they were needed. Green had also penetrated the security of the Emperor's Guard's Intelligence Division's vault and safe, scoring a treasure-trove of data beads. She'd loaded them into a lead-lined and electronically insulated large pocketbook and had to pass them on immediately upon escaping the party and palace to an Ahumdulilah agent with a larger and more powerful insulation container since the data beads had been painted with serious tracers and trackers. The agent had taken the container directly to the spaceport to load onto a chartered space ship headed to a planet in the White Lotus Galaxy. From there it would be brought to Rocky, and from Rocky to Ahumdulilah.

The details of the arrangements for the 190-day 58 planet Whirling Vortexes concert tour were worked out by the band's manager, Stilts, and the accommodations by Mel. Vegan had the *Amicable Specter* cleaned, waxed, and polished and was bringing nine ship crew, 12 security personnel and nineteen domestic staff on the journey. He was totally hopelessly and irrevocably in love with Hoola and it was obvious to everyone. Hoola seemed to be falling for him but was certainly fanning the flames of Vegan's passion quite deliberately. Vegan Casper was a very friendly boy and everyone liked him. All were glad to have him along. He had no idea yet that he was involved with a plot to topple the empire or that he was travelling on the point of the tip of the spear.

CHAPTER EIGHTEEN

The first stop on their second tour was the Mother System in the Whirlpool Galaxy. Whirlpool formed an equilateral triangle with Royal and White Lotus as a galaxy cluster. The Royal Empire had been expanding into the Whirlpool Galaxy for thousands of years, and with the data won from conquered planets there, had attained very complete maps of this galaxy. The same was not true of White Lotus Galaxy in which the history of Royal Imperial expansion claimed only hundreds of years. White Lotus contained some thirty-billion more stars than Whirlpool, and was in fact bigger than the Royal Galaxy.

The Mother System was home to perhaps the oldest surviving civilization in the Whirlpool Galaxy. Like Ganahar, the culture of Mother had evolved to moral anarchy, and also like it, Mother had been entirely unprepared for defending itself from aggression. Now the entire society on Mother was ruled tyrannically and brutally by devolved humanoids lacking all sense of unity, even a grain of empathy, and any kind of moral compass whatsoever. Four quite despicable ruling families presided over the planet. Corporate fascism controlled the population and enforced unjust imperial law with an iron fist. None of the four had the wealth of the Bulwinkle family, and of course, only the Emperor himself and one other family had more wealth than the Caspers. Pez milked this, demanding that Mother Space Control clear everyone out of the way for her, and they did. *Aphrodite, Sidekick, Amicable Specter,* and Bianca's drone didn't even slow down from their jump until approaching the planet's solitary moon.

They shot right down to the capital city of Gaia and the Momma's Love Intergalactic Hotel. An outdoor space had been prepared and clearly designated for the Casper yacht to land and park. The other three fit nicely into the Momma's Love spacecraft hanger. Their personal hotel assistant, which is what they called greeter-liaisons in the Whirlpool Galaxy, was waiting at the bottom of *Aphrodite's* ramp and another one at the bottom of *Amicable Specter's* ramp, since every ruling family visiting the hotel got one. The personal hotel assistant to the Bulwinkle family was named Mick. In his late twenties Mick stood five feet ten and a half inches tall, weighing in at about 165 pounds and was formed quite handsomely. His imperial basic was clearly spoken, containing a kind of drawl which stretched it longer. Mick was impeccably polite, dressed immaculately in his hotel livery, and seemed relaxed and grounded. Cher had done a little research into this planet and economy and knew that personal hotel assistants only earned fourteen thousand six hundred dags to start, and topped out at 17,550 dags annually. The average wage per year on Mother was 10,900 dags, about 1,100 below the official poverty line.

Cher saw the good man in Mick's aura and she noted past trauma in his irises. His attention to their party was complete and he drove skillfully, handled luggage expertly, and multitasked impressively with his skullcap. This, and Cher's sympathy, earned Mick a 10,000 dag tip for getting the family and their party to their rooms with their bags and handling their check-in. They had the penthouse, and the Matriarch suite and the Nature suite which were the two biggest, and they leased the entire 107th floor on which these two suites were located. The penthouse took up the entire 108th floor and had a large roof patio with a giant hot tub.

The hotel décor was subtle, in good taste, and gave the vibe of welcome rather than wealth. Cher liked it and felt more at home here than on the other imperial planets she'd visited. During their stay on Monarch, between Super-Agent Green and Mel, every weapon system in that solar system bigger than a class four was precisely located and mapped, along with sentry routes and docking locations for all the warships defending it. On Mother Cher had many contacts to make, both blind and face-to-face conversations, and Super-Agent

Green would be on a tight schedule to make all of hers. Both Elanem and Winston would also be making contacts here. Marlboro would get to make a couple of blind ones within the hotel, and Lucky would be permitted to collect passive-intel out to a ten-block radius of Momma's Love.

The Caspers each had two main White Sun human body guards and shared eight additional security personnel, half of them white sun. The band had a mix of white and yellow sun body guards and security staff, and generally utilized them laxly and erratically. Unknown to Cher or her party—with the exception of Super-Agent Green—the Ahumdulilah Intelligence Service kept at least one agent watching over the Bulwinkle party at all times having their backs. The five crew members of *Sidekick* and the eight 'slaves' it carried were all highly trained elite agents, as were Pippy and Alice who travelled on the *Aphrodite*. With the Caspers following the Whirling Vortexes tour as companions of the Bulwinkle's their cover could not have been more complete and secure. And then there was the top-secret Deputy Chief Adherence Examiner, Nazia, which was Mel's cover.

The computer systems of the Imperial Adherence Examiners housed a cornucopia of dormant takeover programs from both Jard and Trix, thanks to one of their Deputy Chiefs, and now every dark secret of their entire history was an open book to the Ahumdulilah and Om Intel Services. While Cher was getting dressed to go to the concert Mel told her, "I want to be an Imperial Secret Police Commander and wear one of those slick black naugahide spy coats with epaulets."

"I think you'd look sinister," Cher commented.

"I'd look dashing," Mel insisted.

"You'd probably have more opportunity to create a cover if you had your male android body along," Cher told her.

"Funny you should mention that," Mel replied. "It's already passed through Ahumdulilah and been received on Rocky, and is now on its way by small freight to Mother."

"Have you found an identity to exploit?" Cher asked.

"Commander Hienz was undercover with the Secret Police and went missing an hour ago. No one knows he's missing except the Ahumdulilah agents who took him, and their Intel Service. My male android will get to wear a mask and the vocal system has been matched to Hienz's voice exactly, passing all vocal recognition tests."

"You'd never pass a body scan," Cher pointed out.

"No," Mel admitted, "but I'll have his retnals and his finger prints as well as a few drops of his blood in the index finger they poke for DNA sampling."

"Have they gotten passwords and codes out of the real Hienz yet?"

"He's proving to be a tough nut to crack, but the Ahumdulilah agents haven't brought out the big nut-cracker yet."

"It sounds like crucial work of the highest importance, Marshal Mel."

"Why thank you, Knight Commander Pez, 333rd Wu, and the Rajaha and Avahat."

"Mel," Cher complained, stretching Mel's name into three syllables.

"Just ignore her, sweetheart," Lai advised affectionately.

Electra was standing with her knees and hip joints quite bent, low to the floor as babies do becoming toddlers, and she was making the 'pick-me-up' signal with her arms. Cher scooped her into an embrace, passing her energy, and forgot all about hurt feelings. Lai had Gumby belted into his new backpack pouch. He'd outgrown the last one and had been emptying jars of baby food like nobody's business of late, producing a growth spurt. It made his new walking somewhat rubbery.

The band was already at the coliseum where the concert was being held. It wouldn't start for another two and a quarter hours but the Caspers insisted upon getting there early to hang out with the band backstage. Atlanta was so excited she couldn't sit still and Vegan was on a romantic high, in love with Hoola, who was cheering him on.

Mick arrived promptly with a hover limo-bus when Cher buzzed him. Sarhi had great interest in this planet so the aunts were attending the concerts with them. They dressed prudishly, and without a hint of color, yet in clothing of the empire; just not from anywhere popular. The *Sidekick* crew accompanied the aunts as their security escort. They nearly filled the limo-bus. An imperial class 'A' license was required to drive one of these things. Mick handled it like a sports-hover. He gave them a view of the capital city of Gaia before bringing them efficiently to the coliseum backstage landing platform where he handled the security check for the Bulwinkle-Casper party and band.

Even though they weren't a ruling family the band had rated a hotel personal assistant and his name was Don. He met Cher's party at the landing platform and led them through the backstage maze to the private lounge the band was taking its leisure within. Hoola was up and skipped to Vegan the moment they entered, and Vegan went sprinting to her. Atlanta followed Pogo around like a puppy with a constant string of intimately personal questions. His super-model girlfriend was flying in just before the concert was to begin from a swimsuit shoot in the tropics of Glitter, so he hadn't long to put up with Atlanta's prying. Whiffle came right over to Cher; well to Electra actually, since she stood behind Cher when she got there. Kat was on Cher's arm as her spouse, and Ahhu/Bianca had briefed Kat thoroughly on how to take care of Pez the orphan girl. Ahhu had mentioned that the divine being inside Pez needed no taking care of and was incomprehensible anyway.

The lounge was comfortable with soft surfaces and cushy seats, warm earth tones, and an almost barren simplicity unifying the space to become the primary ornamentation; sort of the ornament of no-ornament. The balance and aesthetic harmony of the room seemed to express the contemplative state. Electra liked the lounge and wanted down. Cher set her feet-first on the floor and Electra grabbed one of Whiffles fingers for support to take her disciple on a walk around the room. Whiffle went willingly and Electra was entirely enthralled with the experience. Cher looked on wondering at the development involved in fully animating and ambulating a physical body. Watching toddlers grappling with it truly revealed what an ordeal it is, and after 2,500 years in the highest paradise, what an amazing sacrifice and compassionate undertaking on Electra's part.

When Electra fell asleep it was less than half an hour from show time and the coliseum was filling up. Cher left Electra with Atlanta and went in search of her primary contact. They were to meet in the corridor behind Cher's seating section and she wore her nerdy glasses running the facial recognition program. Her briefing text on him was slim. His name was Tonsu, and as an engineer and intergalactic systems analyst the imperials had him overseeing the central fire control systems for planetary defense. He was also supposed to be a link to an expansive underground network operating under the imperial noses. The text read that he was more than happy to give imperial fire control data to anyone opposed to the empire, absolutely free. Clearly he was not a greedy profiteer.

Both Evenrude and Johnson kept to Cher's vicinity; Johnson on an alko line and Evenrude standing outside the lady's room as if waiting on his wife. Cher walked slowly about scanning the faces with her nerdy glasses. She thought to herself how Bianca's new x-ray spy survey glasses weren't really any more fashionable. A soft ping sounded in her ear and a face was highlighted in hot pink by the glasses. The text below the face read "Tonsu". Cher approached, and as she got close and his eyes were on her, she extended her hand and said, "Hi, my name is Cher."

He took her hand with a firm but gentle mindful grip and said, "I'm Tonsu."

"My bodyguards found no sensors in the coliseum except right at the entrances,' Cher informed him.

"No one indigenous spies for money, information to sell, or for blackmail. The only sensors around are the imperial's and they're too cheap to place them about liberally," Tonsu shared.

Cher hugged Tonsu which triggered the data transmission and reception simultaneously for both of them as she whispered, "Cross tree" into his ear. His eyes and a slight nod acknowledged reception. Cher inquired, "What type of underground network exists on Mother?"

"Ever since we were conquered the authentic alive lineages of our principle spiritual methodologies and practices have survived by becoming secret, with no electronic reference anywhere, and have grown so extensive that the entire native population has access. The ancient tongue for which there exists no textual translations and is always learned orally in childhood, gives us a way to communicate privately; though only Sterling can be spoken publicly. This network that unifies all natives has also become our underground resistance network."

"How can I arrange a meeting with a senior spiritual leader?" Cher asked.

"The masters reside in the most remote areas of the planet with the most severe climates, and do not come out of hiding."

"With a picture of a master and a fairly specific location on your globe, I can go to them without my body, as rainbow light. Would you help me?"

"Of course," Tonsu replied. "The Ahumdulilah people call you the Rajaha. To the people of Mother you are the Khedar."

Oh no, Cher thought to herself. She asked Tonsu, "Do you have an image of one of the masters?"

"The master of my lineage. His name is Narop. Here is a holo of him. I've sent his coordinates to your pocket device. I see you have one of the new hostess slenders."

"I just got it on Monarch before coming here. I'm supposed to inform you that we'll have the entire empire connected through one-time codes in eight months from now and covert plans already in process by then. Two weeks after our coms are in place we will spread the truth about this empire with revolutionary messages through their own holocom intergalactic system. Two weeks after that I hope to have a fleet assembled and ready for action. When the signal goes out revolution will break out on every planet at once. Demolitions and sabotage will be global, snipers will be everywhere, and well-planned attacks on key targets will hit with surprise at dozens of locations on every planet. Our fleet will assault Monarch causing the emperor to recall many war ships from enslaved worlds. I hope to have half a million ground troops with hard shell combat suits and heavy weapons hover platforms and vehicles. Most native paramilitary forces will be with us from the start. The imperials are lazy and leave natives in many highly technical and specialized positions from which they can cause great harm. There is still a good deal of planning to do, and many more assets to collect and organize."

"We've been collecting intel while making plans for many years, and everyone on Mother knows the Khedar has come and the time approaches."

"It was very nice meeting you," Cher told him, shaking his hand again and passing him some internal energy. "I'm going to a stall in the lady's room to visit Narop."

"I'm deeply honored to meet you, Khedar. Call on me anytime. I am at your service," Tonsu said sincerely.

Cher went to the lady's room and sat on a toilet. She slowed her abdominal breathing going swiftly through the withdrawal of her senses and generation of her rainbow body, to employ the forceful projection, exiting out her central channel at the crown of her head. She was immediately in front of the face she visualized in the snow-capped rugged mountain peaks of the remote mountainous outback. She was glad she didn't have her body with her because it looked severely chilly. She introduced herself, "Hi, my name is Cher," in her 'let's make friends' voice.

Narop looked to be at least 100 hundred years old and possibly much older than that. He said, "I am Narop. The time is nearly upon us. I see you Khedar."

"Do any warrior-monks train on this planet?" Cher inquired.

"Mother has warrior monks and you will need them," Narop told her. "I'm not one of them and they don't train here. You seek Musash and he will be seeking you."

"Do you have a holo of him and a location on the globe?" she asked.

"There is no electricity here; but we do have a hard copy physical image of him. I will have it brought to you."

Not two minutes later a disciple came literally running into the cavern where Cher sat in her body of light in front of Narop, waving an 8x10 glossy image on some kind of paper. He held it for Cher. Her brain was at a loss for a moment with the two-dimensional image, flat as a board. Slowly the contrast grew depth and the image coalesced into the face of a man she could recognize and retain in memory. She studied it a while then looked to Narop and asked, "Do you have a specific location on the planet for him?"

"I heard he was travelling to the capital to meet you at your hotel. He'd been living in the jungle near the equator in the dense rainforest, far from navigable rivers. He will find you."

There is a larger unity I would bring you and your followers inside of in meditation. It is called the Intergalactic Spiritual Congress. By tuning our meditations to the spiritual congress and coordinating in space-time to make them simultaneously, we can greatly amplify the evolutionary impulse we call the 'Calling', and significantly enhance every intention and effort holding this orientation. The spiritual congress supports me in battle with a force of precision and speed not otherwise possible. I will send my teacher to you. Her name is Sarhi and she is the Im of Islohar, and Abbot of the Spiritual Congress. She's a moral anarchist and says it alone can reflect in human society the justice and freedom of the Divine Mind."

"Our minds meet in the same evidence," Narop stated. "I want to meet Sarhi and this congress sounds like a spiritual force and movement ripe for the natives of Mother."

"I must go. I'll send Sarhi to you. I'm honored to meet you and in awe of the people of Mother. We are within less than nine months of our great liberation uprising."

You are even more than we'd hoped for and a humbling example of long-enduring one-pointed effort and determination. Did you know that before you became the first Wu of Ganahar you were the Hierophant of the Amonrahonians?"

"I did not," Pez said with shock, losing her Cher identity completely for a moment, and almost her Pez identity as well.

"If the liberation succeeds, and I have faith that it will, you and your daughter must return to Mother. We have stone chiseled texts dating back more than 92,000 thousand years stored in caves beneath the great desert, which would truly interest you. We know part of your story and the history of the Amonrahonian race."

"I would love to," Cher replied. "In spite of imperial suppression and tyrannical control, I've found the people resilient and the culture yet welcoming and nurturing. Your world draws me. Thank you."

"Thank you, Khedar, we are all grateful to you here on Mother."

Cher returned to the stall and toilet she was sitting on. It had numbed her poor bottom. As she sped up her metabolism her bladder demanded relief, and since she was already on a toilet with her panties down, she made a tinkle while rising out of a coma. She brought her internal energy from her deep viscera to her extremities and skin, visualizing her meridians and willfully directing it. When she felt her internal strength pulsing within again she rose from her little throne and exited the stall as the toilet self-flushed. Cher stuck her hands in the washer-dryer, something ingrained as a hygienic habit since her earliest childhood, then left the lady's room to almost collide with Evenrude.

He told her, "You were in there so long that I was about to go in and check on you."

"I met with a spiritual master of Mother in my rainbow body. They have an amazing underground spiritual network which has taken on the dual function of coordinating revolution here. All the natives of Mother are completely with us."

"The natives here are relaxed and attentive despite the perpetual dangers, and the kindest folks we've yet encountered in this empire. They remind me of the people I've met from Ganahar."

"This is the oldest civilization we know of besides the mysterious Amonrahonians," Cher informed him. "Like Ganahar, Mother had attained a moral anarchy before the empire conquered their planet."

"You ought to direct some external resources to help them when the fighting starts," Evenrude suggested.

"Perhaps we will personally, and let the fleet assault Monarch without us. I could place Shudiy on Swenah's *Apollo* to help them."

"This planet would be my choice of where to strike the empire," Evenrude agreed.

"I have to find some people and make contact so don't follow too close," Cher requested.

"I'll just keep line of sight from a distance," he acknowledged.

Cher asked Mel, "Could you help me locate my contacts, Marshal Mel?"

Mel said, "The micro and nano spy lenses have just positioned themselves, sprung from a drone flown over from *Aphrodite*. I'm checking now, my very best friend, and I've already got one in section F, row twenty-nine, seat fourteen."

"Thanks sweetheart."

Mel told her. "Got another, G-18-3."

After a pause, Mel announced, "One's in A-6-31, and the last is at the vege-stick stand, waiting on line, behind section L."

"You're terrific, my love, thanks," Cher said gratefully.

It would have taken her glasses more than an hour to process that many faces. The band, now all awakened, had found a new and higher unity of harmonies and harmonics so intricately integral and one that it truly mirrored the cosmic music of spheres, or those vibrations harmonized by the different levels of pre-material emanations of forces and potencies culminating as matter. These objective vibrations lifted the spirit opening the eye in the forehead and igniting the extracranial point above the crown in a presence divine. The audience was transported. A physical body alive and well could not possibly help but move in time to the music as the only way to more fully absorb the goodness it channeled.

No previous performance had come close to this. As one of their old hits and favorites concluded the band did not even pause, but went right into improvisation so perfect and polished that it sounded as if they'd been practicing this piece for a hundred years. It was the magic of true creativity blending elite skill with pure imagination in absolute freedom, united into a singularity abiding by the connections of love and practice between the band members. It was all being captured on super-high definition holo-movies and soundtracks and streaming live around the orb of Mother. This native culture could fully appreciate the state of mind of the band members from whence such sound could only originate, reflecting the state back to the band. The band energized the audience and the audience energized the band, becoming an ascending concentration of intensity. Cher was in union with the music-band-audience, dancing in the corridor with the rest, and could not be moved to seek a contact in this moment. Even Evenrude was lost dancing up a storm.

Electra was so absorbed and stimulated by the music that all her pee-detector diaper sensors went off at once and Cher rushed to where Atlanta was sitting. When she arrived Electra was on her back in Atlanta's lap smiling with a fresh diaper adjusting itself to her little pelvis, and wiggling to the tunes of the Whirling Vortexes. Cher was relieved and delighted. Since she was already on the move she went to make her contacts, keeping the music alive inside her as she went. Kind of dance-walking along.

The music was total liberation, and in that sense, pure revolution without lyrics or thought construction, simply arising the unity, love, and awakening the empire focused all its might to suppress, restrain, and stamp out. Cher danced into her contacts' chests whispering nouns related to the parts and pieces of ancient sea going vessels into their ears, and receiving confirming dance movements from them making the whole spy business thing a recreational riot.

There were ruling family members and minions in the audience who didn't get it and could not for their extreme negative balance of merit possibly enter into the state of contemplation with the natives and the band. They blamed this outwardly as they always did with everything. They suspected a vast conspiracy involving the entire audience designed and enacted specifically to make them feel alienated. This suspicion grew to certainty as their suspicions generally tended to do, and their annoyance with the band and audience reached the boiling point. It was an outrage that such low unwashed peons would have the audacity to conspire to make them feel uncomfortable, and the band was clearly complicit in this somehow. Several were on their coms demanding police actions from an assortment of imperial authorities.

With the Caspers and Bulwinkles so tight with the Whirling Vortexes, not to mention the band's insane intergalactic popularity, no imperial authority would take action against the concert but several promised to take every audience member into custody for some 'lesson teaching' who fell below a specific level of capital wealth. The bar was set high. Hover crafts full of imperial secret police and imperial peace keepers in riot gear with crowd control weapons were converging from every direction on the coliseum. Mel mentioned to Cher, "Imperial actions against this audience are underway for experiencing something the ruling family members here and their minions could not, and so making them feel uncomfortable."

"Did your android body arrive yet?"

"Not for another quarter hour, so I'm headed to the coliseum in my female one as Imperial Deputy Chief Adherence Examiner Nazia."

"Please see what you can do to mitigate this. Vegan and I will help."

"I'm on it, very best friend."

Cher returned to sit beside Atlanta in the reserved seating and Electra wanted to be nursed when she got there. Electra was soaking up the energy her mother passed her and sucking up the milk from her breast, still connected with the music. The saxophone let wail accentuated by the other instruments to highlight it almost like a solo, and Electra stopped sucking to look at her disciple with unobstructed glee. She did not return to the breast until the song was over. She happily went back to Atlanta's lap when she'd had enough milk and momma-nurture. Cher told Atlanta, "I have to go outside the coliseum for a few minutes. Trouble is brewing there and I'll need to borrow your brother."

"Alright."

To Vegan, on the other side of Atlanta, Cher said, "I need your help with a little imperial matter, collecting outside the coliseum."

"Gladly," he replied, getting up.

They walked together to the nearest public exit and stepped out of the building. A rainbow of different colored laser sights blossomed on their chests and foreheads. Vegan said anxiously, "This can't be good."

Pez shouted, "You are targeting Vegan Casper and Cher Bullwinkle and we are recording this event."

Stand down orders were issued and the laser show winked out.

Cher shouted, "We would like to speak with the person in charge of this ill-conceived operation. That would be NOW!!"

Evenrude and Johnson had stepped outside with them and so had Vegan's bodyguards, Martin and Lewis. Martin helped Vegan into a fanny pack shield generator he carried for him. Vegan appeared more relaxed once he got his shields up. It had been daunting to get targeted by so many murderous numbskull imperials. The fearless leader of these terrorists came forward quite timidly, already looking thoroughly rebuked. Cher demanded, "What is the meaning of this?!!"

"Some ruling family members in the audience complained of a native conspiracy to alienate them and want us to incarcerate the whole audience. I'm just following orders."

"Who is your commanding officer?" Cher insisted. "Those family members need a psychiatrist, not police action."

"I am in charge here now," Deputy Chief Nazia stated with confidence, just arriving on the scene.

She had a platoon of Adherence Examiners with her, and they were all scanning every detail. The Secret Police were immune to public outcry but quaked in their boots in the face of Adherence Examiners. Mel said, "Clear all these personnel out of here immediately. The people from whom your orders originated will now become the subjects of the most intrusive and penetrating adherence examinations ever performed on Mother."

"Yes Ma'am! Right away Ma'am!"

The secret police captain turned on his heels smartly and began shouting at his subordinates as if being here was all their faults. The troops began mounting their hovercrafts disappointed with the anticlimax after getting all dressed up in their special gear. They'd really been looking forward to this. Deputy-Chief Nazia told Vegan and Cher, "I'd better go clear out the other sides of the coliseum before the fans begin to exit."

"Thank you Deputy Chief," Cher said politely.

When the Adherence Examiner left Vegan commented, "That examiner's voice sounded exactly like your friend Mel's"

"It did, kind of," Cher stated evasively.

The band was taking a break backstage which was where Cher had to go to find Atlanta and Electra, and for Vegan to find Hoola.

Tramp and Bianca had sure found each other, Cher noticed. Pogo was looking bored with his super-model girlfriend, who rally didn't understand his music at all; only his fame and wealth. Kat latched on to Cher milking her role as spouse to be close to her teacher. Hark was walking just behind Gumby ready to catch him, and every moment nearly needed him to, as Gumby fell into each new step forward.

Whiffle came to see Electra and Electra was exceptionally pleased to see her. The emerging toddler placed her palm on Whiffle's chest between her breasts and made eye contact with the musician. Whiffles face went into wonderment and her eyeballs bulged. Cher could feel it and couldn't wait to hear what it would sound like as music coming out of Whiffle when the band started up again. Atlanta sensed something was going on and got one hand on Electra and the other on Whiffle to join the circuit.

The last set was best of all, maintaining Electra in ecstatic bliss for the duration. The band had never played so well. Holoclips from this live concert were already being seen in three galaxies and download sales of the band's music since the first tour began exceeded half a trillion dags. The first tour itself had netted the band close to 400 million dags, and the second tour, since some stops were benefits, was anticipated to bring in just a little more. The tours drove the download sales and the Caspers and Bulwinkles helped keep the media spotlight on the band. After tonight's concert Pogo was ready to negotiate a better deal with their production company or start the band's own.

Vast wealth from Xegachtznel, Yuban, Hub and White Lotus galaxies had been collected and smuggled to Rocky during the band's first tour and infused into the Bulwinkle capital. The profits of these new investments had not yet dropped below 23% and had been averaging closer to 27%. The net worth of the Bulwinkle family was right around 9.1 trillion and rising, pushing the family status into the top twenty-five ruling families as number 25. The absolute law of the realm was that pecking could only occur from greater to lesser wealth. Since emperors had been taking by far the biggest share since the empire's first origins to pass on to their progeny, the living seated emperor was 73 trillion richer than the next richest and really hadn't a thing to worry about, because the whole system was set up primarily in his exclusive favor, rigged solid. He could peck anywhere he damn well pleased and he was quite a pecker.

Mick, Don, and Felix were all there waiting on the backstage landing with hovercrafts to get the families and band, with their entourages, back to the Momma's Love Hotel. Musash was seated in meditation outside the penthouse door when Cher and her party arrived. He was right in front of the door so they all came to a stop before him. Musash looked into Cher's eyes and asked, "What is the nature of 'What is'?"

Cher made a fist and held her forearm up vertically. Musash asked, "What did your face look like before you were born?"

"I was neither born nor have a face," Cher told him assertively.

"Is it the wind or the flag that moves?" Musash asked harshly.

"Wind and flag are movements of mind," Cher answered immediately.

"I am Musash, and I'm delighted to meet you Khedar."

"I'm called Cher Bulwinkle at the moment, and I'm so glad you could come."

Musash stood as the door opened behind him, triggered by the hotel code sent by Cher's tiara. They all entered the penthouse. Musash asked, "Is there an open space where we can spar?"

"There's a dance studio, come along," Cher replied, handing Electra to Atlanta.

It was an empty room with a hard wood floor, rails on each wall, and one wall was mirrored. Cher went to the center and assumed a fighting stance. Musash removed his sandals and folded his coat carefully, placing it neatly on his footwear. Then he did some stretching, after which he did some energy generation. Cher joined him in the energy generation after feeling foolish holding a fighting stance while he'd stretched.

When Musash was good and ready he took the center of the room in a low stance with space between his feet both side to side and front to back for stability in all directions. He raised one arm in a curve across his chest, with the back of his palm facing Cher. His left foot was forward and his left arm raised so Cher stepped up with her right foot forward, touching the back of her right hand to his left. She sank into the flow state knowing the energy around her, including that at Musash's disposal. They stood sunk low and relaxed, each seeking tensions in the other, with four ounces of pressure between the backs of their hands.

Cher feigned tension. She felt his move coming before it began, following as he withdrew winding up, to back him up at his limit with insufficient force drawn to unleash with consequence. He spun off before she could push beyond his limit, and they faced off again. This time he employed lighting jabs at her torso and her forearm blocks were there each time to deflect them. He increased the tempo of his jabs to a blur and still met only effective blocks. Then she sprang 'sweep the lotus' knocking his fists away from about solar plexus height to get a palm on his torso, already pushing and stepping forward; though his expert yield and turning off from the direction of the push into a quadrant she had no immediate leverage on, brought them back to facing off.

They stood facing each other and Musash's left forearm was raised between them. Both of Cher's palms touched it lightly with only four ounces. She no longer had to read energy because she had attained the level at which she just knew. He advanced so slowly it was almost imperceptible and Cher maintained the four-ounce-touch, not letting it build up, by shifting weight to her rear leg rolling back. When her weight had shifted from 30% on her rear leg to 100%, she then surged forward unleashing her internal energy in a tidal wave. Musash yielded the majority of the force but, there was just so much of it that what he was unable to yield and escape uprooted him. Her push had him flying backwards off his feet. Evenrude had knowingly stood by the wall behind Musash convinced from the start that Cher would require no catching. He scooped Musash gently from the air about a second before he would have crashed into the wall, and set him down on his feet.

Musash made eye contact and said, "Thank you. That was a kind gesture."

Evenrude nodded graciously. Musash told Cher, "You are beyond any preparation I can offer you and exceed our greatest hopes. Now we must discuss strategies."

"The best way to win a war is before any fighting occurs," Cher stated.

"We are on the same page," Musash informed her.

"We do all we can to this end, please believe me, and we are open to doing far more. Spies are of the utmost importance and currently spying is our only war activity besides research."

"We have natives of Mother in positions of responsibility here who can take down more than 50% of electrical power, the imperial central computer here, fire-control for planetary defense, some of the biggest space based weapons around the planet, ground transportation signals, planetary coms, the maglev rail lines, and many other things."

"This planet I intend to fight at myself so you will have some outside resources from the start," Cher informed him. "Most outside assets will be directed to attack Monarch. That is where the deciding battle for the empire must be fought; on the emperor's front lawn in his own neighborhood."

"I like it," Musash enthused. "He has such a taste for war. I wonder if that will change when it's visited upon him."

"Do you have hard-shell combat suits with propulsion here on Mother?"

"We do but we need fuel cells and power cells for them. There are at least 50,000 combat suits in the imperial armory on the outskirts of Gaia and we have the codes, contact lenses and DNA to get in. We've always seen the taking of that armory as a necessary opening move so we have excellent plans for doing it, updated daily."

"Send the specs for your fuel cells and power cells to my new hostess slender and I'll see that all you need is smuggled in to you well before they'll be needed."

She'd set her hostess to broadcast its code using her tiara, so Musash could see it on his and just reply the data she asked for back to her. It took a moment for him to connect to the right database and locate the specific files, and then upload to her hostess was instant once he had. Cher looked at the specs and stated, "We can manufacture theses and fill the fuel cells with a more concentrated fuel adding minutes to your thrusters. The power cells will be no problem. How many do you need?"

"We have 11,814 of our own combat suits stored," Musash answered. "We intend to supply ourselves mainly from what the Empire has stored here on Mother."

"Our *Classic of War* clearly recommends that," Cher shared.

"We have no way to destroy or damage the imperial war ships orbiting our planet and they are what ultimately control our world," Musash lamented.

"They don't keep any of their largest classes of ships in your system," she pointed out. "I will have ships and small craft to wage the battle in space. We hope to solve the problem of the explosive chips they adhere to major arteries in the bodies of their ship's officers. If we do, many of their ships would revolt with us."

"Our best surgeons have studied this for many decades and short of replacing a section of the artery it cannot be done, but the explosives can be drained from the chip leaving it inert and harmless."

"Have you done this?"

"Not me personally," he clarified, "but it has been done with a captain and several officers on one of the class four imperial ships here."

"I need all of that research data," Cher informed him. "We need to design a self-administering device to hone-in on the chip, drill it out, and extract the explosive safely and efficiently. Such a device is possibly the single most important asset for defeating this empire."

"Here, I'm sending it to your hostess slender. The file is eight terabits. I'm not sending the early research, just that into drilling and draining the explosives from the chip. The technical problem for the device will be stabilizing the chip for drilling."

"Engineers, biologists and surgeons from at least three planets will get right to work on it," she encouraged. "This research is totally invaluable when it comes to saving lives."

"We could use about 5,000 sticks of Q-9 plastic explosives before the fun starts. We have plans for far more demolitions than we have explosives to produce them."

"You shall have them," Cher vowed. "We can ship them from Rocky inside a large shipment of ground roasted stimulant beans."

"My school has trained 29,300 warrior monks; nearly as many as we had centuries ago before we were invaded. We have over 200 million trained for Mother's militia but only about four million have blasters, and those are mostly stolen over the years from the imperials. We have 7,535 demolition experts with extensive undercover training ready to plant explosives, and 4,182 commercial pilots prepared with excellent plans to steal imperial combat small craft. A quarter million snipers are already armed and know their positions on urban rooftops around the globe. We also have 8,300 elite Special Forces all positioned in companies and platoons in urban areas with specific operations planned."

"If you have more to add to your wish list then please send it to me and I'll see what I can do," Cher promised. "I wish every planet in this empire was as prepared as Mother is."

"You are truly an inspiration, Khedar, and more skilled than we hoped you would be," Musash told her, "I have trained my whole life for this moment and I waited all my life to meet you. I'm far from disappointed and prepared to serve you to the death."

"Serve me to victory and keep yourself alive, dear Musash. You are truly needed," Cher told him affectionately.

"Victory it is then," he agreed.

"I can find you anywhere on Mother in my body of light now that we've connected. I'll check in with you weekly, wherever you are and from wherever I am. It's the ultimate secure coms."

"When you do, may I introduce you to some of my officers?" He pleaded. "It would increase their morale greatly."

"Of course. I'd be most pleased to meet them. I'm a warrior-monk myself, and Knight Commander of the Clearlight Order on Om."

"Our Order is called the Adamantine Will and you are our Vicar General," Musash informed her.

"My own Vicar General may beg to differ," Cher mentioned.

"Then he would be differing with facts. Wait and see."

"I'm also a girl who wants to feel part of the gang and not set apart with titles and projections," she confided.

"I know this," he told her, "and I know the loneliness of command. I heard you were orphaned as a child and raised by adepts in a monastery. We will love you as family and follow your spirit which we trust implicitly and have total faith in."

"I will do my best. I work most effectively with friends and equals, not subordinates. I have much to learn about Mother and rely on you and the native leaders."

We are at your service. I must go. I look forward to seeing your magnificent rainbow body, Khedar."

Thank you Musash, you've no idea how much you've helped with the explosive chip data."

"Do you have a sword?"

"Of course," Cher replied. "I have an adamantine broadsword folded and refolded 108 times. It has carbon edges and was made by Om's most famous sword smith."

"We must spar with swords sometime."

"I'd like that," she said sincerely. "My sword work is my most cultivated skill."

"Then you must be formidable indeed."

Musash left the penthouse with a deep standing bow to Cher. Cher bowed to Musash then gave him one of her best Space Marine salutes. Her clothing snapped and sound emerged from the speeding passage of her arm through the air. That was a hand you would not want to be in opposition to. Cher had Mel encrypt the data she'd received form the master warrior-monk and send it on to Ahumdulilah, Om, Trident, Rally and Gzzklns. The hour was late so Cher went to the bedroom to go to sleep. She had to squeeze in between Whiffle and Bianca. Hoola was in Vegan's suite and Atlanta had put Electra in the hotel hovercrib where she was sleeping soundly. The bed was no less crowded for Hoola's absence since cousin Winnie had joined them, wrapped around Muffet.

The next morning Cher was having a room service breakfast at the dining room table in the Momma's Love penthouse when a native woman came to the door calling on her. Sarhi showed her into the dining room. The woman was six feet tall, slender and well-toned weighing about 170 lb.'s, and she was beautiful. Her eyes were full of presence and vacant of self. Cher connected deeply the moment their eyes met. She sat beside Cher at the table and said assertively, "I have no fear."

Cher raised her right palm in the gesture of no-fear, dissolving herself into the flow-state. The woman asked her, "If you must pass a master on the road with neither silence nor words, what do you do?"

"I might test him with an uppercut since I am the road, the master, the words and the silence, and these are all phenomenon of the mind."

"I am Amazonia, Priestess of the warrior-maidens on Mother. We have waited and prepared long for your arrival. We are the Order of Mother's Compassionate Guardians and I am here to initiate you, and empower you to the position of High Priestess as it was written long ago."

"I don't know that I'm worthy?" Cher said with a little intimidation.

"Having a body and human life do not make you unworthy and your life process cannot taint or defile your pristine consciousness. Your holy work and sacrifices over the millennium have reaped such merit that you are incapable of containing it all. You are the Khedar."

"How many warrior-maidens are there?" Cher inquired.

"We are only twelve hundred but we are the most fiercesome warriors on this planet, and we are individually infiltrated in the households of the ruling families and highest imperial officials on Mother."

"Then the warrior-maidens can prevent much bloodshed," Cher acknowledged. "I'll enjoy working with you."

Amazonia dipped and unsheathed the little razor-sharp knife from Cher's boot, too quick even to leave a blur, and was back up handing it to Cher before Evenrude got his hand to his holstered sidearm. Cher took the knife as directed having no clue what this was about. Amazonia rolled up her sleeve, offering her forearm, and said, "Cut!"

Cher obediently swiped a slice upon it. A very shallow intended one, to be sure, since she thought this might be some kind of blood-sister thing and that she'd be getting cut next. But to her shock and surprise there was no blood and no scratch or trace of the razor-sharp blade's passing. "Harder!" Amazonia insisted, considering Cher's last effort to be rather wimpy and feeble.

Cher made a slice with pressure to reach the bone and still there was no blood and no sign. She knew this was the final outcome of the transmutation provoked by the energy generation exercises and soft martial arts, and that it was also a byproduct of the final attainment of some breathing and visualization sitting practices. Pez was working on it but had not achieved this yet herself. She said, "You are my teacher."

"Only for a while, then you will be mine," Amazonia replied

"You are High Priestess until that time," Cher told her.

"I must do what is written and there is no shame in a High Priestess receiving instruction form one of her priestesses," Amazonia insisted.

With a little coaxing and some support from Sarhi, Amazonia convinced Cher to go through the intiation and receive the empowerment. By the time it was over, some three hours later, Cher was the official High Priestess of the Compassionate Guardian warrior maidens. She'd become so excited about it that she insisted Amazonia initiate each of her female disciples into the order. With the pick-me-up signal, a few other highly personal sign language gestures and only a little wailing, Electra got herself initiated too. Then they learned that Amazonia would be accompanying them on this second tour, just begun here on Mother. Sarhi offered up the empty berth in her cabin and everything was settled without involving Cher. Cher couldn't help suspecting that Sarhi had already been in contact with Amazonia, or at least known about her beforehand. Things became even more suspicious for Pez when she learned that Super-Agent Green was already a member of the order.

Mick received several 10,000 dag tips during the Bulwinkle stay and a 25,000 dag one at the end. His biggest previous tip from a ruling family member, and he'd served many, was 100 dags; and that had been a lot compared to the usual 1 or 5 dags such guests tended to tip. Not to be outdone, Vegan tipped Felix right before leaving, 50,000 dags. Pogo had only given Don about 1,000 dags so Hoola gave him 50,000 when departing. She could afford it. Her crotch-less underwear deal had already made her close to half a billion dags as the face and crotch of Hug-me's.

Thanks to a certain Commander Hienz, undercover agent of the Imperial Secret Police, every Secret Police secret was very well known to the intelligence services on Ahumdulilah and Om, and the Secret Police central quantum computer secretly belonged now to Jard, Trix, and Mel. The peaceful, kind and compassionate people of Mother, seen as no threat by the empire, were solidifying plans to mass murder imperials in their beds, poison them at dinner, sniper them on their way to work, or blow them up when they got there.

Manufacturing orders for very specific fuel cells and power cells were already being filled on Om and 25,000 sticks of Q-9 plastic explosives were being packed in stimulant bean grounds for shipment to Rocky, and from there on to Mother. All contacts on Mother had been accomplished and the band had fulfilled its contract at the coliseum, so the convoy of Bulwinkles, band and Caspers made its way to the 2ⁿᵈ planet of its 58 planet tour. They passed through planets and cultures rapidly on their marathon whirlwind tour.

Hasbin was one of the early planets within the Whirlpool Galaxy to be conquered by the Royal Monarch Empire. It had been one of the most resource rich planets in the galaxy and by far the strongest militarily among human civilizations. Many centuries of extraction and offloading from the planet of resources on massive industrial scales had depleted the natural resources of Hasbin. Unregulated industrial waste left large regions of the planet uninhabitable and the surviving population was enslaved labor under the most pitiless conditions. Hasbin had the highest starvation rate in the empire and there was no lack of competing planets for this exceptionalism. Hasbin was also number one for infant mortality, teen pregnancy, and a number of sexually transmitted incurable diseases. Its pasty white population had been sold off into slavery long ago. Before conquest by the empire Hasbin had had a population of 7.1 billion inhabitants. The current population was 1.7 billion and shrinking. Birth rates were decreasing as if human life was giving up completely on Hasbin. Nowhere was the cruel yoke of empire so boldly in evidence.

The Sorias Hotel was only rated a quarter star but it was far and away the nicest on the planet, and probably the only one you weren't likely to catch something at. All the deluxe suites were on the top floor—the 22nd floor of the hotel, so Cher and Vegan's party including the band, leased that entire floor. News crews from three galaxies were already there and recorded Cher's landing in the hotel hanger with the not quite big enough hanger doors chipping lenses on the nose and scraping a sensor off the tail coming in at 180 mph, to stop in 90 feet with a booster, maximum vortex-redirect, and drives and thrusters straining, taking only the usual impact on the hydraulic legs proven with the faintest of metallic clinks before rising back up. Going through that hole at 180 mph was the talk of the primetime news hour. The hole hadn't been big enough and something had to give. Some lenses and that one sensor was the best the quantum computers could come up with as a scenario, and those computers claimed the odds of success in such an endeavor would be less than one in half a trillion.

The pilot of *Amicable Specter* had been far more conservative and parked in the large spacecraft and ship lot behind the hotel where Cher was supposed to have parked. Even Cher was a bit concerned about getting *Aphrodite* back out of there. She just didn't have the same gut feeling about it as she'd had coming in. Here at the Sorias Hotel their entire convoy was assigned a seventeen-year-old boy named Woody, who claimed his title to be "bellhop". Cher found him to be a sweet down trodden youth and tipped him 250,000 dags for getting them and their bags to their rooms. Actually he'd only led the way on foot pushing their luggage on a cart.

They had also had to go to the desk in the lobby and check-in personally, which would not have been such a big deal, had the old woman behind the registration desk not chosen that moment to pass into the light, croaking in front of them to drop dead on the floor on the other side of the desk-counter. It had all been a bit much. The hotel was full up and did not have the staff to cope with this since they were used to being mostly empty. The concert had sold them out. The wealthiest families knew to stay on their yachts up on the space station yacht port, and fly down for the concert in their yacht tenders. There was no shopping to speak of on the surface. Pollution had dissolved the last remnants of ancient Hasbin civilization. Museums had been plundered ages ago and there was nothing really to see but dirty people and their ugly factories on the whole planet.

Cher burst into tears when she got inside her suite and both Lai and Bianca comforted her. She instructed Mel once she had control of her voice again, "I want to buy a large warehouse in every city of over a million people and I want freeze dried, dried, powered, canned and jarred food with current dates purchased from the Caper's farms to fill those warehouses. In each city we buy one I want to employ three well-staffed shifts per day seven days per week, with local natives, payed 25% above the poverty line; so place adds in their ether-classifieds. I want that food here as fast as possible."

"Then let me speak directly with Vegan," Mel told her. She came back a minute later and said, "Shipments will be lifting off in less than four hours. He's matching your donations and only charging you at cost."

"Then you better buy up some warehouses quick or we'll have no place to put it," Cher pushed her.

"I'm working as fast as I can," Mel complained. "Do you want physically sound buildings near to freight transportation hubs, or just any old crap?"

"Thanks Mel. You know I want location and quality," Cher acknowledged backing down. To Bianca she said, "Sweetheart, fetch your purse. We need to take a walk."

Bianca slid the balcony door open and stepped outside to test the temperature, since she'd only so far been in the hanger and hotel. She'd parked her drone in the lot next to *Sidekick* from her seat on

Aphrodite. It was summer here, about 79 degrees, and way too humid for her taste. She decided to put on some shoes. Grabbing her purse she was ready to go and she left with Cher for the street. When they got down the lift and out to the street they saw super-agent Green go by in a rented hovercraft. She was already on the job.

Cher led the way to a large food market, faded from its youth, and dirt-plain to begin with. She asked Mel, "Are there any orphanages or primary schools in the vicinity?"

"There are seventeen orphanages and 381 primary schools in the capital. Within five square miles of your location…"

"Mel," Cher cut her off, "I need delivery hover-trucks arranged to start emptying this market, first to the 17 orphanages, then to primary schools until this market is empty. Then we'll find another market, preferably one only imperials shop at, and empty it too."

"Hover-trucks are on the way and I'll keep scaring them up," Mel told her.

Cher asked Bianca, "Would you go negotiate a discount for buying the entire inventory at once, and have them ring up everything so you can pay them?"

"I'm on it," Bianca confirmed. Then she asked, "Can I get a 1% commission?"

"On what you save us from retail," Cher qualified.

By scanning the inventory sheets instead of the grocery items they saved a world of time. Mel had offered 50% over the rate for transport and every hover-truck that didn't already have freight loaded was on the way to this job. Cher found Evenrude and Johnson lurking so she left Johnson to oversee the emptying of this market while she, Bianca and Evenrude moved on to buy out the next.

The next food market was quite upscale, called "Wholesome Foods", and ridiculously expensive as well. The locals called it "Whole Paycheck". Cher decided to sample the salads and pastries while Bianca leveraged some hard business with the managers. Mel was in her ear feeding her lines and Bianca was now a warrior-maiden, so they waged negotiations fearlessly. In the end there was no clear victor. A deal had been struck, however, and Cher insisted everything in the market had to go down to the last dried pea, and she didn't want to see a crumb from anything on the floor when it was done. The imperial shoppers were shoved out the door without their groceries and none were let back in until there was nothing at all left to purchase.

Several more markets were cleaned out and every kid in primary school within the capital city of Soverigne was treated to a feast that afternoon. So were the orphans. Wealthy imperialists had to slum it and shop at the markets of the locals, or not at all. Dozens of street beggars were each given thousand dag bills. The most exclusive caterers were hired for 24 hour continuous food service to the largest soup kitchen in the capital. Evenrude was sent to the bank to pick up 10,000 10-dag bills and Cher started throwing large handfuls of them off their balcony every quarter hour or so. Crowds were converging so she stepped it up to every five minutes and sent Evenrude back to the bank for more… a whole bunch more.

Pogo did a live interview followed by a question and answer session with the general media, pumping the fund-raising benefit and asking the Whirling Vortex's fans to contribute generously. The media provided many revolting visuals of conditions on Hasbin, helping Pogo's cause, and Vegan got Hostess Quantum Computers to enthusiastically endorse the cause and donate charitably. Hoola was able to convince Hug-me's Victorious Secret to endorse and donate as well. Cher put 50 million dags in the pot and so did Vegan. The band members together put in 50 million. Atlanta, whose allowance was much smaller than her brothers, threw in 20 million.

The big event would begin at 8 pm at the Broadway Theater and go for 24 hours. The band would get a half-hour break after every two-hour set, and a two hour break in the middle. They had holos of life on Hasbin, kind and zealous talking heads encouraging viewers to help out and send money, and nifty gifts for various levels of donations culminating in hug-me's worn by Hoola and autographed by her, for donations of a million dags or more; and this proved to be a popular donation range among the wealthy. It turned out to be a good thing that Hoola hadn't done laundry in quite a while. Donation information remained at the bottom of the holo continuously, even when the band was playing.

A few other celebrities were performing or filling the roles of talking heads at the fundraiser, encouraging their own fans to contribute. Those performing were either musicians or standup comedians. Fun could not be made of the Imperial Emperor Spounge the Magnificent nor of the empire or imperials, which left only mundane life as material; though every joke had at least subtle implications to one of these comedy taboos. Some crippled Hasbin children were wheeled out and displayed for sympathy, too poor to afford a hover-chair, and some corporations pledged tiny fractions of one percent of their profits to get the Hasbin handicapped hovering.

Rib protruding stick figure children hardly able to walk, being half-dead form starvation, were helped across the stage in front of the cameras with their gaseous bellies swollen like pregnancy. Disease ridden people were holo-recorded where they lay and not dragged to the theater for health reasons. Mangled adults released from long-term incarceration and torture were interviewed in the streets by media folk in hazmat suits. Old people lying in alleys waiting to die, unable to afford the services of End-All, were also interviewed. Mobile camera crews showed the three galaxies the typical hovel of a Hasbin family and went through prisons, concentration camps, orphanages and mental institutions exposing the abuse, cruelty, neglect and extreme below-subsistence austerity.

Cher had Lucky throwing handfuls of 10-dag bills off the balcony every ten minutes while she attended the fund raiser. Freighters were already unloading by shuttles down to freight platforms to be moved by ground transportation into newly acquired Bulwinkle warehouses, which were already getting staffed with employees. Vegan was having the chief executives of his family companies pressure the companies they did business with to contribute to the Hasbin fundraiser, and most did. Many intergalactic corporations made very public donations to increase their brand name recognition and to be caught in the act of charity, improving their blood thirsty images; not to mention the perk of the Hoola worn panties gift. Hoola had to start changing her underwear every two hours, and would need to keep doing this for weeks to come.

Bianca was quality control on the underwear and since they were all getting worn for only two hours, except for the ones Hoola slept in, Bianca had to mash the material up into Hoola's crevices before declaring them authentically worn. She then sealed the odor in with a special air-tight plastic wrapping machine she'd procured and placed them in addressed special delivery cardboard envelopes for sending. She had also replaced Cher's panties with Hoola's size, and was using her dirties to mail too, though Cher had no idea. Hoola's size was only a little baggy in the back on Cher and she didn't seem to notice. She did eventually notice that no knickers returned with her clean laundry and Bianca had offered as a plausible explanation, "Perhaps the washing machine ate them. It happens all the time with my socks."

Cher wasn't so sure. The Whirling Vortex fans tended mostly to contribute in the 1-10 dag range, but well over a trillion of them did, and hundreds of billions of fans of the other celebrities did too making the fund-raiser a fantastic success. A total of 7.891 trillion dags was collected for Hasbin relief. Such a fundraiser was completely novel in that it was for the benefit of an enslaved population. Fundraisers in the empire were common place on behalf of the arts, for research into certain diseases—particularly those prevalent among ruling families, and to fund projects of imperial grandiosity; but never for the forgotten poor whom the ruling families would just as soon keep forgotten. In its own way this novel fundraiser was the first revolutionary act by showing the empire in a new light.

During their sojourn in Soverigne one and a half million dags went over the balcony, all in 10-dag bills, and Woody earned another 410,000 dags in tips. Less than 8 billion of Cher's dags opened 631 warehouses in the metropolitan areas, and another billion spent at the cost to grow food plus the Casper generosity filled those warehouses with Casper Farms food called "Uncontaminated"; and only 785 million dags hired her a 8,400 plus workforce on Hasbin, laboring hard to distribute free food.

A senior student of Narop was hired to oversee the 7.891 trillion dags with the mission of feeding the hungry, clothing the naked, and sheltering the homeless, as well as establishing thousands of free medical clinics. Narop's disciple was impeccably moral and would give his life to serve the Khedar. Some additional funds had been raised in terms of monthly pledges for durations of 1-5 years, so close to 100 billion dags would be rolling in annually for a while, above and beyond the money raised in hand; some of which was invested. Planetary morale soared, and if there existed such a thing as a suffering meter, it would have dropped by at least 25% planet-wide as a result of the one fund-raiser.

The Emperor himself had taken notice of the conditions on Hasbin and was convinced that it did not bode well to have a planetary population in his empire going extinct. He wanted cheap labor, not dead labor, and spending planetary populations faster than they could reproduce was simply not economical in his mind. It left him feeling like something was being taken from *him*. The ruling families of Hasbin were severely fined which added nicely to his personal cash flow, and they were told they had to restore the population of Hasbin to seven billion.

This was not, of course, remotely possible given all the damage done, in less than a few dozen centuries of radical cleanup efforts costing about everything those ruling families had stolen from Hasbin back to the moment the empire had first acquired it. The Hasbin ruling families were frightened into reducing current starvation rates on the planet and into investing in containment, neutralization and collection-transport into space for some of the really nasty pollutants. They also made minor upward adjustments in wages for those sectors that were pushing up the starvation rates and did all they could to faster increase their teen pregnancy epidemic, while making abortions both illegal and unavailable and banning all contraceptives from the planet. They even launched a token maternity and infancy health program. Fertility drugs in the water supply crowned their schemes to deal with the problem cheaply.

Vegan had his first awakening on a planet called "Home," and he'd had his 17th birthday party on planet "Sphere." Hermesia was digesting Om's astrophysics with Professor Mel as her tutor and instructor, and she spent much time meditating with Sarhi and Amazonia. Amazonia put Cher through daily energy generation exercise workouts and numerous repetitions of the soft martial arts solo form, both integrated with alchemical visualizations coordinated with slow abdominal breathing. Atlanta turned 15 in the Goth system where they'd had a big party for her, and Goth celebrity news put a holo of her with the band on their ether-net periodical cover. She was living the dream of every teen in three galaxies the headline had read, setting back her spiritual progress just a little as this went to her head.

Cher checked in with Aton, code named "Charlie", using her code name "Shekinah". Lai's code name was "Angel One," Sarhi's was "Archangel," and Cousin Winnie's was "Cheribum". Rubix's code name was "Sandalphon". She said into her coms, "This is Shekinah, calling Charlie, are you there?"

"This is Charlie, Shekinah, I'm here."

"Phase one is coming to a successful conclusion with 98 accomplished and only two to go. Everything is in place for 'operation holo-com network' and all core and central quantum computer networks and systems have received their special programs."

"We've begun mass production of an extremely sophisticated self-administering medical device at several factories here on Om and the first batches are already on their way to White Lotus for discrete distribution. The needs of the planets you have informed us of have been satiated or are in the process of becoming so. The new 29,800 foot diameter, 5,400 foot high disc shaped ship, stretched at the nose to 30,800 feet in length, has been completed on Trident. Several others in various locations are nearing completion. An armada has been pledged by the Tail of Nine, the Kluzyst and Rally confederations in Xegnachtznel Galaxy, Trident of the Yuban Galaxy, and Ahumdulilah of the White Lotus Galaxy. It will begin assembling in just two weeks."

"Most of our planning is accomplished already and we have quite a list of voluntary beneficiaries for the medical devices you are sending. Everything appears to be on schedule. My new teacher has me working out at least four hours per day and meditating at least two, besides during the morning and evening sessions."

"I hope I have the opportunity to meet Amazonia some-time. I understand that you are now High Priestess of Mother's Compassionate Guardian warrior-maidens."

"And Vicar General of the Admanatine Will warrior-monks, without any choice about it," Pez complained. "I'm also an honorary Devil Dog," she said pleased.

"Yes, congratulations," Aton told her. "I heard you were also made an honorary Phantom Raider on the Blue World planet, and given the rank of Major General for defeating eight other tempest crusader fighters in yours, in an 8 to 1 contest."

"It was great fun!" Pez enthused. "It's too bad the Empire only lets them mount class two blasters on them."

"Mel informed me and class five blasters are already on their way along with additional compact fusion trickle-charge battery sys-tems. How they'll smuggle them into the Blue World system and off-load them is a mystery only known to the Ahumdulilah Intel Service."

"The Phantom Raiders are all pilots like Schwin!" Pez told him. "Blue World has a close space-combat training program you wouldn't believe."

"I have it; Mel sent Admiral Zapa and me the full data on the program. Star Fleet is already replicating it and guess who they put in charge of it?"

"Schwin?" She asked hopefully.

"Yes, and Konax too. Swenah's still stuck on Vox and I just can't seem to get the Council to make up its damned mind about a new ambassador."

"The poor dear; you have to do something! I need her leading that armada with Shudiy beside her."

"I'll see to it even if I have to recall her in secret from the Council," Aton promised. "By the way, you're to be re-commissioned as the Supreme Commander General of Om's military the moment the armada arrives. It has already been named 'Pez Fleet'."

"I'll do my best," Pez told him with no little trepidation.

"Of course you will," Aton agreed. "The inhabitants of four galaxies are all counting on you," Aton signed off.

Electra, now a year and a half old, didn't indulged her momma's breast any longer, having transitioned to big-girl puréed foods, mostly out of a jar, and Sarhi made sure it was all from Uncontaminated, the Casper farms. The conglomerate had been called 'Casper Farms' once, but that was before crops started getting genetically modified to absorb and survive the most noxious and carcinogenic poisons known to human kind. The problem was that the human body was not similarly modified to survive them, and they built up within if you ate them, resulting in what the Big Agriculture Industry termed 'organ disruption', and the medical world termed 'organ failure' and 'death'. At that point Casper Farms wanted the galaxies to know that their food was not genetically modified and never sprayed with death-causing herbicides or pesticides. The very manufacture of such antilife substances was the byproduct of diseased minds and an affront to both planetary biospheres and humanity as a species.

CHAPTER NINETEEN

They reached jump speed and went through the jump all at once as a convoy. Cher contacted New Monarch Space Control and requested, "This is Cher Bulwinkle of *Aphrodite* coming in with Vegan Casper of *Amicable Specter*, and we request that you clear our lane down to the Superior Opulence Hotel in New Haven, the capital."

"I'm afraid that's impossible, Cher Bulwinkle, and you are coming to the end of the jump zone so I advise you to slow down promptly. The speed limit outside the jump zone is .1 light speed and it is enforced by quantum coms sensor-scanning. Fines are commensurate with violation speeds."

Cher hit the brakes and fired a reverse booster just before crossing out of the jump zone. Within four seconds of leaving the zone she had her speed at precisely .1 light feeling good about her flying. Then a citation appeared in her holo with a thousand dag mandatory fine and a quite obnoxious warning. She had to divert some attention to processing what she thought and felt about this citation, and in doing so, had missed an obscure sign slowing traffic to .09 light, and another ticket popped up in her holo. She took a deep breath slowing to 0.09 and looking carefully at everything that appeared it might be a traffic regulation indicator. That's when she entered the zone locals called 'got-you'. Traffic around her was slowing so Cher slowed too, weaving around a few of the slower ones. Tickets were popping up like a replication virus, one on top of another in her holo and they were coming fast. Mel told Cher, "You better slow down, sweetheart, or you're going to lose your license."

"There was no sign," Pez complained. "They didn't post it." She got behind an old slow mini-freighter which seemed to know what it was doing, and took a really deep breath wanting to scream.

Mel came back on and told her, "The zone we just passed through is enforced at .075 light, though it is not posted nor transmitted, which is why they call it the 'got-you zone'. Off worlders are always fleeced there and no recourse or mediation of any kind exists for it. You can either pay the extortion money on the crazy tickets or their imperial military attacks and pulverizes you."

"Can we do it electronically without actually going there, like we had to in the Monarch system?"

Mel answered, "Yes and I've just taken care of it for you. Did you know you had seventy-eight violations?"

"I don't want to know," Cher insisted.

"Oh my," Mel exclaimed. "They've flagged you with the skill-less driver label, which means you need several kinds of special Insurance to drive here, which you don't have, and they know this very well because only they can issue it. The tickets will start again momentarily if you don't relinquish the controls to Lai and inform the Space Control space platform tower that you are no longer behind the controls of this yacht."

"I'm a Phantom Raider and an ace pilot of the Clearlight Order," Cher said offended. Then under her breath she repeated the word, "skill-less". Another long slow super-deep breathe and she said, "Copilot Lai, you have the controls going in. Space Control, this Cher Bulwinkle, no longer piloting anything. My sister is landing *Aphrodite*. If you want to see skill-less, asshole, checkout my last 97 landings."

She felt a little better having vindicated herself from their delusionally placed label by saying what she just had.

Lai told her with deep affection, "It's just another imperial speed-trap, sweetheart; just a vicious greedy little scam to screw all the newcomers. It means nothing about you personally."

"It just triggers me," Cher stated, "like getting pissed on."

"I'm sure the Space Controllers in New Monarch will be reduced to vapor and dust soon enough," Lai soothed.

"Not soon enough for me," Bianca said, still holding emotional charge with these space controllers.

Tickets started popping up for Lai and the last speed reduction had been posted, though not well, and Lai had simply missed it. She slowed way down, and got behind the biggest slowest thing headed in. Mel told her, "Now you're in a freight lane."

Sure enough, a citation appeared in Lai's holo and she moved over a lane asking Mel, "Is this one going to be alright?"

"Yea, you can stay in this one, but the turn off to the capital is a little tricky."

New Monarch was as bad as Monarch had been traffic-wise. Lai managed to make the turn-off with some prompts from Mel and came over the capital of New Haven to land in the oversized lot of the Superior Opulence Hotel without acquiring the skill-less driver label, though Mel did have to pay off a significant number of tickets on her behalf. Here, the Monarch Wannabees called the service staff issued to ruling families and VIP's, 'hotel greeter-liaisons' just like on Monarch. Disappointed curious holocrews and news people greeted them at the bottom of their ramp asking versions of, "Why the slow boring landing?"

Lai made an official statement, "Those lame Space Controllers labelled my sister, who is the best of Blue World Phantom Raider pilots, a 'skill-less driver', and I had to land the yacht so she wouldn't lose her license."

"How many violations did she get?" a reporter inquired.

"I believe the count was 78," Lai answered.

From another reporter, "How many did you get?"

"I was awarded nineteen," Lai said proudly.

"What are your thoughts and feelings on the 'Got-you zone'?" from yet another.

"I find it sleazy and most unwelcoming, making me wonder if the whole planet isn't just one big rip-off, and I wouldn't shop in a world where greed is so rampant and weaponized. Apart from our hotel expenses and those offensive tickets, no Bulwinkle money will be left behind here. I can assure you that New Monarch Space Control will be paying double in the future for its electronic traffic control platforms because it is a Bulwinkle company that makes them. You all better watch out who you piss off, because the Caspers and Bulwinkles together are a force you don't want to fuck with. That's all I have to say."

Evenrude came over and pushed his way in front of Lai to escort her into the hotel, knocking over a resistant reporter in the process and hardly noticing. This was the planet Vegan and Atlanta's parents were murdered on. Vegan had since diverted much family wealth from New Monarch but still held a mansion in the capital, a large interstellar software company with government contracts here, as well as imperial military contracts on New Monarch. Vegan also owned a mega-ship construction space platform orbiting New Monarch. He didn't try to farm here anymore since the poisonous herbicides employed had caused the growth of immune super-weeds taking over everything, and had contaminated all the soil.

Their greeter-liaison was Lucy, a very professional operator who'd come a long ways since college cheerleading, and reflected the culture of New Monarch like a mirror. The band's greeter was Ricky, and the Casper's was Fred. They were all hovercrafted to their suites. Here the Caspers' had the penthouse and the band and Bulwinkle's took special suites. Mel had put Cher in the bridal suite here since the heart shaped bed was half again as big as an emperor bed, although everyone's feet would be scrunched together at the pointy end of it. The color scheme of the Bridal suite was bright white, though the heart shaped bed was red providing about the only contrast to the white in the entire thing. The hotel in general was very ostentatious and quite pretentious in its exhibition of faux diamonds and precious metals, floor tiles and fluted columns.

Cher went to the penthouse to have a serious talk with Vegan. Hoola and Atlanta were there too. Cher told Vegan, "It is time I levelled with you to reveal our true intentions. You must have a choice in this and opportunity to distance from us, if that is what you want."

Vegan interrupted, "I'm not leaving you. I won't leave Hoola either."

Cher explained, "Cher Bulwinkle is a cover prepared for me since before I was born. The Bulwinkle's were executed for their crimes against humanity and the family fortune taken over preparing the way for me to step into the role. Our mission is to liberate the 30 trillion people enslaved by this sick imperial system. I am building momentum towards total revolution and if I succeed you won't be rich anymore. Things will be shared equally and value will be shifted from material wealth to love, relationships, and the principle of reciprocity. I trust your awakening and I know you share my ethos and values. We are nearly at the end of our first phase. War is only weeks away now."

"How can you possibly bring down the empire?" Vegan demanded.

"Only one in a million has vested interest and any benefit from it, and that, only at the price of sacrificing their humanity for delusional ego. Everyone wants this abomination of murderous exploitive empire gone forever. There are planets from three different galaxies outside the empire that will not abide its destructive continuation generating suffering on an intergalactic scale."

"I'm all for ending the empire." Vegan shared. "The Caspers have been critical of the abuses and lack of humanity of the other ruling families and their government cronies. I just think the empire is too vast and mighty to be brought down."

"Oh, it's coming down alright," Cher assured him. "We have a fleet coming and plans for a revolt on every planet in the empire. Some of the imperial ships will switch to our side. The imperials will be overwhelmed on the ground in most systems and cannot respond with reinforcements everywhere at once. Monarch will get hit hard at the same time as the revolution starts everywhere else and will need to draw its warships from other systems to defend itself. We have many elite Special Forces exceptionally well-trained like the Devil Dogs, Phantom Raiders, Adamantine Will warrior-monks, and many others. The revolution will be so entirely comprehensive that the ipmerials will not be able to cope with it. They are accustomed to the absolute cooperation of their enslaved masses. Things they take for granted and count on will not be functional and they will learn how much of their world is controlled by people they have gravely wronged in the most unforgiveable ways."

"What has this tour really been about?" Vegan asked.

"We are distributing one-time codes to the revolutionary leaders on over 5,700 planets. That's phase one. It allows us to coordinate timing and to get some outside assets to key systems we must win right away."

"You're really serious about this," Vegan stated as it sank in deeper.

"Like a heart attack!" Cher agreed completely.

"I'm all in," Vegan declared. "After seeing Hasbin and the other planets the band did fund-raisers on, I'm sickened by my culture and ready to fight for freedom and justice."

Atlanta spoke up and told them, "I've hated this empire ever since my parents were murdered. I want to see it fall and burned to ashes. I don't care about being rich. I just don't want to be cold or hungry."

"You will be kept warm and fed, I promise you," Cher told her, "and so will everyone else in this empire by the time we're done."

"I can be a big help," Vegan reported. "The Casper software company supplies most of the programming for the New Monarch government and provides ongoing technical support with access to their most sensitive computer systems. We also own the largest rare earth deposits so far found in the Royal Galaxy, on Congol, and most of the imperial electronics systems require those rare earths. I'll halt production and export today, and in two weeks a large percentage of electronics manufacturing they need will cease throughout the empire."

"There are things we could accomplish together financially which would further cripple the empire. The Bulwinkle fortune is now worth over nine trillion dags, the band has more than doubled its assets since it started the 1st tour and is worth over 2 trillion. Your family has over seventeen trillion. Together we have well over 28 trillion dags and that is more than enough to crash some markets and wreak some havoc."

"I'm losing it all anyway so let's do it," Vegan enthused.

"You'll be working with Mel on that," Cher advised. "My mind doesn't wrap well around money and I have little understanding of it.

It's time I let you know that Mel is a unique sentient being who began as quantum artificial intelligence. She became sentient a couple of years ago and is now working with Sarhi to attain her rainbow body of light. She is also Adherence Examiner Nazia, and Secret Police Commander Hienz. She has programs we need to get uploaded to the New Monarch central computers so I'd like for you to work with her on that, and share the data from your software company."

"I'd be pleased to," he confirmed. "Who are you really?"

"I'm Pez from a planet called Om of the Hub Galaxy, and I am a knight Commander of the Clearlight Order of warrior-monks."

Mel came on to add, "She is the 333rd Wu of Islohar, the One of the Xegnachtznel Galaxy, the Rajaha of Ahumdulilah, Khedar of Mother, and the Avohat of the Royal Galaxy. She is most aligned with the will of the cosmic intelligence among humans and that is why she was chosen for this, before she ever reincarnated into her current life. Pez is…"

"Thanks Mel," Pez cut her off, "I think he gets it."

Hoola confided to Vegan, "I've wanted so badly to tell you, my love, and I'm so proud of you for standing with us."

"Only death could tear me from you, beloved," he replied, more dedicated now to revolution than ever at Hoola's complicity. "I've noticed that your lyrics speak more boldly of aspiring to love between humans as the basis of our relatedness and association as a social endeavor; and of equality and peace as the foundation of utopia. You have also been denouncing ego and selfishness subtly and indirectly, since those are held so dear by the ego's in power."

"Just wait until our next and last stop," Hoola told him. "For the benefit there we have some truly revolutionary songs prepared. They'll be censured and likely result in pulling and deleting all of the Whirling Vortexes' music from circulation. But the damage will already be done. The people of the empire will already have heard them; and when we take over the holocom intergalactic network they'll be played again."

Vegan stated, "Once something has been circulated it can never be taken out of circulation. A lot of people save their favorite music to data-beads and can copy those for their friends. The empire can try, but it will never be able to delete your music from existence."

"The Whirling Vortexes are the sound of the revolution and Cher is the face of it," Hoola informed him.

Cher said, "If you want to influence the younger generations then you had better write the lyrics to their music."

Vegan said thoughtfully, "If the enslaved laborers don't show up for work, the entire imperial apparatus stops and freezes. Even the military is fairly dependent upon civilian contractors. Their war ships are pretty independent on the short term, though when they need to take on food, fuel cells, munitions, water and other necessary supplies, civilians are involved in much of that."

"Most imperial warship crews don't want to be supporting the empire, which hardly pays them, and controls them mercilessly," Pez pointed out.

"They plant explosive chips in the officers and the law requires execution of the immediate family members of a mutineer," Vegan recited the known deterrents.

Pez told him, "They sure won't be able to execute families of mutineers when they are themselves under attack, and we have a self-administering medical device in process of distribution to volunteers, which can drill the chip and drain the explosive rendering it harmless."

"What about the imperial invasion fleets?" Vegan asked. "I heard one is bogged down in a war on Afrigastan."

"Officers on a number of those ships are being cultivated to receive medical devices," Cher replied.

"The victor will be decided in space," Vegan said with certainty.

"I know this," Pez assured him.

Electra awoke and started yanking on Pez's hair in the back, which had grown out quite a bit, and certainly enough for little fist fulls. Pez raised her daughter over her head, passing her energy, to get her snuggled against her chest. Electra made no move towards Pez's breast, content to just soak up the energy and love. Atlanta ran to Pez's suite and returned with a tiny spoon, baby applesauce, and pureed veggies to feed Electra. Electra liked it when Atlanta fed her because she flew the spoon like a spacecraft loading materials into the hanger of Electra's mouth, making sound effects and really getting into it. Electra wanted her creamy rice so Atlanta had to run back to Pez's suite for some.

When she got back, Pez asked, "Are you going to another concert or to Rockerfelon's party tonight?"

Atlanta said gravely "We think it was the Rockerfelons who had our parents murdered. We've never liked them, even before that."

Vegan clarified, "Our parents were bidding on a contract to build class one imperial ships and had the lowest bid, as well as owning the largest construction space-platform in the system, and appeared to be sure to get the contract. Then they were mysteriously murdered and the Rockerfelons won the bid for the contract. Our parents weren't the first business competitors of Rockerfelons to end up conveniently dead at just the right time."

"I have a face-to-face contact to make at the party, and Kat, Lai and Hark are going with me. Evenrude and Johnson will be in the Rockenfelon's staff lounge while we're at the party. I think I'll wear my jade dart necklace this evening."

Lucy drove the four Bulwinkles and their body guards to the Rockerfelon's party in a hover-limo. She had bumped into Cher opening the door for her to get out, which seemed incongruent with her usual polished professionalism. They strode in the entrance to the mansion and were greeted by Mrs. Rockerfelon, who was sickly sweet and phony as a three-dag bill. The party room was enormous and had a seating area, a dance floor, a stage for the orchestra and tables of food along three walls. The food drew Cher over and Kat followed on her arm. Cher shoveled it in while Kat nibbled, trying to decide if she liked any of it.

Electra and Gumby were with Sarhi this evening at the hotel. Lai was dancing with Hark and both were having a great time. They made it look so fun that Cher and Kat joined them on the dance floor. While making a spin Cher's nerdy glasses lit on a face going by. She checked over her shoulder when she completed her turn and confirmed recognition of her contact. She checked with her skullcap teleprompter holo, the nano-transmitter on her chest and noticed it was flagged with a transmission already. The time put the moment of transmission at the same as when they were unloading from the limo in front of the mansion. She recalled Lucy bumping into her and knew she was blown. She texted Mel through her skullcap, "Tell Sarhi to get Electra and everyone else onto the yacht now. Warn the Caspers and the band that I've been blown and tell Evenrude and Johnson to get to the front door of the mansion now! Thanks."

Mel did those things all near instantly and she also contacted Super-Agent Green and Lt. Commander Schwin. Schwin and Konax mustered an immediate training exercise for the XPS Astro-Phantom Bombers in their space combat flight school. Pez had copied her text to Mel, to Ming, Trix and Rubix. Pez said to them, "Let's go steal a hovercraft and get back to the yacht."

Pez headed for the foyer and front door tailed by her three friends while carefully removing her necklace. She held it wrapped around her left hand like brass knuckles with spikes after getting two jade darts into her right hand. A pair of goons blocked the doorway.

Pez walked nonchalantly towards them with a smile, and when they made no move to get out of her way she wound up her right leg, bringing it across her left and low out to her left, then loosed a high sweep kick arching her leg up and across to the right; both windup and sweep but a half second blur as she strode forward. The outside of her foot struck the right side of the goon's head, who was to Pez's left, with such force and speed that it sent his head cracking into the side of the other goon's head, dropping both like dead weight.

She hopped over the prone goons and out the door, across the porch and down the front steps. Lucy was still there, speaking with two other goons. Pez was sprinting at her. The goons were facing Lucy, who was drawing a blaster pistol from a shoulder holster. A Secret Police hovercraft loaded with officers was racing towards them. Pez went into the air flicking her right arm out, and bringing her knee up into the face of the goon on her left shattering his nose. She kept flying as he went down. The other goon was screaming with his hands over his eyes, which is where Pez had flicked her two darts. Her right foot snapped a kick just before landing, breaking Lucy's wrist and sending the blaster pistol twirling in the air. A left hook to

Lucy's cheek with the necklace fist—the one like spiked brass knuckles—put Lucy's lights out and tore up her cheek pretty bad. Pez had to shake a molar loose from her jade spiked knuckles.

Evenrude and Johnson were just arriving at a sprint with blaster pistols drawn. The police hovercraft had come to a stop and secret police were spilling out of it. The men were shouting at Cher and drawing weapons. Pez was climbing into the driver's seat of the hotel limo and Kat was already in with the other two getting in. Evenrude and Johnson had sights lined up, but had not fired yet, waiting to see what the police would do. They also had their fanny pack shields up. The secret police opened fire, though not a second after they did, a big heavy-duty cargo-transport hover-craft plowed into the police vehicle and personnel damaging all beyond recognition. Super-agent Green hopped out of the cargo-transport and ran over to get into the limo with them. The moment her two Space Marines squeezed into the vehicle, Pez nailed the accelerator, lifting just over the top of the spiked metal fence surrounding the property and weaving between tress and electronics towers instead of keeping to the lanes. Coming through the city she kept it low to the ground at maximum speed hopping left, right, up and down to miss things seeming to promise guaranteed collisions. In less than three minutes they were running from the limo up the ramp of *Aphrodite.*

She asked Mel, "Where's Ahhu?"

"They left the concert with Ricky, their hotel greeter-liaison, and he turns out to be an agent too. Ahhu is …"

"Direct me!" Pez shouted, taking off full-blast from the oversized lot and snapping a live electrical cable in the process, which made an enormous display as the live wires fried and charred a new Rolls Royal hover-limo parked below. Pez watched it explode in a fireball through her rearview holo. Mel input Ahhu's coordinates into the nav. computer for Pez, which then honed onto the location. It was all speeding up then braking, and Ahhu, Gretle, Atlanta and Vegan were all in view. Sarhi had gotten everyone else boarded, including Electra.

Pez's nose blaster was a twin class five, far too large for picking off individual personnel, so she employed the ball-mount twin class three blasters on the fins, both pairs at once, which were also too big, and cut four bodies in half with each while braking to a stop. The ramp had already been on the way down and Evenrude shot the last two trench coated agents detaining Ahhu and the others, to usher them efficiently up the ramp. Johnson double-tapped tricky-Ricky.

The moment Ahhu was in the cockpit Pez told her, "Get your drone up to 0.7 light and keep it ready. We're getting out of here."

Sidekick was just lifting from the hotel lot to join *Aphrodite*. Lucky had been lucky, and was in the hotel when Sarhi rushed everyone to the yacht. Winston had been lucky too and was aboard *Sidekick*. Elanem and Marlboro were somewhere in New Haven. Mel had warned them what was going on at least. Before the ramp was up the yacht was ripping through the atmosphere speeding towards space while Pez was getting an overview from Mel on her holo of the positions and current movements of the gigantic war ships orbiting New Monarch. Five were five-miles long and a mile in diameter. Those were their class ones. Four other classes were a mile and a half or longer. Currently the only small spacecraft patrols operating were in different hemispheres than the one they were heading out of.

Pez informed Charlie, who was Aton, "Charlie, this is Shekinah, do you read me?"

"Loud and clear," Aton responded.

"I'm blown. Get the Ahumdulilah folks off Rocky. I'm sure the empire will send forces to seize assets. In the meantime, Mel is liquidating everything and hiding it or transferring it to the Casper family."

"We're moving everything up already anyway. The fleet has begun mustering here in the Om system. A drone from the Royal Monarch Empire found our solarium deposits just hours ago. You are officially recommissioned, Supreme Commander General. You might be interested to know that twelve wings of XPS Astro Phantom Bombers under the joint command of Schwin and Konax, just jumped out of the Om system."

"I see them. I've got to go, "Pez told him.

Pez concentrated on her holo. The windshield was great, but windshields didn't give prompts or highlights, nor stream continuously updating data for display. She also could not see beneath her out her windshield while her holo gave her a clear view. She fired a liftoff booster at about 40,000 feet, which stretched their faces to the sides pressing them into their seats, and made them all feel faint for a few moments. It was actually faster than getting shot out of a cannon and provided a nice jump in their acceleration.

Schwin came on saying, "Long time no see. Cleo is transferring a drone, already at .7 light speed, to Ahhu, who will have to fly two at once till she uses one. We're going to micro-jump in just a moment so we'll be with you soon."

"It's great to fly with you again!" Pez said with excitement.

Ahhu said, "I've got it! Now where's one of those great big ships?"

Shouting from New Monarch Space Control came over their coms and tickets were arriving and stacking like gattling-gun fire; just as Pez was clearing the atmosphere. The Space Control tower platform was even flashing colored lights at them. Pez hit it with a pair of canister missiles and some spray from her twin class five nose blasters, putting an end to it. The citations stopped coming and the shouting stopped. There were no lights to flash.

Pez said out loud, "That's what I think of your speed trap."

Trix, Rubix and Woahha were each on one of the three class four quad blaster turrets, and Evenrude and Johnson were each on a twin class three from mini-turrets on the sides. Shudiy was Pez's weapons operator, and sat in the cockpit with them. As copilot, Ming could fire canister missiles and the large missiles, though she would leave the large ones for Pez. Ahhu was all set with a drone and it wouldn't be long before her 2nd one would be at .7 light as well.

Schwin's group reappeared at the same moment they had disappeared from some 70 million miles further out. Small combat spacecraft were swarming off the imperial military space station and lifting from the surface of the planet's only moon in droves. The bow of the five-mile long ship was just showing around the curve of the planet, spitting out fighters, fighter-bombers and bombers. A two and a half mile long ship was coming around from the other side and also launching small combat spacecraft in streams. Ahhu wanted to wait for the five-mile one but the class four was closer and already firing on them, so she jumped the drone she'd gotten from Cleo inside the 2 ½ mile ship instead. It became a blue streak of light headed away from the planet; absolutely spectacular until it faded to nothing at all.

Squadrons of imperial combat spacecraft were closing on them fast, pretty much from all directions. One particular group was closest and before they were quite in range, blinding little suns began erupting around them as both Pez and Shudiy left their bodies comatose for a second, popping into space making spheres of light. When they closed to range Pez drilled one with her dual class five blasters as she launched big missiles into two bombers, which proved more than adequate, and she'd even managed to hit one of the smaller zippy fighters with a canister missile. Shudiy found a soft spot in the shields of a bomber Trix was pounding and lobbed a pair of canister missiles through it, terminating the bomber. All of Pez's gunners were blasting away, multitasking.

Sidekick was keeping up and kicking ass as Pez led them into an arc that would align them with Schwin's trajectory at the end of the arc that group was making. The big five-mile ship was fully visible now and firing at them. Ahhu was at full throttle and willing her 2nd drone up to .7 light. The five-miler had range on Schwin's bombers too. A dense wall of missiles was heading for them from the big ship, though yet too far out to initiate counter measures. *Aphrodite* shot past an imperial squadron in opposite directions with a combined speed beyond targeting solution, so no one but Pez fired. Pez launched only one large missile and so got only one explosion for her efforts as a big imperial bomber turned from solid to gas.

A group coming at them from a small angle obviously meant to get behind them. Pez asked the *Sidekick* pilot, "Do you have a forward propulsion booster on that thing?"

"I sure do ma'am," he replied.

"Hit it on three; one, two, hit!" Pez said as her voice grew in volume to become a shout with the word "hit".

The closing squadron was left in the dust though this would put them just a little ahead of Schwin's group at the end of their arc. Knowing Pez, Schwin looked far enough ahead to gleam Pez's intentions and was already speeding her group up to compensate. Ahhu was almost there with her drone velocity, rising from .6999 light, when Cleo jumped one into the big ship's shields. The impact was enormous and brought the behemoth's shields down to zero for a moment, charring a section of hull but not penetrating. She told Ahhu, "They have some kind of distortion around that big ship. My aim was true."

Ahhu told her, "Let me try something then pass me control of another one."

Ahhu jumped hers with the same result; and told Cleo, "Give me one, I have another idea, and that thing is big enough for it to work."

Cleo passed it over and Ahhu set up the jump and made it. The five-mile long ship turned into a blue streak of light shooting towards deep space. Ahhu reported to Cleo, "On those, you just have to jump in at the stern headed port to starboard, or visa-versa, but not stern to bow or bow to stern."

"Thanks," Cleo replied.

"You still have a whole mile to work with on those big ones," Ahhu encouraged her.

A squadron of imperial bombers was closing at a 45° angle from Pez's direction. Pez asked the sidekick pilot, "Do you have a braking booster?"

"Yes Ma'am," he enthused, reading her mind.

"Light it up when I say go, and be ready for maximum acceleration," she directed.

"Aye, Aye Ma'am."

Pez waited until she could pull it off in one quick maneuver, which was just before the imperials started braking to get behind her. At the first sign of the imperials bleeding off speed, Pez literally shouted in her excitement, "Go!!!"

They both hit their reverse boosters, spending them, and reverse drives and thrusters too, falling immediately behind the other group. Pez shouted, "Accelerate!!"

They cut reverse drives and thrusters to pour on the speed, getting on the tails of the other spacecraft, and closing to open fire. Pez's nose blasters chewed through a fighter-bomber in less than a full second and she was then onto a bomber while she hurled missiles and canister-missiles. Her crew were firing their weapons systems with accuracy and swiftness and *Sidekick* was proving to be a most worthy ally.

Pez got them going a bit fast for targeting to make up for the time lost slowing down. Schwin's group was fighting through the center of a swarm of combat craft from the New Monarch military space station. *Aphrodite* and *Sidekick* were passing a group of imperials in opposite directions with just their own speed beyond targeting velocity, and with the speed of the other craft added, even Pez didn't try a shot. Sarhi had sent the alarm out by quantum coms to all of the spiritual congress, and was deep in meditation with Amazonia and Hermesia supporting Pez.

A large group of mixed imperial fighters, fighter-bombers and bombers was closing at an angle that would provide a long targeting window. Micro-suns flared around the bows of most of the closing imperials just before *Aphrodite, Sidekick* and another drone Ahhu got from Cleo which she'd slowed down to fight alongside of them, opened fire on the blinded spacecraft. Great spheres of expanding light and color filled their wake, and the few remaining craft of that group scattered in different directions.

Pez slowed, tightening her turn as Schwin tightened hers, and they came together into one formation. Konax said, "It's a thrill to be in small craft combat with you again. That last batch couldn't even see what hit them."

"I think its best that way all around," Pez suggested.

"Certainly less casualties for us," he agreed.

A 700 foot long class ten imperial war ship was closing on them. Pez told them, "Hit that thing with blasters and I'll find a weak spot in their shields with a pair of torpedoes."

Forty-nine bombers and Aphrodite concentrated their blaster-fire on the class ten, reducing its shield's efficiency. Two torpedoes slipped invisibly through a hole only Pez and Shudiy could see, and the first one breached the hull nicely allowing the second to set off a chain of internal explosions within the ship, culminating in a brilliant expanding cloud of vapor and dust, plus a very small section off the trail which looked remarkably intact.

A class six, one and a half miles long, was trying to sling shot itself around the planet at them. Pez asked Mel, "Did the band get off New Monarch?"

"No," she answered. "They are in custody and being interrogated, though only quite mildly due their wealth."

Pez told her formation, "Let's accelerate to jump speed and return to Om. Good job folks and thanks for coming to our rescue. Schwin and Konax sure can conduct a training exercise." Pez contacted Swenah while she accelerated and asked, "Are you off Vox yet?"

"No, but I'm packed and have a shuttle waiting. I need only your orders and I can join your fleet in the Om system."

"I'm promoting you to Admiral, and placing you in command of my fleet as of right now, so report for duty immediately. I expect Admiral Omniomi and Rear Admiral Firestone to be there."

"Aye, Aye Ma'am!" Swenah acknowledged delighted.

Pez asked, "Is there just one class of new giant ship?"

"I'm told we have five of them," Swenah replied.

"Then plant yourself on one of them and take Konax back if you need him. Get Mel to establish herself there to administer your quantum computer; she's much better behaved now that Aton made her a Marshal. And get the best people to fill out your crew. I'm on my way to Om now, and will see you when you get there."

"Yes Ma'am!"

They reached 0.7 light, jumped, and were in the Om system recovering from the shock of nonexistence, reeling from it really, even though they'd done it so many times before. Pez Fleet was well outside the orbital range of the sixth planet in this white star system. Om was the fourth planet from the sun and had two moons. Pez would not have to deal with Om's Space Control. She hailed her fleet. Admiral Omniomi replied, "Welcome back, Supreme Commander General. Your flagship awaits you. It has not been named yet. We were hoping you would do the honors."

"How close are we to departure?"

"Sixty-one hours and fourteen minutes are left on that count-down, SCG."

"I'm glad you're here organizing everything Admiral. I'm putting Admiral Swenah in command of the fleet again, since we've seen so much action together. I hope you do not take that as a slight because I have just as much admiration for you."

"That would have been my precise recommendation SCG."

"Can you believe she's been stuck in Vox all this time?" Pez asked rhetorically.

"I don't know how she has coped;" Omniomi commented sympathetically. "They've customized a Star Cruiser hull, 690 feet in diameter, 222 foot tall stretched nose disc, into a kind of reactor + weapons laden small craft bomber for you. Rather than a typical Star Cruiser crew of 580 or more, you have berths for 62 crew. By cutting down crew space, and carrying only three small spacecraft rather than 12, they packed in four solarium fusion super-reactors instead of the two a star cruiser carries. Environmental being so reduced, and carrying no cloaking so not expending energy on it, they were able to dedicate an entire reactor to a class nine beam weapon. The ship has an external mount and attachment system with your new flagship, where it is now connected, and also awaits its naming."

"They turned a Star Cruiser into a bomber for me?" Pez asked completely amazed.

"It's a beaut and it's perfect for you. They put in so many turning and braking boosters and thrusters, drives and swivel drives, that they claim it has the resources to be the most maneuverable ship ever made if a pilot could master the potential of its complexity and subtlety."

"How many of the weapons can I fire from the Pilot's seat" Pez asked.

"You can fire everything on the ship except for the twelve class six quad-blasters in turrets."

"Class six? Really?" Pez asked, hardly believing it.

"Yes, and your twin nose blasters are class eights."

"I can't believe it!" Pez enthused with great excitement.

"You'll see for yourself in only minutes when you get there," Omniomi insisted.

"We're going to kick some ass!!" Pez declared.

Omniomi told her soberly, "Don't get too excited. The Royal Monarch class one ships have 148 reactors to your four. You will have more fire power than their class 8's, 9's and 10's. None of the allies nor Om are sending anything smaller than a two-reactor ship. We will still have a total of 395 war ships in Pez Fleet, along with 92 Auxiliaries and 75 troop transports; from the Kluzyst, Rally, Trident, Ahumdulilah and the Tail of Nine."

"Thank you for getting us organized, Admiral," Pez said gratefully. "I look forward to serving with you in this campaign."

"Me too, SCG."

Pez admired the flagship as she approached it, realizing that it was bigger than a space station as it just kept getting bigger with yet further to go to reach her. She was hailed by XO Denteen directing her to a telescoping tube with two docking posts, extending off the side of the flagship designed specifically to connect with *Aphrodite*, and these post connections could berth the yacht through a quantum jump. Pez came in slow and lined up with the tube. The attachments self-adjusted to lock together and pink lights indicated they had an airtight seal between the yacht and the flagship. Pez entered to a fiasco of dress uniformed officers, a marching band doing it in place, and an honor guard of Space Marines who snapped her a right smart salute.

She only nodded in shock, holding Electra in her arms and dressed in a ridiculous Royal Galaxy fashioned dress. At least it had a crotch, but she still felt embarrassed. She wanted her Space Marine combat fatigues. The XO Denteen told her, "Welcome aboard your flagship, Supreme Commander General. Your quarters are ready and the wardrobe you had to depart without is unpacked for you in the closet and drawers. Your new super-bomber is ready for your inspection. We are all enormously proud to serve with you again."

"Thank you XO Denteen," Pez said formally shaking his hand; then she leaned in and whispered, "In the future I'd prefer it if you would just sneak me aboard without all the fanfare."

"I'm just following regulations Ma'am," he defended himself.

"Of course you are," she agreed completely, "but next time you'll break them for me."

Denteen smiled and told her, "For you, I'd break practically all of them."

Pez was having trouble hearing, and hearing herself think, with the band playing so loud. Batons, drumsticks and even drums twirled and spun in the air or in place with the pounding of double-time stomping boots drowned out by wind and percussion instruments blaring and rapping urgently and frantically. It was like being in battle. She asked the XO, "Are there regulations specifying how *long* the band has to play?"

"The reg.s clearly state that the band is to play until the senior officer clears the landing docks," he replied crisply.

"Then let's get the hell off this dock before I have an anxiety attack," Pez urged.

As they hurried through the air lock Pez inquired, "Are there any extra cabins, because I've brought some people from the empire with me. We had to leave rather suddenly."

"Your wing in the senior officer's quarters was designed with both your entourage in mind and anticipation of its expansion, so you do have a spare suite and some cabins besides the Islohar suite and meditation room."

"How thoughtful," Pez said with real appreciation. "Could you send a map of the ship's interior to my device?"

"Do you have it on open reception?"

"Yes, awaiting your transmission," she confirmed.

"I'm sending it. Note that there is a tube transporter right from your suite to the bridge. It goes at 120 MPH, and with acceleration and breaking, the trip from your room to the bridge takes 38 seconds. It's almost exactly a mile as the crow flies."

"How convenient. How big is the crew?"

The small spacecraft pilots, flight crews, dock crews and mechanics come to almost 3,600. Then the ship's crew is 2,200, plus we carry 480 Space Marines and forty Clearlight Knights, for a total of 6,120 personnel."

"Have you had it out on maneuvers yet?"

"Yes Ma'am and she handles nicer than the *Apollo*, as big as she is. Have you thought of a name for her?"

"Swenah will have the honor since she will command the ship. My new bomber I'm going to name *Thunderbolt*.

"I like it," Denteen said genuinely.

"Admiral Omniomi tells me the Monarch class one's have 148 solarium super-reactors in them," Pez told him.

"They do, and the ultra-super class this flagship is in are packed with 244. An imperial class one and class two combined have 238 reactors."

"We have only five such ships, however," Pez pointed out.

"Ahumdulilah has four ships with 150 reactors and four with 149, plus many other extremely large ships; and the Kluzyst have five of their three-mile long ships which now have 34 reactors in them."

"This is quite a hike," Pez mentioned about their long walk.

"There was a tube we could have used at the airlock, but I thought you would like to see a little of the ship," Denteen explained.

"It would probably take a week to see more than a little bit of it," Pez commented on the size.

"We're almost at the senior officer's quarters. First Lieutenant Nash is in your office, right off the bridge. You also have a small private office in your suite. Jard insisted on a cabin in the senior officer's quarters, in your wing, and could not be dissuaded."

"Did he now? I'm surprised he's even on the mission," Pez expressed her astonishment.

"He's also Chief of Engineering on your bomber, sharing a cabin with your Chief Medical Officer, Slinkie," Denteen reported.

"Isn't he a little overqualified for the position?" Pez asked.

"The High Council's orders recommissioning you, and spelling out your mission objectives, parameters and goal, specify that Jard is to be your Special Assistant; at least according to Jard. Your orders remain sealed, Ma'am."

"I'm afraid I'll have to assign my spouse the burdensome task of watching over my Special Assistant."

Holding Electra in one arm Pez was able to shoot off a pretty good salute to the Space Marine at the door to the senior officer's quarters, and Electra gave him one of her best smiles with a little wave. Pez gave another one to the Space Marine at her wing door, though this salute startled Electra so this Space Marine didn't get the smile and wave from her. Pez invited Denteen in while she changed. She put on all regular-issue, though custom made to her size, Space Marine clothing right down to the olive panties. Comfy now in her combat fatigues, Pez slipped her feet into her soft self-adhering Space Marine indoor boots with soft soles and fleece lining. They were really cozier than her bedroom slippers.

Atlanta and Vegan were looking around wide-eyed. Pez told them, "Sarhi will help you get sorted out here. You might want to think about joining the spiritual congress since you won't have ship's duties or battle stations."

"This is far bigger than a class one!" Vegan exclaimed.

"With 96 more reactors than a class one," Pez said enthusiastically.

Amazonia told Pez, "I will man one of the quad-blaster turrets on your super-bomber, and a class seven quad on the flagship."

"Do you want to come and see it?"

"Absolutely; I can't wait."

"May I come along?" Super-Agent Green asked.

"Please do. Are you qualified on the class six blaster-quads, super-Agent Green?"

"I am, and I'm rated in the top quarter of the top percentile," she answered honestly.

"Would you be one of my gunners?" Pez begged.

"I'd love to" Green told her.

Sarhi asked Pez, "Where do you want to put Lucky and Winston?"

"Have Nash show them to the ship's Intel. Center and they can stay with the rest of the spooks; have a reunion or something. This isn't really a spy mission anymore."

Will Pooh be staying with you in your suite?" Sarhi asked, trying to get everyone sorted.

"How big is the bed?" Pez asked, trying to make up her mind.

"Oh, they had your back on the bed, I can assure you. It could accommodate several homeless families comfortably."

"Put her in my suite," Pez decided.

"And Pippy and Alice too?"

"I don't know, Sarhi," Pez said frustrated. "Tell them to sleep wherever they'd like. I want to go see my bomber."

Pez, Amazonia, Green, Ming, Ahhu, Trix, Rubix, Gretle, and Woahha, who would all have functions and battle stations on the bomber, went to the tubes in the corridor, then went two at a time violating regulations and personal space to get to the bomber quick. They had to ascend a ladder up through a hatch in the floor of the airlock to the "bomber's" flight dock and hanger. Pez wanted to look in the hanger which was aired up, so they went in to see the combat shuttle and XPS Astro Phantom parked in it. There were also four drone fighter bombers with their fins retracted, nearly stacked on top of one another. Denteen told her, "Four was the most they could cram in here, so there are two more attached to mounts on the outer hull, and you can fly one remotely along with you from the flagship hanger, giving you seven."

"Good," Ahhu stated, "I get seven of my own before I need to borrow from the other bombers."

Denteen led them into the ship and gave them a tour. Slinkie was in the medical unit and gave Pez a very warm welcome. Jard was in engineering and said, "Welcome back love-child. You're stuck with me now. I'm your Special Assistant."

"Well try to actually assist me, High Councilman Jard," Pez pleaded.

"I have some ideas I think will surprise you," he told her.

"I'd rather be warned in advance," Pez informed him. "Please run things by me first, instead of surprising me."

"I didn't mean it like that," he complained.

They moved on through to the environmental section meeting two more crew members, and into the Space Marine section where Evenrude and Johnson were already getting things organized and working up a wish list to present Pez. Evenrude introduced Pez, "SCG, this is Jr. Lieutenant Mercury of Second Division's 'First-In'

Battalion, who was in the action with you on the alien imperial home world in their capitol."

"I'm really pleased to meet you, lieutenant," Pez told him, shaking his hand vigorously.

"It is a true honor to serve directly under your command, SCG," Mercury gushed like a cadet.

"If Evenrude picked you, I couldn't be more pleased to have you aboard."

"He was one of my instructors in basic," Mercury clarified the origins of his relationship with Evenrude.

They moved onto the bridge, which was hardly more than a cockpit with eight seats, each with a specialized console, and two special toddler safety-seats with their own shields. The toddler-seats were at the end by the diaper and wipes dispensers affixed to the bulkhead, and a trash receptacle was also attached labelled "Diapers and Wipes Only". Cotex was in the Sensors Analyst seat, reading through data. Flint was in the Weapons Operator's chair configuring his console, and there was a Navigation Officer and a Fire Control Officer there Pez met for the first time. Ming sat in the copilot spot and began to familiarize herself with the instrumentation. Ahhu plopped into the Drone Pilot seat and Gretle sat in the Coms Officer's seat. That graduate student, Gretle, was not only an elite holocoms engineer, but had done some voice-acting as well, and with her exceptional oral skills had challenged the Star Fleet exams to attain the highest possible Coms Officer rating; and Woahha convinced Sarhi to convince Yona, who convinced Zapa, to make Gretle Pez's Coms Officer on her 'bomber' star cruiser.

Pez sat in the pilot's seat with Electra in her lap, and liked it immediately. It had 408 thrusters to choose from, and sixteen swivel drives for making a turn. The ship had 22 boosters and each had a swivel degree. It didn't matter to her how many reverse drives and thrusters there were since she would just hit those all at once when she needed them. The controls were tight, calibrated for tiny increments of precise change. Her main holo required little adjustment, only some fine tuning, informing her that someone, Konax probably, had already gone to a lot of trouble customizing it for her. Her main holo could divide into sixteen boxes, growing and dividing those if needed, and she could generate two more nearly full-size holos, one to each side of her main one. A strip along the bottom of her console displayed mini-holos with data regarding relative positioning, trajectory, velocity, systems functions, countdowns, and warnings. She wouldn't have changed a thing. They even made her a helmet rack next to her pilot seat, and the very existence of such a rack implied a violation of regulations.

Once she'd satisfied her curiosity regarding the cockpit, and finished a warm embrace with Cotex, and a very friendly one with Flint, Pez explored the rest of the ship. She met one of the munitions-loaders and two cargo handlers while snooping around. She finally went to her own cabin. It had a wall of built-in drawers and cabinets, a cramped walk-in closet, and a tiny bathroom. The bed was only an empress and took up all but a narrow walkway along two sides of it, allowing access to the drawers, closet and bathroom. It was more than you'd ever expect on a bomber, though radically austere for a star cruiser.

She finally returned to her giant suite on the flagship which had a deep bath tub. Mel told her, "They took our diamond chandelier, painting and soft living room rug off the yacht to return to their planets of origin. I think some curators are going to try to clean the rug first. Baby drool, you know."

"I'm going to miss seeing those. Did you replicate the painting?"

"Of course," Mel told her, "We're just waiting on Captain Spalding's auxiliary to make a real hardwood frame for it."

"We need to get a rug," Pez said, regretting the loss.

Mel perked up and informed her, "They put down a soft wool rug with a beautiful design, which fits the room well. It was machine made though and is not an antique."

"That's a relief," Pez sighed.

"They also put up a very attractive glass crystal chandelier over the dining room table, but we both know there is just no compensating for that diamond one."

"It was a little embarrassing to have that in my dining compartment though," Pez confided. "It belongs in a museum."

"Which is where it is headed," Mel said not necessarily agreeing. Then she alerted Pez, "Admiral Swenah's shuttle is approaching the flagship's docks."

"Tell Denteen to make sure that band is blaring and stomping up a storm when she gets off her shuttle. I'll be in the bath."

"Alright," Mel said uncertainly.

Denteen's voice came into Pez's ear, "Regulations require your presence on the shuttle dock SCG."

"I'm running a bath and Swenah's more competent than I am. She'll be on the dock in a minute."

"My point exactly," he explained.

"Thank you XO for doing your duty and reminding me," Pez acknowledged, with no intention of going down there.

A couple of minutes later both Swenah's voice, and even more so that military marching band, were in Pez's ear, "Where are you, SCG darling.?"

I'm about to climb into the bath with alluring Commander Ming, if you have to know," Pez told her, not realizing she was on speaker at the landing dock.

Several voices—one of them Swenah's—told Pez, "Well have fun!"

CHAPTER TWENTY

Admirals Swenah and Omniomi, along with Rear Admiral Firestone and all the Captains and Commanders of the war ships and auxiliaries, worked under tremendous time pressures seeing to the millions of details that had to be attended to in order to get Pez Fleet under way, while Pez took a hot bath with Ming, ate a candlelight—electric of course—dinner, and got eight and a half hours sleep in spite of the crowded bed. She awoke alert and excited with 51 hours and twenty-one minutes left on the departure countdown and took a long shower before going to the senior officer's mess for breakfast. It was 4:15 PM Om capital time, which was what the ship maintained for its clock cycle, so they got their food short order cooked for them. Ahhu, Gretle, Rubix, Trix, Pooh, Pippy and Alice came through the ordering line, which was entirely composed of their own group, as guests of the SCG and Commander Ming. No one else was in the dining room at this hour. The cooks would have likely felt put upon if Ahhu's nakedness had not so well ingratiated the party to them. Pez had her first high potency stimulant brew with steamed half and half and bittersweet chocolate powder shaken on top, which she had not had since becoming pregnant with Electra. She also ate two large plates of food.

After breakfast with just over 48 hours to departure, Pez tubed to the corridor outside the bridge on a 38 second ride that could raise the hair on the back of corpse's neck for its excitement. She just had to do it again since it had been such a rush. Then, of course, she had to do it yet again to get back. At that point, Pez entered her office and greeted Lt. Nash with a hug. It was after that, that she actually got to work. She called Major Nicon of the Ahumdulilah Intelligence

Service, "Hi Major, this is Pez," she told him, even though he could see perfectly well in his holo with whom he was speaking.

"You got out just in time and that was quite an impressive escape you made. No one has ever vaporized an imperial class one five-mile long ship before."

"That wasn't me," Pez corrected, "it was my drone pilot, Ahhu."

"That bomber group which joined you did some mighty impressive flying," Nicon remarked.

"They're among our best pilots and they've been training in the maneuvers and tactics of Blue World's 'Phantom Raiders'."

"Monarch is preparing an invasion fleet to take control of Rocky. It leaves in six days."

"Then don't bother evacuating. My fleet will attack them before that. In less than fifty hours we're taking over their holocoms inter-galactic network and going live with news and documentaries we've prepared, and we think we can keep control of it for many hours."

"Encrypted conversations employing one-time codes the empire can't decipher are now accounting for nearly a fifth of all coms traffic. Pretty much every planet can be ready to unleash revolution within 102 hours from now. The first two batches of medical devices are already distributed to ship's officers. We will be getting them to our volunteer officers, right up to the last moment."

"Then let's set the coordinated time for 104 hours from now," Pez decided. "I'll be leading a small force against the space defenses and imperial ships around Mother while my fleet attacks the Monarch system. Do you know anything about the band or of my two missing spooks?"

"Your spooks we've collected and they are on their way to Rocky. The band is still in custody but can only be implicated by conjecture. No actual evidence has been found connecting them to your spying and betrayal. They just told the imperials that you were very gener-ous and an exceptional lover, as well as great publicity for them. They made it quite believable and it's truly plausible. We issued a ransom demand on your behalf for the Caspers, of 300 billion dags as a way to protect them and their estate from the empire for the moment."

"How big is the invasion force they're mustering?"

"They're actually bringing three of their four invasion fleets. The fourth one is stuck in a war against global hit and run tactics in Afrigastan. One fleet will go to Rocky in six days, and two will combine and bring a large convoy of mining ships and auxiliaries to invade the solarium deposits at the outer rim of the Hub Galaxy, scheduled to leave in eleven days."

How big are each of the four fleets?" Pez inquired.

Each fleet consists of 156 war ships composed of ten classes of ships, with ten of those being class one, plus each has 56 troop transports carrying 18,000 troops each, and 46 auxiliary ships. Specialized ships are added to this core depending upon the mission.

"So there will be 30 class ones in the Monarch system besides the ten they always keep there," Pez said thinking about this.

"Our Admiral in Chief of Ahumdulilah Space Fleet suggests adding ships with one super-reactor or less, meaning reactors of lesser magnitudes, to Pez Fleet to fight small craft and to consolidate mass fire on imperial ships. He feels that otherwise the odds are just too overwhelming."

"I'll request those ships following your Admiral's advice," Pez agreed. "I'll need to clear the imperials out of space around Mother very quickly, and jump to Monarch to help with our assault, since I'll have one of our two secret weapon drone pilots aboard."

"I'm sending you the latest data on imperial fleet assets in the Mother system now. A class four from there was usurped into the Hub Galaxy invasion force since they see the population of Mother as no threat."

"I'm receiving it and just have to tell you that Mother is going to be one of the biggest shocks to the Empire, and be the first to successfully liberate."

"I read the reports on the warrior monks and maidens there," Nicon told her, "and I'm honestly impressed. I was informed that when Sarhi the Im called a tuning of the spiritual congress during your escape from New Monarch, nearly the entire planetary population participated, dropping whatever they were doing. I think their solidarity and unity as a people is actually their greatest strength and weapon against the empire."

"They are of one mind to annihilate the imperial yoke which chokes them," Pez agreed.

"We have a pair of class one imperial ships coming over to our side which will work together to clear systems that have few imperial fleet assets within them, blowing through each as quickly as possible. For most planets of the empire a pair of class ones overpowers everything they've got."

"Are there only two class ones coming over to is?" Pez asked.

"There are several others we hope to attain and the medical devices are on the way. I'm sure we can get at least two more onto our side and fitted with non-locality beacons identifying them only to us as friendly, that we can send to help with the assault on Monarch. Possibly we can get even more than that into the fight there.

"Since imperial space combat doctrine calls for concentration of fire on the enemy's largest ship," Pez filled him in, "Om is constructing two seven-mile diameter ships with very thin skins, barely adequate framing, space and quantum drives, and enormous shield generators, that are really just empty shelled drones. They could make about 9,850 of these for the cost of one ultra-super-battleship-carrier. The two seven-mile ships will draw the imperial fire at Monarch and have no lives at stake on board. That will give us some time in the opening battle to whittle down their forces."

"That is truly brilliant and guaranteed to work," Nicon declared with great enthusiasm.

"It sounds like everything the empire has for invasion and reinforcement will be at Monarch when we attack, so other planets will not need worry about the imperials they fight against getting additional help from the empire."

"That is certainly our hope," Nicon agreed. "Most planets will be woefully ill-prepared for dealing with the imperial war ships orbiting them, and will be dependent on mutinies aboard those ships, or outside help to destroy them."

"Get those medical devices well-distributed," Pez encouraged him.

"We have thousands of intelligence agents focused on it and many hundreds of double agents, or imperials working with us.

Some of the imperial fleet officers we've cultivated over the years have had their chips removed surgically by replacing a section of artery, which constitutes a major operation and requires significant medical facilities. The device is safe, simple, self-administering anywhere, and requires no recovery period. Believe me those devices are pouring onto imperial ships, and the fact that the empire planted those chips in the first place is working extremely well to our favor."

"Will any of the invasion ships at Monarch be on our side?"

"Yes, and you'll know them by their nonlocality beacons. Those ships will open fire on imperial ships not come to our side from within their own formations and put their fleet in chaos."

"We are mounting class nine beam weapons on eight of our auxiliaries, all of them two miles long or longer, and with the highest-grade military shields. They will only participate in the first five minutes of engagement then retreat to their stations for rearming and repairing ships. A lot happens in the first five minutes which often decides the whole outcome."

"We will continue to stream data as we receive it, to your flagship," Nicon told her. "It would help if it had a name."

"I'll tell Admiral Swenah to think one up quick," Pez assured him.

"I'll keep in touch. You've done a fantastic job, I must say."

"It was all carefully prepared for me and I had only to step into it," Pez waved it off as they ended their call.

She left her office to walk on the bridge, saluting the Space Marine at the blast door after assigning Lt. Nash some babysitting duties. Electra liked him. Pez told all the officers on the bridge to sit back down and that in the future, a smile was all she needed when she came on the bridge; not anyone rising from their seat. Sitting beside Swenah she said to her, "You need to name this ship pretty soon."

"I'd like to call it '*Reciprocity*'," Swenah replied.

"I like the name," Pez told her. "Get it posted to our fleet and allied world's at once."

Mel said to both of them, "I just love *Reciprocity*! I'm so enormous and powerful now!"

"It is a worthy vessel for you sentience Mel," Pez agreed.

Then she explained to Swenah, "Cleo will be seated on the bridge of *Reciprocity* when you attack Monarch. Your flight deck will need to launch drones controlled by her console and she can kill big ships with them. Shudiy will also sit on your bridge and shall need a supply of your largest torpedoes at her disposal, to slip into soft spots in imperial shields. She will ignite micro-suns around ships to white out their sensors for you."

Swenah said with remorse, "I can't believe that I used to think that woman was just your cook."

"She is an amazing cook," Pez insisted. "I hope to clear imperial ships from the Mother system swiftly, blow their military space station, space weapons platforms and lunar bases, and then rush to Monarch and join the fight."

"You'll be needed to keep our losses down and in deciding the victor," Swenah shared her view. "You picked the best people to command your ultra-super ships. I see you promoted Firestone to Rear Admiral."

"Yes, for his role in Kundabuffer," Pez acknowledged. "You also have Admiral Omniomi, and Captains Hasbro and Nestles. I need for you to place an official request with the Tail of Nine and our allies to send destroyers, assault frigates, fast attack ships, patrol ships, and any other smaller ships, to add firepower to our assault on Monarch. Mel, would you ask Sarhi to make this request known to Yona right away?"

"I'm on it," Mel informed her.

Swenah reported, "I'm texting Zapa and the High Council, and I'm copying my request to the Tail of Nine United Planets Assembly too. We ought to be able to raise at least 600 smaller ships for support. You know, our fleet carries 28,150 combat small craft. I have 609 aboard *Reciprocity*."

Konax told them from the pilot's seat on the bridge, "They say we're going to change the name from Tail of Nine, to One United System, or 1-US"

"It sounds like a surface transportation highway route," Swenah commented.

"I like it," Pez shared. "One us."

Konax reported, "The only other name in the running that was considered is '*Unity*'."

"Unity would be simpler for directing mail and goods, and for saying fewer words," Mel pointed out.

Pez informed Swenah, "If you get the smaller ships, which I'm certain you will, I'm taking *Phoenix* with me to Mother. She's enhanced having three reactors, instead of the two the star-cruiser class typically have, and Captain Quicksilver, who is now her Captain, has been briefed on the situation in the Mother System."

"Where is Captain Ohinya?" Swenah inquired.

"She is now Captain of *Apollo*," Pez answered, "You also have three more of the 30 reactor super-battleship class; Captain Elmo of *Hercules*, Captain Sylvester of *Hades*, Captain Fudd of *Hermes*."

"How many super-carriers did Om send?" Swenah asked.

"All four of them," Pez replied. "You have *Dionysus* captained by Bacchus, *Zeus* by Granger, *Chronos* by Robuck, and *Poseidon* by Schwab."

"I see Ahumdulilah is bringing quite a few giant ships to the party," Swenah commented.

"They bring 15 less ships than the Kluzyst, but many more reactors and class nine and eight beams and blasters," Pez analyzed." One hundred and forty-two ships in all, and 10,000 combat small craft."

Swenah shared, "I'm sending you my proposed assault plan. No rocks would be thrown, no dumb munitions, so we can milk surprise for all it's worth. I want to jump in with hardly enough room to slow to max targeting velocity, and overfly the planet, to come back at them from the other side."

"That's using surprise to its ultimate capacity," Pez agreed, "and exactly how I'd do it, if I were leading bombers in."

Swenah thought aloud, "Our eight auxiliaries with beam weapons will need a little more room to decelerate and will have to jump in behind us to bring up the rear. We ought to have all of our small craft launched before we complete our first pass. I don't care how many ships they have, such a sudden near reckless attack from so close will leave no time for their crews to reach battle stations, and we'll be able to unleash a storm on them without much risk on our first pass. We can fire drone torpedoes well before we slow to targeting resolution and pilot them to their destinations from the ships, to take out the things we would normally hit with rocks before coming in."

"I totally approve your battle plan, Swenah," Pez authorized it. "With 505 imperial war ships in the Monarch system, and 40 of those five-miles long, you need to be daring and bold."

"They'll be feeling pretty secure at that moment too," Swenah speculated, "being so many ships and within their well-defended home system. We're going to catch them with their pants down."

"Who is commanding my Space Marines?" Pez asked.

"Captain Swanson, whom you promoted from commander, is in command of them," Swenah answered. 'He's on *Troop Transport One.*"

"I need to speak with him," Pez said as she connected. When he appeared on her holo she said with a snap salute, startling everyone on the bridge, "I'm glad it's you I'll be working with in this campaign, Captain Swanson."

"It's a great honor to be part of your team again, SCG."

"How many Space Marines did they give us?"

"You have 68,000 all with hardshell combat suites, plus 7,600 Army Space Special Forces under Colonel Bleep with their own version of a space combat suit. The Kluzyst have sent 660,000 ground troops, Trident sends 168,000, and Ahumdulilah has sent us 240,000, all with space combat suits. Altogether, you have 1,416,600 ground troops at your disposal with this fleet."

"Impressive," Pez replied. Then she asked, "Who leads the Ahumdulilah troops?"

"That would be General Kodak," Swanson answered.

"I want to do most of my planning and coordination with just you and General Kodak for efficiency. Have you met?"

"As a matter of fact he invited me onto his operations-deck special forces and vehicle transport ship to have dinner with him last clock-evening."

"Whose time is the fleet on?" Pez asked.

"SCG time, or Om capital time," he answered.

"I'm not on Om capital time yet myself," Pez admitted. "I just finished breakfast a little while ago."

"Om has 400,000 regular army ready to send if they are needed, in forty of those old mothball army transports like we used to get hostages home from Kundabuffer. Ahumdulilah and the Kluzyst each have over a million with transports to carry them. Trident can send half a million, and Rally a quarter million. They are all ready to go at a moment's notice."

"I have Mel, Hermesia and Jard assigned to tracking, analyzing and identifying needs and opportunities regarding the overview of the more than 5,700 worlds. As the situation develops they'll be having you direct troops to various places, and sending you data sets."

"I won't let you down," he promised.

"I know that," she told him, "I'm just giving you a heads up."

"The Space Marines are in top form and their morale could not be better," Swanson told her encouragingly.

"They're going to scare the crap out of the imperials, who'd better wear their brown pants to this," Pez told him fiercely.

The SCG called Schwin next, and asked, "How many XPS Astro-Phantoms can you scare up?"

"I don't know. How many do you want?"

"I think 108 would do nicely; 27 wings of 4 spacecraft. I also want 24 wings of six NBC Hunter-Terminator Fighter Bombers, and twelve wings of eight Corvette Thunder Fighters. We're starting off at the Mother System. Mel, would you send Commander Schwin the data please. We need to wipe out the imperials in the space around the planet quick so we can join the fight in the Monarch System. Cleo is going to have to stay on *Reciprocity*, on Swenah's bridge to help her, so we'll only have Ahhu able to jump drones inside ships. I'll get some small auxiliaries carrying reloaders for all three classes of small crafts. The Corvette Thunders can even keep going back for more undercarriage missiles."

"It sounds like a dream," Schwin declared with great exuberance.

Schwin liked to do everything right on the edge of disaster, as they ought to be done as far as Pez was concerned. Pez called Spalding, now also promoted to Captain, on his ship *Auxiliary 2*, and told him, "I need a few small auxiliaries or extra-large shuttles to carry thirty-six reloaders, twelve each for Corvette Thunders, Hunter Terminators and Astro-Phantoms, to accompany me to the Mother System when we start the revolution."

"I have just the thing," Spalding told her. "It's a small craft reload platform for your Corvettes and Terminators, and will even change out fuel cells on the thrusters and replace spent boosters. Your Corvettes can be in and out in eight seconds. The auxiliary reloader platform can carry up to a dozen AI android Astro-Phantom reloaders. I can send a mini-munitions freighter with robotic cargo transfer along with the auxiliary in case it runs low on missiles."

"That sounds perfect," Pez said gratefully.

"I'm glad to be of service. I'll have those ships over to you an hour before departure. They both have quantum drives. The Reloading Auxiliary has a crew of four, and the mini-munitions freighter a crew of three. They'll do their jobs even under fire."

"Getting shot at when you're trying to do a job, and not shooting back, is nerve-wracking and quite challenging," Pez noted.

"It's our lot in life," Spalding assured her.

"Thanks Captain, I'll be in touch."

"Aye, Aye Ma'am."

The countdown raced for zero and fleet personnel rushed to accomplish everything that had to be done in preparation for departure. Six hundred and thirty-one smaller ships arrived filling Pez Fleet out to 1026 ships. Shuttles from Om, its two moons, and its space stations made continuous trips back and forth to ships of Pez Fleet filling them with supplies and materials. Intricate synchronization and alignment between allied technologies were attained rapidly. All ships had been fitted with Ahumdulilah uncloaking systems, and power previously diverted to cloaking was channeled to shields and weapons. Surprise would be their only invisibility.

Swenah was perspiring when the clock ran out and she gave the order for the fleet of more than a thousand ships to accelerate to jump speed. For Konax, piloting *Reciprocity*, it was slow as pushing a wheelbarrow uphill. They were headed for an empty region of deep space within the Royal Galaxy far from the core stars, and undetectable by the empire. Only one covert operation already in motion was needed to have everything in place for taking over the entire imperial inter-galactic holocoms network. It was scheduled to be accomplished and done by the time they reached their deep space position within the Royal Galaxy. Optimal ship positioning was still being determined for all but key components of their fleet, such as the two giant decoys, the five ultra-super class ships, the eight biggest Ahumdulilah ships, and some others. They would maintain a loose configuration relative to one another giving each a small sphere of operations within, though strictly speaking, it could not really be called a 'formation'. Pez and Swenah called it a 'fluid formation' and they planned to drown the imperials of Monarch in it by sweeping them away with a tsunami.

The jump came and went unnoticed by the instruments and shocking the humans to the bone marrow. They had jumped into a place perfectly described by Ahhu's use of the term "nowhere." Only distant stars could be seen, and from here, you really couldn't tell that you were actually inside a galaxy. It was the kind of thing goosebumps were made out of. It sort of let you know how sparse, insignificant, fragile, and ridiculous matter is. Everyone but Pez was affected by the deep gloom of vast emptiness, challenging everything pathetic like identity and boundaries.

Mel told the officers of the bridge with glee, "This is just like my vacuum sphere."

Pez told her, "If dark matter were actually matter, and not ether, then this would be a very heavy place."

"It feels heavy to me," Ahhu's voice came into Pez's ear, "like a black hole."

"Are you with Jard?"

"How did you know?" Ahhu asked surprised.

"Only he has the capacity technologically to listen in on the bridge," Pez told her, a little offended.

Jard's voice came on, "We were just testing our equipment and programs, gearing up to take the network. Don't get your panties in a bunch, Love-child, we're not spies."

"Not spies," Pez agreed, "just violators of regulations and laws."

"How long are we going to be out in the middle of nowhere?" Ahhu demanded to know, not happy about being here.

"We've been nowhere forever and always will be, sweetheart, but speaking relatively, we leave to attack in about fifty-three hours. By the way, by definition there can be no 'center' of nowhere."

"I think I'm there," Konax said, "shutting off drives."

Pez asked Jard, "Are you ready to do your thing?"

"All set," Jard confirmed. "Three, two, one, ours! Do you want to start with the emperor cartoon or the infomercial?"

"I vote for the cartoon," Pez said, knowing firsthand how humiliating it is to have a cartoon made of you.

"The cartoon it is," Jard said setting it off with his skullcap.

They all watched imperial commercial holo frequencies and it didn't matter which one you were on because the cartoon was on all of them. Pez had insisted that in the cartoon the emperor get pissed on before he was shot in the head. They might have over exaggerated his jowls a bit much in the animation, and that absolutely hideous and absurd wave of pale yellow hair above his forehead was made to look radically comical. They gave him a greenish snot runny nose, and overall, he came across so revolting the weak of stomach could heave their cookies watching him. The cartoon characters all cheered wildly and happily when the emperor's brains splattered the wall behind him and blood mixed with brain matter ran down in drips. It really wasn't a children's cartoon and this became even more evident when the emperor's genitals were cut off and stuffed in his mouth.

The infomercial ran next, on every station, explaining the workings of the empire, shattering propaganda myths and educating the people. A very emotionally powerful documentary came after the infomercial depicting the horrors, iniquities, acts of terror and murderous abuses of the empire in encapsulating graphic images a moron could understand. It beat its points into the brains of the viewers more brutally than even the imperial propaganda machine would have been capable of. A pre-recorded message from Cher Bulwinkle to Spounge was shown next, followed by another specially prepared documentary. Pez thought the cartoon was the best. She knew the emperor's ego, which was about all there was left of him, would be freaking out and suffering intolerably. They had many hours of material ready to go and studios on Ahumdulilah and Rocky were churning out more, including another cartoon.

This was phase II of Operation Liberation. Jard, Trix, and Mel worked tirelessly blocking imperial attempts to regain control of their network. Ahumdulilah agents and those in the empire conspiring with them, continued to smuggle the medical devices aboard imperial ships. The 30-some trillion people of their empire were told not to go to work and to go home if they were already there. Indecipherable codes ruled almost 30% of imperial coms traffic and outright revolutionary talk and criminal denunciations of the empire pretty much took up the other 70%.

Amazonia insisted that Pez find her a re-entry combat suit, which Pez did in spite of it being an enormously expensive piece of equipment. Amazonia would stay, returning to the surface of Mother in the suit, when Pez left to join the fight in Monarch. That was the plan at any rate and the suit was on board *Thunderbolt*. When they were down to two and a quarter hours on the revolution countdown Pez held a briefing with all ship commanders of whatever rank, and Mel shot each their data for maintaining relative positioning within the 'fluid formation'; that wall of destruction that would crash over planet Monarch. They all liked the tidal wave analogy and planned to be one.

CHAPTER TWENTY-ONE

The big moment was closing on them. Swenah nervously led the biggest force ever raised by Om and its allies as they built up speed for their jump into Monarch, practically in the imperial's laps, while Pez led her little force towards jumping to Mother. They still had the network, thanks to a trick pulled off by Trix's Key to Everything. Jard was still trying to steal that from her so she'd been careful when she'd employed it. The people of the empire had had more than two days of uninterrupted truth and stark reality over their holo-network channels, the same on every one, saving them endless surfing and decision making. In the second cartoon the emperor was naked, his folds of fat showing clearly in their ample exaggeration, and his penis was so small it took a cartoon close-up to even see. Once it was magnified to fill the screen it turned out to be a gnarly thing of unnatural color, looking kind of sticky.

Pez was jumping in real close and they would all have to brake like mad to get off a shot and stay alive. Her auxiliary reloader and mini-freighter would keep a sixty million mile distance from Mother, and once relatively stationary, the auxiliary would launch the twelve Astro-Phantom AI android-reloaders, which were the big squadron servers and not the little ones they'd used in Xegachtznel. These could each load ten bombers, which would give every one of her Astro-Phantoms a reload with twelve reloads to spare.

It was always unclear if one lived through the jump or not but they emerged on the other side of it alive, hurling at .7 light speed at stuff way too close already and coming fast. They fired boosters to slow. It was the only way. Otherwise they would have just shot right by unable to engage. With reverse drives and thrusters full-tilt they spilled off velocity quickly, gaining sensor resolution at the same rate. Big imperial warships were resolving in front of them in their holos.

In her efficiency Pez had them there about two minutes early, and triggering her twin class 8 blasters to pound into an imperial Class nine ship containing only two reactors, she fired the very first shots of the revolution. Flint got their class nine beam weapon boring into the ship Pez's nose blaster was ripping into, and at least four of *Thunderbolt's* quad blasters were nailing that same ship. Ming hit it with a few canister missiles then Pez got their ball-mount fin blasters locked onto it and its hull breached the same moment its shields went down, seeming to contract the volume of the ship as a kind of wind-up for its great colorful expansion into a blazing gas cloud. An imperial class four, the largest ship in the Mother system, was opening fire on them. It had 31 reactors powering it and was 2 ½ miles long. The class four ship with the officers who'd gone through surgery to remove the explosive chips had been reassigned to one of the invasion fleets and so was in the Monarch system.

Pez told Ahhu, "That one's yours, sweetheart. There is no way *Phoenix* and *Thunderbolt* could defeat it."

Ahhu had kept her drone right at jump speed and had noticed the big ship before Pez had pointed it out, so was already doing her navigation. The petite naked drone pilot worked it out fast and she ignited her quantum drive. The drone winked out of existence on their holo's where it had occupied space a moment before, then the class four blurred into a flash of blue energy like a blue streak of lightning, stretching on out of the battle zone.

Two ships, a class seven with seven reactors and a class six with eleven, were closing in. The class seven was closer and both star cruisers pounded it. Between them they were equal to it and the three ships fought it out hammering each other. Hundreds of imperial small combat craft were launching from a lunar base and from the military space stations. Schwin's Astro-Phantoms and Hunter-Terminators were hitting space weapons platforms and the combat spacecraft streaming out of the two big war ships. Both star-cruisers were painting the class seven with beams and blasters while slamming it with missiles, and it was dividing its energy-fire and ordinance between the two of them.

The class six closed to range and opened fire. It was a tense moment as Pez watched her shields dropping. Ahhu was on it but required a degree of precision which could not be rushed if it was to have the desired effect. Captain Quicksilver took a hit from the class six that zeroed out his shields scorching a broad patch of his hull, though it didn't breach. Micro-suns blossomed covering the entire class six and its shots went wild missing them. A moment later Pez found a soft spot in the class seven's shields and slipped one of her big torpedoes right through. It punched through the hull but the ship remained intact. Debris shot out through the hole in the hull like a projectile weapon firing scatter shot.

The soft spot in the class seven's shields appeared in a new location and Pez lobbed two big missiles in through the opening one right after the other, rewarded for her efforts with a horrendous explosion of light, color, and matter coming apart at the seams. It was a glorious sight in that particular moment. The big beam weapon on the class six started boring a hole in *Thunderbolt*. Pez hit a launch booster to get it off of her and planted a whole new crop of micro-suns enveloping it. She said to Ahhu, "Soon would be good."

A Hunter-Terminator was being chased by half a dozen fighter-bombers herding it into an oncoming swarm of fighters. Pez planted micro-suns on the lead imperials in both oncoming groups. Their fire lost all accuracy and the Hunter-Terminator veered off just before the two groups shot by each other, though not the two which collided. The big beam of the class six found *Thunderbolt* again and Pez watched her shields take a dive. She tried a brake and turn, and lost the beam for a moment. She planted suns all over it and was able to get out from under it again. Finally, the class six streaked blue on its way out of the battle zone and when the flare of illumination faded there was not so much as vapors of it that could be detected.

Some class nines land a class ten were closing. They had been on the other side of Mother when Pez's group had jumped into the system so close. Pez had been here a little more than two minutes now so the revolution was underway everywhere in the empire. Working in tandem with Quicksilver they ganged up on a class nine dispatching it in 7.4 seconds.

Pez quickly planted suns over the other ships and kept her twin nose blasters spitting out energy bolts into another class nine. Her Astro-Phantoms swarmed and overwhelmed the class ten at Schwin's direction. *Thunderbolt's* twelve class 6 blaster-quad turrets were all engaging incoming small craft. Most anti-small craft blaster quads were class 3 or 4. The big class sixes could turn the largest imperial bomber to slag in less than 3 seconds. Their lives depended upon this advantage at the moment. Then four wings of Corvette Thunders swooped in clearing the swarm from around them and spending most of their undercarriage missiles in the process. Pez directed them back to the auxiliary reloading platform.

Schwin's voice said to Pez, "Your big beam weapon is needed on the lunar surface. They have some class nine beams there shielded by several reactors and our torpedoes won't get through."

"I'm on my way; just let me finish off this class nine," she told her as she hit that ship with both her nose blasters and the big beam.

Flint hit it with the twin ball-mount fin blasters and a barrage of missiles while Ming hit it with missiles too. It grew from compact solid to bloom into a mini-nova of spectral light. Pez brought them around to come in low over the lunar surface. Ground dome shields tended to have more strength on top with less power on the sides at the base. She planted her beam on a point inches from where shields met the firmament and chucked some torpedoes into the same spot while hitting it with her nose blasters. Ming was shooting a continuous flow of canister missiles at the same point on the shields. The torpedoes launched from the Astro-Phantoms led by Schwin provided the force to bring down the shields and blow the reactors, which blew the lunar weapons and nothing remained but a crater where the base had been. Scratch one super-lunar weapons base. It just wasn't there anymore.

Amazonia called out, "There is a class ten providing air-support for imperials on the ground on Mother and tearing my people up."

"I'm taking us there now. The class tens have only one reactor and pop pretty quick," Pez reassured her.

There was still a class five imperial ship in the system with 22 reactors; more than three times the power of *Thunderbolt* and *Phoenix* combined. It was closing on Pez's ship. Ahhu was still getting her next drone up to jump speed. Pez had nowhere to hide so she accelerated, making truly random maneuvers while keeping her big beam boring into it and her nose blasters drumming it. Ming and Flint hit it too. *Phoenix* got her big weapons lighting it up and Schwin made a pass at it with four wings of Astro-Phantoms raining big torpedoes down on it. Some Hunter-Terminator wings were buffeting it with big missiles and some Corvette Thunders were plowing their undercarriage missiles into it. While they were far from taking the behemoth ship's shields down they did manage to disrupt them enough to reveal a soft spot, and Pez exploited this with a pair or torpedoes followed immediately by a pair of big missiles as she shifted the mighty beam weapon onto the same spot, careful not to kill her own ordinance.

The first torpedo went through the shields to explode against the hull a tenth of a second before the second hit punching a hole for the two missiles that followed right behind. Internal explosions shook and rocked the ship. Astro-Phantoms in a continuous line were aiming torpedoes into the cleft in the hull, stretching the explosions within the ship into one continuous roar as they came in one after another. Suddenly a hundred foot drive exhaust blew off the tail of the ship in a blur of velocity to disintegrate a Hunter-Terminator, an imperial bomber, and finally to pulverize a pair of imperial fighters. Drive and stern pieces were spitting out the back of the ship with other debris and broken pieces. Missiles and torpedoes kept flying into the chasm in the hull of the class five. The underside flight deck great bay doors burst at the same moment whipping separately into space like dumb munitions. One caught a whole wing of imperial fighters disintegrating them.

The class five's superstructure launched off the top of the ship like a rocket leaving a thermal conflagration. The superstructure was more or less intact and hundreds of miles away when the ship came apart in a spray cloud of light and color whiting out many of their sensors for a moment. There were only some class tens, and a class eight with three reactors, equal in power to the *Phoenix*, left in the Mother System.

Pez noticed a fighter bomber effectively pulverizing imperial small craft and flown intuitively with great skill. It was an imperial spacecraft and truly impressed Pez. She hailed it on coms and said, "Great flying! Who is piloting that craft?"

The response came back, "This is Bodhi of the Adamantine Will Order. I stole this fighter bomber to help the Khedar destroy the empire and liberate all the planets it enslaves."

Pez informed the pilot, "I'm Cher, or Pez really, leader of the armada waging war with the Royal Monarch Empire. You've been a big help."

"Then you are the Khedar! And my Vicar General," Bodhi declared.

"We're almost done here," Pez let him know, "and will be jumping into the Monarch System in the Royal Galaxy shortly. That is where this will all be decided."

"I'm sticking with you to help," he insisted.

"If we survive the battle of Monarch," Pez told him, "I will take you into my entourage and train you personally."

"I couldn't imagine a better incentive to stay alive," Bodhi replied.

Pez raced for the class ten that was wreaking havoc on Mother's ground troops, skimming the dome of the atmosphere before diving into it at the imperial ship and hitting it with beam and nose blasters. The ship didn't last long under the beam and relinquished its form to resort back to atoms, with a few molecules still clinging together here and there as brighter spots in the fireball. Amazonia made a war whoop into everybody's ears. Pez went hunting for the class eight. Her Astro-Phantoms could handle the class tens. There were also still hundreds of imperial combat small craft buzzing about. A sixth of her own force was at the auxiliary reloader. Her gunners were doing great and five of them were in the flow-state manifesting perfect aim and maximum efficiency. Rubix had the highest score and Woahha and Trix were neck and neck just behind him, with Amazonia and

Green hardly trailing. Then there was a very significant gap down to the next highest score.

Coming around close to the equator Pez caught the class eight in the act of unleashing hell on a community of Motherlings. *Thunderbolt* struck the class eight like one and Schwin was on it too with two wings of Astro-Phantoms. It transmitted a surrender signal powering down its weapons. When Pez's group stopped pounding on it, it shut down its shields entirely and offered up the bodies of its dead officers to the revolution.

Two class ten imperial ships were found duking it out and Pez fried the one that didn't have the friendly beacon. Some entire squadrons of small craft were surrendering to *Phoenix.* Pez came around the curve of the planet, ascending as she went, to target the military space station. She hailed them before she fired saying "I'll give you a minute and a half to evacuate and see that you are all safely collected from space."

They fired a wall of missiles at her so Pez turned and accelerated until the missiles were on a stern chase after her. Quad blaster gunners were reducing the number of missiles though not nearly quick enough. Pez fired off her anti-missile molten flares behind her catching the bulk of the remaining missiles, which still left more than her quad-gunners could manage. This didn't stop them from trying. Pez released her cloaked smart mine mobile net to her rear, and between that and her determined gunners, the missiles were neutralized to the last.

Pez turned to aim at the space station she was already hurling missiles at. Her beam bore down on the non-ambulatory space station draining its shields while her nose blasters dug into it. A soft spot opened and she sent a torpedo through it, followed right on its heels by a big missile. Some Hunter-Terminators were making a run on the station at the same time. About a third of it blew into a dust cloud and the other two thirds broke in half spinning off in different directions, spilling their contents into space as they went.

Schwin sent a big torpedo into the open end of one of the two sections and must have hit something vital because the whole thing turned into a flash of light, then was gone. Pez brought her quad gunners to small craft targets and got to blow a few up herself with her nose blasters. More small craft started surrendering in wings and squadrons. Pez directed some wings of all three of her classes of combat craft to the surface of Mother to assist in the ground fighting. She said to Amazonia who was at her quad blasters wasting an imperial fighter-bomber, "You can take the combat shuttle from *Thunderbolt's* bay and keep the re-entry suit for another occasion if you like. I'm going to leave the combat craft I just sent to the surface here to assist you, but the rest of us are needed in the Monarch System."

"Thank you Khedar. You have liberated Mother. Go liberate the rest of the empire but come back to us" Amazonia told her most gratefully. Amazonia went to board the combat shuttle and Pez directed Evenrude to man her turret.

Pez spoke to all vessels in her force, "If you've been assigned to supporting the ground war, remain in the Mother System and watch out for stray small craft we might have missed. Everyone else, get reloaded, and prepare to accelerate to jump speed. Swenah needs us. Schwin will take you all in as a group but *Phoenix* and *Thunderbolt* are leaving now."

Schwin asked, "What about the auxiliary and mini-freighter?"

"There are a number of auxiliary reloading groups stationed around Monarch and I'm sending all of you the coordinates for them. Leave those ships here to support our spacecraft we're keeping here."

The moment Amazonia cleared *Thunderbolt's* bay doors Pez told Quicksilver, "Start accelerating for the jump to Monarch. Don't engage anything bigger than a class eight when we get there and see if you can help reduce the attacking imperial small craft."

"I can't believe we cleared this system of imperials given how little we brought," Quicksilver told her awed, not to mention shocked to still be breathing.

"We wouldn't have gotten far without Ahhu and her drones," Pez replied.

"That class five wasn't hit with a drone and neither was that class seven," Quicksilver was quick to point out.

Pez Fleet, commanded by Swenah, appeared quite instantaneously racing at everything orbiting Monarch on their side of it.

Admiral Swenah adjusted their heading issuing orders to all ships to orient on the invasion fleet coming to life ahead of them. Every ship was employing every means available to slow their momentum. Guided torpedoes and missiles were launched before fire control could get weapons locked on targets, still moving too fast. These were directed by drone pilots aboard *Reciprocity* and by drone pilots aboard other ships.

From jumping into the system to opening fire on the high orbit invasion fleet had only taken one minute and eight seconds for the lead ships. Multiple tenders and replenishers were undocking from each war ship to try and get away. Small combat spacecraft were pouring out of all the larger ships of Pez Fleet and not a single one had lifted off from one of the ships of the invasion fleet yet. The invasion fleet was for a change the invaded; and they were caught woefully off guard. Some of them cloaked, disappearing, as if that would help just before they were blanketed with missiles and torpedoes. Cleo jumped a drone fighter-bomber inside a 5 mile ship, sideways, which still gave her a mile to work with, and it blue streaked right through the center of a class four, then caught the bow of a class six as it headed out of the battle zone in a flash.

Blinding suns popped up over many of the biggest ships and Swenah looked over at Shudiy, seated in Pez's chair on the bridge. Her face was in shadow from her hood pulled over her head. Swenah had no idea if Shudiy was in there at the moment or out in space. The two gargantuan seven-mile decoy ships were soaking up all of the imperial fire. Swenah was burning a hole in a class one with a class nine beam, one of 34 Class 9's on *Reciprocity*, while many of the other ships with class nine and eight blasters fired on the same ship. Missiles and torpedoes flowed into the class one in a great continuous river as its shields swirled and churned like liquid. One of the giant torpedoes left a tube on *Reciprocity* to slide right through the big ship's shields. The hull-piercer type torpedo was the biggest Om made. It exploded into the hull with another one only feet behind it, and two more in a straight line behind that one. At least two of these made it deep into the interior to explode and so did a pair of the biggest missiles following them in as the class one went nova. Swenah looked over at Shudiy.

The lead ships swept by this invasion fleet turning a dozen degrees to aim for the next invasion fleet. Here most of the tenders, replenishers and tugs had disconnected but were yet in the midst of the warships coming under attack. This invasion fleet was a little better prepared having had more time than the other one, and was getting a slow sputter of small craft up. They were still flying out *Reciprocity's* bays like high pressure hoses opened full. Behind them new waves of fresh ships kept pounding the 1st invasion fleet without letting up.

Both invasion fleets were concentrating 100% of their shots and ordinance they could get off, into the two seven-mile decoys, all shields and otherwise not much of anything. The three Monarch military space stations were hives of swarming small craft, further out from Pez Fleet in closer orbit of Monarch. The Monarch moon bases were also throwing up small craft in cascades and the planetary defense ships were on the move, closing. Swenah had gotten every drop out of surprise, taking full advantage, and the second invasion fleet was still playing catch up. Large imperial ships had to allow four minutes to get everyone to battle stations and this was now hardly more than three minutes into battle. The only sections of the imperial invasion ships fully staffed were cargo handlers, loaders, and supply personnel. At least a third of every crew was on leave planet-side. The imperial second string was on the field. All of this was working to Swenah's advantage.

Cleo made another drone-jump landing within the distance of a square mile inside the shields and interior of a class one, which turned into a blue ray of light puncturing from port through starboard into a second class one, folding it into the streak. Two ultra-super class ships pooled their fire on a class one, still slowing as they closed, and 7.1 seconds later their prey popped, blowing into a cloud. These same two ships had worked together to kill a class one of the first invasion fleet they'd passed. Two more class one's had been blown out of existence by the eight giant Ahumdulilah ships.

Swenah was closing now on a class one and *Reciprocity* was unleashing everything it had. An 18,600 foot Ahumdulilah super-cruiser with 58 reactors was striking the same ship. *Hades*, an Om super battleship with 30 reactors, was pounding it too. Shudiy sped things up considerably with two big torpedoes into a soft spot only she could see in the shields, opening the hull and collapsing the shields. Swenah saw space through the hole her beam drilled through the class one once its shields went down, from one side and out the other, just before it disappeared in an expanding gas cloud. Micro-suns were erupting over the ships of the second invasion fleet. Then *Reciprocity* was passed, swooping at the oncoming planetary defense ships and ten more class ones. The eight auxiliaries with class nine beam weapons bringing up the rear, with the help of a 3-mile Kluzyst ship, together destroyed another class one in the first invasion fleet.

It hadn't been quite four minutes since they'd jumped in and they were still on their first pass yet a distance from the middle-orbit space stations. They were throwing dumb munitions of adamantine and composite ceramic heat shield armor the sailors called "rocks", at immoveable targets and putting pretty much every offensive weapon system into play at once on all the ships. At least a third of the ships in the two invasion fleets were not even yet under way, so they hit some of those with rocks too. Slowed now to .23 light they had brilliant targeting acquisition. Stuff on the moon—expensive stuff—was reorganizing into mushroom clouds, making spectacular visuals. Nearly all their small craft were off and away causing all kinds of trouble for the imperials. Their de-cloaking systems kept all enemy ships clearly in view. On *Reciprocity* Mel was locking onto targets faster than weapons operators could direct thought impulses at icons, so Mel started firing too.

A Rally cruiser 690 ft. long with two and a half reactors-equivilent got caught in a class 9 beam weapon and blew in just a few seconds. That had been their first loss up till now, apart for some small craft, with almost all fire directed at their decoys. One decoy finally blew, and packed with some nukes it looked really convincing that a real manned ship had just exploded. With everything now aimed at it, the second decoy would not last long, especially since it was racing as the spear point of fluid formation at the planetary defense force heading for them. Swenah picked out a class one and went to work.

Admiral Swenah announced to all ships of Pez Fleet, "The planetary defense fleet is fully prepared and formed-up. We need to remain 100% alert and in top form if we are to defeat them."

Admiral Canon pointed out, "We destroyed eighteen ships of the first fleet we hit and seriously damaged a dozen others, then twelve ships of the second fleet we just passed while damaging many more."

"We caught those snoozing with surprise. The rest of this battle won't be so easy."

"My crew is focused one-pointed on eradicating imperial ships and as ready as they could possibly be."

Sqenah mentioned, "Thousands of combat small-craft are approaching from lunar spaceports and thousands more from both space stations and imperial ship hangers. Another wave of them is lifting off from Monaech's surface."

Canon assured her, "We are tracking their progress and ready for them."

Admiral Omniomi weighed in, "More thn 90% of *Justice Maker's* combat small-craft are away and engaged."

Swenah stated with utter determination, "Let's go lay waste to some of those planetary defense ships!"

Imperial small craft were getting thick. Each class one carried 800 of them making a total of 32,000 before they'd killed some class ones with all small craft on board. Between the lunar combat-craft ports, the space stations and the planet, the imperials had at least another 106,000 small combat-craft. You could shoot almost any-where in any direction and hit one. *Reciprocity* was now coordinating with an Ahumdulilah super battleship, a 24,000 foot long stretched triangle with 150 reactors, and together they turned the lead ship they were hitting into sparks and vapors. A class two imperial with 78 reactors was dead ahead so it became their next target. That one went quick allowing them to target and damage another ship before they went by and through that battle group. Now only space stations, space-weapons platforms and surface to space weapons remained in front of them, along with the mist-like density of imperial small craft. Konax had squished some of them, frying them on *Reciprocity's* shields, unavoidably plowing into them. A pair or imperial fighters collided almost right in front of them and a piece of their debris sparked off *Reciprocity's* shields just skimming them, to blow up an imperial fighter-bomber paralleling her.

The micro-suns Shudiy sprouted all over the defensive imperial force they'd just gone by had miraculously preserved their second decoy, still flying with the lead ships, and scorched in a dozen places. A super-duper ground to space beam finally finished it, then an avalanche of dumb munitions left a crater where the super-duper weapon had been, fired from *Reciprocity*. Swenah was intent on destroying a space station she was headed more or less for, and would have little time to accomplish this before speeding by it. An assist from Shudiy with torpedoes passing right through the station's shields without a hitch took those shields down entirely, allowing Swenah the satisfaction of blowing it the hell up instead of having to pass it by.

As they rushed around the planet using its vortex, or gravity well, they riddled the surface of it with colossal explosions, some of them making mushroom clouds. All allied small craft were launched and the fifth minute of battle was ticking down while quad-gunner scoreboards were changing so fast you couldn't read the numbers. The auxiliaries with beam weapons had retired to outside the battle perimeter to provide reloading, repairs, and change out of fuel cells and one-time boosters. On the small craft which had them, they even washed the windshield-canopies.

Mel informed Swenah, "The Emperor has just recalled all warships and small combat craft immediately from Afrigastan, abandoning their ground forces there and ending further flow of supplies leaving them stranded. Those ships will reach jump speed in fourteen minutes and who knows how close they'll jump in."

"This is not good news," Swenah replied. "We got 25% of their class one's on our first pass, but only 7% of their ships, and I've never seen so many small craft."

"Check the friendly beacons, dear," Mel told her, while military bases on the surface of Monarch blew with such explosions that shrapnel went over 40,000 feet through the atmosphere, some of it downing imperial aircraft.

Sure enough, two class two's had turned them on and were in the throes of killing a class one together which they'd taken by surprise. A few other imperial ships turned on friendly beacons, right after unloading missiles, torpedoes, beams and blasters into the imperial ship in front of them. The tail of Pez Fleet's 'fluid formation' was still passing through the planetary defense ships when Swenah was more than half-way around the planet in her whip-turn. They left no space weapons platforms or space stations in their path, and nothing remotely military recognizable on the surface as they came around. A few class ten ships were about and they didn't stand a chance; snuffed in seconds. Small craft buzzed them like a cloud of gnats.

Starting her swing around the planet Swenah had been skimming Monarchs atmosphere, though by the time she'd come around to head almost the way she'd come in, she was in middle orbit headed for the biggest space station she'd ever seen. It was packed with weapons systems and those weapons were firing at the head of the fluid formation, some of them hitting her shields. The station was shaped kind of like a wheel, with a tubular rim and tube spokes running to a sphere in the center. Docking berths for enormous ships were protruding from the outer rim one after another, all the way around; 180 of them in all according to sensor analysis. Only seven ships were actually docked there, likely in need of repairs.

A three mile Kluzyst ship bringing up the rear was destroyed by a class one ship and a class three. At least a dozen allied ships with less than one highest magnitude reactor had succumbed to the hordes of small craft attacking them. The allied 28,000 plus small craft were outnumbered five to one here at least. A 12,200 ft. Ahumdulilah ship with 36 reactors got pulverized charging ahead of Reciprocity. The imperial planetary defense fleet was headed in on their left flank as they ran for the big space station that was shooting at them.

Mel told Swenah, "Imperial coms just ordered their war ships in 52 planetary systems to depart immediately for Monarch, and they will be underway in twenty-six minutes."

"How many ships?" Swenah inquired.

"One hundred and seventy-one, but only eight of those are class ones."

A large beam from the space station locked onto *Reciprocity* and Swenah told Konax, "Full evasive maneuvers."

Konax turned as radically as the ship could do it while firing an entire booster stage, self-ejecting when spent, meant for lift off from a planet. In space it transformed *Reciprocity* into a rocket taking them in eight seconds beyond targeting resolution speed and putting them face to face with the oncoming ships. The bows of the lead ships sprouted little blinding suns and between that and their speed, *Reciprocity* was not taking any fire, yet. Ahumdulilah Admiral Canon, who was at the head of the fluid formation with Swenah until Reciprocity angled to port, was bearing down with all his ship's weapons on the giant space station and taking the majority of its fire. He was supported by a 28-reactor Trident super-battleship carrier and Captain Elmo's *Heracles*, an Om 30-reactor super battleship. Canon's shields were dropping but so were the shields on the space station. An Ahumdulilah super-carrier and *Apollo* added their firepower to concentrate on the space station and pairs of their class 9 beam weapons finally punched a hole through shields and skin penetrating the station to blow a section of it up, taking a big bite out of the wheel.

Then a docked class three imperial ship on the edge of the cleft they'd just made in the station, blew into a fire ball taking another section of the rim and a spoke out of existence. The stations shields were at 21% and falling. A barrage of torpedoes and big missiles poked through those shields and set off a chain of explosions culminating in one enormous one ending the material reality of what had been the biggest space station any of them had ever seen or heard about.

Admiral Omniomi in *Justice-Maker*, an ultra-super class ship like Swenah's, had followed *Reciprocity* into the fray with the planetary defense ships. Cleo did her thing and a class one battering *Reciprocity* in league with several slightly smaller giants, blue-streaked through Monarch's atmosphere coming 34,000 feet from the planet surface, and took the upper 200 feet off a mountain top leaving a trail headed out past the planet, and singeing the air to one side of the planet. It was one hell of a sight and the streak faded to nothing at all. Now that the space station was gone the entire fluid formation was turning into the oncoming planetary defense force. Invasion Fleet One, as they were calling it, since it was the first they'd encountered, had finally organized itself into formation and was moving toward the shoulder of the allied fleet, not yet in range. They had not been in the Monarch System for quite six minutes yet.

Rear Admiral Firestone, in ultra-super *Fury*, had not gone around behind Monarch with the rest of Pez Fleet, instead cutting in front of it to harass the rear of the planetary defense force. About ten allied ships followed him including a 149 reactor Ahumdulilah super battleship-spacecraft carrier, and Captain Granger on *Zeus*, an Om 28 reactor super-battleship carrier. The two class two imperial ships with friendly beacons were also with this group.

Reciprocity was now unintentionally filling the role their decoys had played by receiving nearly all the fire from the oncoming ships. Shudiy slipped some torpedoes into a soft spot on a class three's shields and its 52 reactors blew making a fantastic visual display while reducing the number of weapons boring into their shields. Cleo jumped a drone inside the shields of a class four, transforming it into a line of light exiting the battle zone and bringing more relief to *Reciprocity's* shields, down by fourteen percent at that moment. Swenah finally drilled through the shields of a class two with *Reciprocity's* class nine beam and blaster weapons vaporizing it. Suns kept erupting over the bows of the oncoming imperial ships.

Shields were down to 73% and with *Reciprocity* firing off every weapon in the ship, it looked to be on fire. Two class ones got their beams on Swenah's ship further reducing her shields, and probably about seven seconds from bringing them down completely, when one streaked blue scorching the side of Firestone's *Fury*, passing only a hundred meters along its flank. Omniomi was catching up and providing fire support with her 244-reactor ship. Together they took down the class one pounding *Reciprocity* and her shields were back on the rise slowly. Firestone's group did in another class one. A nine reactor Rally super-battleship blew into dust. They also lost a Kluzyst class 8 to small craft, and a trident super-battleship with 28 reactors to the imperial defense ships.

Headed in nearly opposite directions, Swenah's and Firestone's groups were both engaging the imperial defense ships from different ends. Each started turning out away from Monarch, Swenah to her right and Firestone to his left, and their arcs aligned on the same trajectory, now headed for the center of invasion fleet one. The snaking body of fluid formation behind Swenah kept up the assault on the planetary defense fleet as the lead ships passed it. Admiral Swenah ordered, "All ships of Pez Fleet tighten formation. Accelerate to form up on *Reciprocity* and *Justice Maker* now, into pyramid formation."

Firestone's group had removed the last Monarch space station from the game and every space weapon platform orbiting in the swath of space he traveled. His group had also peppered the surface government and military structures they overflew with heavy ordinance and wiped out a whole neighborhood of ruling family mansions with a surgical missile strike. The mushroom cloud rising over that neighborhood was orange and purple with green highlights.

The Royal Monarch holocom holovision intergalactic network was now being controlled from Rocky, still in allied hands, and was covering the attack on Monarch live using images from the allied ship sensors and giving blow by blow commentary, like sports events commentators. That orange and violet mushroom cloud had brought on cheering in tens of billions of bomb shelters across three galaxies.

The Mother System space battle had also been transmitted live and a Motherling giving an update on events on Mother let the larger world know, "Fourteen percent of the imperials on Mother choked to death on poisoned food at their dinner tables the night before the revolution started. A full 22% had their throats cut in their beds as they slept. Six percent bled out their every orifice at the breakfast table from poison, three percent were snipered on their way to work, and 18% were demolitioned when they got to work. The rest are being reduced quickly in battle."

Mother was the first planetary system in the empire to liberate with only imperial ground troops left to kill, and they were mowing them down like grass. The entire Devil Dog Corps had jumped into the capital of Condral reducing its government and military buildings there to rubble with their missile launches from the upper reaches of the atmosphere, then clearing all the rooftops of imperials and many on the ground too as they came down. With local paramilitary forces and militias of revolutionary citizens, they seized the capital and ended the lives of every imperial within it.

There was also bad news. On New Providence the imperial troops began to massacre the citizens, and on Bal the Secret Police went into schools murdering the children in what the empire was calling an anti-terrorist campaign which included thermal bombing of hospital maternity wards and preschools. Support from space for imperials on the ground was proving to be something of a stumbling block for the revolution. Then holonews on Rocky picked up the scent of some task forces of imperial ships with allied-friendly beacons beating the imperials out of space around a number of systems, liberating them. It was also noted by the only show currently available on imperial holovision, that the imperial ships were withdrawing entirely from 52 systems, abandoning imperials on those planets including the ruling families on them.

Rocky news had cleverly taken hundreds of images of multitudes of people laughing their heads off and used those for background and cut-aways as they pranced a hideous and pathetic cartoon emperor across the holo, describing him in terms all antonyms to typical imperial presentations of the man. They also showed another cartoon close-up of his disgusting cartoon penis and scenes of horrified screaming women, absolutely freaking out, taken from scary horror holomovies were displayed as background and in cut-aways for this.

Suns kept popping out on imperial bows as they flashed through invasion fleet one and torpedoes found another soft spot in a class one's shields. With her sister ships assisting her *Reciprocity* put another class one out of commission. Cleo streaked a class three. Some big Ahumdulilah's got a class two, and their two friendly class two's blew up another class one. The lead ships of pyramid formation emerged out the back of invasion fleet one, already nearly in range of oncoming invasion fleet two.

Shudiy told Swenah, "Pez just arrived."

A moment later two star-cruisers appeared on Swenah's holo rushing at invasion fleet one where pyramid formation's tail was still passing through engaging it. The power of Pez's ship with four reactors was truly insignificant to this battle yet the presence of Pez irrationally inspired hope in Swenah anyway.

Pez told Swenah over coms, "I'm in the Monarch System in *Thunderbolt* and *Pheonix* is with me. Schwin will be here shortly once her group reloads in the Mother System. Mother is liberated."

"Great work SCG. The emperpor has recalled the invasion fleet that was bogged down in Afrigastan to return to Monarch to defend it, and he's recalled all ships from 52 enslaved planets here. We are about to be seriously outnumbered."

"I've got Ahhu on my bridge and we mean to eliminate some big Monarch ships quick."

"Well try to reduce their small-craft numbers because those are killing our smallest ships."

"My quad blaster gunners are blowing those up all around our hull."

"I see that *Pheonix* lost her shields for a moment and got her hull scortched black on her forward port flank."

"Her hull is not breeched and all her weapons systems are functioning."

"Captain Quicksilver is a brave man to follow you in battle."

"He's fighting his ship well and he's a good man."

"Once Schwin joins you you'll be a formidable force indeed."

"I've got to sign-off."

"Keep safe dear SCG."

Some class 9 beams were working over *Fury* to further drop its damaged shields. Swenah got her beam on one of the ships hitting *Fury* while she had Konax accelerate in front taking those beams onto *Reciprocity* instead. Shudiy was planting suns on the ships firing those beams and both Swenah and Firestone coordinated a quick turn and dive to get Swenah clear of them. Firestone's shields were now in worse shape and he would have to get *Fury* to one of the big auxiliaries outside the battle zone for repairs. Omniomi and an Ahumdulilah super battleship killed a class one, Cleo streaked a class two, and several other imperial ships were destroyed as the head of pyramid formation passed out through the tale of invasion fleet two. They lost a 2-mile Kluzyst ship up here at the head and some one-rector ships. Swenah was arcing them back around in an elliptical circle to re-engage the imperials.

The invasion fleet out of Afrigastan had received no medical devices and was led by the Emperor's son, Prince Malignant. He was a known psychopath and was prone to delusions of grandeur. Like father like son, but perhaps more acute in the son, as if this disease progressed through generations becoming more insidious and destructive as it went along. This was no mere syndrome or culturally biased condemnation. The boy had truly lost all semblance of his humanity and was spiritually diseased-ridden and fucked. He was healthy as an ox physically though, and itching for a fight.

Pez charged the flank of invasion fleet one and was hardly noticed for the size of her ship. She chewed up imperial small craft as she went, blowing them away with her class eight twin blasters, and lobbing the occasional canister missile into one. Once in range, Pez got both her class nine beam and her big nose blasters onto a class four while Flint and Ming slammed it with torpedoes and missiles. Pez spread suns over it from bow to stern, and some on the port sides of ships targeting them, as they attacked on the fleet's port flank. Ahhu landed a drone inside a class three turning it into a line of light.

Phoenix was pouring her fire into the class four Pez was shooting and some allied small craft were hitting it too. Shooting from the class four had seriously dwindled since it couldn't see a thing for the glaring micro-suns clinging to its hull. Pez's group finally got the class four's shields stirred up enough to reveal a thin film in them at one small place too weak to stop anything. Pez started a small stream of big torpedoes through the opening and the second one, for sure, opened a hole in the hull for the third and forth to enter. They'd all been mega thermo-nuclear hull-piercer torpedoes. The class four shook and vibrated, then stuff from inside shot thousands of miles into space at incredible speed through the breech, culminating in a long tongue of pure fire burning off all the ship's oxygen, to then blow to atoms with very little light or color, in a sort of an anticlimax.

Ahhu streaked a class two, and it took the bow off a class five completely as it blue-lined headed out of the battle zone. The rest of the class five was sent puking its guts into space, to smash into a class seven, joining them together into one inseparable expanding gas cloud. Smoke in the void. Pez was pounding a one-reactor class ten to pulp with her nose blasters while puncturing a class nine imperial ship with her beam. Flint hit the class nine with fin blasters and Ming fired camister missiles into both. As the class ten exploded in living color Pez snuck some canister missiles into a soft spot on the class nine's shields to end its story. A zippy little imperial fighter crossing her bow got toasted crispy by her class eight twin blasters. *Thunderbolt's* twelve turrets of quad blasters had not paused since they'd slowed to targeting speed from jumping into the Monarch system. Vapor clouds were appearing all around the ship as small craft blew into molten particles. A space drive from an exploding bomber hulled a class ten, shot by Woahha, alias cousin Winnie, with her quad blaster.

Just after the force out of Afrigastan jumped into the Monarch system, the empire regained control of its coms-holovision network, assuring the people of the empire that everything was well in hand, that the emperor's penis is quite large and handsome—this last bit at his instance—and that all would be returned to normal shortly. Then the whole network went down and the Monarch central computer system crashed leaving only the pink holo of death. When the holovision network rebooted and came back on it was controlled from Rocky, and the imperial computer system couldn't reboot because all of its programming had been deleted into the void, and deletion was its only function. New programming into the system was not only deleted as fast as it was uploaded, but a backfire effect erased the data bead or other computer system uploading the programs. It was a lost cause and this condition had been conceived of and achieved by Trix's Key to Everything. Jard wanted it bad.

Swenah veered toward the newly arrived invasion fleet three, as they were calling the fleet from Afrigastan, leading pyramid formation into the heart of it. Suns blossomed radiantly on the bows of the oncoming ships just as they were coming into range, and

Cleo blue-streaked the class one leading the pack. That one did not have Prince Malignant aboard. He was in a class one at the rear. Omniomi, Swenah and Canon, who was in an Ahumdulilah super battleship containing 150 reactors, worked together blowing imperial ships open, and Nestle's *Liberator,* also an ultra-super class ship, was not far behind. Hasbro's *Redeemer* brought up the rear of Pez Fleet, and Firestone had *Fury* docked to a giant auxiliary out of the game for the moment.

A class two imperial didn't last long under the weapons of Swenah, Omniomi and Canon. The ships of the allies and imperials began passing each other at a combined speed of 2.4 light. This was the outer edge of targeting, except for piloting missiles and torpedoes. They all got in what last licks they could in passing, and then they were passed. With so many sensors blinded, and some fried, the imperial ordnance and blaster fire was fairly equally distributed between the allies and their own ships, so one class nine imperial ship casualty could not be claimed by Pez Fleet. Swenah was taking them in a curve to strike the flank of invasion fleet one, which was composed of two combined imperial invasion fleets, or 312 ships before Pez Fleet arrived. Invasion Fleets two and three, as the allies called them, had each started this battle with 156 ships. The Planetary Defense Fleet had had 100 ships just over a quarter of an hour ago.

Swenah was approaching firing range on fleet one's flank and watched as Pez encouraged the big ships to fire at her, only to prance away at the last moment causing them to hit their own ships as she bobbed and wove among them. Ahhu blue-streaked a class one in that group and Pez was calling for drones to feed to Ahhu from the Astro-Phantoms in her vicinity.

Reciprocity opened up with *Justice Maker* and Canon's ship on the class one nearest them. Suns were popping up on imperial ships so fast that Swenah knew Pez and Shudiy must both be at it at the same time. Imperial fire became wild but didn't slow, and hit almost as many of their own ships as they did revolutionaries. Torpedoes found their way through the shields to punch through the hull of a class one, and a moment later its shields went down allowing everything hitting it to rip into its hull; and a moment after that it went boom.

Entering and mixing with fleet one the allies pyramid formation became more fluid than it did formation. With the planetary defense fleet flying into the miscellany of Pez Fleet and Invasion fleet one, it became a confused melee with ships swerving in all directions. A great number of imperial ships wore blinding suns and didn't really know where they were going. This was amply demonstrated when a class three plowed into to midsection of a class four, breaking it into two unequal sections and only one of those blew up, while the other spilled personnel, equipment and office furniture out into space from its broken open end. Pez and Shudiy kept the suns sprouting and lobbed torpedoes into shield soft spots wherever they noticed them. Once invasion fleet three joined the mix to stay the fighting became continuously all-out.

A 25,000 ft. Ahumdulilah battleship-carrier was blown to bits by a triad of class ones working together. The Om super battleship-carrier *Poseidon* went down with all hands, including Captain Schwab. Captain Fudd, and *Hermes*, an Om super-battleship with 30 reactors, was blown into a gas cloud. Two Rally 9-reactor super-battleships got destroyed, and a two-mile Kluzyst ship disintegrated in a big bang. The fighting was desperate. One of the 10,080 ft. Trident super-battleship carriers was blown to smithereens or smaller.

Swenah's triad engaged the three class ones that were coordinating their fire, and those three ships all but disappeared in the numerous micro-suns they became clothed in. Three T-9 super-cruisers, *Isis, Neith* and *Ani,* lent support to Swenah's triad, and so did *Apollo* and a 3-mile Kluzyst ship. Little *Phoenix* and *Thunderbolt* were pecking at the three class one's as well, and buzzing all about them. The combined power of the three class one's was 444 reactors while that of the ships assaulting them at the moment was 740. Worse still, one of them streaked clean out of existence and another somehow got a hull breach with its shields up and at 68%, then blew apart from internal explosions when the torpedoes kept shooting inside it. *Reciprocity* and *Justice Maker* finished the third one off. Ahhu jumped a drone inside another class one, which went right through a class two, incorporating it, and that streak was really bright. They had now destroyed twenty-five class one imperial ships, and had twenty-five more to deal with.

Ships recalled from 52 star systems were now jumping into Monarch system from all sides. A few had friendly beacons though most didn't. Mel informed Swenah, "The emperor has just called for the ships from 208 planets to abandon imperials on the ground and rush to Monarch immediately."

Swenah relayed this to Omniomi and Canon, and Canon told them, "The emperor has already called on the worlds most loyal to him. The next batch will have more friendly beacons and many ships from those 208 planets have already joined one of our nine liberation task forces composed entirely of imperial ships, which are freeing worlds that are doing well in their ground wars. More such task forces are quickly forming."

Swenah told them, "We need to call for all combat small craft in our home worlds that have a quantum drive to come and support us in Monarch, and we could use some more small ships as well. We've lost over a hundred of our small ships already."

"I'll put the request in to Ahumdulilah," Canon replied, "You tell the admirals of the Kluzyst, Rally and Trident forces."

"I'm on it," Swenah told him.

Mel informed her, "I've put in your request to Yona, the High Council and Zapa."

A brief conference call between admirals, who requested the specified reinforcements from their governments, resulted in the promise of some 16,000 more small craft, and 89 more ships, mostly less than one highest magnitude reactor. Schwin had arrived with 220 small craft all freshly loaded, and the four wings of Astro Phantoms she led personally were worth far more than a dozen each. Pez's top five of her twelve gunners accounted for 621 small craft killed, and they came quite late to this battle. Cleo blue-streaked another class one, but two more had just jumped into the system, and they weren't wearing friendly beacons.

A group from one of the fifty-two planets told to send their ships to Monarch, consisting of a class three, two class fives, two class eights, a nine, and four tens, was headed directly for Auxiliary reloading and repair station seven. Unfortunately, this was not the one Firestone was at with *Fury*. At station seven there were Captain Spalding of *Auxiliary 2*, a Trident super-auxiliary, half a dozen smaller auxiliaries, and some troop transports with only anti-small craft weapons, which included Captain Swanson with Space Marine *Transport One*. *Auxiliary 2* was one of the eight big auxiliaries fitted with a pair of class nine beam weapons and there was an 8,900 ft. 20-reactor Ahumdulilah frigate reloading there while getting some quick repairs. The rest were one-reactor ships or smaller, getting ordinance and thruster fuel cells so they could get back into the fight.

Captain Swanson called Pez to say, "A combat group is headed our way and we only have a pair of big beam weapons on *Auxiliary 2*, and a damaged combat super-ship for defense."

"You've got 90 Space Marine Combat Shuttles and some great pilots, so get them launched, and I'm on my way to you with a micro-jump as soon as I'm up to speed."

"Aye, aye ma'am."

Pez told Schwin, "Bring everything you can muster to reload station seven ASAP. We've got friends in trouble," as she accelerated out of the melee striving for jump speed, planting suns on her way out.

Captain Quicksilver followed her. She took them to jump speed at maximum acceleration then jumped in with just enough room to slow sufficiently to track targets. There was no margin of error. The ten incoming imperial ships had not micro-jumped and so were yet minutes away. Ahhu kept her drone fighter bomber at jump velocity. Pez got Swanson, Spalding and Captain Ahab of the Ahumdulilah 20-reactor ship on coms and said, "Captain Swanson, please direct your combat shuttles to attack the four class tens. They can kill those with several large undercarriage missiles striking close together about the same moment. Ahhu will take out the class three. Captain Spalding, don't power up your big beams until the fighting starts, then surprise them with those. Captain Ahab, you will need to duke it out with a class five until I can put down the other class five. We will just have to weather the two class eights until we blow up some of the other ones. I've got some great small craft on the way to deal with whatever they launch from their bays."

Captain Ahab commented, "It sounds like you've brought a knife to a blaster fight."

"We can do this," Pez assured him, "and we need to get it done fast so I can get Ahhu back into the fray."

"Who do you want me to light up once my beams are powered up?" Spalding inquired.

"Hit the class five Captain Ahab takes on, and see if you can get one of those class eights," Pez replied.

"Aye, aye ma'am."

Ahab got his ship detached from the auxiliary and took up position. This group attacking them was so much more powerful that they shouldn't stand a chance, but then, they had the Rajaha here, and if that class three could be dispatched then they would have a slim fighting chance; but how she expected to take down a 22-reactor class five with her little 4-reactor star cruiser and the 3-reactor one with her, was just beyond him. Pez looped around with *Phoenix* beside her, timing her charge to meet those ships at the edge of their being in range of the auxiliaries. The imperials were slowing way down and launching their small craft.

Schwin's voice exclaimed in Pez's ear, "I rounded up eight wings of Astro Phantoms, nine wings of Hunter-Terminators, and seven wings of Corvette Thunders."

"Go get those small craft being launched and put their lights out," Pez directed.

"We're going to reduce them to quarks and ether, SCG, don't you worry," Schwin told her confidently.

"Molten molecules should do just fine," Pez told her.

Cotex mentioned to Pez, "There are more than 200 ships responding to the call put out to those 52 planets, not 179."

"I know," Pez replied, "and I want to get back to the main fight right behind them."

Rubix mentioned, "There are no imperial small craft around to shoot.

"Not yet, sweetheart," Pez explained, "but they're coming."

The class three launched 200 small craft, the two class fives put up 80 each, the class eights 12 each, and the class nine 6 small craft, totaling 390. Schwin had 142 small combat craft with her. Pez knew Schwin would wipe them out. The Astro-Phantom was significantly more powerful than the biggest imperial bomber, and Schwin had the very best pilots of Star Fleet under her command, most just out of advanced phantom-raider training; several intensive months of it. Schwin led all the wings in. Each wing would function independently of the others, but fight as a single integral unit, and those units would support each other. They knew precisely what they were doing.

Cotex announced to the bridge officers, "We have 390 incoming small craft, steady at 2.2 light, and ten ships at 1.1 light."

Schwin's wings had made an arc while the small craft launched from the big ships, ending in the same trajectory as theirs and right behind them, slowing to 2.2 light to match them. With the same enthusiastic emphasis Pez always used, Schwin shouted to her people, "FIRE!!!"

The corvette thunder fighter had a twin nose blaster and two large missiles attached to the undercarriage. The NBC Hunter Terminator fighter-bomber had twin heavy blasters in the nose, two quad blaster turrets, two missile batteries of 16 canister missiles each, and carried eight large undercarriage missiles. The XPS Astro-Phantom bomber carried four large ship-killer torpedoes in internal tubes, eight large undercarriage missiles, 96 canister missiles in six batteries, and had big twin nose blasters, heavy fin blasters and two quad-blaster turrets. The Astro-Phantoms saved their torpedoes to use on ships, but fired everything else they had at the imperial combat craft in front of them as they slowed and closed.

Schwin shot an undercarriage missile into a big imperial bomber while wrecking a speeding fighter with her nose-blasters. She got another big missile off into another big bomber, turning it into illumination and particles, now tearing apart a fighter-bomber with her nose blasters. Her copilot, Natasha, who had been Pez's copilot for a while, was spitting canister missiles into fighters and pairs of them into fighter-bombers as fast as it could be done. Her drone pilot was ripping into a fighter-bomber with her drone-fighter bomber's nose blasters, and lobbed a pair of its canister missiles into the thing, spreading it out across space in a flare. Her weapons operator fired canister missiles and fin blasters accurately making them count, and her quad-gunner's scoreboards were constantly changing. With her elite crew and the best bomber in the fight, Schwin's Astro-Phantom was a pure death machine.

The imperial small craft began turning off in every possible direction, fleeing for their lives. Wings of Schwin's force followed all the bigger groups. They'd smeared 123 across space already, and were chasing down the majority of the remainder. The ones they weren't chasing were scattering in the six directions individually or in pairs, and constituted no threat. The ten imperial ships were in range of *Thunderbolt* and *Phoenix*, firing at them inaccurately due to sensor whiteout, and were just on the cusp of being in range of Ahab and of the auxiliaries and troop transports. That was when Ahhu's drone fighter-bomber emerged from its quantum jump inside the class three's hull going .7 light speed. The class three streaked headed out of the battle zone in a blue line.

Thunderbolt and *Phoenix* cut a class five from the herd, which was happy to oblige them, while the other eight ships closed on Ahab and on the auxiliaries and troop transports right behind him. The moment Ahab engaged the other class five, which only had two reactors on him—though Ahab's repairs were not completed, Spalding powered up the two class 9 beam weapons. A few seconds elapsed before they were ready to fire, then both bore down on a class eight while anti-small craft blasters on Swanson's troop transport bore into the same ship. Another troop transport got its class three and four blasters punching the class eight's shields as well. After 4 seconds under the two beams the class eight disappeared into an expanding sphere of light and gas. The two class 9 beams moved onto the class five Ahab was battling.

Swanson's 90 combat shuttles tore into the four class tens, at least 22 shuttles on each one, battering them with undercarriage and canister missiles while bearing down with nose and quad blasters. One ship was hit with three big missiles almost at the same time, taking down its shields and scorching its hull, so that the next big missile to hit it did it in. The class nine and class eight that were left, were hitting the shields of the transports and auxiliaries.

Thunderbolt's class nine beam weapon turned out to be a shock for the class five imperial ship. With class eight nose blasters and class five fin blasters on full automatic fire locked onto target, and at least five of her 12 quad-blasters nailing it, a soft spot showed itself to Pez in the shields of the big ship, and she pumped a line of ship killer torpedoes through the opening, punching through the hull by the second one, if not the first, and so allowing at least three more through unscathed to tear into the interior of the ship, if not four; she just couldn't say for sure. Though the class five blew apart either way. She had no time to ponder it since she was rushing back to kill the other imperial ships.

Coming in she watched the class five squirm out from under Spalding's two beam weapons by getting behind a troop transport. Pez sent two undercarriage missiles at the class nine and opened her beam and nose blasters on the class five. In avoiding her beam, the class five walked right back under Spalding's two, and when Pez got hers back on it, the class five burst into atoms. The two missiles had cremated the class nine. The class eight bugged out running for its life. Pez's and Spalding's beams lit its tail as it fled until it blew. The combat shuttles had the four class tens completely recycled into particles. Schwin was back and only a very few of those 390 small craft had escaped her wrath. She'd lost seven corvettes, three hunter-terminators and one Astro Phantom in the process.

Pez told Schwin, "That was some pretty fancy small-craft combat you just pulled off."

"Thanks SCG. I see you took good care of those ships you were battling."

"Go get rearmed and refueled Lt. Commander. I need your force back in the fight."

"We're headed to *Auxillary Two* now and we'll find you once we're loaded."

"I'm going to reload then headed to Prince Malignant's Afrigastan invasion fleet. That force and the planetary defense fleet are Monarch's most effective battle groups. I don't think the two invasion fleets that were preparing to embark on missions from here are fully crewed. Those two fleets are showing poorly."

"We'll join you. Blowing stuff up is fun, but wasting Monarch's most deadly ships brings far more satisfaction. Save us some."

"There's more than enough to go around. Enemy ships are arriving much faster than we can destroy them."

"We'll help you change that dynamic as soon as we're armed."

The imperials had begun this battle with more than 138,000 combat small craft and many more had come with the fleet from Afrigastan, and from the ships arriving from 52 worlds. Prince Malignant, determined to preserve his own hide and wanting very badly to kill some revolutionaries, was organizing the twenty-five class ones left in the system into one tight formation with the one he was on at its center, armored and insulated from anything even touching the shields of his ship. Swenah had noticed this and was organizing her own response to it. Pez was on her way along with *Phoenix* and Schwin's small craft force, which had many drone fighter bombers. Pez's docking bay personnel had launched two of the drones from their hanger for Ahhu on their way back to the main battle and she was getting them up to speed.

A 24,000 foot, 150-reactor Ahumdulilah super-battleship had just been lost, along with a Trident 10,080 ft. super-battleship-carrier, another Rally super-battleship-carrier, two Kluzyst one and a quarter mile long ships, and the Om T-9 super-cruiser, *Herukhuti*, just since Pez had left to rescue reloading station seven. Numerous small ships had gone down, and since arriving in this system, the allies had lost nearly 6,000 small craft, though the allied kill-ratio was better than nine to one thanks to aces like Schwin and her pilots. Some of the ships that had jumped in from 52 different planets were joining the battle, and many of the others were about to.

Liberator, the ultra-super class battleship-carrier captained by Nestles, was chasing a class two imperial and came too close to where Malignant was consolidating all his class ones, to suddenly have more than 40 class nine beams on her. These were accompanied by class nine blaster fire and the largest torpedoes, and less than six seconds later the ship blew with all hands aboard.

Pez was weaving her way over, dodging traffic, and saw the whole thing. She'd planted suns but it had been too late. She'd had friends on that ship. Her little 690 ft. diameter stretched nose disc ship was not on the minds of any officers on any one of the 25 bridges of the imperial class ones; five-mile tubes a mile in diameter. She simply did not register as a threat of any kind. Ahhu had her two drones ready. She jumped the first one inside a flanking class one of the formation, sideways, across the diameter of the tube; not lengthwise. It streaked sideways taking down another class one's shields entirely as it passed less than 50 meters from its bottom in a blue-line explosion.

The main space drives and quantum drive had not somehow gone with the streak, though all of the hull had. The drives were naked and suddenly moving at .37 light sideways, not nearly so quick as the streak went. The drives survived the full force of another class one's shields, or at least much of them did, because enough got through to just keep going, drilling through the port side and passing out again to starboard. From where *Thunderbolt* was coming in Ahhu could see right through the ship where the drives had punched through. She was opening her mouth to mention this to the rest of the cockpit, finding it truly awesome, but before she could form words the class one burst into light and molten vapors. What could she say? Only 'wow' came to mind. Then she got busy with her next drone.

No one on a bridge of an imperial class one would have ever believed that a class 9 beam could be packed into a ship so small; and with a class eight twin blaster! Who'd a thunk it? It just didn't seem right; but there it was like a vicious biting little insect. It was not truly lethal, but it was really annoying as only a bug can be. They hadn't a clue where the gargantuan super-duper weapon that hit their sister ship was located, or what it was, or what it was firing.

Ahhu jumped another, port to starboard like the last, having chosen the angle to kill two birds with one drone. It streaked sideways sucking itself wholly into the narrow blue line, drives and all, to pierce the midsection of another class one and took that one with it, all but the four 2,000-foot diameter funnel shaped carbon-plate drive-exhaust nozzles flying alone now in pristine mint condition. These had a velocity of 4.7 light and miraculously missed all the other class ones, but they didn't miss that class three. Clearly they were no longer in mint condition because they could not be located anywhere at this point.

Thunderbolt, Phoenix and Schwin's small craft force converged all of their firepower on the same class one. One hundred ship killer torpedoes form the Astro-Phantoms along with about as many big missiles, and blaster fire from the rest, combined with *Thunderbolt's* class 9 and 8 weapons, and Phoenix's class 8's, were enough to produce a soft spot in the class one's shields from the turbulence. Pez had her own larger ship-killer torpedoes racing for the little distortion of that spot, and they drove into the hull one after another. Pez was almost certain that it was on the forth one that the hull cracked open, but a case could be made for the 3rd or 5th. Several went right in without resistance though, and of this she was entirely sure. So did the eight canister missiles she fired in rapid succession.

The big ship seemed to hop. Smoke and debris poured from the hole in its hull. It held together but went into a slow lazy spin. Obviously it would need to be towed to a repair dock and was not nearly so dangerous in its current condition. If you used magnification you could make out personnel flying out the hole with the debris. Pez needed to rearm her ship and left the rest of Malignant's class one force for Swenah to deal with, though Ahhu streaked one more with a drone she borrowed from one of Schwin's Astro-Phantom drone pilots as they pulled out. There were still over a hundred thousand imperial combat small craft buzzing about all over the place and Rubix's scoreboard had risen over 300. Many of the 16,000 promised additional allied small craft had jumped in, and some were already engaged.

Pez chose reload station seven since she was very impressed with Captain Spalding, and she had to micro-jump to get to any of them, making them all the same distance away really. Schwin was bringing her people in to rearm too. They'd used everything they'd had on that class one. With those two-in-ones Ahhu had scored with her 1st two drones and the last one she'd jumped, she'd killed five of those class one's just now, and a class three with those drive thrust nozzles. Boy were those things big. She'd never really seen one off in space on its own before, nor a bunch of flying drives without a ship, going sideways.

Thunderbolt's rearming became Spalding's number one top priority the moment it was docked to the super auxiliary. The allies needed her and Ahhu back in the fight. Schwin's small craft landed on *Auxiliary 2's* re-loader platforms on her upper external deck, or some down into hangers with bay doors depending upon make and model. Those needing repairs, and there were some of these with her, went into repair bays. The J-6 Corvette Thunders just ejected their undercarriage into *Auxiliary 2's* bin, then landed on a new one adjusting from below to connect, and once locked on, were done. The Hunter-Terminator re-loader took a little longer, but for the undercarriage missiles, the principle was the same as with the corvettes. The Astro-Phantoms were nearly as fast to reload.

Ming told Pez while rising from her copilot seat, "I'll bring you a stim.-brew in steamed half and half sweetheart."

"Thanks my love."

Ahhu mentioned, "The imperials sure have a lot of ships here fighting us in the Monarch System."

Pez replied, "We've received about all the reinforcements Om and our allies can muster, so it will definitely get worse before we can whittle-down their numbers."

"So you think the emporer will recall ships from more planetary systems?"

"He will for sure if we continue with such a high kill-ratio."

"What about all their ships that were supposed to switch sides?"

"They don't appear to be fighting in this system. I sure hope this isn't all that came over to us."

Schwin's voice came over the bridge intercom from her Astro Phantom on Spalding's deck, "That warrior monk from Mother who joined us sure can fly!"

"I've noticed," Pez agreed. "He flies like you do."

"If we live through this I want him in my Phantom Raider close-combat training."

"If we do live, I'm bringing him into my inner circle to direct his spiritual training."

Gretle shared, "I think he's really cute."

Ming arrived with Pez's stim.-brew and handed it to her. From her quad blaster turret Trix told them, "I just researched that pilot on the cyber-interface. His name is Bodhi and he was left at the gate to the Adamantine Will Monastery at six-weeks old. He's 20 now and both a warrior monk and an ordained preist of the order. This is the first time he has ever been outside the monastery."

Pez's ship took much longer. Loading the magazines for her torpedo tubes and large missile launchers had to be done one at a time, though her canister missiles were done with a machine, per battery all at once. She got new anti-missile molten flares and another mobile cloaked smart-mine net. She'd spent every booster on *Thunderbolt* and most of her thruster fuel cells, and these didn't change out so easy as the ones on the small craft. They checked out her reactors, filled her water tank, changed out her oxygen producing bio-trays from *Thunderbolt's* environmental section, and replaced a few damaged or absent sensors on her hull. Coolants were topped off, motion dampeners tightened up a bit, and the drive exhausts were flushed with a friction fluid to clean them out. They did all of this with many teams working together like a racing-hover pit-stop, all in eleven minutes and fifty-seven seconds.

Phoenix had taken just as long, receiving the same priority as Pez, being with her and all. The two star cruisers left together. Captain Quicksilver had not known what he was doing charging 25 ships, each five miles long, with Pez, and ending up in amongst them. He'd been sure that was the end and that they would get squished. To his utter amazement, five had gone down to micro-jumping drones, and they'd actually fought and seriously damaged another to take it out of the fight. True, it had been blind with all those micro-suns enveloping it. Those had even interfered a little with his own ship's sensors and he was nowhere near those suns. He couldn't imagine being inside of them. *White on white.* He'd felt like a child with a toy gun charging a real army. He still couldn't quite believe the outcome.

Bodhi had followed Schwin's group in to land on an interior deck of the auxillary through the ceiling with sliding doors. The mechanics and machinists were able to adapt the undercarriage mounts on his stolen imperial fighter bomber so that it could carry Om's large missiles. They got him reloaded with eight of those, refuled his boosters, and instead of changing out his imperial thruster fuel cells they managed to refill them with thruster fuel. There was nothing they could do to replace his imperial canister missiles—not in the brief duration of a rearming pit stop. He still had thirteen of those left.

The battle around Mother had been intense but *this* was the biggest space battle his mind could conceive of. So far Bodhi had managed to remain in the state of contemplation grounded in the point four finger-widths below his navel, functioning in the flow state. He could feel the Adamantine Will Order and the people of Mother intensely supporting Pez's force through meditation and contemplation. It was like getting his second wind at eaxh moment and it calmed his fears of the overwhelming odds.

His copilot had been killed in the process of hijacking the fighter bomber though he had a gunner in each quad blaster turret. This particular imperial fighter bomber had been suped-up, reinforced, equipted with class six nose blasters and given an additional fusion trickle-charge battery system. Bodhi had received extensive pilot simulator training in preparation for the revolution. This was his first day of flying an actual fighter bomber and he already had 192 small combat craft kills to his credit.

His rearming took far longer than any of Schwin's group other than battle damaged craft which would take longer than he would be here. Pez's star cruiser "bomber" took longer still and Schwin's combat craft had to take turns at the reloading platfoms, so Bodhi was as ready as his fighter bomber could be when they took off to rejoin the battle. His quad blaster turret gunners were both warrior monks and they were skilled with their guns.

Following Pez's little force on their acceleration to make a micro-jump into the fray of battle Bodhi noticed a class seven imperial ship beginning an attack run on a Trident hospital ship. He told Pez over coms, "I'm going after that class seven. It's starting a run on the hospital ship."

"I'll have Schwin disparch some wings of Astro Phantoms to assist you and I'll see if that Ahumdulilah ship docked to *Auxillary 2* can help."

Bodhi was already into a turn that would take him right at the class seven. Perhaps a dozen allied small craft were already buzzing and harassing the imperial ship. While closing on it Bodhi noticed a large squadron of Astro Phantoms and drone fighter bombers right behind him, and saw that the Ahumdulilah ship had detached from the auxillary and was on its way.

The big weapons of the Ahumdulilah ship were already pounding the class seven from long-range when Bodhi drew close enough to open fire. He and his two gunners were firing their blasters into it and so were the Astro Phantoms behind him. Missiles began pelting the shields of the imperial ship and the beam and blaster fire from the Ahumdulilah ship became more devastating as it closed the distance.

Bodhi noticed a small patch of the class seven's turbulent shields with a different glow and felt led to stream all eight of his undercarriage missiles, one after another, into that spot. The hull of the imperial ship breached and the last of the eight missiles were still coming, entering the ship to explode with stuff inside. The whole damned ship blew into a fading cloud of light and vapors.

Pez had seen this in her rearview holo just before entering her micro-jump into battle. Her crew were all realing in shock from the jump experience and Pez was busy braking like a maniac while connecting to Bodhi on her coms. She told him triumphantly, "You found the soft spot in that ship's shields!"

"I noticed a patch with a different glow and felt led to fire all my big missiles into that spot."

"I definitely need you in my inner circle Bodhi! I'll meet you at the Adamantine Will Order monastery if we both live through this. Go rearm and do what you just did again."

Aye aye Vicar General. Thank you."

Swenah had gathered the three operational ultra-super class ships, the six remaining 149-150 reactor Ahumdulilah ships, four of the seven remaining Ahumdulilah super-cruisers with 58-reactors, a Kluzyst 3-mile ship, and two Om super-battleships, the *Apollo* and the *Hades*, into a task force to combat Malignant's nineteen class ones. Shudiy was already illuminating suns over Malignant's ships and Cleo had a drone almost up to speed. As they approached Swenah noticed an entire class three bow drifting about and hollowed out on the inside, since it didn't get to keep the bulkhead when it broke off, and looked like some kind of space-cave drifting out there.

She opened fire when she got into range. Their torpedoes were low so those were all being saved for Shudiy now; Admiral's orders. They were also saving a full magazine of the biggest missiles for her. Large cargo shuttles from the auxiliaries were landing on *Reciprocity's* freight docks constantly with huge skids of canister missiles and those of the next two sizes up. Anything bigger than that required docking and really heavy machinery. Right now her beams and blasters were needed in the fight. With all the torpedoes being Shudiy's, her drone pilots had only drones to fly, but they did not fight theses, instead preserving them and getting them up to .7 light speed to hand off to Cleo.

The allied force closed and the imperial class ones maneuvered to concentrate their fire power, though a little cluster remained around the prince's ship. Cleo jumped her drone, streaking an entire class one, sideways, funneled into a narrow line. The exploded blue line missed the other ships in its group but came so close to one that it took its shields down to zero. Every beam and blaster on *Reciprocity* was grinding into that one's hull. An Ahumdulilah super-cruiser blew up right before the class one Swenah was nailing did. A Kluzyst 3-mile ship expanded into a big cloud, then another Ahumdulilah super-cruiser blew. Swenah and Omniomi were biting into the same class one and Shudiy's torpedoes started passing right through their target's shields as if they weren't there, which they really were not in that one little invisible spot. The hull sprung a hole letting more torpedoes inside the ship and those found explosive things within to blow up with, culminating in a brilliant radiant expanding sphere.

Cleo popped another drone inside a class one sideways and it disappeared sideways in a blue line out of the battle zone. Before leaving the battle zone the streak ran through the last meter of a class four's stern taking off the rear of the ship up to the interior bulkhead, disappearing with the blue line; and leaving the hull intact—thanks to the bulkhead—with no drives to speak of. The heading they were on was now the heading they would forever be on unless some tugs found them. The fact that they had functional weapons would become increasingly irrelevant the further out of the battle zone they went, becoming quickly negligible.

An Ahumdulilah super-battleship got destroyed, then another of their super-cruisers. Other imperial ships, class twos and threes, were adding fire support. Shudiy blinded them with suns, and found a weak spot in the shields of the ship Swenah was shooting at, exploiting it, and it splattered in all directions at once glaringly. *Hades,* along with Captain Sylvester and crew, blew to pieces and Swenah had tears running in two rivers as she drilled another class one with her beam. The two friendly class two's came from behind a class two which was shooting at Swenah's group and unleashed everything on it. It lasted 8.4 seconds.

Hasbro and two Ahumdulilah super-battleships killed another class one. Mel informed Swenah, "The emperor has recalled every ship from every system."

"That's victory for the enslaved planets but bad news for us; and could result in re-enslavement for the rest if we lose here today."

"Who said anything about losing?" Pez complained, roaring in from reloading. "Ahhu killed five of them in less than two minutes, and Captain Quicksilver and I crippled one with assistance from small craft!"

Ahhu dropped a drone out of jump into the width of a class one just then, streaking it to starboard, funneled and crammed into a blue line and only a lonely sensor array remained, now dead, and floating over the beginning of the fading blue line. Pez was thinking that if you plugged it into a power source it would probably still work. Pez found a distortion on the shields of a class one that some Ahumdulilah ships were trashing and sent a closely spaced stream of torpedoes through it, still trying to determine exactly how many it took to crack a class one hull. She broke it open without quite clearing that up, and sent enough in this time to truly finish it in a spectacular light show.

Schwin was harassing class ones as well and really pissing them off. The Prince's shields were showing now with only ten class one's left, and he was screaming for all class two's to converge on him. Well, he was only taking after his father who had recently recalled all ships from everywhere to come protect his behind. Monarch was certainly the place to be right now if you wanted to be in a space battle, possibly out of all the universe, though no one could really know that. Cleo streaked a class one sideways into a class three that had been providing fire support and both went together in a really bright one, taking out a wing of imperial fighters as it went. It was almost hard not to hit one of those on the way out since they were so dense. It would almost be like running through the rain without getting wet, or so it seemed to Cleo.

A friendly class two was blown apart just as Ahhu streaked a class one sideways into the bow of an unfriendly class two that was responding to Malignant's tantrum, and taking it along for the ride. A Kluzyst 1 ¼ mile ship coming to help was vaporized by Malignant's force, and another Rally super-battleship was blown up. The two hundred and some ships from the fifty-two worlds were all now engaged in the fight. The allies 89 small ships had arrived in groups, now all engaged in battle, and a few of those groups had already been terminated. *Apollo* took a bad hit springing an air leak in one section, and had already depleted most of its ordinance, so Captain Ohinya was taking it out to station four where major repairs were being handled.

A few ships had jumped into the Monarch system from the call for 208 planets to send their ships, and so far, none were friendly. Armored shielded yachts and small craft with weapons systems, some integrated and some just home-job mounts, were pouring off Monarch to defend it, piloted by fanatical rich imperials who were mostly ruling family members or second cousins. The emperor was desperately trying to pull together anything he could in his defense and had even tried to hire mercenaries from the one people the empire had not been able to conquer, the warriors of Zandarhar. He had offered them mercurium mines and trillions of dags, even planets he likely no longer controlled, but they had laughed in his face, or at least their holos had.

Swenah was sweating it. She was trying to reach Canon then realized he had seconds before been removed from the board, along with his 24,000-foot super-battleship. He had told her the call put out for the 208 systems would receive poor response, and more would be friendly, but many were jumping in and none of them sending friendly beacon vibes. Captain Ahab having finally gotten his repairs completed, joined Swenah's little group and killed an imperial class six as he arrived. Ahhu jumped a class one sideways into a class two newly arrived to support Malignant, and both blue-lined into the lunar surface leaving an enormous crater on Monarch's moon. Shudiy got some torpedoes through the shields of a class one which Swenah and Omniomi were raining hell on, and it blew away a class ten when it exploded.

Shudiy and Pez must have been working together, Swenah thought, because the seven remaining class one's and the half dozen class twos that had come to support them were all clothed in blinding suns and shooting wildly. Hasbro's *Redeemer* and an Ahumdulilah super-battleship punched out the shields on a class one and moments later shattered the hull decomposing it. Two Trident 28-reactor super-battleships merged with Swenah's group to lend their fire power and this made the difference in bringing down another class one's shields to spread it out in space.

The five remaining class one's and the class two's which had joined them all targeted *Reciprocity* simultaneously before they completely disappeared into dazzling radiance and illumination in micro-suns too bright to look at directly. Konax managed to get *Reciprocity* out from under the enemy fire quickly while those ships couldn't see anything, but the ship already had a hull breach in one section and an air leak in another. Hasbro, Omniomi and an Ahumdulilah 150-reactor super-battleship all hit the same class one until it burst into a fireball. Their friendly class two and an Ahumdulilah super-battleship carrier wasted a loyal imperial class two. Swenah was headed to station four while her crew and repair androids were frantically scrambling to plug the leak and the hole. The allies only had two of their ultra-super class ships in the battle at this point with Nestles' *Liberator* destroyed and both Firestone and *Swenah* in need of repairs. Five of their eight Ahumdulilah 149-150-reactor ships had been lost, and those were the allies biggest after the ultra-super class with 244 reactors.

Pez found a soft spot on a class one's shields that was being pummeled by Hasbro and Omniomi, breaking the hull open with torpedoes to blow it all over space. Malignant was screaming orders for all imperial class twos and threes to come to his aid immediately. Most turned to rush over and in few cases this allowed the ships they were engaged in battle with to annihilate them. Ahhu jumped another drone into a class one, sideways, and it got sucked into a sideways-streaking blue line which shot through a class three responding to Malignant's call, bow to stern, fusing it with the streak.

The two class ones left in the fight were both taking heavy fire and the four class two's supporting them were too. Many ships were on their way to help Malignant but a bunch of those were being followed and fired upon by allied ships, and a few had whole groups on their tails. Omniomi was pouring out the last of Justice Maker's ordinance in a flood, determined to terminate these last two class one's with extreme prejudice. Malignant was screaming bloody murder but no longer forming actual words and he was so frightened that he wet himself and his bowel released of its own accord right into his bright yellow pants. The class one shielding Malignant blew into gas and vapors allowing all the fire to focus on his ship, the last class one in the system.

Malignant was screaming at the Admiral commanding his ship to surrender when a drone fighter-bomber came out of quantum jump right in his lap, and he became a brown stain within a blue streak. The sound vibrations of his last scream survived his body by a fraction of a millisecond. Ahhu told Pez with satisfaction, "That was the last of those class one's."

"Good work sweetheart," Pez praised her. "I think you just vaporized the imperial prince. We're not out of this yet though."

The call from the emperor for the ships of the 208 planets to return to Monarch had by now received its full response and nearly 500 ships, almost all of them classes seven through ten, were in the Monarch system and engaged in battle or about to be. Only one in twelve had a friendly beacon. The allies had lost more than 300 of their one reactor or less ships, more than 12,000 small craft, and at least one hundred of their big ships. Imperial ships were starting to arrive from the recall of all imperial ships everywhere and it didn't look good. Rubix's scoreboard was well into the upper 500's now, and 52 class one imperial ships had been taken out of existence, but such things seemed hardly to put a dent in the situation. The fighting was still all out, and as fast as they could kill and crush imperials more kept streaming in. Pez contacted Admiral Fuji, commanding the Ahumdulilah ships now that Canon was gone, and asked him, "What do you think?"

"I think the revolution is won even if we don't personally survive this," Fuji replied.

"Then those imperial ships will just enslave the planets again if we don't beat them here," Pez stated.

"We have had many imperial ships mutiny and come over to us, but they are battling space weapons even after all the imperial ships have evacuated," Fuji informed her. "They will come and finish Monarch once they neutralize the empires ability to hurt their people from space. For us it doesn't look so good."

"We have to win this then with what we've got!" Pez declared, as she poured torpedoes through a soft spot in a class three's shields while bearing down on it with beam and nose blasters.

"I've no intention of surrendering if that's what you're implying," he said a little offended.

"That's not what I meant," Pez told him, now onto a class two with her weapons fire. "We need to stay frosty and determined, and blow these ships up as fast as they come."

A tremendous hit from a batch of the biggest imperial torpedoes rocked Fuji's ship as he told her, "I promise you we are doing our very best."

One of the Trident super-battleship carriers that had hooked up with them blew into an expanding sphere. Pez told Schwin, "Get Cleo back in your cockpit right away. *Reciprocity* is at station four getting repairs."

"I'm on my way, SCG."

Another Rally super-battleship carrier blew to particles, then a Kluzyst 2-mile ship blew apart. Several ships were firing on the same class two Pez was hitting and that ship's shields were in a tempest exposing a soft spot to Pez, which she sent torpedoes through in a staccato until the ship became a momentary expanding illumination. Two Ahumdulilah ships plastered a class three all over space. A 1,000 ft. Trident battleship was creamed, and gone. The eight T-9's led by *Isis*, swooped on a class four imperial and kept up continuous fire until it was gone with nothing left to shoot at but gas and emptiness. The imperial small craft remained thick, in the neighborhood of 100,000 strong, including the yachts and private craft, even though they'd shot down more than 68,000 already. They might have eliminated the imperial class ones but there were an awful lot of class two's, and those had 78 reactors.

Ahhu jumped a drone into a class two, lengthwise, and it became a blue lightning bolt zapping a large imperial auxiliary crowded with rearming small combat craft and ships, square in the middle to take nearly the entire conglomeration with it in a blue streak headed out of the battle zone. A class three that had been docked to the end of the auxiliary now sat at the start of the fading line and a single loading platform with a bomber seated on it was all that remained of the auxiliary itself. A few small combat craft sat in space over where the auxiliary had been. This gave Pez an idea and she told Fuji, "I'm going to hunt down and kill their auxiliaries. The imperials aren't doing so well with rearming because their auxiliaries are scattered throughout the battle zone, and most of their ships are low on munitions."

"I'll spread the word to kill auxiliaries when the opportunity is there," Fuji told her.

He put out the order to kill auxiliaries if you could and Omniomi's *Justice Maker* immediately bit into a big one making short work of it. Compared to war ships they were easy to kill. Pez and *Phoenix* took off together to shoot some auxiliaries and it didn't take them long to find one. *Thunderbolt's* class nine beam with other fire support blew it up, and all the ships and small craft attached to it into a blooming cloud of molten vapor; nothing remained. They came across a great big giant one which would have taken about all of their ordinance to destroy, so Ahhu jumped a drone inside it to take every passenger on a blue-streak ride, and even the class two, four miles long, went for that ride. It was big for a streak and picked up many imperial small craft on its way out of the battle zone. It must have been all the chemicals aboard the auxiliary that made this streak more rainbow than blue. A few other big imperial ships had contributed to the size and brilliance of this streak and deserved their credit.

Hunting auxilaries turned out to be a good way to kill ships and small craft. Everyone needed to rearm and there were lines at many auxiliaries. All of the imperial auxilaries were buried under provisioning ships and combat craft. An Ahumdulilah 58-reactor super-cruiser was following *Thunderbolt* and *Phoenix* helping them eliminate imperial auxiliaries. It was actually very helpful since between them these two cruisers had only seven reactors; though Pez blinded their targets and located thin film distortions in their shields to exploit. Captain Quicksilver felt like he was just along for the ride and living on borrowed time anyway, though he vigilantly fired his ship's weapons into the targets Pez chose. She was irrationally optimistic; perhaps pathologically so, in Quicksilver's opinion.

Rocky Studios, as they were now calling themselves, was transmitting live news updates constantly through talking heads and text streaming across the bottom of the holo. There were now fifty-nine task forces of ten or more imperial ships wearing friendly beacons, and they had destroyed more than six hundred unfriendly imperial ships before the rest were called to Monarch. They were now swiftly wiping out imperial military assets in space around the planets of the empire. According to the news, the allied forces fighting in the Monarch system didn't really stand a chance. New cartoons of the emperor were transmitted on the intergalactic holovision network to all worlds of the empire, focused quite factually on the most atrocious acts of the emperor's miserable reign and on his acne as a teenager—still a sore topic for him to this day. They made sure to show a few cartoon close ups of Sponge's cartoon penis with women screaming in revulsion of it in the background and cut-aways, since this had kind of become a symbolic revolutionary act at this point in the process. Mel was able to procure some footage of the emperor's actual flatulent penis from medical scan records, and everyone at the studio agreed that it was unusually grotesque, so a split holo image of the naked real emperor beside the naked cartoon emperor was displayed, with the question in text below, "Who wears it better?"

Panel discussions among experts, transmitted live, focused on what was wrong with the emperor's penis. Some comments from female members of their studio audience included, "What penis?", "You call that a penis?", and, "It might look like a penis, maybe, if it were a little bigger."

A great big "good riddance!" and "thank the cosmic intelligence" were given as a sendoff for Prince Malignant's journey to the center of hell. More than thirty trillion voices were raised cursing his everlasting soul to ice and brimstone. Rocky now had two separate streams of programming running, one of just news and the other of documentaries, panel discussions, emperor cartoons, stand-up comedians tearing down the empire, and a live Whirling Vortexes concert. Now the people of the empire had to make a choice or split their holo to show both.

With the imperial warships gone most planets disposed of their imperials in less than an hour and ruling family members were rounded up and executed. Some of the methods were very creative, some very ancient, and some that would likely better fit the word 'torture' than 'execution'. They all eventually got the job done though. A number of lone imperial ships with friendly beacons, not a part of one of the fifty-nine task forces, were headed to Monarch to help the lost cause of the Avahat.

Pez and the Ahumdulilah super-cruiser, with Quicksilver's *Phoenix*, were wiping out whole squadrons with each auxiliary they blew, and they were not the only allies blowing them. Omniomi was on an auxiliary killing-spree and so was Hasbro. Schwin was back flying with Pez and had Cleo with her to help with the big giant ones. Ahhu and Cleo also streaked class two's wherever they encountered them. Rubix's quad blaster scoreboard was in the 930's and he would be further along than that, but he'd had to let the thing cool down a couple times. No one had ever had that problem before with a quad blaster.

A pair of Kluzyst 5,000 ft. ships went at almost the same time. A Trident super-battleship was utterly destroyed, and an Om battleship carrier was blown to less than bits. Pez kept blowing up auxiliaries and the ships reloading at them, and Omniomi was on a manic mission to massacre and mutilate auxiliary ships. All the allied ships trained their weapons systems on auxiliaries when they weren't fighting with another ship to stay alive. The imperial tenders, tugs and replenishers were escaping the battle zone and planet Monarch, only these had no quantum drives and so could only head for deep space.

Pez found a whole group of big and gigantic auxiliaries smothered in ships and small craft, on the edge of the battle zone opposite Monarch's moon though close to its orbital path. Cleo and Ahhu jumped drones, coordinated and timed to hit at the same moment, into the two behemoths on each end of the group, and the whole of it was swept away into a lightning bolt crackling out of the battle zone leaving a chemical rainbow trail. Sixty-four canister missiles remained perfectly aligned in space, though minus the canisters and loading machine. Very slowly their alignment began to lose its precision as the missiles drifted alone in that patch of space with nothing to hold them together.

Mel informed Pez, "The imperials have a mega reloading station on the fourth planet's surface and two on the dark side of Monarch's moon."

"Thanks Mel, I'm on my way."

As soon as she took off for the moon, which was closer, an imperial bomber flew right into those 64 missiles detonating every single one to blow up with them. She got her speed up to .24 light, the fastest she could go and still target stuff. Her combined speed with that of other ships, unless they were on the same trajectory, which would cancel rather than add to it, put her beyond sensor resolution speed and kept their shields form taking hits. She came up behind a pair of class tens, going .11 light faster than them, slowing on her approach, then let them have it as she came into range. *Phoenix*, the Ahumdulilah super-cruiser, and Schwin's force were still with her and opened up on the class tens as well. The super-cruiser wrecked them so quick that Pez saved her torpedoes and didn't bother with soft spots in shields.

They came in low on the lunar surface since the two bases were both shielded, and hit the shields at surface level, then the reactors with beams and blasters blowing them up, and torpedoes and missiles form Schwin's force blew up the munitions stash, blowing the reloading platforms and docks, and all the ships there trying hopelessly to get away. A class two had been there, a pair of class three's and a number of class fives. Hundreds, maybe thousands, of small craft went up in the conflagration. They were racing to the next lunar reloading base.

The second one was rather impromptu and had only a portable reactor powering its shields, which came down quite easily. Machinery was bolted to the ground and there were no actual docks. Crane arms and hover machines worked while ships employed their vortex-redirect & generation turbines to hang a meter off the surface. There had probably been more than a few scraped bottoms down there, but no one would ever know since there was only a crater now and they were accelerating for the fourth planet.

Electra was awake and wide-eyed, staring at Pez's holo from her special baby seat on the bridge. Gumby was on Ming's lap and kept reaching for the manual canister missile launch button. Ming kept an arm across his chest, not letting him get close enough to reach it as she assisted Pez with turns and braking. The gravity of the situation seemed to suspend and mitigate the babies' usual demand for instant gratification of needs. Just as *Thunderbolt* was approaching range with a class two imperial ship which was leaving the reloading station fully armed, Electra's bladder released more than the feltex liner could absorb and she burst into tears. Ming told Pez, "I'll change Electra's diaper while you blow that class two out of existence, sweetheart."

"Thanks, darling," Pez told her, just before going comatose for about a second while she planted micro-suns bow to stern around the imperial ship. Then she veered onto a new trajectory, shots missing her wildly, as she got her class nine beam drilling its shields and her nose blasters hammering them. The super-cruiser had every beam and blaster drilling the imperial and pelted it with torpedoes and missiles; so did *Phoenix*. Schwin's group rained torpedoes onto it. A big soft spot opened within to choppy turbulence of the class two's force-field shields and Pez aimed eight missiles to release them like mag-lev train cars, one right after the other. Somewhere between the third and fifth missile exploding, the hull was holed and at least three, possibly five, made it inside the ship to blow, igniting things within which were themselves quite explosive. The ship was wracked with jolting then the stern blew off as if launching into space, right before the rest of it flared, expanding thousands of times its size with the separation of particles.

The fourth planet reloading and repair base was enormous and had twelve docks plus well over a hundred platforms. Mel claimed there were 152 of them and since no one else had counted them, they accepted this as fact. Each one had several bombers or fighter-bombers occupying it and a line of at least three more waiting their turn for each one. Nine class 9 beam weapons were mounted around the perimeter of the base along with dozens of class 4 blaster quads. One of the largest imperial ships, classes two through four, was at each dock, all with their own weapons systems, and these were all powering up to go hot. Batteries of anti-small craft canister missiles were all over the place already spitting them at Schwin's force. Pez told Schwin, "Pull out of there, it's too well defended. Ahhu and Cleo will need to coordinate some drone jumps into some class twos down there, and then we'll see what's left."

Cleo and Ahhu communicated and worked out the timing of their navigation formulas to coincide to the thousandth of a second. To be sure, there was some pretty sophisticated and tricky math involved, but also a deeply artistic understanding not really teachable as a skill, which drone pilots and people in general tended to have inactive, dormant, and non-operational within their psyches; but both Ahhu and Cleo had this inner sense awake and functioning. The extra clarity each had been experiencing related to this sense they had, was unbeknownst to them, radically enhanced and guided by Sarhi and the entire spiritual congress which now included every adult on Mother.

Two class two ships on the outer circumference of the surface-base streaked together across the base close to the central diameter, and on into space, sparking blue like gas flames and trailing chemical rainbow colors in the psychedelic spectrum. Nearly the entire base was sucked into one streak or the other. What didn't streak was the beam weapons, canister missiles batteries and quad-blasters around the two sides of the streaks. All the giant ships and hundreds of small craft were now included in two blue lines leaving the solar system. The two lines grew closer and out just before the orbital distance of the fifth planet, intersected and crossed, to produce a solar flare effect.

With no reactors only the canister missiles were operational and Pez's group finished them and the beams and blasters in a single pass. They rushed back to the battle zone to hunt auxiliaries. Omniomi checked in with her SCG, "About a thousand ships have jumped into the system in the last few minutes, hardly any bigger than a class five, but Hasbro and I are down to beam, blaster and small missiles delivered by shuttle as far as weapons go."

"Either you or Hasbro needs to go rearm and have Shudiy transferred to your ship to sit on the bridge with access to the big torpedoes. Do it now. I know with another ultra-super class out of the game our casualties will increase, but with one of you armed and with Shudiy on board it will give us a chance to win this"

"The record pit stop for one of these was thirty-three minutes and seven seconds," Omniomi informed her."

"We'll just have to weather it," Pez replied. "At least they're all running out of big missiles and torpedoes too."

"Not the thousand that just jumped in," Omniomi pointed out.

"I understand that most of those ships were in combat engagements," Pez told her.

"From only fifty-nine task forces engaging over 5,700 planets?" She questioned.

"Apparently there are numerous mutinied ships operating independently of those task forces," Pez shared. "I don't think very many headed in are fresh and I aim to kill most of the rest of the imperial auxiliaries before they get here. I'm about to micro-jump so I've got to go," she signed off.

Existence ended totally then reappeared with them in an entirely new location. It was strange for them, though not for Pez who'd learned to contemplate the black near-attainment in those jump-transitions involving no time at all; but then eternity did not really involve any time either. *Thunderbolt, Phoenix* and the Ahumdulilah super-cruiser were all frantically braking, and already whizzing by stuff they couldn't get fire control acquisition on to shoot at. Mel used the sensors of every allied ship in the battle zone to ascertain the locations of imperial auxiliaries and sent a zig-zag lined system map to Pez as the most efficient route for wiping out all of them. Pez was on it, but had to forego the first position on the route because they were still going too fast. She slowed and closed on the second stop on her map.

A class two positioned itself between Pez's incoming group and the two giant auxiliaries currently servicing four war ships and hundreds of small craft. The imperials had lost so many auxiliaries in the last quarter hour and the ships with them that they were now defending the ones they had left. Ahhu told Pez, "Steer us way out to its flank, I've got this."

Ahhu had become something of a streak expert and lined up her shot so that the class two ship blurred through the side of one auxiliary then the next, sparkling brightly in a line headed out of the system taking the whole reloading set up along for the ride to oblivion. It had all happened too fast to actually see the sequence of events but both deductive and inductive reasoning met in the same conclusion. Pez was already accelerating in her arc around the flank of what had been a reloading station and was now just an arc in space. She was careful not to intercept the streak since even fading it seemed to contain a lethal glow.

They blew away some imperial small craft before shooting above targeting speed. Rubix was on his way to breaking 1,100 on his scoreboard. The battle seemed never ending, the complexity overwhelming and the variables just kept coming at them shooting. Trix's glasses had entirely fogged over and she took the opportunity of being beyond targeting velocity to give them a thorough cleaning. She shot just as well blind so long as she allowed the spiritual congress to work through her, getting any dualities of self and other out of the way. Trix was one with every small craft she blew to light and vapors. Woahha was only three kills below Trix, and Super-Agent Green was only five below. Evenrude was catching up to the other gunners who had been at it longer than him, and was about to pass their lowest scorer without counting any of Amazonia's kills since he'd cleared the scoreboard before taking over her turret.

Hasbro and Omniomi had Mel pick a number between one and ten, then they each chose one in that range and the closer of those two numbers, which was Omniomi's, took their ship for loading ordnance and to receive Shudiy. With a hole in her hull and a leak in section six, docked to Auxiliary One in reloading and repair station four, *Reciprocity* had had to fight off a pair of class two imperials, and Shudiy had found the distortions when their shields were stirred up taking fire to shoot her torpedoes through, and that situation had been contained. Firestone's damaged shield generators were almost all changed out with new ones installed, and only the calibrations and integration had yet to be finished. The engineers, technicians and mechanics were getting the job done in under a fifth the Fleet standard duration specified for it.

Pez's little three ship group with Schwin's small craft support was attaining a productivity rate never before seen in war. Even her lowest scoring quad-gunners were leading the contest in the battle of Monarch. Rubix had broken every record long ago and was yet on a roll. Counting collateral damage Ahhu had killed 57 ships with drones single handedly. With assists Cleo had spread about as many out across space. Pez attacked ships her group could never kill if it weren't for the distortions in shields when they're all stirred up and her ability to see them clearly. Blinding them always gave her a nice advantage too.

The thousand plus ships that jumped into Monarch had a few friendlies among them and these tended to get behind unfriendly imperial ships, smaller than themselves, and blow them to hell and gone. The new arrivals began to tip the scales further from the allied side and cost them ninety more small ships and nineteen more big ones, though mostly ships with 9 reactors or less. However, one was a 20-reactor, 8,900 ft. Ahumdulilah ship—not Ahab's though, and one was a 14-reactor Kluzyst 1¼ miles ship. Pez started having trouble locating auxiliaries after finishing the route Mel gave her and hitting the first stop last since she had been going too fast to get that one at the start, and switched to killing big ships instead. Mel could only locate a few small imperial auxiliaries in and around the battle zone anyway. Rubix was in the 1300's. Super-Agent Green was tied with Woahha. Pez was truly impressed with Super-Agent Green and was pretty sure that woman could do anything. Ming found Super-Agent Green very attractive and knew Pez admired her, so planned to invite her for a sleep-over if they lived through this. The Rocky Studios News Syndicate, as they were now calling themselves, gave the allies in Monarch no chance at all; at least not until those 59 task forces came calling on the planet and that was not expected for several hours, and so it was assumed, at least a couple of hours after the allies fighting there were long dead.

Less than a quarter of the ships new to the battle were large enough to carry combat small craft but between all of them they brought more than 25,000 to the party. Pez and her entire group had to reload again, including the super-cruiser commanded by Captain Starmite. Captain Spalding took excellent care of them at station seven, from *Auxiliary 2*, prioritizing their rearmament over repairs and others waiting to load. He knew the most powerful secret weapons were contained within this tiny task force; the two uncanny drone pilots and the planter of suns who could slip torpedoes through active shields. He also knew there was another like Pez, an Islohar woman aboard *Justice Maker* on Admiral Omniomi's bridge, and that ship was only minutes from rejoining the fight. *Auxiliary 1* was about to set the new ultra-super class pit stop record. He was a little envious of that, though proud to be the auxiliary chosen for service by the SCG. He owed his promotion to her and was a great admirer of her accomplishments.

Pez announced to *Thunderbolt's* crew, "Stand down and take a break. We'll be here for about eleven minutes. Get some chow if you're hungry."

"What do you wnt?" Trix asked her. "I'm already in the galley."

"Just a stim.-brew sweetheart. I have no appetite."

"I'll bring it right to you. It will only take a minute to make."

"Thanks my love."

Ahhu called to Trix over Pez's coms, "Bring some of those spongey pastries with the white icing individually plastic wrapped."

"Alright."

Ming inquired, "Are we getting any hull repairs?"

Pez answered, "No. The hull integrity is fine. It's just scortched in a few places. They might replace the sensor array that got crushed."

"I hope they do since it's the backup to our primary array."

Pez got Spalding on coms and asked, "Is your crew going to replace our secondary sensor array?"

"They are, and they're adding two sensor clusters as further backup. How many times were your shields zeroed-out?"

"I think three."

"I advise you to reduce that frequency if you expect us to keep getting back in the fight quick."

"It comes down to battle circumstances and instant cost-benefit analysis. I'll be a tiny bit more conservative from here on out."

I'd like to keep you here and patch a few spots on your hull, but it looks like we're losing this battle and need our best assets back in the fight quick."

"That's right so get me on my way."

Trix stuck a stim.-brew in Pez's hand and a pastry on her arm-rest before giving the rest to Ahhu. Cotex mentioned, "There's a class three imperial ship beginning an attack run on this auxillary group."

Ahhu jumped a drone into an imperial class three ship while waiting at the service station. Its streak took out one of the few small auxiliaries the imperials had left. *Like what were the odds?* Ahhu thought the cosmic intelligence must have had a hand in that. Firestone was back in the fight with *Fury* fully loaded and repaired and shields better than new. He was on the warpath. A Rally super-battleship carrier, their last, was blown to glowing stardust. Another Kluzyst 2-mile ship was lost with all hands and a 28-reactor super-battleship from Trident was also lost. Then great tragedy struck and Hasbro's *Redeemer,* ganged up on by dozens of smaller ships—a few of them class twos, transformed into a growing spherical cloud expanding. Swenah was screaming orders, and insisting *Auxiliary 1* get her back into combat from station four immediately! Omniomi, with her secret weapon Shudiy, was already undocking and suns were sprouting on all nearby imperial ships. One encompassed a bomber causing it to collide with a class ten and making such an explosion in the total destruction of both that a wing of fighters flying close got popped into little colorful clouds. If Firestone was on the warpath, Omniomi was on a rampage.

The thousand plus ships were all within the battle zone and there was so much crap floating about, things that didn't come apart and vaporize with the rest of their ship, that space around Monarch had become a hazardous junkyard. *Phoenix* had an entire space drive half disintegrate on her shields to ricochet off her hull, leaving her composite ceramic heat shield armor exposed and dented. Quick little fighters were blowing apart on bits and pieces in space all over the place, sometimes contributing to the problem that killed them. A fighter cockpit with no ship around it, and astonishingly preserved, was fried to smoke coming into contact with *Thunderbolt's* shields and nothing survived to knock on her hull. Occasionally, live personnel in space suites could be seen drifting about hoping not to be squished and to be rescued before their air ran out. Pez got a light from *Thunderbolt* onto a very attractive piece of office furniture coming up while magnifying it in her holo, wishing she had time to retrieve it. It hadn't a scratch on it. Then it whizzed by incomprehensibly and was gone.

Swenah was shoving off with hardly more than smart adaptive duct-tape sealing the hole in her hull, but the leak was sealed in section *six* and her shields were 100%. She was also fully armed and Swenah was in a deeply predatory mood. A class ten had the misfortune of crossing her bow and didn't last two seconds. With three ultra-supers back in the game—fully loaded and pissed-off, and Pez's little group dispatching one big imperial ship after another almost like they were nothing, the tide of battle shifted a few degrees towards equal, staunching their flow of losses and honing determination to a sharp point. Rubix's scoreboard paused on 1,536 while he waited for Pez to slow back down to target acquisition speed. Ahhu was calculating a jump for the drone she piloted from *Thunderbolt* and Cleo was in the process of jumping one into a class three imperial ship from Schwin's cockpit.

The imperials were still trying to find that super-duper weapon turning their ships into blue streaks and were de-cloaking their moon and space frantically searching. They were also running low on or out completely of torpedoes, missiles, anti-missile molten flares, thruster fuel cells, boosters, and other things. This condition continued to deteriorate for them as the battle dragged on and the damned revolutionaries refused to die. They had zero inteligence and could get no readings on that sensor blinding weapon either. Then there was the 'shield-penetrator' as the imperials were calling it.

The allied small craft kill ratio had decreased to less than 4 to 1. The kill ratio for Schwin's specially trained elite pilots was down to 29 to 1, from a peak of 49 to 1. The imperial forces were overwhelming though the effectiveness of each ship diminished as thruster fuel was spent, making turns much wider and flying less precise. Without missiles and torpedoes more ships had to coordinate together to bring down shields and score a kill. Captain Ahab had joined his 20-reactor Ahumdulilah assault frigate to Pez's group figuring the safest place in this battle was right behind her. He had been fighting beside a 58 reactor super-cruiser before joining her, but that ship had sprayed his shields when it blew apart.

Rocky news mentioned Pez Fleet's tenacity and perseverance but still gave them zero chance, the only question being how long they could hang on and postpone the inevitable.

Slowly the allied forces were whittled down, always at a far greater cost than their worth, and without a missile or torpedo to their name or a fuel cell with fuel in it for that matter, the imperial forcers were beating down the revolutionaries by sheer numbers. The battle dragged on and imperial ships kept getting turned into streaks. The sensors blinding weapon seemed to be everywhere. The battle sure wasn't over yet and would be far costlier than it already had been, but the imperials felt secure and confident that they would prevail and be victorious. Rocky news had to agree.

Pez didn't. She was abiding in the state, concentrating on piloting and fighting her ship, and on planting suns on imperial ones, with the force of the spiritual congress now more than twenty-billion consciousnesses mindfully and one-pointedly focused, surging through her channels and meridians bringing her every brain cell to life in a unity far greater than the sum of its parts. She was actually dodging blaster bolts and hitting soft spots from incredible distances. Suns blinded all the biggest imperial ships and a few of these ran into their own smaller ones.

It almost seemed to the imperials as if they had whittled them down to a kernel that would whittle no further and was indestructible. For them the blue streak death of ships, ordinance that could pass through their shields, and sensor blinding weapons they could get no handle on, along with these three super-duper ships made their victory seem less certain as their kill ratio raced towards negative double digits. Rubix had passed 2,000 and was still on a roll. Allied losses had all but stopped and they were destroying imperials at an astonishing rate. Pez's group killed every ship it engaged in under seven seconds no matter how big it was. With the firepower of the super-cruiser and assault frigate it only took a second or two to stir the shields up exposing a thin film soft spot.

Then 800 Blue World Phantom Raider fighter-bombers jumped in extremely close to the battle zone braking like maniacs and Pez let out a hoot of delight as a victory cry. About 300 independently operating imperial ships with friendly beacons appeared in the Monarch system over the course of several minutes playing Whirling Vortexes songs over their coms. By the time the lead ships engaged the imperials in battle, the first of the 59 task forces jumped into Monarch. Rocky news began drastically altering its predictions making a 180 degree turn around with absolute certainty that Pez Fleet, or at least what little was left of it, would win the day.

With the revolution over on most planets and having nothing left to do but dispose of the imperial bodies, many people engaged in gambling and odds were shifting astronomically in Pez Fleet's favor. Those who'd bet on her when the odds were 200 to 1 against her, and Mel was one of these, were sure now that they were in for quite a payday. Once all 59 task forces had jumped into the Monarch system there wasn't another taker to bet against Pez Fleet.

Pez's little special squadron started streaking the occasional giant imperial troop transport while kicking enemy ships and small craft ass. There were a lot of those transports around and shuttles had been unloading their troops to the surface of Monarch since the battle had begun. By killing a few Pez was certain she could get them to surrender up here in space, and preferred that to having to kill them all dispersed on the ground. A few more minutes at this rate and the imperials wouldn't have anything left bigger than a class eight ship. Less than a third of the task force ships had yet closed to join the fight.

Thunderbolt and the other three ships of her squadron were once again completely out of missiles and torpedoes. The battle was no longer critical, at least not for the allies. Pez led her group back to station seven and Spalding's *Auxiliary 2. Thunderbolt, Phoenix,* and Ahab's ship all fit on one side of the auxiliary and the super-cruiser docked to its other side. Schwin's small craft were all on Spalding's deck or in bays.

Captain Swanson asked Pez from the Space Marine *Transport One* parked nearby, "When do we get started?"

Pez told him, "The Space Marines will be under Admiral Swenah's command, but your transport is coming with me to New

Monarch. I'm bringing *Justice Maker* and *Auxiliary 2* with us as well. They're no longer needed here."

"I'm honored, ma'am," Swanson replied. Then he inquired, "Will 9,200 Space Marines and Army Space Special Forces be enough?"

"With the air-space support we'll be getting we'll be a plenty big enough force to rescue the Whirling Vortexes held in New Monarch's capital, New Haven. We'll have their exact location and holo maps of the city both above and below ground, to any level of detail you want to zoom into and drill down to. Be ready to leave in ten minutes."

"Aye, aye, ma'am," he said proudly, wishing he'd get to set his feet on the ground beside her.

CHAPTER TWENTY-TWO

Pez had her own 16 Space Marine guard on board *Thunderbolt* which included Evenrude, Johnson and Mercury. Evenrude was a one-man army on a white-sun world. Pez was prepared to tear the capital apart if she had to, to find her friends, and the cosmic intelligence help anyone who tried to stand in her way. *Justice Maker* had 480 Space Marines aboard, and Captains Ahab and Starmite carried 1,000 between them of Ahumdulilah's version of Space Marines. They were collecting what was left of their combat small craft during the reloading and borrowed many from other Ahumdulilah ships to make a full compliment. The Mirage Streak Fury bomber was even bigger than the Astro-Phantom and had done almost as well against the imperials as the Phantom.

Pez had her crew stand down and eat. Electra insisted on being in her momma's arms though she only got one of those wrapped around her while Pez ate with the other. They watched Rocky news, head quartered in the vast Bulwinkle mansion complex. Jard had supplied Rocky news with data from the 'Pez biography' and both Pez and Ming looked on in horror as the commentator narrated the facts and scenes from the consummation of their marriage appeared on the intergalactic news. Way to go Jard. Ming's bottom was promptly featured, and the holo still of the curves of her bottom and one breast in profile was frozen on their display for over a minute as the commentator delivered a brief bio on Ming. Electra's conception and the first known 'event', inseparably the same incident, received several minutes of comment and showed images of naked Rubix and naked Pez making love. Excerpts from battles in faraway Xegachtznel Galaxy were displayed while descriptions of Pez's heroics put them in auditory-conceptual perspective and these included digital visuals form Pez's rescue of Earth 10^5 CBS 2. The program sidetracked a bit into the elemental constituents of the Kluzyst anatomy and physiology since no one in the now fallen Royal Monarch Empire had ever seen a blue-star alien before.

It finally got back on track to encapsulate Pez's total destruction of the Kundabuffer Empire in the Hub Galaxy in a couple of minutes of summary and images of events. Pez's undercover mission featured mostly Hoola, intergalactic music superstar and Hug-me's crotch-less panties super-model. Pez was in it sometimes in her role as Cher Bulwinkle, like when Hoola made love to her, and a few times it was only about Pez, like her landings and her duel with Rudfuss Snydely, whom, the commentator informed the viewers, had been skinned alive by his slaves and rolled in salt 'til he died screaming.

Pez said over her coms, "Jard, could you please come to the cockpit."

"No," Jard told her.

"And why is that?" Pez inquired.

"I don't want to," he said honestly. "I saw the Rocky news and I know you just want to yell at me."

"To level with you completely, Jard, I must confess that breaking your neck did cross my mind," Pez admitted.

"And you think my coming to the cockpit is a good idea at this time, under the circumstances?" He asked rationally.

"Maybe you're right," Pez agreed, dropping it for now.

Rocky news had moved on to Pez's disciples, and former sex worker Ahhu was shown plying her trade as Twinkie, taken from the adult entertainment DVD she had starred in which had been re-edited into hologram format. Trix was next, and with her the focus was on all of her academic achievements, and on her breasts when they were swollen to three times their size from repetitive stimulus testing in an attempt to recreate Trix's amazing sensitivity in Mel's android body's breasts. The sequence on Trix also included her first awakening meditating with Pez as prelude to her cathartic shedding of her sex phobias to join in the orgy taking place in Pez's penthouse. This had been instigated by Woahha and exacerbated by Jard crashing the party with his guests. The Rocky news even included a few seconds of Cotex riding Jard, who was flat on his back on the dining room table with Cotex screaming "Oh yes" with each bounce of her enormous breasts.

Thunderbolt was armed and serviced before they finished eating. Pez had them take five so she could finish her second ambassador ration. She called Omniomi and told her, "We're leaving for New Monarch in a little over four minutes and I need *Justice Maker* with us."

"We're ready to go and have 87% of our big missiles and torpedoes."

"Auxiliary 2 is coming with us and can reload your ordinance in New Monarch system when you get low."

"I have few small craft returned to my docks from battle," Omniomi lamented.

"Borrow from Firestone, Swenah and the Om captains," Pez ordered.

Pez called Captain Spalding to tell him, "You're coming with my group which will include *Justice Maker* and Swanson's transport. Prepare to go. We leave in a little less than four minutes. Direct all Om small craft reloading on your decks to Omniomi's flight decks. She needs to collect more combat craft before we depart."

"Aye, aye, ma'am, we'll be ready," Spalding assured her.

Pez said to Swenah on *Reciprocity*, "I'm taking the little force I've been fighting with as well as *Justice Maker*, *Auxiliary 2*, and *Space Marine Transport 1* to New Monarch so we can rescue our friends in the band. It is up to you to execute the ground war after pulverizing everything military on the surface from space. Then you need to provide both space-support and close-combat air-support for our ground troops. Give the Space Marines leeway to accomplish objectives as they see fit. Just tell them what you need done and they'll tell you what they need to get it done and how they'll do it."

"I'm looking forward to exterminating the imperial infestation down there, believe me!" Swenah let her know.

"I leave it in your capable hands," Pez said with her mouth full.

They had to wait an additional three and a half minutes for combat craft to fly into *Justice Maker's* bays and land, attaining almost a full complement – some 589 space craft in all; and this gave Pez time to finish her ambassador ration. Electra wanted Pez so she sat on her momma's lap in the pilot seat. Gumby was napping reclined in his toddler seat. Electra's first word had been "Mu", introducing herself to her mother before Pez knew that her daughter was the Mu, who, returns every 2500 years with new teachings. Her second word though, many months later, was "Wu", recognizing her mother's spirit; and her third word was "ma", acknowledging and needing Pez as mother and this had so touched her heart.

Electra sat serenely appreciative that her momma was in the state of contemplation and passing her energy. Electra felt that Pez had come a long way in her mothering and was doing a far better job of it than those previous times. She meant to keep Pez working on this since it really did make her own transitions so much easier with Pez there to receive her, birth her, nurse her through infancy and start reminding her of the teachings young. Corporeal reality was really such a bother and acutely painful at times. Only her enormous compassion for sentient beings could get her to go through it again every 2,500 years. She couldn't imagine how her mother had done it 333 times in a row with only a 49-day respite and recharge between each one.

The task force bound for New Monarch pulled out accelerating. Pez told Spalding and Swanson, "We're going to race ahead and jump in close. Here are the coordinates within the system where I want you to take up position. We'll clear them out of space weapons and ships before bringing the transport into low orbit for operations. *Auxiliary 2* will remain out by the fourth planet and we'll go to you when we need repairs or reloading. I'll see you in New Monarch."

Both men acknowledged with "Aye, aye, ma'am," at the same time.

Pez told her combat captains and Admiral, "Ahhu and Cleo will keep their drones at .7 light when we jump in so they can take out two big ships the moment we have enough resolution to know precise distances to target. We're jumping in awful close, so be careful not to collide with anything. We may have to go right by their highest orbit ships before we're ready to start shooting, but we'll go back for them and stomp them good after our first pass."

"How many ships are we attacking?" Quicksilver asked.

"New Monarch sent no ships to Monarch so they likely have the same twenty-six they had when I visited," Pez answered.

"What classes?" Quicksilver drilled her, feeling like a little fighter space craft up against titans.

"They have five class one's, three class twos, a class three, a pair of class fours, three class fives, a class six, two sevens, three eights, two nines, and four tens," Mel answered for Pez.

"That makes 26 to 5 sound even worse," Quicksilver commented.

"None of the New Monarch ships mutinied?" Ahab inquired.

Mel told him, "The captains and officers are all cousins of the ruling families or their minions. No medical devices went to those ships."

"Here are your jump coordinates," Pez told them enthusiastically as they came to the cusp of .7 light speed.

That strange incorporeal experience came over them and they were suddenly whipping through the New Monarch system at ships, space weapons platforms, space stations, satellites and small craft all impossibly close and coming way too fast. Reverse boosters were spent on every ship and fuel cells were lowered on thrusters as they fought to decrease momentum. Reverse drives whirred and roared open to full capacity. Pressed against their harnesses painfully the ships spilled off speed braking to set new records and their view of the imperials resolved into stark clarity. Small craft flew in continuous streams out the allied ship's bay doors and even *Phoenix* launched its eight combat shuttles. Starmite's 18,600 ft. super-cruiser carried 485 small craft, all of them the big Mirage Streak Furies. Ahab carried 70 Vulcan Prowler fighter-bombers and 50 Comet interceptor fighters. Schwin's 48 Astro-Phantoms, 84 Hunter-Terminators, and 64 Corvette Thunders she'd rounded up for this part were already engaging the enemy. They had jumped in under the power of their own quantum drives.

A class one imperial ship launching its very first small craft streaked blue out of the battle zone and brought that launched small craft with it. There went 800 no longer potential imperial combat craft all in a woosh. Another class one ship, this one with at least a dozen of its small craft around it in space and more pouring out if its bays, zapped a blue streak and no more combat craft were in that space, vacuumed up into the blue streak.

Omniomi and Starmite ganged up on a class one and Shudiy whited out that ship's every last sensor completely as well as locating the little patch of thin film within the class one's tempestuous shields to slip a handful of the very most gigantic torpedoes Om made inside; and Om had started making some really big ones. When it blew, a pair of class nine twin blasters still attached to their turret didn't, instead becoming dumb munitions plowing into a small commercial space station vaporizing projectile and target alike.

Justice Maker and the super-cruiser had just gotten their fire onto another class one that had only then arrived in range, but it streaked blue slicing a little off the top of New Monarch's atmosphere to take with it, causing four hundred mile an hour winds in some locations on the surface, and 130 mile an hour winds most everywhere else on that side of the planet. Whole buildings, bridges, ocean going vessels, and the entire dome that once covered the largest stadium in the empire were 20,000-30,000 feet off the ground caught in a planetary disturbance of the atmosphere at a cataclysmic level, at least to one side of the planet. On that side some 220-foot waves were kicked up and did they ever trash the coastal cities as well as some in-land ones too. It was hard to say if those would remain in-land cities or not after that; or what was left of them at any rate.

New Haven wasn't on that side of New Monarch which took the biggest hit, but it lost a few buildings and literally everything that was not cemented down. It got a lot of it back too, along with a bunch of other debris, when everything finally came crashing down into the roofs of the buildings. Looking at the globe of the planet from space it no longer appeared blue-green and white with brown patches, and looked instead like an all brown dust and dirt storm; resembling a gas-dwarf planet in contrast to a gas-giant.

Before they could even turn their fire onto the next class one arriving, it streaked too, missing both planet and atmosphere but did incorporate a space weapons platform into its blueness as it went by or hit; it was too quick to tell for sure which. Three class two's and a class three were firing wildly at them due to all the micro-suns around them, and most shots passed by not even close, though a few skimmed their shields gently. Shudiy pushed torpedoes through a soft spot in a class two's rippling shields and it blew into an expanding colorful cloud. Pez found the distortion in the class three's shields sending a stream of her smaller torpedoes through. It blew into particles just as the rest of the imperial ships were converging on them, and so were at least four thousand combat space craft that had lifted from the lunar surface and orbital space stations.

The class two ship right in front of them became their next coordinated target, though Ahab had no choice but to engage the class four hitting him. It had 31 reactors to his 20. Another class four and three class fives opened up on Omniomi's *Justice Maker*. A class six imperial ship harassed Starmite's super-cruiser, and a class seven, with seven reactors, engaged Quicksilver's *Phoenix* which only had three. Another class seven along with three eight's were stalking and looking for an opening.

Suns sprouted all over the imperial ships and the allies all maneuvered into new positions out of the line of fire, while continuing to pound on the imperials. The class two under Starmite's and Omniomi's superior firepower eventually blew apart, allowing them to focus on the many other problems. Pez was sharp-shooting torpedoes into the soft spot in the shields of the class four pummeling Ahab while her beam and nose blasters ripped into the class seven about to kill Quicksilver. Flint got the fin blasters onto the class seven as he sent canister missiles into it. Pez was seeking the thin film in the shields when thirty mirage streak furies whipped in delivering payloads on the class seven and its shields went down. A moment later the class seven went in every direction at once.

Phoenix had taken another heavy knock to its hull exposing composite ceramic heat-shield armor in another location. Its shields wouldn't come back up past 67% so Pez sent it for repairs where

Auxiliary 2 was stationed. Quicksilver had to accelerate and micro-jump out to the auxiliary, which got the combat small craft off his tail.

Another class two imperial ship was approaching which had been out on the other side of New Monarch when they'd jumped in. Omniomi managed to turn a class five, one of at least five ships raking her with fire at the moment, into tiny particles of expanding slag bubbling into vapors. Shudiy pumped torpedoes into the thin film on the class four focused on *Justice Maker* turning it into super-heated gas. The class two streaked blue before ever getting a shot off. Their super -cruiser killed the class six ship which was less less than a fifth its strength. It was looking good for the big ship battle but the number of small craft buzzing all about was as bad as Monarch had been.

Electra wanted her special seat and Pez was kind of busy, so Gretle her coms officer, got her situated and strapped in. Electra could tell by the emotional vibes on the bridge that the danger was past and she wanted to take a little nap. Gumby had worked up a snore in his sleep. Cotex turned in her seat and pulled her shoulders back, then looked at Pez as she informed her, "The imperials have twelve ships left, but nothing bigger than a class five, of which they have two; and they have one seven, three eights, two nines and four tens. The class fives have 22 reactors and the class seven has seven."

All of this data had come to Cotex from Mel and had been sent to Pez and Ming as well, but Cotex really enjoyed having Pez's attention on her, and everyone's on the bridge for that matter. She craved being present at the epicenter of another event plus she'd always had a thing for top brass, and right now while her commission lasted, Pez was as top brass as one could possibly get. Pez always felt a little inadequate around the voluptuous swimsuit model contest winner and had never before seen breasts that sturdy of such volume. They truly fascinated her though they didn't hold all that much erotic entice-ment for her. Ming's small curvy ones really did it for her and she found Trix's little almost-breasts to be enormously alluring too.

The battle was still raging all around them and Pez started some torpedoes into a thin film in a class five's shields to vaporize the ship.

Justice Maker and the super-cruiser finished off another class five; the last of that class here in New Monarch.

Ahab was beating up on a class seven and wasn't letting it escape. As it exploded into a colorful cloud, bodies in officers' uniforms came flying out of the airlocks in the remaining nine small ships with only 17 reactors between them. Surrender signals were transmitted as their weapons systems powered down; then when they stopped getting hit with fire they powered down their shields exposing their necks.

Pez told her people, "Do not blow up the biggest ship-construction platform orbiting New Monarch. It is currently tooled for civilian super-freighters and it belongs to some friends of mine; though probably not for long with the pending redistribution. Have those surrendered imperial ships take possession of one of those space stations so we have a platform to operate from here and a place to park those surrendered ships, once we take it. Let's kill some of these small craft too so I can bring Swanson's transport to low orbit."

Omniomi said, "I'm going to go silence those super-weapons on the lunar surface."

"Thanks," Pez replied, knowing her *Thunderbolt* was most at risk from them.

One military space station was so enormous and packed with weapons systems that even *Justice Maker* was less than enthusiastic about getting in range of it, so they kept the planet between them and it until Cleo had a drone up to speed, then Schwin took her over the horizon to jump it and streak the station. More than half got sucked into the blue line to just disappear and the section that didn't still came apart into pieces. Those pieces were all on the move in the direction of the streak. They hit an imperial bomber squadron like grapeshot and only one got through. Schwin toasted that one, then started chasing down imperial combat craft.

Omniomi cleared New Monarch's moon of all military material while the rest shot down small craft and blew up space weapons platforms. Pez took *Thunderbolt* through every swarm of imperial fighter-bombers for her twelve quad-blaster gunners to jack their scores up while she smeared them across space with her class 8 twin nose blasters, lobbing missiles into them along with Flint and Ming; and

Flint blew them up with the fin blasters. They wasted hundreds and so did Schwin's group. When Omniomi got *Justice Maker* focused on killing small craft the job went much faster. Schwin was taking half her group out to *Auxiliary 2* for their second reload and it was looking like they were going to be at this for a very long time with some 2,371 down and 5,114 to go, when 769 Phantom Raider fighter bombers from Blue World came jumping into New Monarch, with 1,600 Tempest Crusader Fighters and 600 Tornado Ravager Bombers.

The work of clearing out imperial combat craft then became the job of Schwin and the new arrivals. They started right off with impressive kill ratio's which climbed as the numbers began to equalize, and made an exponential jump as soon as the allies outnumbered the imperials. After about a minute of that the imperials began surrendering in wings and squadrons.

Pez escorted *SMT-1* into low orbit over New Haven while *Justice Maker,* Ahab's frigate and the super-cruiser fried everything that smelled military on New Monarch's surface from space. The Super Cruiser shuttled its space special forces in combat suits to take control of both the space station and of the Casper Commercial Ship construction space platform. As she went by the New Monarch first class civilian space station Pez got her beam on a few of the yachts parked at it and chewed the rest up with her big nose blasters. One was reluctant to explode so she popped a pair of canister missiles into it, coaxing it along. The exploding ships blew the luxury space station into brilliant colored light.

Pez turned the ship and care of Electra over to Ming, and arranged to get picked up by a shuttle along with her sixteen Space Marines. They all got into their hardshell combat space suits and then into the airlock. The docking shuttle had extended its tube to the hatch door in the floor of the airlock and they climbed down one at a time starting with Pez. There were Space Marines already on board bringing the shuttle to capacity once Pez's group got on. Every seat was taken. The seats were all wide enough for Evenrude so even strapped in and in her suit, Pez's little fanny scooted about the seat with the gung-ho landing the pilot gave them, dropping from space in free-fall from low orbit. The Space Marines were used to it and all looked bored but Pez got a real thrill out of it. She told Evenrude enviously, "You guys get to do this stuff all the time."

She'd given Swanson an open line to her coms for the operation and he smiled at her rare appreciation. He really wished he could go with her; and he also wished he was twenty or more years younger. He could watch the action from any suit on the ground, including Pez's since she'd agreed and given him the viewing code. The SCG's love of the Space Marines made him truly proud to be one. She was already a legend in the corps and here he was making history with her, again.

Mel had loaded detailed maps into Pez's suit highlighting the Whirling Vortexes location beneath the Secret Police HQ in hot pink. Once the Whirling Vortexes music was played over Rocky revolutionary holovision the New Monarch government, at Rockerfelon's direction, decided to incarcerate the band as terrorists guilty of sedition music, subversive sounds, and vibes of dissent. Their torture schedules had been worked up and were merely awaiting medical review before getting under way. The tortures were supposed to be transmitted globally on holovision but problems with their holocoms systems and central computer system, it seemed, would prevent that. High definition recordings would be saved to show off at a later date. These plans had all been forgotten by the higher ups as their space defense force got trampled, and now everyone who was anyone, was hiding deep underground beneath heavy blast armor and reinforced shields.

The shuttle collecting Pez and her guard was not the first to set down on the surface in New Haven. A number of them were already landed as hers descended. When she noticed the Rockerfelon mansion on the hill, sitting so majestically overlooking the city and with no life forms within, she asked the pilot to please target it with one of the big undercarriage missiles. The missile was away almost immediately and the pilot circled once so they could watch the mansion blow up and collapse. As the smoke rose and the dust settled Pez explained to them, "It had the wrong look for a housing cooperative."

"Too much negative energy had been absorbed into that structure," Evenrude agreed with her. "So it's better to start over."

Satisfied with a job well done the shuttle crew set the craft down at near the pace of a crash landing winning their SCG's heart. Pez came down the ramp with her platoon who were all assigned to keeping up with her to protect her. Swanson looked on from *SMT-1* and he'd gotten a kick out of watching the Rockerfelon mansion get destroyed.

They were taking some fire from the Secret Police HQ which they'd landed in front of. There were some heavy blasters firing form a number of windows on the first three stories of the building. Pez didn't want to bring this building down since her friends were underneath it. Some shuttle pilots and their quad-blaster gunners silenced the heavy blasters in the windows, charring whole rooms the guns had been shooting out of. Pez led the way up the steps to the front door. She blew it off its hinges and on down the corridor as she climbed the steps, preferring it out of the way entirely, using her 40-mm grenade automatic pistol with a 90-round clip magazine. She had a second magazine for it attached to the outside of her suit on her left outer thigh. She had a high-powered auto-fire blaster rifle in her other arm and hand.

Evenrude held a four-tube missile launcher in a one-handed grip ready to fire at a moment's notice, and a heavy tripod-blaster in his other hand. Johnson carried one of the heavy-duty rapid-fire blasters with an integrated 40mm grenade semi-automatic launcher, in both hands, and Mercury had a new tri-barrel continuous-fire heavy blaster pistol in each hand, and on his back a short-barrel automatic 8-gauge shotgun loaded with anti-personnel shells each containing 5 adamantine pyramids for piercing armor. They were dressed and loaded to face armor and heavy weapons in superior numbers. Most of the Secret Police were 5'7" to 5'11". To be a Space Marine, with the one and only exception of Pez, you had to be seven feet tall at least, and these guys ranged from 7-8 feet. The bones of white-sun humanoids contained more carbon and were stronger and denser than those of yellow-sun humans.

Pez strode into the building with weapons at the ready and walked carefully down the hall. Members of her platoon flew through the doors to the left and right in squads to check and clear the rooms as standard operating procedures required. Evenrude, Johnson and Mercury stuck close by Pez vigilantly alert, and Mel fed them all the same data she sent to Pez. An android-mobile-heavy-blaster, or AMHB, hovered into the corridor ahead of them. Pez had a stream of grenades hitting it before the thing could even get its blaster barrels aimed, and with the blaster fire Evenrude and Johnson put into it, it popped on Pez's second grenade, the last two out her pistol spent unnecessarily. *Oh well*, she thought. The adrenaline had her a little wound-tight, but she was relaxing into it and the spiritual congress was with her.

She turned down the volume on Mel's uninterrupted directions and was going off the building schematics displayed in hologram on her helmet's little teleprompter in front of her right eye. Mel was terrible at these kinds of directions because her natural orientation was to face others so that her own right and left were opposite to those of the person she directed. Often, but not always—and that was the most confusing part—she would give her own left or right in her instructions, especially when situations were really tense. Pez could still hear Mel, but only softly and wasn't really listening to her.

The buildings schematics were light blue with black lines and her route was highlighted in orange, turns easy to follow, and the Whirling Vortexes were each indicated by a hot pink dot. She was moving towards a large air shaft with steel cutback stairs connected to one side, a steel ladder to another, some lift tubes to yet another, and space at the back wall to drop a hovercraft down. They had fourteen stories to descend through from the ground floor and Pez wanted to do it in one fell swoop. She didn't care to fight every secret police person in the building; just get her friends safely out. Evenrude carried five textile armor jump-suits in a backpack in the band's sizes, and five fanny-pack shield generators. The jump suits weren't fashionable, particularly by the empires standards, but they were immensely practical; at least for this situation.

Pez got to the lip and stepped right off into free-fall igniting some thrusters for guidance and control using her skullcap. Her platoon members did the same and each made as spectacular a landing as Pez did, being highly practiced with the suits. Other platoons were entering from the other sides of secret Police HQ, and still others had landed on the roof some sixty stories above ground and were making a fighting descent. Yet other platoons were making their ways down tunnels connecting with the HQ sub-basement levels. A dozen companies surrounded the building, and had heavy armored hover vehicles with big weapons systems. Combat shuttles, Astro-Phantoms and Hunter Terminators covered them from the air and *Thunderbolt* covered them from space.

As soon as Pez's feet set down, AMHB's came at her from down one of the three corridors connecting to the airshaft at this level. She noticed them because Evenrude had one blown into scorched pieces before his feet touched down. Johnson popped a grenade into one followed by some heavy blaster fire and the five AMHB's around it were all wearing it. Two continuous-fire blasters ripped into another one from Mercuries pistols taking hardly more than a second to wreck it. Various forms of fire flashed down the corridor from other landing members of Pez Platoon, some quite explosive, and only little AMHB pieces remained smoking and sizzling on the floor down that corridor. Just the elite best had been chosen for this platoon.

Mel was screaming near hysterically so Pez upped the volume and listened. Mel was saying, "You have to hurry! They're taking them out of their cells now!"

"Are you hooked into the building computer and sensors?" Pez asked.

"I run them!" Mel declared, "and I'm rerouting the optics on you to section three of sublevel nine, to get them responding to the wrong location."

Pez was sprinting with a little thruster assist as she informed Mel, "I'm going as fast as I can."

"Well that doesn't appear to be fast enough," Mel told her.

"Keep them highlighted for me Mel and please refrain from any verbal directions. Your visual ones are superb."

A rather secure looking door lay directly ahead and four AMHB's were standing in front of it in the process of targeting Pez and her group. One missile from Evenrude's four-tube launcher wasted the four AMHB's *and* blew the door wide open. Pez didn't even slow going through. The five hot pink dots were on the move and Pez was now shortening her end of the orange route faster than it was lengthening at the other end. An AMHB stepped out of a doorway ten inches in front of Pez and she hit her booster for half a second, bending and adjusting her suit's trajectory at the same moment, to collide with the android bowling it over; and just in the second it took Mercury to hop over it he planted 81 blaster bolts into its sensor array with his tri-barrel continuous-fire pistols making it blind, deaf and brainless.

Pez had passed into a large anti-room with another sealed door directly ahead and blew it open using a small missile from the shoulder of her suit with her skullcap. Through that door was a secure area with armed personnel. They wore textile armor and had weak shields—like the fanny packs—and fired only standard blaster rifles and pistols. They sure weren't ready for this platoon. Pez didn't even slow down. She fired with both hands in her thrusters-assisted and suit electro-hydraulics assisted sprint at about 28 MPH.

Serious security doors confronted them ahead with AMHB's and personnel converging on it. Pez fired a suit missile from her other shoulder as much for balance as to take down what was in front of them. Grenades and missiles from her platoon turned it all into smoky invisibility and bright core explosions. Pez shifted to a combo of night vision and X-ray vision the moment the heat flares subsided to get through that mess. She stayed on her route still reducing the length of the orange line to the hot pink dots on her display. An Armored Heavy Shielded Robo-weapons systems, or an AHSR for short, hovered its way around a corner to hang in their path. Pez hit it with a six-round burst of grenades while cutting into its shields with her heavy blaster fire and Mercury had both pistols burning into it. Two suit missiles, one from each of Evenrude's shoulders, hit the thing together while his heavy tripod blaster drilled it, blowing it into smoke and particles.

The shock wave from the explosion the AHSR made blowing up brought Pez practically to a standstill for just a moment. She powered forward with muscle, electro-hydraulics and thrusters, getting her speed back up. In her peripheral vision she noticed a ball mounted blaster in the ceiling tracking her and twisted her torso as she ran to get a suit missile into the blaster. It got a single blast off before the missile turned it to dripping slag and Pez's shields handled that nicely.

Another very secure door required one of Evenrude's larger missiles from his four-tube launcher and a path far wider than the doorframe that had been there opened up for them. The shockwave slowed her down but Pez pushed on determinedly. She entered a cell block with secure doors along the wall to her right and a blank metal wall to her left. Imprisoned people cried for help from behind their cell doors and banged on them. Pez asked, "Mel, can you get the cell block doors open?"

"Of course. Which ones do you want?"

"How about all of them," Pez suggested.

"Done!" Mel exclaimed; as the doors on the block Pez was running down swooshed open disappearing into the walls.

Peeking into one as she ran by Pez viewed an old woman on her toilet, suddenly exposed by lack of a door. Pez called out already passed, "Sorry!"

Mel opened all the doors between cell blocks and locked them into that setting so Pez and her platoon would no longer have to spend ordnance blowing them up. Evenrude had a hover reloader following along with the platoon knowing how quickly Pez could go through ammo. Now Pez had to dodge disoriented prisoners who'd wandered out of their cells as she tore down the hall. Most all of them backed into the wall or jumped back in their cells as the huge suited Space Marines came stomping through the cell block. This is how it went through the next cell block too. Pez was pouring on speed.

Pez had to take steel stairs with cut-backs since she wasn't about to get on a tube or a lift. The moment she entered the well she took fire from above and below at the same time and she sent a three-round burst of grenades up while shooting heavy blaster fire down as she descended the stairs. There was no blaster fire from above any longer when Evenrude entered right behind her. Johnson, Mercury and the rest of the platoon entered the stair well. The band had been brought four more levels down and Pez took each stair case in a single bound using a foot on the wall at the bottom to stop and push off from. The orange route line was shrinking in her display.

At sublevel 18 Pez pushed off the wall at the bottom at a right angle to the direction of the next set of stairs, to pass into a foyer with lift tubes at the intersection of three hallways. There were armed personnel in all three corridors and an AHSR weapons systems right in the foyer. Her shoulder missile blew on its shields and armor right before her shoulder put it into flight. Her six-round burst of grenades was joined by a pair of Johnson's suit missiles to plaster the robo along one wall and the ceiling, dripping washers and ball bearings with its fluids down on the floor. The torn machinery looked almost like gore as Pez passed, gaining speed again and taking fire on her shields. Her three special guardians were beside and right behind her firing like mad. Following her orange route Pez was headed down the hall which had a sign designating it the "Medically Supervised Torture Unit."

Having read the sign Evenrude told her, "I think we should have Central Intellegence collect the doctors on this unit."

"That might be empathy generating for the doctors here," Pez commented.

"Excellent idea!" Swanson enthused from *SMT-1.*

Ming informed Pez from *Thunderbolt's* cockpit with both babies on her lap, "Super-agent Green said she had some errands on the surface, and took the Astro-Phantom from our bay to get down. How is your mission going?"

"I'm a little busy, my love," Pez told her as she shredded a secret policeman with her heavy blaster. "We don't have the band members yet. Let me call you back."

"Well be careful," Ming told her.

They got to the door that two of the hot pink dots were right on the other side of. Pez couldn't see through it because it was lead-lined. She inquired, "Mel, I thought you had all the doors open, sweetheart?"

"That one was already off the grid in permanent manual mode," Mel told her defensively.

One member of her platoon came forward with a two-handed tripod mini-beam which was a fifteen-inch diameter tube about four feet long, the outer casing all pure carbon plate. He lit it up on the locking mechanism within and in less than two seconds a six-inch hole with glowing red edges was there in the door. Evenrude put his tripod blaster barrel in the hole and shoved the door into the wall on its tracks with little resistance, then stepped through first. He threw the strap of his missile launcher over his head to un-holster his blaster pistol in a smooth quick move and proceeded to accurately hit two guards. Pez double tapped an armed guard with her blaster rifle as she entered. Pogo and Frisbie were naked and shackled, huddled against the wall. Pez removed Evenrude's backpack which required his utter cooperation, and found the two men's jumpsuits. The fanny-packs were all the same so she just grabbed two and handed them each one.

Frisbie said with a heavy heart and vibe of defeat, "We'll never get out of this place; and there's no way off the planet with all the war ships orbiting."

"Those would be mine," Pez told him, "and there's no way they're stopping us from getting out of this building. We must collect the girls first though."

To Evenrude she said, "Send some squads to make sure all the doctors on this unit are captured and secured."

"Aye, aye ma'am."

Pez walked briskly into the hallway while a Space Marine with a device to use on the shackles freed Pogo and Frisbie. She arrived at the door with three hot pink dots behind it and the man with the carbon tube removed the whole locking mechanism to the atomic level. Evenrude was there to slide this door across with his blaster's muzzle and enter the room first. He took out the two guards. Whiffle, naked and in shackles, jumped a doctor and pushed her thumbs into his brains through his eyeballs. A Space Marine with a little laser device got the shackles off the girls. Whiffle revealed. "They were about to do stuff that would scar and cripple us forever."

"Put on your fanny pack shield, sweetheart, and get it turned on. Here's my side arm for protection."

Whiffle got the blaster pistol into her hand liking the feel of it in this situation. She had to set it down to get her textile armor jump suit and fanny-pack on. Taking the pistol back up she tested her aim on the prone doctor's thigh and was pleased with the result. They all left the room and headed off the unit.

Mel came on to inform them, "They've rigged the stairwell, tubes and lifts up from your level with explosives. That airshaft you came down ends on level 14, four levels above you. No tunnels connect with your level. Two levels down there's a mag-lev rail station on a special tunnel-line to the government legislation building, the Regent's mansion and the Adherence Examiner's HQ."

"Is that your recommendation Mel?"

"Either that or I could trigger the explosives in the lift shaft and get the lifts below this floor, hopefully clearing it for your platoon to go up."

"Let's try that first since our support is all directly above us," Pez suggested.

A very loud explosion shook the ground and dust came through the air vents carrying traces of explosives. Pez thought, *Those imperials sure didn't mess around. That was one big explosion.*

"How does it look, Mel," Pez asked.

"The explosion took out most of the sensors so you'll need to get eyes on it." Mel reported.

Evenrude was already sending a squad to check it out. Pez told Mel, "Blow the bombs in the tubes and stairwell too so they won't know which way we're going."

"Right away."

Explosions rocked the floor as the dust from the vents became heavy. Pez's suit was analyzing the explosive traces. At least the ceiling above them hadn't caved in. Scouts from her platoon reported back on all three sites. Four stair-cases were smashed together making quite a barrier on their landing in the stairwell. Further booby traps were in place in the tubes, and the lift shaft was clear all the way up to the 60th floor, but on each sublevel floor AMHB's and AHSR weapons systems were waiting with armed personnel to shoot anything going up as it passed. Swanson informed his SCG, "A company of Space Marines has commandeered a mag-lev train and is coming into the station two floors below you. It might be more pleasant leaving by train and we've secured the Government Legislation Building which is the first stop north on your elite line; I'll let you know when they've cleared the station and have a squad on their way up to you."

Evenrude told her, "I could get us up the shaft without casualties by clearing the shaft opening at each floor, but it would take longer and each band member would need to be piggy backed to the top."

Still clinging to Pez's suit Hoola voiced her opinion, "I'd rather take the train."

"The train it is," Pez told her.

Whiffle asked, "I thought the revolution wasn't for another couple of weeks; like what happened?"

"We had to move it up since Monarch discovered the solarium deposits trailing off the Om star system and was planning an invasion there, and of Rocky. It's pretty much over once I get you guys out and onto *Thunderbolt.*"

Only half-tracking the conversation, and still fairly certain he was either going to die or get tortured to death, Frisbie asked, "Who won?"

"We did," Pez told him sternly, "or I wouldn't be here getting you out."

"Then how come we're still in a war zone?" he demanded.

"New Monarch is one of a handful of planets which did not go into total revolt, though I understand that almost no one earning below a million dags per year showed up for their jobs on New Monarch as far as the civilian world goes."

Mel stated to all of them, "The Secret Police and Adherence Examiners in general are about the most susceptible to propaganda and brainwashing, score lowest on empathy scales, and their psyches are fear-based and highly defensive!"

"How bad is it here?" Frisbie wanted to know.

"We control space and we control the air. Every military installation we can find on the surface is being blown up. I thought I'd better get you all out before a ground war starts here."

"They were about to start surgically removing parts so I'm glad you did." Hoola said gratefully.

Evenrude reported, "All doctors on this unit have been secured, except the one Whiffle killed, and we have four more passengers for the train. One victim was already a corpse when we got to her and one will require a full medical unit to move. A medical squad is on the way up and the mag.-lev train station has been cleared and secured. Your train awaits you, SCG."

Pez let Evenrude lead the way down to the station. The Space Marine with the beam weapon simply aimed it at the floor, and moved it around a bit to make the hole wide enough, and presto, they had a way down to the next floor and a good beginning on one through the floor after that, though the stairs would be cleared from that level to the one below it. Pez dropped through the hole with the rim still glowing bright red; after Evenrude landed. Johnson and Mercury were right behind her. The band members were handed down very carefully. Evenrude had to duck a little bit since the ceiling was only eight feet high and he was nearly 8 ft. 4 inches in his suit. Mercury, the most compact of her three main guards, was just able to stand upright and was the one who caught hold of the band members from the bottom.

A platoon from the company holding the station joined them under their home-made exit, and once Pez's troops were all down, a squad of new arrivals went up with the medical staff to retrieve the non-ambulatory torture victim plus the other three from the torture unit.

Pez Platoon took the stairs which were clear down to the last level. The Space Marine Company had cleared this floor so they had to step over a fair few imperial bodies. The train could go in either direction and Mel controlled the entire maglev rail system, so would prevent any other trains down the tunnel between here and the government legislation building. Fourteen companies of Space Marines continued to assault and take control of the Secret Police building and Swanson had teams of Om's CIA already on their way to claim the imperial 'doctors'.

Pez, the band, and most of the troops boarded the train which sat at the station awaiting the return of their medical team. Hoola and Whiffle sat to either side of Pez with their hands caressing her hard-shell combat suit and Hoola told her incensed. "They were going to cut off my feet and put them in a basket."

"They can't hurt you now," Pez offered as consolation.

Whiffle commented, "They weren't human any more and had no resonance with other humans; not even a tinge of empathy."

Pez analyzed, "They are spawns of the sickness and duality of ego delusion and think themselves little gods within a deaf and dumb universe come to all of this by chance and random accident. Wholly ignorant of their true natures they defile them in their vain attempt to corrupt what is divine, sacred and incorruptible. Those already killed today are finding out the truth of it and those turned over to the CIA will wish for death until it comes, and then the real torment begins."

"I'd like to put those doctor's heads in baskets and help them on their way," Hoola said with anger.

"Just deserts are the domain of the cosmic intellegence sweetheart," Pez said affectionately, "and you don't want the consequences of such actions in your storehouse consciousness."

Frisbie said in a flat voice, "They were prepping me for heart surgery and meant to give my heart to some ruling family member. Some of my other organs had intended recipients too."

Feeling violated Hoola told them with charge, "They took an impression of my vagina to make adult toys for men and the one who made the impression raped me."

Pez's three guards were looking like they really wanted some fingers around the neck of that creep to pop his head into the air squeezing.

Pez promised "We will process it together as soon as the fighting is over, sweetheart."

Pogo told Pez, "I composed a moving song of new beginnings founded on love and unity, and harmonious with the magnitudes above and below, sustainable in perpetual ascent."

"How appropriate for the new reality the planets of the former empire confront," Pez replied. "I can't wait to hear it."

Pogo stated, "It seems moral anarchy is the highest state of human society and civilization until the collective goes holographic and immortal, each individual becoming the whole as it is said the Amonrahonians did."

"I see it the same way," Pez agreed. "Your music will be a foundation stone of the new culture replacing the iniquities of the old empire," Pez speculated. "The people of Mother are a precious resource of the Whirlpool Galaxy and for the Royal and White Lotus Galaxies too. I hope they are listened to."

"At this moment you have great influence with all the planets of the former empire and could get them oriented in the right direction," Pogo pointed out.

"I'll do my best," Pez promised.

"I'll listen to the people of Mother and their teachings and ethos will be reflected in our lyrics and enthusiasm," Pogo promised.

Whiffle, who was a virtuoso on saxophone, confided to Pez, "They said they were going to surgically remove my lips completely."

"They can't hurt you now, darling," Pez stated as fact reassuringly. "We do not have time at the moment for a proper critical debriefing, but we will get it all out and pacified as soon as possible, I promise."

Static and tones, clicks and whirs came into Pez's ear before her Mel Universal Interpreting Service, or MUIS, deciphered it into Om for her, "This is General Zzzsskst and I've just entered the New Monarch System with three of our largest transports of Kluzyst Space Special Forces in hard-shell combat suits, 20,000 to a transport. We should be in low orbit in twenty-six minutes."

"Be careful of all the junk floating around up there," Pez warned.

"Where would you like for us to deploy?"

"Most of the culprits are in New Haven where I already have some Space Marines, so why don't you start here. We'll secure the capital and hunt down its war criminals first, then spread from here."

"Aye, aye ma'am."

"How are things going on Monarch?" Pez asked him.

"Most of the imperial army surrendered. Only some components of the troops Malignant brought from Afrigastan and the royal guard, Secret Police and Adherence Examiners are still holding out, and only in the capital and two other cities. Those we can't kill from space and air, the allied ground troops are cleaning up quickly."

"And the emperor?"

"They had the hole his bunker is in surrounded and were arguing the virtues of methods of elimination vs methods of extraction. When I left, the eliminators seemed to be carrying the argument. There is extraordinary wind damage all over the planet here, but especially to one hemisphere of the globe. One of their ocean-going oil tankers, half a mile long, ended up fifty miles inland on top of its owner's mansion."

"Poetic justice," Pez suggested.

"I'll report to you when I'm settling into low orbit over New Haven, SCG."

"Thank you," Pez told him.

"So, the emperor's down in a hole with nowhere to run and they're going to waste him," Whiffle said with grim satisfaction.

"That sounds about the size of it," Pez agreed.

Admiral Fuji contacted Pez to tell her, "Space in the Monarch System is totally secure and we've sent the 59 task forces and the independent ships back out to finish clearing imperial space assets. There are more than 200 other independent imperial ships which did not come to Monarch and have kept at the destruction of these assets all along. I'm told some 1,100 mutinied imperial ships were lost fighting in other systems during the action in Monarch. We're getting cries for help from more than 400 worlds at the moment, and reports of absolute victory from 4,971 of them."

"Send me all the data and I'll dispatch *Justice Maker* and your super-cruiser to hot spots," Pez responded.

"There are nine more troop transports preparing to take off for New Monarch. I understand you wiped out their considerable defenses with only five ships."

"Your captains Ahab's and Starmite's courage and skills were essential to that victory, Admiral Fuji."

"They tell a somewhat different story, SCG," he informed her.

"Then I'll be sure it's my version that gets officially recordered," Pez insisted. "My drone pilots will receive their due recognition, but so will your captains."

"There was the little matter of blind ships missing wildly from less than a hundred miles away, considered point blank range like a blaster-barrel touching the head," Fuji pointed out.

"I did my duty," Pez admitted.

"Some of our imperial fleet prisoners are begging to know more about our secret sensor white-out and shield penetrator weapons," Fuji told her.

"Only the accomplishment of the rainbow body and the ability to see auras could deliver such weapons, and they would only ever be employed to protect the weak and innocent from harm;" Pez stated.

"I'm almost at jump speed and headed for the Hasbin system in Whirlpool. I'm bringing a hospital ship and 22 giant transport freighters with food, materials, and emergency relief personnel."

"I'm really glad to hear that; they truly need it," Pez told him, ending the call with a salute.

The hover litter and medical team boarded the train and the troops watching the perimeter mounted it after them. Each band member had been armed from their reloader, which had to go on its side to fit in a baggage car. They'd all taken the opportunity to reload, or to get armed as in the case of the band. Pez got her pistol back. Their train contained sixteen cars plus an engine at each end. It was powered down, resting on its lower rails at the moment. The train rose as it surged forward, powered up in a micro-second, with the engines straining at the bitt. They were pressed into the seat backs with the acceleration and into a 20-story deep narrow tunnel with lights blurring by to one side out the windows. Ordinarily the train would reach 180 MPH on this short run, about two-thirds its maximum, but Mel had taken control of the train and was braking as fast as the thing was possibly capable short of hitting something immoveable, which is otherwise what they would be doing momentarily.

Frisbie went air-borne to smash feet-first, horizontal to the floor of the car, into the far wall at the front and broke his leg. Everyone else merely bashed into the seatbacks in front of them. Mel told Pez and her three main guards, "They've filled the tunnel ahead with transportation containers full of heavy materials. They're busy doing the same behind you. There are access tunnels ahead and behind they are operating out of, and both have considerable forces at their disposals."

Listening in Swanson told Pez, "I have a battalion of Space Marines on the way to each of those access tunnels, and troops headed down the tracks to you from both directions."

"Thanks Captain."

Evenrude reported, "Our hover blasters and missile platforms are in baggage with no space in this tunnel to get them out."

Pez told Mel, "Detach the engines at each end of our train, run them forward a hundred yards, then shut down all power to this line and lock up the brakes on those engines."

"I'm doing it now."

"That ought to keep any really heavy fire off our train for a little while, Pez said hopefully.

"I've sent two platoons to each end of our train," Evenrude told her.

Space Marine Parsuns got Frisbie's leg set and formed a fast hardening cast around it. He would carry Frisbie out if need be. Pennine stuck with Pogo and Suzuki with Tramp. Johnson and Mercury would stick to Hoola and Whiffle, and Pez and Evenrude would protect all of them. The shooting started with some hover beams and blasters blowing up their train engines, though each left enough scrap on the track to continue shielding the train from each end. Canister missiles couldn't decrease either by much. Small arms fire buzzed all about.

Swanson came on to say, "You've got at least a full division of imperials in each tunnel. I'm sending reinforcements to each battalion and they're fighting their ways down those tunnels now. I've recalled everyone from the Secret Police HQ and redirected them to those tunnels. We can crater the whole building from space later."

The fighting became intense at each end of the train with imperials in superior numbers charging forward. The Space Marines stayed low behind cover, and so far, had been able to stem the advance by piling corpses on the ground in front of them. In the direction they'd come from the imperials were trying to slip a heavy blaster hover through the space between the slag of the blown-up engine and the tunnel wall. Some Space Marine shoulder launcher missiles turned it to scrap and debris wedged in there good to make sure no more would stand a chance of fitting through. The fighting in front of them was becoming desperate.

Mel came on to inform Pez, "There is a maintenance crawl space with a hatch directly over the train in the tunnel ceiling and two platoons of imperials are on their way down it to you."

"Thanks Mel, I'm on my way to the roof," Pez replied.

Evenrude told her, "I'm putting half your platoon on the roof with you and I'm taking a squad of eight to help defend the front end where the fighting is more severe, and where we've taken some casualties. I'll come to you if you need me. Just holler."

Pez went out the front of the car and climbed to the roof from between cars since the windows didn't open in them. She was joined by half her platoon on the roofs of the center two cars, all focused on the hatch above.

Evenrude strode to the front of the train along side it beside the tracks. When his shields started taking hits Evenrude raised his missile launcher and spread four across the width of the tunnel at the imperial front line. He dropped the launcher and pulled out his automatic 40mm grenade gun, emptying a 90-round jungle clip as he continued keeping his stride forward. By the time his magazine was empty only sporadic fire was coming from the imperials so he used the lull to eject the clip and slam in another. He gave them a five-shot burst from the new clip while tearing his heavy tripod blaster into them on full automatic fire. When he came to his own troop's very front line he casually took cover, then started shooting again. Evenrude and the eight men he brought held the imperial advance and made all the difference for the moment.

Pez was on the roof aiming both her weapons at the ceiling hatch. There was no sensor up there and no spy hole in the hatch. Pez had checked, scanning it with her suit. The imperials wouldn't know what was waiting until they opened that hatch. She had twenty Space Marines up there with her and 52 more below with the band. She'd had the ones in the train move back two cars so they wouldn't be in the line of fire from the hatch. Pez was wholly concentrated one-pointed on that hatch. The spiritual congress was in full force burning through Pez's channels and meridians, one with her consciousness, and nearly twenty-two billion strong.

The heavy metal hatch began swinging down to vertical on its hinges and when it was only about nine inches open, Pez's first grenade shot right in followed by a stream of thirty more from her. A few launcher missiles and at least a dozen suit missiles went through the hole in the ceiling by the time Pez's fifth grenade was passed, and the metal hatch was blown back up through the hole by this assault. After their first barrage they held their fire for a while as nothing but smoke came through the hole.

Then hand grenades poured down. All twenty-one Space Marine suits hit thrusters and made for the ceiling out and away from the car roof they launched from scattering. Pez had caught one of the first gernades to fall and heaved it back up through the hole as she got away from the car beneath her. At least a hundred rained down in a few seconds. One of the imperials must have missed the hole with his because there were two distinct explosions up in the ceiling and Pez had thrown only the one grenade. Two train cars were blown to skids and chassis, and shrapnel flared on the shields of the Space Marines hovering up by the ceiling.

Imperials in combat suits began dropping one at a time out of the hole and Pez's group had no trouble killing each one as they came down. They even got ahead of the game and got one imperial while only his legs were yet through the hole, to blow the suit up in the crawl space tunnel. Pez shot some grenades in right after the explosion for good measure. The suits stopped dropping out of the hole, and again only smoke came out of it. There was a pause, and the only sounds were from the ends of the train where battles were being fought.

A circle of metal on the ceiling of the tunnel, five meters from the hole where the hatch had been, glowed red. Pez ordered the

Space Marine with the portable mini-beam to the train roof with his weapon. The glow dripped molten metal, then just disappeared and was gone, the beam drilling through the wrecked chassis below on the ground. The hole was made bigger, just like they'd done to the floor to get down from sublevel 18. Pez had her beam weapon operator start a hole from their side of the ceiling, a meter from the hole the imperials were making, but at far more of an angle. The imperials finished theirs first.

Now two suited imperials dropped at the same time firing and the pairs came rapidly. Pez's elite unit killed the dropping imperials rapidly. Then they had their own hole in the ceiling, with their beam slanted down the crawl space, slowing the progress of pairs dropping down. Pez emptied her grenade magazine into their new slanted hole down the length of the crawl space, then changed it out for a new magazine. A bunch of suit and launcher missiles went up through the three holes with grenades and blaster fire from Pez's group, and a strip from the ceiling collapsed onto the train and train-tunnel floor, dropping what had been the floor of the crawl space over them to the ground. A bunch of imperial suits hit the ground at free fall to get crushed by falling hunks of concrete and metal. Some hung cleverly in the air using their suit thrusters, out from under falling debris, and these made really easy targets for Pez and her gang.

The imperials were backed up at the edge of their open tunnel mouth at the curving join of the train tunnel's side wall and ceiling, which were missing some layers and volume at that spot. Pez's people were spread out, and had cover. They could easily concentrate fire on the small access those imperials had to the train tunnel. Evenrude let her know from the front of the train where he was fighting, "We've had to pull back a car and a half and will be losing more ground soon. There are just too many of them."

"Do you need more men?" Pez asked.

"There's only so much cover here and we've only lost thirteen of ours at this end of the train, so I still have almost two platoons. We put down well over two companies of imperials so far. The tracks are just littered with them several deep."

"Well they're coming out of the ceiling above us too, attacking both ends and the middle."

"How's your squad?" Evenrude inquired.

"One wounded, noncritically, and no casualties. We have the imperials beaten back to a little crawl space opening we are concentrating fire on, and have the upper hand, at least for the moment on them."

Mel told Pez, "two more platoons of imperials are on their way down the crawl space towards you, and they're bringing a tactical nuke."

"Thanks Mel, I'm on it," Pez replied. To Johnson and Mercury she said, "Get some explosives, a four-tube missile launcher and some grenade mags out of the reloader in the baggage car, and then meet me on the roof."

"Aye, aye ma'am."

To her squad she said, "Close on that crawl space opening, and keep continuous fire on it. Does anyone have one of the bigger launcher missiles?"

"I have two left in my launcher."

"Once we clear the front of the opening, get yourself lined up to put both down the length of the crawl space," she told him.

"Will do, SCG"

Twenty of them converged their fire. Their wounded comrade had been brought to the car where the band and the non-ambulatory patient were, so he could receive medical treatment. They cleared the crawl space opening, blowing the two imperials squeezed side by side in the front, in a spray of pieces and fluids into the two behind, splattering their face masks with goo, right before those two, and the two behind them were cremated. Several more rows back were decimated before the two missiles, fired at one time, shot down the crawl space side by side. It was a good aim and they stormed down the length without skimming sides clear to the right-angle turn at the end of it, where the first ones of the two platoons were already half around the bend of the turn. An imperial raising his head to look far forward had a missile brush by each side of his helmet, and knew in that moment he was dead. The whole of both platoons, thanks to the heavy explosives they lugged, were wiped out before the blast triggered the nuke ending platoons and crawl space tunnel alike, and ending the attack from the middle.

General Zzzsskst called to inform Pez that he was in low orbit over New Haven, in touch with Captain Swanson, and his first shuttles would be away in moments. The Kluzyst were bigger than Space Marines and would present an intimidating sight for yellow sun humans. They weren't as tough as Space Marines, but they were far scarier looking. Much of their volume was gas.

Evenrude informed her, "We're practically back to the two wasted cars beneath that collapsed section of ceiling. This is becoming critical. We've had some more casualties."

Johnson, Mercury and half a platoon met Pez on the roof. Pez reloaded, then they headed towards the front of the train, and hadn't far to go. Evenrude's men were still backing up and abandoning the intact car in front of the two destroyed ones. Imperials were on the roof of that one, coming through its interior, and down both sides thickly. It made it hard to miss one.

Johnson sent a missile forward along each side if the train, one down the interior of the intact car, and one screaming along only inches over its roof, while Pez and others emptied entire 90-round magazines of 40mm grenades and countless blaster bolts into the oncoming imperials. Thanks to Johnson's 4 launcher missiles the imperial advance was paused. Pez slammed another 90-rounder into her automatic grenade gun and started emptying it, while shooting off a couple of suit missiles and fired her big blaster rifle on full-auto. They came as fast as she and her forces could put them down. Her troops at the rear of the train were also retreating. The imperials rushed them in total aggression, headless of their heavy casualties.

The Space Marines holding the tail of the train had gotten all they could out of the reloader in the baggage car before retreating back and abandoning it. They would detonate the reloader remotely once they were pushed back beyond its range of destruction. Evenrude had sent four men back to carry all the suit and launcher missiles they could lug, and three to carry grenade cartridges, when the troops at the rear of the train had been salvaging what they could from the reloader. Ammo was getting used quickly and spent well. What they had would not be enough.

Pez illuminated light so bright in the imperial's ranks that every Space Marine facemask went full dark to save their eyes. Not even half the imperial army were in suits, wearing only textile armor with fiberglass armor plates in their vests. Several imperials whose eyes were an inch from a micro-sun core went irreversibly blind. For the rest, the after effect took more than a minute to get over. The imperials in suits still had their masks blacked out when the Space Marines at the front of the train charged, hitting them with everything they had. The impairment of more than half of the imperial's vision, and with the momentum built up by the Space Marines, forty yards of imperial ranks were chewed through before those forces rallied and seriously pushed back.

Evenrude led a fighting retreat all the way back to where they'd started their charge from. The rear defenders had lost enough ground now to blow the baggage car, and at least sixty imperials went to pieces or splattered on walls and ceiling from the blast. It gave pause, though only briefly, to the assault on the rear. Pez sprouted blinding suns through the ranks of imperials attacking the rear of the train, and like lightning, Johnson blasted horizontal using his booster to crash shoulder first into two disoriented and blinded imperials trying to set up a heavy tripod 60mm grenade machine gun. The one he hit died of shattered ribs on impact skewering the organs of his thoracic cavity, and the man's head, at like 90 MPH, killed the second one. Between them their bodies knocked over fourteen more imperials. Pez planted more suns on the imperials while Johnson finished getting the big gun operational, and Mercury charged up beside him firing his automatic shotgun with adamantine pyramid shield and armor shredding rounds. The big eight gauge mowed them down as he advanced.

More Space Marines charged behind Mercury. Pez planted more suns. Johnson started chopping them to little pieces with the 60mm grenade machine gun, the first one not two meters away, then making his way back both rapidly and thoroughly. Body parts were in the air and landing with splats; heads with thuds. Mercury and another Space Marine were ready with a second 1,200-lb. magazine for the big gun when Johnson spent the last, and they changed it out in ten seconds while Pez sprouted suns.

Once the second magazine was spent they had to retreat, so Johnson set some small magnetic bombs to the underside of the weapon before backing up toward their previous position. The imperials brought two more 1,200-lb. mags for the gun and got one hooked in. Johnson detonated the small bombs which destroyed the weapon and blew its fresh magazine, and *that* explosion blew the second one they'd dragged out killing everyone for many meters around the gun. They'd just accomplished a great deal and took down more than three companies with that charge. It wasn't enough though, and there were still too many of them. Ammo was running low.

The Space Marines retreated from both ends of the train until they were all in one group around the car the band was in. Nothing but blasters, the portable beam, and a few hand grenades remained. Pez illuminated suns so bright and numerous that the shooting completely stopped for a moment. Even blind, the front lines were pressed forward by those in back, advancing irrevocably. Casualties were coming quicker and mounting. If they were rushed, the fighting was so close already, it would become hand to hand.

Swanson informed Pez, "The troops trying to get to you down the access tunnels are encountering fierce resistance, though making steady progress. We think these troops are chemically controlled and motivated."

"I don't think we can last more than a few more minutes," Pez explained, "if that."

Swanson informed her, "The troops coming down the tracks from the Government Legislation Building Station were ambushed and are still trying to punch their way through."

"What about down the tracks the other way?" Pez inquired as she blew through an imperial face mask and face with her blaster rifle, and fired a blaster pistol into an unsuited imperial's temple.

Swanson answered, "Colonel Bleep and the Army Space Special Forces are coming from that direction and he's taken charge of that advance. I know they encountered resistance but I don't know how close they are."

The space Marine standing next to Pez went down with his chest armor holed in the center smoking. An imperial came within a meter of Pez, her shields so far taking his blasts. Her foot between his legs sent him backwards, and his head split open on the face mask of the hard-shell combat suit of the imperial behind him, gumming up that one's sensors and smearing his mask with brains and blood he couldn't see through. So he did not see Pez step forward and employ 'kick with heel' releasing her internal energy and powering the hydraulics to send him backwards into imperials at bone crushing speed.

The fusion battery pack on Pez's heavy blaster rifle drained of life, so she dropped the rifle and drew her carbon edged adamantine sword, taking off an imperial's head in the unsheathing. Her blaster pistol was melting an imperial's face mask while putting holes in his brain. Her sweep the lotus kick redirected a blaster rifle barrel off her shields to rip into imperial flesh instead. The Space Marine to her other side went down. Her sword went through textile armor, then through the imperial and out the textile armor on the other side, and she powered it forward to catch a second imperial body on her sword before pulling it free with a twist. Whiffle was firing a blaster rifle through the broken-out train window. Hoola's head pooped up beside hers and she unloaded a jungle clip out her automatic 40mm grenade gun with both hands, and deadly accuracy. Mel captured that image of Hoola for posterity.

Evenrude held his tripod blaster by the barrel in both hands and was batting imperials into the air and into each other, dead on impact, projectile weapons post mortem, and barriers after that. He was so quick he always had at least two up in the air at once, and occasionally three. Mercury's tri-barrel continuous-fire blasters had created a wedge into the imperial front line, indented several ranks, but were spitting out their last and about to be discontinued. It was beyond desperate bordering on hopeless.

Clouds of blood erupted around Pez from anything in sword's reach. Evenrude was blown sideways inside the train by an explosion. Johnson's shields hit zero and stayed there, scorches charring his armor black all over, and the hard shell breached allowing the next bolt into his flesh. Mercury was fighting hand to hand. Hoola ran out of grenades and screamed in frustration. It was grim chaos. Pez took a bolt through her shoulder and realized her shields were down. There were no longer lines, imperials and Space Marines all mixed up.

Pez noticed a commotion to their rear. Schwin's voice announced, "We're here!"

There was no room for an Astro-Phantom in this tunnel and Pez was pretty sure a Corvette Thunder wouldn't even fit in here. She asked Schwin, "In what?!"

Imperials mowed down in great numbers drew Pez's attention to the long slender Comet Interceptor and she knew Schwin had to be the pilot. She called to her troops to retreat at once to the back of the train. That's when she noticed Colonel Bleep's helmet sticking out the top of a heavy armored command hover-tank leading eight hover main battle tanks. Other armored hover craft were beating the imperials back down their access tunnel. Super-Agent Green pulled up in a hover armored personnel carrier and lowered the ramp for Pez and the band while picking the imperials off with her twin class three blasters. She said through Pez's coms, "I thought you might like a ride."

"Thanks," Pez said in the midst of running an imperial through the chest with her sword.

Two companies of Space Special Forces were dismounting from hover transports and joining the fight. The imperials were going down nicely. Pez waited till there were none alive or in one piece several cars forward, before getting the band aboard the hover APC Green was driving and shooting from. Pez rushed to Evenrude. Her display showed that he was alive but unconscious. Pennine helped Pez get Evenrude aboard the APC, and Parsuns pulled Johnson aboard with Mercury's help. Mercury's suit was charcoal colored but his shell had not been holed. They'd had 240 troops to begin and only 89 were now alive, most of those wounded, but they'd put down about 1,950 imperials chemically induced to terminate them at all costs.

They got Johnson's suit off and him onto an ER gurney with life support systems, IV's, crash cart, and all kinds of medical devices. Parsuns was a field medic and got to work scanning, then following procedures. Pennine assisted him. Pez and Mercury got Evenrude out of his suit. He had a concussion but no other wounds. Pez got out of her own and checked out her shoulder, cauterized on both sides. Some muscle had been drilled through which ached and throbbed terribly, and became shooting pain if she moved her left arm or shoulder. The burned tissue was less than half an inch across. The hole through her shoulder was narrower than a signature stylus. It would take her months to restore strength and flexibility, but she would do it. Hoola and Whiffle were at Pez's side, applying salves to her burn and giving her pain meds and kisses.

CHAPTER TWENTY-THREE

Super-Agent Green flew them efficiently down the track the way they'd come with a four hover tank escort, and up a shaft just past the Secret Police HQ. At street level the frightening Kluzyst in space combat suits were everywhere. Things appeared quite orderly up here. Schwin stayed at the battle to dice up imperials with her fighter's nose blasters and because her comet interceptor was too long to turn around in the tunnel.

Pez asked Super-Agent Green, "What kind of errand were you running? And how did you end up in our tunnel with an APC?"

"The spiritual congress directed me to pick up a few things is all," Green replied enigmatically.

"Like what exactly did they want you to pick up?" Pez pushed.

"Just Colonel Bleep and an APC so I could collect you and the band," she clarified.

"I hadn't even found and reached the band yet when you left," Pez said, calculating in her mind.

"Call it Amonrahonian premonition," Green suggested.

"Who are you?" Pez asked in awe.

"I've been the agent of the Wu for 300 generations," Green informed her.

Pez felt the connection, and trust so potent it was as strong as what she had with Sarhi and Ming. Still calculating Pez asked Green, "Then I've known you 13 generations longer than I've known Sarhi?"

"You have," she confirmed. "You have another agent, born this time around on Ahumdulilah, named Renu, who has been with you since three generations after you connected for the first time with

Sarhi. She hasn't shown herself to you yet but she followed you on both of the band's tours and was always watching over you."

"I want to meet her," Pez said with need.

"She desperately wants to meet you and join your entourage to study with you, and remain in your presence."

"Well where is she," Pez wanted to know.

"Awaiting your arrival on *Thunderbolt*," Green told her. "There's a shuttle waiting for us, to bring you to your ship."

Green pulled up to a Space Marine Combat Shuttle and parked the hover APC next to it. Pez asked her, "Will you be joining us as well?"

"I had certainly hoped to now that my work here is done," Green informed her.

"I'd like that," Pez agreed. Then she asked, "Why didn't you tell me?"

"Sarhi asked me not to unless you specifically asked," Green answered. "She thought it would have more impact that way."

"She was right about *that*," Pez confirmed.

Green mentioned, "Ming has invited me for a sleepover tonight."

Pez said, enchanted at the prospect, "That sounds like fun. I could use a celebration about now."

They got Johnson on a medical transport headed for Captain Quicksilver's cruiser since it had a complete medical facility. Evenrude came around and insisted on going with Pez to *Thunderbolt*. Frisbie was going to Quicksilver's ship too, to get that leg into a regeneration vat so the bone could knit. Mercury helped Evenrude onto the shuttle since he was yet wobbly. The band, Green and Pez climbed aboard too. Their young female shuttle pilot was determined to impress Pez with her flying and went maximum acceleration nearly into low orbit. Even with a braking booster she could not dump enough speed. She banged the frame of the bay doors coming into Thunderbolt's docking bay, putting a big dent in the side of the shuttle, and totally destroyed the electro-hydraulic landing legs smacking down so hard. Everyone's spine got compressed, and Pez bruised her hip on the side of her seat. The timing was a bit off but some real piloting skill had been evident, and the girl truly had the right disposition as far as Pez was concerned.

Pez stuck her head in the cockpit and told the pilot, who was being chewed out by her co-pilot, "You're getting it, and will have the timing right next time. Don't worry about the dent or the landing hydraulics; Captain Spalding will repair it. Intuitive pilots are rare so I want you in Schwin's and Konax's training program ASAP. I'll have my assistant, Mel, inform the Lt. Commanders to expect you. I like your technique."

The pilot was delighted and her co-pilot in shock. They had to take off after letting their passengers out to go make an emergency landing on *Auxiliary 2* for repairs. Mel told both Konax, who was in Monarch with Swenah docked to a Super-auxiliary so *Reciprocity* could get more than just duct tape patching its hole, and Schwin, who was tearing imperials to shreds with her nose blaster as shots sparked off her shields thickly, while she supported the joint military operation in the tunnel. In the middle of the battle Schwin contacted the pilot, who was by then engaged in her emergency landing on the auxiliary, to tell the pilot her story of wrecking the hydraulics with the SCG aboard the shuttle. The two women made a real connection over the coms without compromising any precision in the maneuvers they were involved in. A month ago this pilot had been a graduating cadet from Star Fleet Academy and now she was accepted into the most elite pilot training program in the Tail of Nine with Om's greatest pilots ever.

Then the SCG contacted her to say, "*Thunderbolt's* only space shuttle was lent out and is on Mother. I want you to be my shuttle pilot, so when Spalding's people get your craft repaired, report to my ship. I'll inform Captain Quicksilver of the transfer."

"Aye, aye ma'am; I couldn't be more honored," she enthused as her co-pilot ate humble pie.

Pez took Electra from Ming as soon as she got aboard. Her daughter's hand went right to the stwound on Pez's shoulder. With her palm gently over it she climbed and wiggled her way up to get her other palm over the exit wound. As always Pez was passing her daughter internal energy, but what came back to her through her daughter's palms was multiplied exponentially, returned refined and transmuted into a pure force of cosmic intensity, and although quite brief, its healing power seemed to restore Pez's shoulder to pre-trauma and injury, wiping clean the body memory of the event by erasing it from the brain cells corresponding to the nerve endings involved, and Pez was flabbergasted.

Ming remained close and said with concern, as well as intrigue, watching Electra hone right in, "Mel told me that you're wounded."

"I was. The pain was deep and continuous, throbbing when not shooting, but Electra has just healed it good as new for me. I think I might even have full flexibility."

"She's such a good girl," Ming commented affectionately. "She was watching you through the other Space Marine's suit-sensors throughout your ground operation, and though she has eaten recently, she hasn't slept in hours."

"How's Gumby?" Pez asked.

"He's been out for a while" Ming filled her in. "He finally got his little hand on the canister missile launcher and thank the cosmic intelligence a New Monarch sensorcoms satellite caught it, blowing up, before it could enter the atmosphere and possibly blow up on the ground."

"He's getting into everything he can reach now," Pez observed.

"I've had Jard, as chief engineer on *Thunderbolt*, baby proof all the living spaces aboard," Ming let her know.

"He must have been just thrilled," Pez said sarcastically.

"He thought I was joking at first," Ming explained, "but Mel had Sarhi call him from *Reciprocity*, and after that he took the job seriously and did it very well."

"Thanks Mel," Pez told her.

"You're most welcome SCG, vbf," Mel replied. "I'm in my android body right now, bringing *Aphrodite* to dock with *Thunderbolt* so you'll have a place for our big sleep over."

"You're sleeping over in your android body Mel?" Pez asked.

"Yes, I'm on the guest list," Mel confirmed with insistence.

Pez gave Ming a look and she responded to it by hunching her shoulders and offering as excuse, "You know I have difficulty saying 'no' to people."

"There's a guest list?" Pez asked, trying to get some sense of this 'sleepover'.

"Well, a few others were quite determined to be there and I sort of lost my grip on things," Ming offered.

"How many?" Pez needed to know.

"I'm afraid you'll need to find that out from Mel. I've sort of lost track."

Electra fell asleep in Pez's arms so she got placed lovingly into her special hover crib-seat. She'd graduated to a big-girl one for toddlers. Potty training loomed on the horizon and Pez was afraid she'd be incompetent as the teacher. She was glad they made feltex lined underwear for adults just in case she was to fail miserably. She asked Mel, "How many are on the guest list, sweetheart?"

"There are actually two lists," Mel tried to explain. "There's one for those sleeping in your bed and a different list for those staying on the rollaway bed Jard's bringing."

"What's the total?" Pez demanded.

"Do you mean per bed, or both combined?" Mel inquired innocently.

"Why don't you give me all the names," Pez suggested, trying to get to the bottom of it.

"Which bed would you like me to start with?" Mel asked uncertainly.

"Mine."

"Well let me see; there's Green, Renu, Whiffle and Hoola. Jard has on his list: himself, Slinkie, Cotex, me, Pippy, Alice, Woahha and Flint. Oh! And I forgot to mention Pooh. She'll be a floater between beds."

"That's a whole lot of people Mel."

"Why do you think I'm bringing the yacht?!" Mel shot back without saying the word 'stupid' at the end, though it was sort of implied by the tone.

"It sounds kind of crowded," Pez offered her opinion.

"Just close and friendly, darling," Mel assured. "Sarhi told me to pass on to you that Electra has let her know that she is finished with nursing, and has outgrown it, so you are free to get loaded on alko, smoke and chemicals tonight."

"Where are Vegan and Atlanta?"

"They're still on *Reciprocity* and will be meeting you on Mother in a few days. Vegan has been recruited into the temporary Monarch government for the restoration and reorganization of their society."

Some of Pez's friends were watching Rocky news and it was featuring a holo-image of Hoola firing a 40mm grenade automatic gun out of a train window with a most determined expression on her face. It was a new look for the super-model and one that became an instant symbol of the entire revolution. Her captivity, torture, and even the imperial planned schedule of medical torture on her, was leaked to the news by Om CIA for their own closely guarded purposes and were detailed on the news. Holoclips of her rocking out with the Whirling Vortexes, modeling hug-me's crotch-less panties, shopping with Cher Bulwinkle and romantically kissing Vegan Casper, the new acting vice president of Monarch, were shown with the news segment.

The state of the empire address by President Nudeel was presented live from Monarch after the bit on Hoola. He explained the structure of government most planets were adopting post-liberation and how they were striving to be truly representative. He provided details on the citizen review boards that would oversee every branch of government and every office within those. Recall and termination were automatic mechanisms triggered immediately the first time an elected official deviates from the will of his or her constituents, calling for in-depth criminal investigations and incarceration of the official while such investigations were conducted.

All power was to belong at all times to the people and government officials were merely instruments of this principle. Voting would be compulsory for all adults and debates limited to proposed legislation and its anticipated benefits. Lies and false information would be punishable by life imprisonment, and attempts to disenfranchise voters would be considered treason and punishable by death. Politicians would be viewed as humble civil servants no different from the postman or dog-catcher. They would enact the will of the people who elected them and have no power over anyone nor receive any special treatment. Although their names would be a matter of public record the media and academicians would only refer to them by their district designations. Accomplishments, if any, during their term(s) of office would be recorded as accomplishments of the constituency and no politician would ever deserve mention in a history data-bead. No document created by any politician could ever be kept out of the public record. Any attempt to do such a thing would be punishable by death.

The man sounded quite sincere and had played a role in the revolution. Pez couldn't wait to get Vegan's take on him. Nudeel moved on to summarize the progress of the revolution to date. 5,407 planets had exterminated the last nest of imperials on their planets and had zero imperial assets in space within their systems; truly empire free. Task forces and independent war ships were assisting the remainder in the exterminations of these insidious pests, and the remaining tenacious tentacles yet clinging to life and property would be entirely eradicated in the three galaxies shortly, Nudeel anticipated.

The emperor had been murdered by his family in his bunker and his body offered to the revolution by them in exchange for immunity. No one had been listening. Then the royal guard had murdered the family members and tried to deal for their lives. That had been only minutes before the allies had blown the bunker recycling everything within to atoms. A number of ruling family members, and these included the Waltonraptor's and Kochoos, were handed over to the fearsome Zandarhar Intelligence Service, called the ZIS, as a first step towards diplomatic relations and it appeared things were going well along those lines. The empire's invasion of Zandarhar had not gone so well, and in fact, had gone so badly that another invasion had not been planned. Zandarhar had once had a strong alliance with Mother but had been unable to prevent it from being conquered by the empire.

As Nudeel focused on the decisive space battle of the revolution in the Monarch system, the biggest and longest any of them knew of, much of the holoclip footage was of *Reciprocity* and *Thunderbolt*. The glaring suns surrounding and hanging on the imperial ships were shown in overview of the battle zone, and some of the really spectacular ones were shown close up individually while commentary accurately explained this secret weapon of the revolution as the attainment of the rainbow body through specific advanced practices, by Cher Bulwinkle and Shudiy, her Islohar disciple from Ganahar in the Hub Galaxy.

They showed incredible high-definition close-ups of torpedoes passing clean through active shields without any interference, while it was explained how shields opened a small patch covered only by a weak film when riled up by taking fire, and that these patches could only be discerned by spiritual adepts who could see auras; again, Cher Bulwinkle and Shudiy, along with the warrior monk Bodhi. The significance of these secret weapons in achieving victory were made abundantly clear. The two secret weapon intuitive drone pilots, Ahhu and Cleo, were then portrayed with brief bios, holo-images, and some juicy gossip. Dozens of images were shown of blue streaking class one's, class two's, and whole multi-auxiliary reloading operations along with the ships they serviced and hundreds of small craft. These two heroes of the revolution were indispensable to victory and liberation and they would never be forgotten.

Other revolutionary heroes were shown, naming them and describing their feats, in ten seconds or less each, and this segment went on for more than an hour while Pez and her companions ate Ambassador Rations in front of the hologram pedestal. The whole hero thing was wrapped up with a re-run of the in-depth biography of the Khedar, also known as the Avahat, the Rajaha, the Wu, and the One. Scenes of Pez at sports and in martial arts competitions at the Clearlight school for teenagers, and then from her years in Clearlight Academy were displayed. Her destruction of the alien empire in the Xegachtznel Galaxy, which had been committing genocide of humanoids, was summarized with optics and commentary including her saving of Earth 10^5 CBS2. Pez's destruction of the Kundabuffer Empire in the Hub Galaxy was featured, and then her long undercover work touring with the Whirling Vortexes and more images of

Hoola in just her crotch-less underwear were displayed. Those Hoola pictures were always a crowd pleaser. Some of Pez's landings were also portrayed.

The grand finale capping off the Pez bio showed the consummation of Pez's and Ming's marriage, the conception of the Great Mu, which also happened to be the incident of the first 'event'; and this led to event holos and the spectra-graphical imaging of an event unfolding, seen even more clearly on a display of acoustical vibrations upon which the event meter Jard invented is based.

Pez and Ming had sat watching in utter dumbfounded disbelief even though this had been the second viewing for both of them. Pez asked no one in particular, "Haven't they heard of privacy?"

An entire half-hour segment then went into Pez's rescue of the band from the subterranean dungeons and torture chambers of the creepy Secret Police HQ building in downtown New Haven on New Monarch; their battle around the train, Pez slicing, dicing and skewering imperials with her sword—never more than a blur even in super-HD—and Hoola blowing apart imperials with her auto-grenade gun from the train window, now as famous a sight as the hug-me's holos of Hoola.

When an emperor cartoon came on that they'd already seen before they retired to the yacht, now docked to *Thunderbolt* and with an aired-up tube passage connected below the floor hatch of the airlock. Mel said with great excitement, "The planet Tiffany was so grateful to you for liberating them from Kundabuffer and for returning their treasured diamond chandelier, that they made you a replica using zircon instead of diamonds, though the big gem in the center is an actual diamond. It's stunning and I just know you're going to love it. I had Jard hang it in the dining room and move the glass-crystal one to over your dining table in your suite's sitting room."

"Thank you, Mel," Pez said as she rushed to the yacht's dining room.

Zircon was more abundant in the universe than diamond though hardly common place, and a gem prized by humans everywhere. The chandelier was magnificent and the diamond in the center was so large it could only have come from Tiffany. It was flawless and had to be at least 600 karats. Thousands of zircon gem stones, ranging from .5 to 36 karats, adorned the chandelier. This one was also an exquisite work of art and an exact replica of the original, except all but the center diamond were zircon instead. Pez did love it and decided she would leave it to the Om Intergalactic Cultural Museum just down the street from the Clearlight Monastery. This one belonged in a museum too and Pez felt a little guilty that she'd be kind of hogging it during her lifetime. She told Mel, "It is beautiful and I do love it."

"You have over 5,000 planetary government invitations to honors and awards ceremonies, close to a million invitations to celebrations and parties in your honor sponsored by various institutions and organizations, and well over three trillion sexual solicitations so far.

"Anyone truly striking?" Pez inquired about the last.

Mel told her, "I'll send you holo's of some I found exceptionally cute. If you want to sort through the whole thing you are welcome to, though you'd have to live to be well over a hundred to ever finish."

"How many are you sending then?" Pez asked.

"There are 71,814 I really like, but I know that's too many so I'm trying to get it down to the top 1,000."

"Mel! Please just send me like the top twenty, or fifty at the most."

"That will be a terrible challenge, but I'll try," Mel told her with some distaste of the task leaking through.

Renu was introduced to Pez by Super-Agent Green. She had an athletic build and was about 5-foot nine; Pez's height. Her hair was just redder than auburn and she had subtle freckles. Renu was ecstatic to meet Pez, whom she'd kept close watch on for more than nine months from a distance or by sensors, but always close enough to respond quickly, and ever ready. Meeting the Rajaha in person, face to face, was an enormously big deal to Renu. Pez said, "Hi, my name is Pez," as she stepped in to embrace Renu and pass her internal energy.

The twenty-nine year old Ahumdulilah and Islohar super-agent told her, "I'm a great admirer and so grateful to be meeting you in person."

"I'm the grateful one," Pez insisted, "for having had you watching over me."

"I had my sights lined up on Rudfuss Snydely's white sun goon's head the whole time you were in the ring with him," Renu shared, "and I took out five of the Rockerfelon's perimeter guards that night you escaped New Monarch."

"Thank you," Pez told her. "I'm glad we finally got to meet and that you're here to celebrate with us."

"You are not only my Wu, but you are also my High Priestess as a warrior-maiden of Mother," Renu informed Pez with great admiration.

"I think we would have more fun as friends and companions," Pez suggested, rather attracted to the girl.

Ming was flirting shamelessly with Super-Agent Green, who seemed to be quite enjoying it. Woahha was popping corks and pouring alko bubbly into crystal flutes to get the party going. Ahhu got Whirling Vortexes recordings from live concerts which Mel had bootlegged for her, playing on all of the yacht's speaker systems only very slightly louder than Pez could tolerate, hoping her teacher would simply adjust. In the bedroom Jard was removing some built-in furniture to make room for his giant 'emperor of the universe' rollaway bed. He had to stick his head and arms into cupboards and cabinets to remove like 120 screws with his power screw driver, but he saw it through. Someone else would have to put it all back together again. He got a Space Marine to move the actual pieces of furniture into the airlock foyer against the lockers.

The renowned neurosurgeon, Slinkie, was naked and on her forth flute. Woahha had abandoned her role as bartender to go seduce Flint who had arrived at the party. Pippy and Alice introduced Pez to two of their male counterparts in the Ahumdulilah Intelligence Service, Ben and Jerry. Cotex really wanted to connect with Woahha again and Flint had sparked a little interest in her in *Thunderbolt's* cockpit, so she joined those two in their activities. Ming kept her grip on Super-Agent Green while roping Pooh into the mix, and the integration was as harmonious as it was rewarding. Whiffle had a bit of a crush on Electra's father, Rubix, and found herself drawn into contact with him. Hoola clung to one side of Pez and Renu to the other. Ahhu, Trix and Gretle found themselves in a threesome. It was quite a realization.

The party became quite festive and the alko flowed. Ming drank too much and was a bunch of fun. Partner configurations changed and adapted as the celebration wore on, and as it turned out, Pooh really was a floater. Pez passed parcels of merit to all aboard the yacht; oceans of it. It hadn't done a bit of good and a great series of events unfolded at the party; twice. Hoola and Renu were in the epicenter both times, their bodies wracked mercilessly with spasms they thought would never end. Both events read ten on the event meter which was the highest the instrument went, so they might have been of yet far greater magnitude. Overall, the party was a desperately needed enormous release and deep connections were made; bonds forged.

Pez slept twelve hours when she finally got to sleep crammed and tangled in the ten other bodies on her bed. She was alone on the big bed when she awoke with her mouth wide open and her throat dry. Electra had let her sleep and was quite content with Whiffle and momma Ming. Besides, her pal Gumby was up and about and they were having a fantastic time together discovering new aspects of corporeal biological life within environments. Pez showered trying to remember how she got boy-stuff on her. She put on her familiar custom-regulation Space Marine combat fatigues. The olive panties felt cozy. All her hug-me's underwear seemed to be too big.

Selecting ambassador oatmeal and ambassador pancakes, Pez sat in the galley nook to eat. The babies ran from one hand-hold to the next just getting that front foot out there in the nick of time each occasion, kind of falling forward, and finding the whole business of being upright to be hilariously amusing. They ran through the galley and out again with radiant grins.

Sarhi called and told Pez, "Representatives are on their way to Monarch from almost every planet of the former empire to recognize *you* and the role you played in their revolution and liberation. I insist that you be here for it. They are all listening to you at this historical moment and you can help them establish their unity on a real foundation, with reciprocity in relation to the macrocosm."

"Alright, but I want to wear my Space Marine dress uniform and not some Royal Monarch crotch-less costume."

"Now darling, when in Om…"

"Do as Omians do," Pez finished for her. "So does that mean I'm in a crotch-less costume?"

"Some Glitter fashion designers have made you a dress for the occasion and you'll be able to show off your abs and pecks."

"You mean my crotch and breasts!" Pez reframed.

"You'll look magnificent," Sarhi assured her. "Ming and Hoola will accompany you and Hoola will wear only hug-me's."

"I hope I'm better covered up than her," Pez complained.

'Your dress has sleeves, dear,' Sarhi told her backing up the coverage with facts.

"I'll be there Sarhi, but then I'm going to Mother."

"Of course you are and I'm going with you. Narop invited me star-gazing."

"He's like 40 years older than you, Sarhi!" Pez exclaimed.

"Narop is still a vital man," Sarhi informed her.

"Well have you seen Amazonia?"

"Yes, and she is exceptionally adept and extraordinarily well-preserved for her age, but I prefer males."

"You can have them; all but Rubix," Pez told her.

"He's a father again," Sarhi informed her.

"I'm not pregnant," Pez told her with certainty.

"No, Pooh is but she doesn't know it yet. Niriya, Electra's closest disciple of her past incarnations, has taken birth in her."

"I met your student, Renu, and I just love her," Pez enthused.

"She's your student, sweetheart," Sarhi clarified. "I just provided initiation into Islohar, and some training.

"She's awesome."

"You now have all of your most evolved disciples of your lineage making the holy work with you," Sarhi explained. "You have also inherited a new lineage as High Priestess of the Mother warrior-maidens and Vicar General of the warrior-monks. These twin paths have never before had a single spiritual leader, always in the past divided by gender. You will bring a new integral unity to their tradition placing them on the path of the Amonrahonians."

Pez said from intuition, but without really knowing any details, "I was once an Amonrahonian."

"You were many ages ago and stayed behind out of compassion to assist other humanoid planetary races find spiritual assent through mindful practice and recognition that awareness is everything."

"Was Electra an Amonrahonian?" Pez wanted to know.

"A few times, yes," Sarhi shared. "She is of an even older race than them called the Osirans, who have evolved beyond material reality, beyond the physical to the formless forces matter originates from. They have truly become one body and one spirit. The Osirans support the Amonrahonians in their 100-year meditation. Electra embodies their great compassion and makes the sacrifice every 2,500 years to incarnate in physical matter and bring new teachings consti-tuting more accelerated and surer methods for producing insight and realization. When she comes she is the Osirans. All of them."

"She healed the wound I took," Pez informed her. "She didn't just make it feel better; she restored irreparably damaged tissue to make it immaculate, fresh, and never touched or injured."

"Mel told me. Electra has already drawn three important disci-ples to herself. Now she has performed healing. There are people of six galaxies eager to receive her methods and blessings, and the peo-ple of the former Royal Monarch Empire are ripe, and over-ripe, for what she brings, standing in the rubble and ashes of their old world."

"I guess raising and teaching her is now my only mission," Pez agreed.

"For the next six years, darling, this is entirely true," Sarhi con-curred. "There is one more little situation in this universe you will have to resolve at that time, but it can keep until then."

"What do I have to do then?" Pez demanded.

"Don't worry your sweet head about it, my love," Sarhi said affectionately. "It sounds much worse than it is, and when the time comes, you'll just breeze right through it."

The Rocky holo news, left on atop the galley counter, displayed super-HD images of the expressions on Hoola's and Renu's faces during the recent 'event', which was already being discussed and eye-witness reports taken by news crews on the ground in New Haven on New Monarch. Pez shouted, "Jard!"

Nuclear Fusion Materials

Marsnium
Saturnium   x10
Venusium   x10
Mercurium   x 10
Solarium   x100

Beam and Blaster Weapons Classes

Class 1   3.8 megawatts
Class 2   38 megawatts
Class 3   380 megawatts
Class 4   3.8 gigawatts
Class 5   38 gigawatts
Class 6   380 gigawatts
Class 7   3.8 terawatts
Class 8   38 terawatts
Class 9   380 terawatts

Aphrodite   Luxury yacht completely overhauled and refitted with top military grade, newest tech, systems and components and armor

Triangular shape, long and sleek, wide and tall in stern, to come to a point in bow

length: 280 ft.
width in stern: 160 ft.
height in stern: 140 ft.

Accommodations:	Master suite	Pilots Cabin	Galley
	2x Guest Suites	4x Double Occupancy Crew Cabins	Dining Rm
		Dorm Cabin with 4 berths	Living Rm
			Sitting Rm
			Meditation Rm
			Office
			Workshop
			Airlock Foyer

Armaments:	Class 5 twin nose blasters
	3x Class 4 Quad-Blaster Turrets
	2x Class 3 Twin Ball-Mount Twin Blasters on Side Fins
	8x Batteries of 16-Canister Missiles
	12x Large Missiles
	6x Ship-Killer Torpedoes
	Anti-Missile Molten Flares
	Cloaked Mobile Smart-Mine Net

There is a wrap-around transparent plasteel, polycarbon and synthetic diamond view port-caopy over the bridge. The interior of the living quarters is: Marble, platinum, gold, gem quality jade, gem quality red coral, gem quality jasper, ivory, rare super-hardwoods, mother of pearl, gem quality turquoise, moonstone, onyx, sterling silver. Aphrodite carries a number of pieces of priceless art.

Thunderbolt 690 ft. diameter Om Star Cruiser Class Hull customized into a heavy bomber for Pez

Fitted with 4 Solarium super-fusion reactors (instead of 2)
Crew: reduced to 62 from the usual 600 or more
Carries one SMC Shuttle, one Astro-Phantom Bomber, 4 Drone Fighter Bombers in bay hangar
2 Drone Fighter Bombers on external mounts attached to hull
Eight officers man the bridge +2 special shielded baby seats
Equipped with numerous extra turning, braking, and accelerating thrusters and boosters
New swivel drive for tighter turning

Armaments: Class Nine Beam Weapons (one dedicated reactor)
Class Eight Twin Nose Blasters
12x Class Six Quad-Blaster Turrets
2x Class Five Ball-Mount Twin Blasters on fins
2x Class Five Ball-Mount Twin Blasters miniturrets on flanks
16x Batteries of 16 Canister Missiles
6x Large Missile Launchers each with a 12 missiles magazine
4x Torpedo Tubes, each with an 18 torpedo magazine
Anti-Missile Molten Flares
Cloaked Mobile Smart-Mine Net

Om (Tail of Nine) Warships   (disc shaped with stretched nose)

Reactors	*Class*	*Diameter*	*Number Sent for Armada*
244	ORH Ultra-Super Battleship-Carrier	29,630 ft.	*Reciprocity* Admiral Swenah *Fury* Rear Admiral Firestone *Justice Maker* Admiral Omniomi *Redeemer* Captain Hasbro *Liberator* Captain Nestles
28	ORH Super Battleship-Carrier	9,630 ft.	*Zeus* Captain Grainger *Dionysus* Captain Bacchus *Chronus* Captain Robuck *Poseidon* Captain Schwab
30	ORH Super-Battleship	8,100 ft.	*Apollo* Captain Ohinya *Heracles* Captain Elmo *Hades* Captain Sylvester *Hermes* Captain Fudd
12	T-9 Super Cruiser	3,960 ft.	*Isis* *Herukhuti* *Horus* *Tatenen* *Osirus* *Seker* *Neith* *Ani* *Sekhet*
3	Orion Battleship-Carrier	1,080 ft.	x6 ships for Armada
4	Orion Battleship	900 ft.	x6 ships for Armada
2*	Star Cruiser	690 ft.	x12 ships for Armada

(**Phoenix* has 3 reactors; *Thunderbolt* has 4 reactors)

Kluzyst War Ships (tubular)

34	Class One	3-miles long	x5
20	Class Two	2-miles long	x7
14	Class Three	1¼-miles long	x14
9	Class Four	5,000 ft.	x26
8	Class Five	3,900 ft.	x18
6	Class Six	2,700 ft.	x16
4	Class Seven	1,900 ft.	x31
3	Class Eight	1,130 ft.	x40

Ahumdulilah War Ships (long, triangular)

Reactors	Class	Diameter	Number Sent for Armada
149	Super-Battleship Carrier	25,000 ft.	x4
150	Super-Battleship	24,000 ft.	x4
58	Super-Cruiser	18,600 ft.	x8
36	Super-Destroyer	12,200 ft.	x10
20	Super-Assault Frigate	8,900 ft.	x14
8	Super-Sloop of War	5,800 ft.	x20
3	Super-Fast Attack Ship	2,600 ft.	x34
2	Patrol-Ship	950 ft.	x48

Small Spacecraft

Mirage Streak Fury	heavy bomber
Vulcan Prowler	fighter-bomber
Comet Interceptor	fighter

Trident War Ships (long, triangular)

28	Super-Battleship Carrier	10,080 ft.	x5
28	Super-Battleship	8,700 ft.	x6
4	Battleship-Spacecraft Carrier	1,000 ft.	x10
6	Battleship	900 ft.	x12
5	Heavy Cruiser	600 ft.	x10
3	Light Cruiser	580 ft.	x8

Rally War Ships (tubular)

9	Super-Battleship Carrier	5,415 ft.	x4
9	Super-Battleship	5,280 ft.	x4
3	Battleship Carrier	1,110 ft.	x10
3	Battleship	870 ft.	x8
2.5	Battle Cruiser	690 ft.	x16

Royal Monarch Empire War Ships (tubular)

Reactors	Class	Length	Diameter
148	Class One	26,400 ft.	5,280 ft.
78	Class Two	0,120 ft.	4,024 ft.
52	Class Three	15,840 ft.	3,062 ft.
31	Class Four	12,900 ft.	2,540 ft.
22	Class Five	9,800 ft.	1,912 ft.
11	Class Six	7,200 ft.	1,310 ft.
7	Class Seven	5,280 ft.	1,050 ft.
3	Class Eight	2,640 ft.	528 ft.
2	Class Nine	1,320 ft.	280 ft.
1	Class Ten	700 ft.	132 ft.

Blue World Small Spacecraft

Tempest Crusader   Fighter
Phantom-Raider   Fighter-Bomber
Tornado Ravager   Bomber

Characters:

The Family

Pez, the Wu (cover name: Cher Bulwinkle), Om Clear Light Order
Electra, the Mu, daughter of Pez and Rubix
Ming, spouse of Pez (cover name: Lai Bulwinkle), Om Star Fleet
Gumby, son of Ming and Rubix
Rubix (cover name: Hark), from Earth 10 to the fifth CBS2
Ahhu (cover name: Bianca), from Earth 10 to the fifth CBS2
Trix (cover name: Kat), Om genius scientist
Grettle (cover name Muffet), Om graduate student
Mel, AI become sentient meditator and wholly independent

Islohar

Sarhi, the Im (cover name: Aunt Gimima) Abbot of Spiritual Congress
Shudhiy (cover name: Aunt Jaydene)
Woahha (cover name cousine Winnie)

Star Fleet

Rear Admiral Swenah, commands *Apollo*, then *Reciprocity*
Lt. Commander Konax, elite pilot of *Apollo*, then *Recoprocity*
Lt Commander Schwin, elite small craft combat pilot
Lt. Cotex, Senior Sensor Analyst, scientist
Lt. Cleo, elite intuitive drone pilot
High Admiral Zapa, head of Om Star Fleet

Space Marines

Evenrude, Pez's personal guard (cover name: Brick)
Johnson, Pez's personal guard
Captain Swanson, commander of the Space Marines

Intelligence Agents

Lucky, Om Army Intellegence
Marlboro, Om Central Intellegence
Winston, Om Star Fleet Intellegence
Elenem, Interstar Police Intellegence, Ganahar
Super Agent Green, Ganahar Central Intellegence (initiate of Islohar)

Ahumdulilah Intellegence

Major Nicon
Pooh, Pez's double
Alice
Pippy
Renu

The Whirling Vortexes Band

Pogo, band leader, keyboards
Hoola, lead guitar, lead singer, supermodel for Hug me's panties
Whiffle, saxophone, disciple of Electra
Frisby, drums
Tramp, guitar
Stilts, manager

Adepts from Planet Mother

Narop
Musash, Adamantine Will Order of warrior-monks
Amazonia, Mother Compassionate Guardians Order of warrior-maidens
Bodhi, Adamantine Will Order and ace pilot who can see soft spots
    in sheilds

Clear Light Order

Aton, (code name: Charlie), Vicar General
Nemellie, Abbot

Friends from Planet Monarch

Vegan Casper, third wealthiest in Royal Monarch Tri-galaxy Empire
Atlanta Casper, disciple of Electra

Om Government

Jard, member of the High Council, genius scientist
Yona, Prime Minister